'*One generation passeth away, and another generation cometh; but the earth abideth for ever . . .*'

As do the wild dreams, the unslakeable desires, the fears and secrets that combine to inspire and haunt each succeeding generation . . .

Can it be a fair exchange to barter ancient Aboriginal values for the suppurating corruption endemic to the pursuit of enormous wealth and power? Is it even an exchange at all?

This question is faced – though rarely satisfactorily answered – by a host of characters, sometimes separated by generations and continents, but bound by bonds of love and greed, loyalty and fear. The astonishing stories of their lives – and deaths – are woven skilfully into this brilliant tapestry of adventure, romance and intrigue. This is the world as it really is, not as each generation might wish it to be . . .

Andrew MacAllan's previous novel, *Succession*, is also available from Headline.

Also by Andrew MacAllan

Succession

Generation

Andrew MacAllan

HEADLINE

First published in 1990
by HEADLINE BOOK PUBLISHING PLC

First published in paperback in 1990
by HEADLINE BOOK PUBLISHING PLC

10 9 8 7 6 5 4 3 2

ISBN 0 7472 3441 8

Typeset in 10/12¼ pt Plantin
by Colset Private Limited, Singapore

Printed and bound in Great Britain by
Collins, Glasgow

HEADLINE BOOK PUBLISHING PLC
Headline House
79 Great Titchfield Street
London W1P 7FN

For Joan
who went walkabout
with me

FROM THE WRITER TO THE READER

I would like to thank many people in Australia, England, Hong Kong and the Bahamas for their generous help in my researches for this book.

I would also like to acknowledge my debt to the following published sources:

Said K. Aburish *Pay-off, Wheeling and Dealing in the Arab World*, Unwin Paperbacks

Paul Albury *The Story of the Bahamas*, Macmillan Caribbean

Ken Auletta *Greed and Glory on Wall Street*, Penguin Books

Bruce Chatwin *The Songlines*, Picador

Computers and Security, Elsevier Advanced Technology Publication

Computer Fraud and Security Bulletin, Elsevier Science Publishers

Confucius *The Analects*, Penguin Classics

Hugo Cornwall *The New Hackers' Handbook*, Century Hutchinson

Samuel B. Griffith *Sun Tzu, the Art of War*, Oxford University Press

John Hersey   *Hiroshima*, Penguin Books

David James   *The Rise and Fall of the Japanese Empire*, George Allen and Unwin

Robert Jungk   *Children of the Ashes*, Heinemann

Douglas Lockwood   *I, The Aboriginal*, Ian Drakeford Publishing, Australia

Nick Lush   *Australia*, Cadogan Books, London

Winsome Maff   *Katherine's No Lady*, Katherine Municipality and National Trust of Australia (Northern Territory)

Douglas K. Ramsey   *The Corporate Warriors*, Grafton Books

A.W. Reed   *Aboriginal Tables and Legendary Tales*, Reed Books, Australia

Mamoru Shigemitsu   *Japan and Her Destiny*, Hutchinson

Ben-Ami Shillony   *Politics and Culture in Wartime Japan*, Clarendon Press, Oxford

Sir Baldwin Spencer   *Wanderings in Wild Australia*, Vol. I, Macmillan, London

Lao Tzu   *Tao Te Ching*, Penguin Classics

Chitoshi Yanaga   *Big Business in Japanese Politics*, Yale University Press, New Haven & London

ONE

The Present

Now that I am older and have more time, I would like to set down how it all happened and where, and when, and – possibly most important – why.

There have been other accounts, and maybe more are to come, but none have told the whole truth, nor can they, because no one except me knows that truth. I was there. They were not.

I want also to explain my own actions, many of which, with hindsight, now seem foolish, sometimes ill conceived or motivated by self-interest.

I was born in Katherine, a modest, unpretentious town in the Northern Territory of Australia. My parents ran a general store. Over the years this gradually grew until now it is dignified by the name of supermarket, although it is still basically a general store. I was brought up in the shadow of astonishing financial achievements by my half-brother, on the other side of the world. He was twenty-odd years older than me, but by the time he was twenty-eight, he was already a multi-millionaire and spoken of in the hushed voices people use when mentioning the very rich and powerful. I never met him until I was in my mid-twenties, because he lived in England, the United States, anywhere but back in Australia.

He was my mother's son, born during the Second World War, before she married my father. Some people have the gift of words or can paint or compose; he had a much rarer ability, shared with the Rockefellers, the Mellons and, among Australians, Robert Holmęs à Court. Some antennae of his mind enabled him, like them, to spot a splendid commercial opportunity in a ruined company, a bankrupt concern, even a huge, unsecured written-off debt. Out of dross the alchemists of old sought (and failed) to create gold. He succeeded – every time.

He was my hero. I could recite word for word articles about his business successes in newspaper cuttings sent from the United States and England, and the rather stilted letters he wrote to my mother, or had a secretary write for him; he never seemed to me to be a very affectionate or generous person. I lived through all his successes, if at second hand; I was the mirror, he was the man in that mirror. And what he had done, I yearned to attempt – and then surpass.

Just as the son of a farmer or a doctor or a schoolteacher may be brought up to believe that his father's career is also for him, I wanted to follow in the footsteps of a man who had become so famous, so wealthy, that he was not even known by his real name, but by a nickname the world press and TV bestowed on him like a title. To everyone, cartoonists, interviewers, financial institutions, he was simply the Australian.

I have here set down the steps I took along my own private journey, first to meet him, then to march with him, and finally to overtake him, as a young bull seizes the herd when the old bull can no longer claim supremacy. Most of all, I wanted his title, the Australian. I wanted to go out there into a world about which I could only read in Katherine and become richer, more powerful, more famous than the first holder of the title, in whose tall shadow I had lived my life. If there was no room for the two of us at the top, then I wanted to be the one at the top.

When I was a little boy, books were not as plentiful in Katherine as they are now, from the splendid library off the main Stuart Highway. Many of the books I read then were written by Victorians who had the habit of addressing their readers as 'Dear Reader', or 'Gentle Reader' as though they were personal friends. Anyone who reads my story becomes, by proxy of print, my friend and, more, my confidant. Just as the religious need priests to whom they can confess sins and guilts not for other ears; just as the rich or irreligious engage psychiatrists to provide the same service, if at rather greater cost, everyone needs someone to trust. But trust is a valuable commodity, far rarer than rhodium.

How many times have you, dear reader, told someone in strict confidence of a personal problem, desperately seeking their advice as a friend, and within days heard it repeated to you as news by someone else? But in telling my own story, I need only reveal what I want others to know, a very great advantage.

You may also ask how I, born and brought up in such ordinary surroundings, can know of the astonishing prophecy an old man made to Emperor Hirohito in his Imperial palace in Tokyo at the end of the Second World War, which would change the world – and all our lives for ever?

How could I discover that the rape of a shy, young Eurasian girl by her drunken stepfather could so fire a hatred in her of all men that from beginnings far less propitious than mine she decided to beat men at their own game, and become, next to the Queen of England, the world's richest woman?

Or how, again, did I learn that on the death of one of that country's most noble baronets, the last of a distinguished line of chivalry and honour that stretched back unbroken to the thirteenth century, the body of a woman – not a man – would be buried in an unmarked grave?

All these things happened years before I was born. I learned about them from others, because it is one of life's sadder revelations that a secret is almost never kept inviolate. It will burn, corrode, consume the thoughts of its keeper, so that finally it bursts out of the mind and consciousness of the person guarding it. He or she feels an imperative, overwhelming need to confide in someone else, or write it down in a diary or notebook. Once they are no longer the only person with the secret knowledge, the weight of responsibility for its safekeeping seems eased.

Maybe they place their version of events in what they feel is the safe custody of a bank, forgetting that banks are not just buildings, but hives of people working with and by other people's money. I have learned long since that, with enough money, you can discover almost every secret that interests you, no matter how cunningly it may be concealed. Cash is the key to all secrets. For a bribe in cash or kind, for the compliance of a pretty girl, for an honour; introductions to amenable and effeminate boys, the gift of a new car, expensive school fees paid for a son or a daughter; these are routes that lead inexorably to the exhumation of deeds the rich and famous and ungodly trustingly assumed they had buried for ever.

This is how I put my account together, bit by bit, step by step, like the pieces in a jigsaw, until suddenly, at the end, the whole picture of past and present was vividly revealed. You may not like what I have written or how and why I came to write it, but it is true, and truth can be too strong a medicine to take in all but the smallest doses. You may not like me, either, but at least you will know me and, in knowing me, it is just possible you may also discover some unknown facts about yourself.

I was brought up among Aborigines, the ancient and original inhabitants of the world's greatest continent and island. They believed that, at some time in their history, a balance of understanding and knowledge existed between every living thing, embracing men, women, families, friends, animals and birds. The spirit within each person, each living thing, did not drift away to heaven or nirvana or paradise beyond the earth when they died, but remained as a powerful force guiding those left alive – if they were attuned to their guidance and were willing to take their advice.

Everyone in those faraway days was held securely in their allotted place in this unique conglomeration of the living and the dead by what is known to the Aborigines as Dreaming or Dreamtime. This has nothing to do with sleep. It has everything to do with living. In giving my version of events, I have, like they do, ignored the artificial frontiers of time. One moment we are in the present, at another in the past, for life is not lived on one dimension and events of long ago cast shadows on the decisions of today.

From time to time, Aborigines will simply disappear for weeks or months from their homes and their jobs. They have gone, as they say, walkabout. They have felt some imperative ancestral urge to walk – or nowadays to drive – across seemingly uncharted routes over the vast land once known as *terra Australis incognita*, the unknown country of the south. We do not know how they find their way, only that they do, that they must leave when the instinct tells them. Some similar inner force drove me to do what I did.

I went walkabout from Katherine across the world in search of a dream. This is the story of my journey, and of many people I never met, who yet played their own essential part in my wish to become the Australian.

TWO

The Present: Perth, Western Australia
The Past: Calcutta, India, 1945

For some years, it had been the custom of Lady Myrtle Mackenzie, Sir Hilary's widow and hence the majority shareholder in Mackenzie Transworld, the immensely wealthy multinational group, to spend each October at her house overlooking the Swan River that links Perth with the port of Fremantle to the south of Western Australia.

She could, of course, just as easily have stayed in any of the equally splendid houses she maintained, fully staffed, in Connecticut, Lyford Cay in the Bahamas, and Cap Ferrat in the south of France, but this would have been a break with established routine, and as she grew older she disliked departures from an accepted practice which could arguably upset other equally sacrosanct arrangements. She was a creature of habit, and would quote from the early nineteenth-century poet, George Crabbe, whose works had been given to her as a prize for punctuality at school: 'Habit with him was all the test of truth, it must be right; I've done it from my youth.'

So, each October, Lady Mackenzie's private 747, painted in the Mackenzie livery of deep blue and green and bearing the clan's crest of a volcano and the motto *Luceo non uro* – I shine, not burn – transported her to Perth with her constant companion, Mrs Irene Loxby, a woman of indeterminate age and shadowy background, her secretaries and personal maids.

With an estimated annual income of around £40 million sterling Myrtle Mackenzie was one of the world's wealthiest women. No one really knew her background, and with the enormous power and political muscle her money commanded, newspaper references to her were deliberately discreet and flattering. She was invariably described as 'Mexican-born', or as 'looking heavily tanned' from a recent holiday on her private islands in the Philippines and off Cairns in north-eastern Australia. Reporters, normally not notably deferential to the rich, respected her because their editors feared her. After all, she could well be the ultimate financial power behind their newspaper or TV station.

No one intruded on her privacy, wherever she might be; indeed, it would have been difficult to do so. Guards with Doberman Pinscher dogs patrolled the grounds of every house she owned and hidden electronic devices abounded. These alerted the guards to the arrival of any uninvited visitor before they had passed through the outer screen of wire-mesh fences. And some of her male staff, of unusually powerful physique for butlers and footmen or chauffeurs, could clearly double effectively and willingly as her bodyguards, should such services be required.

When in Perth, it was Lady Mackenzie's habit every Sunday afternoon after a vegetarian lunch to relax in the agreeable sunshine on her lawn overlooking the river. She had always liked rivers. Something in their slow, graceful but irresistible progress seemed to parallel life. A few people would plunge in, intent on reaching the far shore or some distant target of their own, upstream or down. But there were far more who preferred to stay safely on the bank. They were the schoolteachers of the world, who loudly urged others to do what they did not care (or dare) to attempt themselves.

Now, from a chaise longue, a glass of iced orange juice at her right hand, her wide-brimmed straw hat shading her face, Myrtle regarded the river, dotted with wind-surfers and sailing boats, their triangular white sails sharp as the fins of giant sharks. When she was young, she never had the opportunity to engage in such activities. Now, as so often through her life, she enjoyed them by proxy.

Sometimes, on these long Australian Sundays, she would imagine what this river must have looked like to the seventeenth-century European navigators who had seen it for the first time. Two Dutch voyagers, Dirk Hartog and William de Vlamingh, had apparently anchored their ship near an island at its mouth. They went ashore and in disgust named it Rottnest – rat's nest – because it appeared to be swarming with giant rats. The Dutchmen could not stand these animals, which were actually quokkas, a species of marsupial, and so they sailed on towards the mainland. Here, in a vast stretch of water, they saw black swans and named the river Swarte Swanne Drift – Black Swan River. As a girl, Myrtle had regarded herself as being an ugly duckling. Now, her jewels, her clothes, her money made her a swan, and if not a black swan, at least a dark one. She therefore thought it fitting and symbolic she should have a home here.

A century after that first Dutch visit, a British sea captain, James Stirling, also explored the river. The British were concerned then by the presence of French expeditions in the South Seas. They posed a possible threat to British settlements already established on the south-eastern coast of Australia, in New South Wales. Stirling sent back an optimistic report to London. Grants of land were made and emigrants sailed from England to found the Swan River Colony. A highway in Perth was later named after Stirling, and others after people and places settlers wished to honour: Nelson Avenue, Adelaide Terrace, Victoria Avenue, Windsor and Aberdeen Streets.

Lady Myrtle wondered what Captain Stirling would think

now if he could sail up the river again and see the powerboats, the forest of masts outside the Royal Perth Yacht Club on Pelican Point, the splendid University of Western Australia with ten thousand students and ten faculties.

Where she sat, in Peppermint Grove, and on round Fresh-water Bay, black swans were now few in number, but along the river banks was another greater tourist attraction: the opulent houses of the very rich, her own, of course, being one of the finest. Two splendid houses belonged to Lang Hancock, who originally developed the vast Pilbara iron ore deposits, which, it was said, earned him 25 million Australian dollars every year. He had given the second house to his daughter as a present on her twenty-first birthday. Her birthday party then was said to have cost a million dollars, and that was years ago.

Then Ric New, head of the Midland Brick Company, had an immense property built on a series of brick arches. The house was designed on a grand scale; the chandelier in the lounge weighed eight hundredweight and required an electric mecha-nism to lower it for cleaning. Alan Bond, largely responsible for Australia winning the America's Cup, owned a house in the oriental style with a green roof. But the bright medal of success sometimes had another, darker, side. One property was still known as 'James Clay's House' although James Clay had never actually lived in it. This building had a white roof with a long balcony and a glass front, and had been built in the mid-1960s by Mr Clay, an extremely successful car dealer. Before the house was finished, however, Mr Clay disappeared in his own aircraft with his young secretary and two million Australian dollars in company funds. Twenty-odd years later, the wreck-age of his plane was discovered in northern New South Wales, with two skeletons still strapped in their seats. The paper money and the documents had long since disappeared, possibly eaten by termites.

Lady Mackenzie returned to this story time and again: it pointed a moral – several, in fact, and she liked morals; they took her back to Sunday school Bible lessons. Although she had never lived by their teaching herself, she set store by them in other people's lives. First, life was short. Next, the risks attached to making a fortune could be enormous. Third, good or evil deeds could bring their own reward.

Not that she had much to fear. Her days of struggle and poverty were long behind her. When she overheard people ask in whispers, 'How did she ever make so much money?' Myrtle was always amused to hear the stock reply her secretaries and public relations executives were instructed to give: 'She married it.' 'Ah,' the inquirer would say knowingly, 'then it was easy.'

This answer was always accepted. It instantly absolved the questioner of any self-criticism: Lady Mackenzie was not cleverer than they were, only luckier. But it had not been luck, nor had it been easy. Only she knew the price she had paid for her wealth; sometimes she still wondered if it had been too high.

No one knew how she felt about that, just as no one ever suspected the reason she had built this house on Swan River, looking west. Here she was nearer to Singapore than to any other capital city in Australia. And beyond Singapore lay Calcutta and Rawalpindi, where her past lay all about her, not here. The past remained a secret; it was hers and hers alone. She had not always been happy then – sometimes she had been miserable, even desperate – but those feelings, so sharp and cruel at the time, had moulded her and helped to make her rich. Without them she would now only be an impoverished and elderly half-caste, marked by brittle bones and the lilting, almost Welsh accent of her kind, the product of parents from two vanished empires, one coloured, one white.

Every evening, as the sun went down over the Indian Ocean and turned the Swan River first to silver then to gold, Myrtle would peer through the warm deepening darkness and hear the crickets and other insects of the night, and imagine she was back in the house which in her secret heart she would always identify as home.

She had not been born in Mexico, although now she had a house in Durango and another outside Mazatlan. The fiction of being Mexican or part South American suited her. When she was young, anything was better than to be known as an Anglo-Indian; East then was East and West was West, and she was the result of their ill-matched union in a bed.

Now, of course, no one thought there was anything shameful in such a thing, any more than there was disgrace in a girl being pregnant and unmarried. But when Myrtle was young, rules were harsher, and she always remembered the lessons of her youth and lived by precepts laid down then, although for her they had long been no more than empty words.

Looking back, her happiest time as a child was probably in Rawalpindi, 120 miles from the Afghanistan frontier. The air felt clear and fresh, and every evening and early morning it was loud with the excited chatter and chirping of unnumbered birds. They rested silently in the cool leaves of the trees during the heat of each day, and only sang briefly at dusk and dawn.

Rawalpindi was proud of its cantonment where the Europeans and richer Indians lived. Here were well-laid-out wide streets lined by the large bungalows, with whitewashed walls and tiled roofs, set back at the end of long gravel drives, and lawns where bullocks pulled lawnmowers. From such elegant homes Indian chauffeurs drove the English *burra sahibs*, the very important people, to their offices every morning. Their cars were always shining, and newly starched cotton covers protected the leather seats. She liked to walk through the cantonment; sometimes she watched smart weddings at St John's Church, and read the memorial inscriptions to past bishops, clergymen, soldiers buried in its cemetery. She believed she belonged to this agreeable world, and although she was not rich, she was English; that was the main thing, a fact to be proud of. Her mother was slightly dark-skinned, of course, and she had no father. At least, he did not live with them.

'Where is he?' she would ask sometimes and her mother

would reply gravely, always in the same words, as though she had learned the answer by heart.

'He was a brave man. A sergeant in the King's Own Yorkshire Light Infantry. He could easily have been an officer, he often said, but he would rather stay with the rankers. A fine body of men, he called them.'

'Why were they light infantry?' she asked.

'It's a description. Nothing to do with their colour, Myrtle, but they carried light equipment so they could march very quickly. If there was any trouble they'd be first on the scene.'

'And what happened to him?'

'He went away,' said her mother sadly. 'He went home.'

She would never elaborate on this, and after Myrtle was rich she paid researchers to discover what really had happened to her father. It was not an unfamiliar story, nor was it difficult to unravel. He had met her mother at a dance in 'Pindi, held in the most modern hotel, Flashman's. The floor sloped slightly towards a stage where the band played; couples waltzed slowly up to the rear of the hall and then raced down towards the front where the band sat. It was difficult to imagine her mother doing this; she had always seemed tired and middle-aged and worried. The sergeant had returned to England after five years in India, and then he left the army, married, sired two children, and ran a public house outside Bradford.

Myrtle's mother was dead by the time she learned this, and even if she had been alive, Myrtle would not have told her. She realised that her mother still loved the man, and love was something rare in both their lives, not to be despised, never to be tampered with. Only once had she experienced it herself, briefly and long ago.

'He was a lovely man,' her mother would say after a few drinks of Carew's East India Gin. 'Lovely. Blue eyes, fair hair. Upstanding. Dashing white sergeant to a T. But he was posted to England. Home.'

'Couldn't you go with him?'

'We weren't married. Oh, he asked me to marry him many times. But I didn't want to, not out here. I wanted to go home with him to live his life in England. He said he'd got a big house, a motor car. Everything. Promised when he was out of the army he'd either come back here to take me to England, too, or send me the money for my fare. First class, of course.'

'But he didn't?'

'No,' said her mother shortly. 'He didn't.' Then her face would cloud. 'I'm sure he *wanted* to. I *know* he wanted to. I feel it in my bones, Myrtle. It was his parents, probably his mother. Mothers are funny about sons. Jealous. Too possessive. You'd be surprised. But anyway,' she added brightly, 'you bear his name, an English name. Gibson. That's something.'

Her mother was given to moments of nostalgia, usually after several glasses of gin, when she pondered on what could have been, might have been, instead of what had been. And then, just as quickly, she would be perkily optimistic. Looking on the bright side, was how she described it.

She usually wore a thin white dress, loose shoes, and her hair in a bun. The light dress accentuated her dark skin, which seemed to darken with the years. Money was always short; she worked as a filing clerk in the local office of an insurance company, and the pay was poor. Myrtle had to turn down the hems of dresses, and wash everything extremely carefully herself – not let the *dhobi* do it in case the worn fabric frayed under his rough handling.

Then one day Myrtle's mother told her excitedly, 'We're moving to Calcutta. Uncle Jem wants to marry me.'

'*Marry* you?' replied Myrtle in amazement.

'Yes. Are you surprised?'

'Well, yes, I suppose I am.'

Uncle Jem was a guard on the railway, their neighbour for several years, not an uncle by blood, only by association. He had no children and had been married to a much older woman who died. He was being moved to Calcutta; promotion, he said proudly.

Myrtle was sorry to leave Rawalpindi, to exchange its clean streets and the grace of a hill station for the stink and bustle of Calcutta – sometimes described unflatteringly as a low-lying city filled with low, lying people. On Chowringhee, the city's main street, trolleys bearing professional beggars with legs swollen to grotesque size, some without arms, others blind, or displaying huge suppurating sores like badges of honour, were pushed into the paths of passers-by by little Indian boys begging for an anna, one-sixteenth of a rupee. This minute coin could mark the difference between food and hunger to the wretched destitute human hulks who cried endlessly, like gramophone records gone mad, '*Baksheesh*, sahib, *baksheesh*!' Pyramids of over-ripe mangoes stood at each street corner. Black crows dug their long greedy beaks into the fleshy, rotting fruit, and the stench of sewage and mud from the great river Hooghly hung like a heavy, evil-smelling miasma in the humid air.

Uncle Jem was a short, wiry man with grizzled grey hair. Myrtle thought him unattractive with his sharp, beady eyes and dark skin, but did her best to appear friendly. After all, he was her mother's choice, not hers. He was a relief guard on the Deccan Queen, a prestige train that ran weekly across India. Its air-conditioned First Class coaches contained saloons the size of drawing rooms, each with its own private bathroom.

One evening during the Second World War, when Myrtle was about fifteen, she went down to Howrah Station to meet Uncle Jem as he came off duty. She was waiting for him near the ticket barrier when three British soldiers, who had clearly been drinking heavily, approached and began to argue with the ticket collector, one of Uncle Jem's colleagues. He told them they needed platform tickets before he could allow them through the barrier onto the platform. They replied angrily that they did not.

'It is the rule,' the ticket collector said mildly. 'I am just now telling you, we must all obey the rules.'

'Bugger the rules!' retorted one of the soldiers. 'No bloody chi-chi is going to tell me what to do.'

Then they saw Myrtle.

'Even if she has got good tits, like this one, eh?'

The soldier winked at Myrtle as though he had paid her a compliment and they all lurched away along the platform. The ticket collector made as if to say something and then thought better of it. How could one middle-aged half-caste impose a company rule on three fit, young and drunken white men?

On the walk back with Uncle Jem, Myrtle asked him what a bloody chi-chi was.

'You really don't know?' he asked her in surprise.

'No, Uncle.'

'It's what we are, Myrtle. Your mother, you, me, and nearly all the people who run the railways. It's the only job we can get. We're neither one thing nor the other. Neither fish, flesh nor good red herring, as your father used to say.'

'You knew him?'

'I met him once or twice, that's all. We're half-castes. There are all sorts of other words for it, and you'll come across them, I don't doubt. Half past eleven. Nearly midnight. Chi-chis. Milk with your coffee. That sort of thing. We don't fit in anywhere, with either the Indians or the British. And now there's talk that after the war, the British may all go back to England and India will become independent or a dominion in the empire. And then God knows what happens to us. When the British are here we can manage – just. But if they go . . .' He shrugged.

'Is that why sometimes people laugh at me? At school. The English.'

'Possibly,' he said. 'Or maybe it's just because you are a funny little thing.'

'I don't feel funny.'

'You don't look funny,' he said. 'You are very pretty.'

He was regarding her now in a way she had not noticed before.

'Anyhow, why have you come to meet me?'

'Because Mother is away until tomorrow night.'

She now had a job with the Calcutta office of the insurance company, and the manager had taken her out of town to visit a sub-branch.

'Oh, then *you're* my little wife,' said Uncle Jem teasingly. 'You're cooking for me, are you?'

They had no cook or *khansama*, as they would have had if they were British or Indian, because they could not afford one.

'Yes,' she said. 'I've got some bekti and rice and vegetables.' Bekti was a river fish with a delicate flavour, a treat they did not often have.

They reached home and Uncle Jem changed into a pair of white slacks, a grey shirt and leather chaplis. She noticed then for the first time how the soles of his feet were curiously white. If only their whole skin were that colour, they could easily pass as white. If only things were different. But then Uncle Jem used to quote another saying of her father's: 'If only wishes were horses, then beggars would ride.'

They sat down in the kitchen, facing each other across the table. An electric fan on the ceiling beat the air into warm humid eddies. Night moths and other flying insects hurled themselves suicidally at the naked electric bulb above their heads, and dropped dead on the tablecloth.

'Seeing as we're alone,' said Uncle Jem, 'and you've cooked a special supper, I've got a drink for both of us. Toddy.'

He poured out two half-glasses of thick, dark, treacly liquid, pushed one across the table towards her, raised his in a toast. A little of his toddy spilled on the cloth. Myrtle guessed he had been drinking already, perhaps in the staff canteen at the station. She remembered the drunk soldiers; her mother had warned her about drink. She feared its consequences and had never tasted anything alcoholic. But she did not want to offend Uncle Jem. She did not like him, but after all he was married to her mother. She sipped the toddy cautiously. It tasted like liquid fire, burning her throat. Uncle Jem was watching her closely. His eyes suddenly seemed very moist.

'Drink it,' he urged in a hoarse whisper, as though he feared he might be overheard. 'It'll do you good.'

'I've never had it before.'

'First time for everything,' he assured her. 'First time, best time, eh?'

Uncle Jem moved his knife and fork and spoon and sat down by her side, so close that she could smell the sickly honeysuckle scent from the cheap pomade on his hair. She had never been alone with him before, at least not close like this. There was something disturbing in his nearness in this small hot room with the beating fan blades and the drink, and the insects dropping dead around their plates.

They ate in silence. Then Uncle Jem poured himself another large toddy, indicating she should have another glass too. Myrtle shook her head. She had drunk enough.

'Well, let's go and sit on the verandah,' he suggested.

This was a little wooden balcony with a mosquito screen. They sat down. In the distance, the amber glow above Calcutta turned the sky to flame. Traffic rumbled in the distance, punctuated by the high-pitched beep-beep of motor horns and the tinkle of tonga bells. Afterwards, Myrtle could never hear these familiar sounds without unease. They recalled a night she would have given a fortune to forget.

They talked, but she could not remember what either of them said. The toddy was fuming in her blood. She felt confused, vague, dizzy, as though she was somehow floating weightlessly a foot above the ground. Was she tiddly, squiffy, as her mother would say?

She was glad to plead tiredness and go early to bed.

Under the mosquito net, her head throbbing, with the dim nightlight beyond the net revolving in an extraordinary way, she realised she was drunk and firmly resolved never to get drunk again. Some time later, she slept.

She awoke to feel a slight draught. Someone had lifted the mosquito net, and the night air, stirred by the big fan above the bed, felt pleasantly cool.

Uncle Jem crawled into the bed with her. In the dim glow, she could see his bare brown chest. What had happened to his clothes? Why was he here? she wondered drowsily. The reason became instantly apparent. He put out one hand, clutched a breast roughly and forced his mouth on hers. She could smell tobacco, the rich sugary scent of toddy on his breath and his peculiar hair oil, and then he was groping down her body, between her legs, forcing them apart, lying on her. She felt him thrust against her, hard and hot, like a throbbing serpent. She screamed with horror and dismay. Instantly, he held a hand tightly over her mouth.

'Don't cry, ducky,' he told her hoarsely. 'First time it may hurt a little, but not much. And you'll get to love it. All girls do.'

Myrtle shook herself free and bit his fingers. He cursed her angrily.

'Get out!' she shouted, now fully awake. 'Get *out*! What would Mother say? It's wrong.'

'Mother's not here and no one's going to tell her. Certainly not you.'

Uncle Jem was in her then, forcing blindly up through her body. She screamed with pain and pummelled his back, hating him, hating the indignity and horror he was inflicting on her.

He thrust like a beast, back arched, panting with his exertions. Then, after what seemed an eternity of raw, red pain and humiliation, he gasped and collapsed. She felt her body suddenly full of warm alien liquid. She turned her face away and wept.

'There, there,' he said clumsily. 'Don't take on so.'

She did not reply.

He sighed and swung himself out of her bed.

When Myrtle was certain he had left the room, she stood up,

locked the door and examined herself by torchlight. She did not
dare to go to the bathroom in case Uncle Jem was waiting for
her out there in the darkness. She washed herself as best she
could with water from the ewer in the hand basin. She was
bleeding and raw; worst of all, she felt violated, diminished. She
was no longer her own person. Something had happened that
could never be explained away; the pain and memory would
never be entirely eradicated.

Myrtle went back to bed, curling up like an embryo in an
instinctive attempt to find comfort, and tried to sleep. When
she heard a tapping on the door and Uncle Jem's voice calling
softly: 'Are you awake? Are you awake? It's me,' she did not
reply, and finally she heard him go back to his own room and
slam the door.

That was the first time. There were other times, of course.
She had known there would be, that there must be, but she did
not know how to prevent them, because her mother was away
more and more. She never imagined that her mother was in fact
having an affair with the insurance manager; her so-called business trips were only as far as a double room in a cheap hotel on
the Alipore side of Calcutta.

When Myrtle learned this years later, she vomited with despair. How could any woman like, even welcome, the degrada-
tion she was forced to endure with Uncle Jem? Then her period
was late, and despite doses of Glauber salts liberally laced
with gin, and baths so hot she could hardly bear to enter them,
it was clear she was pregnant. She was carrying her stepfather's
child.

She was desperate. She knew no one with whom she could
safely discuss the situation. It was impossible to tell the family
doctor. She feared he would inform her mother, and that was as
unthinkable as telling her mother herself.

Myrtle worked as a shop assistant, unrolling bales of cloth
for haughty *memsahibs* who came in, inspected ten or twelve
bales, sniffed and said they saw nothing they liked, and went

away, leaving her to roll them up again neatly and heave them back onto the shelves.

An older woman, Irene Loxby, also a chi-chi, worked at the same counter. One afternoon, when they had ten minutes off for tea (the time of day when the trade was slackest), Myrtle told her. She could not keep her secret any longer; she had to confide in someone.

'Can you help me?' she asked Irene desperately. 'I'm having a baby.'

'Boy friend?'

'No.' She paused, then took a deep breath. She was not quite sure whether to tell the truth. But why not? This was surely a time for truth if ever there was one.

'My stepfather,' she said quickly. 'I'll kill myself rather than have his child.'

'No need for that, dear. I know someone.'

'A doctor?'

'Well, sort of. He's Portuguese. Mr da Leppo. Nice man. He was a medical student in Lisbon. Came out to Goa on holiday and never went back. He knows his stuff.'

'How can I pay him?'

'We'll think of a way.'

'He won't attempt to do what my stepfather did, will he?' Myrtle asked anxiously. 'I couldn't bear that.'

'No, no. He's not interested in women. Says he's seen so much of them – from the wrong end. But never mind about paying him. Let's see if he can help you first.'

Mr da Leppo lived in a flat on the eighth floor of an old-fashioned block off Park Street. The lift wheezed up reluctantly. Irene beat a tattoo on a varnished door, paused, beat half the tattoo a second time. The door opened cautiously on a chain.

A small swarthy man, smoking a cigarette in a holder, regarded them without enthusiasm, then released the chain.

'Hi, Irene,' he said. 'And a friend. In need, are we, then?'

'In need,' Irene agreed.

'Come inside.'

He closed the door. Myrtle noticed that he locked it with three locks. He slid back the chain and led the way into a cramped, shabby room.

Canvas covers on chairs and a settee needed washing. The air smelled sourly of stale sweat and old clothes. The windows were closed, their panes flyblown.

Mr da Leppo looked at Myrtle inquiringly. She explained her predicament. Could he help her – *would* he help her?

'Of course, my dear,' he said at once. 'Delighted to help any friend of Irene in trouble. That's what friends are for, isn't it? You want to be helped now?'

'I don't know,' Myrtle replied, suddenly nervous. 'I should go home. They're expecting me.'

'Them? Live with your parents, do you?'

'My mother and stepfather, yes.'

'Well, tell your mummy you've got a bad period. She'll understand. You'll only be off work for a couple of days.'

'Is that all?'

'Should be, dearie. Now, just come into the surgery. We'll have a look and see what the trouble is. In my experience, all troubles are little ones – unless we let them grow bigger, eh?'

Myrtle lay down on a hard truckle bed. She could see nickel-plated instruments, some none too clean it seemed to her, and bottles of fluid, pads of cotton wool, and an Angle-poise light.

'Take your knickers off and your skirt, dearie. We don't want to make a mess. And here's a towel.'

He spread a towel under her. She lay back. Irene came in and held her hand.

'Will it hurt?' Myrtle asked Mr da Leppo apprehensively.

'Not to notice, dearie. We'll give you something to stop that. A little jab in the leg.'

'I don't want to look.'

'Then I wouldn't, dearie. It'll all be over in a flash, believe me.'

Irene brought another towel, folded it over Myrtle's eyes. She felt the coldness of a swab damp with spirit on her thigh, the jab of a needle, and then a numbness spread through her body. She could hear a clink of kidney-shaped basins and the rattle of unknown instruments on the porcelain top of a side table.

As da Leppo had promised, she felt no pain – then. That came later, when she was home. She sat up shakily. Da Leppo poured her a brandy in a beaker. She wrinkled her nose in distaste at the smell; it reminded her of Uncle Jem's toddy.

'Drink it,' da Leppo said shortly. 'And wait here while your friend calls a taxi.'

He looked strained now, almost worried.

'You take it easy. For three days, I'd say, not two. Irene will come and see you, and she'll tell me how you are. We don't want any complications.'

'Could there be complications?' Myrtle asked. 'What kind? I'm not pregnant any more, am I?'

'No. Not any more. But you're a little weak. Lost some blood. It takes time to make more. Like money.'

Myrtle realised he wanted to be rid of her quickly. She sensed that something had gone wrong, but she did not know what and could not bring herself to ask him. As the effect of the local anaesthetic wore off, her whole body seemed to ache like a gigantic violated bruise. Her heart fluttered and she felt sick and unbelievably weak.

Somehow, she reached home. Irene explained to Myrtle's mother that Myrtle had collapsed at work, and the manageress had given her a brandy. Her mother believed her.

Myrtle went to bed and lay there, bleeding slowly but steadily; the haemorrhage continued for several hours. She did not dare to tell her mother how bad it was in case she called their doctor and her visit to da Leppo was discovered. She tried to plug the leak with hand towels, rinsing them out in the bathroom, carefully washing away the pink water. Gradually, the bleeding slowed and then stopped.

Myrtle was off work for a week, and for a long time after she went back she felt weak and dizzy as she stood behind the counter. Irene arranged a chair for her.

At the end of the following week, the manageress said, 'I've been watching you, Myrtle. You're not at all well. This job's proving too much for you, my girl.'

'I can manage, miss,' Myrtle answered. 'Just had a bad period.'

'You've had more than that, I think. Something else is wrong with you. We can't have you working here if you're not well. You can go at the end of the week.'

'But I don't want to go, miss. And I've nowhere to go to.'

'You'll find something.'

'Where?'

'Oh, in another shop, or a café. You work hard and you're pretty.'

'*Please* let me stay,' Myrtle begged her.

'Sorry, dear. It's the boss's decision as much as mine.'

And so Myrtle was out of a job.

She was afraid to tell her mother and would leave home every morning as though she was going to the shop, and then walk the streets aimlessly, lacking enough money to buy lunch. She tried to find other jobs in other shops, but without any success. She was half-caste, Anglo-Indian. Too many girls like her, unskilled and untrained, also wanted jobs.

One day, in Chowringhee, she saw da Leppo, or rather he saw her first and greeted her warmly.

'How are you, dearie?' he asked.

'I'm all right,' she told him. 'But I had a bit of a bad time. Anyway, you haven't sent me a bill.'

'I know it's difficult for you to pay. I know where you live, and things are not too easy.'

'They're desperate,' Myrtle admitted. 'I've been sacked. I don't know what I can do.'

'I think I can help you,' he said. 'You know the restaurant, Ruggiani's, here in Chowringhee?'

'Well, I've seen it,' she agreed. 'It's near the Grand Hotel and the other swanky Italian restaurant, Firpo's, where all the British officers go.'

'Well, Ruggiani's isn't really Italian. They're actually Indians who run it. With a Goanese backer, a friend of mine. They're looking for people to help.'

'You mean waitresses?'

'Not actually waitresses, more dancers. For the customers. They have a little floor show every night.'

Myrtle did not know what a floor show was. She looked at da Leppo, trying to conceal her bewilderment and ignorance.

'What could I do there?' she asked him.

'You could dance,' he explained. 'You've got a good figure. You're light on your feet. I'll introduce you.'

'Thank you, but I don't know if I could dance well enough.'

'We'll let them decide.'

He took her arm, led her along Chowringhee into the restaurant. She had never been in such an imposing room, with potted palms around the walls, and cane tables and brightly painted chairs. On a stage at one end was a microphone and decorated music stands for a band, smarter than in Flashman's. A few waiters were setting tables. They did not look up as da Leppo and Myrtle entered.

An older man came out of a booth near the stage. He had a sharp, pointed face and very small bright eyes. He reminded Myrtle instantly of a rat.

'Hullo,' he said. 'Who've we got here?'

'A new hostess for you,' da Leppo replied. 'Myrtle Gibson. This is Mr de Souza.'

He looked Myrtle up and down closely.

'Can you dance?' he asked her.

'I have foxtrotted and waltzed.'

'With people you don't know?'

'Of course not. How could I?'

'Easily. I mean with guests, cash customers. Mostly officers on leave. British, I would add.'

'I could try.'

'Good. Then open your coat and let's have a look at you.'

She was wearing an artificial silk blouse and a thin cotton jacket. He unbuttoned it before she could move, ran his hand over her breasts casually, impersonally, not making a pass, just checking she did not need padding. Myrtle felt as though she was meat being appraised.

'Right,' said Mr de Souza, but without enthusiasm. 'You'll do. A hundred rupees a month and a meal every night. Plus a bonus on any drink you persuade a patron to buy. He may offer you the same – whisky, champagne, whatever, and you'll always accept. But actually you'll get ginger pop for champagne and cold tea for whisky. You may have to drink a lot of tea every night, but we're paying you for it. What do you say?'

'I'd like the job. What are the hours?'

'Start at eight every night, sharp. You've got to sit at tables with other girls, or around the walls, until the punters ask you to dance or sit with them. Ends here, three in the morning. Then maybe they want to take you home.'

'Oh, I can find my own way home.'

'I didn't mean that. They may want to take you back to *their* home. But that's up to you. If you do a deal with them, that's okay. But we have an honesty box. Twenty-five per cent. We trust you. If you screw us, then we won't trust you and you won't work here again. Ever.'

'Why should they pay me?'

'Are you kidding?'

The man looked at her sharply, his tiny eyes narrowed to points of light.

'She's very young,' da Leppo explained hastily. 'Just had an unfortunate experience with a much older man.'

'Oh, I see,' said de Souza. 'One of those, eh? Well, you'll see a lot of much older men here, so you'll soon learn. Right. See you tonight. Eight. Those the only clothes you can wear?'

'I've got a dance dress.'

'Come in that, then.'

He turned away from her. The interview was over.

Da Leppo said brightly, 'Well, that's better than walking the streets.'

'Yes,' she agreed. 'Thank you very much. But I still haven't paid your bill.'

'Don't think any more about it,' he said easily. 'One day I help you and one day maybe you can help me. That's the way of the world. Give and give alike.'

He took her arm, propelled her out to the street. After the dimness of Ruggiani's, the sun hurt her eyes. She hurried home to her mother.

'I've found a better job,' she explained. 'As a dancer.'

'Don't do it,' warned her mother earnestly. 'You'll be with men then, and they're all beasts. They only want one thing. They'll tell you any lie, make up any story, cheat you every way for it. And when they've got it, they just drop you. Walk away and leave you. And by then maybe you're pregnant, like I was. I was lucky to meet your stepfather. He's an honourable man.'

Myrtle turned away so her mother would not see the revulsion on her face. At least working so late would give Uncle Jem less chance to visit her at night. She could not bear to think of his body pressed against hers again, inside her, legs entwined, mouth like a sucker fish on hers, the sickly smell of his pomade strong as poisoned honey.

'Still, perhaps it's not such a bad move, after all,' her mother said more cheerfully after a few moments; so much of her life had been grey and unsuccessful, a perpetual struggle to survive, that she always tried to make the most of any situation. 'You might become a famous dancer, maybe an actress. Look at Merle Oberon.'

She was the prime example held up to every half-caste girl as an Anglo-Indian who had successfully broken the mould and escaped from the rut of obscurity as Muriel O'Brien to become a famous film star in Hollywood. She had made her own way out of this no man's, no woman's land where you did not belong to one race or another; where you only drifted, without a past you could admit to; where you told lies, pretending to be someone you weren't with a background you didn't know. And where you could make terrible and mortifying mistakes. When a British soldier asked where you lived in England, you told him the first town that came into your head, Basingstoke, Sheffield, Manchester. Then he'd ask what part, and you panicked and replied desperately: 'The cantonment'. He would look at you first in amazement and then with realisation, and he would say, 'Oh, a chi-chi', and all too often that was the last time you saw him.

Myrtle started work that night. De Souza had been a civilian clerk in the office of a British regiment and had run off with a corporal's wife. Someone had advanced him money – or perhaps he had helped himself to it – and he had started this café. There were other rumours about his past, with possibly an element of truth in all of them. The girls didn't like him, but at least he didn't interfere with them, never touched them up. His wife saw to that. She was tough and hard and kept as cold an eye on them as on her husband.

The turnover of dance hostesses was high. By day a few of the more fortunate girls worked as shop assistants in the Army and Navy Stores or Davichand's Emporium, or at any other job that would accept girls with coffee-coloured or alabaster complexions, and no qualifications. Most, like Myrtle, had to rely on what de Souza paid them, although they boasted to each other of rich and unbelievably generous men friends, and of future starring parts in revues. The restaurant's main attraction were two White Russian dancers, Romanov and Julia, who made three fifteen-minute appearances every night. They were unrelated and unmarried, both twenty-three, and shared a background of penury in Paris where their parents had fled after the Revolution. They did not possess passports, only League of Nations papers that allowed them to travel to whatever countries accepted such scanty documentation. This meant they were doomed to work the world's dreariest theatrical circuit: second-rate restaurants, bars and seedy cellars optimistically described as night clubs in Rangoon, Shanghai, Hong Kong, Calcutta – and then back again to Rangoon. But now, with the war, they were limited to India: Calcutta, Bombay, Delhi.

On some afternoons, when staff were off duty, Myrtle made a few extra rupees preparing vegetables, washing dishes, laying tables and emptying ashtrays. This meant she had the chance to see Romanov and Julia rehearse. Their dedication impressed her. When they finished their routine, sweating and out of breath in the airless room, she would make tea for them and sometimes join them in their tiny dressing room in the brief interval before her night job began. She was excited by what seemed to her a glamorous way of living; at least it was better than sitting at an empty table until a customer asked her to dance.

'You put everything into your act,' she told them once.

'We have to,' Romanov replied simply. 'It's our life. All we've got. We've nothing else, no skills, no letters after our names.'

'But it's such hard work, so hot in here, and you make it look so easy.'

'It's easier than being cold, sleeping on the pavement with an empty belly,' Julia pointed out quickly.

'But what happens when you grow old?' asked Myrtle.

'What happens to you when *you* grow old?' Romanov retorted. 'Oh, I know all you dancers hope to become famous film actresses or marry rich husbands, but do you personally know anyone who has done that? No? I thought not. We hope to save enough money to be independent, though to be honest that doesn't seem likely from what these bastards pay us here.'

'You were born in Calcutta?' Julia asked Myrtle.

'Rawalpindi.'

There was no point in pretending otherwise. So many Anglo-Indian girls felt obliged to claim they were born in the Argentine, or that their parents were Scottish landowners who had sent them to India because of their huge investments in local jute firms.

'You want to get out of here,' Julia advised her solemnly. 'This is a very small town.'

'It's the second city in the British Empire,' replied Myrtle proudly.

'People praised Rome as the first city in the Roman Empire – until that collapsed,' replied Romanov drily.

Myrtle did not argue. She did not really know what he meant, but their cynicism worried her. What *would* she do when she grew old? Her stepfather had a pension; the railway was good about these things. But she did not work for the railway. She tried to shake the horrible thought of future poverty from her mind, but like a tapeworm it sank hooks into her and would not let go.

One day, Myrtle was late – her mother had influenza – and she arrived at the restaurant just before it opened for the evening. She had promised to bring Julia a cup of tea before the first show and hurried along to her dressing room to explain the delay. Julia was sitting at her dressing table in front of a mirror festooned with shadeless electric bulbs, her face in her hands. She was wearing tights and a crumpled ballet skirt. Sticks of make-up, open powder boxes and pots of cold cream without lids littered the table.

Julia raised her face briefly as Myrtle entered. Her make-up was streaked with tears.

'What's the matter?' Myrtle asked in amazement. Julia was a

heroine to her, a beautiful dancing butterfly. She had never seen her like this, weeping, defeated.

'They're not renewing our contract,' Julia explained.

'But why not? You're so popular.'

'That's nothing to do with it. We came here initially for three months. That was extended to six, and we assumed we'd get another extension. But the work permit people won't allow it.'

'What are you going to do?'

'We had the offer of two months in Bombay last week, but we were so sure we would be staying on we turned it down.'

'Have you any money saved?'

'Only a couple of hundred chips. Nothing, really.'

'So what will you do?'

'I don't know. Romanov doesn't know, either, and he's usually pretty good at finding something.'

'But you've lots of rich friends here, haven't you?'

'Acquaintances,' Julia corrected her.

'But they take you out to the races on Saturdays. And you have supper at Firpo's with them on Sunday when this place is closed. You've told me so. Won't they help you?'

'How?'

'Surely one can put in a word with someone who counts at the permit office?'

'I've asked several, but they all say they can't help. They're afraid of their wives, really. If they found out their husbands were helping us, they could put two and two together.'

'What do you mean exactly?'

'Have I got to spell it out? Look, I've been to bed with everyone who *could* help me. *That's* what I mean. And understandably, they want to keep that quiet. They're all married, you see. Big people. *Burra sahibs*, as they like to call themselves. And all yellow inside, bloody cowards.'

Myrtle stood looking at Julia, an idea forming in her mind.

'Maybe I can help you,' she said at last.

'How can you possibly help us?' asked Julia sharply, looking up at her through narrowed, suspicious eyes. Was this kid having her on?

'I have an idea.'

'This wants more than an idea, girl. This wants a job, a contract. Think you can give us that?'

'I *may* be able to give you something better,' said Myrtle.

'Really?'

Julia turned her back on Myrtle without waiting for an answer. She opened the table drawer, took out a medicine bottle of vodka, drank two draughts neat. Outside, beyond the room's thin wooden door where her faded dressing gown hung on a nail, the band was tuning up. They began to play the opening number, 'Three Little Fishes', as Myrtle took her seat at her usual table.

The first regulars came in, flush-faced, sweating, slack-bellied men in creased lightweight suits. They ordered large John Collinses or double whiskies and sat, smoking, each at an individual table. A few younger men came in and sat drinking Murree beer; then some British officers on leave, red-faced, short-haired.

The band played on. Other hostesses arrived, to sit on a bench along one wall or at tables, eyes flitting across the room, trying to look attractive to potential customers. Myrtle caught one man's eye. He was in his late forties, pale-eyed, red-faced, his hair yellow like greased straw. She had danced with him on several occasions but only knew his name because she had once seen a letter addressed to Mr Sidney Crossman drop out of his jacket pocket. He nodded to her inquiring gaze. She crossed to his table, sat down.

'Have a whisky,' he suggested. The waiter brought her an iced tea.

'You're very quiet,' he said, turning towards her, expecting conversation, wanting to be amused.

'I've something on my mind,' she explained. He looked at her in mock alarm.

'Not expecting, are you?'

He meant the remark as a joke.

'No. Nothing like that. It's just about my friend, Julia, the dancer. She and Romanov have got to go.'

'Why? Been some trouble, has there?'

To Mr Crossman, the word 'trouble' could mean only one thing. Some wife had discovered a husband's infidelity and Julia was blamed. Calcutta wives possessed an uncanny knack of knowing when husbands had been even passingly unfaithful.

'No. Their work permits are not being renewed,' Myrtle explained.

'They'll be back,' said Crossman confidently, relieved that it was nothing more serious. He had entertained Julia on a number of occasions in his office on Sunday afternoons when the building was officially closed. It was safer there than in an hotel room where someone might see them arrive and tell his wife. There had been several similar incidents in the past, and his wife had taken them very badly. Another could be serious, and he had to be careful. A lot was at stake. He was a rich man with a position in Calcutta society to maintain.

'I'd like to help them,' Myrtle told them.

'How?'

'I know you've taken her out,' she began tentatively, and saw Crossman's eyes narrow warily. How the hell did this chi-chi kid know that? He did not realise she was only guessing. If he had denied it then, Myrtle would have instantly apologised, but he did not deny it.

'Well?' he asked her sharply, defensively.

'Lots of others also take her out.'

'I don't doubt that. She's attractive. No harm in that.'

Crossman's voice was edged with belligerence. She sensed alarm churning just below the surface. She had seen his wife once, a woman of uncertain age and even more uncertain temper. Myrtle felt calmer now, in control; she was on the right track.

'What I am going to suggest,' she began hesitantly, not really ready to put forward her plan but throwing everything on the gamble, 'what I am going to suggest is that you and all your friends help her.'

'You mean have a whip-round, eh?'

'No. Something more. Something that will help you, too. You're a very successful businessman.'

'I have been called that, yes. I happen to be managing director of one of the largest jute concerns here in Calcutta.'

'I know. So why don't you all join together? Each put down some money, and between you start a club? Romanov and Julia could run it and appear every night, but it would be *your* club. You'd all have a share in the profits.'

'Who else would come in?'

'Well, people you know, who she knows. She has lots of friends, I'm told.'

'Dozens, I'd say. And all – ah – intimate friends, if you understand me?'

'I understand you. Say she knows a hundred – just for the sake of argument. You could call it the Century Club. Then they can stay on. You could still take her out – *and* draw a dividend.'

'You're pretty sharp. For a chi-chi.'

'I don't know about that. I'd just like to help her. She's my friend. I like her. Admire her, really.'

'So do I. Well, that's an idea, certainly.'

'It's going to be more than that,' said Myrtle quietly. A thought had come to her, an easy way to persuade Mr Crossman to agree, to push him firmly over the cliff of middle-aged married indecision.

'What do you mean?' Again, caution and concern sharpened his voice like a whetstone.

'Romanov keeps a list of all Julia's friends,' she said. '*And* the dates and times and places where they meet.'

He didn't, but the words added weight and a slightly sinister edge to her proposal.

'You mean he'd try and blackmail them – us?' asked Crossman in horror. 'I wouldn't stand for that. No way. I'm an easygoing chap. Ask anyone who knows me, they'll tell you that. But I will not be threatened.'

'You are not being threatened. No one is. All I'm offering you is a chance to make some money and at the same time remove all risk that anyone would even guess you had ever been, well, friendly with Julia. You might even put your share in your wife's name. Give her a present on her birthday, or on an anniversary or something. You can't lose, Mr Crossman.'

'This is bloody blackmail.'

'Not at all,' Myrtle assured him earnestly. 'Just a suggestion to help two friends – and a lot of very, very successful men.'

'Did she put you up to this?'

'No. I've just thought of it myself. When I sat down here with you. But it *is* a good idea, isn't it?'

Crossman nodded reluctantly. He could see its attraction, its possibilities.

'I thought it would interest you,' Myrtle told him triumphantly, and when he ordered another whisky she asked him for champagne. She was tired of cold tea.

Five weeks later, the Century Club opened. Romanov and Julia held a party on the opening night and champagne flowed, so guests assured them, exaggerating as people do on such occasions, like the fountains of Rome, which, to be accurate, none of them had ever seen. Ruggiani's customers had all heard about the party and were there; some men will go a long way for free champagne. Drinking and dancing continued through the night until the dawn came up, pink and clear, across the Hooghly River.

Myrtle did not see this. She stayed for barely half an hour. She had not liked to ask for time off from Ruggiani's, and she was due there as usual at eight o'clock. She was secretly surprised how easy it had been to persuade a number of middle-aged men with more money than courage to invest 10,000 rupees each in a venture which they could see for themselves would succeed. The money could be paid out of company funds, so that even the most inquisitive and suspicious wife, searching through the stubs of her husband's chequebooks to discover where he spent his money, would not find any tell-tale evidence.

What had hurt and amazed Myrtle had been Julia's totally unexpected reaction to her good fortune. At first, she had been amused at Myrtle's proposal; she did not imagine that she could carry it through. Then she adopted the whole idea as her own. Myrtle had only helped marginally to set it in motion.

'You will both be able to stay in Calcutta now as long as you like,' Myrtle pointed out.

'I know. All those friends *and* our own place. It's marvellous.'

'I'd like something out of it, too,' Myrtle told her awkwardly. She had not liked to ask before; she had assumed that Julia would offer what she must guess Myrtle wanted.

'What, exactly?' asked Julia, her voice now sharpening with surprise. Was this little chi-chi girl about to ask her for money?

'I'd like to work at the Century, instead of at Ruggiani's.'

'But we've got enough dancers,' Julia replied.

'How? Where from?' Myrtle was surprised.

'Oh, round about,' Julia said vaguely. 'They're European girls. Not a bit, well, dark-skinned, like you.'

'You won't get English girls dancing in these places,' Myrtle retorted hotly. 'It's beneath them. And they don't need the money. And, remember, I started the whole thing off. If I hadn't thought of this way to raise money, you and Romanov would be out of Calcutta by now *and* out of work.'

'Don't think I'm not grateful, child, for your help. But it's really for *me* that these men are doing this, not for you. I've known them all, well, intimately, as the newspapers say when they report divorce cases. Anyway, the dancers aren't English. They're Italian, French, Spanish, Rumanian, Russian like me.'

Now Myrtle understood. They must be whores from the high-class brothels in Coraya Road. There, in large houses screened by high walls and sheet-metal gates, women of many European nationalities plied their ancient trade. Julia was one of them at heart; the only difference was she did not work in the Road.

'Aren't they, well, busy at night?' Myrtle asked her.

'Not all of them. Afternoons are their busy time.'

'So there's no place for me at all at the Century Club, then? *Nothing* I can do?'

'We'll always be glad to see you, of course,' replied Julia carefully. 'But not in a working sense, dear. You must see that.'

'I do now,' said Myrtle bitterly. 'But I didn't. For if I had, I would never have tried to help you. Never.'

She walked back to Ruggiani's close to tears with disappointment and disbelief at such ingratitude. She went straight to the cloakroom the girls used beyond the kitchen, washed her face in cold water, checked her make-up, smoothed down her dress. Then she walked out onto the dance floor. The band was tuning up. She was early, the only hostess there. De Souza called to her from the back of the room.

'So you've come back, have you?' he asked her sarcastically.

'Of course. I'm on duty at eight.'

'Not any more, you aren't,' he retorted angrily. 'I hear you put that old fool Crossman up to raising money for this new Century Club.'

'I wanted to help Julia.'

'Wanted to help your bloody self, more likely,' he said sourly. 'We've lost all our customers tonight. They've taken every bloody one away. We've not a single booking. I've never had that before. Never. And all through you. You're fired. Here's your week's money.'

'But—'

'No buts. You're out. Now. Get your things and go.'

Myrtle walked out into the warm, steamy August evening.

Taxi horns blared like trumpets. Sweetmeat sellers on the pavements hoarsely called their wares. Tonga bells jingled as the horses trotted by. She heard none of these familiar sounds, but walked slowly and alone in a daze of misery. She had been let down by a woman she had tried to help, and then sacked by a man to whom she had been loyal. She had made a cardinal mistake, of course. She should have made it clear from the start that the price for her help was a job if her idea succeeded. Instead, she had trusted someone she admired. That was an error she would never repeat.

Standing beneath the colonnade outside the Grand Hotel on Chowringhee, tears now running unchecked down her face in her misery, Myrtle reached a conclusion that would change her whole life – and the lives of thousands she would never meet, whose names she would never know.

Never again would she be used. Never again would she do anyone a good turn unless a reciprocal favour was agreed in advance. From now on, her own interests would be her sole concern. She would not waste time or energy in anger at Julia's ingratitude; she would not get mad, but one day – and soon – she would get even.

The following morning, wearing a freshly ironed blouse and cotton skirt, Myrtle set out determined to find another job – anything. At first, she answered advertisements in *The Statesman* and *The Times of India* for office juniors, shop assistants, waitresses, but always without success.

Day after day, with a list of addresses in her handbag, she visited offices and shops, and each evening, tired, hungry and dispirited, with a headache from walking so far in Calcutta's enervating heat and humidity, her feet sore from climbing so many steep staircases, she came home still unemployed. She was not quite right for this job; she had arrived too late for that; another was no longer vacant. No one gave her what she believed must be the real reason for their refusals: she was Anglo-Indian.

Late one afternoon, as she left an insurance company's head office in Coraya Road after hearing that the job advertised had been unexpectedly filled from within the organisation that morning, she noticed a smartly dressed Englishwoman in her early forties paying off a taxi. She looked Myrtle up and down, not unsympathetically.

'You look tired,' she said as Myrtle approached, one woman stating an obvious fact to another.

'I am,' Myrtle admitted miserably.

'Come in and have a cup of tea.'

The idea was tempting, but Myrtle made a token protest for the sake of politeness.

'I can't do that. I'm on my way home.'

'You can, and you will,' the woman told her firmly, and led Myrtle into a house set back a little way from the road.

The hall was larger than any room Myrtle had ever seen, except in films, and furnished in an agreeably luxurious style, with silk covers and cushions on the chairs, and on the walls oil paintings of voluptuous, foreign-looking women wearing long flowing robes.

A gramophone was playing in another part of the house; not the dance tunes Myrtle had heard every night at Ruggiani's, but softer, gentler music. A slight and soothing scent from burning joss sticks hung sweetly in the air. Myrtle experienced an instant sense of relaxation. Here was none of the tension of home, with her stepfather coming in at odd hours, hanging his uniform jacket up on a nail behind the door, eating a supper as European as possible – two eggs and bacon, a mutton chop – regardless of its unsuitability in the heat. For the first time in her life, Myrtle came face to face with elegance; and later she would unconsciously model at least one room in all her houses on this hall.

They sat down and the woman rang for a bearer and ordered lemon tea and sandwiches. These arrived almost immediately – no waiting for a kettle on the electric ring, no listening to a mother's regularly repeated aphorism about a watched kettle never boiling.

'Looking for a job, are you?' the woman asked.

'Yes.'

The sharp clean taste of the scented tea revived her. She began to feel at ease in a way she had never known in the cramped conditions of a railway house. Thinly cut cucumber sandwiches were a revelation after crude slices of bread and melting margarine; they did not have a refrigerator at home.

'You've been working, of course?'

'I was a dance hostess. Ruggiani's. I got sacked.'

Myrtle told her about Romanov and Julia.

'Doesn't surprise me,' said the woman, shaking her head. 'If you help a lame dog over a stile – or, in this case, a lame bitch – you must expect to get bitten. Tell me, what is your name? I'm Eleanor Ransom. Mrs Ransom.'

Myrtle explained who she was.

'There could be a vacancy for a girl like you in this profession.'

'What profession is that?' asked Myrtle innocently.

Mrs Ransom smiled. 'What they call the oldest. Giving pleasure. Not altogether an unworthy calling, despite what people say – and answering a universal and timeless need. Otherwise it would never have lasted for so long.'

So *this* was a whore house. Myrtle had forgotten; Coraya Road was thick with them. Yet the house was not at all as she had imagined such a place would be. But then what had she ever thought a brothel would be like? She had no idea, really, except that it must be evil and, well, *nasty*.

'I couldn't do that,' she said quickly.

'Depends what you are asked to do, dearie. Some men want it straight. Others have different ideas.'

'What d'you mean?'

'They want to dress up, put on rubber masks, get beaten, told they're naughty boys.'

'I can't believe it,' said Myrtle incredulously.

'It's a fact. So you don't have to get down on your back if you don't want to.'

'I don't want to.'

'You have a strong reason, judging from your voice. Is it religious?'

Mrs Ransom sounded solicitous. She listened sympathetically as Myrtle haltingly told her about Uncle Jem.

'I quite understand how you feel,' the older woman said at once. 'But there need be nothing like that here.'

'Surely there has to be?'

'Not at all. Some men are simply lonely. They just want to talk. Nothing very wrong in that, is there?'

'I suppose not. But there can't be many who *just* want to talk, surely?'

'You'd be surprised. I see you've a lot to learn. About life and love, and what one can mean to the other. Are you free for an hour?'

'Well, yes. Totally – unfortunately.'

Mrs Ransom had been kind to her; the least she owed her in return was an honest answer.

'Then I may be able to put you right on a few points.'

She crossed to a panel in the wall, pressed a button Myrtle had not seen. The panel slid to one side. Mrs Ransom motioned to Myrtle to follow her up a narrow staircase. Behind them, the panel closed silently. A light glowed above their heads. Mrs Ransom put a finger to her lips and shook her head warningly to stress the need for silence. They reached a small landing, also dimly lit. As Myrtle's eyes grew accustomed to the gloom she could see on one wall a small door of the kind that seals a serving hatch between a kitchen and a dining room.

Mrs Ransom slid this carefully to one side. They were looking through a glass pane into a room with pink walls, a pink couch, a pink, shell-scalloped washbasin and shaded lights. On the bed sat a bored girl wearing a half-open silk kimono. Her breasts were full and soft. Standing by her, grotesque, because his trousers were down over his shoes, stood a man of middle age. He still wore a well-cut alpaca jacket, his shirt and a striped club tie. With surprise, Myrtle recognised the manager of a counting house who, two days earlier, had refused her a job.

She turned to Mrs Ransom in her surprise, but she shook her head violently; Myrtle was not to speak. The girl was stroking the man's penis, which resolutely refused to rise. It was a disgusting sight, Myrtle thought, remembering Uncle Jem. She shivered at the recollection.

Mrs Ransom closed the trap door carefully, and they moved on to peer through similar one-way mirrors into other rooms, where girls and men sat, lay, stood in various sexual poses, but none actually having intercourse. Then they went down the stairs into the sitting room.

'You see,' said Mrs Ransom then, pouring out more tea. 'We don't ask *too* much of our girls. We know what they can't or won't do, and what liberties they will allow. Would you like to join them?'

'No,' said Myrtle firmly. 'I'm sorry, but I wouldn't. But thank you very much indeed for trying to help me.'

'Trying to help myself,' Mrs Ransom replied frankly. 'We always need new girls. Look, don't refuse out of hand. You're tired and it's been a hot day – monsoon due very soon, I think. So why not give this a trial – no more? We'll not ask you to do anything that really offends you. And you'd be well paid. Better than walking the streets.'

'I would only be a streetwalker of a different kind,' Myrtle pointed out.

'Possibly,' Mrs Ransom agreed. 'But as I say, rather better paid. A thousand rupees a month better paid.'

'A fortune!' gasped Myrtle in amazement. This was ten times her pay at Ruggiani's.

'And we will still make a profit on it, I must tell you, because we have to, otherwise we'd be out of business. But it *is* a lot better than serving in the soft-furnishing department of the Army and Navy Stores, or dancing with partners every night and drinking cold tea to their whisky. You can't deny that. And, I still maintain, infinitely better than *trying* to get a job. Is your answer still no?'

'No,' said Myrtle at once. 'It's yes. I'll take it.'

As she spoke she thought ruefully how soon early religious teaching and a strict upbringing could be forgotten, buried, perhaps never to be remembered again. This knowledge, suddenly so clear and sharp, would influence her whole life, her choice of decisions, everyone and everything with whom she came in contact.

So she began a trial period of three months in Mrs Ransom's house. Mrs Ransom was as good as her word, but Myrtle hated the job, hated herself and, most of all, hated the combination of circumstances, totally out of her control, that had made her earn a living like this.

She was thankful she did not have to accept the men as lovers. She dealt with many who could not be lovers in any normal sense, who found brief pleasure and release by manipulating dildoes, in talking rather than doing what they thought about so passionately. Sometimes she stroked them, often without any response to her increasingly expert manipulations; sometimes she took men in her mouth. Always she despised them and their needs, but she found them individually sad and often pathetically inadequate, although some were extremely successful in their careers. She had not realised that men could be like this; the realisation did nothing to lessen her distrust and dislike of them. To her they were not just a different sex; they seemed to belong to an entirely different race.

She told herself she must save money while she had the chance. She opened a bank account, lived on a hundred rupees a month, paying her mother half as always, telling her she was now working as a personal assistant to a lady in business, which, in a sense, was true. But increasingly she loathed the smell of men's sweat and semen, and the whole unhealthy trinity of soft lights and expensive perfume and sex on sale. After three months, she admitted to Mrs Ransom she must leave.

'I don't want you to think I'm not grateful,' she said earnestly, 'but I just can't go on like this. I don't like men, not after Uncle Jem, and I just cannot continue. I'm sorry, but I have to be honest with you.'

'Don't apologise,' said Mrs Ransom sympathetically. 'I admire you for it. I used to feel the same when I started. Going against the grain, against your conscience, is a very insidious thing. You tell yourself you'll save money, and I think you probably have, but no amount of money can pay for some things you may have to endure in order to acquire it. Things that may be trivial in themselves, perhaps a pleasure to others, but hell for you.

'I'm relatively well off now,' Mrs Ransom went on, 'but I still go on, because money takes hold of you. You go after it and then suddenly it's like a race, or a game we used to play at school. It stops running away from you and turns and runs after you. And then, my dear, you run for ever, till the day you die. But keep in touch, and if you ever need any help, remember me.'

'Thank you. I will.'

Neither could guess in what strange and unimagined circumstances Myrtle would keep her promise.

So Myrtle began another search for work, but by now she had become accustomed to pleasant, comfortable surroundings, and good meals. She had even developed a liking for wines, although before meeting Mrs Ransom she had hardly even tasted wine, and after her experience with Uncle Jem, she abhorred spirits. None of the jobs she applied for paid more than a fraction of what she had earned with Mrs Ransom; and more and more she recognised partners and directors in the offices as former clients – and wondered whether they remembered the often bizarre circumstances of their earlier meetings.

She did not tell her mother she was out of work and still left her home every morning at the same time, looking for a job, almost any job, she told herself, but no one wanted to employ a chi-chi girl. One afternoon, after yet another refusal from a shop on Chowringhee, she seriously considered going back to Mrs Ransom. She paused under the colonnade outside the Grand Hotel where she had stood after de Souza dismissed her. Street vendors were selling regimental badges and balloons and stolen medal ribbons to passers-by. A small Indian boy played 'South of the Border' on a bamboo flute.

At least they're all making money, Myrtle thought enviously. I'm doing nothing. I'm back exactly where I started. She had gone full circle and she could not see any way forward. For the first time, she felt such despair she even thought of taking her own life. Her whole existence was a sham. She was reluctant to spend much time at home because of Uncle Jem, and to her mother's surprise had taken to shutting herself up in her room.

Indian boys came running along the pavement carrying bundles of newspapers.

'Special edition!' they called importantly. Her thoughts still on her own problems, she bought one, wondering why they were selling a special edition at that hour. She read the main headline: ALLIES DROP SUPER-BOMBS ON JAPAN: WAR END IN SIGHT.

The news seemed to have no direct relevance to her; against her problems, it seemed insignificant.

As she stood irresolute, her mind in a ferment, she noticed someone leaning against one of the pillars regarding her quizzically through a haze of cigarette smoke. Mr da Leppo.

'I wondered how long it would take before you saw I was here,' he said. 'I heard that Mr de Souza was not very pleased with you. Do I understand right? It was rather unwise, Myrtle, trying to help someone as you did. You must think these things out thoroughly before you act, you know.'

'I will next time,' agreed Myrtle fervently.

'And I hear from my old friend, Eleanor Ransom, that you have also left her establishment?'

'How do you know her?'

'Sometimes my services are called for. Life is a matter of barter, you know. We must all help each other, and the wider our circle of friends, the better for all concerned. Now, I may be able to help you. I have an acquaintance who is looking for a companion. He is a very wealthy man, a baronet, who controls jute companies here, a fruit-canning concern in Sydney, Australia, an iron-ore mine in Canada, a firm making motor cars in England. A very, very successful man indeed.'

'Is he a widower?' asked Myrtle suspiciously. 'Why does he need a companion?'

'As far as I know, he has never been married. Really, I think he's after someone who could be more of a personal assistant. Companion is not quite the right word. He has secretaries in his office, of course, but he's usually only in India for a few months in the year, although with the war on, he spends more time here because passages to England and Australia are very hard to come by – even to someone in his position. He wants someone who is intelligent, good looking, and who can keep his diary, day to day, make appointments, and act responsibly on his behalf when he is here.'

'But I know nothing about business. I can't even type.'

'That is not an essential requirement in this instance. I have formed a high opinion of your loyalty – even if it has not yet been reciprocated by Mr de Souza or that White Russian couple. Loyalty is a rare quality. Never underestimate your own abilities, my dear.'

'I'd like to meet him,' said Myrtle. 'But why are you doing this for me? I still owe you – I don't even know yet how much – for my operation.'

She could not bring herself to speak the word abortion. Even after her experiences in Mrs Ransom's house, it was against all her religious teaching, all her upbringing.

'Well, this will be in the nature of paying off that debt. Mr de Souza would have paid me an introductory fee if things had worked out, but they didn't, and so he didn't. This gentleman will also defray my expenses – if you prove suitable. So, for both our sakes, I hope you do. To give yourself a better chance, I will personally advance you enough to buy a rather smarter dress, shoes and handbag than you have now. If you don't get the job, then I'll bear this expense – which should convince you of my confidence in you. Remember, being smart is as much looking smart as anything else. If you don't *look* the part, you won't get the part. Who would give any credence to an ambassador who was unshaven, with scuffed shoes, or a managing director wearing a suit covered in soup stains?'

Mr da Leppo smiled at the absurdity of such suggestions. He took two 100 rupee notes from an imitation lizard skin wallet, handed them to Myrtle.

'You can pay me back sometime. A bit every month if you like, out of your salary. Or, if you get on with him, and he gives you some tips – he owns a number of racehorses – you might even hear of a certainty and pass me the horse's name. Gambling is my great spare-time interest. Anyhow, here's his address.'

He took a piece of paper from the wallet. On it Myrtle read, 'Sir Hilary Mackenzie, Bt' and an address beyond Fort Belvedere, one of Calcutta's richer suburbs.

'When shall I see him?' she asked.

'At half past five today. I told him you'd be along. So you had better hurry and buy some new clothes.'

'You knew I would leave Mrs Ransom?'

'No. I just thought you would and when I heard you had, I made an appointment for you. You are cut out for better things, Myrtle.'

'Thank you,' she said. 'I hope you're right.'

'I know, therefore I am,' da Leppo replied enigmatically.

Myrtle went into the nearest dress shop, bought herself a new dress – a bargain at the price – new shoes, a handbag. In the ladies' room she washed her face, combed her hair vigorously until it shone, made up her lips, put a little powder on the cheekbones to make her look slightly paler than she really was. Then she hailed a taxi to take her to *The Statesman* newspaper office where she spoke to a sub-editor who had been a regular visitor to Mrs Ransom's house. She asked him whether he could give her any details about Sir Hilary Mackenzie. He produced a folder of newspaper cuttings which she read through quickly. She wanted to know all she could about the man who might offer her a job. As another client, an Army colonel, had told her: 'Time spent in reconnaissance is seldom wasted.'

The Mackenzie Building stood several storeys high, with a smart Indian *chowkidar* in a well-pressed khaki uniform on the door. An Anglo-Indian girl sat at a typewriter behind the reception desk. As their eyes met, each silently queried the other's background. Did this newcomer want her job? the receptionist thought anxiously. Myrtle wondered why the receptionist had not been chosen as Sir Hilary's personal assistant.

She went up in the lift to the top storey. A middle-aged Englishwoman was waiting for her by the door.

'Myrtle Gibson?' she asked pleasantly enough.

'Yes. Mr da Leppo told me Sir Hilary Mackenzie wished to see me.'

The woman looked her up and down, hanging price tags on her clothes, then more sharply at Myrtle's powdered cheekbones, at her skin that was not quite fair.

'Please come this way,' she said more coldly.

Myrtle followed her across the landing. She knocked at a door, opened it. Myrtle went inside. The woman closed the door silently behind her.

Myrtle was standing in a wide room with a richly polished wood floor like decking on an ocean liner. Oil paintings of old men, wearing high collars, sometimes cravats, and all with heavy, dull, brooding eyes looked down on her. There was a strong smell of beeswax furniture polish. At the far end of the room, looking out of the window, stood a man about her own height, his face half in profile. An air-conditioning machine set into the window hummed like a swarm of bees.

'You have come in response to Mr da Leppo's introduction?' the man asked her, not turning to look at her.

His voice was soft and yet had a sharp edge to it; the tones of wealth and power – and something else, she was not yet quite sure what. He turned and she saw that his face seemed curiously soft, as though it was not really flesh but flesh-coloured putty moulded into place. His chin and cheeks were smooth. He looked at her now, and his eyes were hard as stones.

'Yes, sir,' she admitted nervously. 'He told me you wanted a companion.'

'In life's journey, we all need companions,' Sir Hilary allowed sententiously. 'Can you type, or do shorthand?'

'No, sir. I told Mr da Leppo I did not have those skills. He said it didn't matter.'

'Well, what *can* you do?'

He sounded impatient now, as though a little girl with suspiciously dark skin, powdered to make it appear white, was simply wasting his time. The dress, which had appeared so smart in the shop, now seemed cheap and tawdry in the presence of solid wealth. The figures in the portraits looked down at her contemptuously.

'I am willing to learn anything, sir.'

'*Anything?*' he repeated. 'That could be a wide area in which to seek knowledge and instruction.'

She did not know what to say. She had never met anyone who made her feel so small, so second-rate, so poor. Sir Hilary stood looking at her again, as though making up his mind whether to be rid of her now. She was obviously quite unsuitable for whatever post he had in mind.

And yet, watching him, Myrtle felt irritation rise in her as mercury rises in a thermometer on a summer morning just before noon. Why should this man treat her like this? She had come directly in response to an invitation. He must have known she could not type, so why be sarcastic when he had so much and she had so little?

'You live with your parents?' he asked her.

'With my mother and my stepfather, sir.'

'I have made some inquiries. He works on the railway, I understand?'

'Yes, he does.'

'And your father?'

For a moment, she paused.

'He was in the Army, sir,' she said proudly. 'The British Army. A sergeant.'

'I see. And doubtless returned to England before you were born?'

She nodded, surprised. How could he know her innermost secret, facts so carefully shielded from all outsiders, facts that had made her who she was, what she was, an unemployed chi-chi girl from a Calcutta back street?

'Well,' he said. 'If you really want to learn a skill – *learn this.*'

With a quick movement of his right hand, Sir Hilary unzipped his fly buttons. His erect penis seemed to leap out at Myrtle like a thick and rubbery jack-in-the-box. She stared at it in amazement and disbelief. Were *all* men like Mrs Ransom's clients?

'What do you mean?' she asked, her astonishment at his behaviour making her voice sound shrill and unnatural.

'You know damn well what I mean. Get down on it – *now.* Do what I hear you learned to do so often and so well

- and with such enthusiasm - in Coraya Road.'

Myrtle stood, bereft of speech, staring as though mesmerised by the organ protruding from the light duck of his trousers. Inconsequentially, she noticed their perfect crease, a glimpse of white silk underpants. Her hatred of men welled up within her in a soaring, boiling flood. She hated Uncle Jem for what he had done to her. She hated Mr de Souza for dismissing her, and Romanov, who, with Julia, had abandoned and betrayed her. And even though da Leppo had helped her, doubtless he only did so to make certain of his fee.

Memories of all the men - plump, tall, small, bald, hairy - with whom and for whom she had done unmentionable things in Mrs Ransom's house rose up like bile in her throat. The recollection of their expensive aftershave lotions and scented hair oil stank now like raw sewage in her nose. She hated them all. But most of all, she hated this dandified creature before her.

'Don't just stand there, gawking! Get down!' Sir Hilary's voice cracked like a whiplash.

Loathing herself, Myrtle crouched on her knees in a position of supplication - or perversion. She took the organ between her lips, ran her tongue slowly, expertly across the tip.

'Come on!' he snapped. 'Get to it!'

She might have been a dog, a bitch, a slave for hire, and of course that was what she was, except she had not been hired. Sir Hilary was worse than any of the men she had pleasured in Mrs Ransom's house. At least they had paid; he had not even promised to pay.

Then a sudden realisation cut through her rage and hatred. She glanced up at Sir Hilary and saw him looking down at her, mockingly. His eyes were half closed, his lips sneering at her compliance.

She withdrew the organ from her mouth.

'I will do just as you ask, sir,' she assured him politely.

Myrtle thrust his huge phallus gently into her mouth moving forward until she felt its tip touch her throat.

Then, taking a deep breath, Myrtle snapped shut her jaws and bit through it with all the strength she possessed. Her teeth ground together, and she felt the severed end, soft and salty, on her tongue.

THREE

The Past: Tokyo, Japan, 1945

Shortly before eleven o'clock that night, when humidity hung like a damp woollen blanket across the roofs of Tokyo, the Emperor's old Rolls-Royce, all lights extinguished, set out from the Imperial Palace.

Up front, an armed guard rode with the driver. In the back of the car, on a raised brocaded seat that smelled faintly of camphor, sat a tiny man, his head sunk on his chest, eyes closed behind thick pebble lenses already misted by the moist night air.

Emperor Hirohito, direct descendant of Amaterasu, the sun goddess, and thus declared the Son of Heaven, God of the Sun, Divine Emperor of the Sun, as all his ancestors had been and as all his descendants would surely be, was riding to the capital's broadcasting studio to record a message to his people unique in his country's long and turbulent history.

This would be the first time anyone outside his own immediate family and his entourage in the royal household had ever heard the Emperor's voice – or indeed the voice of any other Japanese emperor. It would be revered as the voice of Divinity, awesome, majestic, and now giving tidings not of victory but of unparalleled national humiliation. He would explain that on the following day, or the 14th of the 8th month of the 20th year of his reign of Showa – the word meant enlightenment and peace – the end of his ancient feudal empire was at hand. The Japanese had lost the war they had started so ill-advisedly on a December morning four years earlier. They were defeated and about to be totally humbled. The alternative to such abject surrender was that their country would be obliterated from the face of the earth and become as though it had never been.

The car slid silently through deserted streets littered with rubble from air raids and lined by blackened and burned-out buildings that stood like some enormous theatrical stage against the waning moon. The Emperor lowered his window on its pearl-handled winder and looked out into the damp, steamy darkness, myopically seeking some sign of life, of hope for the nation's future and his own. There was none. Tokyo at that hour, with thoroughfares unlit because the central generating station had been destroyed, lay naked to its enemies, a city of the doomed, the dying and the dead.

Around the rim of some ruined office blocks and shops, tongues of flame still flickered, and he heard the distant crash of falling timber, smelled charred wood from the frames of paper houses and the unforgettable sweet stench of roasted human flesh.

The city was a charnel house in which 200,000 people had already been killed in the barbarous air raids of the Americans. And now two bombs of gigantic and apparently immeasurable size had destroyed whole areas of Hiroshima and Nagasaki. Unless the Emperor's government immediately sued for peace, the whole country could be calcified, reduced within hours to a desert of smoking ash and burned bones.

The Emperor had known privately for many months that the war was lost, but his generals and admirals could not bring themselves to admit defeat, and he lacked the courage to do so.

Like Hitler in his bunker beneath Berlin, Hirohito's staff moved mythical armies and non-existent battle fleets on wall maps, and spoke about secret weapons of devastating power which, even at this late and desperate stage, would bring victory to the Son of Heaven.

He had allowed them to delude themselves, for in such delusions lay some seeds of comfort for him; and they *might* be right; perhaps there *was* an answer to the overwhelming strength of Japan's adversaries. He had hoped so, but hope was not reality, and the two bombs, in which his scientists told him atoms had been split to give to men the power of gods, were a terrible portent of horrors still to come. The three Allied leaders, President Roosevelt, Mr Churchill and Marshal Stalin, had solemnly proclaimed this in a joint declaration issued after their meeting in Potsdam months earlier. Copies of the document, translated into Japanese, had rained down by the hundred thousand from giant B-29 bombers to inform all who could read that the alternative to surrender would be national oblivion, and not at some vague and future date, but now.

'The prodigious land, sea and air forces of the United States, the British Empire and of China, many times reinforced by their armies and air fleets from the West, are poised to strike the final blows upon Japan . . . to prosecute the war against Japan until she ceases to exist.

'The might that now converges on Japan is immeasurably greater than that which, when applied to the resisting Nazis, necessarily laid waste the land, the industry and the method of life of the whole German people. The full application of military power, backed by our resolve, will mean the inevitable and complete destruction of the Japanese armed forces, and just as inevitably, the utter devastation of the Japanese homeland.'

This was fact; all the rest was illusion, wishful thinking, impossible dreams. The Emperor's ministers had already sent frantic messages to the Russians, with whom they had a longstanding Treaty of Neutrality which still had one year to run, begging them to intercede with their advancing Allies. Russia, although an ally of the United States and Britain and China against Germany, had still not declared war on Japan. But no amount of appeals and entreaties could extract from Moscow even the basic courtesy of an acknowledgement. The Japanese leaders could not understand this. They did not know how, at Potsdam, President Roosevelt had promised Stalin great areas of Europe as his fiefdom if he would declare war against a Japan already all but beaten. Stalin, watchful, cautious, cunning as a fox, decided to wait until Japan was about to capitulate; then he would attack. Against such a prize, for such a tiny price, what worth had a treaty with a nation about to die?

The Emperor, his stomach twisted with anguish at the thought of the approaching annihilation of his country, knew nothing of this. Less than four years earlier, he had ridden in full dress uniform on his white charger through these same streets of Tokyo decked then with flags and flowers, and had been applauded by thousands of his cheering subjects. Indeed, it appeared they had much to applaud. Hong Kong and Singapore had fallen. Japanese armies had subdued the Americans in the Pacific, the British and Dutch in Malaya, Burma, and the Dutch East Indies. They stood poised to march into India and invade the great empty continent of Australia.

Control of the whole Eastern world lay within his country's grasp – or so it had seemed. Japan's dream of half a hundred years was about to become reality. The country would emerge from its long sleep in the East to claim equality with the United States, the British Empire, and every advanced European country. Now, this was only an empty, ironic memory, recalled by faded newspaper photographs carefully pasted in a royal album.

The Rolls stopped outside a darkened building that

contained the capital's recording and broadcasting studios.
Sandbags had been piled around the main door, and strips of
paper pasted across windows as a pathetic defence against
bomb blast. The guard jumped down, opened the car's rear
door and bowed to the ground. Hirohito walked past him into
the studio. Behind him, a steward locked and bolted the door.
Was this to keep others out or himself inside? The thought disturbed Hirohito. A pulse began to beat in his neck as he looked
around the small room, heavy with the pungent smell of stale
cigarette smoke.

All windows here were sealed with black paper lest any
chink of light should be seen by an enemy aircraft. Thick
curtains draped the walls to muffle sound. The Emperor had
never been inside a broadcasting studio, and as a man far more
interested in scientific matters than in politics or war, or even
in ruling a country as the Son of Heaven, he would have liked
to question the technicians about the equipment. But this was
not the time, or the place; and yet he might never have another
opportunity.

A court chamberlain, formally dressed in morning suit with
pointed tailcoat and striped trousers, bowed from the waist as
he handed to the Emperor the text of the message he was to
record. This was based on a speech he had made at an Imperial
conference earlier that day, held in a concrete air raid shelter
concealed beneath a hillock in the grounds of the Imperial
Palace.

Only a few in Tokyo were aware of the shelter's existence; it
would not be politic to allow the general public to know that
their Emperor had access to a safe refuge when they did not.
The shelter did not have air-conditioning, and with its thick,
steel door closed and bolted, it quickly became so hot and
stuffy that the Imperial Protocol Section had been unable to
insist on the usual court wear of striped trousers and tailcoats.
Only the Prime Minister, Suzuki, had worn morning dress.
The rest sat in shirt sleeves, but so that some semblance of

dignity could be maintained, a royal servant had handed out a
black tie to each man as he arrived.

The Minister of War and then the Army and Navy Chiefs of
Staff had all made set and expected speeches. In these they
declared that the country should fight on, because the Allies
could not hope to win. Agreed, Burma and Malaya might eventually be regained by the British with the help of Indian
and other colonial troops, but Japan was strong, Japan was
eternal.

The Navy Chief of Staff, however, ended his peroration
with a deliberately ambiguous statement: 'We cannot say that
final victory is certain, but neither do we believe we can be
finally defeated.' Both chiefs insisted that they were personally
prepared to die fighting for their country and their Emperor,
as were all the forces they commanded. Any other decision
would be totally against their training and, more important,
the nation's will. Death, to the Japanese, was always infinitely
preferable to dishonour.

Death, Hirohito thought musingly as he heard these familiar
statements, was the necessary end to every life, but to the
Japanese death was also very much more. They embraced it,
and acclaimed it as a suitable, even welcome end to any
problem they could not otherwise solve. To die meant that
earthly honour, in an individual or a nation, could be kept
bright and unsullied. Westerners could never understand their
closeness with death, the feeling of release that it could bring,
or why men, women, even children announced daily that they
were willing to die for this cause or that, to accept death as a
friend, without complaints, tears or regret. Death was their last
option, the ultimate resolution of every argument. No enemy
could pursue them through the eternal mists, and surely that in
itself must be a victory of a kind.

If anyone failed, in their own opinion or estimation, they
would commit suicide, believing that this deed discharged all
debts and all deceits. Civilians would uncomplainingly take

their lives with a small dagger in the traditional ceremony known as *seppuku*. Men-at-arms would fall upon their ancestral swords and then lie on the ground, the blade within their bowels, biting through their tongues to contain the unbelievable agony as their steaming entrails spilled out of the gaping, pulsing wound.

Every morning, schoolchildren would bow for sixty seconds towards the Imperial Palace in a ceremony called 'worshipping at a distance'. Then, in unison, they would recite the Rescript on Education, which had been issued in the name of Hirohito's illustrious grandfather, the Emperor Meiji, 1890.

'Know ye Our good and faithful subjects, Our Imperial ancestors have founded Our Empire on a basis broad and everlasting and have deeply and firmly implanted virtue . . .

'Should emergency arise, offer yourself courageously to the State, and thus guard and maintain the prosperity of Our Imperial Throne, coeval with heaven and earth. It is Our wish to lay it to heart in all reverence, in common with you, Our subjects, that we may all thus obtain the same virtue.'

Then the teacher would cry: 'What is your dearest ambition?' And, as one, the little boys would reply: 'To die for the Emperor!'

The voice of Foreign Minister Togo scattered Hirohito's thoughts; he was arguing against the other speakers. He declared that surrender was the only course they could conceivably take. His view was that Japan should accept the terms of the Allied Proclamation while they still were offered to them. At this, angry murmurs of 'Defeatist!' came from his colleagues.

The Prime Minister looked at his watch. These men had been talking for two and a half hours without reaching any agreement or decision, or even approaching one, and time was not on their side. He turned to the Emperor and bowed.

'I propose,' he said bluntly, 'to seek Imperial guidance and substitute it for the decision of this conference.'

Such a suggestion was unprecedented; but then so was the gravity of the crisis that gripped their country. The Emperor stood up, impassively wiping moisture from the lenses of his spectacles.

'I have surveyed the conditions prevailing in Japan and in the world at large,' he began in a thin, sing-song voice. 'It is my firm belief that a continuation of the war promises nothing but more and more destruction. I have studied the terms of the Allied reply and I have concluded that they constitute a virtually complete acknowledgement of the position we maintained in the notes despatched some days ago.'

He paused. The Emperor had never been known to indicate any positive personal opinion to his ministers. He listened to them, not them to him. The most he had ever done to influence events had been to express his views to a minister in private audience, but never to give leadership to any policy, or initiate one. Now, with the whole Cabinet present, there was no doubt of his views.

'I cannot endure the thought of letting my people suffer any longer,' Hirohito continued. 'A continuation of the war would bring death to tens, perhaps even hundreds of thousands of persons. The whole nation would be reduced to ashes.

'How then could I carry on the wishes of my Imperial ancestors? The time has come when we must bear the unbearable. I swallow my tears and give my sanction to the proposal to accept the Allied Proclamation on the basis outlined by the Foreign Minister.'

All ministers bowed their heads in acquiescence. Secretly, they knew what none of them dared to put into words: American bombs had already made more than fifteen million people homeless and killed at least another million. No one in that small underground room, lit by throbbing and unshaded lights from a little gasoline generator, knew what lay ahead or how the victorious Allies would treat them. There had been arrests of war criminals in Germany; that could also happen here, with death sentences or, at the best, long and humiliating imprisonment. The only alternative, of course, was the personal way of honour out of this world at the point of a sword or a dagger. At that moment, neither prospect offered any crumb of comfort to these middle-aged men.

Indeed, there was much to cause them grave unease, and the more they knew, the more they feared. It would be simple for even a casual search to unearth secrets that would astound the Allies. One, for example, concerned a small group known for the past nine years as the Epidemic Prevention and Water Supply Unit, or more colloquially Unit 731. This seemingly innocuous force was run by a bacteriologist, Colonel Shiro Ishii, a mild-looking man with thick spectacles. Outwardly he was every inch the scientist. He was a family man with a wife and two children. His interest was the study of comparative religions. His brief was in total contrast to all religious teaching. It was to devise destruction on a vast and unprecedented scale.

The invasion of Manchuria in the 1930s had given him the opportunity to experiment with ways of killing the enemy by infecting them with bacteria. He and his men deliberately murdered thousands of prisoners of war and civilian dissenters by injecting them with cholera, gangrene, typhoid and the plague. Some prisoners were dehydrated until they died. Others, in special laboratory camps in Manchuria, were used for vivisection purposes, or frozen or heated slowly to see what extremes of temperature the human frame could withstand.

During the Pacific and Burma campaigns, Shiro Ishii and his team calculated that most soldiers in action in a hot climate would be dirty, sweating, unable to wash frequently. They therefore bred millions of fleas which they gorged on poisoned blood. The colonel bred rats in vast numbers, covered their coats with the infected fleas and floated them over Allied positions in canisters suspended from balloons. As they landed, the canisters opened and the rats spread the deadly fleas over a wide area.

If the Allies discovered these unpleasant facts, the service ministers, who had sanctioned and supported the colonel's activities, might be held responsible for them. This was a thought they could not ignore. And behind it came another, even more heinous. What if their revered Emperor knew of Unit 731? Could he also be punished for his acquiescence in its activities?

The room was so humid that drops of sweat fell from the ministers' foreheads, noses, chins onto the polished table. They stared at the drops as though mesmerised, and some remembered the old legend about the god Izanagi who had flown through the clouds above the world, and similar drops of moisture had dripped from his spear to the sea where they had congealed to form the islands of Japan. For aeons of time thereafter, these were the only islands in the world. Eventually their rubbish, floating on the surface of the sea, solidified to form other countries, other lands. It was this beginning, by which Japan was clearly the country most favoured by the gods and therefore superior to all others, that had inspired the first Emperor Jimmu, 660 years after the birth of Christ, to believe that the eight corners of the world should be gathered together under one Imperial Japanese ruler. He promised his people to 'extend the line of the Imperial descendants and to foster right-mindedness. Thereafter the capital may be extended so as to embrace all of the cardinal points of the compass so as to form a roof'.

Now the lineal descendant of that first emperor sat watching his ministers sweat at the prospect of surrender and the disintegration of this empire.

Hirohito's brief but extraordinary speech in the air-raid shelter was subsequently closely examined, edited and expanded by three aged scholars, so that the words spoken at this critical moment in Japan's history would be beyond future misinterpretation or criticism.

Hirohito now took off his glasses, polished them with a silk handkerchief, replaced them and looked inquiringly at the chief recording engineer. The man bowed to the ground. Such proximity to the Son of Heaven had put him beyond speech. He could only nod and point a trembling finger to the microphone.

A soft wax disc began to turn slowly, a needle dropped, a red light flickered and then glowed steadily. The technician bowed and the Emperor began to read his speech.

'After pondering deeply the general trends of the world,' he said, 'and the actual conditions obtaining in our Empire today, we have decided to effect a settlement of the present situation by resorting to an extraordinary measure.

'We have ordered our government to communicate to the governments of the United States, Great Britain, China and the Soviet Union that our Empire accepts the provisions of their joint declaration. To strive for the prosperity and happiness of all nations, as well as the security and wellbeing of our subjects, is the solemn obligation which has been handed down by our Imperial ancestors and which we hold close to our heart. Indeed, we declared war on America and Britain out of our sincere desire to ensure Japan's self-preservation and the stabilisation of East Asia, it being far from our thoughts either to infringe upon the sovereignty of other nations or to embark upon territorial aggrandisement.

'But now the war has lasted for nearly four years. Despite the best that has been done by everyone – the gallant fighting of military and naval forces, the diligence and assiduity of our servants of the State, and the devoted service of our one hundred million people – the war situation has developed not necessarily to Japan's advantage, while the general trends of the world have all turned against her interest.

'Moreover, the enemy has begun to employ a new and most cruel bomb, the power of which to do damage is indeed incalculable, taking the toll of many innocent lives. Should we continue to fight, it would not only result in an ultimate collapse and obliteration of the Japanese nation, but it would also lead to the total extinction of human civilisation. Such being the case, how are we going to save the millions of our subjects or to atone ourselves before the hallowed spirits of our Imperial ancestors?

'This is the reason why we have ordered the acceptance of the provisions of the Joint Declaration of the Powers.'

As the Emperor spoke, tension lightened his voice. Sweat glazed his forehead as he went on to stress the need for all to maintain honour, to bear the heavy burden of new responsibilities, and to unite their total strength for the construction of the future.

'Cultivate the ways of rectitude, foster nobility of spirit and work with resolution, so that you may enhance the glory of the Imperial State and keep pace with the progress of the world.'

He stopped, put down the paper from which he had read, and looked inquiringly at the engineer, who turned to his Emperor with tears streaming down his face at the sadness of the moment. The war was over, in defeat and ignominy. He had lost a son, a brother, his home – and for what? He could not speak. He could only bow his head. The disc stopped turning, the metal arm raised its tiny stylus, the red light went out.

'We will make a second recording in case this is lost,' said the Emperor. The wax seemed soft and vulnerable. A single thumbprint on it could easily destroy his speech.

The engineer found his voice.

'There is no need, Your Majesty. It will be pressed perfectly.'

'It is our wish,' the Emperor told him shortly. 'We require one.'

He wanted to play it for his Empress; she might have some valuable comments to make before it was broadcast, but in a totally male-orientated society he could not possibly admit this.

The technician bowed acquiescence. He removed the wax disc and took it into another room. At that moment, a Palace official knocked at the studio door, entered and prostrated himself before Hirohito.

'Your Majesty, I have to say that crowds are gathering in the streets. There is an unusual atmosphere about the city. I do not think it is safe for you to stay here a moment longer.'

A more senior steward now came into the studio.

'Crowds are all around the Palace, Majesty,' he said nervously. 'It would be advisable to leave now – while we can.'

'You think we might be approached here?'

'They are searching for you, Majesty.'

'Who?'

'Members of the Imperial Guard, Majesty. Under their officers.'

Hirohito frowned in surprise and displeasure. These were elite troops chosen to guard his sacred person as the highest honour in all Japan. Was it conceivable that such men could have been suborned? If so, by whom? By misguided if patriotic officers who wanted to fight on, preferring to die rather than to negotiate? Or, more sinister, by unknown others who wished to seize power for themselves or for a puppet leader of their own? None of Hirohito's mental anguish showed on his face, apart from a slight tightening of his facial muscles.

The technician returned. About him hung a faint smell of hot plastic and the peculiar, iodine-like odour of high-tension electricity. He bowed low, handed the Emperor a disc wrapped in paper.

'If Your Majesty pleases, here is the only pressing we have had time to make. If it meets with your Imperial approval, we would need to receive it here half an hour before the broadcast. The news can then be given to the whole nation – and the world.'

The Emperor drove in silence through the city, back to the Palace. The Empress was waiting for him. They sat and drank green tea, together and alone, while he played the record on the Palace gramophone, watching closely for her approval. Both listened with tears streaming unashamedly down their faces. When the disc stopped turning, the Empress went to her room.

There was nothing to say; the war – possibly her husband's reign – was over.

The Emperor sat on his own, listening to the faint crackle of the few anti-aircraft guns still able to fire, and the heavy drone of enemy aircraft overhead. Were they dropping bombs or leaflets? But what did it matter now what they dropped? Why continue the constant and fearful slaughter when the verdict must already be known. How had he, the Son of Heaven, ever descended to this fearful and demeaning situation?

All his life, Hirohito had been lonely, and now he seemed without either friends or hope. He had by nature always preferred the easy way out of any problem. Here, he could see no way out. At last, belatedly, he had to face his future on his own.

Hirohito had never personally wished to declare war on Britain and the United States. His ministers assured him that such a step was essential, and, lacking the courage and stature to contradict them, he had allowed himself to be led by them. Now this was the ultimate result: his country ruined, his public admission of defeat about to be broadcast to the world, and the apparent mutiny of his personal bodyguard.

An ADC came into the room, bowed to the ground and stood waiting respectfully, as protocol demanded, until the Emperor sought fit to permit him to speak.

'I have to inform Your Majesty that troops of the Imperial Guard are already in the Palace grounds.'

'You are certain?'

'I have seen them, Majesty.'

'Have they betrayed us?' asked Hirohito in disbelief. The officer did not reply, but prudently kept his eyes averted. Too often, the bearer of unwelcome news could be personally associated with the news he brought. Safety and survival lay in silence.

Hirohito crossed the room and switched off all the lights. The two men stood for a moment in the darkness, the only sounds their breathing and the distant thump of the Palace generator. The Emperor walked to the wide glass French windows, pulled the tasselled cord to part the curtains, and opened one window.

The smell of distant burning still hung heavy in the air. A humid wind, like warm fog, blew particles of charred paper, parchment, cloth towards them. Hirohito could hear faint cries and shouts of those injured in the rubble of their homes. Nearer, he could also hear men moving across the lawns, the clink of military equipment, metal belt buckles. The ADC was right. Out there, in the darkness beyond the range of his weak eyesight, his guards were approaching the Palace. But for what purpose? To protect him under their oath of allegiance? To kill him? To seize the Palace and make off with royal treasures – or install some usurper as their ruler?

The Emperor had no idea, and at that moment the alternatives seemed equally futile. The last battle had already been lost; the war was all but over. When dusk fell at the end of the day now beginning, the ancient Japanese empire would have fallen with it. What did it matter then who ruled?

Hirohito turned and went back into the room, closed the window, drew the curtains. The ADC switched on the lights.

'You are right,' agreed the Emperor softly, almost thinking aloud. 'There *are* troops in our grounds. Send a message to them. Inform their commander it is our wish that he attends us. Immediately.'

'Here, Your Majesty?'

'Here.'

It would be best to know the position at once rather than wait and worry about what might be happening. For too long he had weakly postponed dealing with unpleasant and disagreeable matters. Now there was no time left for the luxury of delay. The ADC bowed and backed away from the royal presence. The Emperor finished his tea – it was cold now – and went into his study to await the officer's arrival.

At that moment, the commander of the Palace Guard, Major Kenji Hatanaka, was hammering on the door of the headquarters of the Imperial Guard, some distance away. He demanded to see General Mori who commanded all security forces responsible for the Emperor's safety. A junior staff officer opened the door and went to wake the general. Mori was none too pleased to be woken at such an hour, and appeared with his face flushed, eyes heavy with sleep. An ADC came out of an adjoining room and regarded Hatanaka critically.

'I understand you have an important message for me, Major. To be delivered personally,' the general said curtly. 'What is it?'

'Sir,' replied Hatanaka, 'I have word that His Imperial Majesty is no longer a free agent.'

'What exactly do you mean by that?'

'I mean, sir, that he is being forced by weak and craven politicians to broadcast to his people that Japan is surrendering to the forces of the West and the communists. I ask you, sir, as a patriot, as an officer who has loyally served His Imperial Majesty, to stop the broadcast. This will be the first time that the royal voice has ever been heard over the air. It is neither right nor fitting that such an historic moment should be debased with defeat.'

'I know nothing about any broadcast,' the general told him shortly. 'Where did you get your information?'

'We have our sources, sir.'

'We?'

'Members of the Guard who cannot bear to see the Emperor dishonoured. I beg you to address yourself to him on this matter, sir.'

'At this hour?'

'At this hour, sir. It is still not too late. We understand that His Imperial Majesty has been to the studio and recorded the message, which is due to be broadcast before noon. The only record is in the Palace. We must find it before it can be played.'

'And then?' asked the general ironically. 'We fight on?'

'Then, sir, as you say, we fight on.'

'You are out of your mind, Major.'

'I am not, sir. But if you cannot, or will not, use your great influence to dissuade His Majesty from this course, I beg you, as an officer in whom our beloved Emperor has total trust, to put your seal to the order I have prepared, urging all officers of like mind and patriotism to join forces against *any* surrender.'

'I appreciate your motives, Major,' the general replied, 'but what you ask is impossible. You must understand that. Events are now out of our hands, totally out of our control. You know the saying. The cornered mouse fights the cat all the harder. Even so, the end of their conflict is never in doubt. Nor, I regret to say, is Japan's situation. We are on the brink of defeat. Nothing that anyone – even the Emperor himself – does now can change that.'

'No, sir. You are wrong.'

The general shrugged impatiently and opened the door of his quarters as a sign that the conversation was at an end. As he did so, Hatanaka drew his pistol from its holster. The general's aide jumped forward to seize his wrist, but too late. Hatanaka fired two shots and both officers dropped to the ground.

Hatanaka walked over their bodies into the general's office, searched for his official seal. He scribbled a signature on the order, stamped it with the seal and then walked to the main guard house, about a hundred yards away.

The duty officer came out to meet him and read the document by the light of a shaded torch. It seemed official; General Mori's seal guaranteed its authority.

'Turn out the entire guard,' Hatanaka ordered him. 'I will bring them over the moat. We must find the record His Majesty has made. It may be in metal, or wax or black plastic.'

'Where are we to look for it?' the duty officer asked practically.

'First, in the grounds. Maybe it has been hidden there temporarily. Then in the Lord Keeper's office. It is not right to approach His Majesty personally.'

Such a course was in any case unthinkable, even in this crisis; men did not call on gods without a formal invitation.

Inside the secretariat building, on a rush mat spread out on the floor of his office, lay Baron Koichi Kido, the Lord Keeper of the Privy Seal. Kido was a shrewd and aristocratic politician, totally exhausted by the cataclysmic happenings of the previous few days. His task during the war had been to maintain regular contact between the Emperor and his ministers. No appointment could be arranged with the Emperor without Kido's permission and authority – except for those involving the Ministers of War and Navy, who had by tradition the right of direct access at any time.

Kido also maintained an elaborate organisation to provide intelligence about plots, rumours, gossip of any kind that could conceivably affect his master's position – or his own. Now, knowing that the recording had been made, he had undressed for the first time that week, put on a kimono and lay down thankfully to sleep.

During the previous few weeks, whenever the erratic electric supply allowed, Tokyo radio had been broadcasting throughout the night, chiefly to give advance warning of air raids. In between these warnings, the station played recordings of music and talks. Kido kept the radio switched on out of habit, with the volume turned down, providing audible proof that the station was still functioning.

Suddenly, Kido stirred uneasily in his slumber, opened his eyes and then sat up quickly, all tiredness gone. It took him only a second to realise what had wakened him. The station had gone off the air. What could that mean? A direct hit from an enemy bomb, or, worse, the seizure of the transmitter by the mob? He spun the tuning dial. The pointer crossed and re-crossed the dimly lit list of stations. The set could still pick up foreign broadcasts through a haze of static, so there was current and the set was not at fault. But nothing was being broadcast on the Tokyo wavelength. The Emperor's message could not go out unless the transmitter was working. It was Kido's urgent duty to find out why it had gone off the air.

He dressed hurriedly. As he finished, someone beat on the door and an official rushed in, trembling with fright.

'What is the matter?' Kido asked him sharply. Such manifestations of alarm were anathema to him. Men did not conduct themselves like frightened spinsters.

'The Palace Guard has mutinied, sir. They are swarming over the grounds.'

'What do they want?'

'They are looking for the record His Majesty brought back. They want to stop it being used for the broadcast.'

'It is not here,' Kido told him firmly.

'They do not know that. And they will not believe us if we tell them. They are in an ugly mood. They will kill us to get it.'

Kido ripped open the drawers of his desk, gathered up his most important papers, handed half to the official, kept the rest himself. Together, they ran along the corridor to the nearest lavatory, tearing papers into pieces as they went. They flushed them down the pan, but most refused to disappear. Flecks of paper, like oversized confetti, stuck to the sides of the bowl or floated in the water.

This was a complication neither of them had envisaged. But if they could not destroy the papers, at least they could save themselves, if they hurried. There was only one possible place to hide – inside the Palace vaults, and Kido held the master key.

He led the way down stone steps and along corridors, dimly lit and damp smelling, between walls streaming with moisture, deep beneath the cellars. At last they reached the vaults. Kido opened the double door, motioned the official inside, followed him in, and then locked the door behind them. The steel tongues of the vault locks slid into their slots with well-oiled ease.

Then the Lord Keeper, possibly the second most powerful man in all Japan, sat down, out of breath, on the damp stone floor in the darkness to ponder the horror of surrender.

Several storeys above, the Emperor paced up and down his study floor. He was at first astonished and then infuriated that the guard commander had not instantly obeyed his order. In normal times this negligence could mean death, and not necessarily a swift or merciful one. Why, a common thief caught in a warehouse of one of his ancestors had been put to death by slow torture. First, all hair on his head and body was burned away and his fingernails and toenails pulled out, one by one. Then the tendons of his legs were severed and his body bored with woodworkers' drills, the flesh sliced into strips with butchers' knives. The thief was then stretched on a rack and squeezed in a press but, amazingly, the man still lived. His back was broken by a club and the body boiled in a vat of soy sauce. Why should a disobedient and mutinous guard commander at such a time of crisis expect more lenient treatment?

Hirohito knew he was now living on the sharpened edge of anarchy. He sat down at his desk, head in his hands. For the first time in his life, or in the lives of any of his illustrious ancestors, an unknown and unimportant underling was keeping the Emperor waiting – and he could do nothing whatever about it. He was powerless.

The Empress came into the room and stood looking at the man held to be a god, seeing him shrunk in on himself, more like a manikin than a man, the single reading light reflected grotesquely in his thick spectacles.

'I have brought you the record of your speech,' she said gently. 'You may need it.'

Hirohito looked up at her for a moment, not quite comprehending the significance of her remark. He had not seen her remove it from the turntable.

'You must get rid of it at once,' he cried. 'Mutinous troops are out in the grounds. They feel it is a symbol of Japan's surrender. They will do anything to find it. They imagine that if they can stop my broadcast, we can still win the war. Madness! They do not realise the total hopelessness of the situation.'

'I will give it to a lady-in-waiting,' the Empress replied calmly. 'She has a secret safe in her room, hidden behind a Chinese scroll.'

'Then hurry,' he told her. 'The troops may be here at any moment.'

Outside, the sky was already streaked with pink. What would this new day hold for him and his country? The question was too terrible to contemplate, too awful even to attempt to answer. He switched off the light, went to the window, parted the thick curtains.

He could dimly see men milling about on the lawn, searching under bushes and through flower beds. How could they imagine such an historic record would be lying there? And then, as he watched them draw closer to the building, he saw a burly figure run across the bridge over the moat, and recognised General Tanaka, commander of the Eastern Army. He was shouting furiously at another officer, a major apparently leading the troops on the lawn. What did the major mean by daring to humiliate the Emperor by doubting his decision to seek peace? Had he lost all sense of honour and decency? Had he descended to the level of brute beasts and anarchists, men without minds or reason?

Major Hatanaka stood meekly, head bowed, as he listened to this tirade. All his anger and intentions had suddenly deserted him. He was no longer a leader, determined to fight on, he was simply a not very successful officer who had acted in what he believed were the best interests of the Crown and the country. Now he felt drained of energy and endeavour. He had intended no insult to his Imperial Majesty. Instead, he had hoped to save him from the total humiliation and disgrace of national surrender.

The Emperor listened as Hatanaka admitted humbly that he had been wholly misled by his feelings. His emotions had temporarily overcome his good sense and training. He turned to his soldiers and ordered them back to barracks. Then he called to the other officers he had persuaded to follow him.

Hirohito stood, unseen and in silence, as the small group marched smartly in step across the lawn. They came to a halt beneath the Palace wall. As he watched, drawing back slightly from the window so he might remain unseen, they bowed ceremoniously in his direction. Then, at a sharp command from Hatanaka, each officer unsheathed his long sword from its polished leather covered scabbard.

In a drill movement, they directed the points at their own stomachs, and stood thus for a moment. The rising sun glittered off a dozen polished blades. Another barked order and ceremoniously, as their Emperor watched, the officers fell forward on their swords in the final act of Japanese honour. Their bowels burst out, steaming like a nest of pink and writhing snakes, cascading down over their uniform tunics. Slowly, the officers' legs gave way and they collapsed on the grass.

The whole grotesque and suicidal pantomime had been carried out in total silence. Despite their agony, not a sound escaped their lips. They had all maintained their honour. They had died undefiled, facing the Emperor they could not see.

Hirohito turned away from the window. He swallowed several times to prevent himself from being violently sick. Then he closed the curtains and sat down at his desk. His legs were trembling. He bowed his head in his hands, unable to concentrate on what he should do next.

Elsewhere in Tokyo, mercifully out of his sight, officers of senior rank were also atoning in like manner for what they believed had been their own deficiencies in his service. The

War Minister, General Anami, wrote a long apology to the Emperor for his lack of success in the field of battle, and then ordered his personal servant to bring him a bottle of sake. He sat down and drank this steadily from a small china cup without a handle. He drank without any pleasure, but in the hope that so much alcohol in his stomach would accelerate bleeding and so speed his imminent journey from this world to the next.

When he had finished the bottle, he stood up and regarded himself in a wall mirror. His face was slightly flushed from the spirit and sweat shone like varnish on his forehead. He took a deep breath, unsheathed a ceremonial dagger, felt the point carefully with his thumb, and then, bowing in the direction of the Emperor's palace, he plunged the blade through the silk shift of his kimono and into his soft, plump belly.

He turned the blade slowly in the ritual act of *suppuko* and collapsed, gasping in a terrible extremity of pain. His brother-in-law came into the room, knowing nothing of the minister's intention, and found him writhing, half dead, on a floor red with pumping blood. With instant understanding of the situation, he despatched him with a swift thrust of his own dagger.

Elsewhere, Vice-Admiral Onishi, who had commanded the Kamikaze Corps, lined up his officers to apologise to them for his failings as their leader. Then, standing in front of them, he disembowelled himself. He did not utter a word as he died, and they in turn did not speak or express any emotion as they watched him.

These men thus missed the Emperor's broadcast shortly before noon. Hirohito sat motionless in his study, listening to his own voice. When the speech was over, he waited for a moment in silence, and then summoned the Court Chamberlain.

'We wish to see Amaranda,' he told him.

The Chamberlain bowed. Amaranda was the royal palmist, an old man long versed in the rare and complex skills of reading a person's future from the pattern of lines on their palms. Just as the human face becomes the map of past experiences and emotions, so the palms contain a plan of what is to come if the lines can be read aright.

Amaranda and his son regularly read the palms of members of the royal family, and also the palms of others in positions of peculiar responsibility. Every member of the armed services who volunteered for a kamikaze mission was always interviewed by Amaranda or his son before he was accepted for such a task. The reason for this was, of course, never explained to the volunteer concerned. The palmists carefully inspected each young man's life line. If this was short, signifying an early death, he could go forward for selection. If his life line was long, however, then he would not be allowed to join the Kamikaze Corps, because if it was already written on his hand that he was not going to die young, he would be useless in any mission that, to be successful, must cost him his life.

Amaranda came into the royal presence, a small and wrinkled man, and stood in front of the Emperor, head bowed.

'Today, our country faces its most grievous crisis in ten centuries of history,' the Emperor told him frankly. He trusted the palmist; he would no sooner be evasive to him than to his personal physician. He sought accurate advice and so had to explain the desperate background to his request.

'In a few hours, all resistance to the onslaughts of our enemies will cease. No one can fully foretell the future – if indeed there is a future that we can dare to contemplate. That is why we have asked you here. We seek your guidance. We wish you to read our hand.'

As he spoke, Hirohito held out his right palm to the old man. Amaranda put a magnifying glass, the kind that jewellers use, to his right eye and examined the web of tiny lines on his ruler's hand. He frowned in concentration. For a moment both men stood in silence. Then the Emperor spoke.

'Have no fear,' he said. 'Speak of what you see, however painful this vision may be. It is our command.'

'I see a long life, a continuance of Your Majesty's rule. But changes – great changes – will be made in the future.'

'So we will not die yet? We will not be killed as if we were criminals?' asked the Emperor, watching the old man closely.

Amaranda shook his head. 'Your Majesty's life will be long and illustrious. Look for yourself, sir. This is the line of life, of honourable achievement. As you can see, it is unbroken and very long. You are not yet half way through your life's journey.'

'We hope you are right,' said Hirohito thoughtfully, but not yet convinced. 'Proceed.'

'Other signs do not augur an easy future. There will be hard days immediately ahead,' replied the palmist gravely. 'But Your Majesty must remember the proverb, "In the month of storms, flowers appear".'

'Flowers can wither,' the Emperor reminded him.

'In the end, Your Majesty, every living thing must wither and eventually die. That is the law of nature, just as the tide of every sea has its ebb. But equally every tide flows again. So will it be for your people.'

'What of the hopes and plans of so many generations to make Japan a power of world renown?' the Emperor asked him. 'We have striven to achieve this ambition several times over the years, and it seemed we could do so. But now we have been defeated.'

'Not defeated, Majesty, but deflected. Turned aside into another road that can also lead to the same destination. Indeed, it will provide a wider, straighter way. And in the end infinitely more successful – if I interpret your hand correctly.'

'What do you mean?'

'Forty years ago, your illustrious grandfather, Emperor Meiji, saw that Western countries used war – attack, subjugation – as an instrument of their policy and diplomacy, and he determined to do likewise. Our forces humiliated the Russians and then the Chinese. But now more recent reverses to Your Majesty's forces show us that a different way to achieve a nation's aims should be found.

'We must accept that your people have suffered a setback, not through any flaw in Your Majesty's inspired and divine leadership, or in the unmatched courage of Your Majesty's armed forces, but because our adversaries have enjoyed certain important technical advantages.

'The most recent evidence of this is seen in the two bombs that have fallen on Hiroshima and Nagasaki. Had we been able to design and build these devices ourselves, then the Americans and the British and the Chinese would be crawling on their bellies to us, as now they will wish us to crawl to them.

'I see in Your Majesty's hand a clash of lines which can mean a collision of personal wills or of ideas in the near future. But they are speedily resolved, and then lead on to power unmatched at any hour in our history. Look, Majesty. Here are the routes to your destiny.'

With a sharpened sliver of bamboo, Amaranda indicated a tiny web of lines. The Emperor regarded them impassively.

'Well?' he asked.

'For many years, Your Majesty, we have copied Western inventions at almost every level. We have built bicycles after their design. Cars. Wireless sets. Aircraft. Ships. Guns. But to copy is not to create, to follow another is always to be in second place.

'On 18 August 1932, Your Majesty, almost thirteen years ago to the day, a Scottish pilot, Jim Mollison, took off from Portmarnock Strand in Ireland, in a little monoplane and thirty hours later landed in New Brunswick, in Canada. He had flown on his own across the Atlantic – but he was not the first man to do this. He was the second. On 20 May, five years before, Charles Lindbergh had flown the other way, west to east. Everyone knows about Charles Lindbergh. Very few have heard of Jim Mollison.

'By the same token, one day they will honour the first man to fly to the moon – but no one will remember the name of the second man to do so. That is fitting, because he is not the pioneer, he is only a follower in the footsteps of the leader – a very different and subordinate role.

'We have been deflected from our god-given purpose to rule the world because we have attempted to achieve this aim through force, and against very powerful enemies.' To emphasise his point, Amaranda used the words *shido minozoku* meaning the first or leading race.

'We used, as the Westerners say, brawn instead of brain. But then so did the great animals of ages past, which became extinct because they could not recognise fundamental changes in their world – and adapt to them. Japan must learn from these examples for I see every indication in Your Majesty's hand that we will reach our aim of world domination in the span of your lifetime, if not in mine.

'For fifty years, we have struggled to prove that we were militarily powerful, not only equal to the strongest nation individually, but against *all* the strong nations combined. We fought the Chinese. The imperialist British. The Dutch. The capitalist United States. Then communist Russia. Against one of these adversaries we could have prevailed, perhaps even against two, but not against them all. That is an impossibility in terms of arms alone – but not in terms of technical skills and abilities.

'We will take the best that others have achieved, and examine the results, follow their successes, build on their foundations – and improve them. We will leap two, three, four paces ahead, while they plod on, believing in their own abilities, and following their comfortable teaching that their ways must be best because they have been best in the past.

'But the past is dead and the present is dying. The future still waits to be born – and it can belong to Japan, Your Majesty. Once we move ahead of the West, they can never catch us up. Our lead will increase inexorably, as a young runner in a long race leaves behind older if more experienced competitors. And this lead will make us rich. Japan will become bankers to the world, and so will control the world economically. By the time other countries realise this, it will be too late for them to react.'

'And you see all this in my hand?' Hirohito asked him, slightly sceptical.

'I see the signs clearly, Majesty. I see the road ahead. You lead an industrious people. They are ingenious, they are skilful, they work hard, and under your wise guidance they are united. The West will rely on what it calls a military victory. The Americans are blind to the dangers from their ally, Russia. The British see these dangers, but they are weakened by more years of war than the Americans, and they have paid all their treasure to the Americans to buy weapons they should have produced themselves. And if they had done so, it is very likely there would never have been a war at all.

'The Americans were cunning. They would only supply weapons and tanks and aircraft if the British built factories to produce them in the United States. Thus, at the end of a long and exhausting war, the British have provided their chief competitors with new factories full of new machinery, while their own are bombed or, at best, old and out of date. As a result, they are in debt and enfeebled and their views count for little – especially since the socialists are in power and Mr Churchill has gone.

'The Allies will argue among themselves as to whether the European empires in the East should be allowed to continue. And while the Americans attempt to undermine the stability of India and Indo-China and Batavia, and connive to seize their markets, we will be working in the background, funded by them, an American colony in all but name.

'We will praise their demands for democracy, and they will imagine we have learned the lessons of military defeat. But we will have learned a different lesson altogether that will lead to economic victory, not just over the United States but over all competitors. We will plead for aid to help us democratise our country. Therefore they will finance research in *our* laboratories, and developments in *our* workshops. And one day they will wake up to discover – too late – that they have foolishly financed a competitor who controls the technological processes of the world.

'Throughout the war they have plundered the wealth of Great Britain, acquired over centuries of trade and endeavour when Britain was the workshop of the world. We will use this finance to fund research and produce goods the West never imagined we could dare to make – and on a vast scale. Radios, cameras, cars – all of meticulous craftsmanship, built in new factories through new processes, and so capable of being sold at low prices.

'We will seem to bow the knee to the United States and so follow the example of trees in the forest. Some have proud, strong branches and thick leaves, but when the typhoon blows, they do not bend. They break and die and are forgotten.

'But there are also more slender trees with long thin leaves, fine as a woman's hair, and when the wind blows, it blows through the leaves and does not harm the tree. So the weaker outlives the stronger. As it is written, Majesty, the willow branch always bends beneath the snow.

'For fifty years, we have struggled militarily, and to no apparent avail. But this struggle has given us strength and courage and impetus for the *next* fifty years. In this span of time, you will see your country triumphant. Japan will become the manufactory of the world's goods, banker to the eight corners of the earth – and all funded by the wealth of enemies too proud and blind to read the signs.'

'You see all that in my hand?' asked Hirohito again, but now less questioningly. He wished to be convinced.

'I see part in your hand, part in your destiny, Majesty. This is the truth. I am an old man. I have no time left to dissemble, to speak the honeyed words of flattery. I say what I see, and I see what I know. And one day, out of this chaos and ruin and weeping and misery that marks Your Majesty's country now, all the world will see what I see now.

'Japan is at present on her knees – but that is a good position for prayer and rest. She will rise and you, Majesty, will lead her to ultimate triumph. The journey of a thousand miles begins with one short step. That is the step that under your divine leadership and sublime guidance we are now about to take.

'When Your Majesty meets the American General MacArthur, it may be that he will appear victorious. Let him do so. Allow the General to enjoy his brief and illusory triumph. He will not realise that already you will be leading your people on the march to wealth and power and greatness among nations beyond his imagining or the desires and dreams of your illustrious ancestors. Then all eight corners of the world will indeed be under one roof – our nation's roof, *your* nation's roof, Majesty.

'All countries will be the economic colonies of Japan. The world will be your new and imperishable empire.

'It is my submission that the word should go out now to men of genius and talent in every area – engineering in all its aspects, banking and finance – that this is *your* heavenly inspired plan and *our* divine destiny.

'This war may be lost, but a far greater and longer lasting victory will be won. We will be the richest, most powerful nation in the world. War will then belong to the past as far as we are concerned, because no country – or even any group of countries – will be strong enough economically to engage us.

'As Miyamoto Musashi has written: "When you know the enemy's plans, it will be easy to gain victory by means of an appropriate response." And their plans are now ours, Your Majesty. Lasting victory is seen in the palm of your hand.'

Amaranda bowed low as he finished talking. For a moment, the two men considered what he had said. Then the Emperor spoke, and his voice now had the power and resonance of a leader, not of the led.

'It is as you say,' he said. 'All will be done exactly as you propose.'

FOUR

The Present: Perth, Western Australia
The Past: Calcutta, India, 1946

Myrtle could never forget that once she had been poor. Nor, when she grew rich, did she ever fail to remind any senior employee or director of Mackenzie International that before she hired them they had also been far less prosperous and, at her whim, she could instantly return them to that unhappy situation.

She paid them considerably more than she thought they were worth, because she despised them and knew that by appearing generous she could command more than mere loyalty; she commanded them. She also allowed them unusually generous expenses, so they rapidly grew accustomed to a standard of life far higher than they could have achieved in any comparable company. And while they might possibly be able to adapt to a lower life style if they lost their jobs with her, Myrtle calculated that their wives would not. Hence, they were her creatures and always voted her way.

Sometimes, but not very often, remembering her religious upbringing, she despised herself for being so ruthless, but these rare stabs of conscience grew more muted with the passing of the years, and never prevented her feeling contempt for men who could be bought so easily – and so cheaply. Subconsciously, she equated all men with Uncle Jem and Hilary Mackenzie – and hated them all on that account.

In addition, she never let pass an opportunity to impress on them the imperative importance of being able to make instant decisions when the need arose. It was a lesson she had learned in circumstances which they had never heard and could probably not even imagine: that cataclysmic moment when she had met Hilary for the first time in his office in Calcutta . . .

Myrtle put her hand up to her mouth and spat the penis head into her palm.

'Rubber,' she said contemptuously, grimacing her disgust and distaste.

For a moment, Sir Hilary stared at her in astonishment.

'How did you know so quickly?' he asked her hoarsely, weakly.

'Because I've had too many real ones – and rubber ones – in my mouth and in my hand. Is this part of the selection test you usually apply when interviewing a candidate for a job?'

'You cheeky little bitch!'

'You evil old swine!' Myrtle retorted furiously. Even as she spoke the words, she felt astounded at her own temerity, but she was so filled with anger at the way he had insulted her, as other men had used her, violated her, depraved her, that her feelings totally overwhelmed all thought of caution.

'You are mad, woman – and unbelievably, disgustingly rude. I will have you thrown out.'

'You will? When?'

'Now, of course. This instant.'

Sir Hilary turned to his desk, pressed a bell-push. The door opened immediately. The woman who had shown Myrtle into the room appeared, shorthand notebook in her hand, its pages held neatly in place by a rubber band.

'Yes, sir?' she asked him, ready to take dictation.

'Before Sir Hilary says anything to you,' said Myrtle before he could speak, 'I have something to show you.'

She barely recognised her own voice. It was as though someone else was speaking for her, through her. Years of uncertainty and misery, of pretending not to hear cheap sneers because she was a chi-chi, had reached their climax. Enough was more than enough. From now on, she would not accept insults from anyone. And what the hell did it matter what happened to her as a result? Her future could hardly be worse than the past.

She smiled bleakly at the ludicrous irony of her situation. Here she was, wearing clothes supplied by an abortionist, without money and out of work, desperate for almost *any* job, and yet threatening one of the Empire's richest industrialists – and all the while holding half his rubber penis in her hand.

She had so much to lose, and yet she sensed instinctively that Sir Hilary had infinitely more.

She held up her clenched right hand. Only she and Sir Hilary knew what it contained. Sir Hilary flushed nervously and pulled at his collar, as though it had suddenly become uncomfortably tight.

'There's been a mistake, Miss Brown,' he said quickly, unconvincingly.

'Not on my part,' Myrtle corrected him coldly.

'You *did* ring, Sir Hilary?' Miss Brown asked, looking from one to the other.

'I did. I – I – wanted to ask you to cancel my lunch appointment tomorrow.'

'But it's with the Governor, sir,' said Miss Brown. Her voice rose an octave in her amazement. One did not cancel appointments with the Governor of Bengal; his social diary was filled for months ahead.

'I know,' said Sir Hilary, 'but tell him—' he paused. 'Tell him there has been an unexpected crisis in our plant at Barrackpore. Most unfortunately I will have to ask him to excuse me.'

Miss Brown's brow creased with astonishment. Only that morning the plant director had telephoned to report a record output. What on earth was Sir Hilary playing at? Could this little chi-chi have something to do with it? Miss Brown pursed her lips in disapproval, bowed and withdrew, closing the door quietly behind her.

'You were saying, Sir Hilary?' Myrtle continued, now holding up the grotesque piece of rubber between her thumb and forefinger.

'The post is filled. I will pay your expenses for coming to this interview, of course. That is all. The end of the matter.'

'You are mistaken. It is only the beginning of the matter. I am quite willing to go. But on rather different terms.'

Myrtle crossed the room, came round the side of the desk, looked Sir Hilary in the eye. His cheeks were smooth, his mouth soft, the lobes of his ears unusually long. She placed the rubber morsel on his desk. As he involuntarily glanced down at it, she took a deep breath, leaned forward and ripped open his silk shirt so roughly that its mother-of-pearl buttons scattered across the room.

Myrtle stood staring at the naked pendulous breasts of a middle-aged woman.

'You are no more a man than I am. I have seen too many of your sort in Coraya Road.'

Sir Hilary pulled his torn shirt together nervously, adjusting his silk tie to conceal the gap.

'So you see,' Myrtle continued, 'if I *did* go from here and accept the contemptible offer you have made, I would feel obliged to tell everybody you are not a man at all – or a baronet. You are a woman – *Sir* Hilary.'

'I have much influence in Calcutta,' Sir Hilary retorted ominously. 'You might have an accident, a fatal accident, if you spread that story around.'

'Of course I might. So I will ask Miss Brown to come in here again and be a witness to your sex – or I could tell her on the

way out, or *The Statesman* newspaper. I know several members
of their staff, editorial and managerial. They used to come to
Mrs Ransom's house.

'This would be a scoop for them. And if you unwisely
attempted to take them – or me – to court for libel, I would
insist that you proved your masculinity. Which, of course, is
impossible. And I should also tell you that before I came here I
found out from *The Statesman* files a great deal about your
company, and how you came to control it.'

'I had a maiden aunt,' Sir Hilary interrupted her. 'She was
the majority shareholder. She left her shares to me when she
died. She wanted to keep the company in the family. It was
quite simple.'

'Not quite so simple as you make it sound. As a spinster, the
last of her line, she was extremely anxious – obsessed,
even – that her family name should be perpetuated. After all,
her father founded the firm and his only son, her brother, was
killed in the First World War. You only inherited because
everyone else in line had daughters.

'Your parents knew this, and from your birth claimed you
were male. They named you Hilary – a boy's name as well as a
girl's – and brought you up as a boy for fourteen years. And
then when your aunt died, you had to stay as a male – or lose
everything your parents wanted for you, and for themselves.
The papers would have a field day out of this. Here and in
England, Australia, the United States.'

'You can't prove it,' said Sir Hilary sullenly.

'And you cannot risk making me do so. Now that we understand each other better, what terms are you offering, before I
state mine?'

'For what?'

'My services. My silence.'

The shock this girl had given Hilary had brought on a pain
he suffered in his chest from time to time in moments of stress
or anger. It felt as though he had swallowed a stone that had

somehow stuck in his gullet. Hilary felt sweat dampen his back, then mercifully the pain eased. It was only nerves or tension, he was sure. But while it lasted he did not want to speak or move. Gradually, it faded altogether and he was conscious of his heart beating heavily as if he had been running uphill, a long way, for a long time.

'Tell me what you want,' he said at last, when he felt the pain no more.

'I will accept five thousand rupees a month to be your personal assistant. I will be loyal to you in that capacity, and I will stay silent about what I know. But because you and your parents conspired to swindle one of your own blood so readily and so cleverly – as Jacob swindled Esau in the Bible story – I have no doubt you may attempt to silence me in one way or another.

'Accordingly, I will lodge sealed letters with several banks and with my contacts at *The Statesman* newspaper. If *anything* should ever happen to me, such as an accident, as you mention, or a sudden, inexplicable illness, whether fatal or not, they will have instructions to open these letters at once and make public the contents. Do I make myself clear?'

Sir Hilary could not speak. He turned away, looking out of the window at a commotion in the street beneath him. A tonga pony had fallen down dead in the shafts. The driver, with the help of some passers-by, was freeing its body from the harness. In the burnished sky above, vultures, scenting death, were already circling hopefully.

'Why did you do that to me?' she asked Hilary softly.

The question scored him like a knife wound.

'I've done it before,' he admitted, slightly surprised at his own frankness. 'I hate women. I like to humiliate them. You might feel the same if, for an inheritance about which you knew absolutely nothing, you had been brought up as a boy, always made to have your hair cut short, forced to wear boys' clothes, play boys' rough games, which you hated. And, of course, you could never ever be seen bathing or in swimming trunks.'

'I can understand,' Myrtle agreed. 'I hate men as you hate women. We both have our reasons.'

Sir Hilary looked at her sharply. Then he made up his mind.

'I will give you what you ask,' he said flatly. 'Five thousand rupees a month for one year.'

'Initially for one year, then rising by one thousand rupees a month for each of the next five years,' Myrtle corrected him. 'With a car of my choice, and expenses which need not be itemised.'

'You are greedy.'

'Not as greedy as you. You stole a whole company. I only seek a minute share of profits to which you have never been entitled. And I might even have some suggestions for increasing those profits.'

Sir Hilary chewed his lower lip, pondering the situation, desperate to find an escape route, but knowing there was none. He had caught himself in his own net.

'All right. I will send you a letter on those terms.'

Myrtle shook her head.

'No,' she said firmly, 'I will take the letter with me. It will save postage, and nowadays deliveries are so erratic.'

Reaching forward, she pressed the push button on his desk to call back Miss Brown to take dictation.

It was impossible to be long in Sir Hilary's company or with his friends and associates, and remain indifferent to the diverse means by which so many of them had grown so rich. Some were simply successful swindlers, or their fathers had been before them. Others had bribed or blackmailed their way to wealth. A few had actually earned a fortune legitimately, but most had simply inherited it, like Sir Hilary, through an accident of birth.

She still thought of him as male, and always referred to him respectfully out of his presence as Sir Hilary. To the outside world he was a baronet, last of a long and illustrious line, holder

of an ancient title of chivalry, not an embittered woman wearing a man's Savile Row suit, bearing a man's name, living a lie
from which only death could give release. Myrtle knew it was
safer to think of him as masculine, otherwise, perhaps after one
glass of wine too many, or in some moment of unforgivable
confidence, she might unwittingly reveal the truth to a third
party. Such an indiscretion could harm Sir Hilary, but more
important to her was that it could also ruin whatever future she
might have with him and through him.

Myrtle was secretly surprised at the speed and ease with
which she became accustomed to money. It was not her money,
of course, and she was by no means rich, but she was infinitely
better off than all her family and relations put together. And
although she might not personally be wealthy, now that she
was living among very wealthy people, by a strange process of
social osmosis she felt she was one of them, not simply *with*
them, an unsatisfying and unsettling relationship. This she
determined to change in her favour at the earliest opportunity.

It was extremely agreeable to be driven by a chauffeur in a
Buick Eight limousine, to be attended by liveried servants, to
order merchandise to be sent to her flat for her inspection
instead of going to the shops, or, heaven forbid, the bazaar. But
Myrtle realised that these were only the trappings of success,
they did not bring the total self-confidence of personal independence. Also, she could not rid herself of a growing, inner unease
that eventually, as with Cinderella, midnight would strike, and
then she would be back where she began, out of work, out of
money and, by that time, out of hope. This interlude had a
dreamlike quality about it; since she neither trusted nor even
liked Sir Hilary, and he had the power to transform the dream
into a nightmare, she was perpetually aware of her precarious
situation.

Indeed, night after night, Myrtle would start up out of sleep,
sweating from a bad dream in which she had lost everything she
had so recently acquired. She realised that the only way to

escape from this horror for ever was to become rich herself. Then she need not be beholden to anyone. The chauffeur, the car, the servants and all the other privileges would be hers by right, not simply on sufferance or on loan. And then, most important of all, she would be her own person, not another's creature. Then no one would ever dare to humiliate her again, and call her a chi-chi to her face or even behind her back.

But how could she achieve this? The task was made more difficult because she was on her own, and without friends. She was not accepted by Sir Hilary's circle. To them, she was simply a little chi-chi girl who had somehow wormed her way into his employ and his favour. They were polite to her because they were uncertain of the extent of her influence with him, but naturally she was not on their visiting lists, nor was she invited to accompany him to social events. Although Sir Hilary was single, he did not appear to have any close women friends. Not that he was homosexual – everyone agreed on that. In the careful description of the day, he appeared the confirmed bachelor, a man totally dedicated to his business interests, and more recently, to horse racing.

As month succeeded month, Myrtle gradually lost touch with her contemporaries in the railway colony. She did not wish to do so, but nothing divides people more sharply and permanently than promotion for one and not for another. When she visited them, she could not help noticing their envious glances at her expensive dresses, hats and shoes, and tried not to hear their edged and critical remarks. When she invited them out to tea, they went to Davico's, an expensive tea room where, to her horror, she actually saw some of her former friends working as waitresses, and where, only a few months previously, she would have been glad to have had a similar job herself. They now wrongly assumed she had deliberately come there to humiliate them, to hear them call her 'mem'. This was not true, of course, but they thought it was, and hated her – and themselves – for not being in her position. So

Myrtle was lonely, and her only contact with the past was Mr da Leppo.

Sometimes they would meet for a drink at Firpo's, or at the Great Eastern, but never at Ruggiani's or the Century Club. Her hurt at Julia's rejection still caused Myrtle pain, like a poisoned wound. She accepted that some might think da Leppo a pathetic character, but he had helped her when she was in trouble, and he could quite easily have refused to assist her. She suspected he was also a half-caste like her, that his story of rich parents left behind in Lisbon was not the whole truth. But then had not Pontius Pilate asked: 'What is truth?' And if he could not provide an answer, how could she?

One evening the two of them sat drinking at a corner table in the faded Edwardian splendour of the Great Eastern Hotel. Long, thin fan blades above their heads beat the air like the stiff wings of huge birds. Waiters hovered silently on the perimeter of an otherwise empty bar. It usually filled up later in the evening, after Myrtle and da Leppo had left; they met early because they both preferred the quiet and solitude where they could talk easily; and now da Leppo had a question to ask her. Although they were alone, he spoke in a whisper, as he might in a cathedral.

'What do you know about your boss's horses?' he asked casually, sipping his drink, watching her reaction over the rim of his glass. Myrtle could sense from his carefully contrived nonchalance that her answer was important to him.

'Not much,' she admitted. 'Except that he has a string of thirty. Some are in training in Ireland, some in England, and half a dozen here. And I saw a note on his desk the other day about two new horses from Australia that are proving to be a great disappointment.'

'Do you remember their names?'

'One was called Merlin. I can't remember the other.'

'Merlin. The Wizard at the court of King Arthur,' said da Leppo thoughtfully. 'I have heard about this horse. He is a gelding and, like his illustrious eponym, he could also have magical qualities.'

'I don't understand you,' Myrtle said, frowning. She had no interest in racing. Anglo-Indians were not welcome socially at the racecourse. Many of Mrs Ransom's girls bet heavily, but when they saw clients in their formal clothes at the races, with wives wearing expensive new dresses and fashionably wide-brimmed hats, neither would recognise the other. Each knew their place, and it was not in a private box. As Mrs Ransom said drily: 'Men look quite different when they are clothed. But then I suppose many of their wives would not recognise them without clothes on – which is why they visit us.'

'Let me explain,' said da Leppo, breaking into Myrtle's thoughts. 'In Merlin, Sir Hilary has a horse that will make a fortune.'

'For him?'

'He doesn't bet, does he?'

'Not as far as I know. He's really only interested in the social aspect of racing. He told me he loves to lead in a winner. Likes to be thought of as a leader in everything he does. Vanity.'

'All is vanity, according to the Bible,' agreed da Leppo. 'But some of us who are not vain have another interest – making money. I like doing that the easiest way of all. Gambling. On certainties only, of course. And I think that Merlin can make me a lot of money.'

'How can Merlin be so good if his performance is such a disappointment?' asked Myrtle.

'That to a non-gambler can be a conundrum,' da Leppo admitted. 'But not to the knowledgeable – at least not to those with inside knowledge. If I *know* a certain number will come up on the wheel at a certain time, then I will bet on it because the wheel has been rigged and all risk removed. And if I *know* that a certain horse, which experts claim is hopeless, will still actually win its race, I bet on that.'

'So would we all,' agreed Myrtle. 'But how could you ever possibly be sure? You have heard something about Merlin?'

'I have heard more than something about Merlin for Saturday's three o'clock race, and from someone whose judgement I trust. Someone who owes me a very great favour indeed, and who would rather repay it out of the bookmakers' pockets than his own. Someone who knows that if his tip was wrong, he would be even deeper in my debt – and who fears my response to such a situation. And on the following Saturday, the two thirty, there's another winning horse – of a different colour. Chameleon.'

'That's the second disappointing horse. I remember the name now.'

'Well, don't forget it. You will never have a double like this again.'

'But how are you so sure they will both win?'

'For someone who has worked for Mrs Ransom, you are still remarkably innocent about the ways of the world, Myrtle. You may even believe what you read in the newspapers that race horses are owned and trained and ridden by honourable people. Sometimes they are, of course, but the chain of involvement is long, and individual links can be weak.

'Bookmakers lean on trainers and stable lads and jockeys. Fortunes can be made or lost on a single race. The favourite can be given a long drink of water – or deprived of one – just before a race and will then, inexplicably, lose its form. A jockey can be paid not to win, but to lose. And sometimes one horse can even be substituted for another which looks exactly the same, but is either much faster or much slower.'

'Are any of these things going to happen in these two races?'

'Calcutta races do not enjoy the highest reputation for fair sportsmanship and probity. All I am prepared to say is that I am assured that nothing short of death will affect the chances of Merlin and Chameleon. Let me explain what has happened about these horses, on the understanding, of course, that – as in my consulting room – our discussion remains totally private.'

'Of course.'

'They have came over from Australia, as you say. They are both damned good, but they did not have their present names in Sydney, and their markings then were slightly different. Some people say it is bad luck to change a horse's name, like changing the name of a ship. In this case, it will be the reverse – for those in the know.

'They have already been raced in Bombay, in Delhi and here in Calcutta, and they have never done a damned thing. They have always finished well down the field – sometimes even last.'

'Doesn't my boss worry about this?'

'It is just a minor facet in a rich man's life,' replied da Leppo. 'He would prefer winners, obviously. But if horses lose, they still provide a conversational point. And if he has to worry that they are costing him a lot of money to feed and train, then he cannot afford to own race horses at all – and he is never likely to admit that.'

'Then why have they done so badly if they are really so good?'

'Because that's how things have been carefully worked out. They may have been fed the wrong food. Maybe one had a sharp stone pressed into the soft part of its hoof, to make it go lame. Or they could have been walked past the stable of a mare on heat before the race and, even though they are geldings, this excites them and they lose. But they are not going to lose their next two races. They may even get a little pep-me-up in their feed. I don't know. All I do know is that betting stands at forty to one on Merlin, and fifty to one on Chameleon next week. And both will win.'

'Those are incredible odds,' said Myrtle, impressed. 'So if I could put a thousand rupees on, I would be rich?'

'Not rich, dearie, but rich*er*, shall we say. But you can't possibly bet on the course. To do that would instantly cause the odds to drop drastically, because it would hint that you might know something that others don't. A very reasonable deduction, you must admit, in view of their showing so far and you being so close to their owner.

'Bet by telephone or telegram, to Bombay or Delhi, but not with a local bookmaker, or you will ruin your chances – and mine. And other people involved would also not take at all kindly to such a situation. This is not Boy Scouts honour stuff, Myrtle. This is real money.'

'I don't know a bookmaker here, let alone in Bombay or Delhi.'

'I can give you some names.'

'Wouldn't they telegraph the odds back here?'

'Of course. But if the bet is placed literally minutes before the race starts, there just isn't time. How much can you afford?'

'A thousand rupees on each,' said Myrtle.

'Is that all? You may never have a chance like this again,' said da Leppo. 'Can't you borrow some?'

'On what security?'

'You mix with very rich people,' he pointed out.

'Possibly. But you don't realise how difficult it is to get money for yourself when you're not rich, until you try to borrow from a bank.'

'You have no insurance policies you could cash?'

'No. Nothing. But I can let you have a thousand.' She paused, the germ of an idea forming in her mind. 'If I could get more, could you handle it?' she asked.

'Yes, I could. But I have to know by each Saturday morning. I must telegraph cash to the bookmakers. I have no credit with them – or, indeed, with anyone else.'

'After this, things may be different,' she suggested.

'I very much hope so. I have waited long enough.'

Myrtle opened her handbag, took out her chequebook, wrote

out a bearer cheque for a thousand rupees, and handed it to him.

'Cash it tomorrow,' she told him.

'I will. Soon as the banks open,' he replied, putting it away carefully into his wallet.

'But why tell me this?' Myrtle asked. 'Aren't you taking a risk?'

'Not a very big one,' he told her, smiling. 'And, after all, we have been through troubles together. It is only right that if there are any good times, we should share them. Who knows, one day you may be in a position to do *me* a favour – as the person is who gives me this information. And on this deal I would like a small commission on your winnings. Say five per cent. Put it down in your mind as my fee for helping you in your little trouble.'

'I see. Nothing for nothing, then?'

'It is the way of the world, Myrtle.'

In the taxi going back to the flatlet where Myrtle lived in Sir Hilary's house, she thought about what da Leppo had told her, and her own idea for exploiting it. She sensed he was being honest with her. There was no point in deception; they were two of a kind, outcasts. If they could help each other, they should. She had trusted him with her operation, now he would trust her with this information. Her plan began to grow in her mind, like a seed germinating, and she reached a decision.

'The Century Club, please,' she told the Sikh driver.

The club doorman was not too keen on allowing a non-member into the building, especially an Anglo-Indian girl. As a *mussulman*, he despised everyone of mixed breeding, but Julia arrived while they were still arguing and she took Myrtle up to her dressing room.

'I was wondering how you were,' Julia said insincerely, secretly alarmed in case Myrtle had arrived intending to make trouble of some kind.

'I'm fine. And the club? How's that going?'

'Business is increasing every week. It was a marvellous idea of mine to start it.'

'I rather thought that was my idea,' replied Myrtle quietly.

Julia looked at her sharply. 'I know we talked about it together. Anyway, it doesn't matter *whose* idea it was. It's working.'

'Tell me something,' said Myrtle, 'a personal matter.'

'Not about sex, I hope?'

'No. Something much more important. Money. Do you bet at all, Julia?'

'Never. No spare cash to bet with.'

'You must have some now, surely. Anyhow, I have a red-hot tip. A certain horse is going to win on Saturday at very good odds.'

'Really? I've heard that so often – but usually *after* the race. So much can go wrong. The horse goes lame – or drops dead. A rein can break, the jockey falls off. Anything.'

'Would you bet on a certainty?'

'There's no such thing in racing.'

'What about Romanov? Would he?'

'Not a chance. Betting on horses is too risky for him.'

'This isn't risky. I have the name of a horse that will win its race. I've put all I can afford on its nose. Would you lend me a thousand rupees on top, just for that one day?'

'How would you pay it back?'

'Out of my winnings.'

'But if it loses? Certainties so often seem to.'

'Not in this case. I've saved a thousand rupees in addition to what I am betting myself. I'd repay you with that if the horse lost.'

'So why not use that money now?'

'Perhaps because, like you, I always feel there *must* be some risk.'

'Exactly. No one can say any horse *must* win. It might die yards from the post, but that is unlikely. You haven't the courage of your own convictions, Myrtle.' Julia was about to add, 'It's the same with all you chi-chis,' but managed to stop herself. 'What is the horse's name, anyway? Not that it means anything to me.'

'I'll write it down for you.'

Myrtle picked up a notepad from Julia's make-up table, wrote the word 'Merlin', then 'three o'clock, Saturday'.

'Remember the name. Even if you don't put anything on the horse.'

'I won't put an anna on it,' said Julia firmly.

'That's up to you. Anyhow, I'll pop in next week – just in case the horse *does* win.'

'Have a drink on me if it doesn't.'

'I'll need it.'

Calcutta racecourse that Saturday was crowded. The Governor of Bengal wore a lightweight morning suit, and a pale grey top hat. Most of the men in his party were in uniform. All appeared tall and young and handsome. The ladies wore filmy dresses and the sun flashed heliographs from their expensive jewellery. The message they sent to Myrtle was that this would be how she would dress and look when she was rich.

An air of frenetic excitement touched the crowds, British and Indian alike. Everyone felt that independence for India was not too far away and this kind of spectacle could end abruptly once the Indian Congress Party took power. Why, there were even strong rumours that they would forbid the sale of alcoholic drinks.

Sir Hilary was in his private box with half a dozen local directors of his company and their wives. Myrtle watched from the five-rupee enclosure. In the twenty-rupee enclosure she saw Mrs Ransom with a tall, grey-haired man. He looked rather like an ambassador – or an ageing actor pretending to be one. She knew that Eleanor had seen her, but no sign of recognition passed between them.

Myrtle had no interest in the first race at two o'clock, but she saw from the bookmakers' boards that the odds on Merlin in the next race had shortened from 40 to 30. She guessed that a bookmaker in another city had after all been able to send the news that some people were betting on the horse, but not putting on enough money to cause any real alarm. Could Julia have decided to back Merlin after all? Whether she had or not would not affect Myrtle's plan.

The horses burst out of their gates and sunlight gleamed on the lenses of hundreds of binoculars and pocket telescopes as spectators followed their favourites.

Sir Hilary's colours were purple, black and green. To Myrtle, one horse looked much like another, but she could see the colours clearly enough. Merlin seemed to her unprofessional eyes to be a very small horse, and he started badly. But soon he began to overhaul others ahead of him, and without any apparent effort. Myrtle could see that he was indeed a cut above the other animals in the race; of a different class, of better breeding, and far faster. He came up to fourth place, then third, still moving easily, with infinite grace and amazing power.

As he drew level with the second horse, people all around her suddenly began to shout excitedly: 'Merlin! Merlin!'

In the last thirty yards, he overtook the second horse, ran briefly nose to nose with the leader, whose jockey began to whip his mount frantically, and then, without even a touch from his jockey's whip, Merlin was past the post half a length ahead of his nearest rival. He had won. Myrtle's stake had increased thirtyfold.

The palms of her hands were damp with perspiration. Her knees trembled. As those around her moved away to the unsaddling enclosure to watch Sir Hilary proudly lead in his winner, she took a step forward to the rail and gripped it tightly. The white painted woodwork felt comfortingly warm as she stood breathing deeply until the racing of her heart slowed, and she could calculate her astonishingly good fortune.

She had made 30,000 rupees and had her stake returned. Subtract da Leppo's commission and she was still left with the equivalent of more than £2,000. And if she could have borrowed enough money, she might have made a sum on which she could retire from work for ever. It all seemed unbelievable, an excursion into fairyland – except that this was true.

Myrtle left the racecourse, walked across the grassy maidan to the road and hailed a taxi. Her first inclination was to drive direct to the Century Club and tell Julia what had happened. Then she realised that this would be precipitate. She wanted Julia to have ample time to realise how big a mistake she had made in not backing Merlin, if, indeed, she hadn't.

On Thursday, Myrtle went to the club where the guard now recognised her and saluted smartly. She walked upstairs to Julia's dressing room and found her going through the week's account book. She was wearing glasses. Myrtle had never seen Julia use spectacles at any time, and was rather surprised at the sight. It was the first intimation of ageing she had ever noticed in Julia, and, with it, her own confidence increased.

'I was wondering when you were coming,' Julia greeted her petulantly. 'I had no address for you or I'd have called. I saw your horse won. Did you make a lot of money?'

Envy sharpened Julia's voice. Myrtle looked at her closely. Behind her spectacle lenses, Julia's eyes appeared smaller and meaner than without glasses.

'You didn't back it then?' Myrtle asked her, simulating surprise.

'No. What did you make?'

'A profit, at least,' Myrtle admitted carefully. 'But nothing very dramatic, I didn't have that much money to put on. You could have made a lot – if you'd listened to me.'

'I know – now,' agreed Julia. 'But the way you went on about having a certainty, it just didn't seem possible.'

'Years ago,' replied Myrtle, 'it didn't seem possible that the world was round. However, I have an even better tip for next week.'

'What's the name of the horse?' Julia asked her eagerly.

'Ah! I can't give you that. I took a risk giving you the first. If you'd put money on it locally, the bookies would have cut the odds even more than they did.'

'How did you put it on, then?'

'I telegraphed the bets to bookies in Bombay and Delhi.'

'Sounds very complicated.'

'Not really. Not for a thirty to one win. Do you want me to put something on the other horse for you?'

'What's your stake?' Julia asked her sharply.

'I am putting all my winnings on this second horse.'

'The whole lot? *Everything?*' Julia sounded impressed.

'Every single anna.'

'What are the odds?'

'I can't tell you exactly, but rather better than for Merlin.'

'So if I put on a hundred thousand rupees, I could literally make millions?'

'Or you could lose it all. Those are the two ultimates. Win a lot or lose *the* lot.'

'I can't put any money on in my own name,' said Julia firmly. 'Romanov would kill me if he thought I was gambling. He's drinking a bit, you know, and then he gets melancholy. We're both Russian. I suppose that's why.'

'He's been through a lot,' said Myrtle sympathetically. 'Do you want me to put it on in my name?'

'What if it loses?'

'What if the world ends? I can't *guarantee* that it will win. But I have that assurance from the same person who gave me Merlin.'

'I see Merlin is owned by the industrialist, Sir Hilary Mackenzie.'

'Is that so?' Myrtle asked her innocently. Julia had no idea she worked for Sir Hilary; Myrtle saw no reason to enlighten her.

'I'll tell you what I'll do,' said Julia. 'I'll give you all I have for you to put on.'

'It's a risk,' said Myrtle. 'Don't forget that. As you said, there can never be an absolutely certain certainty.'

'But if I had taken your advice last week, I could have made a fortune.'

'*If*,' Myrtle told her. 'Small word, but it can mean a lot – sometimes everything.'

'Don't you want me to put the money on?' Julia asked angrily. 'Last week you were all for it, and now you're not. Do you want to keep it all to yourself?'

'It's immaterial to me whether you back it or not. That must be your own decision.'

'Of course. I'm sorry. I'm a bit het up. We've got problems here I won't go into. You're very sweet. Well, I've got some money in the safe.'

'How much money?'

'Ninety thousand rupees in cash. Or do you want a cheque?'

'No, cash.'

'Be sure to put it on in your name in case Romanov finds out. How long before the winnings are paid out?'

'I had my cheque on Tuesday for last Saturday's win.'

'Then I'll see you here as soon as you get the cheque. Tuesday, hopefully. I couldn't bear Romanov to find the money had gone. He'd kill me.'

She handed Myrtle a canvas bag of money. It felt strangely small, but the notes were of huge denomination. Myrtle counted them out, put them in her handbag and turned to Julia.

'You'd better call a taxi. I don't want to walk the streets carrying this amount of money.'

'No one would believe someone like you had so much,' replied Julia sharply.

'How true,' agreed Myrtle meekly.

She drove to Grindlay's Bank, paid in the cash, and then telephoned Mrs Ransom.

'I would like to come and see you,' Myrtle told her.

'Delighted,' replied Mrs Ransom warmly. 'When?'

'Now.'

Myrtle took a taxi to the house in Coraya Road. As she entered the hall with its smell of burning joss sticks and the muted sound of Brahms, she felt once more the strange feeling of peace she had experienced on her first visit. But Mrs Ransom had changed, aged in a few months; she was clearly worried.

'I hope this is a social call,' she said, 'because if not and you want to come back and work for me, I should tell you in advance that the owners are closing the place down. India is bound to be independent within the next year or two, and with most of the Europeans going, there will be too few clients to make it pay. The owners want to sell the property while house prices are still high. When the Indians take over, they're certain to drop.'

'I'm sorry to hear you're closing,' said Myrtle. 'You were very kind to me at a time when not many others were. Where are you going when you leave?'

Mrs Ransom shrugged. 'England I suppose. But it's years since I lived there, and I hear everything is so expensive, and rationed and dreary with a Labour government. However, I can't stay here, I'll have to get a job there of some kind. But being an ex-madam isn't exactly the best qualification, is it?'

'I may be able to help you,' said Myrtle. 'I've been given a tip on a horse that is bound to win the two thirty on Saturday.'

'I can't afford to bet,' Mrs Ransom replied at once. 'And if I could, I wouldn't. The only winners are the bookies.'

'Not in this case. I can't give you my source of information, obviously, but this is too important for me to fool around. Put everything you have on the horse, and you will clean up. The odds are fifty to one. They may drop a bit, but not much. The horse is Chameleon.'

'I always liked you,' said Mrs Ransom slowly. 'Tell me, this *is* genuine? I can trust you?'

'Absolutely, a hundred per cent. But on no account bet with a local bookie. If word gets around about how much is going on, the odds will drop like a stone.'

'One of my clients – former clients, rather – is a bookmaker in Bombay. I can telephone him.'

'Do so. Make the arrangements you need for credit now, but only ring him with the horse's name ten minutes before the race starts, in case they wire or teleprint back to Calcutta and the odds drop.'

'I don't know what to say,' said Mrs Ransom. 'Except thank you.'

'Say nothing until you've cleaned up. Then we will have a drink together – but not at Ruggiani's or the Century Club!'

Myrtle then telephoned da Leppo at his flat.

'I have some more money for you,' she told him. 'Are the odds the same?'

'They've dropped a bit, but that's to be expected. They're still forty to one.'

That evening they met in the Great Eastern bar. Myrtle handed him her cheque for 120,000 rupees. He glanced at the figure in surprise.

'Where did you get all this?'

'Last Saturday's winnings, and another source.'

'No questions, no pack drill, eh?'

'Exactly. As you said, it's the way of the world.'

'You're a sharp one,' da Leppo said appreciatively. 'And yet you look so meek and mild.'

'I've had a lot to be meek and mild about,' she retorted, and they both laughed.

On Saturday, Myrtle could not bear to go to the racecourse. She felt she would faint, whether her horse won or lost. Instead, she stayed in her flat, listening to All-India Radio which broadcast a commentary laced heavily with fashion details about clothes and who was wearing them. This meant nothing to Myrtle. All that mattered to her was which horse won the two thirty. At two fifty she knew the answer: Chameleon.

She calculated she was now worth something like £350,000. The sum was beyond her immediate comprehension. She wrote down the figures, unable to believe that so much money could so quickly be within her grasp. She hoped that Eleanor Ransom and da Leppo were also rich. Without her, Myrtle might now be starving. Without him, this astonishing transformation would never have happened.

On Monday morning Myrtle went back to the shop where she had worked. A girl she had never seen before stood behind her old counter.

'I'm looking for Irene Loxby,' Myrtle told her.

'She's left, mem,' the girl explained. 'Can I help you?' She was another chi-chi, thin, tired, anxious to please.

Myrtle took a twenty rupee note from her purse, folded it, pushed it across the counter concealed beneath her palm.

'You can give me her address.'

The girl told her. It was a block of flats, old and decrepit, near Howrah Station. Myrtle hired a taxi and told the driver to wait outside the building until she returned; it would be difficult to find a cruising cab in such a rundown area. She climbed the stairs, carefully keeping away from the peeling, greasy walls, alive with bugs. She knocked on a door.

'Who is it?' Irene Loxby called out cautiously.

'Me. Myrtle.'

The door opened.

'I thought it was the rent collector. I'm a bit behind. Got the sack,' she explained. 'But look at your clothes, Myrtle. Why, you're so *smart*. Come in, if you don't mind the mess. Can't offer you more than a cup of tea, but you're welcome to that.'

'I heard you'd left the shop,' Myrtle replied. 'Have you another job?'

'No. I'm too old. The jobs are all for young girls now.'

'Not mine,' said Myrtle. 'I want to offer you a job as a kind of companion.'

'Who to?'

'Me. More than a companion, really. A friend, a confidante, if you like. You helped me when I was desperate. Now it's my turn to help you. I will pay you four thousand rupees a month, with a guarantee of two years' work. If you like the job, it could be yours for life.'

'Doing what, exactly?'

'Keeping an eye out to protect my interests.'

'What do you do now then, Myrtle?'

'I made a lot of money very quickly. I mean to make a lot more, much more. And I need someone I can trust and rely on with me. To see I don't get stabbed in the back, if you like.'

'For that money,' said Irene Loxby in amazement, 'they can stab me all over like Saint Sebastian was stuck with arrows. I just can't *believe* it, Myrtle.' She began to cry with relief and gratitude.

Myrtle opened her purse, took out a banknote, handed it to Irene.

'Here's one thousand rupees on account,' she said, scribbling her address on the back of an envelope. 'This should help you to believe.'

Myrtle's cheque from the bookmaker arrived in a plain envelope on Tuesday morning. She paid it in to her bank immediately, then drew another cheque, sealed this in an envelope, and took a taxi to the Century Club. As she paid off the driver, she thought suddenly and inconsequentially that from now on she could have her own car and, if she wished, her own personal driver. If she invested the money wisely, she need never work again. The thought seemed incredible, but it was true, it was true. And only a few days previously she had been grateful she could afford a taxi rather than a tonga or a rickshaw.

Julia was in her dressing room, again going through the accounts.

'Chameleon won,' she said tensely. 'Was that the horse you had the tip for?'

'It was. At forty to one.'

'A fortune,' Julia breathed. 'A fortune.'

'Agreed. But before I pay you back, I want to ask you something. Do you remember when you first started this club?'

'Of course I do. Why?'

'It *was* my idea.'

'So you have already told me. I won't argue over it now. Let's have the money. I don't give a damn whose idea the club was.'

'I do. It meant everything to me at the time. Do you remember, I desperately wanted a job here with you? I went to endless trouble with Ruggiani's clients, almost blackmailing them to help you out. And when you turned round and told me you hadn't a place for me at all, I just couldn't believe it, after all I'd done for you. And then, when I got back to Ruggiani's the night you opened, de Souza sacked me on the spot. Said I'd been disloyal. So I lost my job, and you wouldn't employ me. Nor would anyone else. I had nothing. I actually had to work in a brothel to get enough to buy food.'

'I heard something to that effect,' said Julia quickly. 'But that's old hat now. All water under the bridge.'

'Not to me, it isn't.'

'Oh, well. How much did you put on the horse?'

'Everything,' Myrtle told her. 'Here's your cheque.'

She handed the envelope to Julia. She ripped it open, unfolded the cheque Myrtle had made out to her, then peered at it closely, her brows furrowed, lips moving in amazement, disbelief.

'But you said the odds were forty to one. I also saw that in *The Statesman*. I made more than a quarter of a million pounds.

This cheque is only for ninety thousand rupees – just what I put on. You've made a mistake, girl.'

'No. That's what you gave me to put on. I am giving it back to you. With my thanks.'

'But you've won bloody millions. With *my* money.'

'And this club was *my* idea. Without me you wouldn't be here. Not just in your club but in Calcutta. Your permit had expired. Remember?'

'But we had a deal over this. It was agreed.'

'That I would place the bet in my name. I did so. And I won.'

'*You bitch!*' screamed Julia hysterically, throwing her account book at Myrtle. 'You bloody little chi-chi whore!'

'Possibly,' said Myrtle calmly. 'But consider. If you had only been just slightly more grateful to a bloody little chi-chi whore who once desperately wanted a job from you, you could have been rich now, too.'

She opened the door, went down the stairs. When she was outside the building, on the pavement, Myrtle could still hear Julia screaming uncontrollably in rage and frustration. The doorman looked questioningly at Myrtle.

'You have upset her, yes?' he asked nervously.

'In a sense, she upset herself,' Myrtle replied.

'She has a bad temper, that one,' said the doorman. 'It is written, whoever lives in a cave with a tiger must never ruffle the tiger's fur.'

'Agreed,' replied Myrtle gravely. 'But first you must recognise a tiger when you see one.'

FIVE

The Present: Alice Springs and Katherine, Northern Territory, Australia

I was probably the first – and almost certainly the last – person in Katherine to speak to the man I will always think of as the Stranger. And although our meeting had no significance at the time, later it seemed to have been pre-ordained. Certainly, my life changed as a result, and so did the lives of many others. I simply saw a rather ordinary, middle-aged American wearing a suit that had doubtless seemed a good buy in the Midwest or even on the East Coast, but here in the Northern Territory, where the temperature in the shade – if you could find any – was 41 degrees, it must have felt cool as a camelhair overcoat.

He stood, sweating and dabbing his damp forehead with a silk handkerchief, in the departure lounge of Alice Springs airport. He had just flown in on the Perth plane and I had arrived by coach from Ayers Rock, and we both faced an hour's wait for the connection to Katherine. Most of the transit passengers spent the time restlessly walking up and down the lounge, reading and rereading notices on the wall about Rotary Club and Lions meetings, and that day's weather details chalked on a board with the brusque comment: 'Fine. What else? Yesterday was 41. Tonight, 27.'

A shuttle bus came in and disgorged the usual mixture of middle-aged to elderly American, European and Japanese tourists, slung about with the modern essentials of every package tourist: cameras, video recorders, tape recorders. They had been on a trip around the Alice, as we call it. They thought, as tourists often tend to on their first visit, that the town must still look just as Nevil Shute described it in the 1950s. It has changed since his novel was published, and so have they, of course, yet somehow they do not expect to find freephones on the airport wall to White Gum Holiday Inn, or Heavitree Gap Motel, or modern shops like Sports Girl and Plaza Men's Wear. The splendid Ford Plaza, a walk-in covered shopping centre on a palatial scale, with escalators and water cascading on either side past tropical plants, also comes as a surprise.

Instead of bars with corrugated-iron roofs, there are leaflets and advertisements for such diverse activities as Aboriginal Tours, Balloon Safaris. The Frontier Camel Farm invites visitors to 'take a camel out to lunch' and agencies provide escorts ('class and discretion assured'). Here, as elsewhere in every modern town, notices warn motorists 'No standing at any time' or 'Ten-Minute Parking' on the road from the Bistro Tavern to the Stuart Arms. This hostelry took its name from John McDouall Stuart, the first man to cross Australia from south to north. It took him three attempts, until, in 1862, he succeeded. Stuart Highway is called after him, and was about all he got out of it, which, in my book, was very little.

The old Alice has, of course, been emasculated, sanitised, totally obliterated. Now, thin-hipped young wives wearing trouser suits push prams or climb out of Mitsubishi or Mojo four-wheel-drives to buy ice-cream sundaes or have their hair permed. Alice is pretty well right in the geographic centre of Australia, what we call the Red Centre, because of the colour of the soil. When the wind stirs the dust of the desert, it still blows red, like dried blood, but the Outback does not start here any more. Alice is civilised nowadays.

I had better introduce myself and explain why I was in Alice. I am Ian Bruce Crabtree. You may have heard of me now, but then not many knew me outside my home town, Katherine, about 1,183 kilometres to the north. According to the last census, Katherine has a population of 3,715 – which makes it about one-sixth the size of Alice. I was twenty-three, single, and not quite sure in which direction my life was going, if indeed it (or I) was going anywhere that really mattered. Looking back, I guess I was also naive; dumb could be a better word.

Even then, though, I liked to be thought of not just as *an* Australian, but *the* Australian, although, as I have explained, that description belonged to my elder half-brother who, by the time I was born, had already made half a dozen fortunes in Britain and the United States. I admired him, and although we had never met I determined to show him I was not just a kid relation from the Outback but at least as clever as he was, and eventually would be much, much richer.

This was easy enough to say, but even in my most optimistic moments I realised I would have a struggle. Every day I read the financial columns in every newspaper I could find to try and piece together the bones of his career and especially details of his present, most ambitious undertaking: an audacious takeover in Nassau of Trinity-Trio, one of the world's greatest multi-national companies.

Trinity-Trio had been founded by an English doctor, Richard Jackson, an American sea captain, Marvin Ross, and a Scottish remittance man, Alec Douglas, in Calcutta and Hong Kong in the last century. It had recently moved head-quarters to Nassau in advance of the Chinese taking over Hong Kong.

Like many other firms founded in the East, T-T had grown rich in its early days through what was then known as the Forbidden Trade, running opium into China. It branched out into more legitimate activities: manufacturing patent medicines, publishing newspapers and magazines, running timber companies and distilleries, and engaging in worldwide building developments on a prodigious scale.

Each of the three founders had held 100 voting shares: holders of other shares received a dividend but had no power to influence the running of the company. Over the years the successors of these founders had unwisely sold some of their master shares to pay gambling and other debts. Lord Jackson, however, great-great-grandson of Dr Jackson, still held 151 voting shares out of the total of 300, so what he said went. But Jackson had fairly recently formed an attachment of some kind – I did not know what this was, although I could guess – with a young Chinese-American girl, Anna Lu-Kuan. The hint in several financial columns was that he had given her two of these shares.

This might not matter greatly – as long as she voted with him. But then two seemingly unconnected circumstances had suddenly and unexpectedly complicated the situation dangerously. First, my half-brother, apparently with financial backing from an Italian-American consortium led by a Mr Carlotti, had somehow acquired 149 shares. If he could also get hold of Anna Lu-Kuan's two, he and his backers would control Trinity-Trio, and to hell with the noble lord.

The second circumstance was that after the opening ceremony of Trinity-Trio's new headquarters in Nassau, Lord Jackson had fallen from a high window in the office block. There was no suggestion of attempted murder or suicide, or even that he was drunk. By all the accounts I read, he appeared a most abstemious character, if an unhappy one. His wife was American and a wildly compulsive spender; their only daughter was in England in a clinic for drug addicts. That someone whose ancestors had risked death to force China to accept imports of opium, against the orders of the Chinese Emperor who was horrified by its pernicious qualities, should now be a dope-head seemed an astonishingly cruel irony.

Anyhow, Lord Jackson had apparently leaned against a

window after the reception. The window had opened unexpectedly and he fell. The good news, as far as he was concerned, was that he had not been killed instantly; a canvas awning over a lower window had broken his fall. The bad news was that for weeks he had been in a deep coma, kept alive with the help of a life-support machine.

I glanced over the newspapers in the news stand for any further news, but none carried any reports from Nassau, so I had no idea whether my half-brother was any nearer to gaining control of the company.

Most of the other punters waiting for the Ansett NT plane to Katherine were with tourist groups. They stood together, as such people tend to, exchanging non-experiences, making talk so small it was barely noticeable. They also sat together on the aircraft. So I sat next to the Stranger; we were the only two passengers on their own. There is a No Smoking rule on airlines across Australia but not all visitors realise this, so when the Stranger took out a packet of cheroots, I shook my head, and he put them away with a sigh and a shrug.

He had a small face and narrow shoulders. His eyes were set close together, and there seemed something altogether thin about him, I guessed in spirit as well as body, as though he was built to squeeze through a closing door or a gap between planks in a fence. I wondered whether he could be a newspaper reporter; they sometimes have that same ferrety look. Certainly, he seemed out of place in the Northern Territory, which is three times as large as California with no more than 150,000 people, and many times that number of buffalo and camels and crocodiles. All this space for everyone and everything gives us a different outlook to city folk; we think big and most men are built big, as though nature realises there is a lot of space to fill. The Stranger would be more at home in a small town than here among Territorians.

'You live here?' he asked me.

'No,' I told him. 'Katherine.'

'Yeah? I'm saying there a few days. Nice place?'

'It's growing,' I said, which was true. The Royal Australian Air Force was building a new base nearby to house two thousand men. This was going to make a big difference – a boost of about seventy per cent to the total population.

'So what's it like, Katherine?'

'Used to be a big railway junction,' I told him. 'During the Second World War the Japs bombed Darwin and Katherine pretty heavily and most of the women and children got out. The Stuart Highway, the only north–south road across Australia, goes right through the town centre. It became a vital route then and was sealed – tarmaced I expect you'd call it – to take convoys of troops and supplies. That opened up the whole of the Territory. Before, things there hadn't changed much since the first white settlers arrived.'

'How come Alice and Katherine are both named after women?' he asked. 'That a custom here? Feminist politicians?'

I shook my head. He probably knew as little about colonial customs as any of his countrymen.

'No way,' I told him. 'Towns in any new colony – sometimes whole counties and provinces – were often originally named after a king, a queen, the person who discovered them – or his wife.

'Back in the eighteen seventies, a surveyor, working out a route for the overland telegraph line between Adelaide (named after the wife of the English King William IV) in the south and Darwin (named after the scientist, Charles Darwin) in the north, discovered a spring or waterhole in a dry river bed. This seemed a suitable site to build a repeater station to boost the signals. He named the river after the chief South Australian superintendent of telegraphs, Charles Todd. Alice Springs was called Alice after Mrs Todd.'

'And Katherine?'

'Stuart, the pioneer, was backed by a southern business man, James Chambers. When Stuart reached a big river, he called that Katherine River after Mr Chambers' daughter. The town followed.'

'So they licked asses then as now,' said the Stranger, as though voicing an original theory. 'Apart from that, much happen since?'

He was looking out of the window, not at me. He might not have been listening, but he was.

'Not a lot, I admit.'

I did not want to repeat stories my father had often told me about old days in the Alice and Katherine. Some he had heard as a boy from Grandpa Crabtree who in turn had probably heard them from his father; others he knew from his own experiences. Life in those early days was solitary and tough, which it still can be, but not unhappy. Alice then was 500 kilometres from where the railway ended in Oodnadatta. From there on, all stores needed for everyone in the repeater station and the town had to be carried north on camels and carts.

The man in charge of the repeater station had a very important job. He ran the Post Office as well as the station, and was responsible for all Aborigines in central Australia. He was also the magistrate, and held his court in the station. He would even act as an emergency doctor, following instructions tapped up over the line from a doctor in Adelaide. This wasn't a speech line then, of course, just Morse, but it was always manned, for from Darwin the line went under the sea to Java and so on to England. A message could travel from Adelaide to London in hours rather than taking weeks or even months by ship.

On a table in the office stood a curved box that amplified the incoming signal, making it loud enough to wake the night-shift operator. He slept in a cowhide bunk right next to it in the winter, or out on the verandah in the summer, but always within earshot. Lives could depend on a message; it was the staff's pride that none was ever missed.

The station master kept around sixty horses at the Alice, mostly for linesmen who would ride out regularly to check the line for breaks. He had a blacksmith, a cook and a governess for his children. On Sunday mornings, the station master would take his family by horse and buggy fifty kilometres to Simpson's Gap for a picnic – and then back again.

In Katherine, one of the main streets, Giles Street, was named after Alfred Giles, who helped to lay the telegraph line. Giles calculated that up at the Top End they would need sheep for food, so he decided to drive five thousand sheep from the south right up through Alice on to Katherine, a distance of 2,856 kilometres. The government promised to pay him 2/6d a head – but only on delivery.

Giles thought he would lose a lot of sheep on such a long trek, so, as a sideline, he also drove horses for Chinese working in the gold fields. He took fourteen months to reach Katherine. By then, he had seven thousand sheep, more than he started with, because so many lambs were born on the journey. He had also been attacked by Aborigines, and hundreds of sheep had died through eating poisonous plants, but he had achieved what he set out to do. That was the main thing. My father reckoned this was the only real success in anyone's life: set yourself a goal – and reach it. Or as my old schoolmaster used to write on the blackboard after showing us how to solve an equation, QED. *Quod erat demonstrandum* – which was to be proved.

Quite a few White Russians forced out of Manchuria used to live in and around Katherine. One was known as Galloping Jack because he rode everywhere at full gallop; he never let his horse walk, or even trot. In my father's memory, the area where he lived is still called Galloping Jack's. My father would recount the trials an Englishman, Bert Nixon, experienced in the 1930s. Nixon bought himself an Essex car, and although he had never driven any car before, he loaded it with water and food and set out to find a place to farm. When he had a blowout, he discovered the dealer had not included a spare tyre, so he simply stuffed the burst tyre with rope and grass and set off. He became a peanut farmer, but the crop didn't take. After a whole year's work, his total profit was £2.12.0. But Bert Nixon did not complain; people didn't then. There was no one to complain to in any case.

The point of this story for me was not what Nixon put up with, but the fact that he hadn't checked things out properly before he started. That is a lesson easier to learn from someone else's mistakes than your own. It certainly impressed me – as did the experiences of Edward T. Collins, known as 'Cowboy'. Before the Second World War, he ran a butcher's shop in Katherine and sold blocks of ice to his customers so that people out of town, without refrigerators, could keep their meat fresh. Once, out in what we call the 'Never-Never', a bull charged Cowboy, who jumped for a tree. The branch snapped, and he fell. He was badly gored in the stomach, and a testicle was ripped open.

Cowboy's injuries were so serious that he could not move but he had an Aborigine, Shadforth Paddy, with him and he instructed Paddy to pull a hair out of his horse's tail, find a needle in his swag and boil both for ten minutes to sterilise them. Then Cowboy threaded the needle and stitched up his wounds himself. It was either that or lying out in agony in the heat and the red dust until he died.

Cowboy faced a long hard ride home, and the stitches burst on the way, so he sewed up the wounds a second time. He reached home and made a complete recovery. This experience proved to me the wisdom of another saying in our family: if you need a helping hand, there's one at the end of your own right arm. It also helps to have a friend handy.

Whitefellows and Aborigines treated each other as equals then. You can see their easy relationship in old photographs where they are working together, getting on well together, which is how it should be, and not as a result of legislation by people in cities who know little about the real Australia, except what they read in articles by people who often know even less.

I didn't tell the Stranger these things; I felt about them too deeply. As far as I was concerned, they were almost private matters, to be revealed only when you knew someone well enough to be sure he'd understand them and appreciate the strength of character Territorians possessed.

So all I said was: 'Yes, it's a pretty quiet place. But it's got a good library, a fine museum, restaurants, motels, a cemetery.'

I don't know why I added that, but the Stranger turned and looked at me sharply.

'Is the cemetery far out of town?'

'No. About a mile. You know someone buried there?'

He shook his head. 'Never been here in my life before. I'm just trying to locate someone. Alive, I hope, not dead.'

'Oh,' I said. 'Who?'

As I asked the question, I sensed that somehow his answer could affect me, although I had no idea what the answer would be, or who this stranger was, or who he was looking for, or why. Sometimes, maybe once or twice in my lifetime, I have had this gut feeling that what someone is going to say next will be important to me. Georgie, the Aborigine who has worked for my father for the last forty-odd years, tried to explain it once to me in terms of what he and his people believe – that time somehow is elastic, all-enveloping. What has already happened casts a shadow behind you, and maybe what will happen, another shadow in front, and the two meet with you in the middle.

'I'm trying to find a guy, give him a bit of good news,' the Stranger explained.

'What are you, then?' I asked him. 'A football pools rep or something?'

He shook his head. 'Nope. I work for a lawyer in New York.'

'A will, is it?' I asked. This sounded interesting; the sort of thing you see on TV, a lost heir being traced. There was a guy I heard of somewhere in the Outback who was told some relation in England had died and he was now an Earl.

'Yes,' the Stranger said. 'A will. That sort of thing, anyway.'

He was looking over his shoulder through the window. The desert beneath us stretched endlessly, raw and rough, like millions and millions of red-hot bricks, crushed to an angry dust. Here and there, patches of mulga bushes and spinifex grass and clumps of melons sprouted by the side of the long straight strip of Stuart Highway like yellowish footballs. Years ago, before the railways and the road trains, and long before aircraft decimated distance, camel convoys regularly used this track. Their drivers were Afghans and as they trekked they sucked slices of melon and spat out the seeds, which took root. When the railway came in the 1920s, the camel caravans were too slow, so the drivers turned the camels loose. Now about thirty thousand camels are running wild out there in the scrub. Periodically some are rounded up and the best sent to the Middle East for breeding purposes. But in a country as vast as this, thirty thousand is nothing; not when you have stations larger than Wales. As a tribute to the Afghans, the railway that superseded them is still known as the Ghan. Now the only sign of life beneath us was the occasional kangaroo, startled by the noise of the aircraft. We watched them lope off and pause to see whether they were being pursued, and then they were far behind us.

'Kind of hot and empty down there,' the Stranger said.

'If you don't know your way around, you could die in a day,' I told him. 'But you can live there, even if you're lost. See those yellowish plants?'

He looked down through the window without much interest; we were flying low. I could see them easily enough.

'Yeah,' he agreed hesitantly.

'They're honey gravelia. They grow things like yellow fir cones, and between their petals are tiny glistening drops of honey. You can live on them for quite a time. Aborigines do.'

'How do you know this?'

'I was born here,' I told him, which seemed explanation

enough. I didn't go on to tell him about Georgie who had
taught me so much about Australia; not the cities with the
high-rise buildings, not the sights tourists see briefly through
tinted windows in air-conditioned coaches with video pro-
grammes and iced water served at every comfort stop, but the
old country, the real country, huge and secret, the biggest, most
fascinating, most mysterious island in the world.

I did not tell him about Dreaming or the Dreamtime, the
quintessence of everything Aborigines and their ancestors have
ever known and experienced or heard about. Until roughly the
middle of the last century, the centre of Australia was unknown
to anyone except the Aborigines. They illustrated Dreamtime
by painting strange pictures on Ayers Rock and in secret caves
behind it where their women would go to give birth.

In the West, a painting can be judged on aesthetic grounds or
on points of technique. The picture is that artist's statement;
how he or she sees a scene or a person. The characters and
patterns which Aboriginal artists paint restate traditional
truths of the past which, because they are a people without
written records, are otherwise in grave danger of being totally
lost. Most white men are unaware that the paintings exist, and
only a very few can translate them accurately.

Each Aboriginal artist knows some traditional stories and
tells them in colour, linking the present with the Dreaming of
his ancestors. Up in the north, in Arnhemland, the Mimi or
Birirrk were the most important ancestral beings. They formed
mountains from dust, made the rivers, and then designed animals, and grass and trees, so that the animals could eat the grass
and drink from the rivers.

Water played with us, they say now, and we played with it.
The currents carried us along, and the ripples danced and the
spirit of the water touched us. The same spirit taught people to
know where water lay beneath the earth, essential knowledge in
a desert land.

The colours they used were primitive and sometimes

symbolic; paints then did not come from tubes. Red was made from blood and symbolises fighting and hunting. White, which denotes something sacred, came from pipe clay. Yellow marked cliffs, and black came from the ashes of the great fire out of which men and women originally took form. The Aborigines believe that they can always keep the Dreamtime if they paint their pictures on rocks; then there will always be food and children and Dreaming places.

If anyone sang or danced in those places, Georgie would tell me that the spirits would hear them and come back through the songs and the dances and the paintings and the stories. One day, they would all come back. They were here once, and then they disappeared, but they left knowledge behind, much of which is concealed in the paintings preserved in caves. The circles and curving serpents and fish and animals with their bones delineated, like X-ray plates, and yellow and red dots, are not like any other type of painting, for their painters do not work simply on one level, but on three.

First, the paintings are decorative. Second, they tell a story in code; a circle of dots may mean a waterhole, a serpent may represent an angry man. The third level, the secret hidden level, lies deep in the mind of the painter, and can only be revealed to those taught to recognise the secret clues each picture contains. The message concealed in every painting is the ultimate secret essence of the artist's life and soul. This is never spoken of to non-Aborigines, any more than they would explain to Westerners how they can foretell weather, or find water or food in a place where others will see nothing but a red desert beneath a baking sun.

The Abos take these secrets very seriously. No one who has not been fully initiated ever knows them all, and no one save a full-blooded Aborigine can be initiated, although some, like me, have been privileged to see part of a ceremony, if not the main part. Just as we know things that Aborigines don't, so they possess powers that we have lost, or as 'whitefellas' maybe never possessed.

For instance, I have seen prospectors in the latest four-wheel-drive go-anywhere vehicle so worried at the prospect they may run short of water that they festoon their truck with cans and containers. But Georgie only smiled and said: 'If they'd just walk fifty metres to the left and dig down a foot or two, they'd find a big stream right under their feet.'

No rains means no water, which in turn means that stock dies, trees wither, grass turns yellow and brittle like straw and the land becomes bare beneath the pitiless vertical sun. At times like that I have asked Georgie when the rains were due, and sometimes he would tell me and sometimes he wouldn't. He never told me how he knew but (I think as a kind of cover for the real clues) he would look at the ground and then squint at the sun, walk about in a circle and say in three weeks, or two months, or half a year. And always the rains arrived when he said.

Water is so important to the Aborigines that they do not waste it by washing overmuch, or at all. In the Outback they will sleep near a dying fire and in the morning stand over the hot charcoal so that the smoke kills all bugs and bacteria on their bodies and seals in the natural oils.

The Aborigines will use water for medicines, however, or for painting, to mix up the colours. My father told me how way back in the last century, an explorer, Walter Christy Goss, arrived at Ayers Rock and was so thirsty and dirty that when he saw a waterhole near a cave he jumped right into it to wash away the dust of his journey. As far as Aborigines were concerned, this polluted the water for ever. They painted a picture of circles and dots on the cave roof to show what had happened. The waterhole remains unused to this day . . .

The Stranger brought me back from my musing on the past.

'So you must know a lot of folk in and around Katherine?' he said, looking at me closely.

I nodded. 'Some,' I agreed. He wasn't giving much away, so why should I?

'Know a man called Crosby? Ronald Richard Crosby. He's the guy I'm looking for.'

'No. I've never heard of anyone of that name.'

The Stranger shrugged. 'He's an American. Unmarried now, though he has been married and divorced. I've searched for him in the States and in Europe,' he explained. 'He was in Bangkok once, then in Hong Kong, and finally I heard he was in Alice. Spent three days there, but no sign. Then someone said he'd heard that Crosby moved to Katherine.'

'When was this?' I asked him.

'Hell, years ago.'

'Before my time, probably. I can't help you. Sorry.'

'So am I.'

It was growing dark outside now, the hour of evening we call heaven time, when the flies fall asleep and just before the mosquitoes wake up.

'You've lived here all your life?'

'Yes. My father and his father were born and brought up here.'

'And your mother?'

'She's English. Or was. Came out here in the Second World War. Went back to England for a while and then came out again, and stayed.'

'What's your father do?'

'Runs a general store. Well, it's a supermarket now, but it started off in a pretty small way.'

'You work there?'

'Sometimes,' I agreed, and paused. It was no business of the Stranger where I worked, but he prodded on doggedly, just like a reporter.

'So what do you do mostly when you're not working in the store?'

'I buy and sell things on my own account. I started with a bicycle I bought at school. I painted it bright red, sold it for a profit, and then bought another, and so on. Then I went into motorbikes and cars.'

This was how my half-brother had started, so my mother

told me. I figured that if he could grow rich from such small beginnings, I could do the same.

'You run a garage?' the Stranger asked.

'I rent a building I use for spraying cars and so on. When I've saved enough capital, I may start a garage. Get an agency for a Japanese car – Honda, Toyota, Mojo.'

'Good idea. Well, I've got a five hundred dollar bill in my pocket that could have your name on it to help towards that.'

'What have I got to do to make sure it does have my name on it?'

'Find Crosby.'

'No deal,' I said at once. 'I tell you, I've never heard of him. And I can't spend time knocking on doors.'

'Five hundred dollars now. And the same if you find him.'

'You don't sound very hopeful I will.'

'I'm not,' he agreed. 'But I was always told two heads are better than one. Even if they're only sheep's. Interested?'

'To an extent.'

I didn't want to appear too eager, but five hundred Australian dollars down was a useful sum. He handed me five one-hundred-dollar bills.

'I can't spend much time on this,' I told him, trying to sound busier and more important than I was. In any case, I didn't want it to be a long drawn out affair. One can grow old and lose hair trying to solve other people's problems. I couldn't imagine the Australian doing that or wasting any time at all.

'Suits me,' the Stranger said easily. 'Two or three days here should clear it up. One way or the other. I'm staying at the motel. Contact me there if you have any news.'

'But I don't know your name.'

'Because I haven't told you. I want to give Mr Crosby a nice surprise.'

'He knows you?'

'No, sir. If we knew each other, it would be easy. Or at least easier.'

'But how can I contact you at the motel? I won't know what room you're in.'

'Check. Just ask for the American stranger who's arrived. That'll be me. The Stranger. Like the guy Clint Eastwood plays in those Westerns. He rides into town, does what he has to do, and rides out again. And no one really ever knows who the hell he is. But at least I've given you five hundred bucks – which is more than Clint Eastwood does in the movies.'

This explanation didn't convince me but his money did. And did it matter who or what he was? I could always check with the airline office – if he had given his real name to them, which I somehow doubted.

We shook hands. His hand felt damp, as though he had washed but not dried it. Almost unconsciously I rubbed my palm against the side of my trousers. I don't like damp hands.

I gave him my name, telephone number and address; then the seat belt sign came on and the aircraft began its long climb down. We streaked across the darkened runway, past a cluster of small buildings seen briefly in the plane's landing lights like a film being rewound on its spool. Someone down there wheeled out a set of steps and opened the aircraft door. Evening air blew in, hot and so damp it felt like a steam room as we crossed the concrete landing ground. All the other punters were going on to Darwin. The Stranger and I were the only two who stayed in the reception lounge, a bleak and otherwise empty room, with deserted car-hire desks and a wall map of Katherine.

Outside, in the darkness, lizards and frogs and other unseen creatures croaked and whirred and ticked. The man who wheeled out the steps had also guided in the aircraft. When it took off again, he came in, removed his earmuffs and put down his bats. Then he carefully turned off all the lights, one by one, locked up the lounge, closed wire-mesh gates that led to the tarmac, padlocked them, and climbed into a Mojo ute – all without uttering a word.

We sat behind him as he drove towards Katherine along the wide, dark Stuart Highway, empty as a dead man's eyes, with the bush stretching to infinity on either side. He dropped the Stranger off at his motel, and then took me round to the supermarket. I asked him in for a cold beer, but he was new – at least, I hadn't met him before – and he explained he never drank on duty, and anyhow he had to get back to his wife who was poorly. We said goodnight.

It was too early to go to bed. My parents were in the lounge. Crabtree – I don't know why I called my father that, but for some reason I have always called him by his surname – and my mother sat watching a soap on the box. They nodded to me, not wanting to be distracted from the captivating vision of rich homes, huge cabin cruisers, red Ferraris; a glimpse through an electronic window of a perfect world of youth and wealth and beauty that did not exist anywhere except on the box, and which even then vanished from the screen with every commercial break.

I went up to my room, dumped my bag on the edge of the bed and stood looking out at the dark sky, pricked with the huge stars you only see in Australia. I wondered about the Stranger and Crosby, whoever he was. I hoped I could make my second five hundred bucks. Odd, giving so much to someone he had never met, but maybe it was on expenses. At any rate, his money seemed as sound as anyone else's – and A$500 was a lot better than a kick in the crotch. I decided to look for Mr Crosby, and if at all possible to find him.

I did not tell my father or mother about the Stranger's payment to me, any more than I told them the real reason I had to go to Alice. They thought I had been generous in offering to go and see our wholesaler about some goods that had been delayed, en route from Adelaide. That was one reason I went, agreed, but not the main one.

I did tell Georgie about the Stranger, however, *and* why I

went to Alice. I knew he would understand. As an Aborigine, Georgie is directly descended from Australia's original inhabitants who are believed to have migrated from Asia over a land bridge, or isthmus, long before history was ever written. Some say they arrived thirty thousand years ago, others forty thousand. But those days are still fresh in their minds, handed on, father to son, as part of the long ago.

In my opinion, Abos are not only different people, but almost a different species. They belong to a far older race than other white or brown or black people. Their beliefs and traditions stretch back far beyond the beginnings of other religions. They came from lands to the north of Australia, which is where they first settled, in what is now the Northern Territory. There was presumably no need to venture south. Distances in Australia are so vast they are almost incomprehensible to Europeans. From Sydney to Darwin, for example, is 3,154 kilometres, roughly the distance between Moscow and Madrid. From Perth in the south-west to Cairns in the north-east is like going from New York to London.

Much of the Northern Territory is desert, surrounding the Red Centre where the gigantic Ayers Rock, 9 kilometres in circumference, 3.5 kilometres long and 348 metres high, and other large rocks nearby, the Olgas, burst out of the desert. They are like monstrous eruptions from the earth's innermost heart; as though they just had to surge free.

Ayers Rock was named in the 1870s in honour of Henry Ayers, then Prime Minister of South Australia. The Olgas are named after Queen Olga of Würtemberg. It was thought then that these formations could perhaps form the focus of a white settlement but, apart from Aborigines, hardly anyone ever went there. It was too hot, too dry, too far away, on the borders of Western Australia and South Australia and the Northern Territory, virtually in the centre of the country. In the 1920s, a reserve was made here for Aborigines who believe Ayers Rock is sacred. Their name for it is *uluru*, which means a shady place.

The Aborigines have many legends about the Rock's origins, which show its importance to them. When the earth was originally fashioned, in the Dreamtime, gods in the shapes of men and animals moved easily across the face of the world and possessed extraordinary powers. Uluru, for example, was partly fashioned by the *Kuniya* or the carpet snake creatures, and the poisonous snake creatures, the *Liru*, who fought a battle on this site. There was another battle here between the hare wallaby people, the Mala, and the devil dingo. The great rocks remain as battle scars of these epic conflicts and play an important part in Aboriginal thinking and beliefs.

One truly extraordinary feature of the Rock is that on top lies a lake which, despite the heat, never runs dry – and this in the centre of a vast, baking, burning desert that trembles at noon like a furnace, with open-air temperatures of up to 50°C.

I went to Alice mainly because I wanted to visit Ayers Rock again. I agree with the Aborigines that it possesses a strange power. This draws me back, time and again. It also has an electrical aura which can stop watches or make them race ahead, so time here can really lose its meaning. Other matters that seem of great importance elsewhere – wealth, status, the colour of your skin – seem to shrink to their true perspective when one faces the Rock.

The Four Seasons Hotel and the Ayers Rock Sheraton nearby look like ships in the desert, great galleons that have somehow become landlocked. They are shielded from the worst of the heat by a complex mass of huge horizontal canvas sails, each held taut on white metal poles by rods and wires. Tourists here are served excellent kangaroo soup and buffalo steak in the Desert Rose restaurant of the Sheraton before being shepherded into air-conditioned coaches to see the sun set over the Rock.

The road from the hotels soon sheds its smooth tarmac surface and drivers have to wind up their vehicles to over 70 kilometres an hour in order to ride out its harsh corrugations, otherwise their cars could be shaken to pieces. The road is in any case rough enough to make your false teeth drop out, and the guides advise older tourists – not altogether jokingly – to put false teeth in their top pocket or their purse in case they lose them.

On either side, as far as anyone can see, which isn't very far because the land falls away, little trees stand alone under a sun that throws no shadows; it always seems directly overhead. Often, drivers cannot see approaching vehicles, only a moving cloud of red dust. The ground shimmers like a mirage. The few leaves left on the trees are still; so are the blades of grass, and as one approaches the Rock its latent strength pounds like a living heart. It is as though the earth is pulsating, breathing.

Shaped and corrugated like a gigantic human brain, the Rock is more than a sacred place, a natural altar to forces older than organised religions: it is a source of power, inspiration. No one really knows how old it is, but I have heard that six hundred and fifty million years ago some kind of mammoth volcanic eruption disgorged the Rock from the centre of the earth at the same time as the Macdonnell Ranges around the Alice and other mountains that sun and rain have since washed out or burned away. Ayers Rock has survived because it is made of harder rock; and while there's so much of it sticking up out of the ground, several times as much again lies buried beneath it. Its red colour comes from oxidised iron in the soil.

Larger than any sphinx, the Rock is carved and grooved by rivers of rain and time into the likenesses of faces and muscles. One is called the Kangaroo Man, because from a certain angle it does look like a kangaroo's head with one hand held up against an ear.

'He's had an ear-bashing from his wife,' guides will tell foreign tourists, and they laugh and say, 'Isn't he quaint?' Other rocks have their red surface striped and scored by green or black lines, made by algae and lichen, baked in the sun. The hills are everywhere pocked with giant holes and caves. Bushes and small trees sprout in their shade like hairs in an old man's nostrils.

Everywhere, the heat beats back as though from an open furnace door. When the car stops, everything is instantly covered in red dust and there at the centre stands the Rock, throbbing with heat, maybe making the heat, or so it seems, like a gigantic fire coal. A track stretches up one slope with a chain for climbers to grasp as they move very slowly uphill. Tourists flock to the Rock to attempt this ascent. The Abos call them mad white ants. Around twenty have died so far on this climb, either from heart attacks or because they foolishly wandered away from the chain. They think they know a quicker way up, but they don't, only a quicker way to their graves. Except for early morning, before the wind starts, a very strong breeze blows higher up, often to gale force. Some people have literally been blown away when they tried to go after hats or cameras that the wind took.

I have climbed it myself, many times, and placed my hands on its rough, lava-like surface and felt warmth come up through my palms into my body, my blood, my own heart. And I have come down fresher, fitter, because I feel I have recharged the secret batteries of my body and brain. I have briefly become one with the earth, the real earth, not the tilled, over-cultivated, over-nitrated, insecticided stuff they call earth in Europe and North America, but earth from the centre of the world, that was there before time began, that will be there when time has ended and all the clocks run down.

To me, the Rock is symbolic of life. It is just as deceptive and it can be just as deadly. It looks smooth, polished by millions of years of rain, and easy to climb, just as life can also appear easy, but both are actually very rough. And when you do finally reach the top of the Rock, what do you see? A desert, except for the Olgas in the west and Mount Conner in the east. Like many things in life – success included, as I will tell – the effort can be more worthwhile than the reward. Robert Louis Stevenson discovered, long before me, that to journey is better than to arrive.

But to arrive at the base of the Rock at sunset as I had done on the previous evening is an unforgettable experience. The Rock changes colours as quickly as a woman changes moods. It can be blood red, then orange or green; blue as electric lightning, purple or gold. And when all the air-conditioned coaches have left, taking tourists back to air-conditioned hotels, when all the cameras that have been pointed at it have been put away, the Rock remains as a deeper darkness, old as the night that was here before ever the sun was born.

This to me is a holy place, possibly the oldest shrine in all the world. I have been to many other holy places: St Peter's in Rome, Canterbury Cathedral, Jerusalem; in each I have found a sense of peace, as though a gentle spirit still lingers there. But at the Rock I feel a strength we all crave for. People go to other holy places to pray, to light a candle, because the outside world can briefly pass them by. I go to Ayers Rock to feel its strength flow into me. I know that this pulsing rock reaches down towards the centre of the earth, to molten fires that will never be seen, and never extinguished. It touches the core of all volcanos and fiery mountains of legend and myth. Here is a strength more powerful than anything I have ever encountered anywhere in the world. When measured against this timeless steadfastness, against the throbbing, beating power of the heart of Australia, maybe the heart of the whole world, the importance of one's own worries and concerns falls smartly into place.

It was the same after this trip. I went to the Rock, made a pilgrimage, if you like, because I did not know what I was going to do with my life. I wanted a sign, to point me in the direction I should take. I did not want to have a life like my father, running a supermarket in the Outback. I knew I could make money; I had already done so on a modest scale. I was probably as well off as any of my contemporaries, but that was achievement on a low level, life with a small letter.

I wanted something different; I wanted to beat my half-brother at his own game. I came back to the Alice feeling convinced that somehow a sign would present itself, just as there had been signs for other journeyers in doubt in the ancient days of all religions. Thus, when I saw the Stranger in the airport, standing out from all the other tourists with their guides, I sensed he was going to be important to me, so I had to speak to him; and I did.

I tell you these things about the Rock and about me so you will not think it unusual that I should confide in Georgie. He may have difficulty in reading and writing – although I think he exaggerates this – but he can read the signs of the bush and write of the past in paintings that only his tribe can ever truly understand. Georgie also taught me many things I would never have learned at any school.

He told me about the Malanugga-nugga, for instance, the Stone People, who long ago lived in the north and whose ghosts still haunt the area. They could move as silently as spirits of the night, lighting fires that did not smoke, marching so stealthily that as they approached their enemy not a single bird would fly away to give warning of their approach. They lived in haunted caves, because, of all Aborigines, they were born to kill, and they practised many means of murder, even how to deal death from a distance, without even seeing their victims as they killed them.

Such secrets are handed down from the earliest days when men would walk across a world without frontiers to fence them in. Aborigines still feel this urgent, imperative need to go walkabout. They may drive in cars now, but Georgie has often told me how, when he was younger, he and others would walk for miles, sleeping at dusk, moving off again at dawn. The urge to travel can be so strong that Aborigines will abandon jobs and homes and leave without even a word of farewell. Sometimes, they will return in a few weeks or months, and pick up their lives where they had left them, as though they had only been out for a cup of coffee. Birds possess the same imperative urge to migrate across great distances and if they are prevented by being caged, they will beat their wings and bloody their breasts against the bars, trying to break free. But among humans, only the Aborigines possess the need so strongly that it must always be obeyed.

I know from what Georgie has told me of life before the arrival of the Singing String, as they called the overland telegraph line, that many Aborigines possessed strong psychic powers that seem impossible to explain in Western terms. I therefore felt he would immediately understand my instinctive doubts about the American stranger, whereas my father might not.

I found Georgie in a shelter he had made of dried twigs plaited to form a kind of thatch over a frame of wire netting. He was sharpening a knife on a stone.

'An American I met in the Alice has come here looking for another American called Crosby,' I told him. 'He wants to find this bloke so badly he's offering money to anyone who can help.'

Georgie went on sharpening his knife. When he looked up at me, his face was totally without expression, but I couldn't help feeling he was more interested than he let on.

'Why you tell me this?' he asked, testing the blade on his thumb.

'Because he gave me a tip.'

I did not tell him how much, I was ashamed to say that I had accepted so much from someone who had been willing to give me money but not his name.

'He hoped I could help him find this man Crosby. You've been here longer than anyone, Georgie. Ever heard of him?'

He shook his head.

'No Americans living here,' he said slowly. 'Not that I know of. Except tourists. There were, of course, during the war. But afterwards they all went home.'

'Would there be any lists of American soldiers who served here then?'

'How can I say? This stranger fella should try the American consulate in Darwin. I don't know anything about any Crosby. Where is this man staying, in case I did hear something? I could use a tip.'

He smiled, his teeth very white in his black face.

'The motel. But he hasn't given me his name. He says he has some good news for Mr Crosby and wants it to be a surprise.'

'So if I hear anything, I will tell him – or you. But I think it's unlikely.'

I then tackled my parents.

'I flew back from Alice with an American, looking for a man called Crosby,' I told them.

My father shrugged his shoulders. 'No one here of that name, son,' he said shortly. 'I would know. I've lived here donkey's years – all my life, apart from the war.'

'Could he have been a soldier working here in the war, when you were away, so you wouldn't have known him?'

'I was here during the war,' my mother interrupted. 'I don't remember anyone of that name. But then they were all passing through, on their way north to Darwin or down to the Alice. They might spend a night or two here – the railway station was a big camp – but I didn't hear their surnames. It was mostly Joe and Hank and Jim in those days.'

I knew that my mother had been a singer and dancer with a services concert party in Colombo in the early part of the Second World War. The group had split up and her party came to Katherine just before the Japanese attacked Pearl Harbor and Singapore. My mother was married then to an Australian sergeant who was later killed in New Guinea. She never talked about him, and once, when I asked what he had been like, she did not reply directly but fielded the question.

'That's all in the past now, boy,' she said. 'It's a long time ago, and I was very young. We both were.'

And then she looked sad and wistful, almost as though she was about to cry, and I guessed she had loved this man, and maybe still did. Her son by him, Robert James, my half-brother, was born months after his father was killed.

Of course, my mother had to leave the show when it became clear she was pregnant, and she stayed on in Katherine, helping Mrs Crabtree run the store while her husband, my father, was away. He had been taken prisoner in Singapore, so it was some years before he came back.

In the 1950s my mother and her son went back to England where she had relations. Mrs Crabtree was older than her husband and had been in poor health for years, and when she died my father wrote to my mother and asked her to come back to Australia and marry him. I was therefore sure that my mother would have known – if anyone did – whether someone named Crosby had been in Katherine during this period, so I reckoned the Stranger was wasting his time. I felt sorry about this, not so much from his point of view, but from mine. Another A\$500 would come in very useful to help me overtake my half-brother.

The Stranger booked into the motel, collected his key, walked to his room. It was on the ground floor, reached by a covered walkway round the inside of the building, overlooking a small kidney-shaped swimming pool. Palm trees planted round it shook their branches against a full moon and cast trembling shadows on a lawn. The walkway led to a side entrance opening on to a car park. He checked it out thoroughly, because anyone could enter or leave the motel through this doorway without the receptionist knowing. The Stranger's room, like the motel, was neat, clean and impersonal. In an automatic action, he carefully drew the curtains before he switched on the main light. In his shadowy world it could be inadvisable, possibly even fatal, to be in a brightly lit room with the curtains open.

Once, in a small motel outside Santa Barbara in the States, he had been shot at by a philandering husband whose wife had foolishly and hysterically informed him she had hired a private detective to inquire into his affair with the wife of their next-door neighbour. The man's aim was as inept as his infidelity, but there was no guarantee that every other punter who might dislike him for one reason or another, but mainly for one – his interest in their activities – would be an equally poor shot. Not that he expected that sort of thing here in Katherine, which seemed a quiet enough town, but Crosby's enemies – or friends – might want to pay off old debts. He knew nothing about Crosby, or why the attorney in New York wanted him found so quickly, but he guessed that when expensive lawyers demanded speed, large sums of money were generally involved, not least to them as fees. His explanation to young Ian Crabtree was totally fictitious, of course, but he reasoned that the guy was more likely to help him if he thought a handout of some kind was included. At heart, most people were romantics.

The Stranger had not worked on any previous case for this particular attorney. As an investigator who specialised in finding missing persons, often people with no great wish to be discovered – husbands or wives who had vanished with other partners, company directors who had gone over the hill with a suitcase of funds – he was usually engaged by attorneys who specialised in this kind of case. One of these had passed him on to Mr Goldfarb, who was clearly not experienced in dealing with private investigators. His law practice, the Stranger guessed from looking around his sumptuous office in the Rockefeller Plaza in New York, dealt more with trusts and commercial matters, where fees were enormous and work undertaken in a seemingly gentlemanly fashion.

Mr Goldfarb was more at home in formal meetings with men who wore dark suits and bio-chemically clean white shirts, men with button-down collars to match button-down minds. Such meetings were held in panelled board rooms, in exclusive

gentlemen's clubs, or in splendid apartments overlooking
Central Park; not in seedy, squalid bars where investigators met
less formally dressed informants who wished to make a few
bucks by betraying a friend or a friend's friend.

The Stranger remembered the interview with Mr Goldfarb
very clearly. The attorney sat in his black leather chair facing
him across a totally empty, black leather-topped desk edged
with gold tooling.

'I understand you have a pretty good track record in finding people where others have failed,' Mr Goldfarb began
tentatively.

'I endeavour to give satisfaction,' the Stranger agreed.

'I have a client who wishes to discover the whereabouts of an
American citizen whose name I will give you. There is nothing
known about him except that he must now be fairly mature, in
his late sixties, maybe even in his seventies. I don't know what
part of the country he was born in but all that can be found from
records. He was, I understand, in one branch of the armed services during the Second World War.'

'Is this a criminal investigation?'

'Certainly not. An investigation to find someone with whom
my client has lost touch.'

'He is a rich client?'

Mr Goldfarb bowed his head in assent. All his clients came
within that comfortable category. The question was manifestly
absurd. What would an attorney of his distinction be doing
with poor clients?

The Stranger's experience with the very rich was limited.
They seemed invariably to be parsimonious and to have few
friends. To him, they were like men who owned golf courses
but then had no one to play with. On their journey to success
they had lost any friends they might have had at the beginning;
they had either screwed them or moved out of their league. But
as the shadows lengthened in their lives and the past loomed far
larger than the future, they sometimes attempted to renew lost

contacts. They had known people once, when they were poor, and had liked, maybe even loved them. They did not want to be alone on the golf course any more, for the greens were growing dark. They imagined foolishly that time had stood still for those they had abandoned; they could pick up a relationship at the point they had broken it off. They forgot that their former friends had also aged and changed, and might not wish to renew their acquaintance. In the Stranger's experience, the rich remembered only when it suited them; the poor never forgot.

'Expenses?' he asked Mr Goldfarb curtly.

'We'll be generous, but you must submit an itemised account regularly. It will be paid at once and not scrutinised overly. And your fee. I understand you charge by the day?'

'That's right, sir. By the day.'

'Because we are anxious for quick results, I will not ask what your normal fee is, but I will offer you two thousand dollars a day, starting now. If you take the assignment, our discussion here will count as your first day's work.'

'I'll take the assignment,' said the Stranger quickly. Business was not so brisk he could refuse too much of it, and sometimes he had been down to $100 a day. Also, the challenge appealed to him. He would find this guy as quickly as he could and then coast for say a week, maybe a month, bumping up expenses, until he deemed Goldfarb's client would stand no more. And if he was successful, as he had every hope of being, who knew what further commissions Mr Goldfarb might give him?

'My client wishes to discover the whereabouts of a Mr Ronald Richard Crosby,' Mr Goldfarb continued. 'It's no good asking me anything about him, because I know nothing. If I did, I'd obviously tell you. I don't know if he's married, divorced, single, has children, relations, brothers, sisters. I don't even know if he's still alive.'

'What if he's dead? What about the fee then?'

'The same. You're not responsible for life and death.'

'Some would tell you different,' said the Stranger.

Mr Goldfarb smiled. 'Not my client, I am sure,' he said smoothly.

So now the Stranger sat on the bed in his motel room, on the other side of the world, as he had sat in so many other equally impersonal bedrooms, pondering his next move. He lit a cigarette and thumbed through the local telephone directory, the first step in any strange town. On the inside cover he read a stern notice: 'During thunderstorms, the telephone, in common with electrical appliances, can be a source of electric shock. The likelihood of this happening is remote, however it is possible during a thunderstorm, so keep these simple precautions in mind.

'Don't use the telephone unless it is absolutely urgent and keep it as brief as possible. If you must use your telephone, keep clear of electric appliances and metal switches such as stoves etc. and avoid standing in bare feet on uncovered concrete.'

That said much about the extremes of climate in this area, he thought, but he could not see any Ronald Richard Crosby listed in the book. He sighed. Such a lucky break was too much to hope for, but still he had hoped. He had come a long way: he could use some good luck. He replaced the directory on the bedside table and swung his feet up on the bed.

He would have to hoof it around all the stock places; the local registrar's office to check for any marriage, move, or death of anyone of that name. If this produced nothing, then it was on to the local museum, the local library, the local newspaper office. Then came the churches, in case Mr Crosby belonged to any religious denomination. He did not have a photograph of the man, only a drawing made from the attorney's description. According to the Stranger's information so far, Crosby was most likely a wanderer, a man without roots, without possessions, without any permanent address. Such lonely, single men did not always enjoy long lives. Early on he should therefore check out the graves in the cemetery.

At the start of his assignment he had traced Crosby's earlier life through American service and health records to a rooming house in the low Forties in New York. The landlord was an ageing fag with tinted hair, made-up cheeks and silver earrings. He wore a pearl necklace and painted his fingernails bright orange.

'I've got some good news for Mr Crosby,' the Stranger told him.

'Mr Crosby doesn't live here any more. Not for years and years.'

'I am sorry to hear that. It could be good news for you, too, if you can tell me where he does live.'

'What sort of good news?' asked the fag, one hand on his hip, shifting his weight from one foot to the other as though sizing up the Stranger as a possible customer.

'I'm working for a rich lawyer,' the Stranger explained vaguely. 'If you can find him, you could have a thousand bucks up your shirt.'

'A change from some other things I've had up there,' the fag replied with a leer.

'No doubt. Any idea where I can find him?'

'Nope. Not now. He *was* here. Then he moved.'

'When?'

'Hell, as I said, years ago.'

'You know where he went?'

'Nope. No address. But he *said* he was going to Cleveland. I think he had relations there.'

'Of the same name?'

The fag shrugged; this conversation was boring and he had no chance of collecting any money if he couldn't give an address. 'Just don't know.'

'What job did he do? Had he one to go to?'

'He worked part-time in the winter here, helping to clear snow. Then I heard he was working on one of the switchbacks on Coney Island. Had private money, I guess. He was an educated guy. Had travelled. Been in Bangkok, he said. Singapore.

Australia. Hong Kong. You name it. He kept moving around.'

'But he still just took on casual jobs?'

'You could say that.'

'I could. But what are you saying?'

'The same.'

'Did he have any letters, visitors, friends?'

'Nope. None. He was a loner. You couldn't get through to him. He didn't want anyone to try, either.'

'You tried?'

'Oh, sure. But he wasn't my type. Or maybe I wasn't his. Like they say, he just kept himself to himself. But he sure as hell travelled a lot.'

Cleveland is a big city and seems bigger still when you are trying to find one man, without an address, apparently without friends, who moved there many years earlier. None of the Crosbys in the telephone directory knew him, and newspaper advertisements did not produce a single reply. Eventually, and after spending more money than he cared in these circumstances (because when the Stranger added his own 100 per cent mark-up to expenses, almost everything looked a serious sum), he discovered that years previously a man named Crosby had picked up some cash playing the numbers game and bought a standby flight ticket to London, England.

A systematic combing of back issues of provincial newspapers in the British Library in North London brought to light a small news item: an American citizen of that name had been found drunk and disorderly at Dover. The magistrate discharged him on condition he caught the next ferry to France. There the trail died, but a contact in Marseilles reported that a number of foreigners, mostly middle Europeans but including apparently a Canadian and a United States citizen named Crosby had been given permission to enter Australia as immigrants because they possessed special skills. What these were, the Stranger did not know.

Because the Stranger had no better lead to follow, and

because Mr Goldfarb was now pressing for results, the Stranger flew into Perth, the nearest capital city to Europe and so arguably the one where an immigrant from France would land. His first chore was to examine back copies of the *Western Australian* newspaper and the *Australian Enquirer*, one of Trinity-Trio's worldwide publications group. Here he found that a man called Crosbie – the spelling was different and there were no first names – had been run down by a car in St George's Terrace, but had not been seriously injured. He had given an address in Alice Springs. The Stranger followed him north but the address was of a commercial hotel, long since demolished. One old-timer said he vaguely remembered someone of that name who said he had a friend or a relation, he wasn't certain which, in Katherine.

So now the Stranger was in Katherine and as he could have anticipated after so long, the trail lay cold as a dead fish. He stubbed out his cigarette and opened the refrigerator, which contained a mini-bar. He emptied the tiny bottle of whisky into a glass, added ice cubes and then lay back on the bed, wondering whether that young guy Crabtree might just come up with something.

His profession did not encourage optimism; tomorrow, like yesterday, would most probably be another day of drudgery. And yet to judge from TV series about private eyes, they enjoyed a glamorous life, laying beautiful women, solving mysteries by making one crucial telephone call, never short of a drink or a wisecrack. Well, he had the drink, at least. He drank the whisky, emptied another of the bottles into his glass.

There must be better ways of making a living than trying to trace people across the world, he thought. It would be a change to have a wife, a family and a home, a nine to five job and a new Chevvy in the carport, and trips to the Caribbean in the winter, like his neighbours. He was too old for this job; he had been for years. But as he drank, he knew he had left things too late to change. He must go forward, seeking, searching, hunting –

and hoping his quarry could be found. So then he could go back to his office and worry about what the next assignment might be.

He enjoyed beefing about his job, but in a perverse way he also enjoyed the freedom it gave him, the opportunity to drink a great deal of whisky every day at someone else's expense. In fact, he drank steadily, and in recent months this seemed to have brought on bouts of indigestion. He sucked stomach tablets after each meal, but they did not always help him: maybe he should have a medical check-up. He promised himself that he would after this assignment was over, win or lose.

Someone (an attorney or a cop probably, because he saw more of them than any other class of person) had once told him, not altogether admiringly, that he was like a gladiator, older at each new encounter, while the lions in the arena were always new and fresh and young. The comparison was apt; so was the fact that the people who hired him were like the audiences at Roman gladiatorial encounters, not at all concerned at the risks and setbacks he had to endure. All they wanted were quick results as cheaply and as favourable to themselves as possible. How the hell could he supply quick results in this dead-and-alive hick town? He opened a third bottle to drink to ways and means.

Next morning, early, the Stranger walked slowly along Katherine Terrace, enjoying the warmth of the sun on his face. He had made up his mind. If he failed here, he would give up the assignment. Better to resign than be fired, and that darned gut ache, higher now it seemed, in his chest, was nagging him again. He had made quite a sum out of Mr Goldfarb; he could afford a rest.

Katherine reminded him of many anonymous Midwest towns in the United States: wide, straight thoroughfares laid out on the grid system – First Street, Second Street, Third Street. Single-storey shops and buildings on either side of Stuart Highway (which became Katherine Terrace while it ran through the town centre) had familiar Midwest decorations of plastic pennants and posters and signs. Even the names could be interchangeable: Dreamtime Motel Inn, Paddy's Ice Cream and Take-Away, Rod and Rifle, Happy Corner Store, Bill's Trading Post.

The local newspaper office was closed, but in a general store a girl sat behind a counter taking advertisements for it. No, she had never heard of anyone called Crosby, not *Crosby*. Cross*ley*, yes. She checked that no one of that name with the right initials was listed in the street directory. Unfortunately, the newspaper's files only went back a few years. There you go.

The Stranger paid for an advertisement to appear in that week's edition due out on the following morning: *Wanted urgently. Anyone who can help with the whereabouts of Mr Ronald Richard Crosby, US citizen, will hear something greatly to their advantage if they contact Room 14, The Motel, Katherine.* He then bought a street guide, hired a self-drive car and drove out along Giles Street to the cemetery.

Katherine Memorial Cemetery stood on the left of the road, opposite the Gardean Holiday Village which advertised motel cabins and a swimming pool. Houses were built up on stilts, originally because of ants. He guessed that animals used to be tethered underneath where now utes and little Japanese cars were neatly parked. It seemed odd that in so vast a country people lived in such small houses each with its own little patch of garden.

The gravestones in the cemetery also seemed unusually small. Many were no larger than a book standing on end, simply engraved with the briefest details of the dead they commemorated. Here and there, above a newly made grave, he passed a small pyramid of flowers, already fading in the sun. Some people had remembered, but experience had taught him that memories of the dead faded as quickly as flowers. He walked along each row, and paused to read the names.

In a far corner, he saw a new grave covered with a handful of wreaths. Next to it, half a dozen bunches of flowers were piled at the head of a much older grave. He bent down to read the cards: 'To dear dad, in loving memory', on one. On another, 'To Jack, always remembered'. On a third, 'To Eileen, from your grieving husband'.

So who was buried here? A man or a woman? The Stranger moved the wreaths carefully to one side. The grass beneath them lay undisturbed, but the headstone had been removed and the earth around it trodden in hastily. He noted the position of the grave, the number of the row, replaced the wreaths, walked back to his car. Someone had taken the stone and concealed their theft by covering the raw earth with wreaths lifted from other graves. But who – and why?

The clerk in the local Municipal Office was very helpful. He produced records of citizens who had left Katherine or died there, but none of the man he sought.

The Stranger said casually: 'I was looking in the cemetery to see if maybe he could have been buried there. I saw a grave in one corner where the stone has recently been removed.'

'Yes? Well, there you go,' said the clerk easily, as though this happened all the time. 'Here's a plan of the cemetery. Can you point it out?'

'Sure. Here.'

The Stranger instantly put his finger on the plot.

'I can easily find out who's buried there,' the clerk promised him. 'Set your mind at rest.'

He pulled down another book from the shelf.

'We'll have all this on the computer soon,' he explained as he turned its pages. 'Meanwhile, this has details of every plot.' He paused, frowning.

'Except this one?' asked the Stranger softly.

'Right. That page has been torn out. See for yourself.'

'Any idea why?'

'None. I've worked here for three years and this is the first time I've ever known that to happen.'

'Well, there's a first time for everything.'

'I suppose so.'

'Thanks, anyhow. Bit of a mystery, eh?'

'Seems like it,' the clerk agreed, and put away the book.

'I don't want to take up too much of your time,' the Stranger said hesitantly, as though he actually meant what he said, 'but do you have a master list, in alphabetical order – to show if the man I am looking for was buried in the cemetery, even if not in that particular grave?'

'Why, sure,' he said. 'Who are you after?'

'An American, though he might have become an Australian national. Name of Ronald Richard Crosby.'

'I'll find it,' said the clerk. 'No problem.'

He went off, returned with a big loose-leaf folder. Reading upside down, as the Stranger had taught himself to do early on in his business, he read 'Cadell, husband and wife' and 'Cowell, J. Miss'. The clerk turned over the page. Crosby should have been there, but the next name was Crudwell.

'That's odd,' said the clerk, frowning. 'There's a page missing here. Look, you can see the numbers and names.'

'So how could that have happened?'

'Maybe someone wanted a photocopy or something.'

'Does that often happen?'

'Can't say it does.'

'But there's got to be an explanation. Could someone have stolen it?'

'Why, they could, but they would have to know where to find it before they could steal it.'

'You found it.'

'But I'm in charge of the department. I know where these things are.'

'Perhaps someone else knew.'

'Why the hell should they?'

'If we could answer every question,' replied the Stranger philosophically, 'we would both be very wise men.'

'Sorry I can't help you,' said the clerk.

'You've no further copy of this that might not have a page gone?'

'Nothing. There's no call for it. You can see all the sheets are loose. When someone is buried there, we just add their name under their initial. No problem.'

'It seems to be one for me,' said the Stranger.

'Well, there you go,' replied the clerk cheerfully. 'Enjoy your stay in Katherine.'

The Stranger had lunch in a bar and then walked aimlessly through the streets, killing time. Half a dozen Aborigines passed in an open pickup, waving cheerfully to friends coming out of a takeaway. The side of their pickup carried a painted sign: 'Landscape Gardeners – Katherine NT'. The Stranger raised his camera to photograph the words. He sometimes found it useful to have such pictures to prove to his employer he had actually been where he said he had been.

A man in a shop doorway shouted at him. 'Wouldn't do that, mate! Abos don't like their pictures taken.'

'I'm photographing the truck, not the guys in it.'

'They won't know that. They believe that if they're photographed, when they die their spirits will still haunt this place. When an Abo dies, relatives destroy every photograph of them they can find just so that won't happen.'

'Odd custom.'

The man shrugged, neither agreeing nor disagreeing. 'There you go.'

The Stranger hoped that someone would telephone him when the advertisement appeared in the local newspaper, but although he sat in his room all next day when the paper was published, no one rang. That night he decided to admit defeat. He had come to Katherine on what now seemed to be the flimsiest evidence, and clearly it had been too thin. He had found a grave without a headstone, and a page had been torn from a list of the dead, but that was inconclusive, although he could dress it up a bit in his report. Young Ian Crabtree had not turned up with anything, either. In fact, he had not turned up at all. Five hundred dollars down the john.

He bought a full bottle of whisky in the bar – the miniatures barely gave him a glass apiece – carried it back to his room and sat drinking it neat from a toothglass. His stomach ached with each beat of his heart, partly with the whisky, partly with the realisation he was quitting. Whatever else he was or might be, he had never been a quitter. Nonetheless, he would fly back to Alice next day and then telephone Mr Goldfarb in New York. For some reason he could not explain, he did not want to do this from Katherine. He felt something almost hostile and inexplicable here; he was unwelcome. Maybe the dead guy Crosby had been a killer. Maybe he was bad news of some other kind, and no one wanted to remember him. Or maybe he was a good guy and some important citizens hated him. Maybe a dozen reasons, but none of them seemed helpful or reassuring.

As the whisky ran like fire through his veins, the Stranger felt he was becoming melodramatic, which was the last thing a private dick could ever afford to be. He tried to rationalise his concern. Because someone unknown had removed a headstone and put wreaths from other mourners on the grave, that did not mean that the person buried there was the man he sought. Other pages might also be missing from records for all kinds of reasons. And because a young kid hadn't contacted him, it didn't mean he was unwelcome in town, now, did it?

The Stranger had finished half the whisky when he heard a faint scratching noise, like an animal's claw, outside his door. He travelled with a weapon wherever possible, but with all the security checks at overseas airports now, it was unsafe to attempt to smuggle through the smallest pistol. Instead, he kept a thick stick with a leather loop in his suitcase. He put down his glass, gripped the stick in his right hand, loop round his wrist. As he did so, he wondered why the reception clerk had not rung on the house telephone to say someone wanted to see him. Then he remembered the second entrance to the motel. Maybe this was someone coming in response to his advertisement?

The Stranger switched off the light so as to present less of a target to whoever might be outside in case they were hostile, pulled back the curtain and, in the same motion, wrenched open the door.

The moon was riding high. A single very bright star lay reflected and trembling on the ruffled surface of the pool. Palm trees shook their fronds gently, like upturned feather dusters, in a wind blowing from the great empty desert around Katherine. At first the Stranger could not see anyone, and then he saw a figure move towards him; an elderly woman, an Aborigine, wearing shabby clothes, her face in shadow under a scarf.

'You are advertising for news about Mr Crosby,' she said flatly, making this a statement rather than a question.

'Sure. Who are you?'

'My name is Nora. Nora Blackfellow.'

'You know anything about Mr Crosby, Nora?'

'Yes,' she said, and now her voice was only a faint whisper. 'I know something about him. Probably more than anyone else in the world.'

'How?' the Stranger asked her suspiciously. This could be a con of some kind.

'I loved him,' the old woman said simply. 'That's how.'

SIX

The Present: Hong Kong
The Past: Hiroshima, 1945
The Present: Katherine, Northern
Territory, Australia

Dr Sen paused for a moment outside the black and gold lacquered door of the penthouse on the fiftieth floor of the highrise, blue glass Mojo building overlooking Causeway Bay in Hong Kong. He waited, breathing deeply and slowly, until his racing heart had steadied; it was always imprudent to appear short of breath. To show that he had hurried here from his home on Peak Road, the richest area in the island, would intimate his concern and unease, which a successful and fashionable physician should never do. As British policemen used to be taught years ago, when life was more leisurely, they must never appear to hurry, for speed could provoke needless alarm.

Although Dr Sen had come up in the express elevator, his heart was beating as fast as if he had run up the hundred flights of stairs. This was because, without a prior appointment, he now had to face his most illustrious and wealthy patient and admit an error he had never previously experienced with any other patient in thirty-five years of successful specialist practice. He had no idea how this particular patient would react. He could quite easily use his immense power and influence to publicise an inexcusable mistake, and then Dr Sen would face professional ruin. In that unhappy situation, he would have to concentrate on his other patients in Cairns on the north-east coast of Australia. So many Chinese and Japanese and other Asians lived there now, controlling thriving businesses and owning large stretches of land, that the potential encouraged him. But here in Hong Kong there was old money as well as new. It would be tragic to lose his foothold here. He moistened his dry lips with the tip of his tongue at the thought. Then, wiping a hand across his eyes as though to blot out the vision of what might happen, he pressed the doorbell.

A Chinese butler wearing a starched white jacket, its polished brass buttons bearing the Mojo logo, opened the door. Dr Sen explained he wished to see Mr Mojo urgently, but without an appointment. The servant recognised the physician, bowed obsequiously, opened the door.

He led Dr Sen into a sumptuously furnished room overlooking the Bay. Through tinted, double-glazed windows which deflected the sunshine and muffled the constant grumble of traffic far below, the sea glowed blue as a cobalt lake. Toy sailing boats slipped their moorings gracefully outside the Royal Hong Kong Yacht Club. On the edge of the water, and pointing across the Bay, a cannon, shrouded in a canvas cover, stood on a small spit of land. This was the noonday gun, whose history went back to the mid-nineteenth century when Jardine, Matheson, the great trading company, had their headquarters here on East Point. Now they had moved to Bermuda, just as the multinational conglomerate, Trinity-Trio, had transferred their headquarters to Nassau in the Bahamas.

In the early days, companies trading with China were forced to arm their ships against pirates. When these vessels moored off East Point, their weapons were usually stored on shore. Jardine's had maintained their own shore battery with a detachment of guards, and when a *taipan* of their company arrived or left Hong Kong the guns would fire a salute in his honour. One day, a Jardine fast schooner overhauled a becalmed British naval ship and as the schooner approached East Point, the customary welcoming salute thundered across the water. This unexpected salvo angered or alarmed the senior naval officer, who was new to Hong Kong. As a penalty for what he considered eccentric behaviour, Jardine's were instructed to fire a gun henceforth at noon every day, a custom immortalised by Nöel Coward in the words of the song 'Mad Dogs and Englishmen': 'In Hong Kong they strike a gong, and fire a noonday gun'.

Dr Sen heard the distant crack of the gun now, muted by the double layer of glass. He checked his watch – exactly midday. In a changing world, some things did not change.

On the other side of the room Mr Mojo sat in an upholstered black buttoned-leather chair. His feet, their tiny size accentuated by loose alligator-skin slippers, rested on a matching stool. He did not turn as the servant announced his visitor; he might not have heard the man speak.

The servant left and Dr Sen crossed the white Aubusson carpet cautiously. He was relieved to be able to meet his patient without making an appointment for days or even weeks ahead. What he had to say would best be said quickly and at once.

Mojo at last looked up at him incuriously, his yellowish face utterly without expression. He was small and wizened. His skin was leathery and wrinkled like a giant walnut. He wore an expensive lightweight silk suit, a white shirt and a black tie embroidered with the motif 'M', which appeared on every one of the millions of cars that bore his name. The Mojo Automobile Works, which he had founded and in which he was the majority shareholder, was one of the three largest motor manufacturers in Japan.

Mojo put on a pair of black-rimmed, yellow-tinted spectacles to regard his visitor quizzically, but still he did not speak. He was making it clear he did not relish visitors who arrived unannounced, no matter who they were or how personal their business might be. Clearly, Sen's presence gave him no pleasure. On one side of his chair stood a glass-topped table with a bottle of mineral water, a bowl of ice with silver tongs and a crystal goblet. He sipped a drink and then raised his eyebrows slightly.

Sen cleared his throat nervously.

'I did not telephone you, sir,' he began hesitantly. His voice, usually smooth and confident, sounded hoarse with embarrassment. 'I felt I had to come at once and tell you what I have to say, in person.'

'You have bad news?' asked Mojo. 'I assume so, because people, even physicians, rarely hurry with good news. But it could hardly be worse, whatever it may be, than the verdict you gave me in your consulting rooms yesterday. That I have a rare, advanced form of leukaemia, of so pernicious a kind that you were forced to admit it was unlikely I would live beyond the end of the year. I have, of course, kept this diagnosis to myself. Many thousands of employees and their families are directly dependent on my factories, with hundreds of thousands of shareholders, and as many more who work for companies supplying my group with components. Any hint that I might be terminally ill would send our stock plummeting. So what other bad news have you to tell me now that brings you here with such speed?'

'I have come, sir, to ask your indulgence for a most grievous error. I could blame my staff, but as the captain of a ship must accept responsibility for any disaster, whether he is physically on the bridge or not, I assume the same responsibility now.'

'Come to the point,' said Mojo curtly. 'My time is limited.'

'All our time on this earth is limited, sir, but I am thankful to be able to tell you that yours is not circumscribed by the narrow margin I gave you yesterday.'

'What precisely do you mean, Dr Sen?'

'I mean, sir, that in examining the clinical details and giving you the opinion you have just mentioned, I was reading the wrong file. My patients include many political leaders in various countries and the heads of many international financial and manufacturing conglomerates.' Sen hurried to explain. 'If confidential details of their health should ever reach the media, the impact of public confidence could be – as in your case – catastrophic. For security reasons, therefore, no medical information bears the names of patients. Each patient has a special codename which is fed into a secure computer, which is in a lead box and contains no metal wires but optic fibres, so that it is totally impossible for any unauthorised person to hack into it and read its secrets.'

'I am aware of these details,' interrupted Mr Mojo, frowning. 'You appear to forget that one of my companies manufactures this equipment and I know you use a Mojo computer. The type of which you speak is totally secure.'

'Unfortunately, one of my staff made a human error and printed out the medical details of another patient.'

'Then I am *not* going to die so soon, after all?'

'That is what I have come to tell you, sir.'

'So. I have been granted a reprieve.'

'I am very happy indeed to say that is so, sir. And most unhappy, beyond all expressing, that I should have been the bearer of such a false and grievous earlier opinion. I beg you to accept my abject apology for this error, which I can only say has never, *ever* occurred in my whole career.'

'I am glad of that. On two counts, yours and mine,' replied Mojo, but no evidence of pleasure or relief showed on his face; it remained expressionless, bland as a bladder of lard. 'In every career, people make mistakes. But not all admit to them. You, as a man of distinction in your profession, have had the rare courage to do so at once, and I honour you for it.

'Now I will tell *you* something, Dr Sen, which I would not have told you had you stayed silent. As soon as you gave me your prognosis, I sought three other medical opinions from American, Chinese and English specialist physicians practising here in Hong Kong. They told me exactly what you tell me now. That I am not ill. I am in good health, if a little tired by the exertions of the life I have been forced to live. You are therefore the fourth physician to give me the comforting news.'

'I am sorry, sir, more sorry than I can express in words,' the doctor began again, wondering whether this rich old man was bluffing and, if not, who these other specialists were and whether he had told them he had made such a completely wrong diagnosis.

'I accept your explanation and your apology, Doctor. That is the end of the matter. But I admit I was disturbed, as you can appreciate. However, my life has disposed me to take a philosophical view of news, good and bad. How wise was the Lord Buddha when he wrote, "If a man conquer in battle a thousand times a thousand men, and if another conquer himself, he is the greatest of conquerors. One's own self conquered is better than all other people conquered." '

'Very true,' Sen agreed; it was always prudent to concur with the opinions of the powerful.

Mojo sat up, pressed a bell-push concealed in the arm of his chair. The servant materialised at the door.

'A bottle of champagne for Dr Sen and myself,' Mojo told him. 'Taittinger.'

The two men drank in silence, Sen sweating with relief, Mojo now barely able to conceal a smile at his visitor's discomfiture. The servant refilled their glasses, then Mojo motioned him out of the room.

'I have to tell you, Doctor, that this is the second time in my life I have enjoyed such a reprieve,' he began conversationally. 'It is good to know that, as the Christians say, my soul is not yet required of me. In my first reprieve, many years ago, I survived while literally tens of thousands of people all around me died the most terrible, agonising deaths without dignity or honour or meaning. And many more thousands have died since, often after years of suffering, as a direct result of events on that day.'

Sen bowed his head, accepting the information but not fully understanding what the other man meant. He was, however,

too successful a physician to make such an admission. Mojo
regarded him quizzically.

'I was at Hiroshima,' he explained gently.

'I know you have a factory there, sir, as in Tokyo.'

'I hadn't either when the atom bomb landed,' replied Mojo
drily. 'They came later – with much else. Mojo cars, trucks,
motor cycles, lawn mowers. The TV and electronics division.
Much, much else, Doctor.'

He sat for a moment, watching bubbles rise in his petal-
shaped glass, suddenly transported back in time and distance to a
moment etched in his mind with adamantine clarity; eight fifteen
precisely on the morning of 6 August 1945 . . .

He had been standing on the third rung of a set of steps to replace
a fuse high on the wall of the shack he called his workshop. The
electric motor that powered the lathe in the hut on the edge of
Hiroshima, was old and its wiring suspect. In addition, the
motor's brushes were dirty; oil leaked constantly from a defective
bearing seal, for which a replacement was unobtainable at that
stage of the war. As a result, the main fuse kept blowing. The
building was surrounded by larger factories, convenient for him
in his business of repairing bicycles because sometimes a
friendly storekeeper would give him a few odd nuts or bolts or
cotter pins, without which he could not continue his trade, for
supplies of all kinds were very short.

In the early years of the war, during the invasion of Malaya,
Mojo served in the 116th Cycle Regiment. He and his comrades
cycled so far and so fast from their original landing place near
Kota Bharu on the east coast that they wore their thin, synthetic
rubber tyres to shreds and were forced to trundle south on the
bare rims of their wheels. When the defending British and
Indian troops, already demoralised by the Japanese army's
apparently inexorable advance, heard the rumbling of hundreds
of metal wheels on the road at night they wrongly assumed that
enemy tanks were approaching – and retreated precipitately.

Mojo was wounded in his left leg during the last battle for Singapore and was sent back to Japan for treatment. Here he was informed that as a result of his injury his left leg would always be slightly shorter than his right. He was discharged from the army forthwith and given a small financial grant to start his business.

Petrol was severely rationed in Japan and cars in the cities were in any case relatively few, so the demand for bicycles was huge. To help people cycle to and from offices and factories was considered work of high national importance. And so Mojo, with two other men, both too old for the services, established a repair shop.

As he reached up to remove the fuse that morning, all the windows suddenly shattered around him. The glass had not cracked but simply crystallised into tiny pieces, like diamonds. The shack leaped like a living thing a couple of feet off the ground and then crashed down, its doors falling open. The wooden uprights cracked, and the roof sagged and fell. Tools on the bench inexplicably took on a life of their own and flung themselves against the walls with extraordinary force, as though possessed by malevolent demons. A blast of air, hot and fierce and unexpected as an out-of-season typhoon, tore Mojo's spectacles from his face and smashed them against his lathe. At the same time, the whole wrecked room blazed with a light so bright and incandescent that it temporarily blinded him. Once, as an apprentice, he had foolishly stared at a welding arc without wearing his protective goggles, and its brilliance had affected his eyes so seriously that for days afterwards, whenever he closed the lids, he still saw the blue, blazing flame. This light appeared immeasurably brighter, like a second sun that scorched away all shade.

He staggered blindly back from the steps and fell to the ground, breath blown from his body. He was still holding the fuse in his hand and stared at it stupidly, unseeingly. At first he thought that a wire inside the motor must have come loose and shorted. But then he realised that the light had been infinitely brighter than any a minor electrical fault could cause. Gradually, his sight returned, but dimly as through a grey mist.

He reeled about, disorientated, searching frantically for his second pair of spectacles. When he found them in an overall pocket, he discovered that his two workers had been flung against the far walls as if by a demented giant. They stood upright, arms and legs rigidly outstretched as though crucified. Then slowly, while he watched in horror, they slid down to the floor and lay among the litter of glass, plaster, wooden roof laths, cycle frames and wheels that had fallen from hooks around the walls.

There must have been an earthquake, he thought, trying to find a reasonable explanation, and failing. Then he heard the belated thunder of an explosion so loud and hollow that he guessed the shock had been caused by a bomb, though he had not heard an air-raid warning. Had the warning siren even sounded?

On several previous mornings, very early, Mojo had first heard and then seen a single small American aircraft circling the city, high up in the sky, always well out of reach of the anti-aircraft guns. This, he and his neighbours assumed, must be a spotter plane for the B-29 bombers which, for weeks past, had flown regularly over Hiroshima, night after night, but which had never attacked the city. They had flown on to other targets, and Hiroshima had been spared. Now, apparently, the enemy had decided to attack the city.

Mojo knelt down by his two colleagues. They were breathing, but unconscious. He slapped their faces, threw water over them from a fire bucket, but he could not rouse them. They lay as though drugged, both snoring loudly, oblivious to all his attempts to revive them.

Now he heard screams and groans from the street and ran out to see who was injured. He was stunned to discover that all the buildings on either side of the road had simply disappeared.

Where they had been, a pall of dust hung in the air like a choking fog. All that remained of houses and factories were piles of wood and tile and paper. Here and there, rafters and beams stuck up from the ruins like the ribs of a beached and stricken ship.

He heard faint cries for help and water from deep beneath heaps of rubble. People lay in the roadside, their backs, legs, arms broken by the force of the explosion, scorched by the fiercely burning wind that followed it. Some were clearly dead. More writhed feebly, limbs moving without any co-ordination, as if manipulated by hidden springs.

Miraculously, his workshop still stood, lopsided and shattered but recognisable as a building. As he stared, transfixed with horror and disbelief, flames began to erupt from shredded paper walls around him. A heavy sickening odour of boiling sewage and burning flesh hung thickly in the air, laced with a choking stench from stocks of noxious chemicals on fire in the ruined factories.

A naked old woman came down the street towards him. She walked unsteadily, arms stretched out before her as if she could not see her way. As she drew nearer, he saw that her eyes had liquefied. They had literally melted, and thick black fluid, laced with blood and slime, streamed down her cheeks from empty sockets. Instinctively, he put out his hands to try and help her, but as his fingers touched her bare arms, folds of warm, decomposing flesh came away, soft as strips of damp chamois leather.

He turned away, retching in disgust, unable to comprehend what had happened. What kind of bomb could be so deadly? The woman walked on, seemingly too stunned to feel the pain of her unspeakable injuries.

Now a platoon of soldiers came marching down the road, but not briskly as soldiers usually marched. Like the old woman, they were all blinded, with huge, gaping, bleeding sockets in their heads. Some had the flesh burned off their faces, and

Mojo could see charred bone and teeth beneath shreds of blackened tissue. They held on to each other tightly, while one, less incapacitated, led them. Mojo had no idea where they were going, and neither had they: they moved like robots, without aim and in silence. Pain had passed them by; they were beyond help or comfort.

Other people now came staggering out of the ruins in underclothes, or naked. Huge burns disfigured their faces and hands, yet they also seemed oblivious of them; they all moved like the walking dead, their ability to feel pain masked by shock or delirium.

'What is happening?' Mojo asked one who appeared less mutilated than the rest.

'Air raid,' the man replied. 'Must be poison gas.'

But what gas was so strong and deadly that it could blind and disfigure and lay waste a whole city in seconds?

Mojo went back into his shack. He could do nothing for anyone outside; they were all beyond his help. His two employees lay where they had fallen. He knelt down between them, felt their pulses. Both had stopped breathing. In the few minutes he had been outside, they had died. Their faces had been lacerated by a paper packet of hacksaw blades that had flown from the bench. As Mojo stared at them in disbelief the cuts began to ooze thick yellow pus and stinking matter that bubbled and spread over their faces, moving slowly like poisoned honey spilled from a jar.

Mojo plunged his hands into a canister of white spirit he kept for thinning paint in an attempt to cleanse himself and erase the terrible smell of rotting flesh. Then he went out of his shack and started off up the road, no plan in his mind, no aim except to escape the horrors all around him.

Hiroshima city, with a population of around 250,000, was built in the shape of a giant fan, incorporating six islands in rivers that spread out from the main River Ota. He reached one of these minor rivers and paused for breath; his chest felt tight and constricted as though bound by invisible bonds. He was glad to rest, but even here, half a mile from his workshop, fires were burning. New tongues of flame kept starting up from heaps of wood and paper. It took him some time to realise that these piles of rubbish had, only moments before, been houses.

A wide open space outside the city hospital was packed with people. Some stood or squatted, others lay dying or already dead. No one in the huge crowd spoke or moved. It was as though the fearful force of the explosion had destroyed their power of speech – or, even more terrible in Mojo's opinion, their wish or will to speak. These were not people, neighbours, fellow citizens; these were waxworks in a grotesque tableau. He was staring at hundreds of men, women and children drawn together by a catastrophe beyond comprehension.

All windows had been blown out of the hospital building, and on the side of a bridge nearby he saw the perfect imprint of a man's body. His likeness might have been carefully carved in the wall or embedded in it when the concrete was still soft instead of being flung there in an extremity of force and heat. Trees took flame and burned like living torches, branches crackling. Mojo had never seen green, living wood blaze so fiercely; their trunks might have been filled with petrol instead of sap. He could calculate the general direction of the explosion, because all telegraph poles were scorched and singed and smoking on one side.

He walked away, towards the river bank. Here, hundreds more people stood up to their thighs in water, apparently in the hope that flames could not harm them if they were in the river. Some had struck out to reach a small island in the centre, away from the chaos, and the smell and sight of death and mutilation. To die in an air raid might have become an accepted risk in time of war; to putrefy first then to die was too horrible a fate to imagine. The island, green with bamboo clusters and laurel bushes, seemed to offer peace, safety and security. But the effort required to swim so far was too much for most survivors in their dazed, enfeebled condition. Humped bodies drifted downstream on the tide, and the drowning lacked the strength or willpower to lift an arm or even utter a cry for help. The men, women and children crowded on the river bank stared at the island in silence, as though they could somehow will themselves on to its shores. From time to time, someone would sink down in the water, and as their companions moved away from them they would lie where they fell. The feet of the living trampled the dead and dying into the mud of the river bed . . .

With an effort Mojo dragged his thoughts from his first deliverance to the present. Sen was speaking.

'You never told me about your experiences there,' he said solicitously. 'You were extremely fortunate not to suffer any ill effects. The effects of radiation at Hiroshima and Nagasaki have resulted in many cases of cancer or leukaemia that are only now appearing.'

'As you say, Doctor, I was fortunate. People were dying all around me, their flesh literally melting away. Others had suffered the most terrible injuries. But somehow I was saved. It may be, as I have often pondered, that perhaps a different destiny had been ordained for me. Perhaps I was chosen, by whatever gods there may be, to play a part in the regeneration of my country. I do not know. I can only wonder.'

'Was there any medical aid?' Sen asked him.

'Very little. Most of the doctors in Hiroshima were dead, and those who weren't had lost all their drugs. Men and materials, houses, vehicles just disappeared, vanished, vaporised. One doctor, I remember, however, still had a drum of iodine, and he bathed serious cuts and lacerations with this because he had no other medicaments. The worst open wounds he sewed up as best he could with a sailmaker's needle and thread a woman found somewhere, but the flesh would not join. Within an hour these cuts were oozing matter, and stinking like rotting bodies. There was no medical help worth the name. But, even so, I *was* saved. Not by a doctor, but by a prisoner.'

'You mean from the gaol? I suppose in the chaos all the prisoners escaped?'

'I never noticed,' Mojo replied. 'The man I refer to was not a criminal, a prisoner of peacetime law, but a prisoner of war, an American. He was stronger than the rest of us, and mercifully he knew Japanese. I knew a little English, even in those days, so we could understand each other to a limited degree.'

'How did this man help you?'

'First, by exercising discipline. I joined the crowd standing on the river bank, hoping we could somehow reach an island which for some reason appeared to be unaffected by the atomic blast. If we could reach it, we felt – probably quite wrongly – that we would all be saved. But only a few could possibly swim that far – maybe sixty or seventy metres – against a very strong current. And we were all dazed, incoherent in our thinking. We did not know what had happened or was happening. The explosion had destroyed our powers of reasoning.

'We just stood there, wishing we could escape, but seemingly unable to do so. This American found a couple of punts moored by the bank. After the bomb landed, an immense whirlwind sprang up and these boats filled with water and sank. We just stood looking at them. He said we had no time to stand and stare, and organised working parties to bale out the water, using cups or cans or hats, or even just our hands.

'When the punts were floating again, he got us fitter men to paddle with branches, poles, anything. There were no oars, of course. He packed people in, ten at a time, and we ferried them to the island. The river was full of dead bodies and dead fish, floating on the top of the water, already bloated and rotting as though they had been dead for weeks. Their eyes bulged in their heads, big as golf balls.

'Many of the people had not eaten since the previous day, and they were hungry, and there would obviously be nothing to eat on the island. They started to devour these fish. They just picked them up out of the water and began to chew them, fins, heads, scales and all. The American literally snatched the fish out of their hands and threw them away. He told them they could be eating their own death if they swallowed so much as a mouthful. Some believed him and spat out the disgusting rancid flesh. Others didn't – and died.

'He then sent foraging parties from the river bank into town to bring out any bags of rice or sugar they could find, indeed anything edible. For four days and nights, he kept us going. He was tireless, an amazing man. On one of those trips I brought back a portable radio set from my workshop. My company now makes them the size of matchboxes, but I remember that this one was like a suitcase. No matter, it still worked. The American thought it essential for us to learn what was happening elsewhere in Japan and the world, for we were totally cut off, absolutely on our own. We might have been the last people left alive in our country, perhaps even on earth.

'We rigged up an aerial in the trees, and that same morning we heard His Imperial Highness, our most gracious Emperor, make his historic broadcast from Tokyo. The war was over, he told us. Our nation had been vanquished. For all of us, Doctor, that broadcast was the most important event in our lives. Not so much for the terrible news it brought us, but because we all heard our Emperor speak to each of us *individually*. This had never happened before in all our country's history. I can still remember the words he used. As the bomb imprinted human bodies on the walls of buildings, his words are imprinted on my mind. And will remain so until the day I die.'

'A remarkable story,' said Sen. 'Did you ever find out who the American was?'

'I was told he was one of several prisoners of war who had been moved from town to town at that time. He had probably been captured in the Philippines, or maybe he had been moved from a camp in Singapore or here in Hong Kong. I do not know. But it is odd to consider how we might have been on opposing sides at Singapore, ready to kill each other, and then in Hiroshima he saved my life and the lives of many, many more.

'It was our High Command's custom at that stage of the war to move Allied prisoners back to Japan and put them in gaols in towns and cities which they feared might be bombed. They broadcast this intention on all wavelengths in the belief that then the Allies would not bomb these places in case they killed their own people. That, however, proved a totally false hope. But then the war was a time of false hopes for both sides, Dr Sen.

'The British and the Dutch hoped that they would keep their Eastern empires. The Americans hoped to frustrate this intention – which, with Russian help, they succeeded in doing – with the aim of seizing these markets for themselves. This, however, they failed to do because we stole them from under their noses. It is said that only the hungry think constantly of food, and the poor of growing rich. You have to be beaten to long for victory – as we did.

'But, to return. Most of the Allied prisoners in Hiroshima died – there were not very many of them – but this American survived. And instead of thinking of his own situation he helped people who would willingly have killed all prisoners of war as enemies. Feelings ran so high he could easily have been lynched, literally torn apart by angry mobs, simply because he was American, but I suspect that they were so dazed from the explosion they lacked the strength to do so. And that was a blessing, because I owe my life to him, as do so many others of my countrymen.'

'Did you hear what happened to him? Did he go back to the States?'

'I have no idea. He never knew my name and I never knew his. Everything was so chaotic then that we had no time to wonder what happened to anyone else. It was enough to stay alive ourselves. It grieves me that I have never been able to repay the debt I owe the American. We lived from hour to hour. And we were not sure how the American occupying forces would treat us. They could have herded us all into camps or executed us as war criminals. That first year in Japan after the war was very tense.'

'And then, Mr Mojo, you built up your business, I suppose?' said Sen politely.

'Yes. In some respects my life and career parallel that of my rival, Soichiro Honda. Mr Honda was the son of a blacksmith; I was the son of a handicraft teacher. He challenged all kinds of established traditions in his career. So did I.

'Both of us realised at the end of the war that if we were going to create anything, we would have to do so on our own. No one else would help us. I went back to repairing cycles in another shack. Then, like Mr Honda, I had the opportunity of buying a number of small petrol engines that had been built for some wartime purpose and, of course, were quite useless when the war ended.

'Unknown to each other, we both fitted them into strengthened bicycle frames, ran a chain to the back wheel – and were in the motor cycle business. These little motor cycles became very popular. They could carry a rider and quite a bit of luggage, and were cheap to run. When the supply of wartime engines ran out, we made our own, and soon we improved them and built proper motor cycles.

'Of course, we were helped by the Americans. They claimed to hate the colonising influence of Europe because they were once a British colony, but they speedily colonised Japan. We made use of their help and their willingness to back our projects with almost unlimited finance. We despised them, naturally, as you Chinese despised the British traders when Jardine, Matheson and Trinity-Trio were beginning years ago. You called them red-bristled barbarians, as I recall. But you traded with them, and you used them – while they thought they were using you. So it was with us.

'The Emperor's own astrologer foretold in the last days of
the war how the future could still belong to Japan. We would
control it not by force but economically, and financially. This
intention was passed on by word of mouth because, at the time,
it was too dangerous to write down. Also, word of mouth has
somehow a greater impact and importance than the written
word because it *is* secret and there is no record. The message
lives between the speaker and the hearer, and all over Japan
people like me, starting their little businesses, became determined to prove this prophecy true. It was our Emperor's wish,
his command. And we succeeded. Whereas in the past we
simply copied Western ideas, now we improved them – and
produced infinitely better products.'

Mojo fell silent, and sipped his champagne. Through the
tinted windows he watched the sails of yachts beat into the
wind like the wings of seabirds. The red neon Mojo emblem on
the roof of the building was reflected in the water as though
written in blood. Mojo thought the scene seemed somehow
symbolic of victory for his company, his country.

Sen, watching him, congratulated himself on having survived what could have been a catastrophic embarrassment. To
the doctor, the present must always be more important than the
past, and his own affairs were most important of all. He determined to discover how Mojo's medical history had been confused with someone else's file. He had been most fortunate that
the error did not seem to worry Mojo unduly. But the same
could not be said of many of his other equally powerful
patients. The nearness of ruin shocked him. This must never
be allowed to happen again; no matter what the cost, he would
ensure that it did not.

The old Aboriginal woman Nora hurried along Katherine Terrace, at this hour totally deserted under the street lamps. She
passed the Golden Bowl Chinese restaurant, the Happy Corner
Store, Cash for Scrap, all empty. From a bar she could hear the

sound of singing and then a burst of raucous masculine laughter. Through a slat in the window blind, she saw men crammed into the room, shoulder to shoulder, sweating with heat, holding glasses or stubbies of lager. A television screen suspended from the ceiling was tuned to an American soap. The floor was littered with trodden cigarette ends and scraps of paper. Outside the door lay two dogs, heads between their front paws, patiently waiting for their masters to come out. Above them was a printed notice: 'No work clothes. No thongs.' This, Nora knew, effectively excluded any Aborigines, whose only clothes were frequently what they wore to work, and who favoured thonged footwear.

Further along the road, a neon sign flickered above the Randy Rooster, and at the all-night self-service garage a transistor blared rock music and a man was filling the tank of his Mojo ute with lead-free petrol.

Nora noticed these things instinctively, without attaching relative importance to any of them but as a camera records a scene impersonally or a radar installation monitors movement. All her kind had been schooled to read tiny signs in a desert that a whitefellow would never notice. A few blades of grass crushed this way or that meant an animal of a certain size had passed by; examination of a paw mark a whitefellow would never see could provide the animal's name, possibly its size and weight. Blackfellows knew these things because they had to. Once, their survival depended on reading them correctly.

She hurried on silently, wondering about the American whitefellow she had just seen in the motel. He had known very little about the man for whom he was looking, and at first she had been reluctant to speak, not knowing why he was inquiring about Crosby. She believed him when he said he did not know why; he was just acting for someone else in New York, in another country, another world. So she had told him what she knew; not all, but some. It was unwise ever to sell all your belongings to anyone, and knowledge of Crosby was about all she possessed. She had always been poor, but now she was richer by the $500 he had given to her for her help; a fortune.

Nora crossed the road. In Zimin Drive, houses stood several storeys high with wide verandahs. Boats on trailers had been pulled up under the shade of trees. On several lawns, sprinklers still played. There was money here. She passed St Paul's Anglican church, the St John Ambulance office, the Pizza and Chicken Palace, and then other houses with smaller, shabbier utes and old caravans parked outside, some with flat tyres, and big blue gas bottles which in the moonlight looked like huge Ali Baba pots.

The road degenerated into a rough track. Houses here had been abandoned and their metal frames stood like rusting skeletons. She reached her own house, small, single-storeyed, with a corrugated-iron roof. She took down the key from the nail where it hung above the front door, went inside into the main room, and switched on the light.

Six old men were sitting in a circle, backs to the walls. Her heart leapt like a hooked barramundi as she recognised the elders of her tribe. They regarded her with cold, unfriendly eyes.

'How did you get in?' she asked the nearest, as though that mattered now. They were here, and they would not go away until they had done what they had arrived to do; words would never move them.

'A friend gave us the key, and locked the door afterwards when he went away,' explained the oldest man. He was the most senior, the leader, the spokesman. He gave no excuse for entering her locked house, and she did not ask for one. The matter they had come to discuss was clearly too grave for such inessential small talk.

'What do you want?' Nora asked them nervously, looking from one to the other so that she would not need to meet anyone's eyes for more than seconds. Already she guessed the answer and dreaded what they might say, what they might do.

'You have been to see the American stranger at the motel?' the man asked her.

'What is that to you?' she asked, trying to sound defiant, but fear had already thinned her voice. These old men with their coal-black skin, their oddly sloping foreheads, lined faces and grizzled hair literally held the power of life or death over her.

In the old days, she knew, if a man transgressed against the rules of his tribe he would be killed. But the whitefellows' law forbade this, so generally he was given another punishment. He could be beaten about the body with sticks so severely that while he might appear to recover, he would never really be as he had been. He could still breathe, but that is not the only mark of life, and he would remain a living warning to others not to do what he had done. She could not recall that this had happened to a woman, but it might if these men were so minded.

'What did you tell him?'

'Nothing much,' she replied.

'How much is nothing much?'

'He wanted to know about Crosby. I told him.'

'Everything?'

She did not reply.

'Do you know why he wanted this knowledge?'

She shook her head.

'Do you know he has already paid five hundred dollars to Ian Bruce Crabtree to see if he can help him with any information?'

'I had no idea,' she said, genuinely surprised. 'But Ian knows nothing.'

'Nor did the stranger until you told him. Now maybe he knows too much. Men who know too much often talk too much. Especially American whitefellows. What did he pay you?'

Nora shook her head and instinctively held her tattered handbag more closely under her arm.

'Nothing,' she lied hoarsely and unconvincingly.

The man held out his hand, its flesh dark and withered as the claw of an ancient and predatory bird. For a moment she thought of refusing to let him have her handbag, but she knew that if she did it could be taken from her by force. She handed the bag over to him. He opened it. Inside, they could all see the folded $500 bill. Why, oh why, had she not concealed this elsewhere about her body or hidden it outside her house?

'You have betrayed us for this?' the old man asked.

'I have betrayed no one,' she replied stoutly. 'No one.'

The elder did not reply but picked up the bill, unfolded it, struck a match, held it to one corner. The widow Nora watched the flame eat her money away until only a crinkled black wisp of paper remained. The old man crushed it within his palm.

'I did nothing wrong,' she said sullenly, near to tears. 'That money was mine.'

'What you have told the stranger was not yours alone, but ours,' the old man corrected her.

'Burning the money does not solve anything. The American can do what he likes with what he knows now. Nothing *you* can do will stop him.'

The others did not reply but, as though on cue, they all stood up and walked past her into the warm darkness outside. She stood for a moment in the brightly lit room that smelled strongly of male sweat and wood ash. Nora had always found the peaty aroma attractive; she had grown up with it. Now she felt it stood for poverty and loneliness and notices outside whitefellows' bars about working clothes and thongs. She sat down at the table, put her head in her hands on the oil-cloth cover. She had lost the largest sum of money she had ever possessed. She had made enemies of the elders of her tribe. So she wept now, not just for the loss of her money but also for the loss of her dignity, and for the memory of a man she had loved, whom she would never know again.

The Stranger sealed the envelope carefully, wrote Mr Goldfarb's name and address on the back and front, took it out to the reception desk. Behind it a door opened onto a small room where the fat, middle-aged night manager sat drinking Fosters from a stubby and watching TV. The Stranger rapped impatiently on the desk with his knuckles. The manager came out slowly, resentfully, half looking over his shoulder so as not to miss the action.

'What time does the mail go?' the Stranger asked him.

'It's gone, mate.'

'Well, tomorrow?'

'There's a pick-up here at nine.'

'That's the earliest?'

'Right. Everything's shut now.'

'Perhaps you could air mail this for me then?'

'She'll be right,' the manager assured him, taking the envelope, tossing it from one hand to the other as though to guess its weight. 'It's heavy. It'll cost you.'

'Charge it to my room.'

'When are you checking out?'

'In time to catch the morning plane to Alice. Then, on to Sydney. Then home.'

'Short stay?'

'Yes. Very short.'

'Successful?'

'I hope so.'

'Then I've got news for you, sport. All Alice planes are grounded. Checking some mechanical fault.'

'Hell!' said the Stranger in disgust. 'For how long?'

'Twenty-four hours, so it said on the news. Got a ticket?'

'Not confirmed.'

'You'd better get down to the airline office then, in the morning. But if you're delayed here, you should visit Katherine Gorge. Great place for tourists. They love it.'

'I can imagine,' said the Stranger. 'Thanks for telling me.'

He went back to his room, sat on the edge of his bed, opened the refrigerator, emptied the last miniature bottle of whisky into a tooth glass, added ice. If he could not fly out then presumably the letter would not leave either, unless it went by road. Somehow, he did not want to ask the manager about that. If he showed any concern about the letter or hinted it could be important, the manager might suspect it contained valuables and open it. You never knew in these outback places; and trust no one was always a wise motto. Anyway, the letter should be safer with the manager than with him. He did not take to these Aborigines, black as coal, odd, restless people, right out of the Stone Age. There was something sinister about them, hostile. He felt they resented him being there – absurd, of course, because Nora was the only one he'd even spoken to. Maybe all the locals resented him, because he was a stranger, not someone born and reared in this hick town. The sooner he was on that aircraft, the better.

Something about this whole town – or maybe his assign-ment – depressed him. Usually, whisky cheered him, but now he felt unaccountably morose, as though he had received much worse news than a delay to his flight. Was he sickening for something? Perhaps he should have had another malaria jab before he came here. He tried to shake off the feeling of melancholy.

The old Aborigine woman, Nora, had told him more than he had suspected, or imagined. Mr Goldfarb should be pleased. Shit, he'd like to see *him* dig out all the stuff he'd discovered. That meant he could easily bump up his expenses to hire a car tomorrow to go and see the Gorge, if he wanted to. He would charge it to visiting his informant.

He sat drinking, and as he drank a dull ache seemed to spread from his stomach through his body. He had never in all his life experienced such a strange feeling. As he put down the glass on the bedside table he noticed that his hand shook very slightly. No question, he was sickening for some goddamned thing, some fever. Must be. The Stranger loosened his tie and collar and lay back on the bed, still wearing his shoes. Gradually, he drifted into an uneasy sleep.

I was late home that night. I had been halfway to the Gorge to look at a car belonging to a stockman who had been advertising it in the weekly paper for the previous six weeks, without finding a buyer. It was an early MGB, the type with chromium bumpers, and I offered him a price which he accepted so quickly I guessed there must be more wrong with the car than I could discover in a quick glance. No matter, I was sure I could deck it out and make a few hundred dollars clear on a resale. Small time, agreed, but didn't the Rothschilds point out that no one ever goes broke taking a profit?

My trip paid me another and altogether unexpected dividend, for if I had not been driving back after dark I would never have seen a faint flickering glow of fire out in the bush. The moon had not yet risen, and it was impossible to tell where the flat lands ended and the hills began; all seemed dark and empty, a world without people, as it must have appeared to the first pioneers; vast, brooding, unforgiving. The fitful glow, probably less than a mile from the road, intrigued me. Either some people were camping out there, which they would be unwise to do when there was the Gorge Caravan Park up the road and another camp for backpackers even nearer, or a forest fire was starting.

The rain was overdue and sometimes a fire, begun by accident from a match or cigarette end thrown away, could burn miles of bush and scrub and trees so fiercely that the whole area would still be steaming after the rain had come and gone. I felt I should find out, if only to raise the alarm, so I parked my car off the road and walked towards the faint light.

Maybe there was another reason for my interest, nothing to do with checking on a fire risk. I am Australian born and, like all of us in the Northern Territory, proud of being a Territorian. As such, I respect the earlier culture that claimed the land long before white settlers arrived. I knew the strange rules by which many of the older Aborigines still lived. If you ate a wild turkey, or its eggs, they believed you would suffer from premature old age. If you ate a lizard or its fat, you could become deformed or diseased. If you ate an eagle hawk, you would grow thin – but not if you ate the eagle hawk's legs. These were supposed to make you strong. When I was a boy, Georgie had often tapped me lightly on my calves with an eagle hawk's leg bone, explaining that in this way strength would pass from the bird's bones to mine.

I half wondered whether the firelight was something to do with an Aboriginal initiation ceremony, part of the complex ritual when a boy is accepted by his tribe as a man. Most races and religions have these, from the warrior customs of the Masai in Africa to the purely religious ceremonies that mark the moment a boy becomes a man: Bar Mitzvah, confirmation, first Communion.

Or perhaps the fire might signify some other tribal ceremony which it was not thought fit for outsiders to see. I had never considered myself an outsider. Georgie had sponsored me through an abridged initiation ceremony years before and I considered myself to be at least an associate of his tribe, if not a fully paid-up member.

Even so, I approached the light cautiously in a wide circle, moving nearer and nearer to it with each step, but not making for it in a direct line. There was no need to advertise my arrival. Strangers were unwelcome at such private rites, and I might be severely beaten up before I could explain who I was and why I was there. I bent down, flattened my hands in the reddish dust by the side of the road and smeared it on my face to darken my skin. Then I began to walk, very slowly, very carefully, towards the fire.

As I drew closer, I could see a young Aborigine frantically stamping out the fire. I guessed he had been sent to watch it did not spread and somehow had let it grow too large. A small fire with tiny flames would not be seen through the thick net of bushes, but fire is necessary for most of the old secret ceremonies and in the dry its size is almost impossible to control.

I passed close by, silently and downwind; Aborigines may smell to us very strongly of wood ash, sweat and smoke, but we smell equally obnoxious to them. Their noses are as sharp as their eyes, and they can pick up the approach of unwanted strangers from an unbelievable distance. The young Aborigine could also be a sentry to warn of intruders. In that case, there might be others on watch. It was unlikely he would be on his own.

I walked more slowly now, putting each foot down carefully to avoid stepping on a twig that might crack or touching an unseen branch that could rustle. This was fortunate, because I was closer to whatever was happening than I had realised. As the moon came up slowly, I saw four Aborigines, naked except for their shorts, on the far side of the fire. One wore a *kuruurkna*, a girdle made from hair taken from a dead man – hence of great magical importance. Two other men crouched on the ground, one on his knees with his hands spread out on the earth in front of him. His companion knelt at right angles to him, with his elbows resting on his back. Clasped in his hands was an *irna*, a small pointed stick or bone. In the dim light of the fire I could see that it was scored with notches and had a fine spiral groove gouged into it. The far end was sharpened like a skewer and the end closest to his body decorated with white and red bird down. Attached by a blob of resin, a strand of human hair trembled in the firelight.

None of the men moved. They could have been a group of statues. The glowing fire turned their black, oiled bodies the colour of new-spilled blood. I heard the pointer of the stick utter the incantation: '*Ita pukalana purtulinja appinia-a* – May your heart be rent asunder.' And then, after a pause, a second incantation: '*Okinchincha quin appinia-a ilicha ilicha-a* – May your head and throat be split open.'

I knew the words because Georgie had taught me, but never

had I seen the Aborigines use the magic stick or bone in what is the most private and deadly ceremony of a dozen secret rituals, and hence the most feared. It is, quite simply, a means of delivering death from a distance, without any visible connection between the killers and whoever it has been decided to kill.

There is no rational explanation for its success that I have ever heard. No one seems to know how it works, except perhaps a handful of Aborigines who have been given the secret, handed down, mouth pressed to ear, generation to generation, but who knows who they are? And even if one discovered them, how to prove that they knew what has confounded scientists since the days of Captain Cook?

I remember how Georgie once took me to see an Aboriginal man, about thirty years old, ill in bed. He was gibbering like a monkey, his lips flecked with white saliva. He was beyond the power of speech or reason. Within hours after we had visited him he was dead – yet medically he had appeared perfectly fit.

'I showed him to you,' Georgie told me afterwards, 'so you could see for yourself the power of us blackfellows' law. That man was sung to death. He did not know by whom, or why, or where the singing took place. That made it impossible for him to appeal for mercy to those who wish him to die. He must have offended someone who has the power to kill, or who knows who in his tribe possesses it.'

'Is there *nothing* that could have saved him?' I asked Georgie.

'Yes. But only if you can find another blackfellow with even stronger magic. That is difficult because who under the whitefellows' law will admit to knowing any of these ancient and deadly rites?'

I knew that these two men, guarded by the others, were killing a man at one remove. They might not have met their target; it was possible they had never even seen him, and he had probably never heard of them. I was watching an act of murder – and doing nothing to stop it. I kept silent because if my presence was discovered I feared I might not leave the bush alive.

There were, I had been told, other ways of singing someone to death. One magic means is called *ungakura* and needs a strange mixture of bones, the claws of eagle hawks and a strand of human hair about two metres long. At one end are tied five small pointing bones and at the other the bird's claws and a single pointing bone. Like the method I was watching, this needs two men to operate it properly. First, they throw up a little heap of earth between them and their victim, whether they can see him or not. This shield is to protect them while they prepare to kill him. They believe that if this protection is not made, then the intended victim will dream, and in his dream he will see the mother of the man using the bone. This will warn him that one of her sons is trying to kill him – and then he could take his own action against them.

Singers using this method of murder at a remove claim that the claws and bones contain deadly magic which, when they are jerked on the hair, somehow leave the bones and travel into the body of their victim. Figuratively, the claws tear his bowels to pieces and he dies in agony – but without an outward mark of any sort. There is no physical attack; it is, as fashionable psychiatrists would say, all in the mind.

Aborigines in the Western Macdonnell Ranges use human hair plaited to a length of two feet and covered with red down from a bird. To this is fixed a lump of resin from which two front teeth of a rat protrude. It is called *tchintu*, which is the local Waiinyuri name for the sun. When the secret incantation is repeated, heat is drawn down from the sun. The singers place the string and teeth and resin in the footprint of the victim in the belief that the sun's heat will thereby pass from their primitive apparatus into the foot of the man or woman and he or she will then die of fever.

It is easy to laugh at these claims and to ask how teeth, resin, hair, bones or claws can possibly possess any evil power, or, if they do, how it can have sufficient malevolent strength to harm, let alone kill, anyone. I think the bones, teeth, hair and all the rest are simply to conceal whatever the real and deadly power may be; they draw curiosity as a magnet attracts iron filings, they are the screen for something too secret to be seen.

It is easy to deny there is a force of evil in the world as well as a force of good. To some people, compositions of otherwise apparently innocent artefacts can increase the force of evil, just as the Christian cross – or even only making its sign – has proved to be strong enough to drive out hauntings from houses in the Western world. I do not know how these spells and incantations work. I only know that they do, and anyone who tells you differently is either deluding themselves or attempting to delude you.

I wondered now who their victim was, and tried to project my eye along the line of the stick, which, to be effective, would have to be pointed towards their target. And I wondered whether the modern phrase about pointing the finger at someone, or putting the finger on them, fingering them – a term of accusation – had its roots in this Aboriginal rite. The stick was pointing towards Katherine and to an expensive residential area where no Aborigines lived; they could not afford to. Then I remembered Georgie's reaction when I mentioned the Stranger and his inquiries about Mr Crosby. I felt that Georgie knew something about Crosby he did not wish me to know. Could it be that he did not wish anyone else to know either?

The stick was pointing in the direction of the American's motel. At this realisation I felt nausea sweep over me like a dark and fearful tide. I did not know how long the incantations would last, or whether the spell could be broken. I knew I did not dare to interrupt these men on peril of my life, for no one outside a hallowed few who witnessed such sacred events was allowed to live; that was how they remained secret. But the least I could do was to warn the American myself, and tell him to move out of the path of these evil invisible rays which emanated from the sharpened point of the stick.

I backed away from the scene as quickly as I could, skirting the dull, glowing embers of the fire. In my haste and eagerness to be away, I foolishly forgot the basic rules of the hunted against the hunter: silence, stealth, cunning. I trod on some tiny branch I had not seen. It cracked like a whip. I sensed rather than felt hostile movement near me. Then someone was on my back. He brought up his knee in my left kidney and I was down in the dust on my hands and knees, gasping with pain.

I knew that somehow I had to escape. If I didn't, I could be dead. I rolled over in a paroxysm of agony and anxiety, kicked out wildly, and dug my left elbow back into a stomach, hard with knotted muscle. I heard a surprised gasp, a grunt of pain and for a second the iron hold on my back loosened slightly. Then I was up, facing my adversary. He was an Aborigine youth, naked except for a pair of shorts. I could see his face, grey with ash, under the travelling moon, sweat shining like varnish on his bare body.

I hit him hard. He hit me just as hard, and we slugged it out, both silent, both keeping quiet for different reasons. He, because he feared that if the elders realised he had allowed a stranger to approach so close his punishment could be as harsh as mine. I, because I needed all my strength, my energy, my breath, to overcome the burning pain in my kidney, and I guessed what could happen to me if he won.

He didn't win. I used all the guile, all the blows I had seen employed by stockmen in drunken fights. The knee in the groin, the elbow in the guts, the edge of my right hand across his throat. The Aborigine also landed some heavy blows on me; my left eye suddenly swelled, so quickly and totally that I could not see out of it. But I fought more scientifically and with the energy of despair, and gradually he fell away. I staggered back, gasping, all pretence now at silence lost. I had to run or die. I ran.

I raced like a frightened steer, careless of any noise, leaping obstacles, bushes, tree branches until I reached the car. My pounding heart did not ease until I was well on the road to the motel. Even then I kept looking back but the road behind me lay straight and empty under the moon. No one was following me. My anxiety diminished with each succeeding mile. It was unlikely I had been recognised; I could be any rubberneck, not Ian Bruce Crabtree.

The hour was late, so I used the side door of the motel which I knew was left open for the use of regular travellers, salesmen and reps who might break their journey here at unsocial hours. A few nightlights burned on the shaded verandah, and reflected stars trembled in ripples on the pool.

The Stranger's room was in darkness. I tapped gently on the door. I heard a grunt and a sleepy 'Yes?' from inside. So I was not too late. At the sound of his voice, my fears for his safety receded. I told myself that I was being a fool, an idiot, to think that some almost naked native men in the bush miles away could conceivably harm this healthy and successful American visitor by pointing a piece of stick or bone in his direction and muttering some mumbo-jumbo.

'Who's there? What's the matter?' came his voice, clearer now, edged with irritation – or could it be alarm?

'It's about Crosby,' I told him through the closed door.

'Who are you? I was asleep.'

The Stranger's voice now sounded slurred, either from sleep or drink, or both.

'It's Ian Crabtree,' I explained in a hoarse whisper; I did not want to wake anyone who might be asleep in the next room. 'I *must* see you.'

He shuffled towards the door, unlocked it, held it open for me. All the windows were shut against mosquitoes or intruders, and the air felt stale, used up, like air in a sick room. By the light of a bedside lamp I stared intently at the Stranger's face. It was damp with sweat and puffy, yet not with the puffiness of a sleeper suddenly awakened. He was ill. I could see this from the droop of his shoulders, the dullness of his eyes. Yet he appeared to be fully dressed.

'What the hell's the matter?' he asked, blinking sleepily at me. 'You've got a black eye. You're sweating like a hog and covered in red dust. Are you stoned? What's happened to you?'

His voice was thick. He sounded like a man dredging for words in the deep recesses of his brain.

'I got into a fight,' I said.

'Jeez! You could say that again. What happened to the other guy?'

'I don't know. It's what's going to happen to you that worries me. You've got to get out of here.'

'Why? What the shit have *I* got to do with it? You said you wanted to see me about Crosby.'

'It's because of Crosby you've got to go.'

'I am going, soon as I can. But the goddamn plane's not flying. I'm going to take a trip down the Gorge and leave as soon as that plane's back in service.'

'That could be too late,' I said desperately.

'What the hell do you mean, too late?'

'What I say. You *must* leave before then. Now. I can't explain here, but someone means to do you harm.'

'Like who?'

'Like some Aborigines.'

'I've just seen one goddamn Aborigine, an old woman. I gave her five hundred bucks.'

'She helped you find Crosby?'

'Nope. As I thought, Crosby's dead. But she told me about him, how he died. Told me a lot about him.'

'What was her name?'

'She told me and I've forgotten. No, I tell a lie. My memory's all to hell. She was called Nora. Without an H. I don't know her other name. My God, boy, I feel ill.'

'You crook?' I asked him.

'Crook? I'm not a crook. If I were, I'd be rich.'

He tried to grin at the feeble pun and then grimaced as though the effort had hurt him.

'Crook here means ill.'

'Yeah, I know. Got a touch of fever. When I went to bed my head was thumping like a steam engine.'

'Get out now,' I said urgently. 'I'll help you to pack. Come and stay with me. We've a spare room in our house.'

'What the hell for? I'll have a slug of whisky now I'm awake, and I'll chew a clutch of aspirins. I'll be fine in the morning.'

I couldn't tell him he could be dead in the morning. If I explained that I believed he was the victim of some local form of black magic, he would laugh at me. People are always reluctant to believe in events outside or beyond the narrow parameters of their own experience. Doubting Thomas proved this conclusively long ago, in another country, at another time.

'No. You must go *now*.'

'Shit! I'm going soon as I can. I've told you.'

'Look,' I said as patiently as I could. 'There are all sorts of things here you don't know about, undercurrents of evil you don't understand, and you wouldn't believe if I told you.'

'Try me,' he said.

He sat down heavily on the bed. A shaky hand reached out for a glass. He poured four fingers of whisky and drank. I noticed that a lot of the whisky ran down his chin. He did not seem to notice this, but sat there staring at me, bleary-eyed. I knew I was looking at a dying man, and he didn't believe he was even in any danger.

'It's a sort of voodoo thing,' I said. This was the only word I thought he might understand.

'You mean, like in Haiti? Native crap?'

'If you like, yes. You've disturbed something. You got up people's noses here.'

'Like who?' he asked. 'I paid you. You produced sod all. Similarly, that old Abo woman, Nora. How could I get up her nose? You mean she wanted a thousand bucks instead of five hundred? Greedy bitch.'

I shook my head. I was talking a different language, and we did not have a phrase book between us. I was calling across a gulf of thousands of years. He couldn't begin to understand, and I couldn't begin to tell him. But I tried. All my life, I'll know I tried.

'Listen,' I said desperately. 'I don't know what you've disturbed, or who or why, but some of these black fellows want to do you harm. So get out, *now*! While you can.'

'Balls! I've paid for the room.'

'I don't care what you've paid for. You can pay with your life if you stay. Come round to my place. I live with my parents. There's a spare room. I'll put you up till you can go. Better still, hire a car and drive out of town, down to Alice – anywhere. *Now.* Before it's too late.'

'Too late for what?'

'Too late to leave,' I said.

'Shit!' he said. 'This is a con. I should never have given you five hundred bucks. You want more. You're like everyone nowadays, gi'me, gi'me, gi'me.'

He was becoming belligerent. He could feel unease moving sluggishly through his body. He did not know why he felt like this, but he knew he was in an alien country, among alien people he did not understand. He wanted out, but he did not wish to show fear.

'Come on,' I said more gently. 'Come with me now.'

'No, I'm staying here. You come in here, stoned, beaten up after some fight, and give me a load of shit. I'm staying.'

'Those your last words?' I asked him. Even as I spoke, I thought that this seemed unintentionally prophetic. Ironic, maybe. He didn't see that, of course.

'I'm staying,' he repeated. 'I served in Vietnam two years. Nothing happened to me there. And nothing's going to happen to me here in this hick town. But thanks for trying to tell me what I didn't want to know.'

'I'm sorry,' I said. 'At least I did try.'

'I just don't understand you. I think you're out of your god-damn mind.'

'No,' I said. 'I wish I were.'

I got up to go. The Stranger stood up, too, but shakily. He put down the empty glass on the side table with all the slow, desperate deliberation of someone very ill or drunk, or both, trying to steady a trembling hand.

'You're a nice kid,' he said, more gently. 'But don't try to frighten me. I've been frightened by professionals.'

'Maybe,' I said. 'But not by people like these. Their art of frightening goes back forty thousand years.'

'Mine goes back to Adam,' he retorted.

He followed me to the door. I went out into the darkness. The moon's reflection trembled on the pool in the evening wind and the fronds of the palms brushed against the stars. A shape materialised by my side. Georgie.

'You saw what you weren't meant to see,' he said. He didn't have to spell out what he meant.

'Only a little,' I said.

'It could be too much. You broke a young black fellow's jaw.'

'He could have broken mine,' I retorted.

'Maybe he still will – or his friends.'

'You were pointing the bone at that American in there, the Stranger, weren't you?'

'I was just there,' replied Georgie, neither confirming – nor denying the charge. 'What others do is their affair. What I do is mine.'

'But why point at that guy? He's harmless.'

'You know nothing about him.'

'He paid me some money to look for a fellow called Crosby. I couldn't find him.'

'Crosby's dead.'

'Who was he?'

'No one you need know about. He came from the States.

He travelled through Australia, and he died.'

'Here in Katherine?'

'In the desert.'

'Where's he buried?'

'That's immaterial. It's where his spirit was that mattered. His spirit has left this place. Now listen, Ian.'

He leaned towards me, so close that I could smell as well as see the burnt ash still on his face.

'I heard you through the door, warning the Stranger to get out. I'll give you the same advice.'

'Why?' I asked him foolishly as though I did not already know.

'Because it is dangerous for you to stay here.'

I thought about this for a moment. He was giving me the same advice I had given to the Stranger. He hadn't taken it. I decided I would.

'I could go down to Tennant Creek,' I said. 'Bloke there has offered me a couple of old cars.'

'Go there then for a few days. Meantime, I'll do my best to make it blow over for you. Now, good night and goodbye.'

As quickly and silently as he had arrived, Georgie was gone and I was in the dark, alone and afraid.

SEVEN

The Past: Calcutta, India, 1945
Coventry, England, 1947
Nassau, Bahamas, 1947

When Myrtle Gibson became used to the astonishing fact that she was rich, she took a week's holiday from Sir Hilary's office. She bought a small house outside Alipore and arranged for it to be converted into two flats so that rent from a tenant in one covered all outgoings on the second, which she gave to her mother.

She then rented an apartment for herself in Park Street, threw out all her clothes and ordered new ones. But even this expenditure, which a few weeks earlier she would have considered impossibly extravagant, did not diminish her fortune to any significant extent. More, she became aware of a curious feeling of discontent, absurd as it seemed. Was this success? If so, it seemed inexplicably empty, just as it had been unexpectedly easy to achieve.

Before the week was out, she bought herself a Pontiac car and hired a Sikh chauffeur, a cook and a bearer. But even a week seemed too long a time without any real work which would have somehow added spice to her freedom. She was a great one for remembering quotations she had once learned at school, and now a line from Shakespeare took on a totally new significance: 'If every day were making holiday, to sport would be as tedious as to work.' He was right. It was. Myrtle felt she was simply idling, marking time, not going anywhere. She invited da Leppo to dinner to seek his opinion.

'How do you plan to spend your money?' she asked him bluntly.

'I didn't make anything as much as I assume you did,' da Leppo replied. 'And I'll probably never have a chance like that again. Also, I owed quite a number of people for all sorts of things. At least I've got them off my back.'

'I thought you were well off,' said Myrtle, surprised at this admission.

'I'm glad,' da Leppo replied with a wry grin. 'When you have little money, it is important that you appear wealthy. It is only when you are rich that you don't give a damn how you look, or what you wear, or how shabby your clothes are. What are you going to do now you are in that happy situation?'

'It's very boring, having nothing to do. I think I will go on with my job, working with Sir Hilary.'

Mr da Leppo noted that she had said 'with' rather than 'for' but did not remark on it, and Myrtle did not explain her plans further. Money had released ambitions she never previously realised she could possess. Before, it had been enough to have food to eat, clothes to wear, a regular job. Now, everything was different. Having always been on the outside, looking in, it was rewarding to be on the inside, looking out.

Money, she knew, could be frittered away, as silly middle-aged men spent it in Ruggiani's or the Century Club, or it could be used to make more money. More money brought you more power and with sufficient power you could reach a position where nobody could ever mess you about, as she and her mother had been treated in the past. Money did not talk; it shouted. People always listened to its voice with respect and deference. Then, no one voiced concern about the colour of your skin; all that mattered was the colour of your money.

Hilary Mackenzie had no idea that Myrtle had won so much on his two winning horses. He had made a few thousand rupees himself, but nothing important; he had always been wealthy, so making more money seemed unnecessary. However, he did notice that Myrtle's clothes seemed smarter, and she exuded a new air of confidence, but he assumed that this must be because he was paying her a very good salary.

During the next eighteen months, Myrtle set herself to learn all she could about his business, for this seemed to offer her the best chance to become a person of consequence. At every opportunity she studied documents relating to his factories in Calcutta and elsewhere. Most surprising to her were the details she discovered about the steel mill and iron ore mine the group owned in Canada.

The Second World War had brought a huge demand for steel, but the company still reported heavy and steadily increasing losses. Indeed, the more steel they produced, the greater was their loss, which seemed to her to be an impossible situation – and quite untenable now that the war was over and car manufacturers could buy steel from any source.

The group headquarters was in Coventry, England. Before the war the Mackenzie factory there had produced a range of dull but worthy saloon cars; during the war it had turned out hundreds of light tanks and four-wheel-drive trucks. They were produced on what was called a cost-plus basis – actual costs plus a profit of ten per cent, a system the government introduced to stop profiteering. Sir Hilary's directors now reported that the huge Canadian losses were affecting the whole group and they sought Sir Hilary's return to Coventry as a matter of extreme urgency.

After some delay, he was given passage on a troopship carrying two thousand British soldiers home after several years overseas. Myrtle accompanied Sir Hilary. They joined a handful of other civilians, mostly senior civil servants travelling to Britain on government business.

Life in England just after the war was not as Myrtle imagined it would be. Her expectations derived chiefly from brightly coloured calendars illustrated with pictures of farm wagons, Shire horses, winding country lanes, and rolling fields heavy with yellow corn. She imagined that England was still like this; thatched cottages, farmhouses, and Palladian mansions. People took afternoon tea on their lawns (Earl Grey and thinly sliced cucumber sandwiches) or spent summer afternoons strolling along the banks of small, gently flowing rivers.

Instead, she found a sad, war-damaged land; vast areas of Liverpool, where the ship docked, and Coventry had been bombed and then bulldozed flat. Rows of houses had totally disappeared but here and there grotesque façades remained, empty windows gaping like blackened eye sockets. Strips of contrasting wallpaper still flapped on the remaining walls of a bathroom, a bedroom, like flags of a forgotten army. Everything seemed grey, black, cold and very small, and without the redeeming benefit of a warm, burnishing sun. The only vehicles on the roads were trucks or buses or shabby pre-war cars. She was dismayed at the lack of grace and elegance; at the meagre rations and an apparently national acceptance of mediocrity in what was still the heart of the Empire and, as such, should surely be a shining citadel of power.

Myrtle had been surprised when Sir Hilary suggested she accompany him but immediately accepted. This was an opportunity she could not afford to miss to learn about the workings of the Mackenzie group. She realised she was becoming useful to him, and that her opinion counted – largely because he often had no opinion of his own to offer. When one was asked for, he would look blankly at other directors in a board meeting, as though trying to gauge from their expressions what their views might be, and then align his accordingly. Also, she guessed he did not trust her completely. If she was with him, his secret would be safer than if she was several thousand miles away. Publicly, of course, Sir Hilary was in total command.

Newspaper reports described him as 'the leading industrialist', a man of boundless patriotism who had given unstintingly of his time and his treasure to help the successful prosecution of the war. According to the Press, his visit to England was to discuss financing a huge extension of the factory to restart production of cars now that wartime contracts were ending. The real reason for it, as Myrtle knew, was less optimistic.

Oil paintings of past Mackenzies looked down on the group of dreary, dull-faced men assembled in the factory boardroom. Apart from a stenographer of about her own age, Myrtle was the only woman present. The room was cold – years earlier, an air raid had destroyed part of the heating system – and a coal fire burned smokily in the black-leaded grate. The other directors looked tired and ill fed. She was surprised at their shiny suits and threadbare collars. She had not realised until she landed at Liverpool that clothes were still tightly rationed; at the most, one suit and a new shirt could be bought in a twelve-month. She had the curious feeling of being at the death of something, either the company or the spirit that had inspired its founders. To her, the directors seemed like mourners gathered for a will to be read.

As the chief accountant made his report, the full gravity of the group's situation became apparent and Myrtle understood the reason for the atmosphere of gloom.

'I have to report to you, gentlemen,' he began, ignoring the presence of Myrtle and the stenographer, 'that Mackenzie Industries worked at full capacity throughout the war. Even so, this factory, making trucks and armoured cars, working three shifts, day and night, in common with our other factories in the Empire, has been – and regrettably still is – trading at a serious and daily increasing loss.'

The accountant nervously fingered the knot of his tie. He was a grey, lacklustre man. He glanced quickly round the table and continued.

'The Canadian steel mill is the sole cause of our huge losses.

Before the outbreak of war, as you are no doubt aware, many hundreds of thousands of dollars were spent on the mill and the mines which supply the ore. Today, the mill produces two hundred thousand tons of steel ingots every year and roughly as much pig iron and coke. Only Algoma is bigger than we are, and both of us are in the position of having steel mills virtually alongside our main source of ore. This would seem an ideal situation – and with the war machine demanding more and more steel every day, it should have been immensely profitable. But in extracting the high-quality ore we need, our company also has to produce enormous amounts of sinter. It seemed they could not have one without the other, but before the war the sinter was, so I am informed by the company's technical experts, a new product.

'Local blast furnaces had not used it before, although our technicians reported that it was perfectly adequate for their purposes – and a lot more economical. But their directors were conservative men and distrusted change. So we could not find buyers for it. Remember, too, that in the late nineteen thirties – as compared to now – the steel industry in Canada was not very prosperous. Companies were therefore reluctant to experiment – and in many cases genuinely could not afford to do so. If the result was a fiasco, they could be ruined.

'More steel was being produced then than could be used, and we were all in direct competition with much larger American companies which could afford to cut their prices just to beat off any competition. In some cases, they undercut us so severely that we were in danger of being run out of business altogether. Only the fact that other companies in our group were profitable saved us.'

The accountant paused, as if inviting comments, but no one spoke.

'Just before the war,' he went on 'we had hundreds of thousands of tons of sinter piling up, because we could not convince blast furnace companies they should buy it. Moreover, our

sinter also contained manganese, which is now extremely valuable. Just before the outbreak of war, when our steel company
was literally on the edge of bankruptcy – and in danger of
dragging the rest of the group down with it – we signed a
contract with a United States company. For the next fifteen
years the American company would market on our behalf all
the sinter we produced. The price agreed was low, but remember it was the only price we could get. The contract had a
subsidiary clause which at the time seemed so unlikely to be
acted on that no one gave it a second glance. It stated that
if at any time we should not have enough iron ore left for
our own steel production, we would buy from them at the going
rate.

'We were in a cleft stick, gentlemen. Obviously we would
not have signed the agreement if we had realised war was
imminent, for the war meant that the demand for steel
increased overnight. At the time the contract appeared provi-
dential, like a lifeline to a drowning man. Now it has become a
noose around our necks.

'With the outbreak of war, the Canadian government's War
Measures Act prevented us from increasing our price – even if
our buyers would have allowed us to do so. We were – and still
are – committed to the American contract at pre-war prices.
We cannot raise the price of our sinter, and we still get nothing
for the manganese which the Americans sell on at a great and
ever increasing profit.

'During the war, iron ore of every quality, good, bad or
indifferent, was in enormous demand. It still is. Moribund
North American factories began producing again. Prices rose,
wages increased, the cost of operations soared, yet we were
bound by our contract. We are locked into it for another ten
years, gentlemen, bound by agreement to sell all the sinter we
produce, millions of tons of it, plus manganese – and on every
ton we make a loss. Meanwhile, our mill is producing more
steel than we can provide ore for, so, under the subsidiary

clause, we have to buy in higher grade ore from the American company. Also at a steadily increasing price.'

'Bloody madness!' exclaimed one of the directors, a large, red-faced man.

The accountant blinked at the interruption. 'At the time and with full board approval – I have the minutes here – it was agreed we were very fortunate to find a buyer,' he pointed out. 'After all, any price seemed better than none.'

The red-faced man studied his blotter.

'Although every branch is making a profit except for the steel mill,' the accountant continued, 'the whole group is being dragged down by the mill's steadily increasing losses because all our companies are controlled by the holding company of Mackenzie Industries. A loss by one is therefore set against the profit in another.'

'Can't we sell off the steel part, mill, mines, the lot?' asked another director.

'Who would want it, burdened with such a debt?'

'What do we owe?'

'Several million dollars.'

'You have an exact figure?'

'Yes. As of the end of last month, in round figures, five and a half million dollars. And remember, that is on top of all the profits that have already been eaten up.'

'Why did you let it go so far?'

'With war conditions and Sir Hilary being in India, it has been difficult to get decisions. I have kept Sir Hilary, as the chairman and principal shareholder, informed by letter every month of this increasingly serious situation. I had no reaction, so this extraordinary meeting was called because we *must* have a decision – or consider winding up the whole group.'

The accountant looked across at Hilary now who blinked, flushed, and began to sweat. Myrtle felt scorn for him, and saw her contempt mirrored in the faces of the other directors. They had been working seven days a week on set salaries throughout the war, and the man who controlled the whole organisation had not even bothered to respond to warnings about the company's solvency given to him regularly for years. She wondered whether Hilary had even read the letters, or, if he had, whether he understood them. Seemingly not, or he would have acted before this. Certainly, she had not seen them in any of the files she had consulted. Perhaps he had read them and then destroyed them, hoping the problem would somehow go away.

As Sir Hilary tried to stare them down, to pretend he had an answer to the problem, he felt long hard searching fingers of pain squeeze his chest in an iron clasp. He held his breath until the grip loosened and then he breathed slowly, carefully, in case the pain returned.

He hoped no one had noticed his discomfort – only a spasm of indigestion, he told himself. He glanced at the directors individually, but none seemed to be looking at him; they were all looking at Myrtle as she asked a question.

'Have we approached the Americans to ascertain their views?'

She guessed that none of the directors were quite sure of her position. They might think she was Hilary's mistress, or a sort of Girl Friday, perhaps even a high-caste Indian, the daughter of a maharajah, someone like that. They had never been to India; they did not know about Anglo-Indians. But they knew she must be important; that was obvious, or she would never have been given a passage to England at that time.

'Of course,' the accountant replied. 'We have tried on several occasions to renegotiate the contract.'

'With what result?'

'They won't budge. What they really want is to take over the mine and the steel mill, for they can get them for virtually nothing. They would then, as an American company, have a very considerable foothold in Canada's steel industry. Algoma Steel is the biggest producer in Canada, as you know, but even Algoma had a rough passage before the war. We are second in size to them. They'll never buy Algoma, but they can take us over – they know it, and mean to do it.'

'Then why don't we sell before they do?' asked the red-faced man. 'Cheaper in the long run to cut our losses. Any price must be better than giving everything away, surely?'

'No!' said Myrtle sharply. 'That reasoning brought us to this pass now. We must do better than that. Where are these people to be found?'

'In the Midwest or the Bahamas. Their company has just been registered there to gain tax advantages.' The accountant rustled some papers. 'In fact, Mr Walter P. Cowan, the managing director and chairman, who, with his family, holds the majority of the voting shares, is in Nassau now. On holiday. He owns a house on Cable Beach which I understand is a most exclusive residential area.'

'Can we get to Nassau these days?' Myrtle asked.

'It's difficult, Miss Gibson. No liners are sailing regularly yet, but banana boats still make the passage. They did all through the war, not even in convoy. Their owners gambled the U-boats wouldn't waste a torpedo on a banana boat. They sail from Bristol to Kingston, Jamaica. From there you can reach Miami. Pan American have an air link on down to Nassau. Why, are you thinking of going?'

Myrtle looked at Sir Hilary. 'I think we should. You and I,' she told him.

'What can we hope to achieve when for years experts have been unable to find a solution?' he asked her petulantly.

'Perhaps, because we are not experts, we might employ some lateral thinking – approach the problem obliquely. Please put it to the meeting that we should go.'

Sir Hilary looked inquiringly at his fellow directors. They shrugged their shoulders. They had nothing left to lose in letting him go, the situation seemed lost beyond redemption. Myrtle could see their low opinion of Sir Hilary. He was a cypher, not a chairman. He had inherited the firm, while they had all worked for years before they were appointed to the board.

The motion was put to the vote. It was passed unanimously.

Myrtle and Mr da Leppo sat on the terrace of the best hotel in Nassau, watching the evening sun drown in a sea of lapis lazuli. Above them, tiny bulbs twinkled in the painted ceiling like captive, coloured stars. In front of them stretched a long and bone-white beach, combed and re-combed every day, now empty, pale and ghostly in the gathering dusk. Beyond this beach, waves sighed on the sand, breaking in a long spume of phosphorescence. Mr da Leppo lit a cigar and blew expensive Cuban smoke towards the ocean.

'Reminds me of those evenings we used to spend in the Great Eastern Hotel bar,' he said conversationally. 'Except the view is better here. Remember?'

'I can never forget,' replied Myrtle. 'It was good of you to come.'

'My dear Myrtle, your wish is always my command. In any case, I was growing tired of administering to the needs of very rich, very old women in Santa Barbara and all points north up the California coast. You have no conception how wealthy some of these widows are – or how stupid. Their husbands killed themselves making fortunes out of breakfast cereals, soft drinks, selling motor cars, you name it. Now they have so much money they simply cannot spend it all, though they do try very hard.

'They flock to join any new religious cult or follow every new health fad. They want to believe in *something*, anything, and the more they have to pay, the more they imagine it must do them good. Money is simply of no consequence to them, they have so much. And at heart they're all lonely and miserable and afraid of dying, because then even their wealth won't shield them from reality. Death is the only real democracy, dearie. And when you're lousy with money and very, very old, who wants to vote Democrat for that?

'But I was right to go there. They had a scare just after I arrived from Calcutta, thought the Japanese were landing. It was amusing to see them. After all, we can both remember Japanese air raids in Calcutta. Then, I had no money to buy the houses and shops and other possessions the rich and terrified Bengalis were almost giving away. In California, I was rather better placed to take advantage of the situation.'

'I'm glad to hear that,' said Myrtle, sipping her orange juice. 'I can remember everything about Calcutta. But not very often. Not now.'

'I understand. But it is wise sometimes to remember that we were not always as we are today. I have my clinic, you know. That keeps me busy and is very lucrative.'

'But you're not qualified, are you?'

'Not in medicine, agreed. But I don't have to be. I had cards printed: Professor of Medicine, Sexual Biochemistry and Medical Thought Therapy at the Royal Portuguese University of Macau. Licentiate of the International Medical College of Portimão, Portugal. Fellow of the Institute of Applied Psychiatry, Goa.'

'But you're none of those things?'

'There *are* none of those things. I made them up. But they sound impressive, you must agree. And that is the most important thing. Anyway, no one has queried them so far.'

'But they could easily check you are not on any medical register and are not qualified to practise medicine.'

'I have never said otherwise. And I don't practise medicine in any accepted sense, although sometimes, you will admit, I have helped a lady in distress.'

'Touché.'

'I remember a famous circus in England called Lord George Sanger's Circus,' da Leppo continued. 'He was never a peer. He just liked the name. I've registered my name, too, as *Doctor* Luis da Leppo. It's all legal. I explain that because of the delicate nature of my treatment I dislike publicity. People stay out of *Who's Who*, you know, for the same reason. In fact, I give them this explanation before they can ask why they can't check me out in any medical directory. It disarms them at once.'

'All of them?'

'Sufficient. Those who doubt, don't come back. And, after all, I try never to treat any real illness. But what is so urgent that you summoned me to this delectable spot?'

'Maybe I wanted to pay back a debt I owed you. Remember the bill you never put in? And the tip you gave me over two horses?'

'Of course. But I seem to remember I took a percentage of your winnings. It's a long way for me to come to collect a debt that has already been paid, or to remind me of a long forgotten good turn.'

'There was another reason for inviting you here,' said Myrtle, and told him.

Da Leppo listened carefully, drawing thoughtfully on his cigar. His face in the dim light was fatter now and fuller. Success had changed him. But then success had also changed her, in the way it changes everyone who feels its golden touch; and, of course, years had passed since last they met.

'I need someone I can trust,' she said simply. 'As you see, I'm playing for very big stakes. And I can't possibly win on my own. Irene Loxby is very loyal, but this sort of thing is quite out of her league. And the fewer who know about it, the better. I can offer you a share in the deal – if I can pull it off.'

'How big a share?'

'It depends on what you do,' replied Myrtle carefully.

'What would I have to do for five per cent of Mackenzie Industries?'

'Exactly what I tell you. But only if my ploy for the other ninety-five comes off. You can't have that in writing, but we'll shake on it. You put a lot of money my way on those horses.'

'My sadness then was I had so little to put on for myself. But I had so many debts and I needed most of what was left to set myself up in the States.'

'But you couldn't use your rupees there. India is in the sterling area. Exchange control regulations would have stopped you.'

'Agreed, dear lady, but I travelled west by way of Nassau here, like Christopher Columbus, who was their first tourist. Here, all money can be changed – for a price. This is the home of the moneychangers. All through the war, the banks along Bay Street were happily changing millions of Deutschmarks, Dutch guilders, Austrian schillings into whatever currency the client wanted. These notes came in bags, sometimes damp with sea water where they had been dragged out of wrecked ships or taken out of flooded bank vaults in countries the Nazis overran. They all went through the mill here – and came out fresh and new in any currency the depositor needed. A remarkable process, dearie, that still goes on.'

'But the Duke of Windsor, who was the Governor here then, didn't he know about this? Didn't he stop it?'

'The Duke of Windsor, dear lady, needed a lot of money to keep his Duchess happy. And not just in sterling. He was no longer so attractive to her – if indeed he was ever personally really attractive to her. Remember, he gave away what she wanted most of all – a royal position in life.

'Imagine what it would have been for a twice-divorced, middle-class, middle-aged American woman, the former wife of an obscure naval officer, with little in the way of looks but with great ambition and very greedy appetites, to be the consort not of a king emperor, but *the* King Emperor. To have a Royal Navy destroyer follow any ship in which she sailed. To eat off gold plate in a Scottish castle or in Buckingham Palace. To be able to delay any express train until *she* was ready to board it. To divert airliners, seaplanes at her whim. To be met by kings and queens as their equal. My dear, when he gave up all that, he gave up her respect. She wanted what he had – not what he was.

'They spent most of their time in America, anyway, not here.

That kept her sweeter than she might otherwise have been. Especially when they would take over a whole floor of the Waldorf in New York, and needed a special rail coach on the train just to carry their baggage. She may not have been a king's wife, but she certainly lived like one – and still does.'

'But the Duke needed dollars for that. He couldn't get any in the war, surely?'

'He had his contacts. In Mexico. They supplied him with all the dollars he wanted.'

'But Mexico was in the Nazi camp. Britain hadn't even an ambassador in Mexico then.'

'Maybe not. But deals were still being done there and bargains in currency exchange, totally illegal and reprehensible, were still being struck – at very special prices. The Duke got his dollars in a roundabout way. Let's leave it at that. I got mine as well – and now you're offering me more.'

'Because I need your help.'

'As good a reason as any other,' da Leppo agreed. 'And you are honest in admitting it. Now, shall we have supper and discuss the matter further? I am told they do a delicious lobster thermidor here. Or there is conch, the local delicacy which is dragged from its shell, a white, soft, fleshy shellfish which I find very attractive. To me, it is somehow symbolic of dragging money out of the reluctant clutches of bankers and trustees who would like to keep it for themselves.'

'You haven't changed.'

Da Leppo shook his head.

'I have,' he corrected her seriously, as he stubbed out his cigar. 'So have you.'

On the top floor of the hotel, Sir Hilary lay uneasily between pink silk sheets in a huge double bed in the Princess Suite.

Ever since the board meeting in Coventry he had been feeling unwell – possibly before, if he was honest with himself. The trip across the north Atlantic in mid-winter had not helped him. With all portholes bolted shut against the anger of the waves, and the little pot-bellied banana boat rolling like a log, he had brooded on his company's problems, and his own, lying awake night after night in his narrow bunk.

The thump of the propeller and the creak of the ship's metal plates against rivets destroyed sleep, and in the lonely hours of darkness he had frequently endured the same sudden unexpected twinge of pain. From Jamaica he had managed to secure passage for Myrtle and himself to Miami, and then they came on to Nassau by flying boat. Now he had arrived safely – to do what? To argue with experts on subjects about which he knew nothing and had no wish to increase his knowledge. How could Myrtle Gibson conceivably help him where his own experts had failed? She was only a chi-chi with a high opinion of herself; no knowledge of finance; no qualifications of any kind. He had been an idiot to agree to come here at all, but then he had always agreed to do what others of stronger character told him. That was the story of his life.

The unease Hilary felt now focused on the pain in the centre of his chest, as though he had swallowed something hard. Perhaps a piece of crusty roll or a fishbone had lodged in his gullet? But surely this could not be the cause, because he always ate very lightly and carefully. He should see a doctor, but how could he possibly do so? He would immediately be revealed as a woman and a fraud. What possible explanation could he give to any strange doctor that Sir Hilary Mackenzie, Baronet, was actually Hilary Mackenzie, spinster?

He could see only one way out of this dilemma: he would send out for women's clothes, put them on, and then call the doctor, claiming to be someone sharing Sir Hilary's suite. He did not trust Myrtle to help him with this. The less she knew about his plan, his pain, about everything that concerned him, the better as far as he was concerned. She was too clever by half, and he knew he was not clever. He had just been fortunate, though he had his doubts about his good fortune. Would any fair-minded person really judge it fortunate to be forced to spend life dressed as a man, although he had been born a woman, simply to inherit a business?

Hilary sat up, poured himself a neat rum from the bottle on the bedside table, picked up the slim booklet which contained telephone numbers of local shops and restaurants. He selected Ibrahim's General And Fashion Store, dialled the number. A woman answered in the sing-song tones of the Bahamas.

'I am in the Princess Suite of the Centurion Plaza,' Sir Hilary explained in his most feminine accent. 'I wish to order a summer dress. I have a thirty-eight-inch waist, forty-four-inch bust, height five foot ten inches. And I'd like a pair of canvas shoes. I go by men's sizes, because my feet are large: size nine. I don't mind what colour the dress is, but something plain and discreet for preference. I am in my forties. Please have it wrapped and delivered here, with your bill, and I will pay on receipt.'

'Your name, madam?'

Hilary was not expecting the question and could not immediately think of a name. He stared wildly around the room for inspiration, then saw the name Craven 'A' on a cigarette packet.

'Miss A. Craven,' he said. 'Care of Sir Hilary Mackenzie.'

He replaced the receiver and lay back thankfully. He'd feel better when he had seen a doctor; there must be some medicine or treatment that could relieve his pain. As he sipped his rum, he heard a knock at the door. Myrtle came into the room.

'Are you all right?' she asked him, surprised at the pallor of his face, damp with sweat. 'You don't look well.'

'I'm a little tired,' Hilary admitted. 'I think I must have eaten something that has disagreed with me. I have indigestion.'

'So you won't be coming down to dinner later on?'

'No,' he said. 'I think not. I may have something light sent up here. But enough of that. You wanted to see me?'

Myrtle nodded and sat down. It seemed easier to say what she had to say sitting rather than standing.

'I have been speaking on the telephone to the Canadian government in Ottawa about the latest figures on the mine,' she said.

'But the papers were all locked in my briefcase.'

'Yes,' she agreed easily. 'That was where I found them. And you left the key on your dressing table, where I have replaced it.'

'You shouldn't go poking around into my briefcase,' Hilary exclaimed angrily. 'That is private.'

'Considering you never read the figures yourself, although they are vitally important to your entire organisation, there could be another view on that. Your company is in a very serious state.'

'I know that. They told us as much in Coventry. And remember, if it goes down, you go down, too. Your job would end immediately.'

'Of course. But I have a plan.'

'What sort of plan?'

'That, like the contents of your briefcase, is private – for the moment. But I can tell you I have access to considerable sums of money. They are in rupees and pounds sterling, but that presents no problem in Nassau. Money can be changed here into any currency in the world.'

'Well?'

'I could bail you out – if I had to.'

'How can you possibly claim to have enough money to do that? I pay you five thousand rupees a month. You had nothing, not a cent, not one single anna, when you came to see me in Alipore. What you are talking about would need *millions*. And not just rupees, but pounds. We're running at an enormous loss every year. The Americans would still go on squeezing the group, no matter who owns it or how much money you claim to have access to. They'd simply take all that and then squeeze harder. Remember we're tied to them for the next ten years.'

'That, again, is one viewpoint. It may be right, or it may not. Either way, I can help you. On two conditions.'

'What two conditions?'

'The first is a personal one. Important to me, if not to you, or indeed to anyone else. At present, no one knows what position I hold in the company. Maybe they think I'm your secretary or your personal assistant, or even your mistress. I don't know. I am not content with that. I want to be Lady Mackenzie. I want to marry you. That is my first condition.'

Hilary sat up in amazement.

'Marry me?' he said incredulously. 'You're mad! How can we possibly marry?'

'Quite easily. We may not have time to get a special licence from the Bishop of Nassau, but there are many other religious denominations here whose pastors or ministers or whatever they call themselves are licensed to solemnise matrimony. I have made inquiries.'

'But we're two women. It's insane – and illegal.'

'Nobody knows you're a woman except me. And obviously I won't talk. I also promise to make no demands whatever on you, sexually or financially. I just want to change my name. After all, you changed your sex.'

'What you propose is ludicrous and totally impossible.'

'You were born into a rich family, Hilary,' Myrtle pointed out. 'Agreed, you had a very strange upbringing, but in a material sense you have never wanted for anything. You have always been deferred to, treated as someone important. I have always been treated as a third-class citizen. A half-caste who didn't fit into any world but was used by both – Indian and British. Penny plain, tuppence coloured. I was both. I've had enough of insults and brush-offs. I want to change my whole background.'

'What good would it do you to be called Lady Mackenzie?'

'A great deal of good. Money, I have. Status, position, a social place is what I want. So that is my first condition.'

'And your second?'

'I want to give you a wedding present.'

'A *wedding* present?' Hilary's astonishment sharpened his voice.

'Yes. It is the custom in India for the fathers of brides to pay a dowry to their daughter's new husband. My father is not available, so I will give you a dowry myself, my present to you.'

'What is it?' he asked, mystified. Was she joking or being insulting? It was sometimes difficult to tell with her. He felt events were overwhelming him. Was he imagining all this? The pain began to throb again in his chest, like the measured beating of a sombre drum. He sank back wearily on the pink pillows.

'It's a piece of paper I want you to sign. It will be binding on both of us, and it will give me the muscle I must have to negotiate on behalf of Mackenzie Industries. Without it, I am nothing. With it, I think I can save us all.'

'So what is on that piece of paper?'

'A statement that you have made over to me all the shares you hold at the centre price of five shillings a share. I will pay you cash when the meeting with the Americans is over – if I fail to persuade them to renegotiate the contract.'

'What the hell do you mean? That will cost you the earth.'

'I told you, I have access to money. This document gives me authority to negotiate because, technically, I then control the shares. I must deal from strength. Otherwise I cannot deal at all.'

'It doesn't make sense.'

'It does to me. It is also my way of returning the compliment you have paid me by marrying me and giving me a title. I am promising to take the shares off you even if I can't carry the meeting.'

'Let's wait till then, shall we? See how it goes.'

'No. It's now or I cancel the meeting.'

'But you promised!' Hilary wailed.

'I only promised that I would do my best to get you out of the clutches of the American company. I can't promise that I will succeed.'

'And you want to buy the shares?'

'If I fail, those shares are worth nothing to you.'

'Then how are they worth anything to you?'

'That is my affair. But either way, you win, Hilary.'

'But how did you get all this money you keep mentioning so casually?'

'How did you get the whole company?' Myrtle retorted. 'By some means you would not like others to know. Maybe that's the same in my case. But this is an offer you cannot beat – or fault. A double-headed penny.'

'So win or lose, you will control the company?'

'Yes. That is my fee for saving you. But don't worry, you will still be chairman. It is written here. Read it, and then I must see the banks. I don't want to be late. There's an American saying, "Never keep the vanman waiting".'

'But the meeting's not till the day after tomorrow.'

'I know. And we have to be married tomorrow at the latest. Not too easy to arrange so quickly.'

Sir Hilary sighed, held out his hand for the paper, read it.

'I want a lawyer to look at this before I sign,' he said stubbornly.

'You won't find one here.'

'Haven't you organised lawyers to be at the meeting when we see the Americans?' he asked Myrtle in amazement. 'Cowan will come with every kind of legal and financial expert. Who have we got to put our case?'

'Me.'

'You?'

'Yes. With the same equipment David had when he set out to beat Goliath. Brains.'

'Are you saying these Americans haven't got brains?'

'Not at all. But we're just talking round the subject – and

against the clock and our own interests. I am saying nothing about them. I've not even met them. Just sign this form.'

'And if I don't?'

'You could lose the steel mill, the mine, everything. And you will, if I don't save you.'

'But if I do sign it, I'll lose the company.'

'Only a majority shareholding. A capital gain, remember. No tax.'

Hilary peered at the paper again as though doubting what he read. It seemed a very reasonable document. He would still be rich – if this extraordinary woman actually had the money. But what if she didn't? He could not imagine how she could suddenly be wealthy. If she was, then why was she still working for him for so little? The effort of trying to reason this out brought on the beginnings of a headache – all concentration did. And that oddly nagging pain grew stronger, more insistent. He gave a sigh, took out his gold-topped pen, scribbled his signature on the two copies.

'So now all I have to do is marry you?' he asked sarcastically.

'That's enough,' she assured him.

Hilary swung himself off the bed, took another long drink of rum, considering the proposition. He hated having to make quick decisions or, indeed, any decisions. Others had always been willing to do so for him – for a fee, of course – and now his mind sagged like a tightrope-walker on a slack high wire.

It would not be a legal marriage, he thought, it could not possibly be, but it need not necessarily be a disaster on that account. If this chi-chi bitch could help him and this was her price, it might be worth paying. And after all, she had guaranteed to bail him out. *If* she had the money she kept on about.

'All right,' he said wearily. 'Fetch a minister here. We can be married in this hotel. But if you can't help me after all this talk, I'll divorce you. Now let's get it over with.'

'A romantic approach,' said Myrtle drily. As she spoke, a

bell tinkled. They looked at each other, surprised. A voice called, 'Special delivery.'

Myrtle opened the door. A messenger boy stood holding a large parcel wrapped in coloured paper and tied with pink ribbon.

'For Miss A. Craven. Care of Sir Hilary Mackenzie,' the messenger explained.

'I'll deal with it,' said Hilary. 'How much do I owe you?'

The messenger produced a bill. Hilary paid it, added a tip. The boy saluted. Myrtle looked at Hilary inquiringly.

'Some things I ordered,' he said noncommittally, and threw the parcel onto a chair.

They were married in the sun lounge of the hotel at twelve o'clock on the following day. It had taken Myrtle longer to arrange than she had anticipated, although generous gratuities expedited everything. Da Leppo gave away the bride. Sir Hilary walked with a stick; under the strain of this new complication in his life the pain in his chest had not eased, and now he also felt a tingling down his left arm, like pins and needles.

He loosened his watch strap and was surprised to see how deeply it had dug into his flesh. It had never felt so tight before. Must be the heat and all the worry. And this ridiculous ceremony meant that he had still not been able to see a doctor.

The marriage was conducted by the pastor of the First Revivalist Episcopalian Church of the Next Generation, New Providence Island, a cheerful, black Bahamian with a bald head that gleamed like a polished ebony ball. He gave a homily on the blessings of marriage as opposed to the single state and then gladly joined the bride and groom for a lunch of cold lobster, salad and champagne.

'Well, I've done my part,' Hilary told Myrtle grimly when they were on their own. 'Now you do yours, or I promise you, the next ceremony you'll be involved in is divorce.'

'You're joking,' said Myrtle, only partly in jest. 'Do you

really want to stand up in court and admit that a baronet, holder of a title that goes back to the thirteenth century, originally given for deeds of daring on a battlefield in France, is not only not entitled to it but is actually not a man at all?'

'That won't be necessary.'

'Then put it out of your mind. In any case, we meet Walter Cowan tomorrow.'

'So short a honeymoon?' said Hilary sarcastically.

'We have a life together to look forward to,' Myrtle told him. Hilary childishly put out his tongue at her. Myrtle saw with distaste that it was furred and white.

When Walter P. Cowan first learned that Sir Hilary Mackenzie was in Nassau and anxious to meet him personally, he at once cabled to his office in New York for attorneys and accountants to fly down. Such a request must surely mean that at last Mackenzie realised the gravity of his group's position; the mine and the mill were as good as in Cowan's control.

He made inquiries and learned that Sir Hilary was in Nassau with a woman executive. No one seemed to know her background, but she was apparently not an attorney. That meant that the only lawyers Sir Hilary would be able to field would be local men. Anyhow, even if he had brought the Lord Chief Justice of England himself, Mackenzie could not win. He had no case. Cowan's company had a firm, unequivocal contract with ten more years to run at a fixed price. That was agreed in writing, and watertight as a fish's ass. They were on a hundred per cent winner.

Cowan arranged their meeting for ten o'clock in the morning in a private room of the Royal Victoria Hotel, a little way from the beach. Furniture was moved so that chairs could be set round a centre table, with carafes of water, blotting pads, notebooks and pencils at each place, to give a businesslike ambience. Just before ten, the hotel manager came up to his suite to see him.

'I thought you might be interested to know, sir, that yesterday Sir Hilary Mackenzie married Miss Myrtle Gibson, the lady who is travelling with him. A colleague in their hotel has just told me.'

'So she's now Lady Mackenzie?'

'That is so, sir.'

'They are on their honeymoon in fact?'

'That would seem to be the case, sir.'

Walter Cowan had not become chief executive of his company by making hasty decisions or reaching quick conclusions; the fact that he had married the daughter of the firm's founder had not a little to do with his promotion; but something about Mackenzie's marriage seemed strange to him, although he had no idea why it should.

'Was this a sudden affair of the heart?' he asked.

'I cannot tell you that, sir, but they appear to have known each other for some time. In India, first of all, I believe. And she accompanied him to England.'

'And now I am going to meet them both?'

'Yes, sir.'

'In that case, perhaps you had better put some flowers in the room. And maybe something to drink other than water. I do not drink alcoholic beverages myself, but they might like the idea. Add a bit of dash to things, show it's not all business, eh?'

'As you say, sir.'

Walter Cowan greeted the newly married couple effusively, a champagne glass of sparkling ginger ale in his hand.

'I give you a toast – the bride and groom,' he said expansively.

'Thank you,' Myrtle replied. 'And in return I give you a toast to the successful outcome of our negotiations – now and always.'

Walter Cowan's lawyers exchanged quizzical glances as they followed the Mackenzies into the room. Cowan indicated that Sir Hilary should be seated at his right hand. Myrtle was across the table. As the men pulled back their chairs and waited politely for her to sit down first, she turned to Cowan.

'I would be grateful if I could see you outside for a moment before we start the formal meeting,' she told him in a low voice. 'I think we might be able to resolve this matter more speedily together than if we debate it with all your experts.'

'If you wish, Lady Mackenzie, certainly. I am totally at your disposal. But I must say, I personally cannot see the point of a private preliminary discussion. My accountants and my attorneys are *au fait* with all the points of the contract. I presume your own experts have been delayed?'

'No,' she replied. 'I have also read the contract closely, and while I obviously defer to your colleagues' legal and financial knowledge, I would still appreciate it if you could spare me a few minutes. On your own.'

Cowan turned to his colleagues.

'Please, gentlemen,' he said, 'pass the champagne round, or the coffee. Or order whatever else you feel like. Remember, this is a celebration as much as a business meeting.'

Cowan opened the door for Myrtle. They went into an anteroom. She sat down in an easy chair and looked closely at the chairman. He was in his late fifties, tall, grey-haired, wearing a magnificently cut lightweight suit. He regarded her enquiringly.

'So what have you got to say to me, Lady Mackenzie?' he asked, trying to weigh her up.

'Several things. But first, I want to make certain you know what will happen if you hold Mackenzie Industries to the terms of your contract to buy sinter – a contract which, of course, is perfectly legal, and which the company must honour.'

'I know exactly what will happen, Lady Mackenzie. Honouring our agreement is costing the Mackenzie group too much money – far more than they ever anticipated when they signed it so eagerly before the war. And because the mine and mill are an integral part of the whole, not a separate entity, the losses in

Canada are bringing down the entire Mackenzie enterprise.'

Myrtle nodded in agreement. 'That is correct, and you, Mr Cowan, quite understandably hope to gain control of the mine and the mill. However, I am informed by my sources in Ottawa that in the event that the company founders, the Canadian government will immediately take it over – nationalise it, is the word they use. Then they will run it as a state-owned enterprise rather than let it fall under the control of a United States company. This is a matter of Canadian national policy – and no doubt of national pride. I can give you the names and telephone numbers of the senior officials in Ottawa with whom I spoke. They have told me that they will be at their desks this morning should you or any of your colleagues care to call them. But for the moment perhaps you would take my word for what would happen.

'Equally, I note that our company, under the terms of the agreement, has to buy higher grade iron ore from you at the market price, rather than from any other supplier.'

'I know that,' said Walter Cowan testily. The possibility that the Canadian government might take over the mill and mine disturbed him. This possibility had never occurred to him.

'What is your proposition for resolving the situation – to our mutual advantage, of course? If you have one.'

'I have one, Mr Cowan. A very simple solution, which is why I wish to put it to you personally. If it meets with your approval, then your team in the next room will agree with you. If, on the other hand, we ask for their opinion first, they may not.

'My experience in business is obviously nowhere near as great as yours, but I think you will probably agree that whenever you ask for someone else's opinion on any matter, great or small, they instantly assume you do so because you are not certain in your own mind which course to take. Therefore, they feel they must give a negative reaction.'

'I am fully aware of the attitude of subordinates, Lady Mackenzie. But what is your proposition?'

'This, Mr Cowan. We cannot alter the basic terms of the contract whereby we sell you sinter and you have the manganese free. Nor can we change the terms of your company's contract to sell higher grade ore to us. What I suggest is that we simply reclassify the qualities of *both* the ores. Upwards. This would release us both from the restrictions imposed by the War Measures Act. The reason given to the Canadian authorities could be that all the original ore has now been exhausted and we are being forced to mine a richer vein. You, in turn, charge more for the ore you sell us, maybe for the same reason. So instead of rigid terms, we have flexibility and profits – and you have even greater profits.'

'An ingeniously simple solution, indeed. And if we do not agree?'

'I hope very much you will,' said Myrtle earnestly. 'But if you do not, as the majority shareholder I would immediately inform the Canadian government of the situation. The matter would then be out of all our hands.'

'Why do you not do that now?'

'Because my proposal makes far better financial sense, and benefits both of us. The Canadian government would wish to control the company itself. That would mean my husband would have to resign – or be kicked out. I personally would not lose because the Canadians would buy my shares.'

'I see.'

Cowan stroked his chin as he considered the matter.

'You have a point,' he agreed carefully at last. 'In fact, two points. I like them. I *had* hoped to take over the company for nothing – in payment of your debt.'

'Even assuming the Canadians allowed this – which I do not believe they will – you would then be liable for all the company's other debts. Now, you are liable only for profits. Do you agree?'

'I agree, Lady Mackenzie.'

'And your experts outside?'

He smiled thinly, a banker's smile. 'They will do as I suggest. Or, rather, Lady Mackenzie, as *you* propose. Now let us rejoin the others. As I said, this is a celebration as much as a business meeting.'

Myrtle followed Sir Hilary into the Princess Suite, closed the door behind them, locked it. At once, he crossed to the table by the bed and poured himself four fingers of rum, added some ginger ale from the refrigerator, took a long swig and then looked at her inquiringly. Myrtle shook her head. She noticed that his hand trembled slightly.

'I felt perhaps this was deserving of some sort of private celebration, as Cowan said,' Hilary explained lamely. 'You've got the company – and me – out of what seemed a ruinous situation.'

'I hope so,' she replied. 'And I have done something else – proved I could manipulate a man like Walter Cowan. It was his will against mine.'

'And against mine,' added Hilary. 'But you offered us both some meat on the bone. A profit for him, survival for me. If I want to survive, that is.'

'What do you mean?'

He sat down on the edge of the bed so heavily that his drink slopped over, effervescing across the coverlet.

'I feel so damned tired,' he said thickly. 'I have, ever since we left Coventry. Probably before, if I'm honest. I've got an almost constant pain in my chest.'

'You should see a doctor.'

'Not as I am, and who I am. I think I can trust you now. I suppose I have to. That parcel delivered here contains women's clothes. I was going to dress as a woman and then call a doctor, as Miss A. Craven. I got the name from that packet of cigarettes. It seemed the only way to avoid discovery.'

Hilary poured out another rum and this time did not dilute it with ginger ale.

'The windows are open,' he went on. 'The sea's just outside and a fresh breeze is blowing – look at the curtains – and yet I feel as though I'm choking. It's like a noose tightening round my neck.'

Hilary rubbed his throat as though he could loosen an invisible rope, raised the glass to his lips. Suddenly, his arm locked, the fingers opened slowly, as though of their own accord. The glass slipped out of his grasp and shattered on the floor. With the speed of a spring trap closing, Hilary's head came down on his chest. He crouched forward, curled up, half standing, half kneeling. Myrtle heard him gasp for breath and then a bubbling gurgle came from deep in his chest. Green bile and rum spewed out of his mouth onto the coverlet of the bed and the white carpet. He fell sideways, rolled over on the floor clumsily, and lay where he fell.

For a second Myrtle stared at him in horrified astonishment. Then she bent down, felt his pulse, searching frantically for the reassuring beat, but there was nothing. She put a hand on his forehead; it came away chilled with sweat. She turned Hilary over on his side, lifted an eyelid. The eye stared out at her sightlessly. Sir Hilary Mackenzie, the last baronet, was dead. So was Miss Hilary Mackenzie. The carnival of deception was over – or was it just beginning?

Myrtle stood up, forcing herself to keep calm, to find a way out of this horror. She should call the hotel doctor, but when he examined Hilary, the secret would be discovered. Not that this mattered to Hilary now, nothing mattered to him. But it mattered desperately to her. She knew Hilary had not made a will. She would therefore inherit everything due to a widow. Her whole future, her whole fortune hinged on concealing that the dead man was not as the world imagined him. Yet her mind seemed numb, almost paralysed from the reaction of dealing with Cowan, and now this. Despite Myrtle's determination never to drink spirits, she poured a measure of rum into a toothglass, added ginger ale and gulped it down, grimacing at the taste but relishing the welcome warmth and life it brought to her.

As she sipped, her thumping heart quietened and an idea took shape. She picked up the telephone, called da Leppo. He arrived within minutes. She locked the door behind him before she took him into the bedroom. He stood in the doorway, regarding the body in silence. His face showed neither surprise nor concern.

'He's had a seizure,' she explained. 'He'd not been feeling well since we left England. He's dead.'

'I can see that, dearie. You didn't kill him, I suppose?'

'Heavens, no. Why should I do that?'

'There are several million reasons. You'll inherit everything.'

'I need your help for that.'

'Again? To do what this time?'

'Arrange the funeral.'

'There'll have to be a post mortem first, or an inquest at least.'

'There mustn't be.'

'Why not?'

Da Leppo listened to what Myrtle told him.

'Are you serious?' he asked in amazement.

'Look for yourself.'

He unbuttoned Hilary's shirt, saw her left breast, the large feminine aureole round the nipple.

'So somehow we have to get rid of the body,' he said practically.

'That's what I had in mind,' she said. 'And I have an idea how.'

'Possibly. But before you begin, let me tell you that to dispose of the body of a millionaire baronet on a fashionable tropical island will not be an easy task, Myrtle.'

'I know. That is why I want you to help me,' Myrtle told him bluntly.

'Not this time, dearie. It's too dangerous.'

'You already have five per cent of the stock,' Myrtle reminded him.

'That was for squaring the banks, dearie, in case you had to buy Sir Hilary out. This is for risking my neck. There could be a murder charge if anything went wrong. You could hang and I'd be an accessory after the fact. Could mean going to goal for years. No way.'

'Right then, a quarter of a million.'

'Pounds?'

'Dollars.'

'In writing, dearie.'

Myrtle tore a page off the hotel memo pad on Hilary's bedside table, scribbled on it, 'I owe Dr Luis da Leppo $250,000 for consultation fees and other help. To be paid on demand.' She signed and dated it.

'Does that satisfy you?'

'Perfectly,' he said putting her paper in his wallet – the same one, of imitation crocodile skin, Myrtle noted with surprise, from which he had first taken a card to give her Sir Hilary's address in Calcutta.

'You discovered his secret and latched on to him then?' da Leppo asked her.

'To save a lot of explanation, the brief answer is yes. But without my help his company would be bankrupt now. So it wasn't all one-way traffic. Now, here's my plan for this problem. There's a parcel on that chair full of women's clothes. His size. He rang a department store and had them sent over. He was going to put them on and then call a doctor as a woman because he was worried about a pain in his chest.

'I suggest we dress him in these clothes and carry him down to the sea. The sharks should do the rest. The tide may bring in the body, but it's just the corpse of another woman, maybe a tourist.'

'And what about Sir Hilary? He can't just disappear.'

'He will. We take his clothes down to the beach, fold them up on the sand. His body is never found. Drowned on a moonlight swim.'

'What's the woman's name?'

'He ordered the clothes in the name of Miss Craven.'

'It's too long a shot,' said da Leppo, turning over the risks in his mind, working out a gambler's chance. 'Also, I doubt whether there are sharks in this sea.'

'You have a better idea, then?'

'I would say an improved version of yours. First, we don't attempt to carry the body to the beach. That would never work. Someone is bound to see us here in the hotel, on the road, anywhere. No, we dress it just as you say and leave it right here, in the room but on the bed. There's some vomit on the coverlet which adds a touch of authenticity to our claim – your claim, actually that Miss Craven had a seizure of some kind while lying clothed on the bed – not *in* it.'

'I follow you,' Myrtle interrupted him. 'Then you dress in Hilary's suit, you wear his hat, his spectacles, and call down to the reception desk beforehand to tell them you want an early call at seven tomorrow morning as you wish to pay your bill before you leave. Then you get them to arrange a taxi. That'll establish he's still alive and has an evening appointment somewhere.'

Da Leppo stood, turning over in his mind what she said, searching for weaknesses. Then he nodded.

'It should work,' he said at last.

'It must,' retorted Myrtle. She picked up the telephone, dialled room service.

'I want half a dozen bottles of champagne,' she told the clerk. 'Conch salad, lobsters, large prawns, for a small celebration party in the Princess Suite. Sir Hilary Mackenzie. In one hour's time. Thank you.'

'What the hell have we got to celebrate?' da Leppo asked her in amazement.

'Victory,' she told him.

'So soon?'

'Of course. And to help establish that all is well here and plans for the future are being made.'

As she spoke she began to go through the drawers of the dressing table. She picked out a bottle of lighter fluid, Hilary's wallet, his driving licence and chequebook, handed them to da Leppo. He peeled off Hilary's lightweight suit, shirt and underpants, stripped off his own shirt and trousers, rolled them into a bundle, and then dressed in Hilary's clothes. Myrtle found a pair of sunglasses and a locally woven, wide-brimmed straw hat of the type sold by old women who plaited them in Nassau market.

'Put your things in his hold-all,' she told da Leppo crisply. 'Now go down to the porter's desk and hire a cab from him. Tell the driver to go along the coast road, past Cable Beach. You'll see several huge houses there. Pay him off at the gates of one of them. Go through the gates until you are out of sight, then cut through the hedge and along the shore until you come to an empty beach. Take off Hilary's suit, fold it up on the sand, with his shirt and socks and underwear. Then put on your own clothes. Don't forget to bring back his bag, but leave the wallet. The money in it is bound to go, but maybe whoever takes it won't steal his chequebook, which is useless. And while you're away, I'll dress Hilary in his – or her – new clothes.'

'Sounds too easy,' said da Leppo sceptically.

'Most good ideas are. But get back as soon as you can. We've work to do. And there's a party organised.'

Da Leppo looked at her, half in admiration, half in doubt.

'You sound very confident,' he said hesitantly.

'I am,' she told him briskly. 'Trust me – and we're both winners, like those horses in Calcutta. Remember, if we fail here, you don't get a quarter of a million dollars – and you'll lose your five per cent stake. It's all or nothing. For both of us.'

Da Leppo nodded, took the lift down to the entrance hall,

crossed to the porter's desk. An American visitor was buying several highly coloured postcards showing Government House, pink and white, like a giant birthday cake, on top of a hill overlooking the town. The porter turned to da Leppo inquiringly. Da Leppo opened Hilary's wallet, took out a five-dollar bill; it was easy to be generous with another person's money. He pushed the bill across the desk. The porter's hand closed on it with the speed of a hungry vulture's claw.

'Sir Hilary Mackenzie, Princess Suite,' he said casually.

'Can I help you, Sah Hilary, sah?' he asked deferentially.

'You can. I want a car to take me along Cable Beach to see a friend.'

'No problem, sah.'

The porter walked to the front entrance, blew a whistle. A Hudson saloon pulled out from a line of waiting cars. Da Leppo climbed into the back.

'Two miles along Cable Beach,' he told the driver as he sank back on the camphor-smelling seat. He paid off the taxi outside a colonial-style house set well back from the road. The short tropical dusk was deepening into darkness. Lights began to glitter as he set off up the drive. Waving palm fronds scattered moving shadows on well-raked gravel. Out of sight of the road, he waited until the cab turned, then he walked back out of the gates and along the road for nearly half a mile until it curved away from the coast.

He left it there and struck out across smooth, flat rocks towards the sea. Dry palm leaves rustled like castanets above his head. He stood beneath the trees for five minutes by his watch in case anyone else was out on the beach, lovers, a lone walker. He saw no one, heard nothing except the restless thunder of the sea and the rattle of the leaves. The moon had not yet risen and the shore lay empty and uninviting. A slight wind carried a strong smell of salty seaweed.

Da Leppo undressed quickly, changed into his own clothes, folded up Hilary's things, carried them down to the edge of the sea. He laid them neatly on a rock, then walked quickly up the beach onto the road. A few cars swung past, their headlamps boring narrow tunnels of light through the darkness. He waited in the shadows of the palm trees until they had gone. Then he began to walk back towards the hotel.

As he let himself into the Princess Suite and shut the door behind him thankfully, the entry bell rang. For a moment he and Myrtle looked at each other in horror. Who could this be? Then a deep Bahamian voice announced: 'Room service, Sah Hilary.'

Myrtle held up a warning finger to da Leppo.

'Play it my way now,' she told him in an urgent whisper. She went into the bedroom, tossed a chiffon scarf carelessly over Hilary's face, in case the waiter should recognise him, then opened the door into the main room.

A waiter in a white monkey jacket and black trousers wheeled in a trolley. On it stood a silver ice bucket, bottles of champagne, dishes of cracked lobster with green salad, prawns, conch.

'Ah, you're catching up with us,' Myrtle told him skittishly.

The waiter looked at her, puzzled. She indicated Hilary on the bed.

'Our friend Miss Craven here has already had a little too much, I think. But a hair of the dog that bit you is a good enough remedy.'

'Sure is, ma'am,' said the waiter enviously.

'Oh,' said Myrtle, turning to da Leppo. 'Have you got a note on you? I've only a few coins. And this poor man's had to push this trolley up goodness knows how many flights of stairs.'

'I used the service lift, ma'am,' the waiter said, looking from one to the other. He was not sure whether these English people were making fun of him.

Da Leppo took out Hilary's wallet. He found an American ten-dollar bill, crackled it expertly between his fingers, handed it over.

'Thank *you*, sah.'

'Have a drink before you go,' suggested Myrtle.

'That's very kind of you, ma'am. Can I get anything to help the lady? We have all kinds of aspirins, Alkaseltzers, pick-me-ups.'

'Oh, she'll be all right. It's the heat. And the rum. A bit too strong a combination. She's just arrived, as a matter of fact.'

Myrtle poured out a glass of champagne. The waiter drank it in one gulp. She poured him another. He drank this with equal speed, saluted and went out, his white teeth making a happy grin in his dark face.

Myrtle opened another bottle of champagne, poured most of it down the washbasin, but left dregs in four glasses. She flushed some of the food down the lavatory pan, broke a glass, and clasped Hilary's dead fingers round the stem.

'Everything go all right with you?' she asked da Leppo, who stood watching her.

He nodded. 'I think so.'

'Right, then, here we go.'

She opened a packet of cigarettes, lit two in her mouth, handed one to him.

Myrtle placed the second cigarette carefully between Hilary's dead, cold lips. A wisp of smoke curled up. Then she picked up the bottle of lighter fluid, unscrewed the top, poured the contents over his pillow and the eiderdown. She struck a match, held it close to the pillow. The lighter fuel took flame with an instant roar. Hilary's hair crackled. The room was suddenly thick with black, acrid smoke and the stench of burning flesh.

'My God!' Da Leppo cried in genuine horror; he had not expected this.

'Someone might have recognised the face,' she explained. 'Now, no one will.'

Da Leppo stood staring at the burning body.

'Get on to the porter,' Myrtle ordered him sharply. 'Call the fire people. A doctor. Quickly!'

Da Leppo opened the door to the corridor, which increased the draught. Flames greedily licked the bed head. The silk cover curled away. Flock in the padding caught fire. Black wisps of blazing cloth floated in the air.

The sudden fierce heat tightened muscles in Hilary's body. The corpse made as though to sit up, as Myrtle had often seen Hindu corpses move on the burning ghats along the banks of the sacred River Ganges outside the holy city of Benares in India. Then Hilary's body toppled sideways over the blazing coverlet, sending up a great shower of sparks.

An alarm bell began to peal in the corridor outside the suite. Someone rushed into the room holding a fire extinguisher.

'A doctor, for God's sake, get a doctor!' shouted Myrtle.

An under-manager appeared, his face creased with horror and dismay.

'A doctor from the hospital is here to attend a civic dinner,' he explained. 'He has been sent for.'

'Thank you very much.'

The bedroom reeked now of the chemicals in the fire extinguisher fluid. Foam covered the bed and the floor. The smoke turned yellowish, like a London fog. The under-manager held a towel to his face and threw open all the windows. The pillows were still smouldering; Hilary's face was badly scorched and totally unrecognisable. His hair was singed, and his cigarette, extinguished now, still hung limp and sodden between his dead lips. Odd, thought Myrtle, I'm still thinking of Hilary as male.

A short fat man wearing a white sharkskin jacket with a ready-made purple bow tie bustled into the room. He carried a medical bag.

'There's been an accident, I hear. Good God!'

He crossed over to Hilary, felt the pulse, took a stethoscope out of his pocket, ripped open her dress. Then he looked up at Myrtle, his face grim.

'She's dead.'

Myrtle nodded. 'I thought so.' It did not require medical qualifications to reach this conclusion.

'Who was she?' the doctor asked Myrtle.

'Miss Craven. A business associate of my husband, Sir Hilary Mackenzie. I am Lady Mackenzie.'

'Of course. I read in the paper you only got married yesterday. What a terrible thing to happen.'

'Yes. Awful.'

'I am Dr Andrew Buchanan. From the hospital. I have just come off duty to attend a function here. What happened, exactly?'

'I've no idea. I must tell you, however, Miss Craven was a heavy drinker. She had only recently arrived and she was tired. Not used to the heat – or the strength of the rum here.'

As Myrtle spoke, she saw that several waiters and maids had come into the room. She recognised the room service waiter.

'You saw her, didn't you?' she asked him.

'Yes, ma'am, I saw her. She'd sure gone right out.'

'Was this recently?' the doctor asked him.

'Yes, sah. Only a few minutes ago, sah.'

'I see. You will have to inform the police, Lady Mackenzie. I am afraid there will be an inquest, perhaps even a post mortem. And your husband, does he know of this tragedy?'

'No. He went out – oh – about an hour ago. He will be terribly distressed.'

She paused, as though making up her mind over some problem. Then she spoke.

'Could I speak to you privately first, Dr Buchanan, before he returns?' she asked the doctor.

'Of course.'

Myrtle looked pointedly at the hotel under-manager. He was used to dealing with the rich; they did not expect to ask for something a second time. He immediately shepherded his staff out of the room.

'Please ring as soon as you are ready to move, Lady Mackenzie,' he said. 'We will prepare another suite for you and Sir Hilary immediately.'

'You are very kind,' said Myrtle. She closed the door behind them all.

'Will you have a drink, Doctor?'

'Thank you, no. I have just left a dinner at which I was guest of honour. I must return as soon as possible.'

'Of course.' Myrtle paused, lips pursed to give the impression she was reluctant to speak, but felt she should. 'This is a rather odd situation, Doctor,' she said at last. 'I would like to speak frankly to you on a delicate matter.'

'Of course, Lady Mackenzie.'

'My husband is over here on an important and secret mission for the British government, involving finance at the highest level. I cannot say any more. Indeed, I only know the basic facts. This poor dead lady was closely involved.'

Myrtle took a deep breath, wondering how high to pitch her story. She gauged her man, and went on.

'During the war, she was a secret agent, under great stress. Actually a citizen of Free France, a countess. She had been in occupied Europe, then in the Blitz in London, and she was passing through here on her way to South America. She has spent years in continual personal danger. She drank, I think, to relieve this strain. I hope for these reasons that it may be possible to avoid an inquest. It would only give our enemies comfort.

'The war may be over, but many of Germany's most evil men fled to the Argentine and Paraguay. If they heard she was over here, they would guess why she was here – and my husband's mission could be prejudiced. I am being frank with you. Totally frank. They might even think – or spread the rumour – that she had not died accidentally, but was murdered. You hold the key to the success or failure, Doctor, of international events on a very large scale.'

The doctor nodded slowly. 'One thing did strike me, Lady Mackenzie, as possibly being worthy of note – if there were to be an inquest. Even a cursory examination shows that the deceased's nostrils are not blackened by smoke.'

'Oh?'

Even as Myrtle tried to keep her voice noncommittal, she realised the significance of this deceptively casual remark.

'What does that mean exactly, Doctor?' she asked in her most innocent voice.

'It means, Lady Mackenzie, that the deceased did not breathe in any smoke from the fire. Her nostrils would have been blackened if she had.'

'Oh? So perhaps she died from the burns – or the shock? Or could she have suffered some kind of seizure, or heart attack, perhaps? I don't know. But I agree, it does seem odd.'

'That's what I mean. It *is* odd. In plain layman's terms, this lady was dead before the fire started.'

'Really?'

Myrtle's voice was loaded with surprise. 'And what do you deduce from that, Doctor?'

'It is not my job to deduce anything, Lady Mackenzie. But it is something I would have to tell the proper authorities. It is, as you say, odd. But then some very odd things happened here during the war.

'You probably read that a friend of the Duke of Windsor, the baronet, Sir Harry Oakes, was found dead in bed in a house which had appeared to be set on fire deliberately? But – another very odd thing – that very night there was an unexpected tropical storm. The rains came – and put out the flames. Otherwise it would have been thought Sir Harry had died in an accidental fire. Perhaps from a cigarette – if, as with this lady apparently, he had smoked in bed.'

'Perhaps Sir Harry had a seizure?'

'Perhaps. On the other hand, he had four very nasty wounds in his temple, and although he was lying on his back, blood from them had not flowed down towards his ear, but up towards his eyes. In other words, he had not been struck down when he lay in bed on his back, but elsewhere, and then put on the bed for a fire to burn away all clues. If it had done so, then no one – except the murderer – would ever have noticed that the bed had been soaked in petrol and the body covered with feathers from a pillow to make it burn more quickly. Odd, wasn't it? And I smell lighter fluid, which is also very inflammable.'

'As a doctor, you must see many inexplicable things,' said Myrtle smoothly. Her mouth felt dry as a warm flannel. What was this idiot going to do? If he called the police, if there was any publicity whatever, then there could be questions about the corpse's identity which she could not stall. She sensed a morass of complication stretching ahead towards discovery and ruin – perhaps even a charge of murder, certainly of falsifying evidence.

The doctor's Scottish voice carved into the turmoil of her thoughts.

'There really *should* be an inquest, you know, Lady Mackenzie. There was for Sir Harry Oakes.'

'But he was not travelling on a mission of this importance, Doctor.'

'That is so. Can you vouch for its importance?'

'You have my word. My husband is chairman and principal shareholder of the Mackenzie group.'

'And where is your husband?' interrupted the doctor.

'I will ring the reception desk and see if he has returned.' She dialled the number. 'Lady Mackenzie here. Did my husband order a car to pick him up?' she asked the clerk.

'No, Your Ladyship. Only to take him out to Cable Beach.'

Myrtle handed the telephone to Dr Buchanan.

'Have you seen Sir Hilary Mackenzie?' the doctor asked the clerk.

'Oh yes, sah. He done gone out under one hour ago.'

'Are you certain?'

'Yes, sah. He was going along Cable Beach. He hired a car.'

'Has he come back?'

'No, sah. Driver set him down outside a house. He saw him go in the gate, sah.'

'I see. Thank you.'

The doctor replaced the receiver, turned to Myrtle.

'I will speak to Sir Hilary when he returns, but I regret I still must inform the police. Purely as a formality, you understand, Lady Mackenzie. I will ask them to use the utmost discretion with regard to any unfortunate publicity.'

'You must do whatever you feel is best,' said Myrtle, as though relinquishing all concern over his decision. 'But if you do have an inquest, I have to tell you that such a public announcement may cause the deaths of other brave men and women who have been involved in this top secret matter. At the very least, it will put them in the gravest danger. Nassau is still not without its Nazi sympathisers in high places. As I am sure you must know.'

'I have heard such rumours,' the doctor agreed, carefully. 'In the Great War, I served in Flanders with the Highland Brigade. I know what it means for people to be placed unnecessarily in danger. Possibly one can become too hidebound in these remote colonial outposts. I will do my best to help you – and the matter on which you say your husband is engaged. I will write a certificate to say that in my opinion this lady suffered a sudden seizure. Cardiac arrest. The cigarette in her mouth could then have set light to the bed. I see there is a tin of lighter fuel on the floor. Perhaps that leaked and caused the fire to burn so fiercely. What I am doing is not by the book, but we live in strange times. We must not be too rigid in our reactions. Now, what was the lady's name?'

'Miss Ann Craven,' Myrtle said quickly.

'That is not her real name if she is French, surely?'

'No. It is not. But it's the name she was travelling under.'

'She had a passport?'

'I have no idea, but in a British colony – and she travelled as a British subject – she would not need one.'

'But if she was going on to South America she would?'

'I presume so.'

Dr Buchanan took a pile of blank death certificates from his case, wrote out the details on one of them, signed it, handed it to Myrtle.

'There it is, Lady Mackenzie. I am very sorry that this should have happened to spoil your visit, and that of your husband. Especially as you are so very recently wed.'

'Thank you, Doctor. You have been very helpful – and understanding.'

Dr Buchanan paused, fiddling with the lock on his medical case; Myrtle recognised the signs.

'Tell me, Doctor,' she said gently. 'How much longer do you have out here before you retire?'

'Nearly two years.'

'And have you any plans when you do retire?'

'None, really. Probably play a bit more golf, I expect. I have no family ties, you see. I am unmarried.'

'I will mention your name to my husband, if I may. His company is international, you know, and expanding. He finds it very difficult to attract mature British medical staff with real experience of the world, even though the pay is very good.'

Myrtle opened the drawer, took out one of Hilary's visiting cards, scribbled her name on the back.

'Write to me at this address in London before you do retire. We will do our best to find you something that could be more rewarding – even than golf. But still leaving you plenty of time for that.'

'You are very kind, Lady Mackenzie.'

'Not at all,' she said. 'It is refreshing to meet someone so understanding. I appreciate your help more than I can say. So will others in high places.'

They shook hands. Dr Buchanan put the card in an inside

pocket, walked to the door, then paused.

'One other thing about this sad case also strikes me as odd,' he said.

Myrtle did not reply.

'Here is a lady of early middle life, wearing an expensive dress but no undergarments whatever. No brassiere, nothing.' Buchanan shrugged. 'Perhaps that is the French way. Good-bye, Lady Mackenzie.'

He went out, closed the door carefully behind him.

Myrtle's knees were trembling. What did he suspect? she wondered. It had been a close-run thing, but she had won – just. Now she had to deal with the disappearance of her husband; two risks, one down, one to go. But she would win. She had to.

EIGHT

The Present:
Katherine, Northern Territory, Australia
Cairns, Queensland, Australia
Hong Kong

Amy Crabtree slid silently out of bed in the darkness and sat on the edge of the mattress for a moment, her feet on the cheap rug, listening to her husband snore; she did not want to wake him. Then she stood up, felt her way carefully and slowly out of the bedroom to the bathroom. She opened the cupboard, took two sleeping tablets from a phial, swallowed them, and drank half a glass of water.

She put on the light and, leaning on the washbasin, examined her face in the mirror. She looked old. The life she led in a world of burning heat or sudden drenching rain, the dull routine of housework and stocktaking had aged her. As a young woman, she had imagined her life as a stage or film star; instead, it had been the life of a drudge. She kept telling herself this was why she felt as she did, trying constantly over the last few months to reassure herself that she was not really ill.

For weeks Amy had been waking up at this hour. She tried to push the reason out of her mind. But as an oyster covers a speck of grit with layers of pearl to cloak the irritation it causes, other more comfortable reasons fluttered through her mind, never the real one: the recurring pain.

She turned out the light, went back to bed, lay awake listening to her husband, thinking of the strange unsatisfactory pattern her life had formed. The Abos painted pictures to show the main points of their experience. Hers would be drab – except for a brief blaze of sunshine and love. She wondered how an artist would see it: a golden sun against a sky of northern grey, perhaps?

From childhood in the north of England, in the gloomy mill town of Stockport, she had desperately wanted to be an actress. That career epitomised everything her own life lacked: gloss, glamour, freedom to be the person she thought she was. She had become an actress of sorts but she was totally untrained – no chance of a RADA course then. An aunt and uncle brought her up after the death of her parents on a day trip to the sea in an accident that would have seemed farcical if it had not also been fatal.

She still kept some yellowing newspaper reports describing how her father had waded into the sea and an unexpectedly strong wave knocked him over. Her mother had rushed into the water fully clothed to help him, and had tripped over a stone. Almost unbelievably, both had drowned in a few feet of water. They had been drinking, the coroner reported at the inquest. Her father was wearing flannel trousers and a sports jacket: no sober man would go swimming dressed like that. The coroner stressed this because he wished to minimise what might be bad publicity for a resort of which his brother was mayor, and which should have posted warnings when the sea was too rough for wading.

When Amy left school at fifteen she worked in touring shows in the winter and pierhead concert parties in the summer. Jobs at this level were not difficult to find, for the routine was tedious, the productions third rate, nothing like the stories about stars which she read in women's magazines. It was different now with TV, of course. Actors and actresses had steady jobs from nine to five in soap operas; almost like going to the office or factory every day. They probably had pensions, too. But then everything was different now, especially her health.

She had been having pains in her stomach for a long time, and had tried all manner of patent medicines and amateur specifics. Some had appeared to help a little at first, but the pain was always there, sometimes quiescent, like a wild beast sleeping. Sometimes it awoke to consume her whole body like a fire within her. Beads of perspiration would start from her flesh and she would gasp for breath; then, as suddenly as it had arrived, the pain would pass.

She might smoke a cigarette to soothe her nerves – she had almost given up smoking – and then the claws would be at her again, tearing at her inside. She would struggle to the bathroom and retch and vomit, leaning over the lavatory bowl, wondering why she felt so ill. The local doctor told her it was stress, strain, her time of life. He did not possess the equipment for tests she read about in newspaper articles about health. He was a good man, though, and she knew she did not tell him all her symptoms and minimised the fierceness of the pain. She was afraid of what he might discover.

The unexpected news Ian had given her that a stranger was in town, looking for Crosby, must have set off the pain this time. She had not heard Crosby's name for years, but, like the pain, it was always in the back of her thoughts, often out of sight, but still there, ready to leap out and attack her peace of mind.

The odd thing was, she had never met Crosby, just heard about him from her husband. Crosby had been in the United States Army on some special detachment in Singapore in 1942. Like Crabtree, he was captured when the garrison surrendered. He was a great character, according to her husband, always willing to help others. He appeared not to have any first name; he was always referred to simply as Crosby.

'One day, we'll be out of this, Crabtree,' Crosby used to say, so Amy's husband had told her many times. 'Then we're going to enjoy ourselves, both of us.'

But it was doubtful whether Crabtree, at least, had really enjoyed himself. He returned to Katherine, to his first wife, older than him and always ailing, and to Amy living in the house with her illegitimate son. Crosby had disappeared, dropped out of sight. Then one day he turned up, unannounced and quite unexpectedly, in the Alice of all places. Her husband had been there that day and came back excited, his face flushed with pleasure at seeing his old comrade again after so long.

'Crosby's here!' he cried in delighted amazement. 'I ran into him in the Todd Tavern.'

'Crosby? You mean the American who was in Singapore with you?'

'Who else? There's only one Crosby. Great bloke.'

'What's he doing?'

'Looking for a job.'

'I thought he was rich.'

'He was, so he said. Anyhow, he spent all his money. Got married. Wife walked out on him. Lawyers put their hooks into him. He married again, then walked out on her. And more lawyers came in for the kill, the crocodile bastards. He couldn't settle down. Told me he'd met several others who'd been in Changi with us and they were all the same. Drifters, unable to settle, trying to escape their memories of the years they'd rotted away under the Japs.

'Everything might seem quite normal with them, and then one night they'd wake up screaming. In their dreams, they'd be back inside, running with dysentery like a tap, listening to the rats crawling over their best mate, who was dying or dead at the other end of the hut.

'They'd start to sweat, pee blood, remembering all those things we all thought we'd left behind us. So they'd up sticks and move on, running away from themselves, if you like. But, Amy, we've nowhere to run to. We carry our memories with us, like baggage. Not wanted on the journey, but impossible to dump.'

Amy had heard this before, many times.

'The Alice must be the last place anyone would expect to find him.'

'Sure. Maybe that's why he chose it. The Outback. The Never-Never. The last place God made. Maybe he heard I was here somewhere, maybe anything. The fact is, he's here, in the bloody Alice.'

'But what's Crosby want here?' she asked Crabtree.

'Help, that's what,' said her husband. 'I've got to give him a job, set him on his feet after all he did for me. Then he'll move on. He won't stay long. He's like the Abos, must go walkabout. Like you'd say, got itchy feet.'

'I'd like to meet him,' said Amy, rather fearing the encounter; why, she had no idea. A couple of days later, she asked her husband when Crosby was arriving.

'Soon,' he told her shortly. 'In his own time. He's got a problem.'

He did not tell her what it was, and she did not ask. If he had wanted to tell her, he would have done. It was no use asking Crabtree questions; he just wouldn't answer.

And then one night, months after Crabtree had first run into him in the bar, Crosby arrived – dead. Amy guessed her husband must have seen him on trips to the Alice but, if so, Crosby had never taken up Crabtree's offer of work. Perhaps he was too ill or footloose, or maybe didn't feel he could work in a store selling eggs and coffee and cans of beer.

Amy did not even know what he looked like, and now she never would. He must have been really ill, because he died in the Outback. The preacher had gone out with Crabtree and the local undertaker in his ute with a coffin knocked down into planks. They put Crosby in the coffin and brought him back and buried him – 'Still with his boots on,' said Crabtree with a kind of melancholy pride, as though this showed the kind of man Crosby was.

'I'd like to have met him,' Amy said.

'I'd like you to have met him, too,' Crabtree agreed. 'But it didn't work out that way. I guess a lot of things in Crosby's life were like that. They didn't work out. He couldn't get his act together. It's Changi that does that to you. But there's something we've both got to do for him, now he's gone.'

And then he had told her, and Amy looked at Crabtree and wanted to refuse to help or have any part of it, but he would not let her speak.

'You're my wife,' he said sharply. 'I helped you when you were down. I invited you back here from England where you and your kid were doing nothing, just drifting. I married you, gave you a home. Crosby helped me so many times I've forgotten to count them. Not with little things like that, but saving my life. Telling me not to lose my temper with the Japs or my faith that we'd survive – oh, lots of things I've never told anyone about, and never will. Now he's gone I have to do this last thing for him. It's the only way I can pay back in his memory what he did for me. You must see that, girl.'

Amy nodded. 'I see that,' she agreed reluctantly. But she hated herself for seeing it, and her husband for what he was forcing her to do. But again, that was long ago. Yet, as with her brief time with James Jackson in Colombo, the memory stayed in her mind, clear as a newly cut diamond – and just as sharp because it hurt every time she recalled it.

Pain gripped her again and she lay, legs outstretched, arms by her side, bracing her body against it. The gnawing ache pulsed, swelling then subsiding like waves pounding tirelessly on an ocean shore. Gradually the sleeping pills dulled the pain, took the edge off it, and she dozed in an uneasy slumber.

Amy Crabtree came out of the elevator on the ground floor of the high-rise block near the Trade Winds Hotel in Cairns, Queensland, where the specialist had his office. She stood for a moment outside the building, looking but not really seeing the wide grass strip that extended along the sea front, dotted with palm trees at regular intervals.

The tide had dropped, and clumps of spiky grass and weeds thrust out of the water like clutches of spears. In the shallow parts, between stretches of mud and sand, platoons of pelicans cruised up and down slowly in the water, then turned as though in a drill movement and moved off in a different direction. Other birds, whose names she did not know, some with brightly coloured feathers and flat beaks, came in gracefully like tiny flying boats, lowering their feet elegantly as they landed on the ebbing tide. She loved the sound of the birds at home every evening, when they would settle in the branches and every tree would suddenly come alive with their song. She loved birds; birds were free to fly away. She was not.

Amy had never realised until that moment, in the sunshine, overlooking the sea, just how beautiful this country was; how lovely the birdsong sounded. But the realisation came late, perhaps too late. In the doctor's impersonal, air-conditioned office, twenty floors up, a room incongruously bright with Sidney Nolans and Arthur Boyds on the walls, Amy had just received a sentence of death.

She had finally asked her local doctor to make an appointment with the best specialist in Australia for stomach ailments, and after some time and telephoning he had arranged for her to see a Dr Sen who lived mainly in Hong Kong but who visited Darwin and Cairns twice a month. His grandfather had worked in the area years before, owning several shops and a laundry, the doctor told her, and on his visits Dr Sen still lived in the family house. Like so many Asians with professional qualifications, Dr Sen had realised the enormous potential Australia offered to him in private practice. Japanese and Chinese nationals were said to own nearly forty per cent of the entire country, and more of them were coming in every day.

Sitting in a leather chair, looking at him across his huge glass-topped desk, Amy remembered how her doctor in

Katherine had spoken of him with respect, even awe. Dr Sen was consulted by all manner of rich and famous people, multi-millionaires, the directors of international companies, politicians, heads of state. He was undoubtedly the best man in his field.

'Well, Mrs Crabtree,' Dr Sen said in his clipped, curiously modulated voice, 'we have made a number of tests, examined the results and the X-ray plates very closely, and I am sorry to have to tell you that there is evidence of something a little unfriendly in your throat and in your stomach. I see from your clinical notes, you have complained of a dryness in your throat from time to time, and of shortness of breath, as well as these stomach pains. You used to smoke quite heavily, according to the records.'

'Not for the past year or two,' Amy corrected him defensively. 'I did before then, yes. Sounds silly now, but there was no anti-smoking propaganda then, and a cigarette always seemed soothing – especially when I was on the stage. There was so much hanging about, so many disappointments. But that's a long time ago. So what is the worst? Please tell me. I want to know.'

'To be blunt then, Mrs Crabtree, you are suffering from carcinoma of the right lung and the stomach.'

'Is there any cure? Any hope, I mean?'

Dr Sen paused before he replied. She saw him purse his lips, glance briefly over her shoulder out at the shimmering sea; a flock of birds was coming in to land.

'There is always hope, Mrs Crabtree. While there is life there is hope. If you had come to me last year, we could possibly have removed the infected areas of your stomach and throat with a very good chance of a full recovery.'

'But it is not last year,' Amy interrupted him nervously. 'It is today. Now.'

'Exactly. The prognosis is not as good now as it would have been then. I must tell you that.'

'At the worst, how long have I got?'

'I do not like to look at things in that way.'

'You don't have to, Doctor. I do.'

'It is really impossible to say. Sometimes there is a remission that lasts for months, even years. Sometimes, for reasons quite beyond all rational medical and scientific explanation, the cancer just seems to lose interest and the patient makes a total recovery.'

'But that's not likely here?' she asked, wishing him to contradict her.

'We must keep all our options open.'

'Apart from that, what are the chances?'

'It is impossible to be specific, Mrs Crabtree. I understand how difficult it is for you to accept that I cannot be precise. Patients sometimes tend to think that we specialists possess almost supernatural abilities. We don't. Unfortunately!

'Is there anything I can do to give myself a little longer?'

'Of course. You should stop smoking and avoid alcohol, especially spirits. I suggest you live quietly and eat as much natural food as possible – uncooked and without any sauces or spices. Fish in preference to meat. Fresh vegetables. Salads. And see your local physician at least once a month. I will write to him. He'll be in touch with you.'

'Thank you for being so frank with me, Doctor,' said Amy quietly. 'I appreciate that very much.'

Now that she knew the worst, she felt an inexplicable feeling of peace. She had feared that something very serious was wrong with her. Now she knew, and surprisingly the knowledge proved less alarming than the fear.

'In view of what you say, Doctor, I had better settle your bill now. If you could tell me how much I owe you?' She opened her purse, took out a chequebook. 'You will accept a cheque, I hope?'

'No,' said Dr Sen. 'I won't accept a cheque.'

She looked at him, puzzled, annoyed.

He smiled. 'I know something of your background, Mrs Crabtree, and you have come a long way to see me. I am sorry I have not better news to give you. But you have borne it very bravely, and I can tell you that some of the richest and most famous people in the world have sat exactly where you are sitting now and have wept when I gave them much less serious news.

'I will not accept your cheque, Mrs Crabtree. I am not a poor man. Sometimes, like the old English character, Robin Hood, I make the rich pay for those who are less rich. I look upon that as their privilege, if you like. You owe me nothing.'

'*Nothing?*' she repeated in amazement. 'But are you sure?'

'I am certain, Mrs Crabtree. Quite certain. Now, I will say goodbye and wish you not good luck, but what I think you already have – good courage.'

Dr Sen stood up and shook hands. His palm felt curiously soft and smooth, almost like a woman's.

Amy walked out of his office as though in a dream, feeling strangely detached from reality, almost weightless; she might already be only a spirit.

A plane to Darwin left within the hour; she could be back in Katherine well before midnight. She walked slowly along the esplanade, listening to the birds; she had never paused to listen so closely to them before. Then, she had time to spare; now, she had none.

Next morning, back in Katherine, a letter arrived for her from the United States. It was delivered as she sat on her own over breakfast of a cup of black coffee. Crabtree had gone into town to chase up a consignment of frozen food which had been delayed coming up from Adelaide. She had not told him what Dr Sen had said to her. She had not even told him she had seen a specialist, only that she wanted to visit a woman friend who had recently moved from Katherine to Cairns. Somehow, the moment did not seem right for her to mention the subject.

Not for the first time, Amy thought how remarkable it would be to share her life with someone to whom she could reveal anything and everything, knowing that they would always be sympathetic and helpful, never sitting in judgement, never criticising. But how many married couples could do that? Surely, like so much else in life, for most that was only a dream?

She opened the envelope. The writing paper was thick, cream coloured, bearing a gold die-stamp of an Eastern pagoda. It was headed Rosael Pagoda Productions, Wilshire Boulevard, Hollywood, California. What the devil was this? A personal letter from a film company? *Now* – when she hadn't acted for years?

'Dear Mrs Crabtree,' she read. 'You may have heard that we will shortly be on our way to Australia to make two films, partly on location on the north-east coast, partly in the Outback.

'The first of these is *Boomerang Two* which, as you may guess from its title, capitalises on the enormous success of our first Australian venture, *Boomerang*, one of the biggest grossers of the year. The second is a comedy, *Captain Cook's Secret Voyage*.

'The Captain Cook of our title is not Captain James Cook, so closely associated with Australia, but a modern seafarer who, like Baron Münchhausen, confuses his dreams with his rather more prosaic life as a ferry boat captain.

'We have followed your career with interest and admiration, and we are writing to offer you a major role in each picture. They have, in fact, been written with you in mind.

'If you are interested in principle, please cable the undersigned with your agent's name and address. We will then airmail the scripts to you and through your agent make you an offer that hopefully you will not refuse and which we trust will also mark the start of a long and fruitful association between us.'

Amy read the letter again, and then for a third time. Was this

an elaborate hoax? She held the paper up to the light and saw
the watermark, ran the tips of her fingers over the heavily
embossed address. The letter was signed Byron Corbin. She
had heard of him and of Rosael Pagoda Films, seen the names
on cinema and TV screens often enough. But how could he
possibly have followed her career? Its peak had been very brief
when she had travelled to Ceylon with a concert party to give
shows to the troops in Colombo for a few months in 1941. And
then her career had virtually ended.

She had danced, sung, taken part in short sketches, playing
anyone from a dumb blonde to a middle-aged landlady. Now,
all that seemed to have happened to someone else, not to
her . . .

Another girl of her age, Esmerelda, was also in that concert
party in Colombo. Amy in those days called herself Barbara,
after the film star Barbara Stanwyck; she'd never asked
Esmerelda whether that was her real name or not. They got on
well and one night after a show they had met James Jackson in
the Galle Face Hotel. Two young pilot officers were bringing
them cocktails, and one knew James and introduced him. Amy
remembered the moment perfectly; even that she was drinking a
horse's neck. That dated her. Whoever drank a horse's neck
now?

James Jackson was older than any of them, not a lot older but
when you are barely out of your teens five years seems a serious
seniority. He owned a car, which was rare, and he took them all
out in it that night. Later, he took the girls out, sometimes
together, sometimes one at a time. Everything seemed new and
exciting, like something out of a Dorothy Lamour film of the
South Seas.

Amy suspected that Jackson went to bed with Esmerelda as
well as with her in the weeks that followed, but she had loved
him from the first time she saw him and nothing he could do
would ever alter her feelings, then or now. He was amusing,
urbane, everything she had admired in men like Clark Gable

or Cary Grant. She had never met anyone like him when she was touring on a theatrical circuit from Ashton-under-Lyne in the north to Woolwich and Chatham in the south.

James wore total confidence like a splendid cloak, while other men she had met through the concert party often seemed nervous, ill at ease. They did not know how to order a meal in a good restaurant because before the war they had been clerks in banks or insurance offices or serving behind the counters of grocery shops, and had never been into a good restaurant. Jackson had, frequently.

Not only did he know how to behave, he had taught her how to love. Now she could never see a beach touched by moonlight or palms bending before a breeze from the warm ocean without remembering him and his expert and caressing hands, his warm, sensual mouth, how his whole body moulded perfectly against her, into her.

Several times he had left Colombo to go to Calcutta and then on to Hong Kong on some special mission, about which he was secretive. He wasn't in the services. She suspected he had some sort of intelligence job, but did not like to ask him. He explained his journeys vaguely by saying that Trinity-Trio, the company for which he had worked before the war, required some important papers to be checked in their Calcutta office and others to be brought over from their Hong Kong headquarters.

He had not added that his grandfather had been one of the firm's three founders; that he personally owned one-third of the company's voting shares; or that he was a lord. All this Amy learned years later, at second hand, and she liked James all the more for not having told her at the time. She would have been over-awed, and he was sensitive enough to have realised that. Did he also realise she loved him? Not that it mattered now, of course, but somehow it would be comforting to know that he had felt about her as she had felt about him; or if that was asking too much, that at least he had liked her – as he seemed to – and might have come to love her one day. Like most women in love, she sought reassurance, proof that her feelings were reciprocated.

When the Japanese attacked Singapore and Pearl Harbor, her concert party split up into two groups; Esmerelda went on to Calcutta and Delhi with one of them. After rumours that Amy's group might go to the Middle East, they sailed to Perth in Western Australia. From there they travelled north by road and rail, and then a short hop in a Dakota – sitting with their backs against the bare rivets of the fuselage – to Katherine in the Northern Territory.

By then, the war in the East was going badly for the Allies. Amy guessed why James had not replied to any of her letters; he must have been captured in Hong Kong when it surrendered. Stories about Japanese atrocities, of their custom of using prisoners as living targets in bayonet practice, of epidemics sweeping their prisoner-of-war camps, she resolutely put out of her mind. The war could not last for ever: not with America in. James would come back, and in spite of her aunt's insistence that girls must be proud, if he didn't find her Amy decided she would seek him out and tell him she loved him. She owed that to him, and to herself.

Amy had the gift, given more frequently to women than to men, of assuring herself that what she wished for must surely come to pass; it could only be a matter of time. The concert party had been due to go on to Darwin, on the north coast, about 355 kilometres north-west of Katherine, but a few days after Singapore surrendered the Japanese bombed Darwin and a few months later, in March 1942, they bombed the airfield outside Katherine.

Everyone who could leave immediately went south. Overnight, Katherine, until then simply a small town of largely single-storey buildings, the end of the railway line, with a population of around 235 people and 600 goats, became a huge and overcrowded transit camp for troops. The company stayed there, presenting their show twice nightly on makeshift stages – the back of a flat-bed truck one night, old packing cases hurriedly nailed together the next.

After a month of these shows, often with a matinée, Amy collapsed. She finished her final dance routine and suddenly the stage began to revolve, its sides crinkled, and she fainted. An Australian army doctor examined her in the cab of the truck which she and the other girls used as a dressing room.

'You know what's the matter, don't you?' he asked, not unkindly.

'The heat, I suppose.'

'When did you last have a period?'

'About six weeks ago.'

'That gives you a clue, doesn't it?'

'In this heat, they've been irregular, Doctor.'

'Not that irregular,' he replied. 'You're pregnant. You're going to have a baby.'

'But that's impossible.'

'Not really. It happens all the time. Especially when there's a war on.'

'Are you sure? I mean, can't something be done about it? Can't I have an operation – or something?'

'Maybe you can in Europe, but not here, that's for sure.'

'But I can't dance like this.'

'It won't show for some time. Four months, maybe five.'

'Then what am I going to do?'

'I don't know,' he admitted. 'But you're not the first woman in the world to find herself in this situation. Ask Mother Crabtree who runs the general store if she can help. Her old man was taken at Singapore. She's not too well and maybe could use another pair of hands in the store. Have a word with her. She's a good sort. She'll help you if she can.'

Amy went to see Mrs Crabtree and explained the situation. This was no time for bluff.

'Been sleeping around a lot, have you?' asked Mrs Crabtree.

'No,' Amy said. 'A few times in England, but that was a year ago.'

'This is much nearer.'

'Well, in Ceylon. A man I liked. He's missing in Hong Kong.'

'If it's got your name on it, that's where it's going to get you. That's what I always say. A bullet or a baby. Never got me, though, more's the pity. Crabtree would like a son or daughter, but it never worked.'

She always referred to her husband as Crabtree; he might have been a stranger or a lodger, someone impersonal who had lived with her and then gone away to the war. His photograph stood on the dressing table of the single downstairs room in her house; a man with a big jaw, tight lips, very short hair, a straightforward face.

'He was captured at Singapore?'

'So they tell me – if he's not dead. There's been no proper word. But there you go. Men go and fight and leave women to weep and bring up their bastards.'

'That's what he or she will be, I suppose.'

'You suppose right. But I wouldn't let that be known around this town. They're a bit prudish here, you know. And you're a Pom, not a Territorian, not a local, which doesn't help.'

'So what can I do?'

'What most other women do in your predicament. Buy yourself a wedding ring. Say your husband was in New Guinea, Singapore, Hong Kong, I don't know where. And he didn't come back.'

'Won't they see through that?'

'Maybe. Maybe not – if you're smart. Any road, they won't say so openly. What would you propose?'

'I've got nothing to propose, Mrs Crabtree.'

'Don't call me that. Call me Jean. I'm older than Crabtree, you know, much older. Maybe that's the trouble. I'll back up your story.'

'Will they try and find out?'

'No. They've got better things to do. Lot of the women here are having a bit on the side themselves. Takes two to tango, you know. You help me in the store, I'll keep you in food and a bit of pocket money. It won't run to much, for we haven't got much. Where are you from in England?'

'The North. Stockport. Near Manchester.'

'Got a mother? Father?'

'No.'

'What were you then?'

'I wanted to be an actress.'

'That's not work,' said Mrs Crabtree scornfully. 'That's play-acting. Pretending. This is real out here. Look at the weather. Burns the hide off you ten months of the year. Then in the wet you get eight inches of rain in a day. Think of that. Eight *inches* in a single day. Got to be tough to survive. But you're going to survive, Amy. You're a survivor. Like me.'

So it proved. Her baby was born, a son. Amy worked in the store, helping Mrs Crabtree, whose health gradually grew worse. When Amy's son was three years old, Mrs Crabtree looked as though she had aged ten years. She had heard that her husband had survived in Changi prisoner-of-war camp and was coming home. This news should have pleased his wife, but instead it worried her.

'When you've been on your own for a long time,' she told Amy, 'you get to like it. You don't have a man fumbling around, wanting to get what he calls his rights when you're not feeling up to it. Always casting an eye over younger Sheilas, staring at their big breasts and tight bottoms. They might be young enough to be his daughter, but men never think of that. They go on and on.'

'Don't you think they should?' asked Amy. 'Isn't it a kind of compliment to us? In a way?'

'Not to me it ain't. I never enjoyed it much.'

'I'd like the chance,' Amy told her.

'You'll get the chance. You'll go back home to England.'

'Home? I've no home there. I've got relations, but that's not home. Anyway, how can I go back? I've no money.'

'Then I've got a bit of news for you,' said Mrs Crabtree. 'I didn't ever pay you much, three pounds a week, but I also put a bit by for you every week, an extra pound in the bank, earning interest.'

'You didn't tell me,' said Amy, surprised and almost embarrassed at the news. She had never realised that Mrs Crabtree even liked her.

'I'm telling you now. There was no point telling you when you couldn't go. But wait till Crabtree comes back. See me through that. Then you go. I helped you. Now maybe you can help me.'

'In any way I can. Without your help, I'd have killed myself.'

'Don't be dramatic. You're an actress, not a dramatist. When I say help me, I mean help me.'

'Of course. In any way.'

'It may be any way. I don't reckon Crabtree will fancy making love to me. I look at myself in the mirror. Breasts thin as razor strops and face wrinkled like a cane toad's neck. He won't want me. I don't want him, either, that's the truth of the matter, but he might want you. You're young and good looking.'

'I couldn't do that. Not after what you've done for me. You've saved me.'

'I'm asking you to save *me*, Amy. He may not want anyone after what he's been through. I don't know, but men are odd. So better keep it in the family. That's what I say. Better to be bunking you in the next room than some little whore from out of town. You follow me?'

'I think I do. I'll make an effort, anyway.'

'So what about your man?' asked Mrs Crabtree, lighting a cigarette.

'He's still in Hong Kong, far as I know. I've not heard

anything else. But then I'm not his next of kin. He may have parents.'

Amy thought, but did not add because the possibility was too painful to consider, that he could even have a wife somewhere.

'You'd better get writing, then. Write to the Army in Canberra, London, all over. He'll probably come back through Australia on his way to England. Then he could stop off here.'

So Amy wrote, claiming to be a relation, but the replies she received were always evasive: it was still impossible to supply information about all prisoners of war. She guessed that they did not want to give anything away to an unknown woman whose claim could not be verified. It was also possible, of course, that some returning prisoners did not wish to go back to their wives or families. They saw this moment of chaos, when no one could say with absolute certainty who was dead or missing, as a once-only chance to disappear and begin a new life somewhere else, with a new identity, as a new person, maybe with a new person.

'He'll turn up,' Mrs Crabtree assured her. 'He'll be back.'

Then one day, in an English society magazine several months old, Amy recognised a photograph of James. The caption described him as the late Lord Jackson. She read on in amazement, mouthing the words as though she had difficulty in understanding them. So he wasn't just James Jackson, he was a peer, a millionaire, holding one-third of the equity in Trinity-Trio. And he was dead. He had fallen ill in Stanley jail in Hong Kong and, ironically, had died on the day the British fleet arrived to reclaim the colony under the British flag. But his title was not extinct. He had left a son, and a widow, Lady Esmerelda Jackson.

That could only be the Esmerelda with whom she had been in the show. How incredible! He must have married her in Calcutta on the last of his journeys to Hong Kong. She had briefly been his wife and was now his widow, and Amy was – nothing. A girl he'd had fun with and left pregnant, without even knowing it. Amy could barely assimilate the news. Esmerelda was now immensely rich, with a title and his son; and she was poor, also with his son, but without any future. And while Esmerelda's son was now an English lord, her son was an Australian bastard.

She had him christened Robert (after her uncle in Stockport) and James after his father, but she always called him the Australian. This was his home, where he was born; Australia was his country. She determined there and then that she would show everyone he was as clever as his half-brother, Lord Jackson. Better, in fact, because he would have to do it all on his own. Well, not quite on his own, she told herself, because I'll be here, pushing him on. And if James Jackson is in heaven, if there is such a place, then he can look down and see his two sons, not a month between them in age, one growing up in England, the other in Australia, not knowing they are related, even that the other exists, or who's going to come out top.

'And I'll tell you, James, I'll tell you now,' she said to herself, speaking aloud, as though James Jackson was actually in the room with her, 'it's going to be *my* boy.'

Amy accompanied Mrs Crabtree to the station in 1945 to meet her husband when he came off the train at the end of his long, tedious journey from Singapore. Relatives and friends of other returning soldiers had draped Australian flags on poles across the line; a number of women stood waiting for their men, and Amy could see concern on several faces. She knew some had been unfaithful, some had even given birth to children, now prudently passed over to relations, at least until the moment of reunion was over. Would their husbands be recognisable or totally changed, alien, even hateful to them? How would they react to evidence of infidelity? With violence – or indifference?

It was difficult to pick up a life together after nearly four years of normal separation. It might be impossible when one partner had been through years of being regularly beaten, humiliated, manacled, taunted, and always hungry; when his only clothes had been a loincloth or a G-string cut from the shirt of a dead comrade. Settling down was not going to be easy for anyone. Four years of different lives alone meant that most had been apart for longer than they had been together.

Amy recognised Crabtree from photographs she had seen. He looked very thin and gaunt, and as old as his wife.

'Here's Amy, who's been helping us,' said Mrs Crabtree nervously. 'Got a little boy. Her husband was killed in New Guinea. A sergeant. She lives with me.'

'Good on her,' said Crabtree without much interest. His mind was still in the past although his body was here in the present, in Katherine. The war was over, but for him and for too many others like him, Amy sensed it might never really end.

As weeks passed, Mrs Crabtree spent more of her time in bed; she was ill and old and somehow seemed to lack the will to live. She had kept the store going while her husband was away, and now that he was home she could relax, and in relaxing she realised how feeble she really was. She pottered about in the shop and cooked some meals, but sometimes she would hand over to Amy and say: 'I can't manage any more today, love. You see to Crabtree.'

So gradually Amy and Crabtree were thrown almost deliberately closer and closer together. Once, when she was alone, washing up the dishes after supper, he came up behind her, put his arms round her body. His hands moved up to cup her breasts. She went on, mechanically wiping soap suds off the plates, as though she had not noticed him, as though this was not happening.

'Put that cloth down,' he told her. His voice sounded different, hoarser. She turned, and dried her hands, and he kissed her. As he kissed, he was undoing her blouse, his hands searching for the clip of her brassiere. Then her breasts were free and he moved his mouth down and kissed them. She could feel him pressing hard against her and instinctively her hands went down and gripped him. She felt the heartbeat in his phallus through the thin trousers. With trembling fingers, she undid the buttons of his fly. There was no way back now. From the moment Amy had first seen him on the railway platform she had sensed that this would only be a matter of time, sooner, later, but inevitable as death.

'Have you got a thing?' she asked him practically. 'I've been pregnant once. I don't want to get caught again.'

'I got one from the chemist.'

So he had planned this. Somehow, the knowledge lessened her own feeling of guilt. He pulled out a rubber and as she watched him, she realised this would be the first time of many. After a long period of celibacy, she felt like a traveller in the burning desert, parched with thirst and dreaming of fountains of cool water, who suddenly sees an oasis and need never be thirsty again.

She had betrayed his wife's trust and kindness but she kept telling herself that this was what his wife wanted. Amy was not sure it was what she wanted. She needed sex, but she wanted love much more desperately, and love was not in Crabtree's gift.

Their affair lasted for several years. Looking back, Amy often felt that it must have happened to two other people, that she had never been involved, that she had never lain naked with Crabtree while his wife was coughing in the next room. She could hear her cough clearly, and wondered whether Mrs Crabtree also heard the sounds of love, Amy's cry as she reached a climax. She did not like to think of these things; most especially she did not want to recall the day when Crabtree made love to her in a side room off the shop. She had turned her head for some reason and could have sworn she saw her son, the Australian, then eight or nine, looking through the doorway.

'Stop!' she told Crabtree urgently. 'He's seen us!'

He lay panting as she got up, straightened her clothes and

ran into the shop, ready to give the boy some explanation – she had just lain down for a minute or two and Mr Crabtree had come in and wondered whether she had fainted – anything except the truth.

The shop was empty but the entrance bell was still tinkling above the door, so someone had been there: it *must* have been her son. Had he seen them? If he had, what had he thought? Amy never knew. She could not ask him, but the thought nibbled away at her peace of mind until she could stand it no longer.

She decided she must go back to England. The strain of this kind of life was growing intolerable. She felt that people in Katherine were talking about the three of them living together. She did not know what they knew or what they guessed, but she was tired of seeing smiles and knowing glances.

So Amy went back to England with the Australian. They lodged where she had lived previously, with Uncle Rob. It would only be for a short time, she told him. She was certain she could pick up a job, dancing, singing, acting, but this proved impossible. Music hall had reached its peak of popularity in the war; now television offered more sophisticated entertainment. One by one, music halls closed or were turned into bingo halls or covered markets, or just boarded up and left to the rats that gnawed at the red plush seats, tattered posters of long-forgotten artistes waving in the northern winds.

Amy drank many gins and limes and gins and lemons with older men of indifferent sex who claimed to be producers or promoters or dance directors, and who were certain they could help her but who somehow never did. Some wanted a quick feel or to take her to bed, but she resisted these crude advances. She feared that if she succumbed to one man, he would tell others, and in the end she would be no better than the other blousy women of indefinite age who called themselves actresses and traipsed around agents' offices with folders of yellowing photographs showing them in sequins or tights or evening dresses against unlikely backgrounds: a country house balustrade, an ocean liner's rail. That was no way to the stars. And yet Amy believed that if only she could get the chance, she could prove she had talent.

Now that chance had come, just as the chance had come years previously for her son, the Australian, to prove he had inherited a most unusual and valuable talent.

In Cairns, on the way to the airport, she had seen a hoarding on top of a boundary fence. Behind this, a high-rise building was going up in a clatter of concrete mixers and power drills, and the incessant blare of workmen's transistors. She read the notice on the hoarding: 'Another residential development by Trinity-Trio'.

How incredible to think that she might have married the man who owned one-third of that gigantic company! The idea was somehow more incredible than the knowledge that she was the mother of a man who was now even more rich and power-ful. Robert James's wealth had no impact on her life. She knew more about her son's activities from what she read about him in the newspapers than she did from personal contact. It was ironic that they should invariably refer to him as the Austra-lian, just as she had called him from childhood.

She had never really understood him. At school, he showed no interest in games, but had bought and sold little items every day, as though the classroom was a market place and nothing more.

If another boy had been given a birthday present he didn't like, the Australian would discover what he would take for it and then auction the present among his classmates and realise double or treble its value. Extraordinary, she thought, because she had difficulty in simply working out what she spent on groceries each week. Ian Bruce was the same as the Australian; she sensed that they both had a gift she lacked, and pos-sessed it in such abundance that to them making money was commonplace.

As a boy, the Australian had taken to visiting Stockport public library to read newspapers, not for general news but, as he explained to her patiently when she wondered at his interest, to check share movements of major companies. Why would one go up three pennies and another drop two shillings?

'If you know *why* people want to buy a share, you can make money. And if you buy enough shares, you can control the company,' he told her.

'But you've got to be rich to do that. Rich and powerful.'

'I'm going to be both,' he assured his mother.

'But how?'

'Well, first of all, I must get some capital. These papers give details of rich people's wills – how much they've left, and what their jobs were.'

'Oh, I see those in *The Mirror* sometimes. Some old spinster in Bournemouth leaves fifty thousand pounds to a cats' home. That sort of thing. Mad, when there's so much poverty about.'

'How other people spend their money always seems mad, Mother, if it's not the same way we'd spend it – if we had it.'

'You think so?' she asked in surprise. This thought had never entered her mind.

'Of course. But what interests me is how the money was made in the first place; presumably not by the spinster who is leaving it to the cats' home. On balance, Lloyds brokers – and I'm not quite sure what they do – and solicitors leave more money when they die than anyone else.'

'So you want to be a broker or a solicitor?'

'Not *want*, Mother. But that could be a means to an end.'

People were frowning at them in the reading room, pointing to 'No talking' notices around the walls. Her son ignored them and showed her two names in that morning's copy of *The Enquirer*. A solicitor in Cheltenham had left nearly a million pounds, most of it to charities and his local church. Another, a widower in Warrington, had left £200,000 to his son, also a solicitor, in Stockport. These were staggering sums of money to Amy who would have been be glad of an acting job at £6 a week.

She looked again at the two names. The first meant nothing to her, but she had heard the name of Pendlehulme, the Warrington solicitor. She pointed to it, not wanting to talk.

'I know,' her son said. He did not care what other people thought of them talking in a silent room. 'His grandson's at school with me.'

'Then you ought to join his firm,' said Amy, half joking.

'Please,' said the librarian primly, coming up to them. She was a middle-aged spinster with an Eton crop and a Fair Isle jumper. She wore a brass wedding ring to make people think she was married. 'I must ask you to desist from talking. Other people require silence to read.'

'I'm sorry,' Amy said, and looked at the other people: middle-aged men in seedy raincoats, old age pensioners wearing woollen gloves with the ends of the fingers cut off so they could turn the pages of the free newspapers on the stands more easily. They only came into the library because here they could have a seat and pass otherwise empty hours in a warm room, out of the sooty rain. They exuded a sour, sad smell of failure. Yet they were not all old; they just looked old because they were beaten, defeated by life, bad decisions, long unemployment. Amy knew how easily she could join them, and shuddered at the thought. She took the Australian's hand as much for comfort and reassurance as for affection when they walked out into the grimy street and the iron clang of tramcars.

When he left school, he took a job as an office boy at £2 a week in Pendlehulme's firm.

'And if you work, you could go on to be a clerk,' said Pendlehulme ponderously, meaning well. 'Then you might even sit your law exams and qualify as a solicitor. Like me.'

'Yes,' agreed the Australian, but without enthusiasm. He did not want to be like Pendlehulme, working in a shabby office with roll-top desks and leather chairs that were splitting and showing dirty cottonwool padding. This was not success to him, but he would use it as a stepping stone to success. He could not understand why Pendlehulme kept on at his boring job, living in a small semi-detached house, driving a Morris Ten, when he had inherited so much money. He could have lived almost anywhere, and in style. Or, much more important, he could have used his money to make more, as a gardener uses a penny packet of seeds to grow an entire bed of flowers. What little respect the Australian had for his employer had evaporated by the end of the first day in his firm . . .

Amy walked on, remembering with pride and almost disbelief her son's first major deal. She had had to sign the contracts for him because, as a minor, he could not sign them himself. He explained exactly what he had done – but only after he had done it.

'Why didn't you tell me when you were starting?' she asked him.

'Because people talk,' he explained.

'I wouldn't have talked.'

'You might have done. Not meaning to, of course. And anyhow, it's a good rule to keep your mouth shut until the deal's done and the money's in your pocket.'

'I suppose it is.'

She had never been in that situation so she did not know, but the rule certainly worked for him, then and in every other transaction he had undertaken. Pendlehulme had taken him to a local recreational club which his firm managed. The club had been adapted years previously from a large house standing in several acres of garden, now hopelessly overgrown. Pendlehulme explained that at its inauguration the club possessed one hundred members, each holding one share, and so these founding shareholders controlled the club. Such co-operative ideas and co-operative societies were popular then in the north of England.

Mr Pendlehulme's explanation gave the Australian an idea.

He paid £5 to a former schoolfriend, Micky Cohen, the son of the local bookmaker, to help him find the owners of the original shares. He told Micky he needed the share certificates to prove a will. He did not tell him the truth; the money spider had also bitten Micky Cohen, and even then the Australian sensed he could not trust him or anyone else where a potential profit was at stake.

The original holders were all dead long since, but some had sons and daughters or other relations still living at their original addresses. The two boys visited everyone they could trace, explaining, if asked, that they were collecting old papers and certificates to sell on behalf of the local Scout troop.

Some relations of the founders still kept the certificates in a suitcase under a bed or in a spare-room cupboard. Others had framed them as wall decorations, a few had lost them, or never even heard of them. After weeks of searching, the Australian and Micky Cohen had acquired sixty-two share certificates. The Australian thus became the owner of the club. He immediately sold half the garden to a speculative builder and kept the rest for himself because he calculated that the price of land must rise. People would always want more houses but no one was making any more land.

Pendlehulme was furious and sacked him at once, but what did that matter? The Australian had made £20,000, a fortune.

He seemed to have the knack of instantly recognising an opportunity that others had overlooked. As soon as he took advantage of it, they realised how obvious it had been – but by then he was on the lookout for the next possibility.

In the 1950s he bought a dilapidated building, once an ice rink, that stood at a crossroads near the town centre. Its walls were plastered with 'For Sale' notices but no one in the north of England wanted to buy an ice rink and the Australian acquired it cheaply. He filled in the great basin of the rink by allowing builders to tip their rubbish into it, charging them £1 a load. Then he concreted this over, erected awnings and rented out

space by the day or week to local stallholders. Instead of having
to set up their stalls by the roadside, wet or fine, they had a large
covered market, a *super* market, as he called it. This was so
successful that he built more in other towns, and called them
supermarkets. Later, when he was old enough to act on his
own, he founded a company to run them, Rink Supermarkets.

The Australian was rising twenty-two when Amy decided to
return to Australia. Mrs Crabtree had died, and Crabtree had
written to ask Amy to marry him. She wanted to accept his
proposal, not because she was in love with him – she doubted
she could love anyone now as once, briefly, she had loved one
man – but because she could not see any future for herself on
the stage in England.

She was tired of skimping and saving and doing without in a
grey, depressing land where even the summer sun lacked heat.
She yearned for Australia, for its warmth, its space. To be
married to a man who owned a thriving general store even in
the Outback must mean a better standard of living than anything she could hope for in a Stockport terraced house.

Her mind made up, Amy asked her son to give her half the
profits he had made on his property deals. She thought that this
was perfectly reasonable and was at first surprised and then
hurt at his response, never realising he was equally surprised
and hurt by her request.

'But it's *my* money,' he said defensively. '*I* made it, Mother.'

'Of course you did, darling. But you couldn't have made a
single penny without me here first to sign the papers to
open a bank account and then all the legal documents, now
could you?'

'No,' he agreed. 'I couldn't, but I've given you everything
you wanted in payment for your help. Clothes. Even a car.'

'It's only a Ford Consul,' she pointed out, mentally com-
paring a few hundred pounds against the thousands he had
amassed for himself.

'That's what you asked for, Mother. It's what you wanted.'

'Well, I still say that without me you wouldn't have got started.'

'I could have found someone else to sign the papers.'

'Like who? If you'd put the money in someone else's name in their bank account, they'd have gone off with it.'

'That's exactly what you're proposing to do now.'

'Only half. I think I am entitled to that.'

'If you leave the money with me, I can double it for you – for both of us – within the next year,' he promised.

He needed the money. Without it he would go down a steep step in the game of financial snakes and ladders. There was another reason, too, which he had only recently begun to understand, and then not fully. He did not only need money, he *loved* it. He did not want money to spend, but to make it work for him, to make more and more and more.

'I promise you I can double it,' he repeated. 'At the very least.'

'I am sure you can, but I have to book a passage, buy clothes, put something towards buying a house. Mr Crabtree thinks he should buy one in Alice Springs. He wants to move from Katherine.'

They had never moved, of course. They could not find any property they both liked, and Crabtree knew so many people in Katherine that they decided to stay.

After long and increasingly resentful arguments, the Australian had given Amy half of his profits, and she put it on deposit in the bank. He had paid with a bad grace, and although she gained what she thought was hers, she realised she had lost her son's affection. The Australian had never been demonstrative or warm. Indeed, she had to admit he always seemed unusually cold and remote, a loner who had few friends and did not seem to need any. He was complete in himself, content in his own company. His only interest seemed to be to make money; friendship, love, these were for others, not for him.

Now, every time Amy read in the papers of the increasingly

large and complex deals he was doing – acquisitions, developments, takeovers – she would mentally divide his profit on
each one in half and think, 'If I'd let him keep my money, as he
wanted, I might be rich now, too.'

But as old Uncle Rob used to say: 'You can't have your cake
and eat it.' Well, she'd eaten the cake now, right down to the
crumbs. Uncle Rob was dead, and when the Australian was not
abroad on a business trip, flying economy class, he still lived in
the little terraced house they had all shared, and where he had
set up the headquarters of his company.

Of course, he maintained houses and apartments in many
other cities around the world, but this was his base. If he had a
home anywhere, it was here, where he had grown up, among
unpretentious people. He was totally unpretentious himself,
totally forgettable as a character. He might be a human
machine that walked and breathed – and calculated. She read
in a newspaper interview that the little house was now
crammed with computers and all manner of electronic equipment, fax machines, and other devices designed to shrink time
and distance between countries and cities and especially
between men like him.

For years she had been forced to rely on articles and TV
interviews for news of her son. His letters to her were always
short and impersonal; his secretary even signed them for him
when he was too busy or out of the country.

They belonged to two totally different worlds, and except for
being mother and son shared virtually nothing in common. She
had never asked him for anything since she had returned to
Australia, and he had never inquired whether she might need
help in cash or kind.

Amy thought about writing to tell the Australian about the
totally unexpected offer she had received to star not just in one
film, but in two. Imagine! And after all these years of waiting. It
would be a change to have something positive to report to him,
to show that at long last she was not going to be a failed actress

but a star. Then she decided against telling him. She would finish both pictures first and then inform him. Deeds were better than words; performance should always outstrip promise.

Amy had momentarily forgotten Dr Sen's sombre forecast. When she remembered, the knowledge lay heavy as molten lead in her mind.

Dr Sen sat out of the sun on the slatted wooden bench of the ferry crossing from the mainland of Kowloon to Hong Kong island. It was late afternoon and he was coming back from Kai Tak airport on his return from Australia. He liked to use the ferry whenever he could; it was infinitely preferable to the slow tunnel crammed with cars that was the other link. The sea – and his house high on The Peak, the island's highest hill and most exclusive residential area – seemed almost the only places where he could escape the heavy miasma of exhaust fumes and diesel oil, and the sour stench of sewage that hung like a poisoned cloud over the city.

Idly, he watched an old Chinese manoeuvring a tiny boat, very low in the water, with one oar at the stern, and was glad he had a profession and style. His ancestors might have earned their living by such manual work, but that was long ago and not for him.

The ferry slowed, churning whitish foam from green water, and then came alongside Blake Pier. A floating palace painted pale green, with a dragon's head on the bows, lumbered away like some grotesque sea beast disturbed in its lair. The sun caught the great high-rise buildings, each topped with a single name: Fosters, Canon, Hitachi, Mojo, Polaroid. A sense of total unreality existed between the prodigious wealth and power they represented and the hundreds of thousands of poor who lived like rats in stews and tenements, sleeping in shifts, three or four to a bed. And they were the lucky ones. Many slept where they were allowed to lie, in doorways or alleys, on pavements.

The ferry bumped against the landing place and Dr Sen walked out through the crowd of afternoon commuters to his

Jaguar. The chauffeur had been instructed to bring the car to
meet that particular ferry, and as ever he had obeyed his master's instructions. The car gleamed like a polished green jewel,
standing out from the cluster of shabby taxis. But of the driver,
there was no sign.

Sen frowned. He could not abide slackness. In his profession, slackness could mean death – not his, but a patient's. He
walked up to the car and was surprised to see the driver's
window open, the key still in the ignition lock. He leaned in,
wondering whether the man might have had a seizure and collapsed across the seat, but the car was empty. It was inexcusable that in a city where thousands had to steal simply to eat,
he should have left the window open and the key still in the
ignition. The car could be driven away to some backstreet
shack, dismantled and sold as spares before the police had even
realised it was stolen.

As Sen drew back, puzzled at this extraordinary lapse on the
part of his driver, two iron-muscled hands gripped his elbows
through his sharkskin jacket. Thumbs bit into his flesh like the
jaws of a bench vice, pinioning him. He turned slowly and
painfully. Two Chinese, taller than him and younger, con-
fronted him with passive oiled faces. One chewed a broken
match. The other, still holding him, said gruffly: 'Get in!'

'I'm waiting for my driver.'

'He's gone. *Get in!*' As the man spoke, he twisted Sen's arms
slightly. Pain shot like daggers through his body. He climbed
into the back seat. The man followed him. His companion slid
behind the wheel. They drove off.

'Who are you? Where are we going?'

The man next to Sen did not reply. Instead, he held up his
left hand, pointing towards the driver, the thumb stretched up
and back, the first two fingers folded away so that Dr Sen saw
the outline clearly against the window. His heart jumped and
his stomach contracted. This was the sign of an official of the
Triads, the international Chinese secret society.

Sen had never had anything to do with them, although once he had treated a senior member who had been brought to him wrapped in a sheet in the back of a taxi with a .45 bullet through his stomach. Sen had operated on the man in a makeshift way as best he could, asking no questions and waiving his fee. Then the patient, still unconscious from the anaesthetic, had been carried away. Had he lived? Sen had no idea, and about such matters it was wisest not to inquire. Equally, he had no idea how they had chosen him in the first place. Perhaps he was the nearest Chinese doctor they could find. If he had refused to help, it would have meant his own death.

He knew that his father and his grandfather before him had always paid their dues to the local Triad when they ran their businesses. It was essential to do so, otherwise they would have had no business. But what could these two men want with him now? It would be useless to ask who they were. Without homes, without roots, they were violent and evil men of the night who arrived from no one knew where, and when they had carried out their task they departed like creatures of darkness, unseen, unknown. He feared them; they were too powerful, too ruthless.

'A friend wants to see you,' the driver remarked casually, as though guessing Sen's thoughts.

The car was going through main streets now. He saw familiar buildings: the Mandarin Hotel, the Royal Navy base. A police jeep overtook them, bristling with aerials, then a taxi; they overtook a bus covered with advertising slogans. All seemed so ordinary, so safe, and yet Dr Sen knew this was only a façade, like a clean bandage on the festering cancerous wound which was the real colony, the terrible city of drug barons, vice, corruption on a colossal scale conducted behind a veneer of smart shops and restaurants.

The car stopped forty yards from the Mojo building. The man sitting next to Sen motioned him to get out and then followed him out, closing the car door. The Jaguar moved off and

was almost instantly lost in a swirl of traffic, one car among a
thousand.

They walked across the pavement towards the entrance of a
block of flats. Each one had long metal-framed windows opening on to tiny verandahs crammed with plants in pots, boxes
and buckets; TV aerials were tied to the railings by pieces
of string and wire. From one verandah, a ginger cat stopped
licking its paws to glance down at them. The stucco of the
building was peeling, its paint scabby and blistered; the railings
had not been painted for years.

Sen's escort pressed a bell push in an elaborate tattoo. An
electronic lock buzzed. The door opened, and they were in a
downstairs hall that smelled faintly of cooking oil and anti-
septic floor polish. Dr Sen followed the man into a lift that
jerked up very slowly, whining, wheezing and stopping at each
floor.

On the twentieth floor, they got out. Across a small, narrow
landing a lattice grille protected the door of a flat. The man
turned a key in the lock, slid back the lattice, opened the door.
Sen noticed that it had steel plates on either side of the wood-
work. They were now inside a small room over-furnished with
icons and gilded Buddhas. Swastikas and dated, yellowing photographs of young men on bar stools, wearing flannel trousers,
holding tennis racquets or smoking cigarettes through holders,
lined the walls. The air was sweet with scented hair oil and
fragrant talcum powder.

Sen guessed that whoever he was to meet did not live here.
These people had borrowed the flat as they had borrowed his
car. A deal had been arranged, a bargain struck. An ageing
homosexual, who did not wish to have his testicles skewered or
the face of his favourite boy branded, had agreed to keep out of
their way for however long they needed his apartment. It was a
fairly routine arrangement, and later, if need be, he could swear
he had been there all the time.

Sen walked towards the window and looked down across

Causeway Bay; the flat was almost directly above Jardine's noonday gun. He could see the twenty-four-hour Shell station, the police officers' club with tennis courts on the roof and a swimming pool where two swimmers swam slowly and methodically up and down, like pale flesh-coloured fish. Near this was the typhoon shelter where fishing boats anchored among power boats. Yachts bedecked with flags were moored sterns in to the shore. Their decks seemed to be deserted but each craft would have its own guard watching it, polishing it, hosing it down. Some of the vessels were so large they carried smaller motor boats on their decks. Alongside the yachts lay the shabby waterlogged craft of the boat people; their grey and tattered washing hung out on strings, dustbins stood on each deck. Sen could imagine the stench from their sewage in the stagnant water at that end of the shelter. Even from this height, he could see plastic bottles floating on the scummy surface. Side by side were the very rich, the very poor; the haves, the have nots. Under Jardine's cannon and the skyscrapers they both seemed to ignore each other's presence. Beyond, yachts of the Royal Hong Kong Yacht Club spread a forest of thin masts like toothpicks.

A door opened and a fat man of middle age came out of an adjoining room. He wore lightweight blue trousers, sandals, a white silk shirt. He was Chinese, with a paunch. His eyes were two olives set in a sweating ball of fat. His face was totally expressionless.

'Dr Sen?' he said. 'We have not met. I am Mr Yeung.'

'Why have you brought me here?' the doctor asked him.

'We wish to make use of your abilities. I should introduce myself more fully. I, too, am a professional man although my profession is not yours. I belong to the 14K group of businessmen.'

This group took its name from the original meeting place of the Triad in Canton at No. 14 Po Wah Road. Sen had heard rumours that they had moved to Kowloon and were now on the island. Other than this, he knew nothing and was content; to know too much could be terminally dangerous.

'You will appreciate, Doctor,' said Yeung, 'that we are willing to pay for your services.'

'In what way? Money?'

'Possibly, if you so wish. Or, as the English saying goes, one good turn deserves another. If you wished to have a good turn some day, we could help you.'

'And if I don't wish to become involved?' the doctor asked, surprised even as he spoke at his own temerity.

Yeung smiled, shrugged his shoulders, inclining his head like a father regarding an erring but still well-loved child.

'I do not think anyone enjoys the luxury of refusing to help businessmen like me when we seek your aid. I will therefore proceed as if you had not asked that question. Do I make myself plain?'

Sen nodded. Far beneath him the swimmers were turning now. He wondered whether they knew that this flat was being used by the Triads. It was quite likely they did; they might even have organised it. In the seventies, Hong Kong policemen had actually run some of the Triads, possibly they still did. There was no escape, no hiding place when they came after you.

'What do you want from me?' he asked in a flat, beaten voice.

'First, to sit down. We will drink some tea and we will talk.'

He clapped his hands. The man who had escorted Sen came out of the kitchen carrying a tray of tea and small cups without handles. Sen sat down, sipped the hot, bitter-tasting tea.

'To business, then, as I am sure you have patients or social engagements to claim your time, Doctor. You will be aware, no doubt, that Trinity-Trio, one of the great trading companies in the East, on a par with Jardine, Matheson, has abandoned Hong Kong and set up their head office in Nassau, just as Jardine's has moved and established headquarters in Bermuda.

'In saying goodbye to Trinity-Trio which, as you may know, started in Canton and then branched out to Calcutta, and so has its roots in the East, we have had to say goodbye to a great deal of revenue. On the other hand, we have held discussions among ourselves to see whether there is a way of recouping that revenue and, indeed, of increasing it. To our relief, there is. To speed this happy conclusion, Doctor, we seek your help.'

'In what way?' asked Sen. 'I am not a businessman, I am a physician, a surgeon. Once I operated on one of your colleagues.'

'Ah, yes. That was a gentleman from a different business group, I think, what we call the Big Circle. Known among us as the *tai huen chai*.'

'He is still well?'

'I fear he is not. He had a most unfortunate accident. He was killed by a hit-and-run driver only a few weeks ago. The roads here in Hong Kong are very crowded. It is difficult when you are growing old to keep out of the way. Especially if, as some unkind witnesses have said, the driver seemed actually to want to hit him.'

Sen picked up his cup of tea. It tasted even more bitter.

'Mind you,' added Yeung cheerfully, 'you are not old. Now, I must draw your attention to a matter that exercised your mind only a short time ago. There was a most unfortunate misunderstanding with your medical records about Mr Mojo, the distinguished Japanese motor manufacturer. Unbelievably, his records had become confused with those relating to someone else, a patient of equal eminence but suffering from a terminal illness.'

'How do you know that?' asked Sen in amazement. 'It was just a ridiculous error, an accident on the part of one of my staff.'

'An error, yes. An accident, no. And not really ridiculous.

But, shall we say, a portent, a swallow in the wind. What has happened once could happen again. I would not like it to, nor would you, Doctor. Such mistakes could ruin the career you have taken so long to build up. And as the saying is, it is easier to consolidate than to acquire.'

The two men sat for a moment in silence.

'What do you want me to do?' Sen managed to ask.

'*Now* we can talk business,' said Yeung, smiling. He had a lot of gold in his teeth and the sight was distasteful to the doctor. 'We wish you to fly to Nassau. You will be given a first-class ticket, a hotel will be booked there, and you will make contact with a young Chinese woman, Anna Lu-Kuan. She is the mistress of an English nobleman, Lord Jackson, who is a direct descendant of Dr Richard Jackson, one of the three founders of Trinity-Trio.'

'Is she ill?'

'No. She is in good health. She does not even know you are coming to see her. You will discreetly make yourself known to her on a social level and then you will be given further instructions.'

'By whom?'

'That does not concern you at this moment. You will get them.'

'How will I know they are genuine?'

Yeung crossed to a small table, opened a black crocodile-skin suitcase, took out an envelope. Inside was part of a white plastic chopstick. It had been broken in two. Sen recognised the name of the restaurant stamped in red on it as one of those in Food Street, a small avenue of eating houses.

'He will identify himself with the other half of this chopstick. Keep it safely. There will be no other identification and no excuses if this is lost.' He took another envelope from the case. 'Here is your ticket, your hotel booking, and some currency.'

He paused for a moment, as though suddenly remembering something of little importance but which nevertheless he wished to pass on.

'You may have the unworthy thought that you can go to Nassau and perhaps even see Miss Lu-Kuan – and then do nothing more except to report she is unwilling or unable to help.'

'No, no,' Sen assured him earnestly. 'I would not do such a thing.'

'I am sure you would not, Dr Sen. But some might tempt you to take this course, so before you go I think you should see someone in the next room.'

'Who?' Sen asked him in surprise.

Yeung opened the door, motioned Sen to follow him into a small bathroom. It had a yellow washbasin of the type fashionable thirty years ago, a corroded nickel-plated shower, yellow and white tiles on the floor. Yeung turned a key in a linen-cupboard door. A body, wrapped in white towels like a mummy, fell forward onto the tiles and lay where it fell.

'Who's that?' asked Sen in horror.

'Have a look.'

Sen knelt down, unwrapped the towels covering the face. The dead eyes of his driver stared sightlessly up at him. He tore away the rest of the towels, felt the man's pulse. His body was already cold.

'Like your former patient in the Big Circle group, he met with an accident. This time, a man with a knife.'

'But he was going to meet me at Blake Pier,' said Sen, as though this had relevance, as though this intention could some-how have saved his life.

'On his way he had a terrible accident. A totally unprovoked attack. There is so much violence about today, Doctor, it is very difficult to know how to combat it. But I am sure you know how you can best serve your interests. Now, I have another appointment.'

'What about this poor man? He was married, he had a child.'

'Then no doubt you will wish to take care of his widow and his child. I am sure you were his main employer.'

'But what can I say has happened to him?'

'I leave it to you. As the saying is, if a doctor cures, the sun sees it. But if he kills, the earth hides it.'

'But I have not killed this man. You know that.'

'Of course I do. It is just my poor attempt at levity. His body will be found in a back street tomorrow. When you're away. I wish you a safe flight, a successful meeting in the Bahamas, and most important of all in view of so many unfortunate accidents these days, a totally safe return.'

NINE

The Present: New York City, USA
The Present: Katherine, Northern Territory, Australia
The Past: Macau, 1840
The Present: Nassau, Bahamas

Mr Goldfarb, the New York attorney – some said that expensive city's most expensive man of law – sat opposite his client, Mr Mojo, in the latter's penthouse in the Towers of the Waldorf.

Mojo, like many other small men, felt an affinity for high buildings. He had been looked down on so often over the years by taller people that he now liked to look down in turn on taller people's smaller buildings.

The room was full of expensive flowers, their scent drenched the air. Mojo found as he grew older that chance odours – an unwashed, sweating labourer, fish, overcooked meat – would bring back with nauseating clarity the smells of Hiroshima on that August morning years ago. He therefore liked the scent of flowers and joss sticks around him. He felt that somehow they could help to cauterise and exorcise the past. Goldfarb, on the other hand, did not like the smell of flowers. He suffered from hay fever and believed that flowers, even such expensive ones, aggravated his condition.

Goldfarb sat now in a cream leather armchair watching Mojo read the report he had given to him. For the most part, Mojo remained totally impassive, as though the news it contained held neither interest nor concern for him. But now and then, as though he found the information disturbing or difficult to accept, he pulled on his lower lip. When he did so, Goldfarb could see a glint of gold in his teeth, but his eyes remained hard as polished cherry stones, his face soft, pallid, bland as beeswax.

Mojo finished the report, pushed it on to a side table, sat back in his chair. He folded his small podgy hands against his small podgy stomach, and regarded the attorney with a cold eye.

'Ah, so,' he said at last. 'That is all?'

'I think everything that could possibly be found is detailed there,' Goldfarb replied defensively. What the hell did this slit-assed bastard expect? He'd got all the facts. There were no more. Nothing. Didn't he understand that? Or didn't he want to? Could he be like some husbands whose divorces he had handled, who were never satisfied with the basic fact of a wife's infidelity, but intent on probing for every tiny detail – where and when and how often?

'What sort of man carried out this investigation?' Mojo asked him.

'A man who built up his own company and who was generally considered to be the best in the field of tracing missing persons anywhere in the world.'

'*Was?*' asked Mojo, instantly picking up the past tense.

'Yes. I regret to say he is no longer with us. He had a heart attack at Kennedy Airport on the way back. He died within minutes of clearing Customs.'

'An old man?'

'In his fifties.'

'But presumably not a fit man?'

'Presumably not, since he's dead. But he sure seemed fit enough to me. Shows you can't judge by appearances. Didn't smoke, drank a bit. Whisky. They tend to in his trade. They have to entertain all kinds of people and there's a lot of hanging about in bars and so on. Divorced. No money worries. Took life pretty easy when he wasn't working. Which wasn't often, I must admit.'

'So. Any dependants?'

'Apparently there is a sister living somewhere in New Jersey, but that's all. Sorry he couldn't come and report to you in person. But there it is. As you will see, his information came largely from one source. A woman.'

'I see that. And this young man he mentions, Ian—' He picked up the papers again and searched for the name. 'Ian Bruce Crabtree. What sort of person was he? Any further news?'

'Nothing more than appears in the report. There's his age, height, occupation, and the fact that the investigator paid him fifteen hundred Australian dollars. Cash. No receipt – and no results.'

'He knows nothing about Crosby, then, judging from this account?'

'Nothing whatever.'

'He speaks well of Mr Crabtree.'

'Very well. Found him extremely civil, as you see. And solicitous, too. You will see in the appendix that young Crabtree became anxious for him to leave Katherine quickly – even offered him a room in his own house. He came to the motel room late one night and found the investigator ill with what he thought was a fever. It could have been a manifestation of the heart trouble that killed him. Crabtree thought some sort of voodoo by Aborigines might be involved. The investigator couldn't make head or tail of that. Neither can I, but he reported their conversation pretty well verbatim. He was a very thorough operator. And according to the records, he'd been passed fit before he left on this assignment. But even with all the electronic tests they make nowadays, doctors can still make mistakes.'

'Too often,' agreed Mojo, remembering his experience with Dr Sen. 'Had he a history of heart trouble?'

'Not that I know of, but there is a newspaper report you might like to see.'

Goldfarb opened a file, removed a newspaper cutting from a cellophane folder. It was datelined Katherine, Northern Territory, Australia, Tuesday night. Mojo read it carefully.

'This is a town of ugly rumour tonight – rumour about an American visitor to Katherine, who flew out last week and died at Kennedy Airport on his way home. Officially, the cause of his death is given as a heart attack, but unofficially people here are saying he was "sung to death" by Aborigines he met during his stay in Australia and somehow grievously offended.

'Such a theory may sound ridiculous to city dwellers in Europe and the United States, but this Aboriginal ability is widely known and accepted here in the Northern Territory. For Aborigines, in common with other ancient peoples – largely in central Africa and the Caribbean – possess the ability, through a complex and secret ceremony, to produce symptoms of serious illness in victims who may be miles away. Some can even cause the victim to die, and this death from a distance is one of the last secrets of Aborigine folk lore to defy modern scientific analysis.

'Recently there were reports that the Chairman of the Northern Land Council faced this ritual tribal death curse for breaching an ancient Aborigine custom.

'He had given to Mr Bob Hawke, the Australian Prime Minister, a sacred bark painting at a festival in which Mr Hawke promised the Aborigines a land rights treaty. A hundred Aborigines claimed that the Chairman was guilty of what they called "displaying secret, sacred and dangerous material" to a white man who had not undergone an initiation ceremony.

'A local resident, Ian Bruce Crabtree, who has lived in Katherine all his life, admitted: "I have heard of such things happening, but I have never really believed them. I met this American several times during his stay here, and at our last meeting I noticed that his health had deteriorated." '

Mojo looked questioningly at the attorney.

'I've checked with the editor, and the original report came from a local stringer in Katherine,' Goldfarb explained. 'It was added to in Sydney by their staff man.'

'Do you give it credence?'

'I don't know,' admitted Goldfarb cautiously. 'I would never sneer at any of these old customs. The fact they are old means they have survived for generations. And if there's nothing to them then my feeling is they wouldn't have survived.'

'Fear always survives,' said Mojo flatly.

'Even so, to be effective fear has to have a basis in fact.'

'How right you are.' Mojo paused for a moment. 'I assume I can keep this?'

'Yes, sir. And, according to your instructions, we will bill you direct.'

'That is so.'

'Knowing how often you are on the wing, so to speak, I brought my firm's account with me.' Goldfarb took out a sealed envelope, passed it over the table.

Mojo did not pick it up. 'I will deal with it,' he promised. 'But first, let me compose my thoughts.'

'Of course,' said Goldfarb.

He stood up, shook hands. Mojo pressed a button. A servant entered and showed the American to the door. In the doorway, he turned and looked back at his client. Mojo was still sitting, hands across his stomach, head on his chest, thinking. For a moment, only a fleeting, brief moment, Goldfarb felt sorry for him. Riches, he had read somewhere, take away more pleasures than they give.

I first heard that my mother was ill on the same day I learned of the Stranger's death in New York. It was difficult to say which of these items affected me most. I should, of course, say the news about my mother, but when you are in your early twenties, your parents seem immortal. They may be briefly off-colour with minor ailments, colds, sore throats, indigestion, but something terminal will never happen to them, any more than it will ever happen to you.

I'd just come back from Tennant Creek, where, as I'd told Georgie, someone had offered me a couple of old cars. One was a basket case but I made what I thought was a silly offer for the other, which he instantly accepted, so I had to drive it 600 kilometres back to Katherine. I parked behind the supermarket and went in through the back door with my pass key. It was about eleven o'clock at night, and I made as little noise as possible because I did not want to disturb anyone. In Katherine, most people keep early hours.

I heard voices in the kitchen and paused because there was something about those whispers, strained and urgent, that made me think the speakers might not wish to be interrupted. And when one hears this tone of voice, one instinctively reacts – at least, I do. It could be something that affected me; I just had to listen and find out. Possibly it was someone who listened like that who decided that eavesdroppers never hear any good of themselves. In this instance, I heard bad news about someone dear to me.

I recognised my mother's voice and that of the Aborigine woman, Nora, who is younger than my mother but who, like many Abos, looked much older. She did odd jobs in the laundry, marked up prices for items on the shelves with that little gun that shoots out sticky tabs, and so on. I had always found her very friendly and extremely loyal to all of us. She was talking now.

'I had to tell someone,' she said. 'I needed the money.'

'So you told this American – and you didn't even know him?' my mother asked in disbelief. 'He could be a newspaper reporter. Did you think of that?'

'He offered me five hundred dollars,' said Nora stubbornly. 'It was a lot of money.'

'Did he pay you?'

'Yes. But the elders found out. They burned the bill in front of my eyes. More money than I have ever seen.'

I heard the snap of a purse opening.

'I can't give you five hundred, but here's a hundred in tens,' said my mother. 'It'll be better than nothing. But don't say where you got it.'

'Before God I promise you I won't,' Nora promised earnestly. 'But it is difficult to live so long with something like this. It's like a stone in your guts. It hurts you physically.'

'I can imagine,' my mother agreed. 'Now I have something to tell you. Not good news, either. I've been feeling crook for a long time and the local doctor arranged for me to see a specialist, a Chinese doctor who flies in once a month from Hong Kong to Cairns. I went to see him.'

'About the pain you have?'

'Yes. It's cancer. There is no cure.'

'Does Ian or Mr Crabtree know?'

'No one knows but you. I'll tell my husband, of course, when the right moment comes. You're the only person I've told so far. It's a very strange feeling, knowing your days are numbered. I know all our days are numbered, but this is nearer the end of the equation than I'd like to be just yet.'

'Truly I'm sorry,' said Nora sadly. 'I will pray for you that you get better. Every day, morning and night.'

'Thank you.'

I managed to squeeze behind the door as Nora came out. She knew the way without turning on the light and had no idea I was there. I waited for a few more minutes and then rattled the outside door and came in, whistling. My mother was sitting at the kitchen table, a cup of tea in front of her. I could see that it was untouched and the tea was cold.

She looked up and tried to smile. I did not want to let on I'd heard what I had heard, but I looked at her closely, trying to find traces of mortality in her face. She seemed tired and had faint violet shadows under her eyes but appeared much the same as ever. I pictured cancerous cells multiplying furiously and uncontrollably inside her and did not like the picture. Yet, curiously, I did not feel personally involved. This was happening to someone else, not to her.

I told her about the old car, and then I said I had to go out and see a man about it. A lie, of course. I just wanted to go somewhere with light and life, not to stay there in that little kitchen with the refrigerator humming and a cheap Swiss wall clock ticking away like a metronome. I wanted to go on pretending I did not know my mother was dying.

I went to the nearest bar; it was almost deserted, only a couple of regulars watching a TV soap on a set high up one wall – out of reach of any drunk who might vent his feelings about a programme by smashing the screen. The credits came up; I saw it had been made by a subsidiary of Trinity-Trio. Their name was everywhere, and while the Australian was trying to take over the company, all I was doing was hoping to sell an old car for a few hundred dollars' profit. I must get out of this league, I thought, and into the big time. But how? I left the bar and outside, on the sidewalk, ran into the motel manager.

'Hi!' he said.

'Hi!' I replied. I knew him slightly, but he wasn't a friend of mine. Now, however, he wanted to stop and talk.

'You know that Yank we had staying with us?'

'The fellow who was looking for Crosby, whoever he was?'

'Yeah,' he said. 'That's the bloke. Well, he's dead.'

'How do you mean, dead?'

'What I say. Kaput, finito. Gone beyond the veil. Stiff. Soon be six foot down – if he's not there already.'

'What happened, an accident?'

'Heart attack, apparently.'

'How do you know? Where did he die?'

'Kennedy Airport, New York. Had a call from some lawyer out there. A Mr Goldfarb. Wanted to know if he'd left any papers here.'

'And had he?'

'Nothing. Nothing at all. Not even a tip.'

He leaned towards me and I smelled beer on his breath. I don't like that smell. If I was hiring staff, I'd never take on anyone whose breath reeked of beer. Whisky, maybe; that at least would show he had more sophisticated taste.

'You know something?' the manager said, becoming conspiratorial with that over-acting way of someone who has drunk too much, or at least more than he can take.

'What about?' I countered.

'About him. We've an old Abo working in the place, cleaning up the kitchen, peeling potatoes, washing dishes.'

'Yes?' I said, guessing what was going to come even before he spoke.

'He says he saw the guy just before he left. Gave him a hand with his bags to the cab. There was something about him he didn't like. He wasn't really crook. He was being sung.'

'What d'you mean, sung?' I asked, although I knew quite well.

'That Abo business. They have it in for someone and they kill the bastard, long distance, without even seeing him.'

'Why should he be sung? Had he offended them?'

'How the hell do I know? You ask bloody silly questions.'

The manager was becoming truculent; I had not been sufficiently impressed by what he said.

'Maybe he saw one of their secret ceremonies,' he went on. 'Perhaps he knew too much – or too little. Anyhow, I've made a few dollars out of it.'

'How?'

'Put it on the wire, the newspapers. You didn't know I've taken on the job of stringer to three papers – one in Western Australia, two in Queensland? One of them's got a tie-up with a London paper, *The Enquirer*.'

'What did you say?'

'Just that a stranger from New York came here and then died suddenly in Kennedy Airport, New York. And that people here are saying it wasn't a natural death or an accident. It was murder, by remote control.'

'Sounds a load of crap to me,' I said, because I had to say something, and most of all I wanted him to keep quiet about it.

'Why,' he said, 'you're jealous. I've quoted you, too.'

'About what?'

'About I dunno what, but I've got to put a name in. Makes the story look true.'

'You could have told me,' I said angrily.

'I'm telling you now. Anyhow, you met the bloke. Flew in with him, actually, from the Alice, didn't you? More than anyone else did around here.'

'But I don't know if the story's true!'

'You don't know a damn thing,' he said contemptuously. 'I wanted to make some money and it seemed an easy way. Stories in newspapers aren't always true, are they? They're only stories, after all. Anyway, care for a couple of stubbies? I can put it down to expenses now.'

'No,' I said. 'I don't think so. But tell me, did that American ever find much on this man he was looking for – Crosby – except that he died?'

'I know nothing about that. But he sent a big letter off, cost a few dollars in postage, before he left himself.'

'So he discovered something, I suppose.'

'Or maybe it was just his expenses. See you about.'

I walked back home, my thoughts turning in my mind like windmill sails. Had the stranger really suffered a heart attack or a seizure or whatever people of his age died of suddenly? Or had he been sung to death?

I wished I did not feel I knew the answer.

Figures moved like misty shapes in Lord Jackson's mind. He

heard voices, saw movements, but all unsynchronised, out of focus, like someone peering through a thick and drifting fog . . .

Distressed at the shadowy tableau he called out, but most of his words were gibberish.

'Lord Jackson's mind is wandering,' the sister reported to the consultant. 'He's delirious. He keeps shouting, "You don't know the whole story." '

'I'm sure neither of us knows the whole story about this man, Sister,' replied Dr Kirkpatrick. 'What I do know is that he is a remarkably successful fellow. Lucky in one way, to be pitied in another. He inherited a third of the voting shares in Trinity-Trio, which is one of *the* great international conglomerates. I was invited to their inaugural ceremony when they moved their headquarters to Nassau, but I couldn't make it, unfortunately. Apparently there was an old last-century penny on show there, electronically protected. They claim it was somehow the start of their whole enterprise. Anyhow, it's their talisman.'

'That's what Lord Jackson was calling it. His talisman.'

'They take it very seriously. The theory is that if they lose it, then they will lose control of the company.'

'Do they really believe that?' the sister asked him.

'People believe anything,' Dr Kirkpatrick replied. 'Mostly what they want to believe. Anyhow, it makes a useful focal point for a company that size. Like the colours of a regiment, a college mascot, or a school tie. A totem, if you like. A relic from the past – as relics of the one true cross once had great value.'

'I would rather have some more modern symbol, like money,' the sister replied tartly.

'So would I. But when you have more money than you and all your family and relations could possibly spend in a dozen lifetimes, then you look for other symbols. You and I are not quite in that league yet. Now, what about dinner tonight?'

A nurse came into the room, glanced sharply at them. Vera

Steele knew the doctor's reputation; it was said he had slept with every sister and nurse in the clinic – except her. She watched him whenever she had the opportunity, trying to sense any electricity of attraction between him and any of the staff on duty. She also knew that his wife, who she heard had private money, was growing more and more disenchanted with her husband's infidelities.

At first, Mrs Kirkpatrick had felt flattered that other women apparently found him so attractive; it underlined her own good taste. Now, she was tired of telephone calls at odd hours, ostensibly on medical matters, of the growing feeling of being excluded by a man whose extravagant tastes in cars and clothes she had willingly and unquestioningly financed. It was said that she had warned him that another involvement would cause her to start divorce proceedings.

'Excuse me,' the nurse said to Dr Kirkpatrick, 'but I think you should know that Miss Lu-Kuan is on her way up in the elevator.'

Dr Kirkpatrick nodded. He had read about Anna Lu-Kuan in the local paper, seen photographs of her taken at the opening of the new Trinity-Trio offices, but he had not yet met her. In the newspaper, Miss Lu-Kuan had been tactfully described as 'Executive Vice-President of Trinity-Trio's aircraft licensing subsidiary in New York'. She was pictured standing on one side of Lord Jackson, with his wife, Corinne, on the other.

Dr Kirkpatrick wondered where Lady Jackson was now. He had been told that immediately after the ceremony she had left to fly back to London. It was clear that her appearance at the ceremony had simply been a matter of duty. Quite probably she had no idea of the fearful accident that had befallen her husband shortly after she left. She would have heard as soon as she reached home, of course, because the newspapers had all made great play of her husband's amazing escape from death.

Anna Lu-Kuan came into the room, a slight figure, her hair tightly drawn back into a glossy bun. Her dress had all the simplicity of a model gown costing $10,000. She wore a flame-red silk scarf round her neck. The doctor realised that if he sold everything he owned, he probably could not purchase the diamond clip through which this scarf passed, although no doubt his wife could. The emeralds and rubies on her rings were clearly as real as the strain on her face.

'I am Dr Kirkpatrick,' he said, introducing himself.

They shook hands. Anna's fingers felt very cold although the room was warm.

'How is he?' she asked.

'Still unconscious, as you see. But his heartbeat is steady.'

He indicated a video screen where a green dot travelled from right to left, jerking up and down in a steady rhythm on its way.

'I don't like talking about him in his presence,' said Anna, wrinkling her face in distaste.

'It is quite all right, Miss Lu-Kuan. He can't hear us.'

'It doesn't seem right, though, discussing him like this. It's as though he is already beyond all help. A sort of human vegetable. And he isn't, is he?'

She looked appealingly at Kirkpatrick, willing him to reassure her.

'Of course he isn't,' the doctor replied easily. 'But come into my office if you prefer.'

He led the way into an impersonal room, brushed aluminium furniture and white walls. Slatted sunblinds at the windows cut horizontal scalpel slices from the morning glare. A cactus grew determinedly in an earthen pot. Anna Lu-Kuan sat down thankfully.

'I have heard varying accounts of what happened, Miss Lu-Kuan,' said Dr Kirkpatrick, 'but only from people who do not seem actually to have seen the accident themselves. You were there, I understand?'

'Yes. I was. It was terrible – and totally unexpected. The Chief Minister of the Bahamas had declared the building open. Several ambassadors and the heads of other international companies were Lord Jackson's guests. Everyone genuinely enjoyed themselves, which is not always the case on such occasions.

'The whole evening was really a remarkable success. It was crowned by the fact that his attorney, Mr Ebenezer, gave him news that some very complex business negotiations had been successfully concluded. The future seemed bright. Not a cloud in the sky. And then . . .'

'And then?' Kirkpatrick prompted her gently.

'And then I think the emotion of the moment temporarily overcame Lord Jackson. He had a lot on his mind. Just before we flew here, he learned that his only daughter, Elaine, from whom he has been estranged for years, had been found lying in a London gutter, a heroin addict. She was also suffering from Aids.

'When Mr Ebenezer gave him the quite unexpected good news about the negotiations, Lord Jackson walked towards the window. I think in his relief he wanted to breathe fresh air. He probably didn't realise that these windows are not intended to be opened, because opening them upsets the complicated air-conditioning system. However, for cleaning purposes, they are split horizontally. The upper part is hinged on a spring, controlled by a lever at one side. I saw him open this and stand for a moment with his hands on the bar, breathing the wonderful, fresh scent of jasmine and honeysuckle that is so much a part of this island at night. He turned to speak to me – I will always remember his words. He said, "This has been the most wonderful night of my life." And I think it was, for both of us.

'Then suddenly he seemed to sag at the knees. I think it was a reaction from the crowded room, the worries he had concealed so successfully for so long, plus sudden relief at unexpected good news. He simply fainted, or felt dizzy, I don't know what exactly. Anyhow, he leaned on the bottom window and it swung out. He overbalanced and fell.'

Anna fought back her tears.

'Please, Miss Lu-Kuan, do not distress yourself,' said the
doctor soothingly. 'I believe in fate. What is written is written,
and if it had been written in whatever celestial records there
may be that Lord Jackson's time was up, then he would have
fallen to his death. Instead, he fell to life.'

'He will be crippled,' Anna said hoarsely. 'No one can fall
from that height and not be crippled.'

'It is too early to say,' Kirkpatrick replied diplomatically. 'I
have asked for two top orthopaedic surgeons to fly down from
New York. I am by no means pessimistic. I have seen far worse
cases – victims of motor accidents, for instance – make complete recoveries. Now, if I may suggest it, would you like a
sedative? You look tired, Miss Lu-Kuan.'

'No, thank you. I must go back to my hotel. I have work to
do. In the meantime, I must ask you, please, on no account give
any interviews to the Press or TV about Lord Jackson's condition, whether it is good or bad. Those people are vultures.
They will only exaggerate any bad news, and denigrate and
disbelieve anything good. Share prices will plummet, and you
may promote a crisis of confidence which, even if Lord Jackson
does make a miraculous recovery, we may not be able to overcome. Do I make myself absolutely clear, Doctor?'

'Absolutely.'

He followed her out of the room and watched her walk down
the long aseptic corridor. Her high heels made no sound on the
plastic floor. She did not look back. He wondered whether he
could lay her, whether he would ever have the faintest opportunity. It wouldn't be easy. But then no worthwhile seduction
ever was. Pondering the possibilities, he returned to the ward.
An assistant physician was examining a print-out from the
cardiograph.

'Any change?' Kirkpatrick asked him briefly.

The younger man shrugged noncommittally.

'He's still in with a chance. That is, if he really wants to get
better.'

'That is always the unanswerable question,' replied Kirkpatrick. 'It never fails to astonish me how many very rich patients simply don't.'

Anna Lu-Kuan walked down the main staircase of the hospital and into the powder room on the left of the entrance foyer. A secretary of Anna's height and colouring, wearing identical make-up and a cotton dress of the same pattern, was sitting in a pink satin chair. As Anna entered, she put down a copy of *Vogue*, stood up, took a floppy white sunhat with a very wide brim from her handbag and gave it to Anna, who in return handed her the red silk scarf she wore round her neck. The secretary put on a pair of dark, gold-rimmed glasses, draped the scarf round her head, and without a word walked out into the foyer, through the swing door, and into Trinity-Trio's waiting Cadillac limousine.

Anna watched the Press reporters and TV men, cameras balanced on their shoulders, their sound operators carrying microphones linked by wires like electronic umbilical cords to the interviewers, surge hopefully towards the car.

'How is he?' they cried. 'How is Lord Jackson? What do the doctors say? Will he live? Miss Lu-Kuan, look this way, please! Can we have a statement?'

The car accelerated away, scattering gravel chips in their faces. The reporters and TV crews shrugged their shoulders philosophically, lit cigarettes, went to find a bar. Clearly, with Lord Jackson's personal assistant or mistress or whoever she was out of the hospital, there would be no more news just yet.

Anna did not trust them; one might still be lurking somewhere to alert the others. She waited for five minutes by her Cartier wristwatch, which bore Trinity-Trio's logo in diamonds on its golden face, and then, with the sunhat concealing her features, she left the hospital by a side door usually used only by staff. As she walked into the bright Bahamas sun, a small hired car pulled away from the car park. She climbed in behind the driver.

'The Eden Roc Hotel,' she told him. Here she had booked a

suite under another name. Even if the Press discovered she was staying there and not in Jackson's huge house in Lyford Cay, she felt relatively safe from their pestering in a penthouse. She sat well back in the seat, looking out incuriously at the crowds of Japanese tourists festooned with cameras, all wearing sunhats with the slogan, 'It's better in the Bahamas'.

Was it? she wondered. What did they refer to, anyhow? The sun, sex, food?

The car swung past the statue of the eighteenth-century Governor of the Bahamas, Woodes Rogers, who had arrived to find the island of New Providence a nest of pirates: Blackbeard, Morgan and a dozen others. The lust for easy money was as great then as now, Anna thought, but lethargy and the effects of strong rum in a tropical climate were even greater; the pirates soon became too lazy to put out to sea in search of victims and instead enticed their victims to them. They organised gangs of runaway slaves to lure merchant ships on to the rocks by putting out false guiding lights. As the ships broke up and the crews swam ashore, they killed them.

Beneath Woodes' statue was engraved the message he had sent to the government in London when, with the help of a handful of loyal, steadfast citizens, he had finally driven out the pirates: 'Pirates expelled, commerce restored.' This was not entirely true, but the statement had a splendid, buccaneering ring to it. The pirates had never really left Nassau. They had only changed their outlook, their means of piracy. Their descendants ran guns during the American Civil War. Later, they ran rum up north to Florida during Prohibition. Then they went into property, selling condominiums, holiday apartments, houses, timeshares, and now the greatest bonanza of all: drugs.

One-third of all heroin and cocaine went through Nassau on its way from Central America to the United States and Europe. Present-day pirates, Anna thought wryly, did not need to carry cutlasses or wear earrings, or make enemies walk the plank.

They wore Savile Row suits and their weapons were lawyers'
pens and fax machines and numbered accounts in banks they
controlled, and they travelled in their own 747s and Lear jets.
They still disposed of enemies permanently, however, and she
remembered Jackson's comment on the changing face of crime:
'Why rob a bank when you can own a bank?' Why, indeed?

And now United Charities, or whatever other name the Italian-American Mr Carlotti and his kind used as a shield for their
real activities, owned the bank where she had deposited the two
vital shares in Trinity-Trio. Whoever held them could control
the company. After Lord Jackson fell from the high window,
Carlotti told her that they now controlled the shares because
when she deposited them with the Occidental-Oriental Bank
she had signed what seemed to her a totally innocuous form,
only required, the manager had assured her, should she inad-
vertently overdraw on her account. The form gave the bank a
lien on any securities, stocks and shares she deposited with
them against any overdraft. Since she owed the bank some
trifling sum and Carlotti owned the bank, he in effect owned
the shares as well. It was as simple and as deadly as that.
Lawyers might argue it either way, and doubtless would do so,
quoting precedents, but the law took time and money, and right
now Anna felt short of both. And, in the last analysis, who
would suborn the judge and jury? There was no need to ask.
She had been an idiot to sign the form, but she had signed
similar agreements with other banks and no harm had ever
resulted.

She knew of Jackson's worries about his wife and daughter,
and she had felt growing concern about her own background.
On the evening of the inaugural ceremony, she had admitted to
him the real reason she had joined the company, and who had
sponsored her. Did he really believe the truth – that she loved
him – after hearing her confess to so much deception? He
seemed to, but she wasn't sure. And now, as he lay in a
deep coma, hovering on the dark frontier between life and

death, it was impossible to communicate with him.

The car moved silently along Bay Street, the main thorough-fare. When white Bahamians, the rich merchants who had made fortunes during Prohibition, held political power, most maintained sumptuous offices here; they were known as the Bay Street Boys. Now black Bahamians held political power and enormous wealth, not infrequently from drugs. On either side of the wide road lined with expensive boutiques and other fashionable stores were unobtrusive doors, painted black, and bearing the names of dozens of shell companies listed in gold letters.

The Nassau the tourists saw was a kind of toy town in the sun. Ancient ceremonial cannon guarded a statue of Queen Victoria, as though her writ still ran. But behind this thin façade of sophistication and elegance lay slums and shanties and dark, odorous alleys where land crabs scuttled and chained guard dogs growled warningly at the approach of strangers. This, in Anna's view, was more representative of the Bahamas.

Policemen in smart white starched tunics and dark blue trousers with red stripes, wearing white solar helmets, moved smartly like toy soldiers which, in fact, was what they were. They lacked power to arrest local politicians who amassed fortunes from drug consignments, flown in regularly from Colombia to remote islands in the Bahamas chain. Often the pilots did not even land. They simply swooped in low and dropped their cargoes in the water, attached to coloured buoys. Fast cruisers did the rest.

If any policeman knew too much or saw too much, he could usually be bought off. If he did not have a price in money, it could be a price in promotion, or, if he still remained incorruptible, in threats of violence to his family. In a world where Colombia had offered to repay to the United States the billions of dollars of national debt it owed if only the US would revoke the present extradition treaty between the two countries for drug runners, such petty bribes were small change, not even worth accounting.

Here at the heart of corruption so rich, so well organised that its annual turnover in crime exceeded that of all legitimate businesses in the United States put together, how could Anna possibly retrieve her two shares?

The car slowed to allow a crowd of middle-aged American tourists to cross the road. They had landed from one of the cruise ships that lay anchored beyond the quay, sparkling in their fresh white, lime green and orange paint. Air-conditioned coaches and limousines conveyed their passengers to the casinos. Then they were allowed a brief and escorted walk along Bay Street to celebrate their winnings or to compensate for their losses.

They peered at Anna now; plump, sweating men with sagging stomachs, most wearing straw hats and overlong Bermuda shorts. They were 'active adults' from a tour advertised as a trip with a difference, but not too much of a difference. Iced water and Thousand Island salad dressing appeared on the menus to calm Americans unversed in foreign eating habits. They watched her with the glazed eyes of people who had spent too many hours in the deliberate gloom of casinos, peering at a turning wheel, the spin of a pointer, at painted apples and pears in a fruit-machine window.

She had always despised such fat, vacuous-faced tourists before. Now, she envied them. They had their little lives, their small apartments, their pets – cats, dogs, birds – maybe each other. She had nothing. No past and now no future.

Lord Jackson, the man she had deliberately set out to ruin, to grasp control of his company on behalf of her masters in communist China, seemed virtually dead. She was not impressed by Dr Kirkpatrick's optimism.

She had betrayed the communists for the simplest reason of all – she had fallen in love with Jackson, just as more than a century and a half earlier, his great-grandfather, Dr Richard Jackson, had fallen in love with another Chinese girl, T'a Ki. The name meant Heavenly Beauty. T'a Ki was already promised in marriage to a Chinese physician who, when he discovered her feelings for Jackson and his for her, took his own life. And then Jackson had betrayed her, abandoned her and their Anglo-Chinese son. He had loved her after his fashion, but had loved money and social status far more; he had been assured that an association with a Chinese woman would not be helpful to his ambitions.

Lord Jackson had trusted Anna Lu-Kuan from the moment they met. So had his executives. Indeed, no one in Trinity-Trio had ever attempted to investigate the enormously detailed background with which her communist controllers had supplied her. People, Anna realised, generally believe what they want to believe, and they wanted to believe she was who and what she said she was. Her controllers had done their work perfectly.

By now Anna almost believed she really was who she was supposed to be, and not the only child of an American father and a Chinese mother, abandoned by both, and brought up in a state orphanage in Shanghai. Her controllers selected her deliberately because her features had a touch of the West about them; she was clearly not pure Chinese. They reasoned this would make her more attractive to Jackson, who was descended from T'a Ki.

They gave Anna the name of a Chinese girl educated at Benenden and Girton, who had died in an aircraft accident shortly after graduating in history. If anyone challenged her identity – which was a very remote risk, but still one to be faced – Anna would claim she was actually this girl's half-sister. Because she admired her academic brilliance, and as a kind of living memorial to her, she had taken her name.

Anna had never been to Benenden, and had never even visited Cambridge, but she was given books of photographs to study and a video of Cambridge and its colleges. If asked, she could say where each one was and which Chinese restaurant was most popular with undergraduates, and so on.

She had been shown the offices of the *South China Morning Post* in Hong Kong and *The Straits Times* in Singapore, studied plans of the buildings, and answered questions about them. Notepaper from their managerial offices was obtained, on which her controllers forged her references. And then, because it was essential that she should quickly become close to Lord Jackson, before any of his associates might question her background, they took her to Macau, the tiny Portuguese enclave on the tip of the China coast. Here, Jackson's great-grandfather, Dr Richard Jackson, had first met T'a Ki.

Anna found Macau a sordid, squalid place. Sitting in a room in a block of flats off the Avenida da Amizade, the Road of Friendship, spelled out on the wall in the Portuguese style of blue lettering against white tiles, she had studied Trinity-Trio's history and then been questioned closely on every aspect of it.

A gate in the wire fence that marked the frontier opened every Sunday to allow housewives from Macau to walk through to China and buy chickens and trolleys of bananas – prices were cheaper on the Chinese side.

Anna crossed into Macau from China through the gate without a visa. It was easy enough to do, despite a giant wire screen with eight strands of barbed wire on high stakes hammered into the rocks round the coast, intended to prevent illegal immigrants from swimming the muddy bay to reach what they called freedom. They did not realise until too late that in Macau, or Hong Kong, without passports, identity cards, papers or permits of any kind they were reduced virtually to the status of slaves. Legally, they did not exist and were driven to take any work offered, at starvation wages, until by theft or even murder they acquired the papers of someone more fortunate, and so legally could begin new lives with new names, new hopes.

Macau was a sprawling mixture of high-rise buildings and shacks made of rusting, corrugated-iron sheets. Above everything hung a fog of concrete dust from old buildings being torn down, new ones going up. The air throbbed with the pulse of pneumatic drills, the bellow of bulldozers' exhausts. In each of the windows of the older properties, under curved Chinese roof tiles, little birds in cages chirped in the dust and the dry rasping wind that blew through the concrete canyons. Roads seemed perpetually jammed solid with traffic negotiating piles of bricks, cement mixers, pyramids of bamboo scaffold poles.

The whole enclave seemed a vast building site, half finished and due within years, like Hong Kong, to be handed over to the Chinese. All this frenetic building seemed pointless to Anna. But this was before she came to know Jackson and realised what wealth, power and influence resulted from such activities.

'I have ordered you here,' her controller explained, 'because in a ship anchored off this miserable colony a hundred and forty-odd years ago, the English doctor, Richard Jackson, met the Chinese girl, T'a Ki, who had such an influence on him and whose influence still lives in the present Lord Jackson. You will exploit and play on this, as the wind plays on the strings of an antique harp. It is necessary to feel the background, to know exactly what Macau is like, for you to play your part to the full.'

When she was in bed with Jackson, in those moments of trust that come after love when neither partner wishes to exploit the other, when confidences can be exchanged in the knowledge they will remain secret, she had asked him about this other earlier Jackson and T'a Ki.

'I feel very close to him,' he admitted. 'Sometimes I dream that I really am him. A sort of reincarnation, if you like. When I have a problem, I wonder what he would have done to resolve it. He was ruthless in many ways, but underneath that hard carapace of ambition was someone far more gentle than many realised.

'He had been poor, you see, Anna. He had been exploited as a young doctor who genuinely tried to help his patients. In doing this, he antagonised a rich man and was forced to flee for his life from England. He resolved never again to be put in such a humiliating and dangerous position. And he never was, of course, although sometimes I feel I have been . . .'

All those years ago, Dr Jackson sat smoking a cigar on the after deck of one of Trinity-Trio's first clippers, *Seasprite*, off Macau, while the crew prepared the ship to sail to Calcutta. The evening was warm and he felt at ease, letting his mind wander over times past. A hesitant cough brought him sharply back to the present. A young Chinese man stood at his elbow. He introduced himself in English as Dr Kuan Chung, a physician from Canton. He had a favour to ask which, he said, would mean little to Dr Jackson but everything to him and to his fiancée, T'a Ki.

'What is that?' Jackson asked him.

'That you permit us to buy a passage aboard your vessel, sir, for Calcutta.'

'It is forbidden for Chinese subjects to leave the mainland,' Jackson replied, fearing the request might be a ruse to entrap him in a dangerous and convoluted labyrinth of law from which he might be able to escape only if he paid a vast bribe to some corrupt Chinese official.

'That is so, sir, but we have to leave for a very personal reason.'

'Which is?'

'My wife-to-be is related to the Manchus, the royal family,' Dr Chung explained. 'By tradition, all ladies of high birth must have their feet bound. Usually this is done in childhood, which means that the bones and muscles of the feet never acquire full strength. This is an advantage from the point of view of husbands, because their wives cannot walk more than a few paces on their own. This prevents them being unfaithful, if only because they can never leave their homes unless they are helped to walk by two serving maids. They are therefore virtual prisoners, totally in thrall to their husbands.

'My wife-to-be managed to avoid having her feet bound as a

child, but now she is ordered to bind them on pain of imperial displeasure. We are both eager to avoid what we consider a mutilation, and we cannot do so unless we leave China. Permission for this, as you say, is never granted. We must therefore escape illegally, and your ship offers us our only chance.'

Dr Jackson drew on his Havana, considering the request. He found it ironic to recall that he had escaped from the West to the East under threat of his life, and now a fellow physician wished to escape from the East to the West for a reason he felt was equally poignant.

'I will take you,' he said.

That night they came aboard. Jackson refused any payment for their passage. He was glad to have companions on the voyage, and enjoyed discussing differences between Eastern and Western medical beliefs with Dr Chung. Indeed, to this chance meeting much of the subsequent wealth of Trinity-Trio could be directly traced.

Dr Chung practised the ancient Chinese art of acupuncture which Jackson later introduced to Britain and even demonstrated to Queen Victoria at Balmoral. As a result, his fame as a healer possessed of seemingly magical powers spread through the land. He soon found it impossible to see, let alone treat, all the sufferers of rheumatism and arthritis who wrote to him seeking an appointment. Instead, he arranged for Trinity-Trio to make and market a cream to his formula, to be rubbed into what he called the acupuncture pressure points. The cream was sold as Dr Jackson's Soothing Balm, and millions of pots were produced in the company's factories and distributed all over the world. The cream itself was of little value; what helped the buyers was the vigorous massage of the pressure points.

From their discussions on the voyage to Calcutta sprang the Dr Richard Jackson Medical Foundation whose aim was to teach Western physicians about Chinese medicine and other branches of healing that had not yet received widespread recognition. But most important, Anna knew, was Dr Jackson's infatuation with T'a Ki.

Their affair began on that long voyage from Macau to Calcutta, and Dr Chung, realising this and despairing at the thought he had abandoned the land of his ancestors and all his family for the love of a woman who loved another man more, jumped overboard to his death. Lord Jackson was descended through T'a Ki's son, fathered by Richard Jackson.

That was the background which Anna's communist controllers taught her by rote. The date, even the exact time, when Anna should meet Lord Jackson had been carefully selected. The communists did not officially believe in astrological significance, but nonetheless they had consulted astrologers for the most propitious day and hour for her to answer an advertisement for a foreign correspondent placed by *The Enquirer*, one of the newspapers in Trinity-Trio's British publishing empire.

The editor was impressed by her qualifications. Not every applicant had a first in history from Girton, nor had they written a most interesting thesis on the rise of Trinity-Trio. He mentioned her to Lord Jackson. As the editor guessed, Jackson asked to see her. And on a day and at an hour all the astrologers agreed were most conducive to success, Anna walked into his office in Fleet Street, overlooking St Paul's Cathedral and the Old Bailey – two separate poles, as he later remarked jocularly, of ultimate human endeavour. And as had been calculated, when Lord Jackson saw Anna, his immediate reaction had been the same as when his great-grandfather first met T'a Ki off Macau.

Anna and Jackson became colleagues, although at different levels of his empire; then confidants; then lovers. He took note of the fact that she really wished to write articles about business, finance, and the people involved, and not about foreign affairs, which was then the only vacancy on the newspaper.

She had been told to learn about this area at first hand so that when the Chinese took over Hong Kong and its very prosperous business concerns she would have direct knowledge of them, unlike other Party officials, who might be put in to run firms about which they knew nothing.

When Trinity-Trio moved to Nassau, partly for taxation reasons and partly because the directors did not altogether trust China's future intentions in Hong Kong, Jackson gave her two master shares as an earnest of his affection. He had offered her ten, but she had refused. She knew that only two were needed, so why ask for more?

'You will play on the fact that Jackson has some Chinese blood in his barbarian veins,' her controller had told her. 'Your ultimate aim will be to secure the balance of power in the voting shares. Two shares will give us as much power as if we owned more than half the equity, because they can swing the balance in our favour.

'It is easy for men who inherit great fortunes or great estates in the capitalist system to waste their bounty and to regard such good fortune as their natural due. In Trinity-Trio, one of the original founders, the American Marvin Ross, was soon rid of his third share. He had devious sexual practices; he went through a form of marriage with a transvestite. His shares fell into other hands.

'The second man of this triumvirate, the Scot Alec Douglas, was shrewd and cautious, but his descendants threw away a fortune on gambling and motor racing between the two world wars, and on any other extravagance that took their fancy. One of them even sold out without telling his partners.

'A company under the name of United Charities Incorporated, a cover for a worldwide criminal organisation run by an Italian-American, Mr Carlotti, acquired one hundred shares. Another company, Beechwood Nominees, ostensibly owned by a half-Australian, half-Englishman who is rarely referred to by his real name – he was born a bastard – but simply as the Australian, holds another forty-nine shares. Actually, the same

Italian-Americans backed him. He holds the shares in his name but he bought them with their money. Lord Jackson has the remaining one hundred and fifty-one and so has voting control.

'We can tip the balance with two shares. When Hong Kong reverts to China in 1997 and we control the company, we will be acquiring nearly one and a half centuries of Western financial ingenuity.

'Trinity-Trio has branches in almost every country. They own all manner of companies people do not even imagine, because they do not change the names of the original owners. Car and truck factories, television stations, film studios, patent medicines, newspapers, book publishers, vast property concerns in the United States, Australia and Britain.

'But always remember that they made their first money selling opium – and we have hundreds of square miles of land under cultivation for poppies. We are also in association with others who have even larger areas in Cambodia and Burma, thousands of square miles in all. We will be able to take on the Mafia, anyone in opposition, because our sources are far greater than theirs in South and Central America, and our costs are much lower. We can undersell them if we have to, but we will preach that there is room for both of us. Better to consolidate than to confront. The first means profit; the second, war.

'You remember what Napoleon said about China? "*Laissez la Chine dormir. Quand eveillera la monde tremblera.*" Now the giant is awake, and you are one of those privileged and honoured to help lead it forward.'

Lord Jackson had laughed when, unable to sustain the subterfuge any longer in view of her totally unexpected love for him, Anna had admitted how she had been deliberately groomed first to attract him and then ruin him.

'I cannot believe it,' he said at first, and then paused.

'But maybe I *do* believe it,' he went on more seriously. 'And maybe I don't care a damn. I didn't make the money in the first place, you know. I only inherited it by several happy accidents of birth. I was like a relay runner who is handed the baton and runs with it. The man working the lift in our hotel, the fellow who drove the cab from the airport, might have made a hell of a better show of things if he'd had half my chances. But he didn't have even one of them.

'You keep the shares, Anna. I gave them to you. I trust you and I love you. My trust and my love may be ill placed, but somehow deep inside me I do not think they are. Anyhow, what does it all matter? We are pawns moved by fate or destiny or genes – or by all three. Whatever will be, will be. Remember, my family motto is "Beyond the dreams of avarice". Perhaps we will go together beyond those dreams, Anna. I pray we will.'

'I want to, more than anything,' she said earnestly, 'But I must get those shares out of the bank tomorrow and give them back to you. I cannot keep them, and I cannot go back to China now. I have betrayed my masters and I have betrayed you.'

'Possibly, but you have been true to yourself. That is by far the most important thing.' Anna shook her head miserably. 'I am a traitor,' she said. 'There is no place for me anywhere, as long as I live.'

'There is always a place for you by my side. Without you, my whole future is grey and bleak. With you, the sun is always shining. You must understand that. You must – if I take the rest of my life to persuade you.'

Anna had kissed him gently then. Her face was wet with tears, and he had smiled and walked towards the window and then . . . and then . . .

She could scarcely bear to think of what had happened next.

She was shocked and sick in her stomach at everyone's instant change of attitude to her the moment they believed that Lord Jackson, her protector, her friend, was dead. To them, she instantly become a person of no importance whatever; not his mistress perhaps even his future wife. She was nothing more than a Chinese-American employee who now belonged to the past.

'I take it the bank will claim them?' The Australian asked Carlotti. Anna had never liked The Australian. He appeared bloodless, like a toad, only interested in making money, not for what it could buy him or bring him, but simply to amass it, as others might collect stamps or coins, simply for the pleasure of owning them. Now, she hated him. They were not dealing here with two pieces of paper but with a world-wide company, with thousands of employees and hundreds of thousands of others indirectly dependent on Trinity-Trio.

'Immediately,' Carlotti agreed.

'But they can't!' cried Anna. 'I promised to give the shares back to Lord Jackson tomorrow.'

'Ah, yes, very possibly. But, dear lady, for that transaction, tomorrow will never come. Lord Jackson is dead – today. Tomorrow is of no concern to him, or so far as this matter is concerned, to any of us.'

Then came the incredible news that although Jackson had been terribly injured, his back broken, and it was still impossible to assess the extent of his internal injuries, he was still alive. That was the main thing.

The Occidental-Oriental Bank was not open yet – it would be at ten o'clock. Anna had already tried to telephone the manager and the vice-president, but there had been no answer from their offices. She would be on the doorstep to collect those shares in person as soon as the bank doors opened. She did not think Carlotti could beat her. He would no doubt be dealing with someone more senior than the local manager. Fax messages would be going to and from the head office in Miami, but with luck she could repay her trifling debt, collect the shares and then close the account before the local branch could act on his instructions.

The car stopped. As she climbed out, she remembered a story Jackson had told her once about Columbus sailing west in his tiny vessel in an attempt, not to discover a new and unknown world, but a new route to the old world of the east.

The mood of his crew grew ugly as scurvy spread through the ship, and amid growing fears that they were going to sail off the edge of the world and disappear for ever they attempted to mutiny. But in his log each night, Columbus ignored all such setbacks and simply wrote one sentence: 'This day I sailed on.' Right now, Anna meant to do the same.

She took the elevator up to her suite, let herself into the hall and locked the door carefully behind her. She went into the bedroom, drank a glass of iced water from the silver carafe on the bedside table.

Beyond the wrought-iron verandah, the ocean glittered. Holidaymakers lay beneath striped sunshades on the bone-white sand and sipped iced drinks. The scene seemed peaceful, yet beneath the surface of that calm, waveless expanse of water lurked venomous creatures of the deep. They gave no sound or sign of their existence to holidaymakers, just as Anna's pale, serene countenance gave no hint of the turmoil that churned in her mind.

She took another sip of water, walked into the drawing room. It was filled with flowers, a gift from the secretary of the company; someone who was hedging his bets in case Lord Jackson recovered, she thought cynically as she read the card. She looked up from the card and started. A man was sitting in a silk-covered armchair near the window, watching her, still as a statue. He stood up and bowed.

'Forgive me for coming in unannounced, Miss Lu-Kuan,' he said, 'but I thought it prudent to introduce myself in the privacy of your room rather than in the entrance hall of this hotel or in some other public place.'

'Who the hell are you?' Anna asked him roughly.

He could be anyone. One of Carlotti's men, a newspaper reporter, someone from the bank to force her to sign some other document. She felt confused, at risk. How had he got in? Hammers of fear pounded alarmingly in her brain.

'I am at your service,' the man said quietly.

She looked at him more closely, eyes narrowed against the sun and the sea. He looked Chinese, bland and smooth and wealthy. He wore a beautiful suit, a silk monogrammed shirt. He stroked his chin with his right hand and she saw his heavy signet ring and the gold Piaget wristwatch, thin as a coin, thin as Trinity-Trio's ancient penny. She also saw the crooked fingers, the curved thumb, and the sight struck like a dagger at her heart. This was the sign of the Triad, the mark of torture, the warning of death.

'Allow me to introduce myself,' the man said softly. 'Dr Sen, from Hong Kong.'

TEN

The Present: Perth, Western Australia
The Past: Nassau, Bahamas, 1947
The Present: Nassau, Bahamas

Because it pleased Lady Myrtle to exercise power over those for whom she felt neither liking nor respect, and to make her feelings towards them unequivocally clear, she invariably held important policy meetings with her directors in one of her houses.

They might meet in the Bahamas under a thatched roof overlooking a pool, or in the panelled first-floor drawing room of her house in Charles Street, London, which had once been the home of King Charles II's favourite mistress. Or, as now, on her terrace overlooking Swan River in Perth.

She contrived these meetings so that her directors and senior executives would be surrounded by immense, sometimes ostentatious luxury: the superb swimming pool with its own waterfall in Nassau; the seventeenth-century elegance in Charles Street; unparalleled views over the Swan, surrounded by the homes of the super-rich. All this was tangible evidence of her wealth, not theirs. It emphasised the gulf that separated them, deeper and wider, she liked to think, than the gulf that had separated the rich man Dives from the beggar Lazarus in the Bible story. Only Irene Loxby had the courage to remind her of the end of this parable: the wealthy Dives had burned in hell while Lazarus had ascended into heaven.

There was another, deeper reason: here, she was on her own ground, not theirs, and this, to her, was of supreme importance. Wealth and luxury had still not obliterated all memories of Uncle Jem and a Calcutta railway house.

After these meetings she always provided her visitors with limousines to take them back to the airport or their hotels. They did not know that concealed beneath the floor of each of these cars was a voice-activated tape recorder with a VHF transmitter. Lady Myrtle frequently derived much amusement, and occasionally information that otherwise could have been denied to her, from listening to the comments they made about her. Their remarks were often quite different from the honeyed sycophancy they used in her presence and under her roof. Sometimes they were not, and she would be pleased, almost touched, when a director she might barely have noticed at the meeting spoke up for her against criticisms from his colleagues.

On this afternoon, she lay on her sunbed facing Swan River. To one side, positioned so that the sun was in their eyes, sat five directors. Each had a file open on his lap. Now and then they dabbed damp foreheads with their handkerchiefs, but no one had the temerity to suggest to her that they moved their chairs into the shade, or at least turned them out of the direct line of the sun.

Lady Myrtle watched them through her dark glasses and found it difficult not to let her lips curl in contempt at their craven acceptance. Had there not once been a Queen of England who, when told that eighteen tailors wished to wait upon her to present a petition, had replied contemptuously, 'We will see both men together.'

The voice of Elmer T. Dawson, the managing director of Mackenzie International's United States subsidiary, droned on like a swarm of nasal bees.

'Taking the global picture, Lady Mackenzie, regarding the ongoing profitability of our automobile manufacturing plant in Coventry, England, the board of that company has submitted for the main board's consideration and assessment an in-depth projection for the future—'

'Cut it short,' Lady Myrtle interrupted him crisply. 'Everything is ongoing unless we are dead. What do they say? And why and when?'

The American cleared his throat nervously. 'In brief, Lady Mackenzie, they have had an approach from the Mojo Automobile Group of Tokyo and Hiroshima. They wish to buy into the company and manufacture their cars in England.'

'That would have the advantage of making the product virtually British,' said his number two quickly, anxious for his voice to be heard. 'Mojo could then benefit strongly from the European Community's arrangements for marketing, and would not be subject to the strict quota system which currently hampers their profitability and expansion.'

'I am aware of that,' said Lady Myrtle. 'I do not wish to be told things I already know. What did the Coventry board decide?'

'They are undertaking a survey, Lady Mackenzie.'

'Reporting when?'

'As soon as possible.'

'How long have they been considering the matter?'

'A week, Lady Mackenzie. We flew a team of our accountants in from Detroit. They will fax the results here by noon our time tomorrow.'

'God made the world in six days and rested on the seventh. These people have had as long to consider a very simple proposition. Let me see all the conclusions – theirs and yours – at one o'clock tomorrow. Here.'

'That's a very tight margin, Lady Mackenzie. We shall have to work out our own assessments. And then it will take at least another hour to get out here, even if the details arrive on schedule.'

'Then tell them to hurry. Is the Mojo company run by a family or a trust?'

'Mr Mojo is still very active and is the majority shareholder. He works mostly out of Hong Kong now. But, like so many other companies, he may move before the Chinese take over.'

'Before we decide anything, I would like to meet him. My last experience of the Japanese was at a distance – in an air raid.' She did not add 'in Calcutta'.

Mention of the Japanese always brought back memories of that hot, fearful summer of 1942 when the Allies were in retreat in the East, and centuries of Western supremacy had begun to bleed away. Roads and bridges in Calcutta were jammed solid with cabs and carts and rickshaws as thousands of Bengalis fled after the first raids. They had been very small raids, in fact, with bombs not much larger than footballs, but in remembering the panic, she also recalled her own first steps towards gaining control of Mackenzie Industries – as the company was called then. The Transworld description came later, with so much else, when she was running things.

'Darwin, on the north coast, and Katherine, about three hundred miles south, had sixty-four Japanese air raids,' Myrtle went on. 'During the first one, after Singapore fell, the telegraph operator in the Darwin post office heard the bombers going over and just had time to send a three-word warning – "Raid in progress". Then he and his wife and daughter were killed. They were the first Australians to be killed on Australian soil. A melancholy distinction.'

'I had no idea,' said Elmer T. Dawson, trying to show interest he did not feel in an event that occurred before he was born.

'Not many people had,' Lady Myrtle agreed. 'But in that one raid, 240 people died, and 350 were wounded.'

'I would not think that Mr Mojo had anything to do with that,' said a third director hopefully.

'Maybe. We will find out when we see him. Well, gentlemen, I bid you good-day until tomorrow at one.'

They all stood up, suits damp with sweat and creased. They bowed clumsily and went out to the stretched Daimler limousine that had brought them from their hotel. Myrtle watched the long car glide down the drive.

Irene Loxby came out of the house carrying a small leather handbag which she put down on a side table. Myrtle opened it and pressed a red button on the minute receiver it contained, tuned to the hidden transmitter in the car.

Elmer T. Dawson was talking.

'Shit!' he said explosively. 'I need a stiff Scotch. That old bag gives me the creepy-crawlies every time I speak to her. How the hell can we get this stuff to her by one o'clock? I don't even know if our people are still in Coventry.'

'Then we must find out where they are,' said another man.

Myrtle recognised his voice; he was a Scottish accountant who had recently joined the company. His name was Keiller.

'We get on the blower to them, wherever they are. Tell them we have to receive the material by eight in the morning or they're out of a job. Better them than us. Let them put their bloody lives on the line for a change.'

'What if they can't deliver? We're asking a hell of a lot.'

'And they're being paid a hell of a lot.'

'She sure scares the shit out of me,' said another director gloomily.

'The trouble is you have too much shit *in* you,' said Keiller contemptuously. 'Better out than in. The fact is, I rather like her. I admire her. She's tough, okay, but in her position she has to be. So it's either their heads or ours. For my money, it's got to be theirs.'

'You thrive on this sort of situation,' said someone else enviously. Myrtle remembered him from his thin, reedy voice; a slight, nervous man with an Adam's apple that shot up and down his neck as though he had swallowed a hard-boiled gull's egg. 'There are other things than money.'

'Name two,' retorted Keiller. 'That was the first time I've

met the legendary Lady M. I took to her – though what she thought of us I can't imagine.'

'What the hell do you mean by that?'

'What I say. We're sitting there like jerks with the sun blazing in our eyes and not one of us has the guts to suggest we move six inches back into the shade.'

The conversation tailed off into details about car production estimates, the profitability of completely knocked down units, duty on imported items and other technical matters that bored Myrtle. It was always wise to leave such dreary facts and figures, the nuts and bolts of every enterprise, to those who understood them. All she needed to know were the main outlines of every deal. She could never be bothered with minutiae; little details were for little people to handle.

She picked up the set, pressed another button on its side.

'Company changes,' she announced to her private secretary. 'Move Elmer T. Dawson sideways, downwards, or out – anywhere and in any direction – as long as we don't have to pay him serious compensation. Give him a bigger car, a better office, whatever he wants. But no executive authority or responsibility. Make him a consultant. As of this day.'

She had done this frequently with other men in middle life who had fallen out of her favour. They still received the trappings of the job, but they had no proper job, for who had ever been known to consult a consultant? They realised they were squeezed out and either suffered a heart attack within a year and had to leave or resigned foolishly in a fit of pique. Either way, they were out of her hair and off the Mackenzie payroll, which was the object of the exercise.

'Mr Keiller,' she continued. 'Move him up. Groom him for a place on the main board. I am impressed with his positive attitude. I like a young man with guts. He will go far.'

She paused for a moment, watching the sun on the white sails of the little boats turning into the wind. Keiller was young enough to be her son. But she had never been able to bear a child. Da Leppo had not only terminated her pregnancy; by an error, he later admitted, he had rendered it impossible for her ever to become a mother. Myrtle vividly recalled that moment in his flat when she sensed in his anxiety to get her home that something had gone wrong. Then, she had no idea what it might be. But when, with wealth and security, she began to yearn for a son who would inherit her fortune, her company, she realised this was a dream that could never become reality.

She abhorred the idea of sexual relations; they were obnoxious to her, for she associated all such activity with Mrs Ransom's clients, or, even worse, Uncle Jem's advances. Even so, she had endured the act with men whom she thought might sire a suitable son. But despite their frequently prodigious efforts and huge payments, with the promise of twice as much to follow if she became pregnant, all attempts had been unsuccessful.

For a time she toyed with the idea of adopting a son but could not find a baby she liked sufficiently. Then she took to looking out for young men in the company whose ideals and ambitions she felt complemented her own. In promoting (and sometimes demoting) such young men who had in some way appealed to her she realised she was acting like a surrogate mother, but what did that matter? They could all be sons she might have had.

Myrtle realised she was still gripping the receiver/recorder in her right hand; the corners were digging into her flesh. She opened her fingers, read the maker's inscription: Mojo Micro-Electronics, Hong Kong. She must meet this fellow Mojo. They might just get on. If she liked him, they would do a deal. If she did not, he could sign with another British manufacturer; the matter was of no real importance to her.

The accountants in Coventry reported on time and Myrtle held her second meeting as planned. Afterwards, she watched the directors of Mackenzie Transworld climb into the limousine parked on the drive and then turned to Keiller, whom she had asked to stay behind.

'Would you like a drink, Mr Keiller?'

'A soft drink, if I may, Lady Mackenzie,' he replied carefully in his deliberately Scottish brogue. He fully realised the importance and significance of their meeting. If he got on well with this curious, dark-skinned woman of indeterminate age and unknown background, his promotion in the company could be rapid. He had heard this had happened to others. He was also aware that he could just as easily be out that same day. He knew her reputation; he admired her, and he feared her. In the circumstances, a soft drink was probably wiser than alcohol in the afternoon heat.

He had no idea that the car was bugged but had thought that perhaps one of the directors who travelled in it with him would give a report to Lady Mackenzie of any remarks that referred to her. He was surprised when Elmer T. Dawson started to criticise Lady Mackenzie and wondered whether he might be her eyes and ears – hence Keiller's vehement defence of her in the hope it would be reported back to her. Now, he felt his suspicion had been correct. Keiller was both cautious and ambitious: with these two qualities, he felt certain he could not fail.

Myrtle led the way out onto the verandah and pressed the bell for the butler.

'A bottle of Taittinger,' she told him. 'And an iced orange juice for my guest.'

He noticed she had not offered him any choice of soft drink but had assumed he would take what he was offered; that must be the way of the wealthy. When he was up there with them, he'd be the same. But harder, tougher, much more ruthless.

The butler brought the drinks to where they sat, just out of the heat of the sun.

'To you, Lady Mackenzie,' Keiller said politely, raising his glass.

'To the future,' she replied shortly. 'Now, to business. You have heard what your fellow directors think – or claim to think – about the proposal to merge our car company with Mojo of Japan, and they are for it. You have not voiced your views on this important matter. Do you hold any? If so, what are they?'

'I speak with less experience of the car industry than my colleagues, Lady Mackenzie,' Keiller replied. 'But experience, I feel, is one thing, and instinct – what in Scotland we call a primitive gut reaction – is another.'

'And your instinct tells you what?' Myrtle asked, sipping her champagne.

Keiller took a deep breath before replying; this was his cue. At the meeting he had deliberately not spoken, nor had he given any indication of his opinions by so much as a nod or shake of his head. He had guessed that Lady Mackenzie was surprised – he had caught her glancing at him sharply once or twice. His plan had worked; she might be brilliant at business, but she had still taken the bait. He was just as good as her; better, no doubt.

He paused, and then, gazing at his orange juice as though this focused his thoughts, he answered her question.

'I think we should go along with Mr Mojo down the road for a certain distance, Lady Mackenzie,' he said. 'Find out exactly what he wants. Discover his strengths, his weaknesses – and then go our own way, capitalising on what we have learned.'

'You mean exactly as we are?'

'Not entirely, Lady Mackenzie. I mean, we go our own way – and take over *his* company.'

She laughed. 'That is an aggressive viewpoint.'

'I come from an aggressive nation, Lady Mackenzie.'

'So I understand. I have come across many Scotsmen in the jute industry.'

Keiller looked at her inquiringly.

'We had interests, you know, in India before independence,' she explained, 'when the jute industry was prosperous. All the

Scots I have known are fighters.' Myrtle put on a pair of dark
glasses so she could watch him more closely without his realising the intensity of her scrutiny. 'What is the basis for your
instinct, Mr Keiller, which is, I feel, not entirely instinctive?'

'It is not, but it is largely so. However, the history of co-
operation between motor industries in different countries is a
long one and has not always brought equal benefits to the
partners. In the mid-twenties, for example, the little Austin
Seven was built in Longbridge, England, and became a tremendous success, saving the company from bankruptcy. It was also
assembled in the Peugeot factory in France where it was called
the Rosengart. In the United States, it was built and sold
as the Bantam. In Germany, it was produced as the Dixi by
BMW. So, in effect, one could say that the little Austin Seven
was the first BMW car. In none of these three instances was the
car anything like so successful as the original. Now, however,
BMW and Peugeot are flourishing, Austin has combined with
Rover and is not in their league, and Bantam is out of
business.

'In the fifties, Datsun obtained a licence to build another
Austin, the A40 Somerset car. This helped to put the Japanese
motor industry on a European course. And look at the result.
Even thirty years ago Britain had thirty-three firms manufacturing cars on a relatively large scale. Now there are less than
half a dozen.

'In the United States, General Motors bought a five per cent
stake in Suzuki. It already held thirty-four per cent in Isuzu and
negotiated a deal with the South Korean firm, Daewoo Motors.
Chrysler imported the Colt built by Mitsubishi, selling it from
Dodge and Plymouth dealers. And, of course, General Motors
own Opel in Germany, Vauxhall in Britain, Holden in
Australia here.

'British Leyland, now the Austin Rover Group, had talks a
few years ago with Renault, but they came to nothing. Instead,
they collaborated with the Japanese Honda. Nissan and Toyota

have their own factories in England for the same reason that Mojo wants one. So there is a considerable history of trans-migration, cross-fertilisation, if you like. But not necessarily in favour of the home product.'

'Agreed. But that need not always be the case. So why would you advise us not to go ahead with this, against the advice of your fellow directors?'

'Because, Lady Mackenzie, I feel that the time is wrong for such a collaboration, which in no sense could be called a union of equals. After the Second World War, British influence in the world was at its peak. We were also the only European country able to produce cars in any quantity. We lost the opportunity to control markets we had never approached before – and against only minimal competition. We never had such a chance again, and we never will. We went on producing what were virtually pre-war small cars intended for running around flat roads on a little island like Britain, but useless here in Australia or Canada where distances are vast and the climate can be cruel.

'Our manufacturers were complacent. They found they could sell whatever they made, so they thought what they made must be the best. They didn't appreciate that their cars only sold overseas because they were almost the only ones on offer. The United States had an enormous backlog of demand in their own country and were not interested in exporting. In any case, their cars were too large and too thirsty to have worldwide appeal. British cars were badly put together, with poor quality control, no real service back-up, and totally out of date. Whereas before the war many Continental makes had indepen-dent suspension and all kinds of other innovations, in 1945 the British were still content with cart springs.

'Canadian importers told them time and again how cold the winter was in Canada, how engines would freeze solid, but the heaters the British insisted on fitting remained far too small. Research was negligible. Trade unions held sway, the tea break ruled. What had been, would be, and so must be. World without end.

'Gradually, Continental makers ate into what had traditionally been British markets. When Britain had an Empire it could impose tariffs on foreign-made goods coming into Empire countries. Buyers in India might prefer the American Ford or Chevrolet to the British Morris, but the Morris was much cheaper and so their overseas sales held up. But as the countries of the Empire became independent they did away with these preference schemes and our markets went with them. The fact that our designs didn't change to suit the new conditions didn't help matters.

'First, the Italians beat us with their motor cycles, when only a few years earlier British motor cycles were the best in the world. Then the Japanese came along and beat the Italians because they studied more closely what buyers wanted. They built up modern service networks. If you tried to find the service station of a British-made car or motor cycle anywhere in the world it was usually in a shed up a back street – and it still is.

'The distance between the Japanese and us now is simply too big for us to catch up. We'll go on producing cars and selling them in very modest quantities when viewed against the sale of other makes from other nationalities. We have some very good specialist makers, Rolls, Bentley, Jaguar, Bristol, but nothing to compete internationally on a mass-produced scale, which is where Mojo Motors score.

'We would always be the junior partner in any negotiations with them. We might make a Japanese car with a Coventry accent, but basically all we'd add to it would be a bit of wood-work veneer inside, a badge on the front and maybe new ash-trays, and give it an English name like the Cornwall Coupé or some such thing. There is no commercial future there, Lady Mackenzie. We'd be running after a past that has gone for ever.'

'I am interested to hear your views, Mr Keiller. You express them very lucidly – although your fellow directors do not appear to agree with them. Why did you not speak out?'

'Because I did not wish to appear to do so simply to catch your attention, Lady Mackenzie.'

'That seems an unusual reason.'

'Truth is sometimes unusual, Lady Mackenzie.'

'I agree. Now, are you sure you won't have some champagne?'

'Well, perhaps one glass, Lady Mackenzie.'

Keiller lifted it in a silent toast. She watched him as he drank. He was quite a handsome young man, if in a rather unpolished way. He reminded her vaguely of someone never far from her mind, the only man she had ever loved. That was one reason, she admitted to herself, she had asked Keiller for his opinions, just as she would have asked this other man's views on all manner of matters – if he had lived . . .

She drank another glass of champagne, recalling their first meeting with the wonderful clarity that only comes with the recollection of first love. Even the roué remembers the first time, while all subsequent sexual encounters are lost in a haze of forgetfulness.

She was sitting in the front pew at the memorial service for Hilary held in St Matthew's Church, the oldest in Nassau. Da Leppo sat by her side, with Dr Buchanan next to him. A week earlier, Hilary's clothes had been found on the edge of the sea, with his wallet, though the money had been removed, along with his watch and his cufflinks, as she had foreseen.

The police admitted that his disappearance baffled them, but then everyone agreed that was no new situation for local detectives. There had been other sudden deaths and accidents which seemed inexplicable to those who knew the victims, riddles which the police had been unable – or, some said, unwilling – to solve. The case of Sir Hilary Mackenzie was no exception.

The body of Miss A. Craven was meanwhile removed to a discreet funeral parlour and buried quietly in a graveyard on the other side of the island. Myrtle did not even pay for a stone to be put above the grave; she could see no reason to draw anyone's attention to its location. As she had been taught in her Bible classes years earlier, the words of Jesus, in the eighth chapter of the Gospel according to St Matthew, seemed apt here: 'Let the dead bury the dead.'

Myrtle had, however, arranged a memorial service for Sir Hilary. This was attended by the Governor and members of the legislative assembly. Some wore morning suits, which not only seemed incongruous in the heat but smelled of mothballs. The ladies wore silk dresses and wide-brimmed straw hats. The Bishop of Nassau gave a moving address on the text from Chapter 12 of St Paul's Epistle to the Romans: 'Not slothful in business; fervent in spirit; serving the Lord.'

Listening to the sermon and hearing the Bahamian choir sing 'Onward, Christian Soldiers', Myrtle felt she was taking part in a charade. She had a sudden urge to stand up and tell everyone what a farce the service was. They were gathered together to honour a man who had never existed, who had been totally slothful and fervent in nothing except perhaps greed. Nor had he ever feared the Lord. What Hilary had feared was discovery and discredit. The title, which would now die, should have expired years earlier. The company was heavily in debt, and on the edge of ruin. Hilary had never undertaken any patriotic duty for the country as the Bishop now steadfastly claimed, as though he could personally vouch for the words, as though the dead baronet had been his friend and companion for many years.

The congregation believed the Bishop, and so fiction was accepted as fact. Once his address, with the names of those present, was printed in the local paper, it became a matter of history, in the records, and so beyond dispute or argument. Myrtle and da Leppo alone knew the truth. Dr Buchanan might suspect that all had not been as was now proclaimed, but suspicion was not certainty, and if he valued the prospect of employment when he retired from the Bahamas he would not investigate the matter too thoroughly.

The service ended and everyone stood up to let Myrtle, as the principal mourner, with da Leppo escorting her, walk down the aisle, out into the bright sunshine where black chauffeurs waited in starched white duck uniforms by their masters' cars. Myrtle had walked to the church and da Leppo offered to accompany her back to her hotel but she replied that she would rather walk alone. He nodded, guessing at the turmoil of feelings in her mind. She watched him walk on down the street, then turned, her thoughts miles away – and bumped into a young man wearing a lightweight linen suit and a floppy Panama hat. She remembered vaguely noticing him in a rear pew, and wondering who he was.

'I am so sorry,' he apologised.

'It was my fault,' she admitted. 'I was thinking of something else.'

'You must have a lot on your mind today,' he said sympathetically.

'Yes,' she agreed. 'I have.'

Myrtle began to walk along George Street; he fell into step beside her. The sun blazed on the baking pavement.

'Forgive me, Lady Mackenzie, but if you are on your own – as you seem to be – and have no other engagements, would you have lunch with me?'

'Lunch?'

She looked at him in surprise. It had not occurred to her that she should be hungry, that it was almost one o'clock. But she was hungry; and suddenly lunch with this young man seemed an altogether good idea. She looked at him now more closely: blond hair, blue eyes, a tanned face, smiling hopefully at her.

His smile was his most attractive feature. Myrtle had almost forgotten what it was to have cheerful, uncomplicated people of her own age around her instead of the rich and ageing and discontented. It was exhilarating just to look at this young man. He seemed so fresh, so wholesome and totally genuine: he was who he seemed, and Hilary had never been that.

'Yes, lunch,' he repeated. 'Somewhere local. Cheer you up a bit – I hope.'

'Well, I suppose so,' she said slowly. 'I hadn't really thought.'

It was a long time since anyone had asked her out to lunch. It made her feel good, wanted. He introduced himself: Peter Hillman, a ferry pilot, flying bombers from United States factories to Britain.

They walked down Bay Street, climbed the stairs of St George's Restaurant and sat on the verandah overlooking the trees along the pavement. She had no idea what she ate, but she was touched by this young man's kindness and thoughtfulness. Alone of everyone at the service, he had offered her friendship.

He still flew the Atlantic regularly, he explained, and had done so for the final two years of the war. Soon, he assured her, when aircraft would be much faster and larger even than they were now, flying the Atlantic would be no more of an adventure than crossing the Channel. The aircraft he flew came down from the United States and landed at Oakes Field in Nassau. Then, refuelled and packed with food which was still strictly rationed in Britain, they would take off, fly the Atlantic, and land in Cornwall.

Although the war was over, the ferrying would continue for some time yet because existing contracts had to be honoured. The main difference between flying in war and peace was the fact that he was now unlikely to be shot down. Mechanical failure was a potential risk, of course, but not a very serious one. Running out of fuel was always a possibility if they met strong winds or made a wrong compass reading but, again, it was not likely, for they checked their positions and speed every hour.

Myrtle had taken nearly two weeks to cross the Atlantic in a banana boat. Now, sitting above the street with its rows of cars parked under the shade of the trees, she thought of young men like Peter flying east above her head, in the clouds. Despite what he said, three thousand miles was a long first flight for a new bomber with tight engines not yet properly run in.

Peter Hillman was staying in a hostel at the other end of the island. Since he could not very well ask her back there, she asked him to her hotel. At first, she felt reticent about being seen with him. After all, she was newly widowed and surely a widow should be in mourning? But she reasoned she had done enough play-acting; it was time for the curtain to come down, time to be herself. Now, at last, she could do what she wanted, how she wanted, when and where. She was rich and, more important, she was free.

And so began days of such intense enjoyment and sheer happiness that, nearly fifty years on, Myrtle would still remember them with a glow of pleasure. Looking back, they appeared like a golden age, when clocks stood still, when she had no worries, no gloom, and they both knew nothing but laughter and almost delirious pleasure in each other's company.

Peter had wanted to make love, of course, but at first she was afraid to agree; the memory of Uncle Jem came back to haunt her at the prospect. She told Peter about her experience guardedly, not admitting how frequently she had been assaulted or how great her dread of sex had become. To her surprise and delight, Peter seemed to understand immediately.

'It would be different with someone you like,' he assured her.

'I like you,' Myrtle told him, surprised at her own frankness. But the admission gave her pleasure, a relief of the spirit she had not thought possible. 'I like you more than anyone I've ever met. But I'm afraid of spoiling it – just yet. Please let's wait. I will be ready sometime. I promise.'

'Tomorrow and tomorrow and tomorrow,' said Peter sadly,

ruffling her hair as they lay on the wide bed in her hotel suite.
'It may never come, you know. Like the notice they have in
pubs in England, "Free beer – tomorrow".'

'You know England very well, don't you?' she asked him. He
had never been to India and had no idea she was a half-caste,
but she suspected that even if he knew, it would not matter.
After all, why should it? Who in all the world could prove that
their blood was totally pure? Wasn't it one of the major flaws in
Germany's National Socialism that its followers claimed to be
one hundred per cent Aryan?

'Of course I know England well,' Peter replied. 'But not as
well as I know – or love – Scotland. I was brought up in
Perthshire in a little village on the road from Scone, home of
the stone on which all the kings of Scotland sat to be crowned.'

'I've read about that,' she said. 'It's in Westminster Abbey
now, isn't it?'

'It is,' he agreed, 'but by all rights it should be back in
Scotland. It's as if they moved Stonehenge from Salisbury
Plain and stuck it somewhere else – say in Swansea or
Edinburgh. It would be all wrong.' He looked at her quizzi-
cally. 'You don't know England, do you?'

'No,' she admitted. 'I've only been there briefly. I was born
in Calcutta.'

Now she had said it there could be no going back. But he did
not show any surprise. He could not have realised the significance of the admission to her.

'A lot of Scots there, I believe.'

'Yes,' she said. 'In the jute business. My husband—' she still
kept to this fiction, even with Peter – 'my husband had business interests there.'

'I have some relations who went out there, years ago. Scots
are great travellers. Dr Johnson said, "The best thing a
Scotsman ever sees is the road south to England." '

'But you've come west.'

'I'm going back east on Friday,' he said.

'So soon?'

The news hurt her like a blow. He had literally flown into her life; now he was flying out of it, and she had a horrible and totally unreasonable feeling he would never come back. Their time together was a magic interlude; Cinderella at the ball. Midnight had still to strike.

'There was a delay in the planes coming in. Now the war's over, they come in dribs and drabs. But they will definitely arrive on Thursday night, so I'm told. Then they must be checked over, loaded, and we'll be out Friday afternoon. You must come and see us off.'

'I'd rather be there to meet you at the other end.'

'That's impossible – this time, at least, because you're here. But I'll give you my address. No. I won't. I'll take yours, because I'm always on the move. Letters are never forwarded.'

'Have you any brothers or sisters?'

'None, I am an only son. No relations of any kind, unfortunately. My parents are dead. They were killed in the first big air raid on Coventry. Ironical, for they didn't even live there. They were only visiting friends. So I'm the last of the line.'

'We have a factory in Coventry. Made armoured cars during the war. Now we're back producing saloons – the Mackenzie Ten,' Myrtle said inconsequentially, as though this had a bearing on what Peter was saying. She only mentioned it because she felt she had to say something or burst out crying, and that would never do. Women did not weep – not English women, at least, and he must still think she was English, even if born in Calcutta.

'We?'

'I mean the Mackenzie group.'

'Ah, yes. Of course, I'd forgotten. My father had a Mackenzie once. Quite a good little car.'

They lay now, gently caressing each other, kissing, drawing apart slowly, savouring the sensation. Perhaps it *would* be different with someone she liked, Myrtle thought. No, not

someone she liked, but *loved*. That was the difference, the real
alchemy that turned everything to gold. Love. As Peter's hands
moved expertly over her body, stroking her breasts, moving
down to her thighs and to her most secret places, she still felt
her body tense automatically at his gentle touch.

Sometimes, even now, when Myrtle tried to sleep without
her usual sleeping pills, she would lie awake remembering that
night; the warmth, the feeling of total compatibility, the nearness of his hard male body. And then it was as though she was
young again, and the future held a hope of happiness bright
beyond all imagining . . .

One day, she knew, she could lose her fear of sex and all
would be well; but not just yet.

Peter sensed this and drew back.

'I must tell you something, Myrtle,' he said as they dressed
and prepared to go down to dinner.

'Something important?' she asked.

'To me, yes. I think I'm falling in love with you. In fact, I
know I am – I have.'

Already she knew in her blood that she was in love with him,
but she could not really believe that he felt the same way about
her. It seemed too much to hope for.

'How do you know?' she asked. It was an absurd question,
but she had to ask it.

'I couldn't tell you exactly.' Peter shrugged. 'It's just something I feel all over from inside, like a warm glow. When I wake
up in the morning I know this is going to be a great day, because
I'm going to see you, be with you. Friday is going to be a black
day for me because I'm going away.'

'But you'll come back,' she said. 'Please give me an address
where I can contact you. There *must* be somewhere.'

'There isn't. When I land at the ferry terminal in Cornwall I
may take a room somewhere until I get a passage back here. Or I
may be put up in a service mess. I just don't know where I'll be;
a letter to the terminal would never find me. At best it would be

pinned up on a board for a day or two and then taken down and thrown away. The staff keeps changing. People are getting demobbed. I'm in a hostel here, and I have been for about ten days. But when I come back the hostel may be full, so I may be in a hotel, or in a boarding house.'

'I could write care of the airfield.'

'You haven't seen Oakes Field. It's pretty primitive. Just a matter of a few huts. Don't send a letter there. Waste of a stamp. You'll have left before I'm back, anyway.'

'So how can we meet again?'

'Give me your address in England and I'll contact you. I promise.'

So she gave him the address of Mackenzie Industries, the only address she had in England. She wrote it down on two pieces of paper, telling him jokingly that if he lost one he would still have the other.

On Friday afternoon she hired a car and drove to Oakes Field. Against a baking blue sky the yellow wind sock hung listlessly from the top of its mast, dejected as her spirits. Waiting on the tarmac were half a dozen bombers, drab in khaki paint, RAF red, white and blue roundels their only mark of colour. Young men she had seen enjoying themselves in restaurants, but now grave-faced and preoccupied, were climbing in and out of them. Fuel bowsers reversed carefully up against the aircraft wings to fill their tanks. Ground crews unloaded trucks packed with cardboard boxes stamped 'This Way Up', 'Fragile'.

Peter Hillman saw her before she saw him, and came towards her. He was in shirt and shorts, carrying his flying suit over one arm, his helmet hung with earphones. His face was tense: he had aged in a day. She suddenly realised the length of the flight that faced him – and its constant dangers. If the slightest thing went wrong, an instrument gave a wrong reading, a wire no thicker than a thread broke, or a tiny blob of solder on a terminal became detached and his plane came down, there was no serious chance of rescue. Each aircraft carried inflatable dinghies, but she remembered the giant waves, thirty, forty feet high, that towered over the banana boat. Who would see survivors, let alone be able to rescue them, if they crashed off the recognised sea lanes? The answer was obvious. No one. When each plane left Oakes Field, it was on its own.

'When are you off?' she asked, her voice suddenly hoarse as though she had been shouting against the wind. She hoped she would not cry.

'Now,' he said briskly, and tried to talk her out of her sadness. 'Lucky you're here. They've brought the time forward. Weather reasons, apparently. A storm's moving east. We go early to try and get ahead of it. Sorry about this. Otherwise we should have had another hour here, at least.'

'An hour gone. It's an eternity,' Myrtle said. 'I feel as though you're going out of my life for ever.'

'Then you feel wrongly.'

He kissed her gently, lips moving softly against lips, tongues quiescent, a kiss of love and warmth and companionship, the sealing of a bond between them.

A loudspeaker crackled on the hot roof of one of the huts.

'Pilots to aircraft, please! To aircraft now!'

'That's us,' he said. 'We're going.'

'You *will* write, won't you?' Myrtle said appealingly. Her eyes moved over his face, imprinting his features on her mind. She wanted to be able to recall him as he was simply by closing her eyes: the scent of his after-shave, the freshness of his soap; the honest, cheerful look in his eyes; how his fair hair caught the sun.

She watched him put on his flying suit.

'I love you,' she said. 'All my life has just been a prelude to meeting you.'

'And all our life afterwards,' he told her, 'will be Acts One, Two and Three. And you know what we're going to do in Act One?'

She shook her head dumbly.

'Think about it,' he told her. 'Think about it. And tell me when we meet. Then I'll tell you if you were right.'

He kissed her again and then he was gone, climbing into the cockpit from an aluminium ladder which RAF ground crew wearing khaki shorts and shirts wheeled away as the door closed above their heads. Myrtle watched the propellers begin to turn sluggishly against the starters, heard the bang as the first engine fired. A gout of blue exhaust smoke blew out across the melting tarmac. The thrust of the propellers as the other engines started flattened grass and bushes around the edge and blew her skirt tight against her body.

She stood, mouth dry with sadness at his going, as the engines warmed up. Then, one by one, the planes taxied up to the end of the runway, turned, and trundled back towards her. It seemed impossible that such heavy lumbering machines could fly. She watched as their great unwieldy bellies rose heavily and reluctantly from the earth, and then, in their element at last, assumed a grace beyond belief. Landing wheels folded up neatly beneath their wings, they looked like large and very powerful birds. If swallows could fly the Atlantic on tiny wings, relying on puny muscles and fluffy feathers, surely four great engines could support these planes across the same distance? Please God, let them. Help them.

They turned once in a wide circle above the airfield, slowly gaining height. The sun was in Myrtle's eyes now. She was not certain which was Peter's plane. It had been the second. Was it now the third, or the first, or the fourth? It did not matter, he was up there in the sky, going east, going home . . .

Myrtle sipped her champagne, watching Keiller.

'You remind me of someone,' she said slowly, choosing her words carefully. 'Someone I met briefly in Nassau just after the war. A ferry pilot flying a bomber to Britain. He never made it.'

That was the fact of the matter, the basic nub of truth. Somewhere out in the Atlantic, deep beneath the waves, Peter

Hillman and his crew lay cocooned for ever in a huge aluminium shell on the bed of the sea.

'I know,' said Keiller gently.

'How do you mean, you know?'

'He was my uncle, my mother's brother. Peter Hillman.'

She looked at him in amazement.

'My mother was actually his half-sister,' Keiller went on.

'How extraordinary. You never knew him yourself, of course?'

'Oh, no, Lady Mackenzie. It was a long time ago. Before I was born.'

'Yes,' she said, watching him closely. 'A long time ago.

'Well', she said more briskly, 'I think perhaps we have spoken enough today. Mr Mojo is on his way here in his yacht to see me. Please hold yourself in readiness at your hotel for another meeting. Mrs Loxby will be in touch.'

Keiller smiled with pleasure.

A car was waiting at the storm porch. Mrs Loxby walked with him to it. He climbed inside and leaned back thankfully on the cushions in the rear seat. It had been a strain talking to the old woman, he thought, but he had impressed her. With any luck he would soon be a director – and then who knew how high he could soar?

For some time after Keiller had left, Myrtle sat on the verandah, toying with her glass of champagne. She watched the bubbles rise, but somehow the drink had gone flat for her. Remembering Peter Hillman and those few idyllic days, so long ago now that it seemed almost another life, always disturbed her. If they had had a son, he might have looked like Keiller.

She put down her glass, crossed the verandah, unlocked a door with a silver key and went into the room beyond it. She stood for a moment, looking about her. The wallpaper was decorated with rabbits, cheerful, red-faced gnomes, and fairies with wands and gossamer, butterfly wings. On a settee lay four huge fluffy teddy bears next to a giant panda and Mickey

Mouse. Their beady glass eyes reflected the sunshine from the window as though they were actually watching her. She walked among them picking one up, stroking the soft nylon fur, holding it closely against her cheek. These were toys for the child she would have liked to bear, Peter's boy or girl.

This was the secret heart of every house she owned. She alone held the key that opened the door on what might have been, what never was, a land of look-behind.

When Myrtle came out of the room she carefully relocked the door. Then she pressed the button for Irene Loxby.

'Please do what is necessary,' she told her brusquely.

Irene nodded. 'He's a good-looking young man,' she said. 'Makes me wish I were young again.'

'Yes, he's charming. Very charming,' Myrtle agreed, and then looked away so that the older woman would not see the tears in her eyes.

Anna Lu-Kuan faced Dr Sen angrily.

'What are you doing here in my suite?' she asked him, reaching for the bell-push.

Sen held up one hand, shook his head deprecatingly.

'You are in no danger,' he answered her. 'I have flown here from Hong Kong to see you because I have an important business proposition to discuss.'

'I don't know you. I have nothing to talk to you about,' Anna told him shortly.

'That is a matter of opinion,' the doctor replied. 'To put it another, if cruder way, I have something to talk to *you* about on behalf of those who sent me.'

'Well?' she asked belligerently. The man looked harmless, more worried than menacing; she could listen to whatever he had to say – always keeping a finger near the bell-push.

She crossed to the table, poured herself a rum and lime juice, added ice. The sugary liquid ran in her blood, cheered her, gave her more confidence. She sat down.

'I'm waiting,' she said.

'My superiors, for want of a better word, have sent me here to impress upon you the importance they attach to gaining control of the Trinity-Trio conglomerate. They believe that you are in a position to help them materially in their intention.'

'Then they believe wrongly,' said Anna Lu-Kuan.

'They are not usually ill informed on such matters. They know all about your communist background, Miss Lu-Kuan, and that in your relationship with Lord Jackson you appear to have become involved beyond the call of duty. More significantly, they know Lord Jackson gave you two of his Trinity-Trio master shares, without which he no longer has voting control. My superiors wish to purchase those two shares.'

'I put the shares for safekeeping in a bank.'

'Which bank?'

'The Occidental-Oriental Bank in Nassau. Here.'

'A very sound bank. My superiors will have friends on the board.'

'They want more than friends, Doctor. The bank is owned by Italian-American interests. Mr Carlotti – about whom you probably know, since you seem to know everything else – controls it. The bank has a lien on all my deposits against a loan. That means the shares are as good as in his hands.'

'I see.' Sen paused, considering the matter. 'What about Lord Jackson? Will he recover?'

She shrugged. 'You're a doctor. You'd better ask your fellow professionals. They give me optimism. They may give you truth.'

'In life, it is good to be optimistic.'

'Sometimes,' she agreed. 'But you have to have a reason. I've no reason. If I get the shares back, you want them. What if I don't give them to you?'

'That is not a situation that can arise, Miss Lu-Kuan. You give them, or they are taken. It is as simple as that.'

She sat down heavily, spilling the drink on her dress. 'How did you get involved in this as a professional man?'

'Because I *am* a professional man. My grandfather was a coolie in an Australian goldfield. Every day he managed to take out one or two grains of gold until he had enough to buy one small shop, and he left the mines. The shop was in Cairns, facing the sea and the land of his birth, China. It prospered and the Triads moved in. They wanted a share of his good fortune, his hard work. He paid up. He had to. But in return they helped him to get other shops, mostly acquired at bargain prices from owners who had been unable or unwilling to pay the price the Triads demanded. He became wealthy, and then my father took over. He went to university and qualified as a physician, and always kept on friendly terms with the Triads. When I went to medical school, they helped with my fees. It was an investment against the day when they might wish to call on my services.'

'And now they have.'

'Yes.'

Dr Sen walked to the door.

'Come on. We'll go to the bank now. With any luck the bank's owners won't have removed the shares yet.'

'No,' Anna said defiantly.

Sen crossed over to her, looked her in the eyes.

'Listen,' he told her sternly. 'If we both want to stay alive, we go to the bank.'

'I'm not taking out those shares for you to have. They were given to me as a gift. They're mine.'

'If you leave them there, they go to the Mafia. Then they are theirs. You have just told me.'

'They are still in my name.'

'You are wrong,' Sen said patiently. 'My information is that they are bearer shares. Whoever holds them, owns them.'

He took her by the arm and they went downstairs. A car pulled out of the park; they climbed in.

'Occidental-Oriental Bank,' said Sen. The car stopped outside the main entrance. Sen took Anna's elbow as they walked inside to the desk marked Enquiries.

'Securities Manager,' said Sen brusquely.

'You have an appointment, sir?'

'No, I am making one now.'

'He's with a client.'

'Then tell him he has a more important client here.'

'Could I have your name, sir?'

'Dr Sen.'

The doctor took a visiting card from his wallet, scribbled some Chinese characters on it, passed it to the clerk.

'Why are you so sure he'll see you?' asked Anna.

'He is Chinese.'

'How do you know?'

'A notice on the wall as we came in lists all the executives of the bank. Mr Li is the Securities Manager.'

'What if there hadn't been a Chinese there?'

'There's a Chinese in every bank in this city,' replied Sen. 'If he'd been in charge of home loans, mortgages, insurance, pensions, deposits, whatever, I would have gone to see him.'

'But then he wouldn't have been any help.'

'He would have put me in touch with whoever could help me. He also wants a long and happy life.'

The clerk returned. 'Will you come this way please, sir, madam?'

The clerk pressed a button. A steel door opened on an electronic lock. They walked along an air-conditioned corridor lined with doors marked 'Manager', 'Vice-President', 'Loan Supervisor'.

The clerk knocked on Mr Li's door. The Securities Manager was standing by a desk; a slightly built man in a silk shirt, lightweight trousers, white shoes. He bowed nervously, looking from the doctor to Anna and back again, still holding Sen's card.

'Please take a seat,' he said. 'Would you like a coffee or a cold beverage? The wine of the country, Coca-Cola?'

'No, thank you,' said Sen. 'We just want your help. We must apologise for interrupting an interview with another client.'

Mr Li bowed obsequiously to show that this was of no consequence.

'This is Miss Anna Lu-Kuan,' explained Sen. 'She holds two master shares in Trinity-Trio. Their headquarters are down near the Sheraton British Colonial Hotel.'

'I know the building well,' said Mr Li. 'I was at their opening only the other day. Why, I saw you, Miss Lu-Kuan. You were with Lord Jackson. What a terrible accident.'

He could not pronounce his Rs. They sounded lilting and odd, as though an impersonator was trying to speak in the Chinese idiom.

'He is making a quick recovery?'

'Yes,' said Anna.

'We're all glad to hear that,' said Sen. 'But what we're here for are those shares.'

Mr Li began to punch out keys on a computer. The screen flickered with green letters, figures.

'The bank has a lien on them,' he said, almost sadly, like a father to an erring but favourite son who should have known better.

'Then take the lien off them.'

'That is very difficult. It is a question of bank policy.'

'It is a question of another more important policy. We want those shares, Mr Li. Do you understand what I mean, or must I spell it out?'

'Please wait one moment,' said Mr Li nervously. 'I will deal with the matter personally.'

Sen and Anna sat looking at each other in the empty room. Three minutes, four, six passed, then Mr Li returned, closing the door carefully behind him. He sat down, his sallow face creased with concern.

'There seems to be some misunderstanding, Dr Sen,' he began nervously.

'About what?'

'About these shares. Miss Anna Lu-Kuan has already withdrawn them.'

'I have not,' said Anna. 'How can I have done?'

'Well, Miss Lu-Kuan, here is the withdrawal form. Taken out only this morning – here is the date, the hour, stamped on it. And your signature.'

Anna looked at the form, at her signature above the typed name. It was indeed exactly as she would have signed it. But she had not.

'This is a forgery,' she said.

'That may be, Miss Lu-Kuan,' said Mr Li unhappily, squirming in his chair. 'But your signature was checked against the specimen you gave us when you opened the account, and it matches perfectly. I am sorry, I cannot help you.'

'Who presented this withdrawal form?' Anna asked him. 'It certainly was not me. I have witnesses to prove where I have been all morning.'

'There is no record, Miss Lu-Kuan. The custom is for the form to be presented, the signature checked, and then the securities released. As you saw in our banking hall, we have twelve tellers. It could have been presented to any one of them.'

'This is a serious matter, a very serious matter,' said Sen. As he stood up, he drew his hand across his chin, apparently stroking it in his perplexity. But Mr Li saw the way he held his thumb, and his face paled at the sign of the Triad.

A couple of miles away, out towards Delaporte Point beyond Cable Beach, three men sat round a glass-topped table on the terrace of Mr Carlotti's magnificent beach house. Speedboats carved white scars in the greeny-blue sea. Pretty girls on skis waved one hand, raised a ski in salute as they turned. But Carlotti and his two guests were oblivious to all attractions of sun and sea. On his left, across the table, sat the manager of the Occidental-Oriental Bank and next to him, Mr Li. Both appeared greatly concerned. Mr Li was sweating with nervousness. He kept dabbing his sallow face with a silk handkerchief. Carlotti viewed both men with displeasure and distaste.

'You mean to tell me that two shares deposited with the bank's lien on them have been withdrawn?'

'That appears to be so, sir,' said the manager.

'Well, is it so or is it not? It can't *appear* to be so. *Is* it so?'

'Yes, sir.'

'How the hell did they get away with them?'

'Miss Lu-Kuan's signature.'

'She came in person for them?'

'She insists she has not been near the bank today. So it must have been someone else who signed the withdrawal form.'

'A man or a woman?'

'We cannot say, sir, because none of the tellers recalls the incident. So many securities are deposited and withdrawn all the time.'

'What about the lien? What about Miss Lu-Kuan's overdraft?'

'A sum of money was paid in.'

'How much?'

'It is a banking matter, sir. We must maintain confidentiality.'

'Shit!' shouted Carlotti angrily. 'I own the bank. How much?'

'Five thousand American dollars.'

'And she owed what?'

'About four thousand, sir.'

Carlotti grunted like a hog in his displeasure. He should have gone down personally to collect those shares the moment Jackson fell out of the window; ordered the bank to be opened up especially, if need be. But there seemed no hurry then. He had a lien on the shares, and so felt certain he could take them whenever he wanted.

'I give you twenty-four hours to find them, gentlemen,' he said brusquely. 'And also to find who collected them. I do not want to see you until you have those shares. I am ready to be rung at any time of the day or night, and someone will go anywhere to meet you or to deal with whoever may be holding them. Now, get the hell out!'

Carlotti pressed a button. A butler materialised and led the two men to the front door. Carlotti lit a cigar, looked out at the sea. He was glad this was the last big deal he would handle. After this he would retire and spend his time between his house here and his other equally pleasant property in Florida. He had worked long enough; it was time for others to take the strain.

As a young man, he had fought his way up with the gangs on the East Side. He had been the brains behind protection for those involved in the numbers game, horse racing and, over the last thirty years, in the drugs business. In the increasingly complex negotiations to launder the vast profits safely he had begun to feel his age. He belonged to an easier time before computers complicated everything; when people were more important than electronic brains.

The plan to capture control of Trinity-Trio had been hatched then, during Prohibition, when he had helped to run motor launches packed with oil drums filled with rum and gin from Nassau into Florida. Carlotti's father had been among the first to capitalise on the fact that the demand for alcoholic beverages far outran such smuggling activities and the production capabilities of illicit, back street distilleries. The sensible move was to buy genuine distilleries and breweries, ship the product into Canada legally, and then run it across the border. People would pay more for good whisky – and since Prohibition could not last for ever, when it ended they would be right in there with their own customers and a first-rate product.

It had taken months of research to find the right distillery, Long Glen Distillery in Scotland. This was owned outright by one Clive Douglas, whose grandfather had been Alec Douglas, one of the three original founders of Trinity-Trio. Clive was a spendthrift; he owed thousands of pounds in gambling debts, had mortgaged his estate several times and was desperate for ready money.

'We can buy into the firm,' Carlotti recalled his father saying. 'This guy Douglas is a bum. He races expensive cars at Brooklands, the English motor racing track, like Indianapolis, only more socially orientated. He owes a fortune to bookmakers and moneylenders, and he hasn't the brain to realise if he goes on like this soon he'll have nothing. The distillery is on his estate in Scotland and is apparently his own property, not owned by Trinity-Trio. Get over there, wait for the big races – and then go and see him. It's ten to one he'll have lost more money and he'll be ready to talk.'

Two operatives crossed in the *Berengaria* and shacked up in Edinburgh for a week until their local contact told them Clive Douglas was back at home, owing more money from that Saturday's races. The two visitors were Mr Logan, which wasn't his real name, and Mr Schoenbach, which was.

They had both done their homework; they knew the questions and the answers, and they offered Douglas what was then a huge sum – £25,000 in cash for the distillery and two acres around it in case they wanted to expand. He appeared willing to do a deal, so they made a proposal to bring him even more money. They offered him a further £15,000 for the option to buy half of Douglas's voting shareholding in Trinity-Trio at any time during the next ten years. Douglas had all the cunning of a fool. He said he would sell them an option on only 49 per cent. That way, he hoped to keep some control over his inheritance. They agreed, on one other condition: the option should be renewable for a further ten years upon payment of £1,000, and it should continue to be renewable, on the same terms indefinitely.

Douglas consulted his lawyer who warned him he should be

very careful before he diluted the company's voting shares, because already one-third had been bought by United Charities Incorporated. Douglas saw the dangers, but more importantly, in his view, he saw the prospect of solvency. His greed overcame his loyalty to his fellow directors. Without telling them he not only sold them short, he all but sold his own birthright.

Carlotti drew on his cigar heavily. What the situation needed now was not nostalgic reminiscence but sharp, hard action. And that was what he intended to provide for this last tremendous coup before he retired to let others run the risks.

He would see the man who, with Family money and backing, had grown very rich. If need be, he would threaten to pull out their backing, which would destroy the reputation of this man they all called the Australian. He was an oddball character in any case, immensely proud of his reputation as a man who never failed in any deal.

Carlotti drew on his cigar until the tip glowed like a red warning light. That's what he'd do. He'd lean on him to discover who held the two vital shares. And with all his weight.

ELEVEN

The Present: Katherine and Darwin, Northern Territory, Australia Perth, Western Australia

So far as many sons and daughters are concerned – perhaps most – their parents appear to be not so much of a different generation but of a totally different race. They accept that they were young once; that they must have loved is obvious, or the sons and daughters would not be here, but their youth seems so remote, so unlikely, that it belongs to a lost and misty past; their lives and emotions, their personal ambitions, triumphs and defeats have little or no relevance to the present.

My mother had been ill before, but nothing serious. Privately, I thought she might like to exaggerate. Women often did, according to Crabtree; it gave them a sense of importance. But despite my initial lack of concern, over the next few days I could see that she really was not well. A strange luminosity shone about her face, as though the skin was stretched too tightly over her cheekbones, taut as the canvas shades that stretched like the petals of giant flowers above the Ayers Rock Sheraton Hotel.

The letter she had received from Rosael Pagoda Films seemed incredible to all of us. This sort of approach was more suited to a film or novel than real life, it was too good to be true – and yet it was true. Crabtree and I knew, of course, that Amy had once been an actress, but we weren't very impressed by that. She had never appeared in any film, and certainly not on TV, and if you are not on the box as an actress nowadays, you don't really count for much.

There was a lot of telephoning, mostly by reverse charge, to California. She found an agent, and the producer and director flew over to see her. They stayed in the motel; one of them actually had the Stranger's room, although I did not tell him this. I did not take greatly to either of them. The producer was plump, sucked a hollow tooth, bit his fingernails, and ran out of breath if he walked more than a hundred metres in the heat. He was not my kind of person.

The director was about ten years older than me and was clearly not on very good terms with the producer, but I guess a bit of friction in any creative project is not a bad thing.

The scripts for both films greatly pleased my mother: the two parts she was to play were pivotal, and she seemed to be in nearly every scene. I could well understand how thrilled she was, and how totally determined not to let illness stand in the way of this tremendous chance. The local doctor fixed her up with some kind of drug – mainly painkillers, I think now – and she set off for location in Darwin up in the north.

Darwin is the Northern Territory capital, a tropical city right in the centre of what we call the Top End. And just to keep you right as to the vast distances involved in my country, Darwin is nearer to Manila in the Philippines than it is to Sydney, and about the same distance to Jakarta as it is to Adelaide.

On the day they flew north, I was offered a chance of buying a fairly rare car, a 1939 Triumph Dolomite roadster which someone had brought out from England before the Second World War. It had spent most of its life in a lock-up garage in Darwin. The seller was a total stranger to me but wrote a very friendly letter, enclosing several colour photographs of the car.

I receive letters like this from strangers probably every month; somehow they hear I buy old cars and hope I will buy theirs. This car looked pretty and was an almost exact copy of the small Mercedes of a previous year, although Triumph strenuously denied its designers had ever seen that model. For some reason, the price had not risen too much. This was a car I could buy and renovate, putting it down like a wine to keep for several years; it could be worth a lot then. When I thought that twenty years ago for a few thousand dollars one could have bought a Mercedes of the type that fetched $5 million at Christie's in London, I saw some potential profit here. In the meantime, I wanted to see my mother act. I had never had the opportunity before, and maybe, deep down I thought that since she was so ill there might not be another chance.

The heat in Darwin was like an open oven with steam added, which may help to account for the fact that a stubby of beer, which holds 375 millilitres of the amber nectar elsewhere in Australia, holds two litres in Darwin. I found the unit outside the Old Post Office, which had been built in 1872 and lasted until the first Japanese air raid on Darwin on 19 February, seventy years later.

Darwin has a mass of citizens of Chinese, Taimorese, Italian, Spanish, Caucasian, Greek, Indonesian and Japanese origin and a whole lot of them, wearing thongs and white cotton tops, were watching the crew. They had built a kind of railway along the pavement, and when I arrived the camera was being wheeled on it by men in shorts. A sunshade was tied to it in case the heat melted the film.

I saw the director and behind him the producer, and the continuity girl with her notebook to check that anyone smoking half a cigarette when they did the first take hadn't switched to a full cigarette for the second. The microphone, held on a long boom like a fishing rod, quivered in the air above a huddle of actors, and at the centre of all this I saw my mother.

It is very difficult to say what a scene will look like when it's being made, because the camera only sees one part, the selective part it wants to see, and the human eye sees everything; trees alongside, cars parked out of shot, onlookers laughing or silent or making ridiculous comments.

The crew made a video tape of each scene as they shot it, and when I saw my mother's face on this small screen I realised she really was a good actress. She wasn't just being herself; she was being someone else, and I also knew then that she was dying. She had summoned up every atom of her life and character and energy and was projecting it through the lens of the camera. I was watching something great and finite, and I felt both proud and amazed.

This wasn't the mother I had seen helping Crabtree with his books in the evening, or checking out stock or sticking labels on cans of beans on the supermarket shelves. This was someone else altogether, someone who had talent of a stature I had never encountered before, and for the first time in my life I felt humble.

I wished above all things that she had been offered this chance when she was fit, but then I rationalised by thinking, maybe, because she was not well, because cells were multiplying crazily within her, this provided some kind of spur that forced genius to blaze like a beacon. The other actors and actresses were all playing parts; she *was* the woman whose part she took. It was a total integration; reality outshone illusion.

The director and the producer did not notice me, and in any case I kept out of their way; I didn't want to appear just another rubberneck. When the continuity girl walked over to a car to get herself a new notepad, I recognised her; she used to live in Katherine. I had seen her often enough in the supermarket, but I did not know her name.

'Going well, is it?' I asked her.

'So so.'

'Who's making it?'

She gave me the producer's name.

'No, I mean, who's backing it?'

'Rosael.'

'I know, but who owns Rosael.'

'An Australian.'

'You're joking!'

'Like hell I am! We've got some good people in this business, you know. In fact, he's so Australian he's called *the* bloody Australian. Works out of London sometimes, New York, the Bahamas, Hollywood. He's bloody well everywhere.'

'Does the star, Amy Crabtree, know that?'

'Why do you ask?' the girl said, looking at me rather oddly.

'I just wondered,' I said.

'No, she doesn't, and she's not to, either.'

'Who said so?'

'The Australian.'

'So why are you telling me?'

'God knows! Maybe 'cos I'm tired and I've seen you around Katherine and you asked a question and I foolishly gave you an honest answer. But if you tell her, I'll deny it. So will everyone on the set. It's instant sacking for *anyone* who breathes a word about that. Do I make myself clear, mate?'

'Abundantly,' I said.

I went away then and walked down the esplanade. Darwin used to be an outpost of the old British Empire, only reached by sea. Now, it is most accessible by air, as the Japs discovered in the Second World War. Thirty-two years later, on Christmas Eve, Cyclone Tracy managed what Japanese bombers had failed to achieve: it virtually destroyed the whole town. More than a hundred people died and goodness knows how many more just disappeared. In the following three months, the population fell from 47,000 to 25,000.

Now, of course, the city is all new. It has five hotels and Australia's only duty free development zone, but still some oddities remain. There's a beer can regatta, for instance, when boats made from empty beer cans race each other over the calm sea off Mindil Beach. At the Humpty Doo Hotel near the Arnhem Highway there's a Brahmin bull named Norman. I'm told he can drink a two-litre Darwin stubby of beer in forty seconds, which is one minute, eleven seconds quicker than his nearest human rival at the bar. Every August there's a crazy World Mud Crab Tying championship. There used to be a Darwin Rocksitter's Club; members would perch on a platform right out on the rocks and watch the great rollers come in, until one day the flagpole caught a flash of lightning and the rock blew up. More lightning flashes are recorded at Darwin airport than anywhere else in the world. Between October and December, they have as many as forty thousand. Darwin also has a suicide season when its very high humidity reaches a peak during the build-up to the rainy season – what we call the Wet.

I walked on past the post office, past what is known locally as Crocodile Corner. Here, a lot of layabouts – in Darwin they call them the long grass people because they sleep rough in the grass or on park benches – were getting up, scratching themselves. It's nicknamed Crocodile Corner because the layabouts like to put the bite for a handout on soft-hearted passers-by.

One in three of the people around here are said to be Aborigines. I walked past them all in a kind of Dreamtime of my own. How could it be that the Australian was secretly financing his own mother in two films, with strict orders on pain of dismissal that no one should tell her he was involved? If she didn't know, I wasn't going to tell her. But I wondered about her and about him and their relationship, and I wondered about his father, the man she had married, the sergeant who was killed in New Guinea. I wondered about him most of all. He must have been a pretty sharp customer to pass on the financial acumen the Australian possessed, but then maybe our mother wasn't such a slouch when it came to figures. I reckoned I had a bit of financial acumen myself.

The Triumph I'd come to see was parked under a tarpaulin in a lean-to shed at the back of a house built on stilts off

Cavenagh Street. This must have been one of the few that survived the cyclone. All around stood new properties and building lots for sale. I knocked on the door and a parrot began to shriek inside, 'Go away, go away!'

The door opened and a Japanese or Chinese stood in the doorway, looking at me inquiringly.

'I'm not selling something,' I told him. 'I want to see your Triumph.'

'Oh. You Mr Crabtree?'

'Yes.'

'I am Mr Hong.'

This seemed unanswerable, so I didn't answer it.

'Can I see the car?' I asked him.

'Oh, yes.'

He led me out to the lean-to, pulled the tarpaulin off the car. and there she lay. Rats or termites or both had eaten into the canvas hood, salt and sun and dampness had dulled the maroon paint, the chrome plating was pitted with rust. Even so, the car seemed complete, including its period accessories such as the two Mellotone horns for town or country driving, the matching Lucas spotlights, the Ace wheel discs. The leather upholstery was cracked and smelled as though something had died in there. Probably lots of things had; rats must have been living there for years, and even rats don't live for ever, whether they run on four legs or two.

'Does she go?' I asked Mr Hong.

'Can be made to.'

'Ah,' I said. 'Everything can be made to happen in this world, if not the next. But it costs money.'

I lifted the bonnet. Cobwebs stretched across the carburettors. The aluminium valve cover was white, as though with hoar frost, from oxidation. But, runner or not, this was worth buying.

'How much?' I asked, as though I didn't know.

'Seven thousand Australian dollars.'

I walked round the car, patted the bonnet, kicked the tyres and shook my head regretfully, the customary pantomime between buyer and seller.

'Five,' I told him.

Mr Hong rolled his almond eyes slightly and said that was impossible. The car had been in his family since new, which was an obvious lie. But finally, after more shaking of heads, more walking to and fro and kicking tyres, I agreed to six thousand.

I peeled off the money, took his receipt. Now I had to transport the car back to Katherine, 272 kilometres away. There was no question of driving it; tyres that old would never make the distance, and the idea of being marooned on the side of the Stuart Highway didn't appeal to me. I had a return ticket on Ansett NT airlines, but that could wait.

I telephoned a few people and heard that a road train going south tomorrow had an empty trailer. I saw the driver. He said he'd be glad to move the car and me as long as I had the car loaded up by noon the following day. He wanted to move off at one o'clock sharp from the loading and turning area, out of town. Mr Hong said he could arrange for the Triumph to be towed there, so that was settled. QED.

Rosael Pagoda had booked Amy Crabtree into an hotel overlooking the esplanade and the sea. She had a bedroom and a sitting room that opened on to a balcony. When she came back from filming, dusk was already falling from the sky. She threw the bag containing her filming clothes on to the bed, slid the glass doors apart and went out, leaned wearily on the rail. Down below, by the side of the storm porch, she could see a heart-shaped pool of water ringed by coloured lights, with fountains that changed colours, blue to red to green. Beyond lay the almost empty esplanade and then a stretch of grass and the indigo sea.

The hotel doctor had just left. He had given her an injection, and told her she was doing fine. She did not feel fine, but he had to say something optimistic; the film company was picking up his fee.

Amy leaned on the warm rail, watching palm trees and casuarinas shake in the evening wind, and thought back to similar evenings at the Galle Face Hotel in Colombo where she had dined so often with James Jackson, a lifetime ago, when she was young and the future was like an unknown country, waiting to be discovered. She wondered what the Galle Face was like now, but realised it was folly ever to attempt a sentimental journey, even in the mind.

She wondered whether, as a prisoner in Hong Kong, James Jackson had also remembered the Galle Face and making love in that wide bed with crisp, clean linen sheets, or out under the stars and the palms, hearing the heavy rhythmic roar of the waves only feet away. But what did it all matter now? He was dead and she was dying. Would they meet again, in some other life? The idea was appealing, but unlikely.

She felt unusually tired. She had never asked the doctor what drug was in his hypodermic syringe and he did not volunteer any information. But she knew that whereas during the first few weeks of filming she had felt immeasurably fitter after one injection, now she needed two injections instead of one.

The good news was that both films were going well; she was making them back to back, as they called it. In one, she was a middle-aged Englishwoman widowed in Australia and now trying to make a go of life on her own. Almost too close to reality, she thought with a wry smile, except that she had never been widowed; she had been a wife only to Crabtree, and that was a marriage of convenience, even despair.

In the second film, Amy played an Australian career woman who had made a great success of her life in terms of money and prestige. She owned a Ferrari, a penthouse overlooking the ocean, a yacht in the harbour, but was still lonely. On the outside, all was gaiety, glitter, glamour, success. Inside, there was nothing; an emptiness like darkness at sea, before the moon came up. Again, she knew how the woman felt; she had felt like that for years.

That afternoon she had overheard an assistant director talking to the cameraman.

'It's odd we've never heard of this Sheila before – and yet she's acting like she was born to it.'

'She's a great actress,' agreed the cameraman. 'And this is her first picture. That I do know. Maybe she's just played towns on tour where we've never seen her. But our producer's sharp. He found her. Got to give him credit.'

Yes, she'd been playing in places where they had never seen her: in Katherine; in Colombo; in Stockport, in the north of England; she and her son, the Australian, and old Uncle Rob, with his clichés for all occasions: 'Nice weather for the ducks'; 'Better fish in the sea than ever came out of it'. All through those years she had played the part of the widow of a husband who never was. The part she played and the player had long ago become one.

A knock on the door scattered her thoughts. She had left it unlocked for she knew Ian was coming to see her.

I came into the room, walked on out to the balcony, kissed her.

'Had a good day?' I asked her.

'Pretty good. We got about eight minutes in the can, which is double what we achieve some days.'

'You look tired, Mother,' I said.

She nodded. 'I am. So I thought we'd eat in tonight. Have something light sent up to the room. I don't feel like a restaurant, people in the unit coming up, wanting to talk about the script, that sort of thing.'

'By all means,' I agreed, but I was surprised. Usually she liked to be out with other people; it was all so different from Katherine.

'Ring down and order what you want,' she told me. 'I'll have two poached eggs on toast with a glass of Perrier, and some fresh fruit.'

I ordered barramundi, the local fish, and a bottle of Tyrrell's Long Flat White wine, French fries and a side salad. I poured a gin and tonic from the mini bar. Amy shook her head when I offered her a drink.

'I've just had my usual jabs,' she explained. 'They don't mix with alcohol.'

'I'm sorry,' I said, not because it didn't mix with alcohol, but because she was in need of regular injections, because we both knew now, but would not admit to each other, that time was running out faster than we had anticipated.

'How do you feel, exactly?' I asked, trying to be cheerful, talking in those false, rather loud tones visitors use in hospitals and sick rooms as though the person to whom they are talking has suddenly lost the ability to hear properly.

'When my old father was about seventy-nine and was hoping to make eighty,' Amy replied, 'people would ask him that, and he always had the same answer. "Well, I'm not ordering green bananas." '

'I see what you mean, Mother,' I said and laughed dutifully, but wished I had not asked the question. 'You've not seen that specialist, Dr Sen, again?'

Amy shook her head. 'No,' she said. 'There's no need. There's nothing he can do. Not now. He was very good, though. One of the best men in Australia and Hong Kong. And he didn't charge me anything. Not a cent.'

'That was kind of him,' I agreed.

'It was indeed. Very kind. And most unusual. The older you grow, Ian, the more you tend to notice people who do you a kindness. Most usually want something in return, then or later.'

The meal arrived. Amy toyed with her eggs, ate a few mouthfuls, pushed the plate aside, drank the mineral water greedily, sat back in her chair. I could see the outline of her skull clearly beneath the stretched skin on her face. I thought that this was almost like looking at a death's head, and I remembered something Georgie had once said to me: 'The living are only the dead on holiday.' For one of us, the holiday seemed all but over.

'What are your plans for tomorrow?' she asked.

'Katherine,' I told her. 'I bought a car here today. It's going back on a road train. I'll go with it.'

'Oh. Well, give your father my love.'

She paused, embarrassed.

'He rings me every night,' she said, obviously pleased. 'He's been a very good husband.'

We both realised that, quite without meaning to, she had used the past tense. It was as though she had already gone, left us, not just to make two films, but for ever.

'I'm glad you looked in,' she said. 'I wanted to tell you something.'

Amy spoke slowly because she was not quite sure how much she wanted to tell, or if she really wanted to tell the whole truth.

'You're very like the Australian,' she said, almost thinking aloud.

'Wish I could meet him,' I replied.

'You will. You're making enough money now. You can fly and see him – though whether he wants to see you may be another matter.'

'Why do you say that? He's always been very pleasant in his letters.'

'You've never spoken to him on the phone, have you?' she asked.

'No. I tried to ring him several times but all I could ever get were secretaries and secretaries' secretaries. It was costing me money, so I gave up. Forget what I wanted to talk to him about now. It was nothing important anyhow.'

'It could be important to him. I never realised this before, but men get terribly jealous, not only about women, but about other men's success, especially in the family. It's like the old bull being leader of a herd. Then a young bull grows up and challenges him.'

'I'm not challenging the Australian.' I said it without thinking. Of course I wanted to challenge him; I wanted desperately to overtake him, to prove there was room for two of us. Or if there wasn't, that there was room for me. But I'd never told my mother about my ambition.

'He may think you are,' Amy said, reading my thoughts. 'He mightn't like that.'

'You haven't seen him for years yourself, Mother.'

'No. But he writes. He's been a good son, too. In his own way.'

I wondered what she would say if I told her the Australian was financing the two films and must have insisted she had the two starring roles. But this was not the moment to tell her.

'Do you ever hear from his father's family?' I asked her to change the subject.

She looked at me strangely for a moment, as though her mind was far away and she had difficulty in concentrating her thoughts.

'No. No, I don't.'

'But you must have met them before you were married, before he went off to New Guinea?'

Amy sipped the mineral water.

'That's really what I wanted to see you about, Ian,' she said. 'I have a confession to make. I owe you the truth. There was no sergeant in New Guinea.'

'What do you mean?'

'What I say. I'm telling you something now that even Crabtree doesn't know. Only old Mrs Crabtree knew. She suggested it. I was in a show in Colombo, giving concerts for the troops. The cast was made up of men and women who had been on the stage or who wanted to go on the stage, or thought they did. We would sing and dance, play in little sketches. There were lots of troops around then with nothing to do and very little money, and we'd give shows to them. The stage was often just the back of a truck. If we were lucky it was in a hall, a hut, a tent, anything.

'In Colombo, I had a friend in the show, Esmerelda, and we were pretty close. We got on, and a lot of young officers took us both out.'

Amy smiled at the memory, and her face was suddenly young, not old and tired and taut. The lines of pain and weariness had vanished. I was looking at a young girl, not an ageing, sick woman.

'We went dancing, swimming by moonlight. The sea was phosphorescent. It was like being covered with luminous paint.'

'You had a particular boy friend?' I asked her.

'Yes. Actually, one we both liked. Fellow called Jackson. James Jackson.'

'Was he in the army?'

'No. He was out there on some special job. There were all sorts of things going on then. A group called Force 136 had people behind the Japanese lines in Burma. He had to go to Hong Kong, just before it fell, on some secret mission. I don't know what, and it doesn't matter now. He was taken prisoner. Died there the day Hong Kong was liberated. Ironic, but then so is life. He was the sergeant, if you like.'

'You mean he was the Australian's father?'

'Yes.'

'Does he know that?'

'I've never told him.'

'What did this guy Jackson do?'

'He was in a company, Trinity-Trio.'

'They're doing a big development here.'

'I know. You see their name everywhere. He was very rich, only he didn't let on in case we'd feel embarrassed, I suppose. He was a gentleman in the real sense – a gentleman. His ancestor was one of the three men who had founded the company.'

'Really?'

'Yes. Really. Actually, he was a lord, an English lord. I never

told you before. He didn't tell me, either. I only found out after
. . . after . . .'

She paused.

'After the war?'

'Yes. After the war.'

We both knew she had meant to say, 'After his death', but
somehow death was not a word either of us cared to use.

'You're kidding?'

'No.'

'What about Esmerelda? You still keep in touch with her?'

Amy shook her head. 'Our concert party split up. I came here
with part of it to Katherine, which was a big staging post on
the Stuart Highway up to here. She went off to Calcutta and
Delhi.'

'Is she still alive?'

'I believe so. She married Jackson before he went to Hong
Kong on his last trip.'

'She got any children?'

'Yes. A son. The present Lord Jackson.'

'You been in touch with him?'

'No. Why should I? How could I? That's all in the past.
I've never met him, and he's probably never heard of me.
Esmerelda, she's Lady Jackson now. She wouldn't want me
coming out of the past where all old forgotten things – and
people – should remain.'

'She might like to hear from you.'

Amy shrugged.

'And Crabtree doesn't know any of this?' I asked her.

'Nothing. His first wife was very kind to me. When I found I
was pregnant, I had to leave the concert party and she gave me a
job, helping in the shop. Gave me a home. In those days, Ian, if
you were having a baby and you weren't married to the father,
you had a pretty hellish time. I owe a lot to her. So does the
Australian. I'm telling you this now perhaps because I am tired
and perhaps also because I'm not very well.'

She sipped the mineral water again.

'Once, when I was in Stockport with the Australian – it's funny how we all call him that – we took a day trip to the coast, to Southport. There was an artificial lake with a lot of little motor boats putt-putting around for children. You'd get about ten minutes in a boat for sixpence then. Because of the noise of their engines, the attendants couldn't tell them when their time was up, so they'd hold up a board. On it was written: "Come in, number one, your time is up." That's how I feel now. I wanted to tell you this, but keep it to yourself, a secret.'

'I will,' I agreed gravely, and as I spoke I remembered that I was also keeping a secret from her.

The road train stood in the loading and turning area some way outside Darwin; three ten-wheel trailers, with a giant Mack six-wheel truck to pull them, all painted in the owner's livery of green, white and red. In front, across the huge radiator grille with its double searchlights and four headlights, a heavy shield of horizontal metal rods rose from the great girders of the bumpers to fend off any buffaloes or kangaroos that might wander into its path; these rods were known as 'roo bars.

The whole train, forty-five metres long, took a lot of stopping, even from a low speed, and road trains generally travelled fast. They could not traverse town or city roads because they could not negotiate any but the most gradual bends. Hence they were driven between loading areas outside their destinations, just as goods trains went to goods stations or marshalling yards.

On either side of the cab, big air intakes for the engine rose high above the roof like submarine periscopes somehow gone aground. The height was necessary to keep them as far as possible out of the red dust that the wheels would churn into a thick abrasive fog which could ruin any engine within a few days. Double air horns lay like trumpets on the cab roof. Behind the cab was a sleeping compartment for the driver, and then the long, slat-sided trailers where sheep or cattle livestock were packed in tiers. The Mack bulldog mascot squatted belligerently on top of the radiator in front of a wide metal strip to deflect insects from the windscreen.

The driver was wearing rubber-soled shoes, shorts, a sweaty, short-sleeved shirt with the legend 'Sex may be bad for one, but it's great for two', and a hat with beer-can rings dangling from strings to keep off the inferno of flies that, when he stopped in the Outback, could cover his entire face and neck. He stood by the cab talking to a smaller man in blue shirt and trousers.

'Well, here's the owner of the car,' he said as he saw me pay off my taxi.

'Got a Pom here wants to see you,' he called to me.

'What about?' I asked.

'About that old car you've loaded on the end trailer,' said the Pom. 'I'd like to buy it.'

'Not for sale,' I told him at once. 'I only bought it yesterday. I want to restore it.'

The Pom seemed to know the spiel well enough; anyway, he paid no attention to it.

'I collect cars,' he went on. 'I've been looking for one of these for a long time. This is the first Triumph Dolomite roadster I've seen out here. I've money that says you might like to sell.'

'How much money?' I asked him.

'Forty thousand Australian dollars. Each one with your name on it.'

I looked at him more closely. This was a very large sum indeed, probably more than the car would fetch when restored. And I would have to pay for the restoration, which would take several months, at best. Also, the Dolomite roadster was not in the Isotta or Bentley class; it was pretty to look at, but not of particularly noble lineage. It just happened to be rare. Even so I had to make a last stand. When it comes to car-copers, Custer simply isn't in it.

'I couldn't let it go for that,' I told him. 'Forty-five and we might be talking.'

'Forty-two and a half,' said the Pom at once. 'Now.'

'Now,' I repeated with as much feigned reluctance as I could command. 'You have a deal. So where's your money?'

'In the bank. Over on the Mall.'

'I want a banker's draft,' I told him. 'No cheques and no cash.'

It was too risky to carry that amount of money in my back pocket. For all I knew the Pom might try to steal it back himself – with a few from Crocodile Corner to help him.

'How long have we got?' I asked the driver.

'No more'n half an hour. Then I'm leaving. You still riding with me?'

'I might as well.'

For a moment I thought of refusing and catching the plane to Katherine, but as he asked the question I had the same feeling I had experienced in the Alice when I first saw the Stranger. I felt it was somehow important – why, I could not imagine – that I rode with him. So I agreed.

We walked over to the bank. There was some toing and fro-ing and telephoning among clerks in the air-conditioned bank-ing hall, then the banker's draft appeared.

'I don't bank here,' I told the teller. 'Please telex it to my account, Ian Bruce Crabtree, at the City and Provincial Bank, Katherine branch.'

We walked back to the road train. The driver had lowered a ramp from the trailer, and let the car roll back. It stood at the side of the road now, tyres half inflated, dusty, forlorn.

'How did you hear about it?' I asked the Pom.

'I told you, I'm a collector. I have people looking out for odd cars. I heard there was a Triumph here and I missed it by hours.'

'I see. Well, I'm glad it's got a good home. It could do with some loving care. What's your name, by the way?'

'Ford,' the Pom replied. 'Dick Ford.'

'Like the car?'

'Yes. But no relation.'

'Well, Dick Ford, glad to have met you. And I wish you well with the motor.'

I climbed up into the cab beside the driver. The Mack engine stirred, fired. The bulldog mascot trembled briefly on the high radiator as gouts of black smoke blew out of twin exhausts thick as a corvette's smokestacks. The entourage moved forward slowly; links to the trailers bit and clanged; the cab chassis shuddered as it slowly took the weight. Then we were on our way.

'What do you make of that?' I asked the driver.

'That you're a lucky bastard!' he replied at once. 'I saw that bloke nosing around. Thought he was a Pom tourist rubberneck.'

'So he was. With a difference.'

'What difference?'

'He had forty-two and a half thousand iron men on him.'

'You could buy me a few beers on that.'

'I will. When are we stopping?'

'I've got an old relation, an uncle who owns Zachariah, a station about a hundred and eighty kilometres south. He's in bad shape there. Widower, got a gammy leg, and there's been no goddamn rain for years. I thought I'd stop the night there, cheer him up. We can park easy enough, and we're in no hurry.'

'Fair do,' I agreed.

We came out on to the Highway and gathered speed slowly and inexorably, like a locomotive. A road train generally chooses the high ground in the centre of the road, and cars and trucks approaching it wisely pull well over to the side to let it through. This was a bit like being royal, I thought; you have a clear run and unobstructed priority.

Gradually, flat-roofed buildings, shops, overhead power lines fell away, and the open, empty road stretched straight ahead, diminishing with distance, until it seemed no thicker than a thread. On either side, the earth burned, brown as blood dried in the sun. Here and there, patches of green vegetation sprouted; bushes, shrubs, lone clumps of trees. As we drove into the afternoon, heat beat on us like a madman on a drum.

Glancing in the mirror, I could see red dust surrounding us, shrouding our whole length with a travelling cloud. My mother had told me how, during the war, before the road surface was sealed, drivers of US Army convoys, possibly half a mile long, would travel with dust up to their axles. They were unhappy about presenting such an obvious target for any prowling Japanese aircraft, so the roads near United States camps were bitumenised. Then bulldozers, trucks, graders and road rollers commandeered from private firms were brought out to make what officials called a sealed road from Darwin right down to Alice Springs.

I thought how different it was to drive in this giant vehicle, sitting comfortably in an air-conditioned cab with the radio playing, to travelling then, or in even earlier times. It is almost impossible now to understand just how rough and tough conditions had been in those days. The only constants remained the immensity of the land, the shrivelling, baking pulse of its raw, red heat; the feeling of total inferiority, man against nature; always against all odds.

When a mail service began, which was the first step in attempting to cut this gigantic island to something like measurable size, telegrams about selling stock would go by packhorse courier from one town to another; this might cost as much as £20. The couriers had to ride carefully because Aborigines could be hostile and hostility could mean death.

The worst problems were either a total lack of water – or floods. In the Wet, flooded creeks and rivers and streams could prove impossible to cross. In the dry season, it was difficult to carry enough water for horses and riders.

One courier, riding to Katherine with two companions, had banked on reaching Koolunjie water hole, but when he reached it the hole was dry. They decided to head on for Corella Lakes, fifty miles away, with six pints of water between three men and six horses. When they did not reach Katherine, mounted constables went out in search of them and found their bodies. They had dug so frantically in the hard, baked clay to try and find water that the flesh on their fingers had been worn to the bone.

'They were tough men then, Ian,' my mother said. 'And no sooner had those poor fellows been found dead than a dozen others volunteered to take their places.'

It had not been easy in the early pioneering days when people fell ill or had an accident. One man my mother spoke of was mustering cattle on Hodgson Downs Station, one hundred and fifty miles east of Katherine, when his horse fell and rolled on him, breaking one of his legs and crushing his ribs. A companion rode back to the homestead for help, but it was still two days before he could return with a colleague on a springless farm cart. All this time, the man lay in agony under the sun and moon. His friends tried to set the leg but aggravated the break so that the jagged bone stuck out through the flesh. In this condition he was taken to Katherine and a message went north to Darwin for a doctor. The doctor could not leave his patients, so a nurse came instead. Meanwhile, the patient travelled for another sixty more miles to Pine Creek on the way to Darwin. His leg was gangrenous by then, and its stench attracted thousands of flies; the ghastly wound crawled with maggots. The nurse arrived and calmly set about dressing it. She accompanied him to Darwin where his leg was amputated – thirteen agonising days after the accident.

As I thought of the stories my mother had told me I felt an immense sadness that I had not been closer to her. There had always seemed so much to do, and so little time for talk. She was stocktaking, sticking price labels on the goods in the shop and later the supermarket, or off to the Alice, buying new consignments. I had been at school or helping in the shop or, latterly, making my own deals.

I suddenly realised that my parents were almost strangers,

and now my mother was dying. I remembered odd isolated incidents. Once, after bathing with her in the river, we sat on the warm rocks, just the two of us, enjoying a picnic. This had only happened once in my whole childhood, and yet the memory stood so clearly in my mind it could have been yesterday. I still felt the afternoon sun on my face and recalled the taste of ham and egg sandwiches, and my mother so happy and young. I remembered asking her then about the sergeant, and her face had closed in as though a cloud had passed over the sun. Now I knew that when she had replied, 'He was a fine man, Ian. But that's all in the past', she was referring to someone else.

'Well, what about the Australian, Ma?' I had asked her, always eager for any news of someone I admired so much.

'He's a clever fellow,' she said. 'And he's a kind man at heart, but he just doesn't think. You see, Ian, you can't buy everything in this world. Some things haven't a price – they're priceless. He'd send me money tomorrow if I asked him. But he knows I would never ask him. It's much better for people to *give* you something, even if it's only a letter, without your having to ask for it. Remember that.'

I remembered her words now, and how she quickly fenced further questions. There was always some excuse to break off the conversation, just when it seemed interesting. And now I realised there would not be too many more conversations. I was shocked by my mother's appearance. When you're close to someone, when you see them day after day, any change or deterioration in their health or appearance can be so gradual that it is almost imperceptible. When you don't see them for a week or a month, and all that time they're going downhill, then they age with the speed of those films that show spring and summer and petals unfolding in sequences that may have taken months to capture but which only last for seconds on the screen.

The driver nudged me.

'Hey, sport,' he said. 'Get a load of that.'

He pointed out of the window, eased his foot a little off the throttle. The train slowed slightly, shuddering behind us. Through swirling red dust and the shimmering distance I could see a high double-decker truck bouncing over the desert. It had canvas sides and a loose canvas flap at its tail that waved like a flag with each dip and roll of the rough ground.

'Who's that?' I asked him.

'Rustlers. On my uncle's station. That poor bastard's losing his cattle all the time.'

'How do they do it?'

'Bloody easy. The cattle are all skin and bone. They can hardly move their arses, they're so weak. No water. They just stand there. Those blokes drive right up to them, drop down the ramp at the back, set up a stockade fence on either side to make a kind of funnel. And then they drive the cattle up the ramp, close the tailgate, and off to the meatworks.'

'There's a lot of rustling, then?'

I knew there was some, but not on a large scale.

'Sure,' he said. 'If the meatworks is still in business, they'll arrive after dark, wake up the foreman, tell him they've got a load to go through. The cattle are de-boned, the hides burned, the meat comes out at the other end. And that's it.'

I knew of several small meatworks dotted around the Outback that had been shut down for years. But what is closed can always be opened – if you possess the key and enough cash to persuade workers to work through the night on rustled cattle and clear up the mess afterwards.

'Your uncle's insured against rustling?' I asked the driver.

'Hell, no! Who'd take that risk? It's almost a certainty out here if you haven't got many men. You gotta live with it. And if you try and mix it with those rustlers you could die with it.'

'What about the law?' I asked.

'Don't give me crap! Law? What's the law – one policeman with a walkie-talkie – going to do against ten or twenty men?

He hauls them up in the court. So who's going to give evidence against them? Do they want their homes burned down next, their cattle rustled? Even if the rustlers are convicted, and that's not too likely, they're not going to be put away for ever. And when they come out, they'll come visiting. Be your age, boy.'

Rustling was not a subject we talked about much in Katherine, and now I understood why. But I felt sorry for the driver's uncle. I wanted to discover whether anything could be done to help him – which must surely show how naive I was then.

The driver slowed and pulled off the Highway. A great cloud of abrasive red dust engulfed us like a sandstorm. The truck and the trailers were too long to turn and he stopped about a hundred yards from the sealed road near an unpretentious house: corrugated-iron porch held up on unpainted posts, a water tank on four poles near some sheds. A shabby Mojo ute was parked in the shade.

A dog began to bark as we climbed out of the cab, and an old man limped out of the house to meet us. His face was grizzled like a lizard's skin, his hair thin. He peered uncomprehendingly at us until he recognised the driver.

'Rupe!' he cried. 'Glad to see you, mate. Here for long?'

'We could make it a night. Me and my friend. Ian Crabtree.' We shook hands.

'There's a dozen Fosters in the fridge got your name on them. Stay as long as you like. Kind of lonely on my own. Be right glad of company.'

I dumped my overnight bag in a back room, all scrubbed boards and pictures that looked as though they had come from calendars: snow-covered ski slopes in Switzerland, Highland glens in Scotland. Nothing was more incongruous out here in the barren desert trembling with heat like a volcano, ready to erupt.

'How many cattle you got?' I asked the old man later.

'Four thousand in the wire. As many outside – or I did have until the rustlers started. Bastards!'

'We saw a truck on the way here.'

The old man nodded, took out a packet of tobacco and cigarette papers, rolled himself a cigarette.

'Double-decker transporter?' he asked.

'Yes.'

'Thought as much. How far away?'

'Several miles.'

'The bastards are getting closer. They'll be at it in my back yard soon.'

'Who's behind them?' I asked.

'Difficult to say. But they're not working on their own. The bank wants me out of here. Maybe it's them. Wouldn't put it past them. You see what the cattle looked like?'

'Skin and bone,' said the driver.

'More bone than skin,' retorted his uncle. 'We've had no rain here for getting on five years. The longest on record.'

'What do the Met men say?' I asked.

'Nothing. They don't know when the weather is going to break. Or they didn't when I last heard a weather broadcast, but the radio's crook and I've not been into town to have it seen to. One of those solid state things. You can't repair 'em, I reckon. Need a whole new set.

'We want a deluge, several inches, just to make up for what we haven't had all this while. I've three bore holes out here, and two are almost dry. There's no money in cattle now, but the bank still want their interest. They're like vultures. When they get a whiff that all's not well, they come in for the kill.'

'What's the land worth?' I asked him.

'Could be sixty dollars a square mile – if we had the rains. Bloody bank wants to cut the loss and make me sell for nothing.'

'What's nothing?'

'Thirty. Bloody rape! And these rustlers don't add to the

value. We can lose a few hundred head in a week, a big percentage, and there's sweet nothing I can do about it.'

We stood on the back porch, drinking stubbies of iced beer.
The old fellow was rattled, and, I guessed, frightened. He
didn't know what to do because, deep down, he realised he was
helpless. I resolved to try. I wanted to help him, though I'm not
sure why exactly. Perhaps because, like him, I was on my own.
And also I felt I had somehow been offered a chance to make
some real money. The opportunity might be disguised now,
but if I gave the matter enough thought, surely I would see it
more clearly.

TWELVE

The Present: Between Darwin and Katherine, Northern Territory, Australia

I accepted that the rustlers would not be the sort of people one would expect to find in the local Sunday afternoon Bible class, but I believed I could take care of myself. I had grown up the hard way, and I wanted to discover whether they were doing this as a one-off operation or whether they were more professional, determined to wear down the old man's resistance by regularly rustling his cattle until, finally, he was forced to accept some ridiculous offer for the whole station. Depending on what I discovered, I hoped I might be able to devise a scheme for combating them.

I calculated that the truck we had seen could now be about six miles north along the Highway. I asked the driver about the locations of any local meatworks.

'There's one at Katherine, as you know,' he said. 'But I reckon that's too far away. There are several small works just north of here, but not active now. When the big companies, Vestey's and Bovril, looked like making profits, all kinds of small operators set up on their own, maybe with a handful of workers. They thought they could make a living out of it, but one by one they went down.'

'What's the equipment like in those places?'

'Fair to rough, I guess. Some of them keep the plant in reasonable order, just in case any work turns up. They may do a small amount for local stations.'

'And for rustlers?' I asked.

'Not legally. The boss man won't know about that if they do, or at least he'll say he doesn't. But maybe you could get half a dozen men who would come in at night for a special job. They'd be paid in notes and be off in the morning. Why d'you ask?'

'I'd like to see what the rustlers are doing.'

'You're bloody mad if you do. They're tough boys, y'know.'

'I know. I follow what you say. And I'll keep my head down.'

That night the generator failed and our only light came from pressure lamps, which seemed to attract flies and mosquitoes like homing beacons. We all went to bed early and this gave me my chance. I put on a pair of rubber-soled shoes, jeans and a dark shirt. Then I found some boot blacking I thought the old man wouldn't be using and rubbed it over my face and the backs of my hands in case the moon was bright. I slipped on my thickest leather belt with a buckle and some loose coins – shrapnel, we call them – in my pockets. A few stuck between the fingers of each hand could make a reasonable knuckleduster if things grew rough, but I hoped they wouldn't.

I let myself out of the house quietly. The dog growled but he recognised my smell and my footsteps, and did not bark. I set off along the side of the road. Dust, inches deep, felt soft as red flour under my shoes; a ragged moon rode up the sky.

I had only gone three or four hundred metres when I realised I was not walking alone. Someone was behind me, dogging me, trailing me. I kept turning, but I couldn't see him; indeed, I couldn't see anyone. When I stopped, whoever was following me stopped, too. I wondered who he was, what he wanted. Did he trust me? Could I trust him? And then, suddenly, he was right up against me, walking so closely by my side I could smell the burned-ash on his body; an Aborigine.

'Who are you?' I asked him sharply, for his face was still in shadow.

'Thought I'd taught you better than to ask,' Georgie replied reprovingly.

'What the hell are *you* doing here?'

'I could ask you the same question.'

'I got a lift from Darwin. On a road train,' I explained. 'We passed some rustlers who are taking cattle off Zachariah Station where the driver and I are staying the night. It's owned by the driver's uncle. I wanted to find out more about them. See how they work.'

'They're bad news,' Georgie said, shaking his head in disapproval. 'They've done over several of our people. That whole station is going downhill. They're slowly ruining the old man so he can barely afford to pay wages. The rustlers will run him right down, and then he'll have to sell.'

'This happen often?'

'Sometimes,' Georgie said. 'What do you expect to find up here?'

'I don't really know,' I admitted. I had to be honest with Georgie. 'I thought that perhaps I could help in some way. Or maybe it's just curiosity.'

'That's what killed the cat, so Mr Crabtree likes to say.'

'Well, I'm not a cat. But what are you doing up here, anyhow?'

'I'd gone walkabout. Saw you come off the truck and thought I'd say hello. You might have wondered what had happened to me when you get back to Katherine.'

'And now you've said hello?'

'It's goodbye. See you about.'

He left me as quickly and silently as he had arrived. I was sorry to see him go. My initial enthusiasm was waning. I guessed I was being foolish, but I didn't like to give up, so I kept on heading north. After about two hours I saw the double-decker truck parked some way off the Highway. Men were swarming around it. They had brought out two sets of paling fences and were setting these up by the rear of the truck. At one end was a steep, ribbed wooden ramp, leading up into the truck; the other end of the fence fanned out like a funnel.

I moved away as quietly as I could and lay down, concealed by patches of rough grass and spiky bushes. It was as well I did so because, with my ear close to the ground, I could hear the distant drum of hooves steadily grow louder, coming closer. Then a great cloud of reddish dust moved across the land, opaque and sinister beneath the moon. Suddenly I saw the cattle, rearing up in terror, and behind them, driving them on, two men on motor cycles.

Even in that dim, diffused light I could see how thin the beasts were; their ribs stood out beneath their flesh like the frames of canvas tents when the wind blows against them. I heard the crack of whips but the men did not shout or race their engines.

The first cattle reached the opening between the fences and hesitated, heads down, pawing the ground. I smelled the sharp stench of their dung, voided in terror, the instinctive dread all animals bred for slaughter experience as they approach the slaughterhouse even though they have never seen it before.

More cracking of whips, like small dry branches breaking, and the leading cattle were forced on by those behind; anything to escape the stinging lash of raw leather. They paused briefly at the bottom of the ramp and a gate slammed shut behind them. Now they were trapped. The terrified steers began to climb up the ramp, some stumbling at its steepness but forced on by the press of beasts behind them. When most were in the truck, those the men could not cram in they let run loose.

The truck started with a bellow of exhaust and moved on down the Highway, travelling without lights along the empty road. Headlights were switched on briefly as a few other trucks came and went. Their lights threw brief yellow paths ahead of them, then they were gone in a swirl of red dust. I stood up and followed the truck, carefully keeping about thirty yards away from the road so I would cast no shadow on its dry, hard surface.

To one side, maybe two miles ahead, a rough, unmade track led to a building three storeys high, with a corrugated-iron roof. Its windows were covered with sheets of newspaper, but I could see chinks of light where the pages did not quite fit the frames. The truck backed up to a wide entrance on one side of the building. The opening was several feet off the ground, exactly level with the rear of the truck.

Fences were again set up to stop cattle escaping, and with a creak and squeak of rusty hinges the truck's tailgate went down. I heard the plaintive lowing and coughing of the beasts in the hot dry night and then the rattle of their hooves on wooden boards as they came down backwards, awkwardly, into the building. A man prodded them so that they turned to walk to their deaths head first. For a moment, the only sound was the drumming of hooves as others came out behind them.

It was too dangerous to remain where I was, so I walked round to the far side of the building. The windows had all been covered, but here, by climbing up a drainpipe, I could peer in through a space.

One man prodded the animals up a steep concrete slope within the building, ribbed and rutted to stop them slipping and falling. They lowed miserably, moaning as they started to climb. The slope was steep; it reached up three storeys to the top floor.

I climbed on up the pipe and found that the windows at this level had not been covered with paper. I could see a man waiting at the head of the slope. He wore a white overall and thick rubber gloves. In his right hand he held a knife like a dagger, but with a slightly longer blade. As the cattle burst up from the slope, the man's right hand moved with a quick incisive jerk, an expert twist and thrust. The blade entered each beast's body just behind the head. One after the other, steers staggered forward for a few paces and then rolled over, dead.

Other men who had been standing out of my line of sight now came forward. They wore yellow hard hats like construction workers and white overalls with aprons that glittered under the shadeless light. The aprons were covered with hundreds of small strips of bright metal clipped together in a kind of protective chain mail. They worked with incredible speed as they split open the beasts and bled them.

Blood poured and spouted everywhere; streaming down walls, spraying up to the ceiling, running in rivulets across the herringbone pattern of the floor. There was so much blood that sometimes the men actually slipped in it. They knew exactly where and how to cut. Amateurs could easily break an arm or a leg, or even be crushed to death as a steer rolled in a sudden, muscular paroxysm.

The carcasses were hauled to a great vat at the far end of the room. This was already steaming like a witch's brew and water slopped over the rim onto the floor. Men wearing thick leather and metal gauntlets ripped off the hides; boiling water made the hair easier to remove.

Another man carried away the hides to be burned elsewhere. Everyone knew his job. There was no haste, no hurry. The carcasses were picked out of the cauldron, and the animal's intestines writhed and swarmed on the floor, as though possessed of a life of their own. They looked like coils of huge pink serpents. So much blood, such an orgy of disintegration, and yet every aspect of dismemberment was carried out with speed and skill. I guessed that this was not the only night the meatworks had been in use.

The bodies of the steers, now appearing curiously naked, were lowered through an open trap door to a lower floor. Here, another team awaited them. These men wore sweaters and scarves under their white aprons. Some even had leather helmets like First World War aviators, in total contrast to the heat and sweat on the top storey. This was the cold zone. Carcasses were easier to carve when cold. The men's breath fanned out like fog as they worked and the still-warm bodies of the steers steamed under bright electric bulbs.

This was to me a vision of hell; Dante's Inferno on several levels, down to the nethermost pit. What only minutes previously had been healthy animals were now reduced to steaks and cuts of meat, and all the time the stench outside grew as the furnace devoured the skins and the hair and the contents of the animals' stomachs.

I knew that at the other end of the factory the offal would come out as sausage meat or in any other of a dozen meat products, such as the filling for pies or pastries. I had eaten these often enough in the past and enjoyed them, but after this they would never taste quite the same. I realised now why meat workers so often refused to eat meat. They'd eat fish, junk foods, rice and beanshoots from Chinese takeaways; almost anything except flesh that had once been on hoof and bone.

I lowered myself carefully to the ground, flexed my cramped arms and legs and stood for a moment, leaning against the wall, feeling through the warm bricks the pound of the generators that powered the freezers in the cold room. Then I walked towards the road, wondering about my next move.

I was barely twenty feet away from the building, maybe even less, when my right instep caught a hidden trip wire in the grass. Behind and above me, under the eaves, an alarm bell clanged its warning. Foolishly, I had not thought that the place might have any electronic security system; it seemed far enough away from a town to be safe from any intruders. I started to run, but too late.

One man raced out of the darkness and brought me down heavily in a rugger tackle. Another kicked me in the groin as I lay gasping for breath on the ground. They picked me up as though I was already a carcass, carried me to the front of a truck parked behind the works, out of sight from the road, threw me down and turned on the headlights.

I lay in an extremity of agony, curled up like a foetus, trying to control the waves of pain that surged through my body with every beat of my heart. Georgie had taught me a way of holding my breath to calm the mind, to force the brain to think of something else. This is easy enough to say, not so easy to do, but I did my best, and slowly the worst of the cramping pain receded. I opened my eyes and I didn't like what I saw. Their faces were rough, hard, cruel. They looked like the original convicts – not the sheep stealers but the ones transported for murder.

'On your feet!' ordered the man who had tackled me first. 'What the hell are you doing here, hanging about?'

'Walking around,' I said. 'There's no law against that, is there?'

'Don't give me that shit! You black up your face every time you take a walk? Where you from?'

'I got a lift from Darwin on a road train, saw some work going on here, wondered what it was, and jumped.'

'Who're you with? Who you working for?'

'No one. I'm on my own.'

As soon as I admitted this, I realised, too late, that I had made an idiotic and dangerous mistake. All kinds of people jump road trains every day, usually drifters, students who have dropped out of their study courses, young and foolish girls out from England and looking for a thrill. Often, no one knows where they are from or where they are going; or even who they are. If they die or disappear, there need be no trouble, no questions asked, because no one knows what questions to ask, or about whom. It was madness for me to allow these men to imagine for a moment that I was one of this vagrant army, rootless, totally on my own.

I took a deep breath, meaning to tell them that if anything happened to me a lot of important people would want to know where and how and why. This was not much of a threat, but it seemed my only one. But before I could speak, the man hit me in the stomach. I fell forward. His companion pulled me upright by my shirt front.

'I'll get Jack,' he said briefly, and ran into the building. Another rustler came out with him. He was built like a solid brick privy, wearing a white overall, now red with blood. He had on red rubber gloves, streaming with blood and fat and slime.

'Who are you, mate?' he asked.

'Bruce is my name,' I said.

'Bruce what? Bruce who?'

I shrugged. He hit me, not too hard, but as a warning, a trailer for violence to come. The blow sent me reeling.

'Anyone know this bloke?'

'No. Never seen him. He's just a bum. But he'd know us again. If he gets the chance.'

'You reckon he's working for someone?'

'Could be. He's all blacked up. He's after something all right, this bastard.'

'What do you think he's seen?'

'He was round the back of the building. The windows are screened there.'

'Not higher up, they aren't.'

Someone else now came out from behind the building. He carried a powerful torch.

'There are marks all down the wall,' he announced angrily. 'The bastard's climbed a pipe. He must have seen the whole damn thing.'

'So let's do him now,' said Jack instantly. There was no doubt who was leader.

'You mean kill him?'

'What else? We can't have him wandering about. We let him

go, he can pick us all out tomorrow or the next day. Why risk that? He's on his own, on the road. No one knows where he's going so no one will know where he's gone.'

'I don't like it,' said someone from the darkness. 'Too many of us would know. One of us might take a bit too much and boast about it, then we're all in the shit. Accessories after the fact.'

'You talk like a bloody lawyer, mate.'

'I'm talking bloody sense, Jack.'

Jack shrugged. 'Well, turn the other way, then you won't see nothing. What you don't see, you can't know about.'

'How you going to do him, Jack?'

'Strip him. Burn his clothes and put him through the mincer. Let the Japs eat him. Potted meat. Sausage toad. Whatever they want.'

'That's murder.'

'You could call it that. But we're going to do time for rustling, years maybe, if this bastard gets out. So let's stop him getting out. There's only one way – keep him here. We can't keep him here alive, so he stays here bloody dead!'

Jack turned towards me. For an absurd moment I thought he was going to ask my opinion.

'You'll not get away with this,' I told him, trying to sound confident.

'Who the hell says not? You, you bastard? You've got a bloody nerve!'

'I got some money,' I said.

'We don't want your bloody money.'

But as though to prove I did have money on me, I put my right hand into my trouser pocket and slipped the coins, the shrapnel, between the fingers, closed my fist. I took my hand out. Jack bent forward inquisitively.

'What you got there?' he asked me.

'This!' I said.

I hit him with all my strength in the face. I felt the sharp edges of the coins smash into his cheekbone. Then someone behind me punched me in the left kidney. I swung round as I fell, brought my right hand across his windpipe. He dropped. Someone else out in the darkness beyond the headlights blew a whistle. Now men came streaming out of the building, moving like shadowy figures in a strange and terrible ballet of violence, half white, half red in the dust and the blaze of the truck's headlights.

'What the shit's going on?' someone cried in amazement, staring down at me as I lay on my back in the red dust.

'This bastard's spying on us. He's done Jack.'

'No, he hasn't,' said Jack, holding up one hand to his face. 'I'll kill the bastard.'

Against one man, even two, I might have prevailed. But against this number I was good as dead. And with this realisation a strange and curious feeling of acceptance came over me. There was no way out; this must be the end of the road.

Through a red mist of pain and darkness, I peered up at them. Some held cleavers or meat hooks, reddened with the blood of beasts; others, knives with hair and flesh still sticking to them, steaming.

Within minutes I'd be stripped and flung into the churning, roaring machinery at the far end of the building, probably not even dipped into the vat beforehand. There was no need for that; my skin wasn't as tough as a steer's coat. No one would ever know what had happened to me. Not my mother. Not Crabtree. Not Georgie. No one. I would have simply gone walkabout and disappeared. Lots of other people did every year; now I would join them.

Jack stood up. The other men parted to let him come through. He kicked me in the stomach as I lay. Then he bent down, picked me up by my shirt, brought his elbow up across my chin. I dodged the worst of the terrible blow but even so I felt my mouth fill with broken teeth.

'I'm going to put you through the mincer all the bloody way,' he said grimly. 'Get his clothes off!'

The others jumped on me, ripped off my shirt, my trousers, my underpants, my shoes. I stood before them, naked as Adam, streaked with blood and dust, bruised, and shining with sweat.

Jack came towards me, grinning now at my plight. He tripped me expertly, then with two others dragged me up the ramp into the building. I fell heavily on a floor already slippery with animal dung and urine, and began to slide forward as rollers set into the concrete between two metal walls carried me on towards the jaws of the machine.

I still had about thirty feet to go and I tried desperately to escape, twisting, turning, attempting to grip the smooth metal sides, but still the gap between the machine and me shrank steadily and inexorably. I strove to jam my bare feet against the sides above the rollers, to grip them with my hands splayed out against the metal, but the walls streamed with water from the vat and were slimy with damp tufts of hair and animal fat. The jaws of the mincer, opening, closing, opening again, loomed closer and closer ahead of me, bright raw metal teeth in the blaze of unshaded 1000 watt bulbs.

I struggled even more frantically, leaping and bucking like a fish on a hook – and to as little purpose. As in a nightmare, I heard men shouting, cheering as they watched one of their own kind about to die. This prospect of a death, a human life being cut down, had the same effect on them as a public hanging used to exert on those who witnessed it a century and a half ago. It was a spectacle, no faking, no special effects, just the public death of a stranger.

Twenty feet, ten, five, four. The stench of hot oil from the bearings, the salty smell of blood and melting fat became almost overpowering. I closed my eyes and prepared to die.

And then, inexplicably, the engine cut out. The rollers stopped revolving. The mincer's jaws locked open. A little blood from the last carcass they had devoured dribbled out from them.

'What's wrong?' Jack shouted angrily in the sudden silence. 'Who's thrown the switch?'

I lay exhausted, watching him as he ran to a control panel on the wall. And then I saw other figures move around him and behind the rustlers. These were dark-skinned men, Aborigines all, their faces covered in grey ash. They rose silently from the bushes like an army of avenging, silent, terrible shadows. Then all the lights went out.

With wild shouts and war cries, they leaped on the rustlers. Knives clattered uselessly away in clouds of red dust. I crawled on hands and knees over the slippery rollers, away from the mincer, until I reached the end of the ramp and could stand upright on a firm footing in the light of the truck's headlamps.

I grabbed a meat hook that had fallen from someone's hand and waded into the rustlers myself. I smashed the hook against skulls, arms, knees. Men hammered at my head and shoulders, but I barely felt their blows. Relief from having stepped back from the brink of eternity poured through my blood like liquid fire. I was drained of all mercy, all humanity. I was an animal, not concerned with right or wrong. I wanted revenge. And I had it.

Gradually, the fighting eased, then ceased. Some rustlers writhed feebly on the ground like beasts with broken backs, or grasped arms bent at unnatural angles. Another held his broken jaw closed against his teeth. I regarded them all without pity or compassion. I didn't care a damn about any of them or their injuries, whether they lived or whether they died. They had been willing to see me murdered. How they fared now was not my concern. But Jack was. Towards him I felt an all-consuming hatred. There was not room in the wide world for both of us.

The engine began to run again. The lights came on. I heard unseen cold-room refrigerator motors pound as their pumps drew heat from the steers' warm flesh. At the end of the rollers, the mincer's steel teeth champed uselessly, waiting to be fed.

Animals jammed on the ramp began to low nervously, or maybe gratefully as though they somehow realised they had also been reprieved.

I did not know who the Aborigines were, where they had come from, or why they had fought the rustlers. All I knew was that they had saved my life. Then I turned and saw Georgie. He was calmly turning the animals round, slapping their flanks to persuade them back and into the truck. When the last one was inside, he locked up the tailgate and crossed over to me. I picked up my clothes, put them on.

'Hurt, Ian?' he asked briefly, as though I had been struck by a 'no ball' in a friendly cricket match.

'Not badly,' I told him just as casually. 'I'm alive. Thanks to all of you. And you especially.'

'I told you those blokes were bad news,' he replied. 'Now maybe you'll believe me. They've made life hard enough for us, but they won't do that again in a hurry.'

'There's one not going to have the chance. Ever again. Jack. The leader.'

'We know him,' Georgie said grimly.

'Well,' I said, 'you'd better say goodbye to him, because you won't know him any longer. He's going.'

'Where to?'

'Through the mincer. What he planned for me.'

'You can't do that, Ian,' said Georgie earnestly. 'That's murder.'

'Who are you to talk about murder?' I asked him roughly, barely realising what I was saying. 'What about that American guy, the Stranger, you lot had sung to death?'

He looked at me sharply.

'You can't prove anything,' he said defensively.

'I don't want to prove anything. I don't need to. But if you let this bastard live, he'll come after you. He'll recognise you again, even with your ash make-up – and me. It's his life or ours, Georgie.'

'Don't do it,' Georgie pleaded. 'They won't rustle again. Some of them can barely walk.'

I turned away. I did not want to listen to Georgie's voice of reason. I still wanted revenge.

Jack was leaning against a tree. He had been hit on the head; he was dazed, but nothing serious. I crossed over to him.

'How are you?' I asked as though I cared.

He looked at me, his eyes not quite focusing. Perhaps he did not even recognise me.

'Crook,' he said.

'Don't worry about that,' I told him. 'In five seconds, you'll be dead. And death's the final cure for all ailments.'

As I spoke, and before he could reply, I tripped him as only minutes before he had tripped me. He fell forward onto the rollers. They carried him, screaming and thrashing about in terror and despair, towards the mincer. Death lay only feet and seconds away. I knew exactly how he felt.

'Help me!' he screamed in anguish. 'For Christ's sake, help me! You're going to kill me.'

'You were going to kill *me*,' I shouted back.

'No,' he gasped. 'I didn't mean it. It was just a threat.'

'So's this,' I shouted. At that precise moment, I realised I did not mean to kill him, just to frighten him, to show him where his best interests lay – as far away from me as possible. As I watched him wriggling, writhing to try and escape, pity began to dissolve my rage. Jack seemed pathetic rather than dangerous; the approach of death diminishes all pretensions.

The rollers steadily propelled him towards the champing maw of the great machine. He was still quite safe, I told myself, only he did not know it. I walked round the side of the ramp to press the red 'Stop' button on the control panel. I had seen Georgie standing by it when he re-started the machinery. I was only feet from the button when suddenly the truck lights went out, and so did the 1000 watt bulbs in the ceiling.

Once more we were in total darkness. I jumped forward to

stab the button, and immediately my arms were pinioned to my sides.

'Let me go!' I shouted. 'He'll die!'

There was no reply. I struggled, kicked, tried to butt with my head, jab with my elbows, but unseen Aborigines held me as tightly as the jaws of a metal vice. Then the lights came on as quickly as they had gone out. Georgie stood in front of me, shielding the button with his body.

I heard Jack scream. He was struggling frantically, his legs flailing out wildly. The rollers inexorably pushed him forward. He screamed again as the bloodied cogs trapped his wrists, his arms, then drew in his whole trunk. Then, mercifully, there was silence, broken only by the pounding of the refrigerator motor and the whine of the electric engine that powered the mincer. One moment a man had been lying on the rollers; the next, the rollers were empty. I turned to Georgie.

'You've killed him!' I shouted hoarsely. 'You've killed him! And after what you said. You're a bloody murderer! I only meant to scare him.'

Georgie said nothing for a moment.

'He would have killed you,' he replied dully.

'I know. But he didn't.'

'He would have come back,' Georgie said. 'You said so yourself. This is a big, rough country, Ian,' he went on quietly. 'The death of a bad man does not diminish any of us.'

I turned away, into the darkness, beyond the headlights and the Aborigines, and the rustlers lying on the ground. All the others had disappeared. There had been no witnesses except the Aborigines and me, and Georgie knew he could count on our silence. All my resentment, my burning lust for revenge, had vanished. I leaned against the wall of the building and was violently sick.

I stood there shaking, and then I saw Georgie near me, regarding me with compassion; an old man whose life had always been hard, who lived by the ancient rules, watching the young man who, he thought, had had it all so easy. In that moment of realisation, I grew up. I had learned at first hand how little one human life matters in the context of the universe, and I felt bereft, bemused. I had lost an innocence I would never again recapture. Others had experienced this irreversible change in war, earthquake, a fire, a flood. I had learned this basic truth in a concrete building off the Stuart Highway. No matter where or what the schoolroom, the lesson is always the same, and one all men must learn.

Georgie must have sensed my thoughts.

'We'd better go home,' he said quietly.

'Yes. We'd better go home,' I agreed. 'But won't the police want to know what's happened – or at least find out?'

'Only if someone tells them. And no one here will do that. They'll see blood, maybe a body or two, and a dead man in the machine. What they do then is up to them. The rustlers will clear up a lot of the mess – when they're able to walk.'

'Won't their mates come after us?'

'How will they know us?' he replied. 'Look at our faces.'

He bent down in the light of the truck headlamp. He was covered with ash, slashed with streaks of black and red dust. It could be a war mask, a death mask. I would not have recognised Georgie myself except for his voice.

'And remember, if they do come after us, we know what *they* look like. And if anyone tries to make trouble, we'll be able to stop him. That answer your question?'

I nodded.

We began to walk back along the road together.

'I warned you to keep out of this,' Georgie said, almost sadly. 'But you are young, and young men always think they know best.'

'I thought I did,' I agreed. 'Now I am not so sure I know anything. I feel like the Hungarian who went to England in the nineteen thirties and made a great success as a film director. He couldn't speak English very well, and one day he thought he was being taken for a sucker by his employees, so he told them angrily: "You think I know fuck nothing. Actually, *I know fuck all*." I feel like that.'

Mojo sat under the scrubbed white awning on the afterdeck of his yacht. He wore a white linen suit, gold-rimmed dark glasses and was smoking a seven-inch Havana cigar. He looked bland as a Buddha and twice as pleased with himself.

Dick Ford sat rather timidly on the edge of a deckchair facing him. On a table by his side was a glass of Pimms, which he sipped nervously. Mojo watched him, gauging his man, no mark of his thoughts creasing his countenance.

'So how exactly did you arrange it?' he asked, as though he did not know. It pleased him to hear other people's accounts of matters he had personally organised. Sometimes he learned something, either about their recollections or his own. Most people, he knew, had selective memories: they selected those that showed them and their actions in the best light.

'Well, sir,' said Ford, thankful of the opportunity to talk, 'I had to find an old car first of all. We managed to locate a Triumph which the owner had owned for some years. He was willing to sell, but it was in pretty poor condition. We put this into someone else's yard, actually one of your own local executives, sir, Mr Hong.'

'I know that,' said Mojo. 'He played his part well, I believe. He is a good man. And then?'

'Then, sir, we advertised the car for quite a time, in Katherine. But the subject didn't respond, so Mr Hong wrote him a letter. That brought him out. He bought it, and I waited for him by the road train and made him an offer which he accepted – forty-two thousand five hundred Australian dollars.'

'A very good offer. So where is the car?'

'Back with Mr Hong.'

'Would you like the car, Mr Ford, or a cash bonus for your work?'

'A bonus, I think, sir. I have really no use for an old car.'

'So,' said Mojo. 'Give instructions to have it renovated by any local specialist in such work. Charge the work to Mojo Engineering as an experimental project. We can then sell it to the highest bidder.'

'Very good, sir.'

The mean old bastard, Ford thought. This yacht cost $10,000,000 if it cost a cent, and here he is trying to save a few thousand. Well, that's probably why he's so rich. He had always heard that taking money from a rich man could be harder than pulling a crocodile's tooth. Both hated to part with what was theirs.

'You discovered what bank Crabtree uses in Katherine?'

'Yes, sir. He asked for the money to be transferred by draft to the City and Provincial there.'

'Very wise. No cheques, no cash. A prudent decision. You have done your part well, Mr Ford. It is fortunate that I found a member of the London branch of our company actually on detachment here. Send all your bills to Mojo Electronics. They will take care of them. And I wish you a pleasant stay for the remainder of your time in Australia. I shall watch your progress upwards through my organisation.'

'Thank you very much, sir. If I can be of any further assistance to you, please let me know.'

'I will most certainly do that,' Mojo assured him.

He pressed a button for a steward to show Ford to the launch alongside and then watched the boat carve a scimitar of foam in the blue water as she headed for the shore.

He drew on his cigar. He was enjoying himself. It was agreeable to be in the situation where he could do what he was about to do. Everyone, he thought, would like to play God at some time in their lives. He was fortunate that for the last forty-odd years he had been able to do just that. But this was the first time he had done what he could have done, indeed should have done, all that time ago.

* * *

I slept well in what was left of that night. After all, I'd had a long walk, been roughed up, as near as damn it come out as meat paste or filling for a frankfurter, and then seen a man who would have killed me go through the mincer himself. I needed my sleep.

When I came downstairs next morning the old man was sitting at the bare wooden table in the kitchen. He had a plate of three cold fried eggs, half a dozen rashers of congealing bacon and about half a pound of baked beans in front of him, but he wasn't eating anything. He was just sitting, looking, maybe at knot holes in the wooden table top, maybe not; his mind was obviously miles away – he didn't even comment on my split lip. Then I saw what had put him off his breakfast; a big, long envelope which he'd slit with a knife was on the table.

'Bad news?' I asked him.

He did not reply, just pushed the letter over to me.

'Read what the bastard says,' he told me.

'What bastard?'

'Bloody bank. They're on my back, like the old man of the sea. If you don't need their money, they're shovelling it at you, can't give you enough. But the moment things get a bit rough, they panic, like a bloke who lends you a raincoat and then wants it back soon as it starts to rain.'

I picked up the letter, read it. The writer went straight for the jugular: 'We are surprised and concerned that, in view of our recent discussions and our various letters of the 17th ult, the 23rd ult and the 4th inst., there has still been no movement on your account. It would appear to us that this is now so seriously overdrawn above the agreed limit of accommodation that there may be no other way of regularising the situation than by foreclosing on your station, the deeds of which you will recall we hold as security.

'As you may know, we have several clients who are looking to buy land in your area, and if need be a sale should not be too difficult to arrange. Owing to the severe drought and consequent deterioration of stock, as well as the amount of rustling in your neighbourhood, I am advised that the price per square mile would be in the region of $25–30.

'The writer will be in your area towards the middle of next week and will take the opportunity of calling upon you to discuss whether you expect any significant inflow of monies from any source. Otherwise, head office is of the opinion that the only solution will be to sell the property. Should it realise more than your indebtedness to the bank, the monies, after payment of essential fees and duties, would, of course, be credited to your account.'

I folded the letter and put it back in the envelope; it wasn't the sort of communication one wanted to leave around for anyone else to read.

'What are you going to do?' I asked him.

He shrugged. 'I've no option. I owe the bastards money and, with compound interest, I owe more every bloody minute. They hold the deeds. I hold nothing. The bloody rustlers are skinning the stock every night, the bank's skinning me, I'm getting older, and I've about had enough of them all. I reckon even if I sold up for twenty-five dollars, which is a giveaway price, I should come out of it with a few thousand myself. Not much, but something.

'But I hate like hell to sell at that price! I had a brother, dead now, who had a college education. I dunno what it taught him, but he taught me a motto: "*Nihil illegitimae carborundum* – Don't let the bastards grind you down!" That's what this banking bastard wants to do. He sits on his arse and adds up sums that represent other people's lives. Like those old buggers who wrote hieroglyphics on the pyramids, he only deals in symbols, plus and minus. In my case, mostly minuses. If he comes up here into the real world, he'll be out of breath before he's walked half a mile. Get him afork a horse, and he'd bloody rupture himself. He's not a man, he's an accounting machine with balls.'

'What would you think was a fair price?'

'Anything above thirty.'

'That means thirty-one,' I told him, trying to cheer him up.

'Hell, you're as sharp as all the others,' he said bitterly. 'Give me even thirty-five dollars a square mile, and I'm out running. Not laughing, mind you, but in the clear.'

'How many square miles have you here?'

'About five thousand, give or take. Pretty good station, this.'

'I can see that,' I said. 'What about staff?'

'Aborigines, mostly, and all going. The others went weeks ago. We had to lay 'em off. We just couldn't pay 'em.'

'So how do the Aborigines eat? What do they use for money?'

'They get a bit of welfare, some of 'em. Do odd jobs, work here and there. But what can I do? We haven't painted the place for years. My old car out there, my old Mojo, all it's fit for is an old crocks race. But there it is. Got no rain, got no loot. Simple equation.'

'Let me think about it. I might be able to find a buyer.'

'You?'

He looked at me in surprise, frowning, eyes narrowed. Was I on the bank manager's side, one of those city slickers who wanted to buy a good station cheaply just to show it as figures on a sheet of paper, a plus on a computer screen?

'I'll do what I can,' I told him.

The old man shrugged and started to eat, but without any appetite. I knew I had cheered him up a little, although he didn't put much faith in me – after all, why should he? We'd only met the previous evening but, to the despairing, any hope is better than none. What he thought was that I was going to look for a buyer. He didn't think the buyer could be me.

I couldn't face three eggs, but I had a couple soft boiled, a pot of coffee, toast and honey, and then I went out into the sun. Heat was coming up out of the dry, cracking red earth like a great oven door opening, and I stood, feeling it flood through my body, rich as wine. I love the heat, but it can kill, and it was killing this man's farm, burning away his whole livelihood as I have seen forest fires burn away a landscape.

I saw Georgie walking past, and called out to him.

'Thanks again!' I said.

He just nodded in acknowledgement. 'What are your plans now?'

'I'm going on to Katherine in the road train.'

'You'll be lucky. The driver's got some trouble with his diesel. Got dust in it. He's cleaning his filters. That'll take a couple of hours yet.'

'So maybe you can help me while I wait.'

'To do what?'

'I want to know if it's going to rain – and if so, when.'

'How should I know?'

'You people know lots of things we white fellows don't.'

'Give me twenty minutes.'

'Will you cast the runes, the bones?'

'Don't ask questions, then you don't get told lies,' he retorted.

I could see a glint in his eye. I had offered him a challenge.

Georgie was back in about half an hour.

'I got news,' he said, without any preamble. 'Rain. It's coming.'

'So's Christmas,' I replied, disappointed. 'When is the rain due?'

'You're like all white fellows – impatient. You want a time and a place and a date. I can't give you those exactly. No one can. But some of my friends can tell from signs they see in the sky, in the desert, in the animals. Within four months is what they say, and that's what I tell you.'

He wouldn't say any more.

I did a few calculations of my own on the back of an envelope, and by then the driver was ready to set off.

We drove down to Katherine, not talking much. We had
nothing worth a fish's tit to say to each other in any case. He
drove fast. Most road train drivers do, right bang in the middle
of the Highway. He chewed as he drove. He didn't offer me
any because he wasn't chewing Spearmint but amphetamines.
Without them it would be too easy to fall asleep, just watching
a wide tarmac ribbon of road, straight as a Roman arrow,
unwind under the wheels, on and on and on, with only baking,
shimmering desert on either side and the occasional wallaby or
kangaroo loping across the road.

One driver, not too long ago, was refused a drink at some
trucking station, so he went back to his train, unhitched the
trailers, chewed another amphy and drove right smack into the
place. Killed half a dozen people, injured twenty more – and
then wisely he went walkabout.

They found him, of course, but they never mentioned the
drugs; they thought he was drunk. Or, rather, they said they
thought he was drunk. People wouldn't like it too much if they
knew that while driving these giant forty-ton locomotives of
the road, bellowing up and down at full bore, horns blaring,
ordering everyone else to get out of the way or get crushed, the
men at the wheel could be high.

We coasted into the road-train park outside Katherine late in
the afternoon. I thanked the driver, rang for a cab, and was
home by dusk.

A week later to the day, I had just finished my car auction in a
yard I rented off Giles Street when I saw Crabtree waiting for
me behind the cashier's desk.

I hadn't seen him for some days – he had been away in the
Alice – and since he never showed much interest in my activities beyond telling me gloomily that making money wasn't as
easy as I thought – or, indeed, as I was proving – I wondered
what had brought him out to see me.

When I was selling cars one at a time, I used to wash and

polish each car and clean the engine with detergent. This took an inordinate amount of time and was a chore I could well do without. When I started selling by auction I used the local car wash, but then I had a much better idea. Why should I pay to clean cars when I could persuade their owners to do this for me?

I offered three prizes of $100, $50 and $25 for the cleanest cars. This meant that every seller cleaned his car, hoping to win a prize, and I had possibly fifty cars cleaned inside and out for a total cost of $175, which was a good bargain by any standards. And they went through at prices 10 per cent above what uncleaned cars would fetch, which was even better.

This week the prices had been higher than I'd expected so I was in a good mood and waved cheerfully to Crabtree.

'Have a beer?' I asked him.

Crabtree shook his head. His face looked lined and grey and somehow sunk in on itself, as though originally the flesh had been designed for a bigger man and fitted only loosely over his bones.

'What's the matter?' I asked him.

'Your mother. She's real crook.'

'When I saw her filming in Darwin she was driving herself pretty hard. I told you. But she was doing what she wanted to do, what she can do best. Acting.'

'She's a good actress,' Crabtree agreed.

I didn't know then just how good she had been, or what he really meant, but somehow I sensed it was a statement on two levels.

'Where is she, then?' I asked him.

'Home. She came back by ambulance. They had her in hospital up there but she wanted to be home.'

'Hell!' I said. 'She must be bad. Couldn't they do anything for her in Darwin?'

'No,' he replied. 'There's nothing anyone can do for her now. She's asking for you, so I came down to fetch you. I guess we humans are like animals. We sense when our time is up. She wanted to come home to die.'

'You mean she *is* dying? Now?'

He nodded, as though suddenly he could not speak. I could see that his lips were trembling and I realised, for the first time, that he loved her. Or maybe he was just crying for himself. Crabtree had been married twice. One wife was dead and the other dying, and soon he would be on his own again. I had a sudden glimpse of the loneliness ahead for him.

'Let's go, then.' I explained to the cashier what was happening and jumped into the car with Crabtree.

The approach of death always casts a shadow on the living. Although the afternoon was still so hot that Katherine Terrace shimmered in the heat, I felt suddenly chilled. I could dimly imagine how Crabtree must feel, as though his heart was packed in ice, but I lacked the ability to reach out and tell him how sorry I was, and how much they both meant to me. Words are a difficult bridge to throw between generations, but I should have tried harder. At the time, however, I was wondering how my mother would look and what life would be like without her.

The sight of my mother shocked me. She had changed beyond all imagining since I had seen her in Darwin a little over a week ago. She did not seem like my mother at all, but someone who resembled her, someone much smaller, a little girl in the body of an older woman. The skin on her face was now almost transparent, her lips blue and bloodless, her hair thin and brittle and faded. She lay with her hands and bare arms outside the coverlet, and plucked constantly at it with fingers thin as the bones beneath the flesh. I was shocked, almost horrified by her appearance, because it was so unexpected.

'How are we, then?' I asked her with that ridiculous boisterousness the healthy display when visiting the terminally ill, as though by being over-cheerful they can somehow transfer excess vitality through verbal osmosis. She smiled and nodded slightly.

'Been better,' she admitted, not showing self-pity, simply stating an obvious fact.

'You'll be better yet,' I answered. She shook her head very gently, as though any more vigorous movement was either beyond her or a needless expenditure of energy.

'I'll make you a drink,' Crabtree told her. 'Milk with honey and rum do you?'

She nodded very slightly. I guessed he was offering to make her a drink to give himself something to do, an excuse to get out of the room, if only for a few minutes, so he would not have to keep watching her grow weaker and more feeble. And, like a good actress, she had picked up her cue.

'You've finished the films?' I asked her.

'Both,' she replied, and for the first time her eyes shone and sparkled. 'The director said he loved the rushes. Byron Corbin, the producer, is already talking to my agent about the third. I told them, like in the song, I should have known them years ago.'

'But you'll go on from here together,' I assured her, misquoting the lyric.

'No.'

'Rubbish! You must get better for that,' I insisted.

She said nothing. We both knew we were playing with words, fencing with optimistic phrases as false as a four-dollar bill.

'I wanted to see you,' she said, changing the subject. 'I have something to tell you, and I would rather you heard it from me than from anyone else.'

Her voice fell away to a whisper.

'Don't tire yourself, Ma,' I said. 'It can wait.'

'It has waited long enough,' she replied. 'But now I can't wait any longer. Actually, I've two things to tell you. I've already told you about Robert James. You know, the Australian.'

She paused.

'I've made quite a bit of money, Ma,' I said. 'I'm going over to

England to meet him and see what I can do there. Then there'll be two Australians, and two Territorians. Both of us right up there where the real money is.'

'Money. There are other things, Ian.'

'I know. And there's one other thing it can't buy – poverty!'

I was trying to cheer her up, and not succeeding. But what did she know about money? She had never had much.

'I know it doesn't always buy health or happiness, for such gifts are priceless. But have those who always imagine the rich must be miserable ever considered how much more wretched they would be without their wealth?'

'You talk just like the Australian,' said Amy, almost sadly, I thought, as though she had expected something different, a less commercial view.

'I suppose I am like him,' I said. 'After all, that's not too surprising. We are half-brothers.'

'He won't like being reminded. He always wanted to be on his own, even as a boy. He's a funny person, Ian.'

'You mean funny ha ha, or funny peculiar?'

'He's not interested in anything except money, and just in making it, not spending it. He lives in a terrace house like a factory worker – and probably one of his companies owns the factory! He's never been a big spender.'

Amy lay silent for a moment, eyes closed. The effort of talking seemed to have tired her beyond all reason. I did not tell her I knew that the Australian had helped her, unasked, by financing the two films. I should have told her in Darwin, but then I didn't want to hurt her feelings or damage her confidence. I knew nothing about her feelings for her elder son, and I wanted her to believe she had been selected on her own merits, not because he had insisted. She was a proud person, and I thought then that I did right. Now, I am not so sure.

She opened her eyes, looked at me and smiled weakly. She began to talk, and her voice seemed a little stronger.

'I have two confessions to make,' she said, and closed her

eyes as though she could not bear to look at me while she spoke. 'About you.'

She paused. I waited.

'It's ironic, isn't it, that the Australian's father was a lord?' she said, as though her thoughts were wandering off at a tangent. 'Perhaps that's where he got his gift for making money from.'

'Why not from you?' I asked her. 'You're my mother, too. And you seem to have survived pretty well.'

'People were very kind to me here. Australians *are* kind. No. Neither of you got the gift from me, Ian – which brings me to my first confession. I brought you up as my son, and I love you as my son. But – *I am not your mother.*'

'I don't understand you!' I cried. 'Of course you are!'

'No,' she said weakly, shaking her head. 'And Crabtree isn't your father, either. That's the second thing. Though he has been better to you than most fathers.'

'Then who *is* my father?' I asked her hoarsely. My safe little world of home was suddenly breaking down all around me. 'Why have you both kept this hidden from me all this time? Why didn't you tell me years ago?'

'Because it seemed best not to,' she replied wretchedly, opening her eyes and looking directly at me as though expecting me to challenge what she said.

'Then who are my parents?'

'I'll tell you. As you know, Crabtree was taken prisoner when Singapore fell. There was a fellow in Changi with him, an American, who apparently saved his life several times.'

'Was his name Crosby?' I asked her. Bits and pieces of a hitherto unimagined mosaic were beginning to fall into place in my mind, soft as snow flakes; but snow flakes can turn into ice and ice can cut like a razor.

She nodded. 'Crosby was moved from the camp with other Americans. Crabtree had no address for him. Then one day he turned up totally unexpectedly in the Alice. He'd been having a fling with an Aborigine woman. They had a child.'

'Me?'

'You. Crosby was dying. Leukaemia. Crabtree helped him as much as he could but, as with me now, there comes a time when no one can help you, when you can't even help yourself.

'Crabtree wanted to pay back his debt to Crosby, so after his death we brought you up. But you were never formally adopted. I don't know why. At the time it just seemed more paperwork and expense. What matters in such cases are not names on a bit of paper. It's the love you can give someone.'

'And you both gave me that,' I told her. 'I just wish I had known earlier. I could have understood so many other things.'

What I meant was that I would have instantly understood my affinity for Aborigines; how Georgie and I got on so well together; how I always felt at ease in their company when other people might feel embarrassed or even try to keep them at arm's length.

So I wasn't related in any way to the Australian. We were strangers. But did he know that? I asked Amy. She shook her head.

'No. He thinks of me as your mother.'

'He doesn't know about Lord Jackson either, does he?'

'Not from me. And I would be careful about telling him. There's no proof. James Jackson is dead. You don't want to rake over old ashes. If you start a fire, you could be the one who gets burnt.' Her voice now was barely above a whisper.

The thought that the Australian and I were strangers brought back to me the American I had met in the Alice.

'Why did that American, the man I call the Stranger, want to find Crosby?'

'I have no idea.'

'Does Crabtree know?'

'I don't think so.'

I wondered whether Georgie knew. I would find out if I could.

Then I heard Crabtree outside the room. He came in with the drink, put the beaker down on a side table.

'The doctor's here,' he announced, not looking at me.

I left them together and went out and sat in a chair on the back porch, feeling the sun warm on my face. My mind was racing like the torrent through Katherine Gorge. I did not want to have to talk to Crabtree just then; I did not want to hear any more explanations, any more excuses.

I wanted to decide who I was and, more important, who I was going to be. I wanted to get away from the sick room and the woman who was not my mother.

I had half promised to see someone out of town about a couple of vintage cars he was selling on behalf of a collector who had gone broke. I had no appointment, but I decided to go on the impulse. I packed my bag and took off.

I was away for three days. I didn't buy either of the cars. For the first time in any deal I did not know whether I wanted to go through with the transaction. I just couldn't make up my mind, and then, as quickly as I had left, I decided to come back to Katherine. And when I came home, I realised I had returned too late.

Amy was dead and Crabtree was out with the boys in a bar, drinking himself insensible.

I was up early next morning and sat on the back porch waiting for Crabtree to come downstairs. I heard him shambling about in his bedroom, and then a door slammed and he came downstairs into the breakfast room, yawning, rubbing sleep from his eyes.

'Hell, I had too much to drink,' he said gruffly.

'Imagine,' I replied, looking at him. I couldn't say exactly how I felt about him. I felt numb inside. The woman I had thought of all my life as my mother had never been my mother, and this man, who I had assumed was my father, was also no relation to me whatever. And neither had told me.

The coffee was still warm in the pot. Crabtree poured out a mug of black, stirred in three spoonfuls of sugar, drank it. I sat down opposite him. He looked at me and then looked away without meeting my eyes. He felt as guilty as I felt aggrieved.

'She told me about myself,' I began obliquely.

He nodded. 'It was bound to come out sooner or later, I suppose.'

'Why did you leave it so late?' I asked him.

He shrugged. 'Hindsight, we've all got twenty-twenty vision. I should have told you, but when you've got a kid around who believes you're his dad and calls you father, and thinks your wife is his mother, you don't want to spoil that. If you do, you're going to hurt him even more than you hurt yourself. Also, I'd always wanted a son. And now I had one. Well, sort of.'

'I'd like to have known,' I persisted. 'Then I might have understood so many things.'

'Like what things?'

'Why I feel so drawn to the Aborigines. Why Georgie is my best friend. Why I sympathise with them when they're up in arms because highways and railways are going through their sacred places.'

'That's all shit!' said Crabtree dismissively. 'They're heathen. Stone Age people. Railways, roads go through all sorts of other people's sacred places. They don't beef like this all the time.'

'Maybe they don't feel strongly about it. But I can't think of any case where that's actually happened. Can you?'

'Not off hand, but it must have,' he insisted. 'When they were building the railways in England in the last century, they cut through people's private estates, through graveyards, cemeteries. Nothing stood in their way. It can't, for a railway has to go in a straight line. Why, they build on cemeteries regularly in England, they're so short of space.'

'Maybe that's a reason there, but it's no reason here. Tell me more about Crosby. I want to know everything. I think I have the right.'

I still could not refer to him as my father. He was only a name. A stranger had come searching for him and now he was dead. Someone knew too much. About whom, or about what?

'Crosby,' said Crabtree slowly, pouring more coffee. 'He was a strange guy. American. My age, maybe a bit younger. College educated. Harvard or Yale, one of those places, I don't know which. Not now. It was a hell of a time ago, boy, a hell of a time ago. It was a different world then, different attitudes.

'We were thrown together in Changi. He'd been on some special mission attached to the Royal Navy. I don't know what it was. I never asked him. What the hell did it matter, anyhow? It had failed, otherwise we wouldn't have been in the bag together. But he was a good guy. He knew Japanese quite well, I don't know how. Maybe he had studied it at college or he'd taught himself it. Anyway he stood up for us. He could negotiate with the Nips when all we could do was try pidgin on them and get beaten with rifle butts for being insolent. Crosby knew the way the bastards thought. He was brave. They admired him for that. There was another thing. He was rich.'

'Very rich?' I asked.

'How the hell do I know? Someone who was rich then could be poor now. Money was different. There wasn't so much of it. And it went a far greater distance.'

'How did being rich help him?'

'In Changi, not a lot, but I reckon if you're rich, you don't have the worry of keeping afloat, like the rest of us. That's taken care of, so you can concentrate on other things. Like Crosby did.

'As months went on, more and more died, older men mostly. They hadn't the resistance. Dysentery, beri beri, malaria hit them, or they just lost faith in keeping alive. They were sure their wives were being unfaithful. They thought their children, families, had been bombed, killed, maimed. Remember, all we got was Jap propaganda. Britain was being annihilated. The Allies were finished, on the run. These blokes turned their faces to the wall. Like it says in the Bible, they literally gave up the ghost, the spirit that had kept them going. But not Crosby.

'There were Chinese on the other side of the wire who remembered when the British had run local firms and had treated them straight and paid them well. They believed that maybe, for all the Nips said and did, those days might come again. Or maybe they just wanted to repay good turns of the past. Anyhow, they'd smuggle in packets of rice in a twist of newspaper maybe, or a rolled-up rag in a tin, mixed with a bit of salt fish. That helped to keep us alive.

'Of course, it cost them money, and maybe their freedom if they were caught. So Crosby gave each of them chits. They'd say what it was worth to them for each little consignment, and after the war he paid up every goddamn cent to everyone. Went back specially to Singapore to do it. He kept his word. He was a gentleman, son. I can't say more than that.

'Mind you, he didn't end the war there. He was pushed off to Japan. They shipped a lot of the brighter ones out, officers mostly, and then other ranks like him, who should have been officers. Maybe he was one, but he never pulled rank, never claimed to be anything but an enlisted man. They dumped them in prisons all over Japan, Korea. And they advertised what they'd done, broadcast it.

'Tokyo Rose, a woman broadcaster – every day she put out her stuff. She'd say where these blokes were, give their names, service numbers, their home addresses. They hoped the Allies wouldn't bomb those places. Crosby was in Hiroshima.'

'When the atomic bomb landed?'

'Yes. I never heard from him. I thought he was dead. I had an address for him in the States. I wrote to it several times, but the letters were always returned, "Gone away".'

That sounded like the old call the huntsmen make in England, so Amy had once told me. Gone to ground. When a huntsman dies and he's being buried, his colleagues blow that call on their horns; it's a kind of Last Post. Gone away, gone to ground, gone walkabout.

'So how did you know he paid back those debts to the Chinese in Singapore?' I asked.

'Got a lot of Chinese in the north, here, Darwin, Cairns, with relations there. When they heard I'd been in Changi they told me how he had come back and paid every cent. A man of honour.

'Then one day in the Alice I was in a bar and there he was, at the other end. Cigarette going, tube of Fosters at his elbow. I couldn't believe it, nor could he. He'd been in most countries trying to settle down – what you kids now call trying to find yourselves.

'Maybe we found ourselves years ago and didn't like the discovery. He couldn't go back to the old life. He'd spent his money; wives, divorce settlements, alimony, lawyers, all that crap. I know he wanted what everyone born in a big country wants – space, to be on his own.

'Have you ever wondered, son, why people from little countries like England, Portugal, Holland were the great colonists? Why they were the ones who set out in their little boats to find new countries? They were quite happy in their old countries, most of them, but they lacked one thing – space. Room to move, to be themselves. And that's what you've got here, what everyone's got here in Australia. You can drive for hours and not see another soul, and that's what life should be like.

'I read once that if you put a lot of rats in a small space, like a box, they start fighting, eating each other, and one rat always comes out on top, the head rat. I'll tell you another thing about them. You put a lot of rats in a box and you make life hard for them, they'll organise themselves into a sort of pyramid. The head rat, the cleverest one, the king rat, sits right on top of the heap, so he's away out of all the danger. You give 'em space, they don't attack each other at all. Always remember that. Keep out of cities, boy. Even Katherine's getting too crowded now to my mind.'

'Tell me about my Aborigine mother,' I asked him. I guessed he was dodging the main issue.

'She was a good-looking woman in her own way. She'd been in the north, met Crosby. Been in Darwin for a time. They came south with you. By then he was real crook – leukaemia, blood cells all gone wrong. I reckon that was due to radiation at Hiroshima. People are claiming all sorts of compensation now, but it was too late for him. He didn't want you to be put in an orphanage or grow up wild in the bush with the Abos. He asked me if I could help him. Heaven knows, he'd helped me often enough, son. I'd have been dead half a century ago if it hadn't been for him. It was the least I could do, and I did it.

'Amy wasn't so keen, but she grew to like you. She was a fine woman. She raised you as her own. Maybe she thought one day you'd show talent of some kind, like her real son. Not that the Australian has ever spent a cent of all his money on his old mother, to my knowledge. He could have revolutionised her life, but there was some argument they had when he was starting off and I reckon he's a bit bent in the mind. All he can think of is making more money. Nothing else matters. Anyhow, this woman came down, just to be near you. Nora Blackfellow.'

'Of course,' I said. 'Saw her quite recently.'

'Yeah. But the other Abos didn't altogether take to her.'

'Because of Crosby? Because of me?' I asked quickly.

'I don't know what reason. They got their own reasons. They don't tell white fellows. You know that, same as I do. She's gone, anyhow.'

'She's not dead?'

'I shouldn't think so. Just gone walkabout. Maybe they pointed the bone at her, told her where her best interests lie. She'll not be back.'

'I'd like to find her.'

'You're wasting your time.'

'Can you tell me anything more about either of them?'

'That's all I know, son. Except Crosby's buried out in the cemetery and some goddamn Yank came screwing around trying to find him.'

'I know,' I said. 'He gave me five hundred dollars if I could help him.'

'He'd have given you a bloody fortune if he'd known who you were.'

'If I'd known who I was then, I'd have told him. Why do you think he wanted to find Crosby?'

'Maybe he was hired by a lawyer acting for one of Crosby's ex-wives. Wondered why he wasn't coughing up his dollars to her. Maybe Crosby had left some money, shares, I don't know what. Private dicks and lawyers only come after you if they want money. They smell money like we smell shit. They buzz round it like flies. He went on his way.'

'He's dead,' I said.

'So I heard.'

'So I guess that trail's cold.'

'Maybe it was never very warm. Well, any more questions, son?'

'No,' I said. 'Nothing, but I think I'll move out.'

'You're of age. I reckon you should. Where are you going?'

'I've got enough money,' I told him, without mentioning how much. 'I'll buy an apartment somewhere. I don't need a back yard. I just want a place to sleep and eat. I can lock it up when I'm not there. Like an animal's bolthole. People get tied by possessions. We go after them and then we can't leave them in case someone else gets hold of them. We don't own them, they own us.'

'That's Abo thinking,' he said. 'I reckon there's a lot in it.'

'I reckon there can be everything in it.'

I left him then. There was a lot in that theory, of course. A hell of a lot, but it still didn't deflect me from my aim: to get rich, to make a fortune bigger than the Australian's, to have power. Maybe I could do some good with it, or what I thought would be good. With enough money no one would ever mess me around again. I'd be my own man. My own ancestor, if you like.

I went out into the sun and did not look back.

I thought I had left everything behind me, my bruised feelings, my pride, my love for Australia, but of course, I hadn't. I carried them with me, baggage for my journey, extra weight on my walkabout.

Amy was buried at the end of the week; I came back for her funeral. As the leading car in the cortège turned off Giles Street into the cemetery, we passed half a dozen elderly people putting flowers on graves. They stood up awkwardly, as though they had been engaged in some peculiarly private, almost secret act and felt embarrassed at being disturbed by strangers.

In the far corner, a man in a dark blue suit who had been photographing one particular grave put away his Mojo camera and came towards us. Amy's plot was almost in the centre of the cemetery. Everything had been arranged with the theatrical precision of professional undertakers; they had even put sheets of plastic grass round the raw, newly dug hole, to conceal the nakedness of the grave.

The cars stopped. Crabtree and I, as the chief mourners, followed the coffin, borne on the shoulders of the undertakers' men. A number of other people stepped out of the following cars. They were mostly women who had helped in the shop or who now worked in the supermarket at the tills or stocking the shelves. I also saw some old customers who, I knew, owed the Crabtrees for goods. This was not the time to remind them.

We were not a very impressive bunch of mourners, possibly

no more than twenty. As the clergyman intoned the sonorous words, 'In the midst of life we are in death . . . thou knowest, Lord, the secrets of our hearts . . . Earth to earth, ashes to ashes, dust to dust . . .', I looked around at their faces.

Crabtree was weeping. He must have genuinely loved Amy, but I guessed that she had never loved him as much as she had loved, briefly and passionately, another man who had died nearly two generations earlier in Hong Kong. Is love a chemical attraction, is it spiritual, or simply a physical phenomenon – or an amalgam of all three? I had never been in love then and so I did not know, but I wondered.

The other faces were all sombre in the moment of burial and then I saw the face of the man in the blue suit. He had come up to our group silently, walking on the cropped grass in rubbersoled shoes. Close to, he seemed older than he had appeared in the distance. He was either Chinese or Japanese, with that peculiarly unwrinkled yellowish skin unique to the East.

Crabtree dropped a single flower on the coffin and turned away as a handful of earth rattled on the brass nameplate screwed onto the polished wood.

We drove in silence to the motel. Crabtree had asked friends and neighbours, whether they had come to the funeral or not, to join us for tea, or something stronger, and sandwiches. It seemed easier to let the motel handle this than to attempt to do it in his small house.

As the youngest there, I ushered the guests into the main room. The manager had switched off his TV for once and put on a tie and jacket. He nodded significantly towards the man in the blue suit.

'He's staying here,' he explained importantly. 'Japanese. Got a kind of Kung Fu fighter fellow with him. Says he's his male secretary. More like a bodyguard, I'd say.'

'Who is he?'

'Name of Mojo.'

'You mean like the car?'

'Yes. Like the car. I saw him down at the Mojo garage poking around the service area.'

'Where's he from?'

'Perth. Hired a plane. A jet. It's waiting out at the airport. Putting up the crew here, too. But he's with your party, you must know him.'

'No,' I said. 'I don't. But I will.'

First, I checked that everyone had a drink and a sandwich and some more than one, according to their needs and capacity. There weren't too many takers for the tea; and most who drank that laced it liberally with whisky. As alcohol loosened tongues, the older women jabbered away about deaths and serious illnesses and complicated internal operations, subjects that spring so readily to mind with the elderly at any funeral, when the mourners secretly congratulate themselves they are not the one being mourned.

Then I approached the man in the blue suit.

'You all right?' I asked him. 'Have a drink?'

'You are very kind,' he said, 'but I already have had one.'

I held out my hand. 'Crabtree is my name. Ian Bruce.'

'Mojo,' he said.

'Like the car?'

'Yes. I founded the firm,' he said simply.

I was astonished, but he was obviously telling the truth. His suit and silk shirt were of a quality I had never previously encountered in Katherine.

'I saw you in the cemetery. Did you know my mother?'

I still called Amy that; the habit of a lifetime is not easily changed.

'No,' he admitted. 'I was photographing the grave of someone I knew many years ago. It is sad, my friend, that when we grow old we often find we have left it too late to renew earlier friendships. Life is like a track across a mountain, steep on one side, a precipice on the other. Behind us, we are always pressed on by other people. We can go forward, we can never go back.'

'And you tried to come back today?'

'I have tried to come back for many years.'

'Can I ask you why you are with the mourners for my mother if you did not know her?'

'I regret I never had the privilege. But from all I hear, she was a remarkable lady.'

'You know my father, then?' I pointed to Crabtree across the room.

'We shared this mutual friend years ago,' Mojo explained.

'Does he know this?'

'I think not. I will make myself known to him in due course.'

I looked closely at Mojo. Had he been in rags he would still have possessed that peculiar dynamism of personality that only comes with real ability. He would never just be a man in the company of men; he would always be a leader.

'Unless I am mistaken,' I said, 'you were photographing the grave of Mr Crosby who died here when I was very young?'

'That is so,' he agreed.

'You were, in fact, photographing the grave of my real father.'

'I am aware of that. But I gained that knowledge only very recently. If I may, I will explain more fully the reasons for my presence here. Your father and I were in Hiroshima on the day the first atomic bomb landed. All around us was chaos and ruin and death. Terrible, unspeakable death.

'Unknown thousands died then, and many, many more later. Your father, an American and a prisoner of the Japanese army, was freed when the jail literally collapsed. But instead of at once seeking his own safety, he stayed to help those who were still technically, politically and legally his enemies. He saved many lives that day, mine included. And in so doing I believe he contracted the disease that eventually killed him.'

I listened in silence. Then I asked him another question.

'How did you lose touch?'

'He went back to his country and I stayed in the ruins of

mine. By the time I could afford to search for him, it was too late.'

'Someone was looking for him here not long ago. An American.'

'Yes. At my instigation. I understand that he also died. But he found Crosby's grave and told me you were Crosby's son. Mr Crabtree – if you still intend to keep that name – I owe your father a debt which now it is unfortunately impossible to repay him personally. But it grieves me not to make an attempt at some kind of payment, however late, however unsatis-factory. I was curious to see the son he had sired. I am without children, Mr Crabtree. It interests me to follow the progress of the sons and daughters of my contemporaries.

'I did not know your father well, but I believe he was of wealthy parentage, and latterly spent all his money. I am told that at the end he lived on credit, on the strength of the memory of a fortune he had whittled away, as one can whittle a stick to the thickness of a match. I also believe he handed on to you a certain shrewdness of mind, which is rare among the young today. I would like to repay my debt to him by helping you.'

'In what way?' I asked bluntly, too intrigued by the conver-sation to put the question in more gracious terms.

'One of my employees, a Mr Ford, bought a car from you in Darwin,' he went on.

'You arranged for him to buy the car?' I asked, making a guess.

He bowed in acknowledgement. 'I understand you hold a regular auction for cars here. I am sure you will do well, but I would like to help you do much better. I will make you an offer which I think your father would have appreciated. I propose appointing you as my sole agent for Australia, New Zealand, Malaysia, Singapore, Indonesia, for a range of products Mojo Electronics are about to produce.'

'I know nothing about electronics,' I said, feeling, quite

possibly wrongly, that I was about to be patronised, given a hand-out as one might give a coin to a beggar, just to be rid of him.

'I am aware of that. You can employ people who do.'

'I have no money for that,' I said. 'What I have got is already tied up.'

I was thinking about Zachariah Station. I had to see the bank manager in the next few days if I wanted to go ahead with that deal, and I could anticipate his unenthusiastic response.

'I do not expect you to have money,' Mojo replied. 'So I will make you an offer that no other of my distributors or agents has ever received. It is the custom of some trades to give thirty days' credit. Others stretch this to sixty or even ninety. I will go further. I will be helping myself through your increased sales as well as helping you.

'I will give you four months' credit on all the stock you buy. That means that if you have a consignment on January the first, you do not owe me a cent until May the first. If you can't sell at a profit in that time, my friend, I have grossly misjudged your abilities, and it is not in my nature to make errors of such magnitude.'

But you don't know me, I thought, bewildered. All around us, people were chattering, holding out their glasses to be filled, picking up sandwiches. Here I was, just back from the graveyard, talking terms with a total stranger who claimed that years ago he knew my father. I didn't even know if he was who he claimed to be. Then I remembered the motel manager's remarks about the hired jet.

'We have a deal,' I said, and we shook hands. 'I would like to introduce you to Mr Crabtree.'

'My pleasure,' said Mr Mojo. 'My secretary will deliver a letter to you confirming our discussion. It is strange to think that out of the ashes of a ruined city, out of the memory of a dead friendship, a whole new dynasty of prosperity will arise.'

'Phoenix?' I said.

'Arizona?' he queried, with a puzzled frown.

'No,' I said, 'the legend of a bird that arose from its own ashes.'

'Ah, so,' he said. 'Perhaps you should call your company Phoenix Electronics.'

'Maybe I should,' I told him, and took him across the crowded room to meet Crabtree.

Next morning, I received a letter from the manager of the City and Provincial bank in Katherine. He would like to see me within the next day or two. Well, I'd like to see him, or rather I needed to see him, so that made two of us. I fixed an appointment for eleven o'clock on the following day.

I never feel too easy in these people's offices. I think that when it comes to making money, real money, too many bank managers and accountants are like eunuchs when it comes to making love. They know well enough how it's done, but they can't do it themselves. Worse, they watch others do it constantly. To spend one's life surrounded by other people's money and to have so little of one's own would be a living death for me, a torture of the damned.

The manager, Mr Davis, a Welshman originally, was almost due to retire. I'd not met him before. I had always dealt through an under-manager, never had need to go to the top man for money.

Mr Davis was a small bloke who had cut himself shaving that morning. A tiny dab of white cottonwool, stained with blood, stuck to his chin. That didn't look too attractive to me. I guessed he used a cut-throat razor, which could make him a bit old-fashioned in his ways. We shook hands.

'I was very sorry to hear of the death of your mother, Mrs Crabtree,' he said.

I didn't tell him she wasn't my mother. It was none of his business. That was my affair, or rather shared between me, Crabtree and my real mother.

'Yes,' I said. 'She was a very brave person. Put up a great fight and never complained.'

'Good on her,' he said. 'I've been looking at the reviews of her two films. They're great. Fancy, a film star in Katherine.'

'Yes,' I agreed. 'A real star. A great actress.'

'Well,' he said, 'I suppose you know that, as the manager of the bank, I am executor of your mother's will?'

'I didn't.'

He looked surprised. 'I assumed you would know, so I asked you to come and see me. She was very methodical. Left everything between you and Mr Crabtree.'

'There is another son,' I said. 'Before she married Mr Crabtree.'

'Is that so? I didn't realise that. There's nothing about him in the will.' He looked at me accusingly, as though I was making it up. I said nothing. This was not my concern, I just felt he should know, though if I had been left out of my real mother's will, I would have felt very sore; not so much for the money, but for the fact that she could ignore me.

'She's left you some savings, and an insurance policy which will bring you the not inconsiderable sum of twenty-five thousand dollars.'

'That's quite unexpected,' I told him. 'I didn't know she saved money, or knew anything about money.'

'Well, not in the accepted business sense, perhaps, but she was very frugal. She had known hard times, like many of us, before the war and during the war, long before you were born. People think they have a hard time now if they haven't a couple of TV sets, two cars, and holidays in Fiji or Hong Kong twice a year. It was very different then.'

I knew. Davis was like all the older people, harking back to the past. But I suppose, when perhaps four-fifths of your life is in the past, that's only natural. I look at things the other way. I look towards tomorrow and the day after.

'Well,' the manager said, 'there will be some formalities,

always are on these unhappy occasions. But I thought I should
tell you personally rather than just setting it out in a letter.'

'Thank you,' I said. 'Now, I want to see you about something
altogether different. And a much larger sum.'

'An accommodation? Buying more cars? You deal in them, I
understand.'

'Up to now I have,' I said. 'But I feel the time has come to buy a
bit of land before the Japanese get their hands on all of it.'

'They're certainly coming in at a great pace. Only yesterday I
had two principals of Japanese real estate companies in this
office looking for stations. And ready to pay cash in any currency, anywhere in the world. No loans, no mortgages, nothing
like that.'

'Well, I've found something I want to buy,' I told him. 'A station with five thousand square miles of land about one hundred
and fifty miles north of here. The price is low because there's
been no rain for so long.'

'It's very hard on the owners,' said Mr Davis, shaking his head
gravely as though the drought also affected him. 'Some of these
stations are as big as Wales and mortgaged up to the last square
metre. Back in Wales, we had farmers on as little as thirty
acres – and making a living out of it. Here, they've got thousands of square miles and they're nearly broke. Extraordinary.
So why do you want to get into that situation?'

'Because the price is right and rain must fall one day.'

'But until it does, you'll be paying interest and not making a
dollar.'

'I accept that.'

'So what is the asking price?'

'Around forty dollars a square mile.'

The manager didn't need to use his calculator to show I
needed $200,000. Perhaps more, when you consider the stock.
Say, $300,000. He looked at me, and dabbed at the cut on his
face. It began to bleed. He grimaced; he did not like the sight of
blood.

'So how are you proposing to finance this purchase?'

'With money from the bank.'

'*This* bank?'

'I've no account anywhere else.'

'It's a very large sum,' he said soberly, stating the obvious, as managers like to on these occasions.

'It's a very large slice of land.'

'But you have no knowledge of farming?'

'Agreed. But I had no knowledge of the car business until I went into it. There's a lot of phoney mystique about these things.'

'This is a very large purchase indeed, Mr Crabtree. You'll have staff to pay, and you'll also need running capital.'

'I understand that.'

'But if the present owner can't make it pay – and presumably he has been a farmer for some time – how can you?'

'The station is owned by an old man living on his own. He's being hounded by some big boys who want to buy his land cheaply. I reckon he's a good farmer but he lacks money, and the bank's on his back.'

'I could be on *your* back, Mr Crabtree,' warned Mr Davis, only half in jest.

'Undoubtedly. That's the banks' natural position – they should all have it on their coat of arms. But I will pay off the loan.'

'But how? When?'

'If it's worth, say, forty a square mile now, what would you say it would be worth when the rains come?'

'Half as much again,' he said instantly. He had done his homework on these things. He must have financed many deals, not with people like me, but for people who really knew about land. I knew nothing about it, not a toss. But I believed I knew about making a profit.

'I think the rains are going to come,' I told him.

'Well, they must eventually, of course, but the Met boys say not yet. No sign, according to them.'

'They always been right?'

'Well, no one is *always* right, but they're not forecasting the weather with a bit of wet seaweed as we used to do down in the Gower in Wales, you know. If it was wet, it was going to rain. If the seaweed stayed dry, it would be a fine day. They do it by radar, satellite signals, every kind of electronic means. What makes you think it's going to rain, Mr Crabtree, if they don't?'

'If I told you,' I said, 'you wouldn't believe me. Let's just say I feel in my bones it is going to rain. Soon.'

'You're serious?'

'Deadly serious.'

'I see. At present in your account you have possibly fifty thousand dollars. With the twenty-five thousand dollars from your mother it comes to around seventy-five thousand. A healthy balance, but not enough to warrant a loan on this scale.'

'What would make it enough to warrant a loan on this scale?'

'If you had, say, some other profitable business you could set against it. Or maybe a portfolio of blue chip shares, equities, that sort of thing. Something substantial, Mr Crabtree.'

'What about this?' I asked, and took out Mr Mojo's letter.

He read it.

'Hmm,' he said. 'A hundred and twenty days' credit. That's unusually long.'

'It is,' I agreed.

'And this is signed by the founder of Mojo Motors, Mojo Aviation, Electronics, everything?'

'That's right.'

'How did you meet him?'

'Through a family connection.'

'And why did he give you this?'

'I think he wanted to pay a debt to someone who had helped him in the past.'

'But you don't have sufficient capital to start such a business, selling videos and transistors and hi-fi sound systems and so on.'

'Agreed,' I said. I seemed to have been agreeing to lots of things. Now I felt it was the manager's turn to agree with me.

'Your business as a banker is to lend money,' I told him. 'Bankers are basically usurers. You pay one set of interest to clients who lend you their money and you lend it out to people like me at a higher rate. The difference is your profit.'

'I would not describe banking in exactly those simple terms, Mr Crabtree.'

'I don't mind how you describe it. But that remains the fact of the matter. I have little capital, as we both know, but I have two very profitable propositions. With this exclusive contract from Mojo Electronics for the southern hemisphere I will not have to pay for any of the goods they supply for four months. In that time I will sell them at a profit. I'm running on Mojo's money, not yours, not mine. But I need some from your bank to set me up, start me off.

'I also want to buy this station, and to do this I need to borrow more money from you – or from someone else. If you're not going to lend me that money, tell me now, and I'll go right out across the road and into that bank I can see through the window here, and put my proposition to them. And if they turn me down, I'll go to the head office in Adelaide of the bank Mr Mojo uses. They will be more sympathetic.

'I'm only coming to you first because you have helped me in the past over small sums for cars and so on. Now I'm giving you the chance to help yourself over large sums, for this is only the beginning of much bigger things. Take it or leave it. Do we understand each other?'

'I think so, Mr Crabtree, I think so. But there really is no need to be so abrupt.'

'I think there is. We can talk round this project for ever.'

The manager stood up, glanced at his watch.

'Give me five minutes,' he said.

He was actually out of the room for ten minutes, not five. But when he returned I could tell from his face that we had a deal.

'I think we can help you,' he said pompously.

'I don't want you to think. I want you to *know*. Yes or no?'

'Yes, Mr Crabtree. Head office has agreed to advance you up to five hundred thousand dollars against the deeds of the station and the stock and all buildings, vehicles and equipment. For six months only.'

'And if the rain doesn't come by then?' I asked him.

'Then we will come after you, Mr Crabtree,' he replied with a rather forced smile. 'Now, if you will give me some details, I will ask my senior mortgage manager to discuss the matter with you at once.'

THIRTEEN

The Present:
Katherine, Northern Territory, Australia
Perth, Western Australia
Nassau, Bahamas

For the next few days I tried to keep my mind off what to me was an important investment and concentrate on what could bring me in an immediate profit – buying and selling cars. When you do something regularly, simply for a profit, the routine becomes automatic, predictable. You buy at one price and sell at another. And what you have to do to make the buyer pay more than you paid is largely a matter of psychology.

When it comes to a secondhand car, this means that the car must be clean and appear well cared for. Whether it genuinely has been cherished may be doubtful, but once it has been washed and polished, tyres painted black, oil stains removed from the engine bay with detergent, a coach line and perhaps one or two spotlights or other simple accessories added, even the most mundane vehicle acquires a personality. Buyers could easily do all this themselves, of course, and save hundreds, maybe thousands of dollars, but they don't. They lack vision, or imagination, or they simply can't be bothered.

Another thing I learned about the human condition is that one must never offer two or three cars of the same type for sale at the same time. A potential buyer will invariably like the colour of one car but prefer the seats of a second, while his wife is taken by the stereo in the third. In the end, you don't sell any of them.

I sold quite a few cars in between my regular auctions and when I wasn't in the bank manager's office signing the proliferation of papers that accompany every property deal. When we completed the sale, I was rather surprised when the manager turned up at the next auction and wanted to buy a car at a knockdown price.

'But it's got to go through the auction,' I told him. 'I owe that to the seller.'

'You owe the bank quite a lot, too,' said Davis pointedly.

'You mean you want a little bit on the side for yourself?'

I didn't know why I spoke like that, but his request surprised me. I know it shouldn't have done, but it did. I felt a sudden distaste for the man, and also for the whole business of making money, which was unlike me. He was receiving a good salary, might even collect a bonus through lending me so much money, while I was paying the bank every kind of fee and interest.

The bank could also seize back Zachariah Station in six months if the rains didn't come – and still he wanted something extra. In the end, I bid for one of the cars myself, using a dummy in the back of the auction room, just to cover the reserve. The manager got his car cheaply, but he lost my respect. I had thought better of him, in a way looked up to him as an example of probity, and he had shown he was only a small-timer, looking for a back-hander. Did money – bigger money than I had been accustomed to – always have this effect on people?

The day we completed I drove out to Zachariah. The old man was amazed when he heard that I had bought the place.

'How d'you get the money, son?' he asked me.

'Borrowed it,' I said. 'Where everyone else gets money. Only a fool uses his own.'

'Then I've been a bloody fool all my life,' he retorted. 'I've always used my savings, never borrowed a cent until I ran into trouble here and the banks put me on the rack. They'll have your balls, too, if you don't watch 'em, the bastards.'

'I'm watching them,' I assured him. 'I reckon I'll follow the motto of the eunuchs of Kabul.'

'Which is?'

' "Eunuchs of the world unite. We've got nothing left to lose." If I can't pay back the money, they take back the station.'

'But you've put some of your own money in, haven't you?'

'A little,' I agreed. 'But I started with nothing. I can go back there tomorrow. Wouldn't worry me greatly. I can always make it again. That's a risk I have to take.'

As the weeks stretched into months and still no rain fell, the risk grew from being a tiny spot in a sunny sky to a very large dark cloud. Despite my brave talk to the old man, I couldn't afford to lose my savings. Every morning I looked out across an incandescent red desert that should have been green but which still burned like a branding iron. I hoped fervently that Georgie had not made a mistake. He knew I'd bought the farm, but he didn't tell anyone. I hadn't told him either – I felt rather embarrassed about it – but somehow he knew.

'About the rain, Georgie,' I said to him when we were coming up to sixteen weeks. 'It had better come soon.'

'It'll come,' he said.

'How do you know? How can you be *sure*?'

'How do you know the sun's going to set this evening or rise tomorrow morning?'

'I don't,' I agreed. 'But I have faith. It always has done, in my lifetime. It will see me out.'

'This will see you out, too, son. It will come.'

A week later I woke up suddenly at two o'clock in the morning. In my sleep I had heard a great boom, an explosion, like a big gun firing. I jumped out of bed and ran out onto the verandah. The mosquito screens were down and night moths and other winged insects beat against the fine mesh as though desperate to come inside. They often did that, but not so many of them, and not so frantically.

The night felt hot and moist, like a steam bath, which was unusual; generally, the air was hot and dry. And then I heard the boom again, closer. This time there was a rattle of rain on the tin roof as though people were throwing shingle at it, and then a crash of thunder. Lightning split the sky with blue jagged daggers and the heavens opened.

The genteel pitter-patter of raindrops was drowned in the cascade that drummed like a regiment on the march. Water streamed off the roof, instantly blocking gutters with dead leaves and the dust of years of heat. Gullies poured in rivers across the parched earth.

Holes like giant pores opened in the red earth, and the force of the rain raised a mist of steam. Within seconds, the desert was drinking millions and millions of gallons of water.

I stood there, sweating with relief. Georgie had been right. Now I could sell the property. I was out of the bank's clutches with two months to spare. Not a desperately close-run thing, I thought, but close enough. In one leap, like Houdini, I was free – and on my road to riches.

I went back to bed but I did not sleep. The roar of the rain, the claps of thunder, the brilliant electric-blue blaze of lightning kept me awake. But I didn't worry any more. I was on my way. Nothing could stop me now. Yet, oddly, I had a strange and totally unexpected feeling of anti-climax. Was this all there was to being rich? You followed a hunch, had a lucky meeting with someone who owed a favour to a relation you had never met, and all your money worries were over? Or were others just beginning?

I remembered reading somewhere that a very rich old man had declared that you either had no money or you could never have enough. Perhaps the price of creating wealth was that in the process you destroyed something else of equal value –

maybe of even greater value: contentment. I did not know, and in puzzling out the problem, I fell asleep.

In the morning, I drove to Katherine to see the bank manager. Roads were flooded, awash with water. Cars and trucks sailed along like ships, throwing up huge waves from their wheels. One or two of the more foolish drivers had ploughed up too much water and their vehicles stood abandoned at the roadside, bonnets raised, or with drivers, up to their knees in the swirling flood, peering into steaming engines, wondering what was wrong. I could have told them but I had business elsewhere.

'Well, the rain has come,' I told the bank manager as though he did not already know. 'I'm going to sell Zachariah.'

'Odd you should say that. We've had an inquiry already.'

'That soon?' I asked. 'How?'

'Companies are always looking for land. The good Lord's not making any more, you know.'

'There's quite a lot here in Australia,' I pointed out.

'Not enough for some.'

'So who wants my land?'

'A company called Sixty-Six Horsa Properties.'

'Means nothing to me,' I said.

'I wouldn't expect it to,' he replied. 'It's registered in the Cayman Islands for tax reasons. They own a lot of land in Australia, but none so far in the Northern Territory. How much are you asking?'

'All my expenses to be paid so far. Your legal fees, mortgage fees. All that, plus a minimum of five hundred thousand Australian dollars' profit to be paid into an account in the Caymans.'

'You have such an account?' he asked in surprise.

'No. But you're going to fix me up with one today.'

'You are a very positive young man,' said the manager, half in surprise, half in envy.

'It's a positive world,' I told him. 'You either push on or

you're pushed down. And tell them they've got one week to complete.'

'That's impossible,' the manager said.

'Nothing's impossible,' I told him. 'The value of Zachariah will go up now the rain's here. A week, or the deal's off.'

'I'll do my best.'

'Do better than that,' I told him sharply, my contempt showing in my voice. 'Do a deal.'

He did a deal. We had the money on the close of business on the seventh day. I was amazed, really, but I didn't show my surprise. I was half a million dollars richer. I was moving on. I paid the money into the Cayman Islands account the manager had arranged. On leaving his office, he stood up and opened the door for me. I was no longer just a young bloke on the make, I was a young bloke who'd made it – and who would make a lot more.

'There's just one thing, Mr Crabtree,' he said, almost hesitantly, as though he did not like to mention it.

'What's that?' I asked him. 'I don't want an overdraft, you know.'

'I wasn't thinking of that – sir,' he added, not sarcastically but because now I had shown I could make a profit he thought I deserved the title. 'There's a lady in Perth who would like you to meet her.'

'I don't know anyone in Perth, lady or otherwise.'

'Probably not. But she is Lady Myrtle Mackenzie, the life president and principal shareholder of Mackenzie Transworld.'

'I've heard of them,' I said.

'I expect so. As a matter of fact, they also own this bank.'

'What does she want to see me about?'

'We make reports on all our larger deals to Mackenzie's headquarters, as a matter of policy. I think she was intrigued that someone – shall I say someone so young, almost inexperienced – should take such a risk in borrowing so much money and then be so firm about the profit he wished to make on it.'

'You've told me,' I said. 'There's no need for me to go to Perth to hear that from her.'

'I think it might be in your own interests if you did, Mr Crabtree. She is a very powerful lady, financially and politically. Not only here in Australia but in the States, in England. All over, in fact.

'When her husband, Sir Hilary Mackenzie, died just after the Second World War, she inherited the business. Many people thought it would just go downhill, for Sir Hilary had not been the most provident of directors. Instead, she took the group by the scruff of its corporate neck, split it up into separate companies and built on that foundation to what it is today. A young man could learn a lot from her.'

'I'm not arguing about that. It's just that I don't want to go to Perth.'

'She has sent an air ticket for you. You'll be met at Perth Airport, and first-class accommodation will be provided at the Sheraton Hotel. This invitation is really a great honour, Mr Crabtree. You're the first customer who banks with this branch she has ever shown any interest in meeting.'

'Hardly surprising,' I said tartly. After all, the accounts of most of the people who banked with him would be pretty small. And then I pulled myself up mentally. Already I was starting to look down on people who had less money than I had, just as those who had more only a week before had doubtless looked down on me. I didn't like that attitude in others; I did not want it in myself.

'I'll go,' I told him. 'Just for you.'

'Thank you. Here's the ticket. It's open. Just advise me before you leave and I will fax your arrival.'

As soon as I reached home, I telephoned the motel and spoke to the manager.

'Ah,' he said. 'What do *you* want? A room for the afternoon or just for an hour, short time?'

This was his idea of humour.

'No,' I told him. 'Something more difficult to arrange. I want to hire you as a journalist, which you tell me you are in your spare time. I want everything you can get me on Lady Myrtle Mackenzie, and as quick as you can. For fifty dollars cash.'

'Like when?' he asked.

'Like two hours ago,' I told him. 'Get your arse in gear.'

He was round the following evening with a folder of newspaper clippings and photostats. I paid him and then sat down to read them through. All references to Lady Mackenzie were very guarded and cautious; clearly, she was not a woman to antagonise. They all mentioned her wealth, her charm, her properties; some, her Mexican background and upbringing. Then I turned up something rather more interesting from *The Australian Enquirer*.

It seemed to me that most of the information in this article had come from a young Scotsman, Hamish Keiller, a director of a Mackenzie company in England. Although he was never quoted directly, it was obvious that the journalist who wrote the piece had interviewed him and added information from old newspaper clippings about Lady Mackenzie. This article actually gave some new facts.

It revealed how she liked to lie on a sunbed in the shade outside her home in Perth while the directors sat in the heat of the sun. It described her custom of presenting a propelling pencil to her directors and senior executives. Each pencil wrote with lead of a colour exclusive to the recipient. If any of them wished to write her a personal memo, but not to sign his name in case it fell into other hands, she would instantly know who had written it from the colour of the writing.

This seemed an ingenious idea to me, and also very simple. I resolved to do the same should I ever chair a board of directors who I suspected might not all be totally loyal to me.

From a news item in the latest edition of the same paper I learned that Mr Keiller had remained behind in Perth when his fellow directors returned to England. The inference seemed that Mr Keiller was being groomed for promotion. Although I had never even heard of the man, from what I read now I did not altogether care for him. He blew his own trumpet too often and too loudly. And, just possibly, too soon.

I read all the items through several more times, and then destroyed them. I sat for some time, thinking about what I had read. If I felt there might not be room at the top for two Australians, there need not be room on the way up for Mr Keiller. I calculated that doing him a bit of harm could only do me a lot of good.

Then I telephoned Mr Mojo.

Myrtle Mackenzie was stretched out on a chaise longue on the verandah overlooking the Swan River. As a girl at school she had learned, among a mass of quotations, many long since forgotten, one that still stayed in her mind: 'The crowd on the Appian Way is always young.'

Who had said that? She must instruct a researcher to find out. The words came back to her now as she looked over the river and saw the speedboats, the sailing boats, the windsurfers. It was ironic to think that at a time when some people could afford a really big yacht – like Mr Mojo's, for instance – they were too old to indulge in more vigorous water sports. The young envied the old their possessions and the old envied the young the greatest possession of all, which diminished every day: youth.

This brought her mind round in an easy circle to the young man she was about to interview: Ian Bruce Crabtree. She had half expected he would refuse the invitation to fly down to see her, but was pleased he had accepted. He seemed to be a man of vigour and strong views. She had discovered he was ingenious, enterprising and courageous, and maybe he also possessed that other essential attribute of every successful man, the quality Napoleon looked for in all his generals: luck.

Irene Loxby came out on the verandah.

'Mr Crabtree has arrived,' she announced. 'Do you want to see him here or in the house?'

'Here. This is an open-air country, and he is an open-air man – if he's the sort of person I think and hope he is.'

I came out through the vast drawing room with its white marble floor, white Aubusson carpets, and the oil paintings much larger than life size that covered the walls. A fountain played somewhere, and goldfish swam in a marble pool. An air of peace and coolness permeated the house; of elegance and luxury; of being completely separated from the rush of lesser lives outside, traffic jams on St George's Terrace, crowds patiently waiting to across at lights on the intersections.

I saw Lady Myrtle before she saw me. An Aboriginal attribute, I suppose: see your enemy first. But why should I consider her a possible enemy?

She was lying on a cane chair, a glass of iced orange juice on the table by her side, just as the newspaper articles had described. She wore sunglasses so that I could not see her eyes, which was one up to her and one down to me. She smiled, extended a hand, warm to the touch. I am not drawn to people with clammy hands; that was one thing I had disliked about the Stranger. Her nails were painted deep red, but they were not long. Lady Mackenzie was a worker; no one with long fingernails can ever be so described.

'Ian Crabtree?' she said.

'An honour, Lady Mackenzie,' I replied. 'I like your house. It reminds me of Katherine.'

'Of Katherine?' she asked, surprise sharpening her voice.

'Yes. Because it is all so different. So hot up there, so cool down here.'

'I see.'

Myrtle looked puzzled. She guessed I was trying to be humorous but did not find the remark particularly funny. Nevertheless, she smiled. She could see I was tense, ill at ease. This was the first time I had stood in the presence of real wealth and power, and my embarrassment showed.

'Do take a seat.'

I sat down, at first on the edge of the chair, my trousers tight over my knees. Then I relaxed and sat back. There were only two differences between us, I told myself. She was a woman, and she was richer than I was. I couldn't do anything about the former, but the latter was entirely up to me.

'A drink?' she asked me.

'I'll have a Fosters, please.'

'A very good choice. But I wish you'd asked for a Malthead.'

'That's a new beer, isn't it?'

'Yes. Have you tried it?'

'No,' I admitted. 'I haven't.'

'A pity. One of my companies has started brewing it. We bought an old brewery just down the river from here. It has quite a nice taste, although I'm not a beer drinker myself.'

She spoke briefly into a mobile phone. A butler brought a bottle of Fosters on a silver tray, poured it out into a cut-glass goblet as carefully as if he was decanting an ancient chateau-bottled wine, set it down on the table beside me, then withdrew. She raised her glass of orange juice.

'To you, Mr Crabtree.'

'To you, Lady Mackenzie.'

'You may be wondering why I've asked you here.'

'The thought crossed my mind.'

'I will tell you. I rather admired two things about you, and I wanted to meet you face to face. First, when you saw rustlers doing what is clearly illegal, you didn't hang back and pretend you hadn't seen them. You didn't look the other way, say it was someone else's business, not yours. You went back to see them. Why?'

'Curiosity, I guess. They were trying to ruin an old man who owned the homestead. I just wanted to see how – and if – I could stop them. He seemed kind of defenceless.'

I was surprised she knew about the rustlers; maybe the bank manager had told her?

'You wanted to ruin him yourself, then?'

'No way. I thought I might be able to stop them from doing that.'

'And in fact you did?'

'With a little help from my friends,' I said, 'who I didn't even know were there.'

'I'm told that some of those rustlers have not been seen since.'

'Is that a fact?' I said easily. 'I wouldn't think they pay rent anywhere. They move around.'

'I heard some are not moving around at all.'

'You heard that?' I asked her innocently, sipping the cold beer, looking beyond the terrace at the brilliant river.

'I heard that,' she went on. 'In fact, they've been moved. In tins. Dogmeat, perhaps?' She smiled with her mouth; I was not sure about her eyes – the shades effectively concealed them.

'Perhaps,' I said. 'You hear all sorts. The more you hear, the less you believe.'

'Your philosophy, Mr Crabtree?'

'I think it's going to be.'

'Well, it could be worse, I suppose. It's at least realistic. The other reason I asked you here was to tell you that you have cost me a great deal of money.'

I was puzzled. 'I don't follow you, Lady Mackenzie.' The last thing I wanted was to antagonise a woman so rich she could buy all Queensland, sell it and not care whether she'd made a profit or a loss.

'You see, I, or rather one of Mackenzie Transworld's companies, wanted Zachariah. Badly.'

'So you put rustlers in to try and persuade the old boy to sell out?'

'In its crudest terms you could say that, Mr Crabtree, but that does less than justice to the situation. In point of fact we offered him a price. He refused. We offered him more. He still refused. There had been no rain for years, the cattle were getting thin, and he was growing old, but still he would not change his mind. I thought that if his cattle started going over the wire he might see where his real interests lay and sell. We offered him thirty dollars a square mile. I understand you paid forty.'

'You understand correctly. I suppose you got that information from the bank your company owns, which lent me the money?'

'We have our sources of information, as you have yours. However, I must congratulate you on taking a risk. It wasn't worth that for us then, but it seemed to be for you, although you had to borrow heavily to buy it. Could you tell me why?'

'Of course. I figured out the rains would come very soon.'

'The Met reports said differently.'

'All sorts of people say differently to every question you ask them. They used to say the earth was flat. Galileo had to retract his thesis to avoid the Catholic inquisition. They said men would never fly. They also said a bumble bee's body is too big, its wings too short for flight. Technically, aerodynamically, weight for wingspan, it is impossible for the bumble bee to become airborne. But no one told the bee that – and it flies. No one told me the rain would not come. I believed it would.'

'But why – how?'

'I've lived among Aborigines, Lady Mackenzie, I feel at one with them.' I was going to add that I was one of them but didn't. I don't know why; I just didn't. 'I gathered from them that the rain would come within a certain time, so I took a risk.'

'I see. The bank telephoned me. They knew of my interest, naturally, and you could offer very little security. Only a letter from Mr Mojo, the Japanese industrialist, I understand?'

'So why did you allow them to lend me the money?'

'I rather liked your style, if you want to know. I understand you made half a million dollars' profit after all legal and mortgage fees. That cost me money too.

'You sold out to Sixty-Six Horsa Properties which is another part of Mackenzie Transworld, a new acquisition which we have not even announced yet. You couldn't know we were involved. So, you see, in two ways you cost me, and I don't like losing money.'

'You asked me down here to tell me that?'

'Yes. And to tell you I admire you – and I think we could do some business together.'

'What sort of business, Lady Mackenzie?'

This seemed so incredible that my voice moved up an octave and I had to swallow several times to bring it down.

'I want your views about how I could prove whether a young man who sat in your chair only a short time ago is as loyal and trustworthy as he would like to appear.'

'If I could ask a question, Lady Mackenzie?' I began tentatively, throwing in the line as a man throws a stone into a pond to see where the ripples end.

'Go ahead,' she said.

'You have cause for suspecting his integrity?'

'I have doubts,' she corrected me. 'No more. I could be mistaken, but I do not think I am. And I never go ahead with any deal – or with any person – if I have doubts. To borrow a phrase from this young man, who is of Scottish extraction, I have a gut feeling.'

I nodded. She had told me what I wanted to know. Keiller was a Scottish name. As I suspected when I read the newspaper cutting, he was pushing too hard.

'Before I came to see you, Lady Mackenzie, I looked through a few newspaper articles that had been written about you. One of them described how you have an unusual custom of presenting to your executives pencils with different coloured leads. Whenever you receive an unsigned memo from one of them you know instantly who sent it. Is that correct?'

She nodded. 'Perfectly. I saw the article myself.'

'I have here a pencil which writes with a fluorescent and very distinctive colour. I suggest it might make a suitable gift for him.'

I took it out of my jacket pocket and handed it to her. She glanced at it briefly, put it down on a side table. She looked pleased, as though some instinctive reaction had now been corroborated.

'There is something else I would like to discuss with you,' she said. 'I believe you have a gift of knowing what deal to pursue and what deal to let go. Some people think that you can work that out mathematically. They used logarithms in the old days, calculators and computers and what-have-you now. To my mind you need what I call a wheel in the mind that sets all these other mechanical or electronic gadgets in motion. You've got to know in your blood, in your bones, in your brain, that if you do this, you lose. If you do that, you win. I think you have this gift. It's like water divining. You either have the knack or you don't. You have it.'

'Thank you, Lady Mackenzie. I'm flattered by such an opinion, coming from you.'

'Don't be. I have the same gift and I can recognise it in others. Possessing it has won me many victories, made me more money, given me control over more companies and people than I ever imagined, than I ever wanted. But there's a price to pay. You don't get this for nothing. The way of the world, as someone once told me years ago, is nothing for nothing.

'There's a price to be paid for everything. Sometimes it's very high. Sometimes you discover afterwards it was too high. I wanted to tell you that, Ian. To warn you, if you like. I've paid a price, several prices.'

She paused.

'Why are you telling me all this, Lady Mackenzie?'

'Because I have no son. My marriage was childless. For

various reasons, I found I could never have any children. And it is the natural thing for women to bear children – or to want them. You are the sort of son I would have liked to have had, Ian. Go-getting, positive, willing to take a risk – like pilots in the Second World War.

'I asked you to come to Perth because I thought if you measured up – and you do – I have a specific proposition to make. I am speaking to you now in total confidence. Do not tell anyone else. If you do, I will probably discover it, because when you are rich and powerful you are surrounded by people who seek favour by telling you facts about others. You may not like such people, but they can be useful. So please keep my confidence.'

'I get the message, Lady Mackenzie.'

'I thought you would. Now, I am of the opinion that Mackenzie Transworld should take over one of two very large international conglomorates. The first is Trinity-Trio, which, as you probably know, started in Calcutta and Hong Kong running opium to China and then became legitimate, as so many of those companies did in the last century. Trinity-Trio is now based in Nassau. The other is run by a man known as the Australian. Have you heard of him?'

'I have indeed,' I said. 'Often.'

'His shell company is Beechwood Nominees. He's a funny sort of man. He lives modestly in England, in a terraced house which is also his headquarters for a worldwide empire. In the 1950s he was without money. Now he is immensely wealthy. Like Midas, everything he touches turns to gold. But gold itself is useless. If you were in a shipwreck and filled your pockets with gold coins, you'd drown. If you were on a desert island with nothing else but gold bars, you could starve. Money – gold, cash, currency – is only useful for what it does, what – or who – it can buy; the pleasure, the help it can give.

'I think the Australian suffers from a disease – gold mania, if you like. He just wants money to own it, not to use it. I think if we joined forces, your youth and enterprise with my experience and backing, we could assume control of one or other of these concerns.

'I have studied the stock markets, and all Trinity-Trio's quoted shares are non-voting. Beechwood Nominees is not quoted. It is a private company. So let us go for Trinity-Trio first. Its capital was originally split into three hundred voting shares, one hundred owned by each of the three founders. Some of their descendants sold them for all kinds of reasons. Beechwood Nominees, I believe, is backed by Italian-American interests. They are rich through gambling and drugs, and want to wash their dirty money. They own one hundred shares and the Australian, through Beechwood Nominees, has forty-nine. Lord Jackson, a direct descendant of one of the original founders, owns one hundred and fifty-one voting shares, so controls the company. He is in Nassau but has had a very serious accident. He fell from a high window.'

'Was he pushed?'

'My investigators are of the opinion he wasn't. He leaned on a window that opened unexpectedly, and he overbalanced. He's alive, legally, but in a coma, unable to speak. How long he'll stay alive, I don't know.'

'So where would we come in?'

'Like this. Shortly before he fell, Lord Jackson gave his mistress Anna Lu-Kuan two shares. She is half American, half Chinese, and used to be his assistant. I am told they genuinely cared for each other. Whoever can get hold of those two voting shares can control the company.'

She looked at me inquiringly, hopefully.

'I'm overwhelmed that you should think of me in this connection,' I told her, which was absolutely true. 'All my deals have been on a very small level indeed compared with this.'

'The man who built Rome had to lay one brick first, you know. What is worrying you?'

'To be crude, what's in it for me?'

'What do you want?'

'A share of the action.'

'You'll have ten per cent of the action if we get a deal.'

'And if we don't?'

'You'll have expenses, unlimited and unchecked, but nothing more. And you will have learned how to play for a big fish – knowledge you can then put to good use in some other proposition. That's my offer. I don't want you to go away and sleep on it, discuss it with lawyers, bankers, all those people. They know nothing about such matters. If they did, they'd all be rich, and they're not. As far as creating wealth is concerned, they're only *accoucheurs*, the midwives to money. They help the birth, but they don't bear the child. So what do you say?'

'I say yes,' I answered, and finished my Fosters.

Mr Mojo sat on the rear upper deck of his two-hundred-foot yacht, *Lady Mojo*, off Cairns. As was his habit, he contemplated his future, his past and his present, and found much to satisfy himself in all three. The yacht stretched elegantly and magnificently ahead, pure white with tinted glass. Above him, the aerials of his Mojo radar system revolved slowly, seeking out any other craft long before they crossed the farthest horizon. At the rear, above the stern, spherical aerials for the Mojo satellite communications systems stood like giant white golf balls ready on their tees.

On another deck, his Mojo limousine was parked. It could be lifted by crane on to a quayside should he wish to drive ashore. A Mojo helicopter had a special launching pad just behind it. A Mojo 400h.p. speedboat, a Boston whaler powered by a Mojo 180h.p. outboard with a Mojo jet ski machine, and two Mojo 49cc mopeds for the crew of fifteen also waited, fully fuelled, ready for their owner's orders. Down in the heart of this superb vessel two 2,000h.p. Mojo diesels provided a cruising speed of 20 knots. Fuel tanks of more than 35,000 gallons' capacity gave a cruising range of around 10,000 miles. Water tanks held

5,600 gallons, and Mojo water makers could produce a third as much again every day.

Aboard *Lady Mojo*, with direct-dial satellite communication, Mojo telephone and telex communication, colour radar, automatic direction finder and weatherfax, and such ancillary novelties as a hot air balloon, scuba diving gear with compressor, sauna bath, jacuzzi, even a Mojo grand piano, Mr Mojo felt at ease, at home – and safe. His bodyguard travelled with him, of course, but any kidnap attempt would be difficult at sea, always in radio touch with land.

Here, in his private floating fortress, he could relax. He lacked only one blessing: companionship. He was always on his own. But then, what really rich man could claim to have genuine friends for the journey? In his experience, they were mostly sycophants, hangers-on, scroungers.

Above his head, the company flag bearing the red Mojo insignia fluttered in a breeze from the Coral Sea, blowing towards the Australian coast. He thought of the factories and office buildings, the high-rise apartments and commercial blocks his company owned which proudly bore that logo as a flag or a neon sign. He thought of all the TV sets, the radios, fax machines, satellite equipment, motor cars, motor cycles, aircraft which carried it to the eight corners of the world, and he marvelled at his own success. He had carried out the wishes of the Divine Son of Heaven; no man could do more. Out of the ashes of defeat he had heard the word and risen like the phoenix, the great Arabian firebird.

One deck beneath him, on the wall of the dining room which could seat twenty people in splendid opulence, was an illuminated photograph of his original cycle shop before the bomb destroyed Hiroshima. Sometimes Mojo would examine it through a magnifying glass, picking out old familiar cracks in planks, scrutinising the faded paintwork of his sign, blistered by years of sun, wondering what had happened to all the cycles stacked outside.

It was a long time ago in human life, if nothing in terms of dynasties or eternity. Yet in the words of the Japanese proverb, 'Every man draws water for his own field'. He had kept his field abundantly irrigated; he had made the most of every opportunity and had reaped the harvest of his own endeavours.

An aide, smartly dressed in white shorts and white silk shirt, came in, bowed obsequiously. Mojo raised his dark eyebrows inquiringly.

'We have had word from our friend in the conglomerate, Mackenzie Transworld, about joining them in their motor works in Coventry.'

'And?' asked Mr Mojo.

'We understand from him, although not officially, that the directors are against the idea.'

'On what grounds?'

'I think, sir, they may be planning some acquisitions of their own. One possibility could be Trinity-Trio.'

'That I understand. It could well be true. That man the media call the Australian has acquired many of their shares, which are not publicly quoted. Perhaps he is their puppet?'

'I do not think so, sir. He has heavy backing from Carlotti's interests.'

'I have heard much about Carlotti,' said Mojo, frowning. 'And I have heard nothing good. Mackenzie will have a hard fight if they face the organised evil he represents. Have you any idea of their plan?'

'Not yet, sir, but we are making most energetic inquiries.'

'Continue,' said Mojo. 'Meantime, if Lady Mackenzie or any of her people in Australia contact me, I will, of course, know nothing, and will endeavour to see them.' He was silent for a few moments. 'Perhaps we should prepare an attack against Trinity-Trio ourselves, or against the Australian personally, or even both. Give that matter our resolute consideration.'

'They would be very serious adversaries, sir.'

'Of course. But as the Chinese philosopher Sun Tzu says, "A victorious army wins its victories before seeking battle".

'When our High Command, under our illustrious and divinely born Emperor, committed themselves to attack the American Pacific fleet in Pearl Harbor in 1941, they decided to use half a dozen aircraft carriers, to win or lose in the first day of a war that had not even been declared.

'Of course, British and American Intelligence knew of this intention. The American admirals argued that aircraft carriers had *never* been used before in naval warfare to such an extent. The battleship was king. But they did not consider that the brontosaurus had once ruled the earth. He could not adapt and so he died. As did the American fleet.

'It is written that in the month of storms, flowers appear and there is no medicine, you know, to cure a fool. But then we do not wish these fools to be cured. We wish to defeat them, take them over, add their wealth and power to ours. And that is what we will do.'

Even as he spoke so belligerently, Mojo wished he could come to an amicable accommodation with Mackenzie Transworld. He had been forced to fight all his adult life, first for survival during the Second World War and afterwards; then to establish his company; finally to make it a world force. Now he was losing his appetite for struggle.

Hamish Keiller sat in the back of the limousine he had hired to take him from his hotel to Lady Mackenzie's home on Swan River. Mrs Loxby had telephoned to ask him to come to see Lady Mackenzie at exactly five o'clock that evening. Keiller was certain that this could only mean good news; it was clearly not a vaguely timed social invitation, but a business appointment.

He fingered the special pencil which a few days earlier Mrs Loxby had delivered to him personally at his hotel. She explained how Lady Mackenzie gave such pencils only to directors and the most senior executives, and he had been flattered and secretly surprised at the distinction.

He wondered whether Lady Mackenzie and Mr Mojo had yet met. If not, they would soon, and it was with a pleasant feeling of anticipation that he stretched his short legs and looked out at the buildings as the car swept along St George's Terrace. No doubt she wanted his advice on Mojo's proposals. Keiller felt he was the favoured son, the only director of the Coventry car firm still in Perth. The others had flown back to Britain.

The car swept past banks, the Anzac Club with its grave inscription: *They only deserve freedom who are prepared to defend it.* Right, thought Keiller. He might adopt that saying as his own, have it on his desk in place of the rather crude motto he had at present: *When you've got them by the balls, their hearts and minds will follow.* Yes, definitely an improvement, especially if he adapted it to read: *They only deserve success who are prepared to risk all for it.* That was his philosophy, he told himself; those were the words he lived by.

When he first knew he would be meeting Lady Mackenzie, he had set about finding all he could on her background. The matter of her husband's death in Nassau, his body not recovered, and the sudden death in his suite of a Miss A. Craven; all this intrigued Keiller.

Early in his career, he had discovered the need for good relations with the media. For an envelope of £10 notes, a reporter friend in London contacted his newspaper's stringer in Nassau for any local paper reports of that tragedy, and of the memorial service in St Matthew's Church to Sir Hilary Mackenzie, with a list of all those present.

Then followed a week of intensive research into what had happened to that congregation of long ago. Most were dead, a few lived in retirement in Dorset or southern Spain. A Dr da Leppo was in Santa Barbara. A bachelor, Peter Hillman, was the subject of a small paragraph in the Nassau newspaper some weeks afterwards, with a photograph and an editorial note on the importance of Nassau during the war, and the irony of his loss in a peacetime flight when he had accomplished so many successful crossings of the Atlantic from 1939 to 1945.

Keiller wondered about Hillman. He would have been slightly older then than Lady Myrtle; they must have known each other – or else why was he at the service? It was not impossible that they knew each other well, and on this theory he had carefully groomed his hair to look like Hillman's photograph. A long shot, agreed, but it had worked brilliantly; he felt he could congratulate himself on that, and he did so, frequently.

The car stopped outside Lady Mackenzie's house. Beyond the well-barbered lawn, Swan River ran like molten glass under the burning afternoon sun. A Filipino manservant opened the door. Keiller nodded curtly to him. He was becoming used to such trappings of luxury. People like Lady Mackenzie were clever to have acquired them, but he was just as smart, just as sharp; and he would start where they left off. He was humming to himself as her English butler led him through the entrance hall and out onto the back verandah.

Lady Mackenzie was sitting where she had sat when they had discussed the Mojo affair some days earlier. Keiller had a sudden, strange thought: had she ever moved? She still wore dark glasses, although the sun was sliding down the sky and soon would lose its heat, and another day would begin to die.

She motioned him to a chair. He noticed with surprise that she did not seem to see his outstretched hand. He sat down.

'I wanted to see you personally,' she said.

'About anything specific, Lady Mackenzie?'

'Yes,' she replied. 'Something extremely specific. I feel that you have not been totally honest with me.'

'*Honest?* I don't quite understand you, Lady Mackenzie.' Keiller frowned in his concern and concentration. What the hell was happening? What had gone wrong? Who had put the knife in? That American bastard, Elmer T. Dawson? He had never liked him.

'As a girl at school I was taught that a man who loses his honesty has nothing left to lose.'

'I am sorry, but I'm not quite with you.'

'Then let me put it more plainly. You are a member of the board of a company which belongs to Mackenzie Transworld, in which I hold the controlling shareholding. Right?'

'Right, Lady Mackenzie. You recently promoted me. I was very honoured.'

'You already received a large salary and expenses, and after our discussion on this very terrace you had reason to believe you might receive further and speedy promotion.'

'Well, yes, that was what I felt *might* happen, Lady Mackenzie. Not that this was promised, of course. It was just that I felt our meeting had gone well.'

'You have the use of an expensive motor with a driver,' Myrtle continued. 'You receive a two per cent mortgage, an annual cash bonus, plus ten thousand shares in the company every year, with an option to purchase more at fifty per cent below their middle quoted rate. And further promotion would bring you even greater pecuniary advantages.'

She paused.

'That is so, Lady Mackenzie. I am very grateful, and I pledge myself to work to the best of my ability in the interests of Mackenzie Transworld.'

'You work in the interests of Hamish Keiller, not Mackenzie Transworld. You have been lacking in honesty, in that you have just told me a deliberate lie – in addition to another lie even more blatant at our last meeting.

'You claimed then you were a nephew of the late Peter Hillman, whom I met many years ago on business in the Bahamas. That is not so, and you know it is not so.

'Mr Hillman died when his plane crashed into the Atlantic while he was delivering it to Britain after the Second World

War. He was unmarried, and he had no relations living. Somehow you discovered we had met, and used that knowledge to attempt to ingratiate yourself with me.'

Keiller opened his mouth to speak but Myrtle held up her hand imperiously to silence him.

'You will have your turn when I have finished,' she told him coldly. 'You advised me, against the advice of all the other members of the board, not to go ahead with a merger with Mr Mojo. You gave the most cogent reasons for it. I was impressed, just as I had been impressed by the kind remarks I heard you had made about me when you and your colleagues drove back to your hotel from the meeting here.

'But I wished to make certain that I was not being falsely impressed. So I made some inquiries. I discovered that you were to be paid a very large sum of money by Mr Mojo, deposited in the Bermuda Bank, to pass on certain information about Mackenzie Transworld to him.

'While you proposed to me that we should string Mr Mojo along and endeavour to take over his company, you were, in fact, giving him all manner of details of the structure of *our* company in the hope and expectation that instead he might take over Mackenzie Transworld. In which case, you had every hope of being appointed chief executive. Judas received thirty pieces of silver. Your fee, in cash and kind, allowing for inflation and exchange rates, would be rather larger.

'I am dismissing you, Keiller. Your employment, and salary, terminate today. You will return to your hotel where you will find a return ticket, economy class, deposited in your name at the reception desk. I have already given instructions for your office in Coventry to be locked and your car to be repossessed from the long-term car park at London Airport.

'You have let me down, but more important you have let yourself down. Sue me if you wish. But think before you start. I have naturally consulted our company lawyers and you will only waste your own money in going to law. And in your present situation, to spend money pointlessly would be extremely ill advised. Now, have you anything to say before you go?'

'I have indeed, Lady Mackenzie. You have totally misunderstood my discussions with Mr Mojo. Your company's interests have always been paramount with me.'

'You swear to that?' asked Myrtle.

'I swear,' Keiller insisted. Sweat was streaming down his back. He had to convince this cow she was mistaken, or he was finished. 'I give you my word of honour.'

'And also that you have not passed on to Mr Mojo confidential information about Mackenzie Transworld?'

'Absolutely and positively not. I swear.'

Myrtle pressed the bell push. Irene Loxby appeared. She was carrying a small tape recorder. She placed it on the table, pressed the activating switch. Against a faint background of static, all three heard Keiller's voice.

'. . . And so, Mr Mojo, the key to the company lies with Lady Mackenzie. She holds a majority of the voting shares, but it should be possible to buy on the stock exchange in London or Hong Kong, through nominees of course, a considerable amount of non-voting shares. When the buyer holds an important enough stake, she could be forced to take him or his representative on the board. From this, I believe the other directors could be persuaded where their future interests lie. And from their decision would stem all the advantages which I have earlier enumerated. After all, everyone likes to be on the winning side.'

Myrtle pressed the stop button.

'You need not enumerate the advantages again, Keiller. They are on another tape. So much for your word of honour.'

Keiller stood up. 'It's a lie!' he cried hoarsely. 'That's not my voice! It's a fake. I can prove it. A malicious fake.'

Myrtle shrugged; the man was going to be tedious.

Keiller began to shout. 'You're mad! I knew it. Bloody mad!

All you rich people are mad! You don't recognise loyalty when you see it.'

'I think we do, Keiller, largely because we see it so rarely. Oh, one last thing. That pen I gave you. It was rather special. I would like it back.'

'Take the bloody thing!'

Keiller flung the pencil onto the terrace flagstones. The plastic barrel split open like a nut being cracked. Inside lay a thin piece of green plastic, a printed circuit, silver transistors, a silicon chip, and, in tiny lettering, the name Mojo Electronics.

'You see, Keiller, that pencil was my ear – and your downfall. Now, get out!'

The Australian did not care greatly for Nassau. It was not his sort of place. He distrusted its glitter and gloss, the pretty pastel colours of the expensive shops on Bay Street which provided a thin veneer of sophistication on a secret world of violence. Three murders a day was the average, and mostly in the streets during shopping hours – a higher figure in relation to population than in the worst areas of New York.

The attackers were usually drug addicts, wild-eyed, crazed young men wearing masks, carrying guns and cutlasses like the pirates of another age. It was unsafe to walk in any street, no matter how brightly lit, after dusk. Clients for the casinos would not risk strolling from their hotels a hundred yards away for fear of being assaulted. But then, when a penthouse suite with a sliding roof that opened to reveal the stars cost £14,000 for a single night, the gulf between the rich and the wretched was of staggering width.

The Australian's hotel suite cost several thousands a week, and although he did not pay it himself, the bill still had to be paid, along with other ludicrously inflated prices for meals, room service, limousine hire. These debits represented money going out instead of money coming in, and this the Australian always set against his own private parameter of expenditure in the terrace house in Stockport. Here, at the lowest possible cost, he maintained the headquarters of his company; and more important, the house represented emotional security and stability.

He had grown up here with his mother and Uncle Rob – who to the Australian's delight and surprise had actually left him a legacy of £50 in his will. The sum was negligible, of course, but the affection and generosity prompting the gift were not. It was tangible evidence that Uncle Rob had liked him, perhaps even loved him, and the Australian could not recall anyone else who had ever shown their feelings for him so convincingly. He had never cashed the cheque, but kept it framed on the wall behind his chair in his office in what had once been Uncle Rob's bedroom, as a reminder of an old man's affection.

The Australian had come to Nassau at the suggestion of Mr Carlotti, who through the introduction of the Australian's former schoolfriend, Micky Cohen, had originally put up money to buy his share in Trinity-Trio – as well as shares in other companies which the public innocently assumed the Australian owned personally. Astute public relations consultants spread and fostered the legend that, as some people have green fingers when it comes to gardening, the Australian possessed the uncanny knack of spotting financial opportunities. He bought companies as other men without his gift might buy neckties. And reading of his deals, his mergers and takeovers, the public assumed that the money required to finance and fuel them must be his own.

Micky Cohen, the son of a bookmaker, had opened the door to such enormous sums of money by starting a betting shop in the 1960s when the British government of the day made such ventures legal. This change in British gaming laws was advocated by well-meaning members of Parliament, many of whom had no idea that such a proliferation of gambling on every level would provide a solid foothold for organised crime. When

Cohen's betting shop was operating successfully, an emissary from Mr Carlotti approached him with the interesting suggestion that, using Carlotti's illimitable funds, Cohen should open a chain of such betting shops, and then casinos, all over Britain. Money from robberies, swindles and, most important, from the sale of drugs could now be constantly laundered through such outlets, where people dealt almost exclusively in cash.

Cohen told Carlotti of the Australian's gift for sensing money-making opportunities where others could only see disaster or failure. Carlotti met the Australian and proposed they should join forces: Carlotti's money plus the Australian's genius.

The Australian did not trust Carlotti, of course. He had engaged his own private investigators and knew from what deadly and dangerous sources Carlotti acquired his money: largely from drugs smuggled out of one country into another, then across a border and into a third. On this tortuous journey a small amount of white powder, almost worthless at its source, could become a million-pound security by the time it reached its destination. The fact that on the way it would alter, ruin and frequently end the lives of those involved was of no concern to him. That was their affair entirely. Neither Carlotti nor the Australian would ever handle the goods personally, nor would they dream of sampling them.

The partnership had certainly been profitable, and efficient. But now something had jarred in the smooth machinery of their joint ventures. Progress in what had seemed a relatively simple takeover, if on a gigantic scale, had come to a sharp and unexpected halt. The two vital shares in Trinity-Trio, which could tilt the balance of ownership, had suddenly and inexplicably disappeared. Anna Lu-Kuan was adamant she had not signed a form to claim them but the under-manager, Mr Li, was equally insistent she had, and moreover had produced the relevant document that bore her signature and so apparently proved her a liar. So what the hell was going on? Maybe Carlotti could provide some answers. The Australian looked at his watch. He should arrive soon.

As he sat in the white leather chair, a glass of iced mineral water at his side, the Australian turned his thoughts to another matter that had been preoccupying him, as a man with a hollow tooth keeps sucking it, almost savouring the discomfort.

On the night Lord Jackson had fallen from the window after his reception to mark the inauguration of Trinity-Trio's new headquarters in Nassau, the Australian had received a letter from his half-brother, Ian, in Katherine, telling him of the death of Amy Crabtree.

The news about his mother was sad, but not altogether unexpected. Although his communications with her had been minimal, he maintained sources of information in Australia and knew she was in poor health. For this reason, and as a belated and secret attempt to make amends for their quarrel years ago over the division of the profit from his earliest deals, he had instructed film studios he had recently acquired in Hollywood to offer Amy the starring roles in two films to be made in Australia. She had never suspected this, of course; and now she would never know. Still, he had helped her – and also himself, for the pictures were already grossing huge sums.

Ian's letter went on: 'Now for something better. I have been following in your footsteps out here as best I could. As a result of a number of deals which I won't go into now, I have made 500,000 Australian dollars clear, so I'm coming to London.

'I don't know half the deals you've done, because you wisely keep your name out of everything. But now, look behind you! Another Australian is coming up in the fast lane. We've never met, but we will, and soon!'

The knowledge should have given pleasure to the Australian; he should be looking forward to meeting Ian, who was about half his age, and who clearly admired him. Instead, he felt dread. This youngster seemed to be making more money much faster than he had at the same age, and a heavy feeling of foreboding lay like lead in his belly. There was no room for two Australians.

A tap on the door interrupted his thoughts.

'Come!' he called.

Carlotti entered the room, instinctively locking the door behind him. Years of living on the edge of danger made this a habit. He crossed to the bar, poured himself a huge Bacardi, added fresh lime and ice cubes, sat down. This annoyed the Australian, although he did not show his annoyance. But the man might at least have the courtesy to ask whether he could pour himself a drink, especially such an expensive one. And then he remembered that Carlotti owned the hotel.

'What have you discovered?' he asked.

'Not a great deal, that's the odd thing. A Chinese physician, Dr Sen, has arrived here from Hong Kong. I'm told by my people he has some involvement with the Triads, so presumably he's not here just to examine a patient.'

'What about the man Li in the bank?'

'We've intercepted him.'

'What do you mean, intercepted?'

Carlotti sighed. How could this guy be so sharp when it came to making money yet be so incapable of grasping the basic facts of real life? The Australian saw Carlotti's eyes cloud with anger and began to feel uneasy.

'I gave him twenty-four hours to come up with an answer to our question,' Carlotti continued. 'He couldn't – or rather he didn't. So one of our cars ran into his car when he was leaving the bank. He wasn't injured, but badly shocked, of course. Another of our cars was right there, and the driver offered to take him to the hospital for a check-up. Actually, we have him in a house on the other side of the island. I want to question him myself.'

'I'd like to be there when you do.'

'You will be,' Carlotti replied shortly. 'Let's get going.'

The Australian followed Carlotti out of the penthouse. As he closed the door, he glanced behind him and frowned with annoyance. Carlotti had not finished his rum. He could never abide waste.

As they crossed the reception hall, a page boy saluted him smartly.

'Telegram for you, sir,' he said.

The Australian opened it: 'HAVE CHANGED PLANS STOP AM GOING WALKABOUT AND FLYING TO LONDON THEN NASSAU AS UNDERSTAND YOU ARE THERE STOP LOOK FORWARD TO OUR FIRST MEETING STOP PUT CHAMPAGNE ON ICE STOP REGARDS IAN'

The Australian put the telegram in his pocket. Champagne on ice; that would cost at least £50 a bottle, and he never drank the stuff. It was bad for you, he thought, and anyhow you pissed it out minutes later. Fifty pounds for a pee. Insane!

Carlotti's Cadillac, with dark glass in the rear compartment, stood blocking the carriageway under a huge 'No Parking' sign opposite the hotel entrance; the man who made the rules could also break them. Two doormen sprang forward to be first to open the car doors. The Australian and Carlotti climbed into the cool, air-conditioned interior.

Up front with the American chauffeur sat another American. His shoulders and arm muscles bulged under his light-weight shirt. He did not acknowledge them as they climbed in, but kept looking from side to side, his head moving slowly with the latent menace of a warship's gun turret.

The huge car accelerated along the coast road, past the imposing gates of big houses where uniformed guards waited, arms folded, night sticks and revolvers at their belts. Notices warned away casual callers: 'Private Property. Keep Out. Bad Dogs.'

'Where is this man staying?' the Australian asked Carlotti. He did not want to mention names. He was not sure he could trust the two men up front. The less anyone knew, the safer for all; especially for him.

'On the south side. You'll see.'

The car swung away from the ocean, going inland, crossing the carefully unadvertised centre of New Providence Island. Trees that had been tamed on the north coast in the gardens of the rich, surrounding artificially grown lawns sprayed by electronically controlled sprinklers, here grew wild. Pines and palms bearing coconuts or huge red berries stood so close to casuarina trees that trunk rasped against trunk. Ahead, the potholed road shimmered in the heat. Beyond the next village, Adelaide – named presumably, the Australian thought, after the same queen as the city in Australia – wooden huts were painted in crude colours: blue, purple, yellow, green. Some lacked windows, most had only primitive front doors made from the panels of looted packing cases or old-fashioned enamelled advertisements for Pratt's High Test Petrol, Lipton's Tea.

Outside one such shack, made of sheets of corrugated iron rusted by the salty air, the driver stopped the car and then reversed expertly and instantly so that it was facing the way they had come – a mark, the Australian guessed, of the trained getaway driver.

Carlotti tapped on the door of the hut. It opened slowly on hinges made from strips of an old leather belt. A black Bahamian stood behind it, eyeing them cautiously. When he recognised Carlotti, he opened it wider. A gust of foetid air from the unventilated interior, foul as a blocked sewer, spewed out in their faces. The Australian coughed at the stench, then followed Carlotti inside.

The room's painted metal walls were hot to the touch. Whoever lived here must cook themselves alive, the Australian thought. They went past a primitive closet, the cause of the smell, into a smaller room made of wooden packing cases. Inside, a Chinese man in his early thirties sat on a wooden chair, his wrists and ankles tied with rope. An American and a

Bahamian stood watching him. The scent of ganja was sweet and strong on the air.

'Is he talking?' Carlotti asked the American.

'No, sir. I've told him it's in his own interest to talk, but I guess he's afraid to.'

'Isn't he just as afraid of what will happen to him if he doesn't?'

'No, sir. It's the Triads. These Chinese are shit scared of them.'

'You a Triad man?' asked Carlotti.

Li shrugged his shoulders. 'I don't know what you mean.'

'Don't give me that crap!' said Carlotti angrily. 'Here you stay until we get the truth from you. You can play it hard, or you can play it easy. If you play it easy, nothing happens to you. We dump you in the hospital Out Patients, where you will be looked after. We've got witnesses who will say your car got run into and you were in shock. Someone very generously picked you up and gave you a lift. No one will ever know what you've said.'

'I'll know,' said Li. 'So will you. So will they.'

'To hell with the Triads! Where are those goddamn shares?'

'I've told these men already. Miss Lu-Kuan signed for them. She must have them.'

'That's a load of crap! Think again, buster! Because we're getting the truth out of you if we have to keep you here for ever.'

The Australian turned away. He could not stand violence and that was clearly the next move. He went out of the hut and stood leaning against the wall, feeling its heat through the thin cloth of his shirt. Carlotti followed him out.

'What's the matter?' he asked.

'You'll never get anything out of him with that sort of treatment,' the Australian replied. 'He'll die rather than reveal what he knows – if he knows anything. Why don't you try it more subtly? Give him a jab of Pentothal.'

'We've done that,' Carlotti replied. 'He just talked a load of garbage. The trouble is these Triads often use deep hypnosis. Their people will sing, but only surface stuff. No truth drug can reach deep enough down into the hidden recesses of their minds. Fear is the only way.'

'There must be some other way to resolve this – just in case he really doesn't know anything.'

'So why don't you tell me what it is?'

'I will.'

'I'm listening.'

The Australian began to speak slowly, incisively. At first he had only a vague idea what he was going to say, but the words carried him along and he could tell from Carlotti's face that the man was interested.

'All right,' said Carlotti at last. 'It's risky, but we're playing for hellish high stakes. We'll give it a whirl.'

Mojo waited to receive Myrtle at the top of *Lady Mojo*'s gangway. A launch had brought her out from the shore at Fremantle, the quaint little town south of Perth. As the base for Australia's successful challenge for the America's Cup, it had been redecorated, renovated and restored to an elegance it had never originally possessed when it was a major port in the nineteenth century. Now it had all the charm of a stage set, a beautifully preserved monument to an age of steam and sail.

As soon as Mojo had received reports that Mackenzie Transworld appeared unwilling to co-operate over car manufacture, he had engaged teams of researchers to uncover Myrtle's real background. As the Chinese sage Chia Lin had wisely remarked: 'An army without secret agents is exactly like a man without eyes or ears.'

Mojo now knew that the widely published and publicised accounts of her upbringing in Mexico were totally false, and that she still felt embarrassment because she was neither fully Indian nor British, but, in the harsh judgement of an earlier generation, a half-breed. He also knew that she had made her first real money through a remarkable betting coup at Calcutta races, and how on the death of her husband in Nassau in circumstances at least as peculiar she had assumed control of the Mackenzie group.

His investigators had discovered an old Goanese, who called himself a doctor, one Luis da Leppo, living in California. He had provided a great deal of information about Lady Myrtle. He had not wished to discuss her at all – indeed initially he denied even knowing her. But Mojo's men were expert, and without any limit on their expenditure, as long as they produced results. They learned that da Leppo had received huge legacies from a number of wealthy, elderly ladies who, shortly before their deaths, had altered their wills in his favour. This had not endeared da Leppo to their families and others who had expected to benefit from their estates. Some had even thought of bringing suits against him for alienating the affections of these old ladies, but since he was not a professional doctor, they found they lacked grounds. Nonetheless, they poured out their theories and thoughts and bitterness to Mojo's investigators, who used the threat of combined legal action to loosen da Leppo's tongue.

Mojo approved of the way in which Myrtle had divided the ramshackle Mackenzie group into totally separate companies so that if one lost money – as the mine in Canada had been doing – it would not affect the profits of the others. He had heard stories of her habit of making quick decisions, regardless of the advice of experts, working on what she claimed was feminine intuition. Mojo did not rate that explanation very highly; he suspected she consulted other sources of information before she reached decisions – sources different from those of her own executives. So she was wise. She was wealthy. She was also probably lonely – as, indeed, he was himself.

He watched her now as she climbed the scrubbed wooden steps. Her skin appeared dark against the dazzling white hull.

She wore a light grey silk frock with a wide straw hat to keep the sun out of her eyes, and this emphasised her colouring. She carried a small handbag, and extended her hand warmly to him as he bowed in greeting.

'I appreciate your request to meet me personally,' he said. 'Like you, I prefer to discuss business matters privately. Two people can reach a decision, one way or the other. Three makes a committee. As Napoleon said, "You cannot make war by committee." '

'Or love,' replied Myrtle. 'I understand that you are very well read in the biographies of the great decision-makers?'

'That is true,' agreed Mojo warmly. So she had also spent some time in research. But then that was to be expected; he would never underestimate her talents. As Sun Tzu had said: 'Know your enemy and know yourself, and you can fight one hundred battles without disaster'.

Mojo led his guest to the afterdeck where chairs were set out under an awning in the Mojo colours, beside a table of drinks.

'We must learn from those who have achieved great things,' he said, as he drew up a chair for her. 'I have studied Foch's *Principles of War* and of course Clausewitz on war. Then there is *The Book of the Five Rings* by my countryman, Miyaoto Musashi, and the Chinese classic *The Art of War* by Sun Tzu. I keep these books by my bedside. If I cannot sleep, I read them. They are my constant companions.'

'All on war,' said Myrtle in mock surprise. 'Nothing on peace?'

'Ah, my Lady Mackenzie, peace is unfortunately only an interlude between wars. We fight to come into this world, we fight for survival, we fight against leaving it. Yet war is not essential. It is, as the Chinese think, a continuation of failed diplomacy.'

'I hope you do not now wish to fight against me?'

'No, Lady Mackenzie. I do not wish to fight, I seek no victory over you. I seek something much more worthwhile. Association.'

Sunlight glittered on the surface of the sea and caught panes of glass ashore, heliographing unknown messages across the water. A steward hovered with a tray of drinks.

'Champagne,' said Myrtle.

'French or Japanese?'

'Taittinger.'

'You have the best taste, madam. My own favourite.'

'It is a taste refined by earlier years, when I could never afford the best. Or, indeed, even the second best.'

'As with me,' said Mojo approvingly. 'You know how I started?'

'Repairing cycles, so I hear.'

'Yes. Like the English Mr Morris who became Lord Nuffield, and whose cars, unfortunately, are no longer made but which for years carried his illustrious name. He started repairing bicycles in a side street in Oxford. Then he began to build them. Next, he equipped them with little engines and sold motor cycles. It was then suggested he should add another two wheels and so he found himself selling cars.

'My beginnings were much the same. But in Hiroshima. In rather harsher circumstances. A small stone rolling down a mountain side gathers momentum and power as it goes. So it was with both of us. And, of course, with you, Lady Mackenzie.'

The steward poured champagne, stood back respectfully while they sipped it. Mojo waved him away.

'I believe what Omar Khayyam wrote: "I often wonder what the vintner buys one half so precious as the goods he sells." '

'I agree,' said Myrtle. 'And also with another opinion attributed to Omar Khayyam: "Take the cash, and let the credit go." '

Mojo smiled. The sun reflected gold on his small and perfect teeth, glinted on his gold spectacle frames.

'Ah, so. I have heard you have a fine business mind, better than a man's, much better. I did not know you also read the classics.'

Neither of them were easy conversationalists. They had met

to discuss business, but without the frills and curlicues of talk
beloved of the East; first, skating around the subject, then
probing it from oblique angles, approaching it in a slow and
circular manner, a stately and set minuet of retreat and
advance. That was for other times, other places, other people
who had more time or the need to prove their superiority.

Mojo and Myrtle had no such need; they had both faced
obstacles of totally different kinds and had overcome them.
They accepted that this proved they must be superior to those
who had faced obstacles and failed to surmount them. Looking
at each other, they felt a mutual admiration, almost – if this
was not too strong a word after such a brief acquaintance – a
liking, certainly a real respect. They were two of a kind; they
understood the rules of the game of life – and instinctively they
felt they understood each other.

'I have come to discuss the possibility of some form of collaboration with our motor manufacturing plant in Coventry,'
Myrtle said, reaching the reason for their meeting without
further preamble.

'I did hear that you had discussed this with your directors,'
Mojo admitted. 'But my information was that as a result you
were not, shall I say, enthusiastic, Lady Mackenzie?'

'Your informant is misguided, Mr Mojo. We have examined
the problem and wish to discuss it further. I, personally, wish
to go ahead. And I am the majority shareholder in Mackenzie
Transworld.

'The history of the British motor industry since the Second
World War has unfortunately not been one of expansion, as it
has in your country. Indeed, wages in the 1980s increased by
315 per cent while productivity only went up by 26 per cent.
Also, our industry has some unhappy reciprocal agreements
with other countries, such as Spain, whereby they can export
cars to Britain, which only levies a duty on them of 4.4 per cent.
But on a British car, the Spanish add more than 36 per cent tax
on top of its basic price.

'Also, when we export cars to your country, Mr Mojo, every car is minutely inspected on landing for slight and frequently unimportant deviations from its specification regulations. This might be the size of a single bolt head or the colour of some totally unimportant wire.

'Britain has been importing 250,000 cars a year from Japan – many Mojos among them, as you know – but Japan in return only buys a handful of ours. This is not a sensible arrangement, especially when French and Italian makers have government help to keep the Japanese share of their car markets down to 3 per cent of their total car imports.'

'Ah,' said Mojo. 'I am well aware of these problems, but of course with the EC we also have our difficulties. Collaboration with your group could be profitable to both parties. Nissan plan to produce 400,000 cars at their factory in Washington, near Newcastle, within the next ten years. Toyota hope to produce about half this number from their plant in Derby, and Honda are building a factory in Swindon to turn out 100,000 cars a year. There is a great future ahead for all of us.

'Now, can I tell my experts who deal with the nuts and bolts of agreements that you, as the principal shareholder in Mackenzie Transworld, are in agreement?'

'You can,' said Myrtle shortly. 'I will tell my people the same thing. Let them sort it out.'

'Provided,' said Mojo, and the shadow of a smile played about his smooth face, 'provided that we both keep our personal and corporate identities.'

'Absolutely. I would not wish that you, as a manufacturer, should assume control of cars produced by Mackenzie Transworld, and I feel sure you also wish to retain your total independence. Cross-fertilisation, a sharing of ideas, and facilities such as research, marketing and production, these are what I have in mind.'

'Your feelings are mine. Sun Tzu tells us that there are but five basic elements – earth, wood, fire, metal and water. But their permutations are so many that they fill the world. The primary colours are also five in number, and their combinations are so infinite that the mind cannot visualise them all. Flavours, too, only number five, but their blends are so various one cannot taste them all. In the same way, the combinations of association are so many that we must find one that suits us both – equally.'

'I entirely agree,' Myrtle replied. 'But unless I am wrongly informed – as you appear to have been – you may have heard that it is my intention to take over your company.'

Mojo looked at her sharply. His eyes narrowed, his lips compressed.

'Are you telling me that is your intention, Lady Mackenzie?' he asked. 'I have heard rumours, yes, but only rumours, to which I never pay much attention. To the wise man they are but whispers on the wind.'

'But you believe this rumour has a basis in fact?'

'Knowing the toughness of the world of commerce today, and the fact that it is only another branch of war, the answer must most regrettably be in the affirmative.'

'I would like to assure you categorically here and now that I have not the slightest interest in taking over your company. If you need to reassure your bankers, directors, shareholders, or any other interested parties involved, please do so.'

'I am honoured by your frankness, Lady Mackenzie. And I must say, having heard of your business acumen and your directness of purpose, I am greatly relieved.'

Mojo smiled. So did Myrtle. And suddenly they were both laughing.

'I think we will get on, Mr Mojo,' said Myrtle. 'To be frank, I rather dreaded meeting you. I was in Calcutta during the Second World War at the time of the Japanese air raids and these prejudices linger in the most inexplicable way.'

'We must forget the past, which has sad memories for both of us, and look to the future, Lady Mackenzie. Our future. I think we will do a lot of business together.'

He poured another two glasses of champagne. They raised them in a toast, not quite sure whether they were toasting the future, the prospect of business they could do together, or simply each other.

Looking at Myrtle as she sipped her drink, Mojo felt a warmth towards her that he had never anticipated, indeed had not experienced towards anyone for years. She was a fighter, like him, and like him she was also on her own. After the death of his wife many years earlier, he had also been alone; childless, without relations, striving to find fulfilment, satisfaction, and meaning in an otherwise solitary and empty life.

In the early years of his marriage, he and his wife had consulted all manner of physicians in their attempt to have a child, but without any success. Only comparatively recently had he learned that in all likelihood this inability to conceive was a side effect of his experiences in Hiroshima. Others suffered from leukaemia or different forms of cancer: he, who had so much to give any child, was denied the right to reproduce. It seemed the ultimate irony of fate. The explosion on which his vast fortune and industrial empire was based had also ensured he would not have any successor in direct line to whom he could hand it on.

Mojo had put work in place of relationships, commercial deals in place of love. He had bought women as he wanted them and found nothing but ashes in his mind and mouth when the relationships ended. He might be envied by all manner of people around the world, interviewed on television by those who sought to find the secret of his success, written about in newspapers and magazines he never knew existed until the press cutting agency deposited acres of frequently inaccurate newsprint in his main office, but none of these reflected the inner man.

Here, next to him, sipping champagne with every evidence of enjoyment as though it really was a treat she could not otherwise afford or justify, was someone of like mind, like background, who had married and lost her husband, and who, like him, was childless.

A waiter appeared with another bottle of Taittinger, opened it, set it down in a silver ice bucket, bowed and withdrew. Mojo poured two more glasses, and then two more after that.

Myrtle removed her dark spectacles. She felt she need not hide behind them any longer. With this man she could be herself. The sensation was rather like removing shoes that had proved too tight – smart in the shop but uncomfortable for hot-weather wear.

'I have a question to ask you, Mr Mojo.'

'Speak on,' he said. 'I have very few secrets in my life.'

'I cannot believe that,' she said.

'That is up to you – if I may call you Myrtle? Please call me Kendo. Now, what do you wish to know?'

'My question is simple and direct. How did you come to believe that my directors were not keen on the idea of amalgamation?'

'We had information,' Mojo replied carefully, smiling.

'I can imagine. And I can imagine it came from one source. Let me ask another question. Did all your information come from a man called Keiller? A Scotsman, ambitious?'

Mojo did not answer immediately. Instead, he sipped his champagne slowly, looked out over the shining sea, past the yachts and the speedboats. He could deny this easily enough and she would have to accept his denial, or at least appear to do so. But to tell a lie was not a sound foundation for a future friendship, or indeed for any alliance. This thought ran parallel with another. He was already planning, if only subconsciously, for some deeper association with this remarkable woman. She intrigued him; more important, he liked her, not as a potential business partner but as a person, as a woman. He made up his mind.

'Yes,' he agreed. 'You knew about that?'

'Afterwards, only,' Myrtle admitted. 'We held a meeting in my house here in Perth. Everyone seemed for an amalgamation, but this young man did not speak, so I asked him to stay behind and tell me why he kept silent. He then expressed strong views against it, which I won't go into now. I was impressed by him. Perhaps because he reminded me vaguely of someone I had known years ago on the other side of the world, who was killed just after the war – when he was about the same age as Keiller.'

She paused.

Mojo bowed his head in understanding. He knew how she felt; his brother and too many of his friends had died in that same war. An image flashed through his mind of crossing the Causeway to Singapore from the mainland. The sudden unexpected thunder of a British shell exploding; the cries and screams of wounded and dying all around him, the slow spread of pain in his leg, blood thick as treacle staining his uniform.

'Possibly because of this I felt drawn to Keiller,' Myrtle continued. 'For a moment I thought foolishly that he might have been the sort of son I could have had. But I had my doubts as to his character, so I decided to test him.

'To show Mr Keiller how impressed I was with him, and as a mark of my confidence that he could go on to greater things, I presented him with a pencil, as I do all my senior directors. I did not tell him, of course, that in his case it had a secondary purpose.'

'Ah, so,' said Mojo, smiling his approval. 'And then he came to me and you heard our discussion?'

'Part of it, yes,' said Myrtle.

'You have asked me a question which I have answered frankly,' said Mojo. 'Now let me ask you one. Did the pencil by any chance come from a young Australian, Ian Bruce Crabtree?'

'Yes. It did,' Myrtle agreed, surprised.

'Ah, I suspected as much. He asked me to give him one. He is a clever young man. The son of someone who, many years ago, did me a very great favour. Tell me, what happened to it?'

'When I dismissed Keiller, I asked for it back and in his rage he threw it to the floor. It split, useless.'

'That is very sad,' said Mojo. He put his hand inside his sharkskin jacket, took out a propelling pencil, handed it to her.

'Would this do as a substitute?'

She glanced at it, smiled broadly. 'The same sort of thing?'

'Of course,' Mojo said. 'You can see the name. Mojo Electronics. I make them.'

'So I see. As a replacement, it may come in useful for future discussions.'

As Myrtle put the pencil in her handbag, Mojo took out a pen from the same jacket pocket.

'This goes with it. They make a pair. You press the top once, twice, three times – like this. Then it gives a warning. A faint buzz to warn you that someone is carrying a listening device.'

'So you knew all along, when Keiller came to see you?'

'I did, Myrtle. But I thought you would somehow discover that he was not entirely trustworthy.'

'It takes a rogue to know one,' laughed Myrtle.

'Ah, so. I agree,' said Mojo, smiling. 'Or a woman to know a man.'

'Which is often the same thing,' Myrtle retorted.

He poured more champagne and they laughed together, liking each other more.

'Now,' she said. 'Would you dine with me tomorrow night?'

'I would be delighted – on one condition. That you lunch with me here aboard my yacht the day after tomorrow.'

'Agreed.'

Myrtle felt absurdly pleased. It was a long time since a man had asked her to lunch as a social engagement, not simply as the excuse for a commercial discussion.

'I am so glad you are free then,' said Mojo graciously, 'because I am off the day after that to Sydney.'

'I've just bought a house on the harbour,' said Myrtle. 'It's being furnished now.'

'You have not lived there before?'

'No,' she said, 'but I have stayed there often, and the restaurants on the Rocks are alone worth the journey.'

She did not add how she liked to see the immigrants, the new Australians, yellow or white or brown-skinned, all enjoying themselves with an equality that had not existed in Calcutta when she was young.

But then, of course, Australia was a land of immigrants. The Aborigines, she knew, were the first by probably 40,000 years; the British came next and after them, since the 1970s, Lebanese, Indonesians, Greeks, Italians, Japanese, Chinese, Vietnamese, Germans, Spaniards, Portuguese. She had read somewhere that now one in five of the population of Australia had not been born in the country.

'I have a rather different reason for visiting Sydney,' said Mojo hesitantly. 'I have never told anyone else of this, but I feel you would understand.'

He paused.

'People go there in thousands to see the Opera House or the bridge, both of which are a symbol of Australia, like Ayers Rock. They go on tours all round the harbour in boats with guides who explain the points of interest. I join these parties, sometimes a different one each day. They don't know who I am. They remark on my yacht which is at anchor, and when they read her name it is interesting – and sometimes illuminating – to hear their comments on Mojo cars, or TV sets or cameras.

'My reason for going on these trips is that they are a kind of pilgrimage. I had a brother two years my senior, Myrtle. He was proud to serve in the Navy and had volunteered for any kamikaze operation his superiors might require. He was selected to sail in a warship towards the mouth of Sydney Harbour. When still some distance out at sea, they shut off their engines and coasted on in total silence. Then they launched midget submarines that could creep in under the metal nets strung across the harbour mouth. But once inside, my brother's submarine developed engine trouble. He managed to surface, sent a radio message to his mother ship, and then submerged.'

Mojo paused, his face suddenly gentle.

'He never reappeared, nor has that submarine ever been found. He was much cleverer than me. Had he lived, his achievements would have far outshone mine. I always remember him when I look out over the sunlit ocean and see the sailing boats and young people all enjoying themselves.

'Have you ever noticed, Myrtle, you hardly ever see *old* people in Sydney? It is a city of the young. And I think of all those other young men in every army, navy and air force in that war now so long ago, who never had these opportunities, who never came home.

'In Burma, at Kohima, where our Japanese army faced its first serious defeat in that theatre of war, the British raised a memorial to their dead. On this is a Greek inscription: "When you go home, tell them of us and say: For your tomorrow, we gave our today."

'I think of that when I think of my brother, and I feel humble. How did I survive when so many, far better, far braver, did not?'

Myrtle reached out and took his hand gently.

'I'll give you my address,' she said. 'I'm going to be in Sydney for at least a couple of weeks. You must come and see my house – and me. Then perhaps we can try to answer your question together.'

FOURTEEN

The Present: Katherine, Northern Territory, Australia
London, England
Nassau, Bahamas

I flew back to Katherine on the next plane. I wanted to consider in my own place, among my own people, the offer Lady Mackenzie had made to me. I didn't really feel at home in Perth. High-rise buildings and wide streets were alien to me. Among them it was all too easy to forget where my real roots lay.

I found a mass of papers from Mr Mojo awaiting me regarding the franchise for his electronic equipment. I had no idea that his companies produced so much and under so many different trade names: television sets, microwave ovens, telephone-answering equipment, fax machines, electric fires, bugging devices, midget radios, radars for yachts and aircraft, military installations, echo-sounding gear – the list was staggering.

And as I read, I realised that I held in my hands the seeds of a fortune that could equal or surpass whatever the Australian was making or had made. Asia was a virtually inexhaustible market. I thought of the millions in India who could afford cheap transistor radios or TV sets. Malaysia was a huge market; so was Thailand. The opportunities in China, if ever they amended their rigid Marxist regime, were without limit. And on all these sales and the sales to sub-agents I would receive four months' credit. It was a chance beyond all imagination. With this, did I need to act as Lady Mackenzie's go-between? I thought not, but the challenge was too attractive to let pass. So was the unrepeatable opportunity to show the Australian I was not simply a young man on the make but someone to be reckoned with seriously.

Looking through Mr Mojo's material, with its complex formulae and a whole new language of computers which meant little to me, I came across the name of Dick Ford. He was an executive in a company in Wales that made some of the gear under licence. I put a telephone call through to him at his hotel. He was on the point of leaving for the airport, and I was lucky to catch him.

I really just wanted to make my number with him, to say that, in a sense, we were now working for the same firm. His voice was breathless at first, as one who feels he should be on the airport bus and not forced to take an unimportant call, and then instantly conciliatory when he heard who I was and what I wanted him to do for me in London; no expense spared, speed and accuracy my only requirements.

'I'm flying to London,' I told him. 'I'll be at the Dorchester. I want the names and addresses of two people with the specialist qualifications I have given you waiting for me when I'm over there next week. People you can personally recommend.'

'Of course. I'll be delighted,' he said.

Maybe he thought he could join me in my franchise. On the impulse I asked him: 'That Triumph you bought – what have you done with it?'

'Well, as you may or may not know, I bought it with Mr Mojo's money. He's going to have it refurbished and then resell it. He never misses a trick, that man. As a matter of fact, he offered the car to me as a bonus, in lieu of cash.'

'And you decided against that?'

'Yes. After all, I wouldn't know how to sell it. What could I do with an old car?'

'What indeed,' I said and put down the phone. I knew Mr Ford had reached the limit of his achievement. One man could use the unexpected gift of such a vehicle as a stepping stone to fortune; another did not even recognise it was a stepping stone.

I felt contempt for Mr Ford, instant and total. And almost immediately I felt the same contempt for myself. Ford might have reached the peak of his career in the sense of making money, but he seemed loyal. He could be trusted, and trust, I had already discovered, was as scarce a quality as integrity which, in turn, was as rare as a man with naturally green hair. He wouldn't knife me in the back or, indeed, anywhere else. This was a big point in his favour. He had helped me, in his way. In return, I would help him on, as far as he could go, as far as he wanted to go – which hopefully might just be the same destination.

I then sent a cable to the Australian in Nassau, and a fax to Lady Mackenzie in Perth. I hadn't got my own fax machine yet but there was a shop in Katherine that did photocopying and advertised the latest kind. I noticed it wasn't a Mojo, and thought I should sell them one later on.

I asked Lady Mackenzie if she could kindly arrange to have all available information about Trinity-Trio ready for me at the Dorchester when I arrived.

The London plane was delayed at Perth for three hours through some electrical faults of the kind that never feature in any airline advertisement. I bought *The Australian Enquirer* at a news-stand and skimmed through the pages. There were more shootings in the Lebanon, in the Middle East, in Northern Ireland. Another nuclear leak was reported at a Russian plant; an airliner had come down in the Arctic with three hundred passengers aboard, and no survivors had been found. There is so much bad news that I often wonder how newspapers managed to fill their pages years ago when there seemed so little. I turned over to Australian news, and a headline seemed to leap out of the page: '*British executive found dead; high flyer takes fatal overdose.*

'Mr Hamish Keiller, a Scots-born 32-year-old director of the British motor manufacturing subsidiary in the Mackenzie Transworld Group, was found dead in bed in his Perth hotel this morning.

'Mr Keiller, who was on a business visit to Perth, had stayed behind when his fellow directors flew back to Coventry, England, earlier in the week after a conference with the chairperson and principal shareholder, Mexican-born Lady Myrtle Mackenzie. Mr Keiller was married and leaves a widow and two young children in Edinburgh, Scotland.

'A bottle containing sleeping tablets was on the bedside table beside a note, on Mackenzie Transworld notepaper, addressed to the Coroner. A police spokesman said that from the contents of this note it seemed that Mr Keiller had committed suicide. An inquest will be held later this week.

'Lady Myrtle Mackenzie, who is at present in her Perth mansion, was unable to be contacted late last night but a spokesperson for her, Mrs Irene Loxby, said: "This is a great tragedy. Our deepest sympathy goes out to his widow and young family." '

I folded up the paper, went into the bar and ordered a double brandy. The sun was shining brightly outside, as it nearly always does in Perth, but for me some of the shine had suddenly gone out of the day.

I had never met Keiller. I knew nothing more about him than what I had read in this same newspaper, and because a rich old woman claimed she doubted he was all he seemed I had shot him down.

I felt ashamed. I was indirectly – maybe even directly – responsible for his death, just as I was responsible for

Jack's death in the meatworks. And maybe if I had tried
harder to persuade the Stranger to leave Katherine he also
would still be alive. I had been playing out of my league with
forces I did not fully understand, and could not control. I felt
again that curious sense of disillusion I had experienced in
Katherine when the bank manager wanted a cut-price car. I
was focusing all my efforts on growing rich, and in doing so I
had lost sight of other values, other aims that might be more
satisfying, more worthwhile. I thought of my father, and
remembered Lady Mackenzie's advice about the price that
great wealth always exacted.

On the impulse, I stepped into a phone booth and telephoned her house. Mrs Loxby answered and put me through
immediately. I could imagine Lady Mackenzie out on the back
porch in the shade, overlooking the sunlit river, watching and
envying the young people in their sailing boats. Ironically,
they probably envied her the luxury with which she was
surrounded.

'I have just read in *The Enquirer* about Keiller's death,' I
told her. 'I take it he was the man to whom you gave that
special pencil?'

'You take it correctly,' she said. 'It is very sad. He took all
this so seriously, this business of making money, while you and
I know it is only a game.'

'One in which who dares, wins?' I suggested.

'Of course. He was out of his league like Phaeton in the
myth, who drove his father's chariot across the heavens and
then found he could not control the horses, approached too
close to the sun, and so nearly set the world on fire. I
sometimes think of Phaeton when I watch the swans on the
river here. Swans were called Phaeton's birds because his
friend Cygnus was so saddened by his death that he persuaded
Apollo to change him into one.'

'Really?' I said. 'A black swan?'

'No,' she corrected me. 'White.'

'You have a great knowledge of the classics, Lady Mackenzie,' I told her.

'Not really,' she replied. 'Just what I learned at school. I like myths. They are always so much more interesting than reality.'

'Always?' I asked her.

'Always, Ian. Goodbye to you.'

She replaced the receiver before I could reply. That was another thing I must learn from the very rich, I told myself. They would invariably cut off any call when they had said all *they* wanted to say. They never appeared greatly concerned about hearing what others might have to tell them. There was much I could learn from the very rich, I knew. But, equally, I was beginning to wonder whether I could not teach them a lesson even more valuable.

When I reached London, I found a thick parcel awaiting me, and an oleaginous letter from the managing director of Mojo's London office asking me to dine with him at the Connaught. I put that on one side and read through the T-T material.

There were photocopies of old newspaper cuttings from the *South China Morning Post*, *The Wall Street Journal*, *The Financial Times*, *The Times*, the *Daily Telegraph*, *The New York Times*, *Forbes Magazine*, *The Enquirer*, as well as expert calculations by stockbrokers and others. I knew the early history well enough. I just wanted to check who held the voting shares.

The later material on this had come from some private and unacknowledged source in Nassau. Lord Jackson was desperately ill – some thought he could even be dead, although such suggestions were strenuously denied by the consultant physician involved, Dr Kirkpatrick. Jackson still held 149 shares; two lodged with the Occidental-Oriental Bank had apparently gone missing, 100 were owned by United Charities Incorporated, and the Australian controlled the remaining 49. It was thought the Australian was a front man for Italian-

American interests. The name Carlotti was mentioned several times; so were other names linked with organised crime.

I rang the managing director of Mojo, thanked him for his invitation, explained that unfortunately I could not accept at the moment, but in the meantime I wanted everything he could discover about Mr Carlotti, apparently now in Nassau. Also, about Lord Jackson's present state of health, his background, and his relations.

The information was brought round by a motor-cycle courier within the hour.

I spread out the cuttings, telexes and faxes on the table in my suite. As I did so, I thought how easily I had slipped into the habit of living well. Why have one little bedroom, as in the Katherine motel, when you could have a suite? The more you spent, the more important people thought you were. And the more important they thought you were, the more helpful they'd be. It was a simple equation – especially when I was not paying the bill.

There were several newspaper cuttings on Lady Jackson. She had been Deb of the Year twenty-five years earlier and was still referred to in one of those unctuous phrases used by ageing chroniclers of the social scene as 'the well-known society hostess', or 'the brightest party-giver in London'. She was interviewed frequently on the subject of her youthful skin and figure, and always gave the credit to skin specialists and herbalists, who in turn were interviewed and praised what they called her classic features.

She was American, the daughter of a professor in the Dr Richard Jackson Medical Foundation which had been set up years ago by Lord Jackson's great-grandfather, one of the company's original founders, to examine what was then bluntly called unorthodox medical treatment by quacks but which nowadays had become dignified by the title of alternative medicine.

By reading between the lines, I gathered that her daughter

Elaine was a drug addict. Little paragraphs in society columns explained that the Honourable Elaine Jackson was missing from this party or that reception; she was resting in the country after her recent illness. Other cuttings referred to her friends who had been arrested on charges of handling cocaine or having marijuana in their handbags. Somehow, she had always gone free. I figured that now she was somewhere lying low having treatment; she could even be dead. I resolved to look into the matter.

There were also several articles about the style in which the Jacksons lived. They must be immensely wealthy, I thought, even by the standards of the ultra-rich. But they did not appear happy. The few pictures of them together showed them standing with some distance between them. I then turned up a report of an incident where Lady Jackson had her car towed away and she had struck a traffic warden. There had been a court case, and she was fined and her licence endorsed. I didn't care a damn about that. What interested me was the name of Lord Jackson's lawyers: Messrs. Lightfoot, Proudbody and Dedberry of Lincoln's Inn. I made a note of the name and address.

It had always struck me as odd that lawyers, from the time of Dickens, seem to have such unusual names. Perhaps all names are unusual, or perhaps those with unusual names gravitate to the law? I decided that if I ever took over Trinity-Trio, I would have *The Enquirer* newspaper, which they owned, do an in-depth series about that. If it interested me, I guessed it might interest others.

Dick Ford had also done his duty. His Wales office provided the names of two men, with their addresses, whom he believed could help me. The first one lived in Notting Hill Gate. I telephoned his number. A woman's voice answered.

'I'm looking for Mr Lockwood, Roger Lockwood,' I said. 'I'm a friend of his from Australia.'

'He's gone away,' she said.

'When will he be back?'

'Goodness knows. He's gone with a crowd of others. They're trekking across India, into Burma. I'm his mother. Can I help you?'

'I want to contact him with the offer of a job. You've no address for him, no number I could catch him at? This could be a very lucrative assignment.'

'No, none,' she said. 'He threw up his job three weeks ago.'

'What was his job exactly? He never really told me.'

'Oh, he was in charge of computer security – in one of the banks. A good job, with prospects. His father and I told him he was a fool but, well, if you know him, you know he's got red hair. He's headstrong, always right, never listens to anyone else if he doesn't want to, and that's that.'

'That's that,' I agreed, meaning that he wasn't getting any trade from me. I replaced the telephone and rang the second man, Mr Ghulab Khan, at an address in Watford. A Pakistani voice answered.

'Khan's Old Rawalpindi Takeaway here.'

'I would like to speak to Mr Ghulab Khan,' I said.

'He's working in his room. Is it his tutor who wants him?'

'No. Just someone who wants to have a discussion with him about a business matter.'

'He doesn't owe you money, I hope?'

I heard anxiety in the man's voice and guessed he was a worried father.

'Far from it. I want to pay *him* money.'

'That'll be a change. Wait a minute. I'll get him.'

In the distance I heard a BBC announcer read the news headlines, and then a younger voice said: 'Yes?'

'Yes,' I said. 'My name's Crabtree. I'm an Australian. Electronics. I hear you're pretty expert in that field?'

'It's my hobby,' he said, as though I was going to dispute it or criticise him.

'I work for Mojo Electronics in Australia,' I said, which was true in a sense. 'When can I see you?'

'Where are you?'

'In London. The Dorchester. Could you come here and have a drink with me?'

'I don't drink: I'm a Muslim.'

'Shall I come to your takeaway, then?'

'No. My father will be here. It's rather difficult. I've got a van. Can I meet you somewhere near here?'

'Sure. I don't know the area, though.'

He described his van, an old Morris 1000 painted white with a red stripe down the side, and suggested we meet in a village, Letchmore Heath, near Watford, at six o'clock that night.

'I'll be there,' I said.

'How will I recognise you?' he asked.

'You won't, as we've not met, but I will look for your van.'

I went down into the foyer, bought an A–Z Guide to London to find the way out, and a map of Hertfordshire. Then I hired a nondescript Ford Escort, ate a quick sandwich, drank a pint of black coffee, and drove out through the thrombosis of rush-hour traffic, up through the Park and the Edgware Road, then right on into Elstree and branched off for Letchmore Heath.

It was a tiny village with a pub, still quaintly and somehow uncharacteristically rural in a mass of housing estates, building projects, walk-in precincts. Billboards advertised new Tudor-type executive-style homes. Not houses, always homes. When did a house become a home? I wondered.

I could not tolerate this crammed-together existence, like ants in one of the termite eruptions outside Katherine; all quiet outside but inside, throbbing and teeming with overcrowded life. More than ever I missed the open spaces, the wide emptiness where one can think for oneself and not be pressurised by the sheer mass of other people's opinions.

This was not my country. I had thought that as the plane came in over London Airport, dipping and turning in a wide circle, stacked seven deep until the others in front of us had landed. Far beneath us, below grey, heavy clouds, lay rows and rows of identical houses facing narrow streets along which rows of toy cars were parked. Minute green spaces, with here and there the glitter of a reservoir or a lake with windsurfers on it, were the landscape's only redeeming features.

I saw Ghulab Khan's red and white van parked in a lay-by. I stopped behind it, walked over to the driver's door. Ghulab Khan was at the wheel. He looked at me in surprise but when I spoke, he smiled. He was a young man, not much more than twenty, wearing jeans and a tartan shirt. I climbed in beside him. The van had no carpets, only a rusty metal floor covered with old newspapers. The seats were split, showing dirty padding and grey horsehair. The cab smelled damp, as though the van always lived out of doors or beneath the surface of a lake, a smell which was probably accounted for by the English climate.

'I'm glad you came,' I said.

'I wanted to hear what you had to say,' he replied.

'I understand you are a pretty good hacker?'

He bowed his head in acknowledgement.

'I want to use you, if I can, for a private job.'

'Nothing illegal?' he asked. 'I've had one or two brushes with the law. They can't sue you for hacking into someone else's program, but they're working on it.'

'Lawyers work on anything if there's a fee,' I said. 'It's a lawyer's private papers – computer disc or whatever you call it – that I want you to look at.'

'In London?'

'Yes. Lincoln's Inn. Lightfoot, Proudbody and Dedberry.'

'That should not be too difficult, so long as you can arrange for someone in their office to put them up on the screen. I can't hack into their discs otherwise. Can you fix that?'

'I'll do my best.'

He wrote down the name, picked up a telephone directory from beside his seat, checked the number.

482   Andrew MacAllan

'When?' he asked.

'As soon as possible. But I know nothing about this business. Is it a long job?'

'Not really. Want to come with me?'

'Why not?' He made no move towards starting his van. 'What do you want me to find?'

'Details of a will. Who the beneficiaries are, when it was signed, how much there is to distribute. Especially in shares.'

'If it's on the computer, I can peel it off for you,' he said. 'No problem. But it will cost you two hundred pounds.'

'What if it's not on the computer?'

'I still have to go through the motions and try. Two hundred pounds, win or lose.'

'You'll go far,' I told him.

'Some say I can't go far enough. I'm one of them,' he said. 'I've hacked into the Bank of England, the Ministry of Defence. Stockbrokers' offices are a joke. A lawyer's should be easy. Like picking a child's money box for a professional thief.'

'Why are you so sure?'

'Many businesses, newspapers, law offices and so forth collect so many files that they just haven't the physical room to store them all, so they put them all on computer. This makes them easy to find, from their point of view – and also from mine, because each file has its own codeword. Find that, and you can read everything it contains.'

'But how do you discover that codeword?'

'By running literally millions of words through my machine. Dictionaries of word names, place names, nouns, anything. It's a matter of trial and error, but very, very quick to do – usually only minutes. And then only very few secrets can stay secret.

'In the early eighties, a nineteen-year-old Los Angeles student hacked into the Pentagon. NASA, the Space Agency, was also done over, and to prove he wasn't boasting, the hacker left a message, "Kilroy was here", on the screen. Another had a look-see into the National Security Agency at Fort Meade, Maryland.

'How I do it exactly is what you pay for me. That is my secret, but, as I say, I don't expect many problems from a solicitor's files. If I'm going into a bank, their computers are covered in sheets of lead. They use optic fibres, all kinds of tricks to make it damned hard to winkle out their secrets. The MOD is the same. A lawyer will have some sort of armour against hackers, obviously, but for every poison there is said to be an antidote. And for all antidotes there's always another poison.'

'You sound like a philosopher,' I told him.

'Actually, I am doing a correspondence course for a philosophy degree,' he admitted. 'When I get that I would like to run an electronics shop.'

'Maybe you will. Ever thought of emigrating? Australia?'

'Is it difficult to get in?'

'I don't know,' I said. 'Maybe I could help you. I know some useful people in the electronics business there.'

'You didn't tell me.'

'You didn't ask me. Now, what's the best time to try this out?'

'They'll be pretty busy all day. I reckon about five, five thirty, should be best. Before they go home. Say tomorrow. It's too late tonight. They'll all have gone now. But first I'll dress up the van a bit.'

He climbed out and so did I. From the back of the van he took two boards that slipped into clips on either side of the vehicle. They read: J. BROWN & SON, ABERYSTWYTH. BUILDERS AND DECORATORS, ESTIMATES FREE, and a telephone number.

'It's unlikely there will be anyone from Aberystwyth in Lincoln's Inn at five tomorrow – I hope,' he said.

'Would it matter if there is?' I asked.

'Not really. That's the phone number of the local vicar.

They'll think they've got a wrong number if they ring him. By then we'll be out of the way.'

'What about the van's registration number?'

'Oh, that's not the real one.'

'But your van's red and white. That's pretty distinctive.'

'It's white because that will take any colour I care to blow over it with an aerosol. I can blow the wings blue, or paint the bonnet green, and stick some other lettering on the side, and then I'm a chimney sweep or a plumber. It's difficult to identify this van, if anyone could be bothered to try.'

'Have they up to now?'

'Not so far,' he said. 'But I like to take precautions.'

We arranged to meet in Park Lane next afternoon and then drive to Lincoln's Inn.

We arrived at exactly five o'clock, and parked two doors down from the lawyers' office. Khan swung round in his seat, went into the back of the van. I followed him. He pulled a curtain over the rear window so that anyone looking in would not see us. He had a set of car batteries bolted to the floor and an old TV set fixed in a corner. I noticed with proprietorial interest that some other black boxes were stamped Mojo Electronics. There was a primitive aerial rigged up inside the roof. He threw a number of switches. Lights glowed, the screen flickered green.

'Right,' he said. 'Now you do your bit.' He handed me a mobile telephone. 'Ring them. Say you want to see the will. You're one of the witnesses, you're uneasy about it. Anything you like. But we have to get that will up on their screen before we can hack it.'

'Okay,' I said, and dialled the number. A receptionist answered.

'I wonder if you can help me,' I said in my best Australian accent. 'My name is Jackson. I understand from a relative, Lord Jackson, who controls Trinity-Trio, that you handle his affairs?'

'I will put you through to our senior partner, Mr Dedberry.'
Another voice came on the phone, hard, querulous, suspicious.

'Can I help you?'

'I hope so.' I repeated who I was, said I needed to see him on Lord Jackson's behalf about a bequest he had made.

'I would need Lord Jackson's permission before I could discuss the matter,' Mr Dedberry said, very correctly.

'Of course. Obviously. But I have with me a letter from him giving me authority to do this.'

'Where are you now?'

'I'm in London at the moment. Just changing planes. I have come in from Sydney, Australia. But I'm flying on to Nassau this evening. Lord Jackson has had a very serious accident there.'

'I read about that in *The Enquirer*. Do you know how he is?'

'I would rather tell you when I see you than on the telephone,' I said guardedly.

'Well, Mr Jackson, it is very difficult to see you today. The office closes at six. But I can understand how you are placed.' He paused.

'I would be very grateful if you could manage literally ten minutes,' I said. 'No more.'

I heard a turning of pages, probably in an engagement diary.

'Could you be here in, say, half an hour?' he asked. 'I can fit you in then, if it really is for only ten minutes. I would like to help if I can. Lord Jackson is a much valued client.'

'I'll be there,' I promised and rang off. Kahn gave me the thumbs up.

'It will be up on the screen in a minute,' he said confidently.

He crouched down and began to tap keys, peering at the monitor, tapping out one set of digits after another, waiting for a few moments, then tapping out another set. Words flooded over the screen in a pale green cascade; five-letter, four-letter, six-letter words, like a moving pattern of letters. Some I recognised, like CASE, CHART, TOAD, then a jumble of consonants or vowels, RZGXG, BTVWZZ, GHLQT, and so on. I could make nothing of them. Then, after about ten minutes, a loudspeaker in the van began to bleep. Ghulab Khan looked at me and winked.

'We've got it!'

The word was PENNY, which, considering the importance Trinity-Trio always gave to the penny which they claimed was their talisman, seemed very apt.

It was stuffy inside the tin box of a van without proper ventilation; the electronic equipment seemed to give off quite a bit of heat.

'Now what exactly do you want?' he asked me. 'And exactly whose will?'

'Lord Jackson's.'

'Where's he live?'

'Right now he's in Nassau in the Bahamas. He has a house in Belgravia, a country place in Dorset. His first name is Roderick.'

I was surprised how many R. Jacksons there were, from a greengrocer in Edgware to a farmer in Cumbria. And then Lord Jackson's name came up with the note: *See also Trinity-Trio share deals, offshore companies, acquisitions.* A whole list of companies moved up the screen as Ghulab Khan went on tapping his keys, peering at the machine as though willing it to reveal more secrets. It did.

'There are several wills,' he said.

'Can you record them?'

'Of course. Which one do you want?'

'All, if you can,' I said. 'But especially the most recent; who he's leaving his company's shares to.'

Lord Jackson owned a lot of property. The screen was littered with details, valuations, prices, lists of insured antiques, paintings, the addresses of freeholds, farms, rows of shops, all of which he appeared to own personally. He was very rich, quite apart from his T-T shareholding. Whoever inherited this money need never be poor again.

Eventually, Ghulab Khan had it all. He switched off the machine.

'I'd like a print-out,' I said. 'Two, if possible.'

'I can't do that here. I'll do it at home for you.'

'Please do.'

He dropped me off at the Dorchester.

'I'll wait for you here,' I told him.

'What about my two hundred pounds?'

'When you deliver,' I said. 'I won't let you down.'

'I trust you,' he said.

'And I think I can trust you. You certainly know your business.'

'I like it, that's why. My old man likes buying and selling. So do I, up to a degree, but most of all I like electronics. Do you know, you can store the whole *Encyclopaedia Britannica* – that's forty volumes – on one disc only a few inches across? The entire Bible doesn't even take that. Amazing. It's a computerised world now.'

'Are people better for being computerised?' I asked him.

'Hell, no!' he said. 'They're all shits. They'll screw you if they can.'

'I hope not all,' I replied. 'Would you like to come in for a drink?'

'No. I told you, I don't drink alcohol. I'll see you later tonight.'

'Have dinner with me?'

'Be my pleasure. But don't forget to ring the lawyers and cancel your appointment. Otherwise they may get suspicious.'

I watched his van drive away, still with the absurd Aberystwyth signs, until I lost him in the traffic. I telephoned Mr Dedberry and apologised for being unable to see him after all. My plane had been put forward half an hour. I greatly appreciated his kindness in fitting me in at such short notice, but I would probably be back in London before the end of the week and would make a new appointment then.

I went into the hotel bar. I felt I had earned myself something long and strong and reviving.

The nursing home stood some way back from a road which had once been a country lane but which year by year had been widened to take more and more traffic from more and more new buildings. The nursing home itself was an Edwardian house of red brick with some Gothic pretensions: turrets, sharply pointed gables, patterns set in stone above an arched porch.

I turned in at the gates and noticed that the drive could do with raking. The lawn had not been cut that week and the edge was ragged. Here and there, in flower beds, lay discarded sweet wrappers and cardboard ice cream cartons. Several cars were parked side by side under a laurel hedge. The place had seen far better days, but as a retreat for very rich patients who did not necessarily wish the nature of their illnesses to be publicly divulged, it clearly had its uses. Few would give the house a second glance.

I parked my car near the others and walked across the drive to the porch. A brass letter slot that should have sparkled with polish was dull. Paint had blistered on the green front door; the blue and red and white pattern of glass panes in the door, once so fashionable, had chipped.

I pressed the doorbell and waited. A middle-aged woman dressed as a nurse but with a sluttish air about her, scuffed shoes and a shiny, sweaty nose, opened the door and stood looking at me.

'Good afternoon,' I said. 'I've come to see Miss Elaine Jackson.'

'We've no patient of that name here,' she replied at once.

'I understood that you are caring for the daughter of Lord Jackson?'

'You understood wrongly,' she said. 'I've told you, we've no one here called Jackson. Are you a reporter or something?'

'Something,' I answered, 'but not a reporter. The fact you think I might be, makes me feel you may also be mistaken about the presence, or absence, of Miss Jackson.'

I put my hand in my inner pocket, took out a wallet, removed a twenty-pound note, put the wallet back, rubbed the note between my forefinger and thumb. She looked at it greedily as though she had never seen a twenty-pound note before. She certainly wouldn't see this again unless it produced a reaction. But, as I knew it would, it did.

She said in a whisper: 'There *is* a Miss Jones here who might be the lady you seek.'

'The lady I seek is in her very early twenties, brown hair, blue eyes. Was of a cheerful disposition until she fell ill.'

'That describes so many of the young women patients we get here,' she admitted. 'Come in.'

She held out her right hand. I placed the note in it. Her fingers closed like the claws of a bird on a grape. She transferred the bribe to her pocket.

'You'd better see the doctor.'

I came into the hall. She knocked on a door. A young man wearing a white coat came out of the room, looked from the nurse to me. A stethoscope hung from a pocket.

'This is Dr Graham,' she explained. 'Our resident physician.'

'Glad to meet you, Doctor,' I said. I shook his hand. 'My name is Crabtree, Ian Bruce Crabtree, from Katherine, Australia.'

'I was out in Australia last year,' he said. 'Sydney. Stayed there three months till my money ran out. Wonderful place. Those restaurants down on the Rocks. Everyone so friendly. Great.'

'Working?'

'No, just looking around. Off to Hong Kong shortly. Got a position there.'

'You should keep on the plane to Sydney again. Australia's bigger than Hong Kong. There's more scope.'

'And there aren't too many more people!' he said jokingly.

'That's true,' I replied. 'We could always do with one more. Now, Doctor, I would like to see Miss Jones.'

'Which one? We have three Miss Joneses here as patients.'

The nurse moved away. She did not want to get involved. She had already betrayed one trust.

'The patient I want to see is really Elaine Jackson, whatever she's called here.'

'You are family?'

'No. But a very close friend. And her father, as you may have read, is very, very ill in Nassau. I happened to be in London and thought I must see her. I leave tomorrow for Nassau, you see.'

'Oh, yes. Come with me.'

Elaine Jackson was in a small room, one of several partitioned out of a much larger room. Three feet of ornate Edwardian cornice showed round the ceiling. There was a bed, still unmade, a chair, and a white cupboard with a Mickey Mouse stencil on the door. Whatever other attributes the nursing home had, they didn't spend much on furniture.

The patient was sitting on the chair, with a book in her lap. When she looked up at me, her eyes were vacant, unfocused. She was only looking at her book, not reading; she had probably slipped back to a mental age that would appreciate the Mickey Mouse stencil more than the printed word.

'A visitor,' said Dr Graham brightly. 'You know each other?'

'We do now,' I said, extending my hand.

She shook hands, but her hand felt damp and soft and unhealthy, as though it had been filleted.

'Well, I'll leave you two people,' said the doctor. He went out of the room and shut the door.

We stood staring at each other.

'Who are you?' she asked me bluntly.

'An Australian,' I told her. 'I heard you were here. I thought I'd just drop in and wish you well.

Even as I spoke, I marvelled how easy it was to tell lies, to begin a whole fraudulent story and, worst of all, to make it sound so plausible; not just to the person to whom I was telling it, but to me, who had made it up. She indicated the bed. The old springs creaked as I sat down.

'Who told you I was here?'

'A mutual friend, someone who didn't want me to mention their name. They thought it would embarrass you.'

'Why should that embarrass me?' she asked. The suggestion seemed to concentrate her mind. 'It would embarrass my father, my mother even more. She's embarrassed by everything about me. Fact one is I'm on the hard stuff and have been for years, and fact two is that I've got Aids. Did you know that?'

'I heard you weren't well,' I replied diplomatically.

'I could hardly be worse,' she said. 'You don't die of Aids but then you catch a cold or get 'flu or some damn thing and there's just no resistance, and you die of that. I don't think it's a new disease, you know. It's just that it's been discovered. Before, people got ill and wasted away.'

'There's nothing new under the sun,' I replied. 'It's probably just a new name, as you say.'

'It doesn't really make much difference, does it? You're still dying. But now in a socially unacceptable way.'

For someone who appeared to be so vacant, Elaine Jackson seemed fairly rational to me; at least, so far.

'It makes some difference to those who love you,' I said. 'And if you're wealthy, it can make some difference to those you leave behind, who have not been so fortunate.'

'Like who? Don't say you're one of these do-gooders who want me to give money to drought victims in Ethiopia or something? If I did, it would only go into the Swiss numbered bank accounts that the rulers of so many African countries maintain. It would help buy them a new Mercedes with air-conditioning, or maybe a Lear jet or just a white mistress. I know some of those dictators in Africa. I've slept with several of them. Maybe I caught Aids from one of them and not from a poisoned needle, though that doesn't matter a shit now.'

'Some things matter,' I said. I wanted to turn the conversation in the direction of Trinity-Trio shares. I didn't think I was doing too well. We were shadow boxing, not landing any blows. I didn't know much about drugs; in fact, I knew nothing about them then, but I guessed if I lost her interest I lost the deal, and the deal was what was important to me, no matter what I had to say or do to get it. The end must always be worth the means employed to reach it. If you don't believe that, then don't get involved – and I was involved. So I came to the point; in with a punch.

I said: 'I've been in the Bahamas with your father.'

This was a lie, but, I told myself, only in respect of time. Within two days I would be in Nassau.

'He came to see me weeks ago,' she interrupted. 'He was sorry I was in here. The police found me in the gutter. I had a bit of paper on me with my mother's address on it. They rang her. She wouldn't get involved, so she rang him, and down he came.

'They don't live together, you see. Well, not really. But they keep in contact. They have to. It would be bad publicity if they didn't. The shares might fall, and that's the worst possible thing that could happen. I was rather touched, really, when he looked in. We haven't ever had much in common. We hadn't at this meeting, either, but at least he made the effort to drive down here – or rather his chauffeur drove him.'

'Do you like your father?'

'So so. Don't really know him.'

'If you had the chance to do good to him – or to anyone else – would you take it?'

'If it didn't hurt me, yes. Why not?'

'I told you I'm an Australian. I'm one of the real Australians. My mother is an Aborigine.'

'My mother was Deb of the Year,' she said.

'Maybe we should talk about these things,' I suggested.

'We are, aren't we?'

'The Aborigines are one of the oldest people in the world. Forty thousand years ago, when Australia was joined to Asia by a narrow isthmus, they crossed it and settled in the north. Maybe the fact that Australia was once part of Asia is why we welcome so many Asians now as immigrants. There used to be a "white only" policy. Not now.'

'What are you getting at?' she asked me. 'You're talking too much and saying nothing. If you've nothing else to say, I'm going back to my book.'

She pouted, like a spoiled little girl. Her eyes were vacant again; her mind had wondered off course. I realised I had simply to touch the right note, with the right accent, and I would have what I wanted. But how could I find the note? I felt like a blind man trying to open a locked keyboard on a piano he'd never played.

I said vaguely, casting around for something to catch her interest: 'The Aborigines are probably the only people left alive in the world who have the right values. They're getting corrupted, of course, as all other simple peoples are. American Indians, Eskimos, all kinds. But the Aborigines less so because the distances are so vast.'

'What's so special about them?' she asked.

'They don't care for possessions. They up and go and move on. They move across the face of their enormous country like birds fly when they migrate. If we could find out what makes Aborigines wander at will, what inner compulsion it is that drives them on and guides them when they go walkabout, we would have learned one of the last great secrets of mankind. We might even have learned the secret of happiness.'

'You see all kinds of people with the urge to move,' Elaine said vaguely. 'They go on holiday abroad, take cruises, fly hither and yon seeking something, never finding it. Do the

Aborigines find it? Do they even know what they're looking for?'

I sensed mild interest in her voice; I was getting warmer, slightly nearer the heart of the argument.

'I think so,' I replied. 'And I want to spend time trying to discover whether what I think is true or not.'

'So you want money from me?'

'No. That's the last thing I want from you,' I said.

'That'll be a change. What do you want then? Everyone wants something.'

'I want your interest.'

'Well?'

'Interest expressed in a way that's better than money.'

Then I slipped in my key question, quickly, when I thought that her fuddled mind was already fully occupied trying to digest my last remark.

'You don't own any shares in Trinity-Trio, do you?'

'Not one,' she replied at once. 'I don't give a damn for T-T. I've heard nothing but that bloody company since I was a kid. Was it making money, losing money, should they buy this, sell that? Shit to the whole thing!'

'A lot of people feel the same,' I said, not adding that I was not one of them. 'If ever you acquired any shares – say your father left them to you, or someone else gave them to you, that kind of thing – would you pass on a few to try and discover this last locked-in secret of the human mind?'

'How many's a few?'

'Eleven,' I said. 'How about that?'

'How about it, then?'

'They would be held for you in the name of trustees. You wouldn't lose them. And they could do an immense amount of good.'

Elaine's eyes were beginning to glaze over; I was losing her attention, her interest.

'I haven't got any, but you can have eleven of what I haven't got,' she said dully, as though the matter no longer concerned her.

'You mean that?'

'I've said so, haven't I?'

'Shake on it.'

I shook her hand again. It still felt cold, unhealthy, like the fingers of a corpse. I tried to keep the distaste from my face and my accent.

'Will you give me a letter that you agree?'

'I haven't got any paper,' she said petulantly. 'Don't you trust me?'

'Of course I trust you. But if anything happened to me driving back to London, say, who would know what we'd agreed? It's the others we can't trust.'

'You're right,' she said. 'Everything you said is right. You can't trust the others. That makes sense. They're bastards. Have you any paper on you?'

I patted my pockets as though searching, and then I pulled out the document Mojo's London lawyer had drawn up for me.

'Here,' I said. 'I've typed out a few lines that give the gist of what we've discussed.'

'I can't read well without my glasses. They won't let me have glasses. This book has pictures and I can see them. They won't let me have a pen or a knife and fork either. Silly buggers! It's in case I kill myself. And I've been killing myself for years on snow. Why should I start again now with a knife or a fork? They don't understand, these people.'

'Of course they don't,' I said. 'They're the others. But we do. We understand, you and I.'

I took a pen from my pocket.

'Sign here,' I told her.

She signed obediently in a rather round, childish signature. A graphologist might have made much of it; I didn't. I just wanted her signature on the dotted line.

'Better get the doctor or someone to witness it,' I suggested. 'You know what these lawyers are like.'

'They're all bastards!' she said. 'I've got a trust fund somewhere, but they don't let me have any money out of it. Whenever we meet, it's a thousand guineas for this, for something else, petty disbursements, travel, miscellaneous costs. They're milking it themselves, but they won't give me anything, the bastards!'

I took a twenty-pound note from my wallet.

'Here's something,' I said, and gave it to her. 'It's not much, but it's all I have on me.'

Again, this was not true, but it sounded convincing.

In a corner of the room a string with a red tassel hung from the ceiling. The string was thin; I suppose if it had not been, some patients might have tried to hang themselves from it. I pulled the tassel gently and heard a bell tinkle faintly in the far recesses of the house. I waited for a few minutes and rang again. This time the nurse who had shown me in opened the door.

'What do you want?' she asked. 'A pot of tea?'

'No,' I said. 'I would like to see Dr Graham and you here for a moment.'

'All right,' she said. 'I'll get him.'

She pressed a bleeper in her pocket. Graham came running.

'No hurry,' I told him. 'I just want you to witness something Miss Jones here has signed.'

'You a lawyer?' he asked, suddenly cold. 'She's in my medical care, you know.'

'I know that, and I'm not a lawyer. But she's over twenty-one. Would you witness it? If not, I'll get two other people.'

'I'd like to read it first.'

'There's no need. It's a personal document,' I told him, and pushed the paper towards the nurse. She signed her name. Her eyes were fixed on the twenty-pound note Elaine Jackson was smoothing out on the arm of the chair. I wondered how long it would be before the nurse got that, after we'd gone.

'I quite understand your reluctance, Doctor,' I said smoothly, 'but it's only a formality, and so I'll ask another nurse to sign, or someone else.'

'Oh, all right, I'll do it,' he said. 'The trouble is she's a rich young woman.'

'Rich?' said Elaine. 'You're joking! The only money I've got is this twenty pounds this kind man's given me.'

'It's just to buy sweets,' I said hurriedly. 'Tins of Ovaltine, little things she may want. Twenty pounds doesn't go far these days.'

The doctor signed his name. I folded up the paper, put it back in my pocket, stood up.

'Thank you very much,' I told him and the nurse.

'You're not going, are you?' Elaine Jackson asked me.

'Yes,' I said. 'I have to get back to London, but now I've found where you are, I'll come and see you again.'

'You're a nice person,' she said. 'You and the Aborigines.'

'I'll send you a book about them,' I told her.

'Thank you,' she said. 'I want one with pictures in it. Reading's so difficult without my glasses.'

I went out of the room, walked down the corridor, round a corner, waited. I heard the clack-clack of the nurse's heels as she turned into Elaine's room. I walked back along the corridor and stood outside the door, listening.

'Give me that money!' ordered the nurse.

'No. Shan't. It's mine,' said Elaine defensively.

'Give it to me.'

I heard a scuffle, and opened the door. The nurse looked at me guiltily, Elaine with relief.

'Nurse,' I said, 'I'll give something to you. Advice. I've already given you one tip in cash. Now I'll give you this promise. You touch that money and you'll regret it every minute of your life. Give her back the note.'

The nurse pushed the crumpled ball that had been a twenty-pound note over the table to Elaine, and then ran from the room. I turned to Elaine.

'Hide it,' I said.

'I've nowhere to hide it,' she said. 'There are only three drawers with my clothes in them. They search through those and under the bed, under the pillow, every time I have a visitor in case they brought me drugs. If she doesn't take the money, someone else will.'

'Give it back to me then,' I told her. 'I'll keep it for you. When you come out of here, we'll have a party.'

'You mean that?'

'I mean that,' I said. And I really did – at the time.

It was only on the way back to London, driving through the thick traffic of commuters going home to their mock Tudor-style executive-type residences that I felt mean. I'd given a mad girl a gift and a lot of talk, and she'd signed away a fortune. I'd taken back the gift. If I hadn't taken the twenty-pound note myself, that nurse would have done so, or if she missed it, a cleaner or perhaps even the doctor would have prised it out of the girl. I rationalised that I was keeping the money for her, but it didn't make me feel any better. The only thing that did make me feel better was that I'd done a deal. No one could beat me on that.

Ghulab Khan had shown me the paragraph in Lord Jackson's will in which he left 140 Trinity-Trio voting shares from his controlling share holding of 151 in trust to his wife for her life-time, and 11 absolutely to his daughter Elaine.

He regretted their estrangement and hoped that before the will would be proved, all disputes and disagreements between them would have been resolved.

There was a further comment that I had noted down especially because I realised I had only to wait for Lord Jackson to die and I would control those shares. The two missing shares would then be totally irrelevant.

I was all but up there with the Australian. Only he didn't know that. Yet.

I had not expected anything like the publicity circus that surrounded me as I came through Customs at Nassau International Airport. I had imagined I would simply arrive quietly, like any other passenger, totally unknown to anybody, and then make my own number discreetly with the Australian. I had reckoned without the incredibly complex web of communications that now surrounded the world, and which one day could throttle it.

A stringer at Heathrow had tipped off an Australian journalist in London that I was flying in. He checked from the passenger list that I was from Katherine, and a paragraph went back to the Katherine weekly paper about the arrival of a young Territorian in London. The Katherine paper immediately responded with a long fax to their London office, explaining I had just made half a million dollars and was obviously someone to watch. Would they send a full interview soonest? The reporter missed me, but to cover this lapse cabled to Nassau that the Australian's half-brother was arriving. Hence the reporters, cameramen, TV and radio crews thrusting microphones at me as in the old days beggars held out their hands for alms. In a sense, I classed these people as mendicants; they also wanted something for nothing. In this case, news of my intentions.

I gave them a smile and nothing else, and took a cab to the hotel. Here, my arrival had already been noted before I even checked in. The reception clerk handed me a sealed envelope and I went up to a room overlooking the sea and banked with flowers. I didn't like these. They weren't the fresh, free wild flowers of the Outback. These were hothouse blooms specially grown to be bought by the rich. I classed them as cemetery plants.

I switched off the air-conditioning, found one window that

opened – all the others were hermetically sealed – and stood breathing in the salty air blowing off the sea. Then I read the letter.

It was from someone I had never heard of, a Dr Luis da Leppo. He was in Suite 171 up on the seventeenth floor. He wrote, 'I believe we have a mutual friend in Australia. Please be kind enough to ring me on arrival. I may be able to help you.'

I wondered who he was and how or why he could help me, and then I punched out his room number on the house telephone. A woman's voice answered almost immediately: 'Dr da Leppo's suite.'

I explained who I was. There was a pause. I could sense that a hand was being held over the receiver. Then she said: 'He is resting, but if you would like to come up now, he would be pleased to see you, just for a few minutes.'

I had a quick wash, took the express elevator up to the top floor. A nurse was waiting for me by the door. She was middle-aged, stern-faced, wearing a white uniform.

'Dr da Leppo has not been very well,' she explained. 'Please do not tire him.'

'I'll do my best not to,' I assured her.

I followed her into the room. Air-conditioning made it very cool, almost uncomfortably chill. Whoever was in here was being kept in what was virtually a cold chamber. I saw an old man sitting in a wheelchair. He wore a striped pyjama jacket. He was probably wearing striped pyjama trousers, too, but his legs were covered by a light cashmere rug and I could not see them. He gripped an ebony walking stick between his knees in the way old, frail people in wheelchairs often do, as if they were in a punt on wheels.

His face was yellow as old vellum and scored with lines, wrinkled like a tortoise's neck. Muscles and veins stood out in bold relief. He offered me a hand to grip, thin, boney, dry and bloodless as a lizard's claw. He indicated I should sit down, so I sat in a chair that had been thoughtfully pulled up near his.

'You are very kind to come and see me so quickly,' he said in a faint whisper, as though he had to drag each word up a long way from some limitless depth. He looked very ill and very tired, but clearly he had something to tell me that was important to him, if not to me.

'My pleasure,' I said, not altogether insincerely.

'As you see, Mr Crabtree, I am no longer as young or as spry as I was, but I have heard from a mutual friend, Myrtle Mackenzie, that you are what she calls a likely lad. It is nice to meet you. I understand from her that you have already made a relatively large sum of money in Australia, and she believes you could go on to become very rich. That is what I wanted to see you about.'

He paused. His mouth opened and shut and opened again, and for a moment he gasped like a fish on the fishmonger's slab. His left eyelid flickered, as though winking at me in confidence; his mind had somehow lost control of the muscle.

The nurse came in and said soothingly: 'There, there, Doctor.' She turned to me accusingly. 'You're not tiring him, I hope?'

'I hope not,' I answered.

The old man waved her off with the feeble, irritated dismissal of the aged. She moved away but did not leave the room.

'I must tell you I am part Portuguese, part Indian,' he said at last in his soft, strange whisper. 'When I was very young, I said I was Goanese. There are a lot of Goanese in India, and I lived in Calcutta where, in those days, such things mattered.

'Lady Myrtle, of course, whatever she says now about being born in Mexico, is half Indian, half English. I am not a real doctor; I never qualified. I only adopted the title as a name, so I am not breaking any vow of medical confidentiality when I tell you she became pregnant in very unhappy circumstances by her stepfather. I was able to help in that situation, but she was innocent and had left it late before she approached me. Things went wrong – they often did then. Death was not uncommon after an abortion. She had a bad haemorrhage. And she could never have a child.'

'She told me,' I said.

'Yes? I am not surprised. That has always been very close to the surface of her mind. I felt guilty about my part in this and tried to atone for what I had done – although from the best of motives. I helped her to become secretary to Sir Hilary Mackenzie. Then I heard that two horses were going to win their races, which had been fixed. She borrowed some money and made a great deal more. But we both discovered there is something much more valuable than money.'

'I don't know what that is.'

'Then I will tell you. You're a young man, you're ambitious, like she was, like I was. We both wished to become very rich because we had both been very poor. We wanted to rise above insults and sneers, and to make a lot of money was the only course we had. If we succeeded, those who had looked down on us would look up to us. That's the way of the world. The rich man's jokes are always funny.

'So we set ourselves aims and somehow we achieved them. But we were like climbers on Everest; halfway up they think they've reached the peak, then they see another peak, and one after that, and they are all false peaks. When you go after money, as we did, you find a whole mountain range of false peaks. And you have to keep on climbing, although by then you doubt whether there really is a true and final peak. You've lost all your old friends on your way up, and you find you're on your own, and it's very, very lonely.'

He paused, and swallowed. His Adam's apple moved up and down in the thin leathery case of his neck, not much thicker than a turkey's gizzard. Tears began to run unchecked down his cheeks from the effort of talking so much.

'I'm an old man, as you can see,' he went on. 'I am not going to live much longer. I'd trade everything, as all rich old people would, to be young like you, knowing what I know. But both those wishes are impossible. So I must do the next best thing, tell you what I've learned in sixty years of, shall I say, business life.

'I wanted to see you because I understand you are a sensitive young man, as well as clever with figures. So remember this. Don't *just* worship Mammon. I did. So did Myrtle. And in the end we found he's not a very friendly god. More like a devil, actually. In Syriac, the word Mammon simply means Money, nothing more.'

His voice trailed away. His chin was now down on his neck. A thin streak of saliva dribbled from his mouth. The nurse came forward and dabbed it away expertly with a white tissue.

'There, there,' she said as though addressing a child, and turned to me. 'I think you had better go, Mr Crabtree. When he's a little better, you can come up and see him again. He's enjoyed the conversation.'

If that was enjoyment, what was purgatory? I remembered a Bible story from one of the few times I went to Sunday School as a boy. It was about a rich man named Dives and a poor man, Lazarus, who begged for crumbs from his table. They both died, and while the rich man went to hell, Lazarus went to heaven. A great gulf lay between them, but the rich man could see Lazarus and Abraham and asked if someone could be sent down to earth from heaven to warn his five children to change their wicked ways or end like him in hell. But Abraham refused. If they would not pay heed to the teachings of the prophets 'neither will they be persuaded though one rose from the dead'.

I felt that somehow I had been warned, if not from the dead, then by the next best messenger, a man waiting at the mouth of the grave.

I had a quick shower and then went back down to the reception desk, handed the clerk a sealed envelope. He opened it. When he saw the hundred-dollar bill I had put inside, he closed it again, put the envelope in his pocket, and addressed me very politely.

'Can I help you, sir?'

'You can indeed. I want a list of all the guests in this hotel and every other five-star hotel in Nassau.' I wanted to know who exactly was in Nassau who could help me and who might harm me.

'It will take a few moments, sir. It's on the computer.'

He went into some inner room. I glanced around the entrance hall, impersonal as an airport lounge, listening to the syrupy piped music; a tape on an endless loop. There's some similarity there, I thought, with the treadmill of life. Someone dies, someone else is born; the carnival is over for one but just beginning for someone else; a song – or a lament – without end.

The clerk came back holding a long computer print-out.

'Anyone special you're looking for, sir?'

'Yes,' I said, not wanting him to guess how little I knew. The names on the list meant nothing to me: Germans, Americans, two English lords, a French count, three Japanese – and one Chinese whose name I did recognise: Dr Sen, Hong Kong, physician and surgeon. He was the specialist who had treated Amy Crabtree and not charged her a fee. He was a long way from home. So was I, but now I felt I could be getting nearer home base.

'Dr Sen,' I said. 'What room is he in?'

He consulted a chart. 'Fourteen forty-four. But he's just gone out, sir. Only moments ago.' He glanced towards the hotel entrance. 'Why, there he is, sir. That gentleman in the light suit.'

Sen was walking slowly because he was worried. He had been in Nassau for several days and he had achieved nothing. Anna Lu-Kuan appeared sincere in her protestations that she had not signed the form; he had questioned her time and time again,

out all his skills as a physician in prising out truth from
a reluctant patient were useless. Her story never changed.
Mr Li, his only contact in the bank, had disappeared.

Sen feared that he might have acted too soon, too precipi-
tously; he was nervous and totally new to this dark half-world of
threats and danger and millions of money. He knew he must
proceed more cautiously.

He climbed in behind the wheel of his car, this thought in
his mind. Someone tapped on his window. He lowered it. A
young Bahamian, tall, clean-shaven, wearing a well-cut light
grey suit was smiling at him.

'Are you Dr Sen of Hong Kong?' he asked. He had no trace
of accent in his voice.

'I am. Who are you?'

'Bamford is my name, sir. Joseph Bamford. I think I have
got something here that really belongs to you.'

He held out a small envelope.

'What is it?' Sen asked him, puzzled. He had never seen the
man before.

Bamford did not reply. Sen ripped open the envelope. Stuck
between two small pieces of cardboard was half a chopstick; he
had received the other half in Hong Kong. He felt the blood
drain from his face at the memory. This Bahamian must be his
contact. He looked up at him, eyes narrowed against the bright
sunshine.

'What do you want?' he asked him.

Bamford did not reply but came round to the other side of
the car, climbed in beside him. Instantly the car was filled with
a very strong smell of jasmine hair oil. Sen kept his window
lowered.

'I thought I might be able to help you,' Bamford now
explained courteously, almost hesitantly. Whatever his choice
in hair lotion, Sen had to admit his manners were certainly
impeccable.

'In what way?' he asked cautiously. This fellow wasn't

Chinese, so how could he be certain he was who he claimed? He might have found this envelope in the street. But then he would not have known its significance, so he must be genuine. At this, Sen felt perceptible relief.

'I believe you are looking for two shares in a certain company,' said Bamford.

'Who told you that?'

'Someone I do not think you would know, so a name would be meaningless. But am I right?'

Sen took a deep breath and closed his eyes, trying to make up his mind. Should he trust this man? *Could* he? Could he afford not to? He opened his eyes.

'Yes,' he admitted. 'Trinity-Trio. Mr Li, a Chinese under-manager in the Occidental-Oriental Bank, claims that Miss Lu-Kuan signed for the shares and took them out. She denies this.'

'I know that.'

'Mr Li has disappeared. He was involved in a car accident. He was not greatly hurt. Some other people in another car kindly said they'd drive him to the hospital. But I have made inquiries and he did not arrive.'

'I see,' said Bamford, but not as though he understood. 'What does Mr Li know?'

'About what?'

'About Anna Lu-Kuan, for instance?'

'I have no idea, except that she is the confidante and probably the mistress of Lord Jackson. Where do you think the two shares are?'

'I could make an intelligent guess.'

'Make it.'

'I think they could have been removed by Mr Li himself. Consider my thesis, Doctor. Anna Lu-Kuan had to sign a form before she deposited the shares, and if Li copied her signature over a piece of tissue paper and then copied that on a withdrawal form, he could remove the shares himself. And no one would know.'

'Have you any proof he did this?'

'None. But they are bearer shares, without the name of the holder. Whoever holds them can vote with them. Other forces are also seeking these shares. The most dangerous is a Mr Carlotti who represents a powerful consortium of Italian and American businessmen. You follow me, Dr Sen?'

'I do.'

'There is also another interested character who appears to be operating on his own but, I understand, with Carlotti's backing. The Australian.'

'I have read about him. You think Mr Li was working for one of them?'

'The thought had crossed my mind. I also think he may have hidden them somewhere until the time was ripe to use them for his own, or his masters', gain.'

'Then they could be anywhere.'

'He may have used the flat of a girl few people knew was his friend. I propose we search there.'

'What, now?'

'There is no time like the present moment. I know the way.'

I had no time to hire a car, with all the performance of producing an international driving licence and credit card. I called up a cab.

'Follow that little car,' I told the driver, 'but don't let them know. Keep a couple of hundred yards behind.'

The driver nodded. He was probably used to this.

The cab was hot and small, with a smell of melting plastic from its cheap seats. A fan up under the roof directed a breeze of warm air into my face. A crucifix dangled from the rearview mirror. On the dashboard was a photograph of a plump Bahamian woman and a child.

'Your family?' I asked him.

'Yessah. My boy. He's six now.'

I took out a twenty-dollar bill, gave it to him.

'Buy him a present,' I told him.

'Thank you, sah,' the driver said, but without real feeling. He guessed I wanted something from him and intended that this should only be a down payment, not the full price. We went along the coast road, turned inland.

'Do you know the man with the driver?' I asked him.

'That's Mr Bamford, sah.'

'Who's Mr Bamford?'

He shrugged. I guessed he knew but did not want to say. I handed him another twenty-dollar bill. He did not even look but slipped it under a spring clip on his sun visor.

'He's a soldier, sir.'

'In the army?'

'No, sah, With Mr Carlotti, sah.'

'Who's he?'

'American gentleman, sah. He controls a lot of things here.'

'Are we heading for his house?'

'Oh, not here, no, this is poor man's area, black man's side.'

'So where are we heading?'

'I think very possibly to Mr Bamford's house, sah. He rents rooms. For an hour, a day, a week. Short time. Rich men with girls, sah.'

'He's a rich man?'

'Not yet, but he will be. He's a very clever man, sah.'

'A friend of yours?'

The driver smiled. I handed him a third bill. He shook his head.

'Not my friend, sah. Not my foe, sah. I just know of him. He's a well-known man, sah.'

I nodded. The driver was being diplomatic. After all, he had to live here and he didn't know who the hell I was.

We passed houses with pink and white and pale blue walls. Beyond them, through a lattice of bright green branches and trellises red with bougainvillea blossoms, the ocean glowed a deeper blue. Dr Sen's car turned off down a narrow road and the closely mown grass verges and regularly watered palm trees were suddenly behind us. Here, clusters of green coconuts like huge eggs of some prehistoric birds hung high in the branches of the palms. Acres of fleshy trees and prickly bushes seemed to crowd in on us, as though nature had gone mad.

We drove past a village school where a giant attendance bell hung on a square wood frame. The houses now were not pink, white and blue but plain wooden shacks roofed with rattling dry palm fronds. Here and there lay the abandoned rusting shells of burned-out cars, without tyres or windows. The rotting keel and ribs of a boat sprouted from a sugar cane field like the skeleton of some beached sea beast.

I read a crudely painted sign, 'Vista Villa', nailed to a post. A goat on a chain regarded us with baleful and wary yellow eyes. A pick-up truck was parked at one side of the house; a Mojo four-wheel drive on the other. Dr Sen turned into the driveway, switched off the engine, climbed out and carefully locked the car.

'Go on fifty yards,' I told the driver. 'Stop and then turn round and wait for me.'

'Will you be long?'

'No longer than necessary. Is there a back way into that house?'

'Yes, sah.'

He pointed through a hedge, some kind of thorn. The car turned, stopped. I climbed out. Heat hit me like a fist. I thought it had been hot inside the cab, but outside, away from the cool breeze blowing off the ocean, I felt I had walked into an oven. This was a different kind of heat from Katherine and the desert; this was steam heat, jungle heat. Sweat soaked my shirt before I had walked ten paces.

I crossed the rough track, went through a gap in the hedge into a back garden. Chickens rooted in the dust, clucked and fluttered their feathers. They paid no attention to me; they must be used to people coming and going.

I saw a narrow wooden staircase that led up to a verandah. I could hear voices upstairs. I climbed the stairs quietly, quickly, glad I was fit. I wasn't the slightest out of breath when I reached the top. I wondered if Mr Bamford was as fit. I feared he just could be, and also that he might be armed. The Mafia would not have much use for an unarmed soldier.

I leaned against the wooden clapboards of the upper storey. Unknown summers had powdered their paint. The planks felt warm. I moved to the left, and the voices grew fainter. I moved to the right. I paused by an unshuttered window and peered through a torn and dirty cotton net curtain into a bedroom.

Sen saw with surprise that his companion had pulled on a pair of flesh-coloured rubber surgical gloves. Why was this necessary? he wondered uneasily but did not like to ask. They climbed up a staircase to the verandah.

The only sound was the bleating of the chained goat. The heat felt so oppressive it became a physical weight on Sen's shoulders. Beads of sweat rolled like tears down his back beneath his white silk shirt. Bamford took a bunch of keys on a chain from his jacket pocket, selected one, opened a door.

The room beyond it was small but tidy. Cheaply printed pictures on the walls showed Chinese scenes: Hong Kong Island, Canton waterfront. One was lit by a hidden bulb and an electric motor drove a series of tiny mirrors to give the impression of a constant waterfall. A desk stood in one corner, with a table, three chairs. Bottles of gin and vodka and tonic with three glasses were on a tin tray.

Sen wondered where the shares could be concealed – if indeed they were concealed here. He saw a diary open on the desk and instinctively glanced at it, then picked it up. The diary was opened at that day's date, and to his astonishment he read his own name, 'Dr Sen, Hong Kong', ringed in red ink, and underneath, 'his hotel'.

'How does she know about me?' he asked Bamford in amazement. But Bamford was in the next room. He returned

holding two large pieces of thick white paper. Sen could see
scrolled writing and under the name Trinity-Trio the legend:
'This share entitles the Bearer to One Vote in decisions
affecting the above company.'

'You found the shares so easily?' he asked in surprise.
'Where were they?'

'Here. Where I thought they'd be.'

'Why bring me along if you were so sure?'

'I thought you wanted them.'

'Of course I do, but you tracked them down, not me.'

'Mr Li did not know his girl friend was one of us.'

'*Us?*' Dr Sen's voice sounded hoarse, alien. What did the
man mean? He felt totally bewildered, lost in a deadly labyrinth of deceit; Triads, Communists, Mafia. Was this how his
rich patients had become so wealthy, by successfully treading
such dangerous, mine-strewn jungle paths? If so, he wanted no
part of it. He would take these certificates back to Hong Kong,
give them to the man who had ordered him here in the flat
overlooking Causeway Bay and then, maybe, he might be free
of this nightmare.

'Yes. She's the one who wrote your name in the diary.'

'But why? Where is she now?'

'Here.'

Bamford opened the door of the bedroom. Lying on her
back on a crumpled bed, totally naked, with a rope knotted
round her neck, was a young Chinese girl. Her eyes, still open,
bulged out like huge onions. Flies buzzed greedily about her
open mouth, her pubic area. Sen was suddenly and horribly
reminded of his driver in the cupboard of the bathroom with
the yellow and black tiles in the Hong Kong flat. He took a
pace towards her with the instinctive professional intention
of checking her pulse, then stopped. Instead, he touched her
hand. Even in this sweaty heat her fingers felt chill and rigid.
She must have been dead for at least an hour.

He swung round on Bamford, rage and bewilderment

overcoming his middle-aged sense of caution. 'Who killed her? Did you know she was here – like this? Just who the hell *are* you?'

'My identity is unimportant. What I have achieved is not. I thought you should come here because otherwise you might get too close to other people's secrets. I heard you were ferreting about, and you could *just* be successful.

'She trusted me. I led her on. She told me about the two shares and I knew who she was working for because I found the chopstick, which is a fairly universal way of identifying friends in that organisation. She also had a telephone call from Hong Kong and afterwards wrote your name and address in her diary. Foolish girl, not versed in the arts of war.'

Sen stared at him. He had been duped and now was all but beaten.

I craned my neck until I could see the girl on the bed. She was not a pretty sight, although once, possibly only hours earlier, she might have been.

I could not help her, but perhaps I could help Dr Sen; I owed him a good turn and unless I moved quickly I would never have another chance of repaying it. I could see him weighing up Bamford. He was older and overweight, but he was not a coward. His eyes had narrowed; he was going to try and jump him. Bamford must have threatened him.

Then I saw the small pistol in Bamford's right hand, held away from his jacket. When he fired, he didn't want any blast to show on the jacket. And he was going to fire unless I stopped him.

I banged the shutter roughly against the wall. Bamford turned involuntarily at the unexpected noise. In that second he lowered his aim fractionally, and Sen hit him hard in the gut. I was impressed. Sen could have been a Kung Fu fighter in his young days. Now, he was strictly a one-punch fighter. I jumped through the window.

Bamford saw me – and fired. I ducked. The shot went over my head. I jumped at him, brought up his right arm. He fired again and again, wildly. The bullets tore harmlessly into the wooden ceiling. I brought my knee up into his groin, the back of my right hand across his throat. He went down. His pistol clattered on the floor. I picked it up, watching him. He did not move. Dr Sen turned towards him. I could see he was trembling.

'Who the devil are you?' he asked weakly. 'You've just saved my life, whoever you are.'

'I know,' I agreed. 'But let's leave the chat till later. Why was this goon threatening you?'

He told me about the Triads, and what would happen if he could not give them the two vital Trinity-Trio shares.

'I get the drift,' I said. 'Now, we've got to get out of here before anyone else arrives.'

I saw that Bamford was wearing surgical gloves. I peeled them off his hands, put them on mine. Then I picked up his pistol and pressed it into his dead right hand, forefinger round the trigger. Then, still wearing his gloves, I picked up a few glasses, pressed them into his other hand. If I was going to leave his fingerprints behind, I might as well do it in a big way. I wanted to give the police every assistance. They might be puzzled by a dead girl on the bed, a dead man on the floor; and a lot of bullet holes in the ceiling; then again, they might not. Such events might not be too infrequent on this island.

'You've not touched anything?' I asked Dr Sen anxiously.

'Nothing,' he said.

He was shaken and moved slowly, like a very old man. All his professional life he had worked to save lives, and now the only life he worried about was his own. For some extraordinary reason, I felt no guilt, no fear. If Bamford was the best anyone could put up against me in this white fellow's world of money power, I was on the winning side.

And then another thought struck me. Did I want to be on *any* side in a situation involving treachery, bluff, blackmail and death? I didn't think I did, but I was already part of the sordid equation. I picked up the two share certificates, folded them, put them in my jacket pocket.

Sen followed me to the hotel in his hired car. I paid off the cabbie.

'You took me along the coast road to look at the beaches, okay?' I said to him, and handed him a hundred-dollar bill on top of his fare to keep his memory clear. He smiled, but only with his big white teeth, not with his eyes.

'God save the Queen, sah,' he said inconsequentially.

God save us all, I thought as I went into the hotel. The doctor followed me into my room. I placed the little gadget Mr Mojo had given me on a table to test whether the room was bugged. It wasn't. We could talk fairly freely.

'You saved my life,' Sen repeated.

'Yes,' I said, 'but only temporarily. At least I have the two shares that so many people seem to want.'

'They're what I came here from Hong Kong to collect,' said Sen flatly.

'Right,' I told him. 'You can have them for whoever sent you. But they are useless unless Lord Jackson dies.'

They were useless in any case if he died. While he lived, their value was incalculable. But as soon as he died they became worthless because I held control.

'I don't understand you!'

'You don't need to. Just believe me.'

'Lord Jackson is dying now. By degrees.'

'How do you know?'

'I have made my dispositions,' said Sen. 'A Dr Kirkpatrick is treating him.'

'How long will he live?'

'Maybe days, maybe weeks, maybe even months. But that is unlikely. He's just a creature. They're pumping nourishment into him, pumping out excrement. He's on a glucose drip, a saline drip, a ventilator to keep him breathing. Electric shocks to his heart. That's not living.'

'But it's not dying,' I said. 'And he has to die.'

'Are you asking me to arrange that?' he said.

'Have you ever heard of mercy killing, Doctor?'

'That goes against the Hippocratic oath,' he said at once.

'Hippocrates isn't here,' I said shortly.

'You jest about the most important possession anyone has – life. Yes, I have helped people over the last barrier when they were racked with pain and there was no hope of any cure or even any improvement. I have helped, in such instances.'

'Could you help here?'

'If I am satisfied that he is beyond all aid, I could. If I have to.'

'You have to. Will you do it?'

The telephone was ringing as Dr Kirkpatrick opened the front door of his neo-colonial house on Cable Beach, the richest residential area of Nassau, overlooking the ocean. He had just come here from the clinic and was in no hurry to answer it; all the maids were under strict instructions never to take a call because they frequently misunderstood, or did not even remember, important messages.

He felt hot and tired, and believed his wife Muriel was at home, playing bridge, as she did most afternoons. She would be nearer the telephone than he was. Do her good to move about a bit; she was far too lazy and fat.

The bell went on ringing with that peculiarly imperative and petulant insistence of an unanswered telephone. Finally, he crossed the tiled floor, picked up the receiver.

'Kirkpatrick here,' he said brusquely.

A voice he did not recognise, thin and reedy and somehow metallic, tones to which he took an instant and instinctive dislike, spoke softly in his ear.

'You have been conducting a tempestuous affair with the senior sister at the clinic, Doctor, despite your repeated assurances and promises to your wife after earlier affairs that such philandering would cease. The sister is also married, but her husband does not know of your association with his wife. Yet. This liaison is in addition to one still going on with a young woman patient. Do you know who I mean?'

'I don't know what you're talking about,' Kirkpatrick retorted angrily. 'Who the devil are you? How did you get my number?'

It was not listed, and was only known to senior hospital staff. If it appeared in the telephone directory, too many holidaymakers with minor cuts or suffering from overexposure to the fierce Bahamian sun might find it and ring him, demanding immediate treatment.

'That is not the question at issue, Doctor. I have your number. I need hardly remind you that the penalty for an affair with a woman patient will almost certainly result in the doctor involved being struck off the Medical Register.'

'I don't know what you're talking about!' shouted Kirkpatrick despairingly. 'Is this a joke or something?'

Who was this bastard who knew so much – and what would he want to keep his knowledge to himself? People were notoriously willing to believe the worst – and, of all people, his wife would give him the hardest time. She distrusted him. She had found him out too often. All she had ever wanted from him was his name and the reflected glory of being married to a successful consultant. All Kirkpatrick had ever wanted from her was continued access to her prodigious wealth. He had grown accustomed to it and had borrowed heavily against her guarantees.

'You're talking crap!' he said inelegantly. 'And you know it. Now, what's your game?'

'No game, Doctor,' the soft voice continued. 'If you care to look on the table in your hall, you will see that a package was delivered to you by hand this afternoon, shortly before you returned. I will hold on while you open it. That will save me making another call.'

Kirkpatrick put down the receiver, crossed the hall. He saw the package and instantly picked up a second telephone. This was connected to the house burglar alarm system with an unlisted number, and it had a mechanism that allowed calls to be made out from the house but not to be accepted, to prevent the line being blocked by an incoming call in an emergency.

He jabbed the digits of the police station number. He would have this blackmailer traced and arrested. Not until he put the phone to his ear did he realise that the line was dead. He replaced the receiver slowly, picked up the packet, opened it.

Inside were sixteen photographs of a kind he had sometimes seen elsewhere but never in his own house, never with him involved, not with that sister and that woman patient. They were fakes, they *must* be fakes. And yet with increasing concern and alarm he recognised the background of his master bedroom, paintings on the walls, ornaments on the mantelpiece. How the hell had they done this – and who, and *why*?

Kirkpatrick's mouth suddenly felt dry as old leather. His heart began to beat too quickly. He picked up the other receiver.

'Are you there?' he asked, trying to keep the alarm out of his voice.

'Of course. I thought you might try the other telephone. I should have told you that would be useless.'

'This call can be traced,' said Kirkpatrick blusteringly.

'It may be traced, but *I* will not be traced. I take it you have had the opportunity, as the lawyers say, to peruse the contents of the parcel?'

'They are bloody fakes.'

'That will be a matter for the court to decide. Or your wife. I have heard she reacted very strongly to the last liaison she discovered. That was with a secretary. What would she say to these?'

'She'd never believe it.'

'Would she believe *you*?'

'Why are you doing this to me? I don't even know who you are.'

'Of course not. But you soon will, because it is necessary to establish a relationship between us. I will meet you in half an hour in the bar of the Diplomat Hotel. I will be drinking orange juice and, in the tradition of spy novels, I will be carrying a newspaper, *The Nassau Tribune*.

'I am aware that you have influential friends here among all classes of the community, but I would strongly advise you against attempting anything foolhardy. I will be on my own in the bar, but friends of mine will be in the vicinity.'

'What if there's someone else drinking orange juice and reading the paper?' said the doctor, trying to keep the caller on the line, hoping he might recognise his voice.

'In that case I will introduce myself to you. I know you by sight. I have seen you entering and leaving the clinic, and in the street, but time is not waiting for either of us. Half an hour. In the bar.'

The line went dead. Kirkpatrick replaced the receiver on its stand; it was damp with sweat from his palm. At that moment he heard the crackle of gravel on the drive as his wife's Jaguar arrived. He had forgotten it was Tuesday; every Tuesday she went out to play bridge. Thank God she had not been here to take that call. He picked up the parcel, pushed it hastily into a drawer of his bureau, locked the drawer, pocketed the key.

His wife came into the room, a blonde, brassy, plump woman. She could have been an inflatable rubber doll, Kirkpatrick thought with distaste. She dressed as a young girl in the most expensive clothes from Nassau's most exclusive boutiques. She was everything he disliked in a woman; her only virtue was that she was stupendously rich and allowed him expensive toys: a Rolls, a Ferrari, a 400 h.p. Mojo speedboat. Her eyes belied her coquettish appearance. They were small and hard and mean; pig's eyes, distrustful, wary, unfriendly.

'You're early,' she said accusingly.

'My deputy is looking after Lord Jackson for the moment.'

'Someone rang you earlier. Twice. Wouldn't give his name.
Man with a funny-sounding voice. Like he was speaking down
a well. Said he wanted to meet you. I told him I didn't know
when you'd be back.'

'I think I've already spoken to him,' said Kirkpatrick
quickly.

'Who was he?'

'Oh, no one special. A nutter, I think, who had somehow got
hold of my number.'

He had to play along with her, otherwise she would instantly
be suspicious. She liked to know what he was doing, who he
was visiting, where he was. Sometimes she would telephone
the clinic several times in a morning just to establish he was
actually there and not simply pretending to be on duty. He
had heard some of the junior medical staff refer to her as
'Kirkpatrick's Keeper'.

He racked his brains to think of some plausible excuse for
going out again. He now had only twenty minutes left before
he must be in the hotel bar.

Anna Lu-Kuan sat by Lord Jackson's bed, watching the thin
green lines on the monitor screens record the feeble beat of his
heart, the weakness of his breathing. His hands, pale as
alabaster, rested on the white bedsheet. Taped to his veins,
thin, plastic tubes fed in drips of saline and glucose and
blood.

He was alive, legally and medically, but in no other sense
could he be said to be living. His hair was neatly combed and a
barber had shaved him that afternoon. The slight movement of
the sheet, helped by his ventilator, seemed almost imperceptible. She thought that it already resembled a shroud more than
a sheet.

Dr Kirkpatrick's deputy was a Canadian in his middle

fifties, a cheerful man with a blue chin. He looked as though he had shaved only an hour previously and would need another shave in an hour's time.

'You are very loyal, Miss Lu-Kuan,' he said now, 'and very good for the patient. It is amazing what comfort a seriously ill person can draw from a healthy visitor. Although they may not be aware of their surroundings, or even that a visitor is with them, some kind of vitality appears to pass from one to the other. I have seen this so often. Some people call it the power of love.'

He spoke with a Vancouver burr. He was very popular, especially with the rich and the elderly. He comforted visitors as successfully as he cured those they visited. He numbered very few poor people among his patients.

'Where is Dr Kirkpatrick?' she asked him.

'He will be here in the morning. Can I help you with any query?'

'Only this. Do *you* think he will get better?'

'Time is probably the greatest physician of all, Miss Lu-Kuan. We call Father Time *the* homeopathic doctor. Little by little, he helps every patient.'

'But can you give me any idea when you think he will speak, open his eyes?'

The doctor looked at her and then at the patient, gauging his answer. Jackson could live indefinitely, classed as a human being but in reality no more than a vegetable. His back was broken and his brain could no longer send signals to any part of the body it had ruled for nearly half a century. There might be a partial recovery, but it would not be soon, if at all. He rather liked this young woman and wanted to be honest with her, or at least as honest as a fashionable physician could ever afford to be. There was so much litigation these days; he always had to be careful what he said.

'I can't give a time,' he replied frankly. 'No one can. But his heart is reasonably strong, considering what he has been through. He is in good physical shape, except for breakages occasioned by the fall.'

'Do you think he will ever walk again?' she asked.

'Orthopaedic specialists from the States are optimistic. It would appear from the X-rays and other tests that certain nerves in the spinal column have been severed, but these have been known to join up and regenerate themselves. Frankly, it's a miracle he is still alive. And in this situation I think we should adopt the motto of the most successful Governor of the Bahamas, Woodes Rogers. *Dum spiro, spero*. While I breathe, I hope.'

'This may sound terrible, Doctor, but he would be better dead than alive like this,' Anna replied. 'If he could speak I'm sure he would say the same. Why prolong a life when all point in living has gone?'

The doctor did not reply. He was not used to such bluntness.

Suddenly Anna could see no reason for remaining any longer in this air-conditioned, aseptic room with its blue windows to filter out harmful ultra-violet rays. This was only a well-furnished antechamber to a tomb, a vestibule on the way to the grave. She was a mourner before her time.

'You have my number,' she said briskly. 'Please ring me any time of day or night if there is any change whatever in his condition, for good or bad. If I am not in, then send a personal messenger to wait for my return. But do not leave a message at the hotel. I never trust hotel switchboards. The Press can bribe the operators.'

'We will inform you personally of any change in Lord Jackson's condition,' the doctor promised.

He watched her walk out of the room, then looked down at the waxen face on the white uncreased pillow.

He left the room, checked with two duty sisters, and walked along the long shining corridor to his chauffeur and his Camaro. He envied Kirkpatrick his Ferrari, but not his wife.

The Australian sat in a corner of the Diplomat Hotel bar. Two young Americans perched with their girl friends on high red leather stools, watching the Bahamian barman mix double-strength Brandy Alexanders. A Canadian family party, greying, middle-aged, speaking in the soft tones adopted by those unused to expensive bars, sat drinking weak rums and Coca-Cola at a far table. The hour was early; serious drinking in Nassau began later.

The Australian sipped his orange juice, glancing at a head-line in the local paper. A young Chinese girl, Miss Mary Chin, had been found in a house belonging to a Bahamian business-man, a Mr Bamford. She had been sexually assaulted and strangled. He was also dead by her side, a pistol in his hand. A police inspector was quoted as saying his fingerprints had been found on various objects in the room. Robbery was not thought to be the motive.

What *was* the motive? wondered the Australian. He did not trust the Nassau police, but then he trusted no one. He had trusted his mother once because she had to sign the deeds for his earliest deals when he was too young to sign them him-self – and then she had demanded half his share of the profits.

He remembered wryly the sign he had seen in the bar of a public house in England, one of a chain he had bought when he took over a brewery. He had never been into a public house before – he did not like the smell of stale beer and cigarette smoke – but the sign he remembered perfectly: 'In God we trust. All others pay cash.' A good motto – if you believed in God.

Dr Kirkpatrick came into the bar, glancing around hesi-tantly. Then he walked across to the Australian.

'We spoke on the telephone?' Dr Kirkpatrick said, as though he was not quite certain.

'We did,' said the Australian. He took from his jacket pocket a small carton of cracked black metal, the size of a matchbox. He put it on the table. A green light, no bigger than a matchhead, flickered briefly.

'What the hell is that?' Kirkpatrick asked him.

'Just to reassure me that we can speak freely, without the benefit of voice-activated receivers, hidden microphones and other electronic evils of our time. An ingenious device. Japanese, of course. Made by Mojo Electronics.'

The Australian left it on the table; the light flickered on and off as though sending signals no one understood.

'Your voice sounds different now.'

'That was my intention,' said the Australian. 'A synthesiser, I believe the device is called.'

'What do you want?' asked Kirkpatrick bluntly, sitting down.

'A drink?' the Australian suggested.

Kirkpatrick shook his head. He desperately wanted a large whisky, but he was afraid that alcohol might loosen his tongue. He needed a cool head.

'You asked me here,' he said. 'What do you want? And who are you?'

'I want to make you a proposition. You have seen some photographs. They will be sent to you, with their negatives, provided you help me with certain medical matters.'

'You want treatment?' asked Kirkpatrick in amazement.

'No. Just help, as I said. Now, you are treating Lord Jackson in your private clinic. I want you to answer some questions about his treatment and condition.'

'That is against the ethics of my profession,' Kirkpatrick replied sharply. 'I have taken the Hippocratic oath.'

'No doubt,' replied the Australian calmly. 'But, consider. You could also be offered the opportunity of taking another oath in court when the husband of the adulterous nursing sister – or even your wife – sues you. I want an answer to my question, or we cannot discuss the matter at all. And we have nothing else to discuss.'

He made as if to stand up.

'Those photos are fakes,' said Kirkpatrick in a heavy dull voice. The Australian sat down again; this fellow was weakening.

'You know as well as I do that that is beside the point. The real question is whether others will *think* they are genuine. Now, to business.'

Kirkpatrick was silent. He felt like a man with a steel noose tightening round his neck.

'I understand Jackson is on a life-support machine?'

Kirkpatrick nodded.

'What would happen if the power failed? If there was a power cut?'

'Nothing serious,' replied Kirkpatrick, finding his voice again, a croak he did not recognise as his own. 'In that circumstance, a back-up generator would start immediately. The pause between the source of one current failing and another taking over would be infinitesimal.'

'And the back-up generator – if that failed?'

'There is a second generator, powered by the wind. This is running continuously to keep a battery of cells at full charge. These cells can keep the equipment working for at least twelve hours. Under no conceivable conditions could power not be restored, either from the mains or the generator, in that time.'

'I am glad to learn that you maintain such intricate and comprehensive safeguards in your clinic. They are as efficient as I imagined. What you are telling me is that no outside accident could stop the life-support machine working? Am I right?'

'Yes.'

'But that does not exclude an *inside* accident – like switching it off, loosening an electrode, or some other relatively simple means of stopping the equipment?'

'I suppose not. But sisters and nurses are on duty day and night. I have a most able deputy, a Canadian physician, who visits the patient every two hours when he is on duty, as I do myself when I am on duty.'

'Since presumably your deputy and the nurses would not interfere with the equipment, that leaves only one possible person who could. You, sir.'

'But why? I'm trying to save his life.'

'It is written that he who saves his life shall lose it. And one day we will all lose our lives, Doctor. But you will lose all that makes your life enjoyable very quickly, unless we come to an immediate understanding on this delicate matter.'

'You are, in effect, asking me to kill Lord Jackson?'

'I am asking nothing of the sort. *You* have made that suggestion. I am asking you, as a matter of common humanity, to see that this distinguished patient does not suffer needlessly any longer. Nor am I alone in this wish. Through the wonders of electronics I have been able to record a conversation between your Canadian deputy and Miss Lu-Kuan, a young woman very close to Lord Jackson, in both business and emotional matters. In this conversation – only moments ago – she said she would rather see him dead – indeed that *he* would rather be dead – than just living as a cabbage.'

'People sometimes say these things,' said Dr Kirkpatrick. 'They don't really mean them.'

'No? Yet how else can we express our inner thoughts except in speech? But I digress, Doctor. If Lord Jackson fails to survive the night, the negatives will be delivered by messenger to your house in an envelope marked "Medical Records. Strictly Confidential". If he is still alive tomorrow morning, I think I have made it clear what will happen.'

'Why are you doing this to me? Do you want to ruin me?'

'Certainly not. I have the highest regard for your skills, if not for your morals. But I need to protect certain substantial interests of my own, and their importance is much greater than my admiration for your abilities.'

'If I did this – and God knows I don't intend to – how could I trust you to do as you say?'

'A good question, with a simple answer. You cannot trust me. But you must. I have no interest in harming you, Doctor. Believe me, this is purely a commercial matter. No more, but certainly no less.'

He pushed a copy of the newspaper across the table.

'Did you see this story of a dead girl and a dead man? That could be suicide, out of remorse, or unrequited love, or lust, as it would seem from the account. On the other hand, it *could* be an accident. Or, Doctor, it could be for none of these reasons.

'Perhaps one or other of these people – or even both – thought they could outsmart someone. And then they failed to match that wish with the deed. But there, we have talked long enough. Those are my terms. The ball, as they say in tennis, is now in your court.'

FIFTEEN

The Present: Nassau, Bahamas

Muriel Kirkpatrick poured herself half a tumbler of Gordon's, added a touch of tonic water, and looked across at her husband. He had been moody for two or three days; she knew the signs, or she thought she did, which as far as she was concerned was the same thing. He was chasing some woman. He must be; there could be no other reason for his silences. And like all suspicious wives, she felt certain she knew who the woman was.

'A penny for your thoughts,' she said, not expecting him to reply but offering him the opportunity.

Kirkpatrick tried not to wince at the banality of the question. He realised he must answer it sensibly, reasonably, otherwise he could precipitate a cataract of accusation. Then would follow screaming and shouting. Muriel would fling her glass onto the floor, storm out tearfully and lock herself in her bedroom. He had enough on his mind without facing such needless domestic histrionics. He tried to smile, but succeeded only in grimacing.

'I'm worried about a patient,' he said unconvincingly. 'Lord Jackson. He's very ill, poor fellow.'

Even as he spoke he realised he was preparing her for

Jackson's death. He had already decided what he must do, but he must act cleverly, without haste, dropping hints here and there about the gravity of the patient's condition. That way, his early death could be anticipated.

'Unlike you to worry,' she replied sharply. 'You've never been one to bring your work home. Come to think of it, you're hardly ever home yourself.'

'Oh, I don't know,' he said, as easily as he could. 'The difficulty these days is that I have to be at the clinic more often than I used to.'

'What about that sister, that blonde with the big tits?'

'That could describe half the female nursing staff.'

'You know quite well the tart I mean.'

He shrugged. 'I don't. Sorry. Anyhow, I have to go back.' He glanced at his watch.

'I'll only be half an hour. Care to come for the drive? We could stop off somewhere on the way back for a drink?'

Muriel shook her head and then wished she hadn't; the gin was getting to her, making her feel fuddled. Soon she would be crying, weeping for a lost love that had never really been hers and so could never be found. She knew her weakness and hated herself for it; almost as much as she hated her husband for forcing her to drink to forget his infidelities, his obvious lack of love for her.

There was only one way to cure him and that was to cut off his allowance. And if she found proof he was screwing that bloody sister, that was what she would do. Not directly, of course; that would be too painful for her, but through her Trust lawyers. There were enough of them; let them earn their money for once.

'No, I'll stay here,' she said curtly.

Kirkpatrick nodded, went out of the room. He had half hoped his wife would accept his invitation. Somehow, it would seem less like murder if Muriel was actually sitting in the car outside the building while he did what he had to do.

Kirkpatrick had rationalised his decision to himself by arguing, as his blackmailer had done, that it would actually be a kindness to diminish his patient's suffering; he would really be helping Lord Jackson. The man lay at the door of death: surely all Kirkpatrick was doing was to open that door and allow him to pass through it peacefully and without pain?

A little voice within him answered that Lord Jackson was not conscious of any suffering; he was not even conscious. Then Kirkpatrick assured himself that Jackson had a wife in England, a half-Chinese mistress, and a daughter somewhere. They would all be suffering because of his condition; he would therefore be helping three other people as well as his patient.

Kirkpatrick switched off his bleeper – he was off duty and he did not want the clinic to call him on some trivial matter; he needed to keep his mind clear. He climbed into his Ferrari (bought, like so much else, he reminded himself bitterly, with his wife's money). The crisp crackle of the car's four exhausts drowned the faint ringing of the telephone inside the house. He was out in the road and accelerating away by the time Mrs Kirkpatrick stood up shakily, placed her drink on a side table with the slow, deliberate movement of someone already heavily intoxicated, and began to walk towards the telephone.

She hoped it would stop ringing before she reached it; each peal of the bell felt like an electric drill boring through her aching head. The ringing continued; she picked up the receiver.

A breathless feminine voice said: 'Doctor, please –'

'I know who you are,' retorted Mrs Kirkpatrick bitterly, her voice clotted with rage. 'You bloody bitch! If you want a man, get one of your own, not my husband!'

That was the way to talk to these people; they understood a direct approach. They were no better than animals. Worse, in many ways.

'Who am I speaking to?' asked the voice at the other end in astonished tones.

'Mrs Kirkpatrick, that's who. I don't know your bloody

name, but I know your voice,' she screamed down the phone.
'And I know what you and my husband get up to. Now *bugger
off*!'

She slammed the telephone back on its stand and stood for a
moment, swaying slightly, breathing heavily, one hand still on
the receiver. Almost immediately, the bell began to ring again.
That whore could ring for bloody ever, she told herself. She
had never heard the voice of the sister she distrusted, but that
was the sort of voice she imagined she would have, one which
would appeal to her husband: soft, feminine, classy. The cow.

Muriel weaved her unsteady way back to her chair. The
effort had dried her mouth. She refilled her glass from the
bottle and began to sip neat gin gratefully.

Out on the evening road, Kirkpatrick thought about the
Hippocratic oath he had taken when he graduated. He had
promised 'to use treatment to help the sick according to my
ability and judgement, but never with a view to injury and
wrongdoing. Neither will I administer a poison to anybody
when asked to do so . . .' The pledge had been quite unequivocal, no sidestepping or argument there. But life in Greece in the
fourth century BC could not be compared with life today; it was
far simpler then. He preferred the nineteenth-century poet
Arthur Clough's advice to physicians: 'Thou shalt not kill; but
need'st not strive/Officiously to keep alive.' That was the real
truth of the matter. There was no need to postpone the inevitable as far as Lord Jackson was concerned; no point whatever in
doing so.

The clinic's car park was almost deserted. He noticed that
the space usually occupied by his deputy's Camaro was vacant.
He sat in his car for a moment, pretending to search for papers
to postpone the moment when he would have to leave. When he
returned, he would have deliberately killed a man. He would be
a murderer; if discovered, he would face a lifetime in gaol.

The evening sun, red as blood, dropped swiftly into the sea
and flashed on the clinic's glass swing doors as two people came

out through them. One was the Chinese Dr Sen from Hong Kong. His face looked set and grim. With him, Kirkpatrick recognised Lord Jackson's mistress, Anna Lu-Kuan. She had been crying. He could see tears on her face, shining in the sunset. She appeared too concerned even to wipe them away. They climbed into a waiting taxi. He watched it drive out of sight. Then he went into the building himself to do what he had to do.

He walked up the stairs to the floor where his three patients lay. It would be prudent to have a word with the first, a retired American diplomat, and afterwards just look in on the third, a rich Canadian widow. If there was any inquiry – and he prayed there would not be – they could both say he had visited them on the night of Lord Jackson's death and had appeared in no way concerned and that his manner was normal. What *was* normal? he wondered. In any life, what was pretence and what was real?

He found the diplomat sitting up in bed, watching a soap on the huge TV screen.

'How are you, Doc?' he asked Kirkpatrick without much interest.

'About as good as you,' Kirkpatrick replied easily. 'You're looking fine. Getting stronger every day, I see.'

'I feel it, too,' the patient agreed. 'I'm much better in myself.'

He glanced over Kirkpatrick's shoulder at the screen: a young couple were riding in a park past a house as large as a municipal office.

'I don't want to appear rude, Doc,' he went on, 'but this show is just getting to its most interesting point.'

'Sorry I missed it at home,' said Kirkpatrick. 'But I expect my wife's got it on the video. See you in the morning.'

He walked briskly along the corridor to Lord Jackson's room, went in, stood for a moment by the bedside.

Jackson lay, eyes closed, his face almost completely

concealed by an oxygen mask. Kirkpatrick glanced automatically at the drips but could not bear to look at the monitor screens with their travelling green lights. They were just out of his line of vision, and for this he felt thankful. When Jackson died, the lights would cease their movement. There seemed something frighteningly symbolic about those green dots, which Kirkpatrick did not care to contemplate. They would be still – but staring blankly, as unseeing as a dead man's eyes.

He looked at the life-support machine, wondering how best to incapacitate it without arousing undue suspicion. There was no point in simply switching it off, the emergency standby would immediately come in. Down on the floor he saw a junction plug where three sets of wires joined; he had never noticed it before – but then he had never had occasion to do so. Technicians always dealt with such complicated electronics equipment, not consultant physicians.

He bent down, wrapped a handkerchief round the plug to avoid leaving any fingerprints, then carefully drew the two sides apart by a quarter of an inch. This should be sufficient to break the contacts inside, while to the casual eye the wires would still appear connected. A nurse's leg or the maid's vacuum cleaner might easily have knocked against the wire.

He went out, closed the door quietly, walked into the next room. The Canadian widow was reading, propped up on pillows. She wore half-glasses which reminded him vaguely of a schoolmistress.

'You're not in often at this hour,' she said almost scoldingly, as though it would be better for both of them if he were. She closed the book carefully on a vellum bookmark bearing the likeness of a saint.

'Just thought I would see how you are doing,' Kirkpatrick explained conversationally. He sat down, glanced surreptitiously at the red second hand of the wall clock. He would give it six minutes, just to be sure; no more, for this woman, he knew from experience, suffered from verbal diarrhoea. Then he would go back to Jackson's room and discover the broken connection.

The woman immediately launched into a long description of new symptoms: unexpected twinges in her joints, a pain behind her eyes; then a long rambling diatribe about the difficulties of getting good house servants, the decline in ethics and standards everywhere.

Dr Kirkpatrick nodded sympathetically. It was nearly ten minutes before he could excuse himself.

He came out of the door, and found suddenly he could not face seeing Jackson dead; a man whose life he should be fighting to save. He went downstairs, nodded to the porter on duty and drove back home.

His wife was asleep in the chair, her mouth open. A little saliva drooled down her Yves St Laurent blouse. Her glass had dropped on to the white carpet which was stained with a damp patch of gin. Her fourth or fifth?

He glanced at his watch – nine thirty. He had been away longer than he imagined. Time was elastic; it could race along or linger with leaden steps. He poured himself a whisky, drank it neat; poured another.

The room suddenly felt stuffy, the air used up, stale, unbreathable. He crossed to the glass sliding doors, parted them, went out onto the stone flags of the patio. Evidence of his wife's wealth lay all around him: the huge swimming pool, its wave machine making it churn like a miniature ocean; the white garden furniture specially imported from Italy; sunshades striped in his old college colours, now folded like the furled wings of brightly plumaged birds; the barbecue area, beyond which lay a secret garden.

As he took a few steps along the flagstones towards this, a figure detached itself silently from the purple shadows.

'Dr Kirkpatrick?'

'Yes. Who are you? How did you get in?'

'I was told to deliver something in person. I was going to the front door, but then I saw you here in the garden.'

This was a lie, Kirkpatrick knew. The front door was on the other side of the house. This man, whoever he was, must have been waiting for him here. Perhaps someone else was also waiting outside the front door? Kirkpatrick did not feel threatened, only surprised, concerned; his privacy had been violated too easily.

The man handed him a white envelope, marked 'Medical Records. Strictly Confidential'.

'You might care to look inside it,' he said.

The doctor put down his drink, slit open the envelope, shook out the strips of negative film, held them up to the moon. Here they were, just as promised – or were they? He counted them. Twelve. There should be sixteen.

'They're not all here,' he said shortly.

'I have been asked to explain, sir, that four have been kept back.'

'But why? The man I saw in the Diplomat bar promised me the lot. I have kept my part of the bargain. How did you know, anyhow?'

'I am not a party to any arrangement between you both, sir. I am only the messenger.'

'And what's the message?'

'They are keeping them for a short time. Just in case they should be needed.'

'By whom?'

'I am not empowered to say, sir.'

'The bastards,' said Kirkpatrick thickly, whisky rising in his throat like bile in the bitterness of his rage. 'The bloody bastards! Get out! *Get out!*'

Only by a great effort of will did he stop himself hitting the man. But what good would that do? As he said, he was only the messenger.

The man retreated into the darkness. Kirkpatrick replaced the negatives in the envelope, put this into his pocket. He would get rid of them. Burn them; that would be the safest thing, along with the photographs in his desk. But what about the four missing? Even if he had received back the sixteen negatives, he guessed that almost certainly there would be another set of prints. And who was he to argue? He had shown himself to be weak – and willing to kill on the promise of a stranger. He must be *mad*.

Muriel was the root cause of all this, of course. If she wasn't such a bitch, there would never have been any other women. Well, that was a bit steep – say, only one or two other women, and then he would have been on surer ground. Now he was a murderer, and they could go on blackmailing him. He could be bled white for everything he owned, and all his wife's money, too.

He drank the whisky quickly. It fumed in his tired body like liquid fire. As he came back into the room, the telephone rang. He picked it up. His deputy's familiar Canadian drawl sounded in his ear.

'Glad to get you,' he said.

'Why, what's the trouble?' Kirkpatrick asked, as though he didn't know.

'Bad news. Jackson is dead.'

'Dead? How?'

'Heartbeat just faded. Did everything I could. Sister Steele tried to get you earlier, but your bleeper wasn't working.'

'I was in the hospital,' Kirkpatrick explained defensively.

'So she says – later. But we missed you. She rang your home and got your wife, who bent her ear a bit. Didn't you get *that* message?'

'No, I did not,' said Kirkpatrick, looking at his wife in her chair. She began to snore. Breath rattled in her throat and he wondered obliquely whether Jackson's breath had also rattled before he died, or had he passed peacefully into the darkness of the eternal mists, from one deep sleep into another?

'Are you there?' the Canadian was asking.

'Yes. I was just thinking. Poor Jackson. He put up a good fight.'

'Yes. I left the ventilator on, just in case he picked up, but it was no use. He just went out. Nothing anyone could do.'

'What time was that?'

'Oh, nearly an hour ago.'

'An hour?'

Kirkpatrick could not believe it. Lord Jackson had died *before* he pulled out that plug. He had attempted to kill a dead man. He should have checked those monitors.

'There's something else I want to see you about.'

'Now?' asked Kirkpatrick.

'No. It can wait until the morning. But can you be in early?'

'Yes. What's the trouble?'

'No trouble. Why should there be? But I would like to have a private word with you before any of the Press get on to you. Something went wrong with the ventilator. We found a loose plug.'

'A loose plug?'

Kirkpatrick repeated the words as though he had never heard them before.

'Yes. And Vera – Sister Steele – said she saw you go into Jackson's room just minutes after she had been in there and it was not loose then.'

'So what about that?'

'Let's agree on what happened, that's what, and tell the same story to the Press if they start snooping around. You know what the tabloids are like. And this story has everything. A lord in a coma. Millions of money. His wife, his mistress. Daughter a druggie. Death and sex and drugs. What more could they ask for – except the mystery of a life-support machine that stopped, eh? The fact is, Jackson was already dead, so it doesn't matter what was working and what wasn't. But we can't expect the media to accept that, can we?'

Kirkpatrick said nothing; these were complications he had

never envisaged. He heard his deputy's voice again.

'You okay? You sure sound a bit odd tonight.'

'Odd? Sorry. I'm fine. Just shocked at Jackson's death. Poor devil. Anyhow, see you at seven thirty.'

Kirkpatrick replaced the receiver. If Muriel *had* taken the message, or if he had kept his bleeper active, would that have helped him? Kirkpatrick could not think clearly. Alcohol began to beat in his brain like the drums of the damned.

He could not face the Canadian in the morning. Or that stupid bitch Vera Steele, always following him about, making sheep's eyes at him. It *would* be her who had seen him – if she had. He could not face the Australian bastard, either. He thought of the four negatives. Where were they now? Were they on their way to his colleagues, his wife? He could not face anyone, not even himself. He was trapped, and the more he struggled, the deeper he became enmeshed.

He poured another whisky, gulped this down, went out of the room and into his study. He unlocked the drawer in his bureau, took out the photographs, held them in the flame of his cigarette lighter with the negatives until they all burned to a dark ash. Then he opened another drawer, took out a pistol. Nearly everyone kept one in Nassau in case of armed robbery. Best to go now, quickly, he thought, than to linger like a wounded lion to be dragged down by jackals, humiliated, struck off the Register.

It would have been better for everyone if Jackson had died quickly, cleanly, not clinging on, kept legally alive by tubes of blood and salt water and glucose and electric wires, even a pump to help him breathe. It had been an act of mercy to be willing to put him out of that twilight world of death-in-life. It would be another act of mercy to put himself beyond the reach of his tormentors.

Kirkpatrick was too tired, too fuddled, too afraid now to think clearly; he wanted peace, escape from his blackmailers, sanctuary from the Press, his deputy, his wife, Vera, everyone. His bemused brain could only offer one lasting solution.

He sat back in his chair, examined the muzzle of the gun as though he had never seen it before. This would be his tunnel to freedom, to everlasting peace. He had never been able to understand how people could kill themselves. Now, he did. Indeed, he was surprised he had not thought of this escape route earlier on; it was so obvious, so easy.

Dr Kirkpatrick took a deep breath, closed his eyes, pressed the muzzle to his temple, and squeezed the trigger.

The telephone rang as I came into my hotel room. I let it ring while I drank a neat rum. I wanted something strong and sweet to wash away the taste of what was happening all around me. Then I picked up the receiver.

The operator asked, 'Mr Crabtree?'

'Yes.'

'I have the Australian on the line, sir.'

So at last, at long last, I was going to speak to the man I had admired from boyhood, the man with the golden gift.

'Hi!' he said, but without any trace of an Australian accent. 'I heard you were in town.'

'I sent you a cable,' I reminded him. 'You didn't get it?'

'Yes, I got it. Now, when are you going to come and see me?'

'When are you free?'

'Now?' he suggested.

'Now,' I agreed.

I went downstairs, hailed a cab and drove to his hotel. The Australian was tall, as I'd always known, but thinner than I had imagined. He also had a stoop. His face seemed lined and sallow, as though he saw too little sun.

I have heard it said that people tend to grow into their jobs so that, after years in the trade, butchers develop beefy faces; accountants, thin lips, tight as a closed purse. I wondered whether the Australian's unhealthy pallor was the colour of the counting house?

'So we meet at last,' he said with forced joviality. 'Glad to see you've got here. Even though it's taken so long.'

'Yes,' I said. 'It's been a long time.'

'I was very sorry to hear about Mother,' he went on.

'Well, at least she lived to know she'd been a great success in those two pictures.'

'Yes. As a matter of fact, I can tell you now, Ian, I had a hand in selecting her for those roles.'

'That was very kind of you,' I said, not letting on I already knew.

'The fact of the matter is, I felt a bit guilty about her. We had a coldness over some ridiculous thing that happened years ago. The details don't matter now, they're unimportant. But I wanted to prove she was as good as she thought she was, and also that I wasn't as bad as she thought I was. But, of course, I never let her know.'

'That was very kind of you,' I repeated dutifully. 'So what are you up to now?'

'This bloody company, Trinity-Trio. I thought I had it all sewn up, but two vital shares are missing. And now the head man, Lord Jackson, is dead.'

'When did he die?'

I hoped my surprise was not too obvious; if it was, the Australian gave no sign.

'Today. I've just had a call. A Canadian doctor at the clinic has been keeping me informed of his condition.'

'He died suddenly, then?'

'Very. But only after a hell of a long time in a coma. Couldn't eat, see, talk, hear – anything. Just a cabbage, but stable. Not getting any worse, apparently. Could have lasted for weeks, months maybe. Then, bang, he's dead. Better than lingering on, a vegetable. And maybe now we can buy some of his shareholding and to hell with the two missing shares.'

I said nothing and tried not to appear too interested. Dr Sen must have worked very swiftly; I hoped that in his haste he had not left any clues that could lead back to him; or, worse, to me.

'This whole business is a rat's nest of troubles,' the Australian said gloomily.

'I heard that,' I said.

'What exactly did you hear?' he asked quickly, suspiciously.

'That you and a Mr Carlotti were interested, and some Chinese bloke, a Dr Sen, was also hunting around.'

He nodded.

'We're like wasps around the honeypot. The Chinese communists want the damn thing. Carlotti and I want it. Now this doctor is in the act – for the Triads, so I hear. Extraordinary. It's enough to warn people off trying to make an honest buck.'

The telephone tinkled.

'Excuse me,' he said and picked it up.

I saw his face tighten, harden. Suddenly, his eyes were no longer blue but cold as chips of polished steel.

'You'd better come over right away,' he said grimly and replaced the receiver. He turned to me.

'You must forgive me, Ian. Someone wants to see me urgently on a most important private matter. I'm sorry. I'll have to see you later. I'll ring you as soon as I can.'

He looked concerned now, almost worried. He must have a lot of problems, I thought. It looked so easy, making money, but one had to keep on running just to hold on to it. Great wealth was like a handful of sand; it could so quickly run through your fingers.

I took out a cigarette packet.

'Cigarette?' I asked him.

'Never use them.'

'Damn!' I said, irritably. 'There's not one left in the pack.'

I threw it into a wastepaper basket.

'Give me a call when you're free,' I said. 'Maybe we could have dinner together? I've a lot to tell you.'

'And I may have some good news to tell you,' he replied. 'I hope so, anyhow. Forgive me for cutting short our talk now.'

'I forgive you,' I told him and went out, back to my hotel.

In my bedroom, I unlocked my suitcase, switched on the midget Mojo VHF receiver it contained. Inside the empty cigarette pack I had placed a tiny Mojo transmitter, the sort used by private eyes.

I heard door chimes sound in the Australian's suite. A door opened and closed, a key clicked in a lock. Activated by the sounds, the tiny spools of my Mojo tape recorder had begun to revolve.

'Give me a drink, for God's sake,' said an American voice. I guessed this must be Carlotti.

The sound of liquid being poured, the hiss of a soda siphon, the clunk of ice cubes in a glass.

'What exactly is the problem this time?' the Australian asked irritably. 'I've never known a deal go sour in so many ways.'

'Well, stay with it. There are still a few snags left. You know that character Li, at the bank?'

'I know.'

'He's croaked. Dead.'

'I told you not to be so harsh.' The Australian's distaste sounded in his voice.

'He got nothing but kindness,' Carlotti assured him unconvincingly. 'But he didn't react. He took liberties. He got up the nose of the guy looking after him. He took Li to the hospital casualty department and dumped him on the steps, but it was too late.'

'Well, at least my idea of leaning on Dr Kirkpatrick paid off,' said the Australian. 'He must have gone right in there and finished off Lord Jackson. So now we can go after whoever inherits his holding, and to hell with those two missing shares. Deal with the other shareholders direct.'

'It's not so simple. My people in London visited Lady Jackson. They gave her a spiel about being investment bankers anxious to keep T-T in its traditional ownership in the sad event of the noble lord not recovering, etcetera, etcetera.

'They promised her all kinds of financial incentives – she's a greedy bitch – and somehow she winkled details of the will out of his lawyers. She inherits 140 shares, but only on trust. The remaining eleven go to their daughter, Elaine, who's a druggie in a home.'

'So?'

'So here's the bad news. The will contains a most unusual clause which shook my Lady Jackson to her elegant core. On Jackson's death, this junkie's eleven shares go to her, no matter who else might claim them. So even though he's given two to Anna Lu-Kuan, they will also go back to the girl.'

'They'll never make that stick,' said the Australian stubbornly, trying to convince himself. 'No court would stand for it. Those shares are still vital.'

'You think? I reckon they're worthless now – because some Australian guy has already made a private deal with this kid.'

'What do you mean, exactly?'

The Australian's voice sounded hoarse, strained, as though he was speaking through a choking fog.

'Elaine Jackson has her own nurse in the clinic. When our people made it worth the nurse's while, she remembered she had witnessed a letter that made over these eleven shares to some guy, Ian Bruce Crabtree.'

'It can't be. He's my half-brother. He's just arrived here from Australia. I've met him for the first time just before you came in. He didn't say anything about this.'

'I wouldn't expect him to.'

For a moment neither of them said anything, and I watched the tiny spools of the tape recorder revolving. Then the Australian spoke.

'I can't believe it.'

'You have to,' Carlotti told him grimly.

'What I mean is, about those two shares. This bloke Jackson

loved the Chinese girl. I have checked on that. And we both were there when he fell from the window. We know how she reacted. She was hysterical with grief. She loved him.'

'That doesn't mean he loved her.'

'But why would he ever swindle her, pretend the shares were of great value, when actually they're absolutely worthless? What would he get out of that?'

'Maybe he had forgotten what he'd put in the will. Maybe he just wanted to impress her, bind her to him. After all, he never thought he was going to die.'

'I checked him out carefully,' the Australian replied. 'He seemed a decent bloke. Had a strange family motto: "Beyond the dreams of avarice." '

'Well, that's where he is now,' said Carlotti. 'I reckon Anna Lu-Kuan will go apeshit when she learns this. But that doesn't concern us. What does, is this half-brother of yours. Can you get on to him?'

'Of course.'

'Well, get him over here. Lay it on the line where all our best interests lie.'

I heard the creak of a chair as the Australian sat down heavily. I had heard and recorded all I needed, and more than I wanted. I switched off the machine and poured myself another rum.

Personally, I didn't give a fish's tit about how this news affected the Australian and Carlotti, but I wondered about Anna. I suddenly realised that, although I hardly knew her, I liked her in a way I had never felt towards any other girl. I wanted to protect her. I didn't want to see her hurt – and when she heard this she would be devastated. She had trusted and loved Lord Jackson, and somehow, by accident, by deliberate intent, or simply thorough total forgetfulness, he had betrayed her.

I couldn't allow her to discover this terrible fact from either of the only two other men who knew it. I must tell her myself – in my own time, in another place, and gently, so she could still keep alive the warm memory of a man she had loved, and who had told her he loved her.

I sat there drinking and pondering the problem for about half an hour, when the Australian rang me again.

'Sorry to break off our conversation so soon,' he said apologetically. 'Do come on over if you're free.'

He appeared in a more expansive mood; I had to admire his calmness.

'I don't usually drink champagne, or indeed any alcohol,' he said when I sat down in his suite. 'But I feel that this does call for some minor celebration. I mean, us meeting and me about to sew up this T-T thing. Would you have a glass with me?'

'Love to,' I told him. While he was busying himself at the mini-bar, I crossed to the wastepaper basket, casually picked up the empty cigarette packet, slipped it into my pocket.

'What are you doing?' he asked sharply, turning to watch me, eyes narrowed suspiciously.

'I know you are a non-smoker,' I explained. 'It was careless of me to forget. You wouldn't want your reputation sullied. I'll take my litter elsewhere in future.'

The Australian closed the refrigerator door and suddenly paused, champagne bottle in his hand. His eyes were fixed on a small black carton, the size of a matchbox, which had been pushed behind a tray of glasses. I had not seen it – and neither had he. Now a tiny light flickered on it, cold and bright as a serpent's eye.

'Wait a minute,' he said slowly, looking at me. 'This room's bugged.'

'What do you mean, bugged?' I asked him, as though I had previously never heard the word.

'You bloody well know. Someone's planted a listening device. That bastard Carlotti. Or *you*! Of course, the cigarette packet!'

He lunged at me, ripped the packet from my pocket, extracted the transmitter, no larger than a sugar cube.

'You *bastard*!' he shouted furiously. 'My own flesh and blood, eavesdropping on me!'

'We're not flesh and blood,' I retorted. 'We're not even related.'

'What the hell do you mean? Who *are* you, then?'

'No relation of yours,' I told him. 'Your mother brought me up, but she was not my mother, although until a few weeks ago I thought she was. My mother was Aborigine.'

'And your father? Old Crabtree?'

'No. An American.'

'I can check,' he said warningly. 'Don't give me shit, boy. I can break you if I choose.'

I shook my head.

'No,' I said. 'You can't. No way. Never.'

I could have added that I could break him and I very nearly did, but even as I started to tell him so, I remembered the rustlers at the meatworks; Bamford dead; Keiller dead; Lord Jackson dead. I wanted no more hard words or actions. In the last analysis, we could probably break each other – and for what purpose? Threats seemed as futile as carrying them out; one act of violence always led to another, and on to a third. As far as I was concerned the show was all but over. When the curtain came down, could we at last go home?

'You ever meet Lord Jackson?' I asked him.

He shook his head.

'You're certain? You were related, you know.'

He looked at me very closely then, eyes narrowed.

'Who told you that?'

'I found out,' I said. 'Did *you* know?'

'Yes. I knew. But only fairly recently.'

He turned away, his anger evaporated. He looked sad and lonely, not exactly defeated, but for the first time in his life not a certain winner.

'How did you know?' I asked him.

'Purely by chance. So many things happen in life by

chance – or maybe that's another word for destiny. When I bought the film studios in Hollywood, I made it my business to read every letter any member of any audience anywhere in the world wrote to the company, criticising or praising any of their pictures. If we had a dozen letters, say, praising some scene, I would know that it had gone down pretty well. If we had a hundred, I knew it had been a great success and we could repeat that scene in another movie, because people liked it and related to it. Remember, barely one person in a thousand will ever write – maybe only one in ten thousand. When our mother – I mean my mother, Amy – starred in those two pictures for Rosael Pagoda, I examined all the letters that came in. One was from a Lady Esmerelda Jackson in Belgravia, London.

'She'd been in a small travelling show in Colombo with Amy during the Second World War. The party split up and they lost contact. Esmerelda then married a man called Jackson who'd also been in Colombo. He died as a prisoner in Hong Kong. Only after the war did she learn he was Lord Jackson. He'd made her pregnant in Colombo, where he and my mother had also been very close. It was all set out in her letter.

'I realised then that her husband, Lord Jackson, was also *my* father, not an Australian sergeant as I'd always been told. It was a strange feeling. Extraordinary, really. At first it gave me a certain edge. As the bastard, I wanted to control Trinity-Trio and beat his legitimate son.'

'And you did beat him?'

'In a sense, yes. At least, I'm still alive and he's not. But he'd be alive, too, if he hadn't fallen from a window. Again, pure chance.'

'But you still haven't the controlling shares. Which means you won't control his company,' I told him.

'Of course I will,' he retorted, angry again that I could doubt him. 'I'll get them. It's only a matter of time, probably only hours. I'll get them, boy. I *must*.'

I knew he felt he must, in order to survive. Not in the basic sense of simply keeping alive, but of keeping himself on top, which was now the only place where he could exist. To the Australian, life on any lower level would be a living death.

To try and acquire control he and Carlotti had killed Mr Li and Lord Jackson, and still control eluded them. Carlotti would not accept this finite situation gracefully or easily. I could also be in for a rough time – except that I held the aces. He knew I could make life hard, even for him.

I guessed the Australian needed time to consider how he could best cajole me, maybe even try to bribe me, to give him control of the shares. But he was too shrewd to bring up the subject immediately, although it must have been burning in his guts like a red-hot coal. I admired him for that, too. Then I wondered whether he realised he had no hope; his hitherto irresistible force had finally come up against the ultimate immovable object.

I sensed from his eyes he realised what I was thinking, but again he gave me no word. I also realised something else I should have guessed long ago: that for this strange, driven man, goaded by ambition, spurred on by the obsessive dream of becoming the most powerful, richest person in his world, there was something even more important than the acquisition of wealth – his own reputation.

He had been immensely astute, maybe sometimes lucky, but always able to convert the currency of any good fortune into cash. The media had loved him, hailing him as a superman, someone who could never fail in any deal, against whatever odds. He had come to believe his own legend. And now I had shown not a chink, but a yawning crack in his golden armour.

He watched me, almost appealingly. He wanted my silence, for he was desperate for the dream to continue; he was the unbeatable. He could not face awakening to reality.

I nodded, as though he had asked me a question, and in a sense he had, silently, almost despairingly.

'I have beaten you over this,' I told him gently. 'But you and

I are the only two who need ever know that. You can still make a fortune from the shares, you hold, you and Carlotti. And you have enough bright public relations people to gloss over any unanswered questions – and even sharper lawyers to prevent them being asked too loudly. You are the top. You are still the Australian.'

He sighed then, and I realised he had been holding his breath tensely against my reply. I could not destroy his wealth but I could destroy the man who had made it – or at least his image, which to him was just as important, perhaps even more important. It did not count with him that possibly most people who might hear of this matter of the shares were likely to forget it within moments. It was right out of their experience, beyond their comprehension, but to him it was life itself. He and the legend had become one. Every man must believe in someone or something. He believed in his own myth.

'Thank you,' he said.

'I have a price,' I replied.

He stiffened.

'What is it?'

'Not in money,' I told him, 'but in *your* silence. I keep quiet on the fact that I have beaten you in the biggest deal of your life, and you make sure that Anna Lu-Kuan never learns Lord Jackson betrayed her.'

'That could be very difficult.'

'Your life could be very difficult – if people ever thought you'd been tripped up by someone half your age.'

We stood for a moment, staring at each other. I thought of many people and many things, and none gave me any comfort. Lady Mackenzie should be pleased with me for what I had done, for what I had achieved at her suggestion. But was I pleased with myself? That was a different question. I did not want to answer it.

The Australian swallowed once, twice. I thought for a moment he might choke. Then he nodded.

'All right,' he said reluctantly. 'It's a deal.'

We shook hands, and I left him standing there, still holding the unopened bottle of champagne in his hand.

Muriel Kirkpatrick stood in the doorway of her husband's study, glass of gin in her hand, surveying the doctor with contempt.

'I tried to kill myself,' he said hoarsely. 'The gun didn't go off.'

'Of course it didn't. I took the bullets out after you had that telephone call from that man with the funny voice. I taped the call and thought he might push you too hard. And then, like the weakling you really are, I guessed you would try to find an easy way out.'

'I don't know what you mean,' Kirkpatrick said, almost in a whisper. He laid the pistol on the desk with a trembling hand. What had happened? How could this bitch know so much? Was he already dead and in hell, imagining all this?

'You know damn well what I mean,' his wife retorted, not even looking at him but watching bubbles rise in her drink. They are like truth, she thought. In the end, it always comes to the surface. And this was the end of her husband's philandering. She found it difficult not to smile.

'Here's something for you to look at. Some pretty pictures.'

She threw an open envelope onto the desk. Photographs scattered over the green leather top. The faces of the blonde nursing sister and the woman patient looked out at him, but they were the same fakes he had just destroyed. Why, their breasts were quite wrong. He was about to point out this obvious absurdity as evidence of his innocence, but bit back the words. To admit that would be to admit everything.

Muriel came into the room, perched on the edge of the desk so that she could look down on him as he sat, slumped back in his chair. How odd to think that she had once looked up to him, admired him.

'Where did you get those?' Kirkpatrick asked her. He had burnt them once: their remains were still grey in the ashtray in front of him.

'From your drawer. I've had spare keys made to all your drawers, all your cupboards. I wanted to know if your women were sending you love letters. I found the photos, got them copied – and replaced them. I had several sets of copies made, as a matter of fact, and deposited one lot with my bank. Just in case you had any ideas.'

'About what?'

'About anything. Because from now on, everything is going to change around here. In my favour.'

She smiled at Kirkpatrick, and his heart contracted in horror at the prospect of his life ahead. He had been prepared to murder a patient, largely because he feared his wife. And all the time she had been watching him, stalking him as a hunter stalks the hunted.

Dr Kirkpatrick covered his face with both hands and wept at his own weakness. His wife watched him and then finished her drink. He was hers now, and hers alone, for as long as she wanted him. If she wanted him.

The telephone was ringing by the bedside in my hotel room. A woman's voice I remembered but could not quite place spoke to me.

'Mr Crabtree?' she asked nervously.

'Yes,' I said.

Then I remembered. She was the nurse I had seen with da Leppo upstairs.

'I thought I should ring to tell you that Dr da Leppo passed away this morning. I have been trying to get you but there was no reply.'

'I am sorry,' I said. 'I was out. But I am glad I had the chance of meeting him before he died.'

'Yes. He was glad, too. It was a great effort seeing you. I

think that really took more out of him than he realised.'

'He died peacefully, I hope?'

'Very. After you'd gone, he went to bed and fell asleep. He never woke up again.'

'Have you informed anyone else?'

'Well, there is a doctor staying in the hotel. A specialist from Hong Kong. A Dr Sen. The reception clerk very kindly informed him. He is with me now.'

'I'll come up,' I said.

I took the elevator to the top floor. The nurse was waiting outside the room, as she had been when I had first arrived to see da Leppo. How long ago had that been? Days, years, a lifetime in the past? She said nothing. There was nothing to say. She let me in. Dr Sen stood by the window.

'You knew the patient?' he asked me.

'I met him once. He was a friend of Lady Mackenzie, who has been very kind to me.'

'Yes. An interesting man, I believe. Unfortunately, I never knew him. Well, I had better hand the details over to the resident hotel doctor. He was out on the beach when this lady telephoned. Someone had had a stroke there, I believe. Too much sun, probably. I was the only qualified physician they could find.'

'You must often find yourself in that position?' I said.

'Sometimes,' he agreed.

We were both polite but distant. No one overhearing us would ever have imagined that a stranger had recently tried to murder him – and I, in turn, had killed the stranger. As actors, I thought we did well; as human beings, I wasn't quite so sure.

In death, da Leppo's face was dark against the whiteness of the pillow. His eyes were closed. As so often happens with the old, death had erased all wrinkles from his face. He could be a man in his mid-forties, resting. All make-believe, all pretence was past; now, at last, he could be what he always had been, not a high-born Portuguese physician, but a half-caste, good-hearted quack.

'Are you going back now?' I asked. 'To Hong Kong?'

'Yes. As soon as I can. On the next plane. New York, then San Francisco. Then home.'

'With the shares?'

'With the shares.'

'Well, you've done what you set out to do.'

'That is so,' he agreed. 'Perhaps I will now have a more peaceful life.'

'I hope we both will.'

We stood in silence for a moment, and then I raised the question I most wanted to ask.

'That hospital patient. No comebacks, I hope? You dealt very quickly with him.'

'Not me, Mr Crabtree. The Almighty. I went to see him with Miss Lu-Kuan – we are both from the East, and she was very close to him. But he died peacefully, literally as we arrived.'

'Was any doctor there?'

'Not Dr Kirkpatrick, although I saw him arrive in his car just as we were leaving. The Canadian doctor had just stepped out to make a phone call.'

I could guess who he was telephoning.

'So Lord Jackson was on his own when he died?'

'I fear so. As he came into this world, so he left it. Alone.'

This seemed sad to me, that a man of such power and wealth should leave on his last journey from this world to the next without one friend to wish him farewell. But life *is* sad and we must find what laughter we may – while we may.

'You know, Mr Crabtree,' Sen continued, 'most of my patients have been rich, very rich. I often envied them their wealth. I did not know how they all acquired it. Nor did I realise then how fiercely they had to fight to keep it. Now I realise that I possessed something greater than wealth – peace of mind. Sometimes, in the past, I would help a patient who had no money or little money – like Mrs Crabtree. But not often enough. I will help people like her more in future. I plan to make great changes in my way of life.'

'I know how you feel, Doctor,' I told him. 'I feel the same myself.'

He looked at me, surprised. 'But you are on your way to being very, very wealthy.'

'That's not the only thing in life.'

'I am surprised to hear you talk like that,' Sen said, and smiled.

I smiled, too. I was surprising myself. We shook hands, and he went out of the room. I never saw him again.

As was the custom in Nassau, an early edition of next morning's newspaper had been placed, neatly ironed and folded, outside my door with a note: 'With the compliments of the management.'

I picked it up, and without much interest read headlines about wars, revolutions, earthquakes, chaos, treachery and death. I turned the pages, half hoping but not really expecting to find some item of better cheer, and a single headline seemed to leap out of the paper: *'Mojo founder to wed Mackenzie chief.'*

The report to which this referred was datelined Sydney, Australia.

'The engagement was announced here today between Mr Kendo Mojo, founder and principal shareholder of the mammoth Mojo Corporation, producers of aircraft, cars, motor cycles, TV and radio sets and electronic equipment, and Lady Myrtle Mackenzie, Chairperson of the equally successful Mackenzie Transworld.

'Lady Mackenzie is the widow of Sir Hilary Mackenzie. On his death after the Second World War she inherited what was then a relatively small British company – Mackenzie Industries.

'Under her shrewd guidance and leadership, this has grown

to become the present multi-national concern with interests
ranging from mining to motor manufacture. It is thought likely
that the marriage will result in these two immensely powerful
and wealthy conglomerates amalgamating. For some time there
have been rumours that the Mojo and Mackenzie car divisions
would combine. This merger seems now virtually certain to go
ahead.

'In the business communities of New York, London, Tokyo
and Hong Kong, rumours have persisted for weeks that either
of these conglomerates might bid for Trinity-Trio. On news of
the engagement, T-T non-voting shares scored gains of up to
10 per cent. (See page 7 for our Financial Editor's comments.)'

I couldn't be bothered to see page 7 or any other page for
anyone's comments. They would not know what I knew. That
through lying to a drug-addicted lonely young girl hidden away
in a shabby clinic in an English suburb I now held the key to
control of Trinity-Trio. I had only to contact the members of
the family who had held on to their inheritance, handed down,
generation to generation, and between us we would be
unassailable.

Even so, I was glad that those two strange, isolated and
ageing people, Lady Mackenzie and Mr Mojo, had found each
other. They might both be in the afternoons of their lives, but
at least now they would not need to go home in the dark alone.

I went out onto the balcony overlooking the beach and the
brightly lit casino. Floodlit palms stood in grotesque silhou-
ette, pink and amber and blue, against the darkness of the sea.
Somewhere, a calypso band began to play.

I felt totally disenchanted with this life. I had fought for a
visa to this golden land, but now I did not wish to make the
journey. I felt punch drunk, almost dazed, as though I had
followed a fallen star. The race was over and I had won all I had
set out to win, but the winning now meant nothing to me. I
experienced a strange emptiness in my heart. Would I have felt
the same if I had lost? I did not know, and in any case the

question was academic. I remembered the rustler Jack standing against a tree by the meatworks, dazed. Maybe he thought then he had won, and yet death waited for him only feet and minutes away. In life there are no ultimate victories, only holding, delaying operations.

Like a child who has been playing in the dark at the edge of a deep and unimagined precipice that he only sees when the lights come on, I realised I was facing dangers I had never previously imagined.

I had set out with one over-riding aim: to become rich, and so prove myself superior to my half-brother who I had admired from the first time Amy had told me about him and his achievements. But he was not even my half-brother. He was no relation whatever, and in attempting to overtake him I had lost more than I had gained. I had paid a high price, as Lady Mackenzie had told me I might.

Three incidents disturbed me especially. First, two doctors, Kirkpatrick and Sen, trained and dedicated to saving life, had both been willing to take it in order to save themselves. Next, the Australian, the man I had once almost idolised, had shown no hesitation whatever in suggesting to Dr Kirkpatrick that, in the bluntest terms, he should kill his patient, Lord Jackson. And, most damning of all as far as I was concerned, I had given the same instructions to Dr Sen.

What was happening to me? Or, worse, what had already happened? I felt I had lost my way and wondered now whether I would ever be able to find it again.

On a lower level, but equally without any alleviating circumstances, I had acted selfishly, greedily, although in the heat and urgency of events it had not seemed that way.

Through tunnel vision, always looking ahead, consumed by my own ambition, I had made an unnecessarily large profit out of the old man who owned Zachariah. Then, instead of repaying my enormous debt in a tangible way to Georgie and the other Aborigines for saving my life, I had thanked them – and then sold the property over their heads. But now I would make amends. I would make it part of my agreement with Lady Mackenzie that she employed all the Aborigines on Zachariah or other stations she owned. I would also see they had firm contracts and job security.

I had found, almost too late, that the fun and the excitement lie in making the journey, in going walkabout, not in reaching a destination which, like a mirage in the desert, invariably turns out to be quite different in reality from the dream. By the time you reached it, you were different, too. Your values had changed, and what had once seemed important no longer had such significance. Equally, what had earlier seemed of little importance, like enjoying a sunset or a sunrise, a swim, a conversation with friends, assumed infinitely greater value. In the longest life, one could only see so many sunsets, only know so few friends. Everyone changed, moved on or away, or died.

I had learned this the hard way, but that was the only way to learn anything. As Louis Armstrong once told a young trumpet player who asked how he could improve his playing: 'If you have to ask, you'll never learn.'

I hadn't asked, and I had learned because I had lived the lessons; I had been both teacher and pupil. Now it was time to put into practice what I had learned so slowly, with such difficulty – and at such high a cost to so many others.

A memory of a text stirred in my mind: 'One generation passeth away, and another generation cometh; but the earth abideth for ever.' I had strayed too far from my roots in the earth; it was time to return.

An early moon threw a silver path across the placid sea, and I recalled other times when I had seen that same moon light up the empty desert, cooling after the heat of a summer sun. My place was there; that was where I belonged, close to the red earth of home.

I thought of Ayers Rock, and at once felt in memory the tingle of vitality pulsing through my body as I placed my hands on its rough carborundum surface. I needed to make contact again to recharge the batteries of my mind.

I did not envy Mr Mojo aboard his yacht, surrounded by artefacts his factories produced; helicopter, car, motor cycle, sonar, TV and radar equipment, electronic gadgetry . . . Myrtle Mackenzie, still carefully keeping her dark complexion out of direct sunshine in case it grew still darker . . . or the Australian, not a couple of miles away from me in distance but now separated by an immeasurable gulf.

The badger, I had learned at school, might not wish to dig in the earth, but if it ceases to do so, the beast's huge claws curve into its flesh, so dig it must, simply to survive. These people were like that: they must go on, they could never go back.

I picked up the telephone, told the receptionist to book me on the next plane to New York, and on to Perth. I would pick up an Ansett flight there for the Alice and Katherine.

I had wanted to do what I had done, and I had done it. But once was enough. For the climber who conquers Everest it is enough to prove he can scale the ultimate peak. I had done the same, but I did not want to live there.

On an impulse, I asked the switchboard operator to connect me with Miss Lu-Kuan's suite.

Anna Lu-Kuan was standing by the window when I came into her room. She had left the door on the latch for me and she stood looking out to sea, as though she could not bear to turn and meet another predator. I coughed slightly in case she had not heard me. She turned.

'You want to see me,' she said flatly, making the question a statement.

'Yes,' I said.

'Do you come here on behalf of your relation, the Australian?'

'No. Actually we're not on very close terms.'

'Am I to believe that?'

'It's your prerogative to believe it or disbelieve it, Miss Lu Kuan. It happens to be true.'

'So what do you want to see me about?'

Anna's face was drawn, but even in the extremity of her sadness she was beautiful, with the serenity of those Madonna figures one sometimes sees in old churches.

'I wanted to tell you two things,' I began slowly, watching her. I paused. Still she did not look at me. Her gaze remained fixed on some object far out at sea. Beneath us, muted by concrete walls, the calypso pulsed like an imprisoned heart.

'Go on,' she said. 'I'm listening.'

'First of all,' I continued, 'I know you loved Lord Jackson, and I am told on very good authority that he loved you. But I am also told that he would never have recovered. I have recently lost someone dear to me through a wasting illness, and it is better to remember those you have loved as they were, as you loved them, than to think of them as someone almost inanimate, just kept alive scientifically because it may be convenient – profitable, maybe – for others to keep them alive.'

'What exactly do you mean?' she asked, turning now to look at me, eyes narrowed, frowning in her concentration.

'I mean that you could not bear to see the man you had loved, whose outlook had changed your entire philosophy, simply existing in this way. Not dead, yet not really living in any sense of that word.'

I could see from Anna's eyes that she guessed what I was about to say; maybe not all, but part of it. I decided to tell her everything I knew, everything I guessed. She might learn something she didn't know before, and I, in turn, might have my suspicions confirmed or totally refuted.

'What is the second thing you have to tell me?'

'Three people, for totally different reasons, wanted Lord Jackson out of the way,' I replied. 'My compatriot, the Australian, was one. He had Carlotti leaning on him. If the Australian couldn't deliver what he believed were two vital shares,

Carlotti's financial backing might have been removed, or at best seriously diminished.

'The Australian is personally too wealthy to be really concerned about such a situation, but his pride was at stake, and that for him is even more important than money. He had always delivered on every deal, always shown a profit. But now he thought he could fail. He blackmailed Dr Kirkpatrick to see that Lord Jackson did not live till morning.'

'I don't believe you,' said Anna stoutly. 'I spoke to Dr Kirkpatrick. He was doing everything he could to save his patient.'

'Possibly. Until he found a greater need – to save himself. Next, Dr Sen. The Triads were on his back and so was I.'

'You?'

'Yes. I saved his life here in Nassau. He told me that Lord Jackson had no hope. He thought, like me, that it could be a kindness to help him go.'

'You? Why you?'

'I will tell you later.'

'I liked Dr Sen,' said Anna. 'I trusted him.'

'Of course you did,' I said. 'You knew that, as a physician, he would not betray *any* secret. And when he told you that, despite Kirkpatrick's false optimism, there was really no hope, you knew you loved Lord Jackson too much to see him condemned to such an existence. So *you* killed him, Anna. Am I right?'

She gave a sigh that sounded almost one of relief. She nodded.

'Yes,' she admitted. 'I loved him. I couldn't bear to see him go on like this. My controllers in Beijing had taught me how to kill silently, without leaving any sign of violence, just the weight of a finger for a matter of seconds on one of half a dozen pressure points on the neck, the back, the body.

'Dr Sen told me the extent of Roderick's injuries. It was quite impossible for him to recover. After all, he had fallen about sixty feet. He was in terrible shape. Dr Sen came with me to the clinic. He had been in touch with the doctors there. A

Canadian consultant, who should have been on duty, had stepped out for a moment, and that was all I needed – a moment. Dr Sen told me he had a way to stop Roderick's suffering.'

'By pulling out the plug?'

'No. A much gentler way. Roderick was on a ventilator pumping oxygen into his lungs. The machine had a two-way tap, you simply turned it over from oxygen to fresh air. He would die gently then, peacefully.'

'But Dr Sen didn't do that?'

'No, he did not. *I* wanted to make sure that Roderick was really out of all suffering and future pain. I wanted this to be a last act of love for him. I killed him – quietly, silently, peacefully, painlessly, as I had been taught.'

Anna and I stood looking at each other. I was thinking about this Canadian doctor, the Australian's contact. Was no one above accepting a fee – a bribe would be a better word – in cash or kind? The bank manager in Katherine; Kirkpatrick; Sen; the Canadian; all professional men with a weakness the shrewd could explore and exploit. I felt a sudden revulsion for money and for what it could do to people, who and what it could buy; the destruction of integrity and trust.

The calypso beat changed to the lamenting cadences of 'Yellow Bird'.

'Now that I have admitted it, what are you going to do?' Anna asked me quietly.

'Nothing,' I told her. 'You acted in the best interests, as you saw them, of the man you loved. That is all anyone can ever do. You also acted in the best interests of his company.'

'I'm sorry, I don't understand you,' she frowned, disbelieving, puzzled.

'I have seen his will,' I explained. 'He left eleven shares to his daughter. Eleven are better than two. They will block the Australian and Carlotti getting control – unless we want them to have it. And I don't.'

'You can't possibly have seen his will. It's with his lawyer in

London. You're lying! You're making this up!' Anna's eyes flashed in her anger and contempt.

'No,' I said. 'I'm telling you the truth.'

'His daughter's a drug addict,' she replied. 'She wouldn't know what to do with the shares. Don't you know that?'

'I know,' I said. 'But I have Elaine Jackson's agreement to administer them in any way I choose.'

'How did you get that permission – if you did? If you're not just making all this up?'

I shrugged. 'It's a long story but briefly, I asked her.'

'I don't believe you.'

'So you keep telling me. But, Miss Lu-Kuan, this is not the time for belief or disbelief. It is a time for action. I am giving you facts. I have nothing whatever to gain by fabricating this story. I have a lien on the shares, and I don't want them to go either to the Australian or to Mr Carlotti which, in effect, means the same thing.'

'There is still Dr Sen. What about him?'

'He is out of this particular race. At this moment he is on his way back to Hong Kong. He was ordered to get two shares and he has them. He has fulfilled his obligation.'

'Why tell me this?'

'Because I thought you should know. You have been loyal to the man you loved.'

'Where do you belong in the equation?'

'Another long story. Briefly, a rich woman asked me to try and gain control of the company for her. Lady Mackenzie—'

'Ah, Mackenzie Transworld. I know about them,' she said. 'And you've done that? You *have* got control for her?'

'I am in a position to give her control, yes. I owe her a debt for sending me here. If I don't honour my bond, then I am no better than the others. But she will have to throw in her lot with the other descendants of the founders – on our conditions.'

'They are not much of a crowd,' said Anna dismissively.

'Inheritors of great wealth are not generally of the same

calibre as those who made that wealth. But they are at least better than organised crime, better than drug traffickers, better than murder, blackmail and the rest.'

'You know what you're talking about?' she asked me.

'I know,' I said.

She moved towards me until she was so close I could smell her perfume. She stood there, tacitly admitting defeat, a proud yet forlorn figure.

I had never had much time for girls. There had been the odd affair with one or two who helped in the supermarket; the furtive almost animal couplings behind shelves or in the back seat of a car, or even in my bed when the Crabtrees were out of the house. But these had been brief, loveless liaisons, which afterwards brought me mixed feelings of guilt and shame.

I had never been in love with anyone. I had been completely obsessed, to the exclusion of all other interests, all other distracting passions, with the determination to grow rich and overtake the Australian who I now knew was only a stranger linked to me by a web of lies. Now I would take a longer view of events.

Looking at this slight and beautiful creature in front of me, with her high cheekbones, almond eyes, her slightly suntanned complexion, I instinctively put out my hands to steady her, to comfort her. I felt she needed a friend, and I wanted to tell her that more than anything I had ever wished for, I wanted to be that friend. For a moment Anna resisted, and then she moved towards me. I enfolded her in my arms, kissed her, smoothed her dark hair, soft as down on a raven's wing.

I kissed Anna's forehead, her eyes, tasting the saltiness of her tears on my lips. For a moment she remained passive in my arms. Then the tip of her pink tongue moved between her lips and met mine. As our tongues touched, she drew back.

'I shouldn't be doing this,' she said. 'I loved him.'

'There is room in every heart, in every life, for many loves, not just for one.'

She looked at me quizzically. 'You're just saying this because you want something from me. To sign a legal document, an affidavit, some damn thing. And then, like all the rest, you'll leave me.'

'No,' I said. 'I want nothing from you that you don't want to give. I have no forms for you to sign. Indeed, I have nothing more to do here. I am returning to Australia.'

'To see Lady Mackenzie? To hand her those shares you have somehow acquired?'

'To see her, yes. I think she will understand. And she may be pleased.'

'About what you have done?'

'And about how events seem to be turning out. I will tell her everything. As I say, she will understand.'

'I wish I did. I can't go back to Beijing now. I don't belong anywhere. And if I lose my job at Trinity-Trio too, I'm finished. Will she understand *that*?'

'I think she will. The three of us have something very important in common, you know. We're all half-castes, if you like. Her father was a sergeant in the British Army; her mother, an Indian. You have an American father, a Chinese mother.'

'You know that?' she asked in surprise. 'And you?'

'My mother is Aboriginal. My father was also an American. I never knew him, but he was captured during the Second World War and transferred to Hiroshima as a prisoner of war. When the atom bomb fell, he tried to help the Japanese locals. One of them was Mr Mojo.'

'You mean the name I see in all these cars?'

'The same. Mr Mojo tried to find my father, for he owed his life to him, but he left it too late. My father had died of leukaemia from the atom blast. So Mr Mojo found me instead. And to repay the debt to my father, he gave me the franchise for his products throughout the East.'

'So you are rich?'

'I will be, relatively so. But I have learned there are other, better ways of counting riches than in cash. It's not the only currency, not even the best. I want to avoid the mistakes I've seen others make because they sought money above everything else. And Mammon was a god that failed them all, every one. Also, I want you to come to Australia with me.'

'In what capacity?'

'As companion, friend, business associate, however you care to describe it. Then, I hope, as lover. Then – who knows?'

'You're asking a lot. We've only just met.'

'I agree, but ask a lot and you may get something. Ask for little and you can get nothing.'

'You may be right. But even if I decided to come, I doubt I could afford the fare.'

'I can,' I told her.

'But what will you do in Australia? You'll miss this life, no?'

'No. I've had enough of it to last me for ever.'

Anna nodded slowly. She believed me. 'And then?'

'Then I will find my mother. That may not be easy. She may have taken a different name now, even have a different appearance. But I intend to find her – eventually. It will be easier if you help me. I don't know much about women.'

'Perhaps I could teach you?'

'Perhaps. Will you?'

She nodded, and smiled, a small almost secret smile.

'It's incredible,' she said slowly, 'but I feel at peace, as though everything has somehow been working towards this.'

I kissed her again, gently, the sealing of a bond between us. I knew that I could love her. Perhaps, one day, she might feel the same about me. I would spend my whole life endeavouring to make this come about.

Together we went out onto the balcony and stood facing the sea, now silver beneath the risen moon.

I had gone walkabout for my own reasons. That journey had taken me further and taught me more than I had anticipated. Now it was time for me to go walkabout again. This time it would be to find out all I could about a father I had never known, a mother I had never acknowledged, a woman I had never imagined I would meet.

The wealthy I had encountered had told me that once you set your foot on the road to riches, you can never go back. They were quite right.

But I was not going back; I was going home – with Anna.

A selection of bestsellers
from Headline

FICTION

THE EIGHT	Katherine Neville	£4.50 □
THE POTTER'S FIELD	Ellis Peters	£5.99 □
MIDNIGHT	Dean R Koontz	£4.50 □
LAMPLIGHT ON THE THAMES	Pamela Evans	£3.99 □
THE HOUSE OF SECRETS	Unity Hall	£4.50 □

NON-FICTION

TOSCANINI'S FUMBLE	Harold L Klawans	£3.50 □
GOOD HOUSEKEEPING EATING FOR A HEALTHY SKIN	Alix Kirsta	£4.99 □

SCIENCE FICTION AND FANTASY

THE RAINBOW SWORD	Adrienne Martine-Barnes	£2.99 □
THE DRACULA CAPER Time Wars VIII	Simon Hawke	£2.99 □
MORNING OF CREATION The Destiny Makers 2	Mike Shupp	£3.99 □
SWORD AND SORCERESS 5	Marion Zimmer Bradley	£3.99 □

*All Headline books are available at your local bookshop or newsagent,
or can be ordered direct from the publisher. Just tick the titles you want
and fill in the form below. Prices and availability subject to change without
notice.*

Headline Book Publishing PLC, Cash Sales Department, PO Box 11,
Falmouth, Cornwall, TR10 9EN, England.

Please enclose a cheque or postal order to the value of the cover price
and allow the following for postage and packing:
UK: 60p for the first book, 25p for the second book and 15p for each
additional book ordered up to a maximum charge of £1.90
BFPO: 60p for the first book, 25p for the second book and 15p per copy
for the next seven books, thereafter 9p per book
OVERSEAS & EIRE: £1.25 for the first book, 75p for the second book
and 28p for each subsequent book.

Name ....

Address ....

....

....